A SHADOW IN THE EMBER

Also From Jennifer L. Armentrout

Fall With Me
Dream of You (a 1001 Dark Nights Novel)
Forever With You
Fire In You

By J. Lynn
Wait for You
Be With Me
Stay With Me

The Blood and Ash Series
From Blood and Ash
A Kingdom of Flesh and Fire
The Crown of Gilded Bones

The Flesh and Fire Series
A Shadow in the Ember

The Covenant Series
Half-Blood
Pure
Deity
Elixer
Apollyon
Sentinel

The Lux Series
Shadows
Obsidian
Onyx
Opal
Origin
Opposition
Oblivion

The Origin Series
The Darkest Star
The Burning Shadow
The Brightest Night

The Dark Elements
Bitter Sweet Love
White Hot Kiss
Stone Cold Touch
Every Last Breath

The Harbinger Series
Storm and Fury
Rage and Ruin
Grace and Glory

The Titan Series
The Return
The Power
The Struggle
The Prophecy

The Wicked Series
Wicked
Torn
Brave
The Prince (a 1001 Dark Nights Novella)
The King (a 1001 Dark Nights Novella)
The Queen (a 1001 Dark Nights Novella)

Gamble Brothers Series
Tempting The Best Man
Tempting The Player
Tempting The Bodyguard

A de Vincent Novel Series
Moonlight Sins
Moonlight Seduction
Moonlight Scandals

Standalone Novels
Obsession
Frigid
Scorched
Cursed
Don't Look Back
The Dead List
Till Death
The Problem With Forever
If There's No Tomorrow

Anthologies
Meet Cute
Life Inside My Mind
Fifty First Times

A SHADOW IN THE EMBER

#1 *NEW YORK TIMES* BESTSELLING AUTHOR
JENNIFER L. ARMENTROUT

A Shadow in the Ember
A Flesh and Fire Novel
By Jennifer L. Armentrout

ISBN: 978-1-952457-64-7

Published by Blue Box Press, an imprint of Evil Eye Concepts, Incorporated

Acknowledgments from the Author

Thank you to the amazing team at Blue Box—Liz Berry, Jillian Stein, MJ Rose, Chelle Olsen, Kim Guidroz and more, who have helped bring the world of Blood and Ash to life. Thank you to my agent Kevan Lyon, Jenn Watson, and my assistant Malissa Coy for your hard work and support, and to Stephanie Brown for creating amazing merch. Mega thanks to Hang Le for creating such beautiful covers. A big thank you to Jen Fisher, Stacey Morgan, Lesa, JR Ward, Laura Kaye, Andrea Joan, Sarah Maas, Brigid Kemmerer, KA Tucker, Tijan, Vonetta Young, Mona Awad, and many more who have helped keep me sane and laughing. Thank you to the ARC team for your support and honest reviews, and a big thank you to JLAnders for being the best reader group an author can have, and the Blood and Ash Spoiler Group for making the drafting stage so fun and being utterly amazing. None of this would be possible without you, the reader. Thank you.

Dedication

To you, the reader

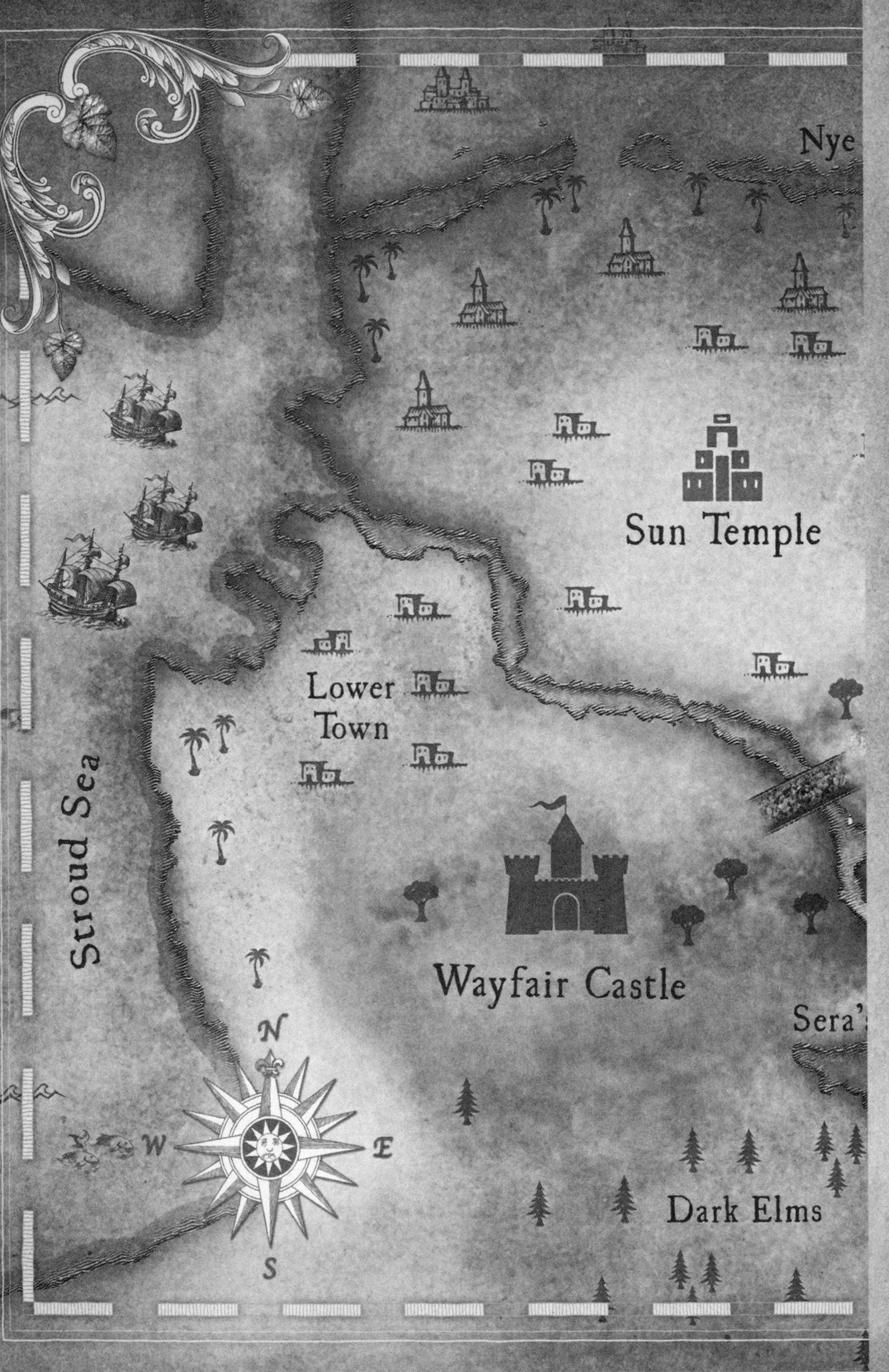
Nye
Sun Temple
Lower
Town
Stroud Sea
Wayfair Castle
Sera's
N
W
E
S
Dark Elms

LASANIA MAP

River

Croft's Cross

Golden Bridge

GARDEN DISTRICT

The Luxe

Shadow Temple

Eastfall

Lake

Cliffs of Sorrow

Elysium Peaks

Prologue

"You will not disappoint us today, Sera." The words came from somewhere in the shadows of the chamber. "You will not disappoint Lasania."

"No." I clasped my hands together to stop their ceaseless trembling as I breathed in deeply. I held that breath and stared at my reflection in the mirror propped against the wall. I had no reason to be nervous. I exhaled slowly. "I will not disappoint you."

I took another deep, measured breath, barely recognizing the person who stared back at me. Even in the dim, flickering light from the numerous candelabras placed throughout the small chamber, I could see that my skin was so pink, I almost couldn't see the freckles smattering my cheeks and the bridge of my nose. Some would call the blush a glow, but the green of my eyes was too bright, too feverish.

Because my heart still pounded, I held my breath again, just like Sir Holland had taught me to do when it felt as if I couldn't breathe—couldn't control what was happening around me or to me. *Breathe in, slow and steady. Hold until you feel your heart slow. Breathe out. Hold.*

It didn't work like it normally did.

My hair had been brushed until my scalp started to burn. It still tingled. The pale blonde hair was half swept up and pinned in place so the mass of curls fell down my back. The skin of my throat and shoulders was also flushed, and I figured that was from the scented bath I had been made to soak in for hours earlier. Maybe that was why I found breathing so difficult. The water had been so heavily perfumed with oils that I feared I now smelled as if I'd been drowned in jasmine and sweet anise.

Holding perfectly still, I inhaled deeply and slowly. I'd been groomed to within an inch of my life after the bath. Hair plucked and waxed from all manner of places, and only the balm rubbed over my legs, arms, and seemingly everywhere in between had soothed the sting. I held my breath once more, resisting the urge to lower my gaze beyond my face. I already knew what I would see, and that was, well, nearly *everything*.

The gown—if it could be called such—had been constructed of a sheer chiffon and little else. The sleeves, which were nothing more than a few scant inches, rested on my upper arms, and the thin, ivory cloth had been draped and wrapped loosely over my body, the length left to pool on the floor. I hated the dress, the bath, and the grooming that had come after that, even though I understood the purpose.

I was to entice, seduce.

A rustling of skirts drew near, and I exhaled slowly. My mother's face appeared in the mirror. We looked nothing alike. I resembled my father. I knew this because I'd stared at the one remaining painting of him enough times to know that he too had freckles, and his jaw was just as stubborn as mine. I also had his eyes—not just the color but also the same tilt at the outer corners. That painting, hidden away in my mother's private chambers, was how I knew what my father had looked like.

My mother's dark brown eyes met mine briefly in the mirror, and then she walked around me, the crown of golden leaves upon her head shining in the candlelight. She studied me, searching for a stray hair out of place or where one didn't belong, for a flaw or sign that I wasn't the expertly crafted bride.

The price that had been promised two hundred years before I was born.

My throat dried even more, but I didn't dare ask for water. A rosy paint had been applied to my lips, giving them a dewy finish. If I messed them up, my mother would not be pleased.

I scanned her face as she adjusted the sleeves of the gown. The fine lines at the corners of her eyes appeared deeper than the day before. Tension whitened the skin around her lips. Like always, her features were impossible to read, and I wasn't sure what I searched for. Sadness? Relief? Love? The sound of tiny golden chains clinking together caused my heart to kick even harder against my ribs.

I caught a glimpse of the white veil someone handed to her, and it made me think of the white wolf I'd seen by the lake all those years ago when I'd been collecting rocks for whatever bizarre reason I couldn't remember now. Based on the magnificent size, I'd imagined that he'd been one of the rare kiyou wolves that sometimes roamed the Dark Elms surrounding the grounds of Wayfair Castle. I'd locked eyes with the creature, terrified that it would rip me apart. But all it had done before loping off was look at the pile of rocks in my arms as if I were some sort of idiot child.

My mother placed the Veil of the Chosen over my head. The flimsy material floated around my shoulders and then settled so that only my lips and jaw were visible, the length flowing down my back. I could barely see through the wispy material as the thin chains were placed atop my head to hold it in place. This veil wasn't nearly as thick as the one I wore whenever I was around anyone but my immediate family and Sir Holland, nor did it cover the entirety of my face.

"*You may not be Chosen, but you were born into this realm, shrouded in the veil of the Primals. A Maiden as the Fates promised. And you shall leave this realm touched by life and death,*" my old nursemaid Odetta had once said.

But, once again, I looked like the Chosen—those third sons and daughters born in a shroud, destined to serve the Primal of Life in his Court. I spent my entire life hidden behind this veil, and even though I had been born in a shroud and treated like most Chosen in many ways, I was also the Maiden. What they were destined to become after Ascension was the highest honor that could be bestowed upon a mortal in any kingdom. Celebrations would be held throughout the lands in preparation for the night of their Rite, where they would Ascend and enter the realm of Iliseeum to serve the Primals and the gods. What I was destined for was the most closely guarded secret in all of Lasania. There were no celebrations and feasts. Tonight, on my seventeenth birthday, I would become the Primal of Death's Consort.

My throat tightened. Why was I so apprehensive? I was ready for this. I was ready to fulfill the deal. I was ready to carry out what I had been born to do. I had to be.

Part of me wondered if the Chosen were nervous on the night of their Rite. They had to be. Who wouldn't be anxious in the presence of a lesser god, let alone a Primal—beings so powerful, they had become fundamental to the very fabric of our existence? Or maybe they were simply thrilled to finally fulfill their destiny. I'd seen them smiling and laughing during the Rite, only the lower halves of their faces visible, clearly eager to begin a new chapter of life.

I was not smiling or laughing.

Breathe in. Hold. Breathe out. Hold.

Mother leaned in. "You're ready, Princess Seraphena."

Seraphena. It was so rare that I heard my full name spoken, and never had I heard it said with the official title. It was like a switch had been thrown. In an instant, the thundering of my heart stopped, and the pressure on my chest lessened. My hands steadied. "I am."

Through the veil, I saw Queen Calliphe smile, or at least her lips went through the motions. I'd never seen her *really* smile at me, not like she did with my stepsiblings or her husband. But even though she had carried me for nine months and brought me into this world, I had never been hers. I had never been the people's Princess.

I'd always belonged to the Primal of Death.

She gave me one more look, brushed back a curl that had found its way over my shoulder, and then swept from the room without saying another word. The door clicked shut behind her, and every sense I had honed over the years heightened.

The silence of the chamber lasted only a few heartbeats. "Little sister," came the voice. "You're as still as one of the statues of the gods in the garden."

Sister? My lip curled in barely contained disgust. He was no brother of mine, not by blood nor bond, even though he was the son of the man my mother had married soon after my father's death. He didn't carry a drop of the Mierel bloodline, but because the people of Lasania didn't know of my birth, he had become the heir. Soon, he would be King, and I was sure the people of Lasania would face a different crisis even after I fulfilled the deal.

But because of his claim to the throne, he was one of the few who knew the truth about King Roderick—the first King of the Mierel bloodline and my ancestor—whose desperate choice to save his people had not only sealed my fate but had also damned future generations of the very kingdom he sought to protect.

"You must be nervous." Tavius was closer. "I know Princess Kayleigh is. She frets about our wedding night."

My fingers unlatched from my sides. I eyed him quietly.

"I promised her I'd be gentle." Tavius drifted into my line of sight. With light brown hair and blue eyes, Tavius was considered handsome by many, and I'd bet the Princess of Irelone had thought the same upon meeting him, believing that no other girl could be as lucky as her.

I doubted she felt the same now. I watched Tavius circle me like one of the large, silver hawks I'd often spotted above the trees of the Dark Elms.

"I doubt you'd get the same reassurances from *him*." Even through the veil, I saw the smirk. I *felt* his stare. "You know what they say about him—about why he's never been painted nor had his features carved into stone." He lowered his voice, packing it full of false empathy. "They say he's monstrous, that his skin is covered in the same scales as the beasts that guard him. That he has fangs for teeth. You must be terrified of what you must do."

I wasn't sure if the Primal of Death was covered in scales or not, but all of them—gods and Primals—had sharp, elongated canines. Fangs sharp enough to pierce flesh.

"Do you think a blood kiss will give you great pleasure like some claim?" he taunted. "Or will it bring terrible pain as he sinks those teeth into your untouched skin?" His voice thickened. "Probably the latter."

I loathed him more than I did this gown.

He moved again, prowling around me and tapping one finger against his chin. My skin crawled, but I remained still. "But then again, you've been trained to carry this through to the end, haven't you? To become his weakness, make him fall in love, and then end him." He stopped in front of me once more. "I know about the time spent under the tutelage of the Mistresses of the Jade. So, maybe you're not nervous," he continued. "Maybe you can't wait to *serve*—" He lifted a hand toward me.

I caught his wrist, digging my fingers into the tendons there. His entire body jerked, and he cursed. "Touch me, and I will break every bone in your hand," I warned. "And then I will make sure the Princess has no reason to fear her wedding night or *any* night she is doomed to spend at your side."

Tension built in Tavius's arm, and he glared down at me. "You're so incredibly lucky," he snarled. "You have no idea."

"No, Tavius." I shoved him back, a reminder that my training hadn't only consisted of time spent with the Mistresses. He stumbled but caught himself before he hit the mirror. "It is you who is lucky."

His nostrils flared. Rubbing the inside of his wrist, he said nothing as I stood there, motionless once more. I spoke the truth. I could snap his neck before he even had a chance to raise a hand against me. Because of my destiny, I was better trained than most of the Royal Guards that protected him. Still, he was arrogant and spoiled enough to try something.

I kind of hoped he would.

Tavius took a step forward, and I started to smile—

A knock on the door stopped him from following through with whatever incredibly foolish thought had entered his mind. He lowered his hands, barking out, "What?"

The nervous voice of my mother's trusted Lady came through the door. "The Priests expect his arrival to be soon."

Tavius's smile was a mockery as he brushed past me. I turned around. "Time for you to make yourself useful for once," he said.

He opened the door, slowly making his exit, knowing that I wouldn't respond in front of Lady Kala. Everything and anything I did in front of the woman would be reported back to my mother. And she, for some godsforsaken reason, cared for Tavius as if he were worthy of such an emotion. I waited until he'd disappeared down one of the many dark, winding halls of the Shadow Temple, located just outside the capital's Garden District at the foot of the Cliffs of Sorrow. The halls were just as numerous as the tunnels underneath, connecting to all the Temples in Carsodonia—the capital—to Wayfair Castle.

I thought of the mortal Sotoria, whom the steep bluffs had been named after. Legend claimed that she been picking flowers along the cliffs and fell to her death after being frightened by a god.

Perhaps now wasn't the most opportune time to think about her.

Lifting the diaphanous skirts of my gown, I turned and padded barefoot across the cold floor.

Lady Kala was very much a blur in the hall, but I could tell that she hastily turned her head from me. "Come," she said, beginning to walk before stopping. "Can you see in that veil?"

"A bit," I admitted.

She reached back, curling her arm through mine. The unexpected contact caused me to flinch, and I was suddenly grateful for the veil. Like any of the Chosen, my flesh should not encounter another's unless related to my preparations. It spoke volumes that Lady Kala had touched me.

She led me through the twisting, endless halls of nothing but doors and numerous blazing candle sconces. I had just begun to wonder if she was lost when the hazy outline of two silent figures draped in black appeared by a set of doors.

Shadow Priests.

They'd taken their oath of silence to all new heights, having stitched their lips closed. I always wondered how they ate or drank. Based on their wraithlike, sunken frames under the black robes, whatever method they used wasn't exactly working out that well for them.

I suppressed a shudder as each of the Priests opened a door to reveal a large, circular chamber aglow with hundreds of candles. A third Shadow Priest seemingly appeared out of thin air, taking Lady Kala's place. The bony fingers didn't touch my skin but pressed into the center of my back. The contact still bothered me, made me want to pull away, but I knew better than to step away from the coldness of his fingers seeping through the thin layer of cloth. Forcing myself to breathe, I stared at the etchings carved into the otherwise smooth stone. A circle with a line through it. The symbol filled each stone tile. Having never seen it before, I wasn't sure what it meant. My gaze lifted to the wide dais before me. The Priest guided me down the aisle, and some of the pressure returned to my chest. I didn't look at the empty pews. If I had truly been Chosen, those benches would be full of the highest-ranking nobility, the streets outside alive with cheers. The silence of the room chilled my skin.

There'd only ever been one throne before, constructed from the same stone as the Temple. Shadowstone was the color of the deepest hour of night, a marvelous material that could be polished until it reflected any source of light and whetted into a blade sharp enough to pierce flesh and bone. The throne was the glossy sort, absorbing the glow of the candlelight until the stone appeared as if it were full of dark fire. The back of the seat had been carved into the shape of a crescent moon.

The exact shape of the birthmark I bore just above my left shoulder blade. The telltale sign that even before I was born, my life had never been mine.

Tonight, there were two thrones.

As they led me to the dais and helped me up the steps, I really wished I had asked for that glass of water. Guided to the second throne, they sat me there and then left me alone.

Resting my hands on the arms of the throne, I scanned the pews below. Not a single soul from Lasania was in attendance. None even knew that their lives and their children's lives all hinged on tonight and what I needed to do. If they ever discovered that Roderick Mierel—the one the histories of Lasania called the Golden King—hadn't spent day and night in the fields with his people, digging and scraping away land ruined by war until they revealed clean, fertile soil… That he hadn't sown the land alongside his subjects; his blood, sweat, and tears building the kingdom… If they learned that the songs and poems written about him had been based on a fable, what was left of the Mierel Dynasty would surely collapse.

Someone closed the doors, and my gaze stretched to the back of the chamber, where I could make out the shadowy forms of my mother and Tavius in the candlelight. A third figure stood beside them. King Ernald. My stepsister, Princess Ezmeria—Ezra—stood beside her father and brother, and I didn't need to see her expression to know that she hated every aspect of this deal. Sir Holland wasn't here. I would've liked to have said goodbye to him, even though I didn't expect him to be here. His presence would raise too many questions among the Shadow Priests.

Would reveal too much.

That I wasn't the beacon of Royal purity, but rather the wolf dressed as the sacrificial lamb.

I wouldn't just fulfill the deal that King Roderick had struck. I would end it before it destroyed my kingdom.

Determination filled my chest with warmth as it did whenever I used my gift. This was my destiny. My purpose. What I would do was bigger than me. It was for Lasania.

So, I sat there, ankles crossed demurely beneath the gown, hands relaxed on the arms of the throne as I waited.

And waited some more.

Seconds ticked into minutes. I didn't know how many passed, but tiny balls of unease formed in my belly. He'd been summoned to *his* Temple. Shouldn't…shouldn't he be here?

My palms dampened as the knots grew, stretching into my chest. The pressure increased. What if he didn't show?

Why wouldn't he?

This was his deal.

When King Roderick had grown desperate enough to do *anything* to salvage his lands ruined by war and save those who were starving after already suffering so much loss, I imagined he'd expected a lesser god to answer his summons—which was far more common for those bold enough to do such a thing. But what had answered the Golden King was a Primal.

And when he'd granted King Roderick's request, this was the price the Primal of Death had requested: the firstborn daughter of the Mierel bloodline as his Consort.

The Primal had to come.

What if he didn't? My heart pounded as my fingers curled against the chilled stone of the throne.

Breathe in. Hold. Breathe out. Hold.

If he didn't arrive, all would be lost. Everything he'd granted King Roderick would continue to come undone. If he didn't come for me, and I failed to fulfill this, I would doom the kingdom to a slow death at the hands of the Rot. It had started upon my birth, first with just a small patch of land in an orchard. Unripe apples had fallen from trees that had begun to lose their leaves. The ground below had turned gray, and the grass, along with the roots of the apple trees, had died. Then the Rot had spread, slowly taking out the entire orchard. In the time that passed, it had devastated several more farms. No crop could be seeded in the soil and survive once tainted by the Rot.

And it wasn't only affecting the land. It had changed the weather, making the summers hotter and drier, the winters colder and more unpredictable.

The people of Lasania had no idea that the Rot was a clock, counting down. It was an expiration date on the deal the Golden King had made, one that had started with my birth. There was a good chance the Golden King hadn't realized the bargain would expire no matter what. That was knowledge gained in the decades after the deal had been struck. If I failed, the kingdom would—

It started as a low rumble, like the distant sound of wagons and carriages rolling over the cobblestone streets of Carsodonia. But the sound grew until I felt it in the throne I sat upon—and in my bones.

The rumbling ceased, and the candles—all of them—went out, plunging the chamber into darkness. An earthy-scented breeze stirred the edges of the veil around my face and the hem of my gown.

In a wave, flames sparked from the candles, surging toward the pitched ceiling. My gaze fixed on the center aisle, where the very air itself had split open, spitting crackling white light.

A mist seeped out from the tear, licking across the stone floor and seeping toward the pews. Tiny bumps erupted all over my skin in response. Some called the mist Primal magic. It was eather. The potent essence that not only had created the mortal realm and Iliseeum but also what coursed through the blood of a god, giving even the lesser, unknown ones unthinkable power.

I blinked. That was all I did. I *blinked*, and the space in front of the dais that had been empty no longer was. A male stood there, garbed in a hooded cloak and surrounded by pulsing, churning tendrils of deep shadows laced with luminous streaks of silver. I didn't allow myself to think of what Tavius had said about him. I *couldn't.* Instead, I tried to see through the wispy mass of smoky shadows. All I could tell was that he was unbelievably tall. Even from where I sat, I knew he would tower over me—and I wasn't short by any means, nearly the same height as Tavius. But he was a Primal, and in the stories written about them in the histories, they were sometimes referred to as giants among mortals.

He appeared broad of shoulder—or at least that was what I thought the deeper, thick mass of darkness was that took the shape of…*wings.* His hooded head tilted back.

I forgot those breathing exercises in an instant. I couldn't see his face, but I felt the intensity of his stare. His gaze pierced straight through me, and for a brief, panicked moment, I feared that he knew I hadn't spent seventeen years preparing to become his Consort. That my tutelage went beyond that. And that the meekness, the *submissiveness* I'd been taught, was nothing more than another veil I wore.

For a moment, my heart stopped as I sat on the throne meant for the Consort of the Shadowlands, one of the Courts within Iliseeum. Looking up at the Primal of Death, I felt real terror for the first time in my life.

Primals couldn't read mortals' thoughts. In the back of my mind, where some bit of intelligence still existed, I knew this. There was no reason for him to suspect that I was anything other than I appeared to be. Even if he'd watched me grow over the years, or if spies had been sent to Lasania, my identity, my heritage and bloodline, had been kept hidden. No one even knew there *was* a Princess of Mierel blood. Everything I did had been carried out in highly planned secrecy—from training with Sir Holland to the time spent with the Mistresses of the Jade.

There was no way he could know that in the two hundred years it had taken for me to be born, the knowledge of how to kill a Primal had been obtained.

Love.

They had one fatal weakness that made them vulnerable enough to be killed, and that was love.

Make him fall in love, become his weakness, and end him.

That was my destiny.

Gaining control of my hammering heart, I pulled from the hours spent with my mother, learning what would be expected of me as his Consort. How to move, speak, and act in his presence. How to become whatever he desired. I was ready for this—whether or not he was covered head to toe in the scales of the winged beasts that guarded the Primals.

My fingers relaxed, my breathing slowed, and I allowed my lips to curl into a smile—a shy, innocent one. I stood in the glow of the candlelight on feet I couldn't feel. I clasped my hands loosely across my midsection so nothing would be hidden from him, just as my mother had instructed. I started to lower to my knees as one would upon greeting a Primal.

The stir of air was the only warning I got that the Primal had moved.

Shock silenced the gasp of surprise before it reached my lips. He was suddenly in front of me. No more than a handful of inches remained between us. Swirling light rippled the air around me. He felt *cold*, like the winters to the north and east. Like each winter here in Lasania slowly became with each passing year.

I wasn't sure I even breathed as I looked up into the void where his face should be. The Primal of Death shifted closer, and one of the shadow tendrils brushed across the bare skin of my arm. I gasped at the icy feel. He lowered his head, and every muscle in my body seized. I wasn't sure if it was his presence or the innate instinct we all had that warned us not to run. Not to make any sudden movements in the presence of a predator.

"You," he said, his voice smoke and shadow and full of everything that awaited after someone took their very last breath. "I have no need of a Consort."

My entire body jerked, and I whispered, "What?"

The Primal pulled back, the shadows retracting around him. He shook his head. What did he mean?

I stepped forward. "What—?" I said again.

The wind whipped from behind me this time, pitching the chamber into darkness as the candles whooshed out. The rumbling was weaker than before, but I didn't dare move, having no idea where he was. I wasn't sure where the edge of the dais even was. The earthy scent disappeared, and the flames slowly returned to the candles, sparking weakly to life…

He no longer stood before me.

Faint wisps of eather wafted up from the now-sealed opening in the floor.

He was gone.

The Primal of Death had left. He hadn't taken me, and in a deep, hidden part of me, relief blossomed and then crumbled. He hadn't fulfilled the deal.

"What…what happened?" My mother's voice reached me, and I looked up to see that she was before me. "What happened?"

"I…I don't know." Panic sank its claws into me as I turned to my mother, wrapping my arms around myself. "I don't understand."

Her eyes were wide and mirrored the storm brewing inside me as she whispered, "Did he speak to you?"

"He said…" I tried to swallow, but my throat tightened. The corners of my vision turned white. No amount of breathing exercises would help the alarm that took root. "I don't understand. I did everything—"

The burning sting of my mother's slap came as a shock. I hadn't expected it—hadn't even prepared myself for her to do something like that. Hand trembling, I pressed it against my cheek, standing there stunned and incapable of processing what *had* happened—what *was* happening.

Her dark eyes were even wider now, her skin a ghastly pale shade. "What did you do?" She pulled her hand back to her chest. "What did you do, Sera?"

I'd done nothing. Only what I'd been taught. But I couldn't tell her that. I couldn't tell her anything. Words failed me as something shattered inside me, shriveling up.

"*You*," my mother said. While her voice was not smoke or shadow, it was just as final. Her eyes glistened. "You've failed us. And now, everything—*everything*—is lost."

Chapter 1

Three years later…

The Vodina Isles Lord strutted down the center of the Great Hall of Wayfair Castle, the soft, steady thud of his polished boots echoing the silent tap of my fingers against my thigh. He was handsome in a rough-hewn sort of way, skin baked by the sun and arms honed from wielding the heavy sword at his hip. The smirk on Lord Claus's face, the arrogant tilt of his fair head, and the burlap sack he carried told me all I needed to know about how this would go—but no one in attendance moved or made a sound.

Not the Royal Guards who stood in a rigid line before the dais, adorned in their finery. They looked ridiculous. Gold fringe fell from the puffed shoulders of their plum waistcoats, matching their pantaloons. Their lapeled coats and thick pants were far too heavy for the hot Carsodonia summer and didn't really allow for unrestricted movement like the plain tunic and breeches the lower-ranking guards and soldiers wore. Their uniform screamed *privilege* that hadn't been earned with the swords sheathed in their bone and stone-encrusted scabbards.

There was no movement from the dais, where the Queen and King of Lasania sat upon their diamond-and-citrine-jeweled thrones, watching the approaching Lord. The golden crowns of leaves atop their heads shone brightly in the candlelight, and while my stepfather's eyes held a sheen of fevered hope, my mother's showed utterly nothing. Standing stiffly beside the King, the heir to the kingdom appeared somewhere between half-asleep and annoyed by the responsibility that required his presence. Knowing Tavius, he'd likely prefer to be at least three cups deep in ale and between some woman's legs by this time of the evening.

Queen Calliphe broke the tense silence, her voice crisp in the warm, heavy air thick with the scent of roses. "I did not expect you to answer the offer our Advisor made to your Crown." Her tone was unmistakable. The Vodina Isle Lord's presence was an insult. He was not royalty. And his actions were clear. He did not care. "Do you speak on behalf of your King and Queen?"

Lord Claus stopped several feet from the Royal Guard, his unflinching stare tilted upward. He didn't answer as his gaze traveled over the dais to the many columned alcoves. Beside me, Sir Holland, a knight of the Royal Guard, tensed, his grip on the sword at his waist tightening as the Lord's survey glossed over me and snapped back.

I held his stare, an act I'd surely be reprimanded for later, but only a handful of people in the entire kingdom knew that I was the last of the Mierel bloodline, a Princess. And even less knew that I had been the Maiden promised to the Primal of Death. This smug Lord didn't even know that the only reason he was standing here was because I had failed Lasania.

Even though I stood in the shadows, Lord Claus's slow perusal was like a sweaty caress, lingering on the bare skin of my arms and the cut of my bodice before reaching my eyes. His lips puckered, blowing me a kiss.

I arched a brow.

His smirk slipped.

Queen Calliphe noted the direction of his attention and stiffened. "Do you speak on behalf of your Crown?" she repeated.

"I do." Lord Claus shifted his attention back to the dais.

"And do you have an answer?" the Queen asked as a rust-colored stain spread across the bottom of the burlap sack. "Does your Crown accept our allegiance in exchange for aid?"

Two years' worth of crops. Barely enough to supplement the farm's loss to the Rot.

"I have your answer." Lord Claus tossed the sack forward.

It hit the marble with an oddly *wet*-sounding smack before rolling across the tile. Something round spilled out of the bag, leaving a spattering trail of…red behind. Brown hair. Ghastly pale complexion. Jagged strips of skin. Severed bone.

The head of Lord Sarros, Advisor to the Queen and King of Lasania, bounced off a Royal Guard's booted foot.

"Dear gods," gasped Tavius, jerking back a step.

"That's our answer to your shit offer of allegiance." Lord Claus edged back a step, hand going to the hilt of his sword.

"Huh," Sir Holland murmured as several Royal Guards reached for their weapons. "Was not expecting that."

I turned my head toward him, detecting what I thought was a hint of morbid amusement in the features of his deep brown skin.

"Cease," King Ernald ordered, lifting a hand. The Royal Guard halted.

"Now *that* I expected," Sir Holland added under his breath.

I clamped my jaw shut to stop myself from doing something incredibly inappropriate. I focused on my mother. There wasn't a single flicker of emotion on the Queen's face as she sat there, her neck stiff and chin high. "A simple no would've sufficed," she stated.

"But would it have had the same impact?" Lord Claus countered, that half-grin returning. "The allegiance of a failing kingdom isn't worth a day's worth of crops." He looked at the alcove and continued backing up. "But if you throw the hot piece over there into the deal, I may be convinced to petition the Vodina Crown on your behalf."

The King white-knuckled the arms of the throne as Queen Calliphe said, "My handmaiden is not a part of the bargain."

Just like my mother, I showed no emotion. Nothing. Handmaiden. Servant. Not daughter.

"Too bad." Lord Claus climbed the short set of steps to the entrance of the Great Hall. Hand on the hilt of his sword, his elaborate bow was as much a mockery as what spilled from his well-formed lips. "Blessed be in the name of the Primals."

Silence answered, and he pivoted, strolling out of the Great Hall. His laughter seeped into the hall as thick and cloying as the roses.

Queen Calliphe shifted forward as she looked at the alcove. Her gaze met mine, and a strange mix of emotions crawled over me. Love. Hope. Desperation. Anger. I couldn't remember the last time she'd looked directly at me, but she did now, and it fueled the kernel of apprehension. "Show him what a hot piece you are," she ordered, and Sir Holland cursed softly. "Show all the Lords of the Vodina Isles."

A near choking sense of sorrow settled in my throat, but I shut that thought down before it could breed and take on a whole new life. I shut it all down as I exhaled, long and slow. Like the countless times before, emptiness seeped in through my skin. I nodded, welcoming the nothingness that sank into my muscles and penetrated my bones. I let the nothingness invade my thoughts until no inkling of who I was remained. Until I was like those poor, lost spirits that roamed the Dark Elms. An empty vessel once again filled with purpose. It was like donning the Veil of the Chosen as I nodded and turned without word.

"You should've just given her to the Lord," Tavius commented. "At least then, she might actually do us some good."

I ignored the Prince's caustic remarks and quickly walked through the alcoves, the skirt of my gown snapping around the low heels of my boots on my way out of the Great Hall.

The corridor was eerily still. I reached up and lifted the hood attached to the collar of my gown. I pulled it into place, an act driven by habit more than anything else. Many of those who worked inside Wayfair Castle knew me simply as the Queen had called me: a handmaiden. To most outside the castle, my features were those of a stranger, just as when I'd been veiled as a Chosen.

I stalked past the great mauve banners adorning the walls. They swayed, caught by the warm breeze rolling in through the open windows. In the center of each banner, the golden Royal Crest glittered in the lamplight.

A crown of gold leaves with a sword through the center.

The crest supposedly represented strength and leadership. To me, it looked as if someone were being stabbed through the skull. I couldn't be the only one who thought that.

I passed the Royal Guards at the doors leading to the wall facing the Stroud Sea, where I knew the ship would be waiting to return to the Vodina Isles. Passing the stables, I crossed the courtyard and slipped out the narrow, smaller gate rarely used since it fed into a less-traveled trail through the bluffs overlooking Lower Town—a crowded section of warehouses and dens, catering to the dockworkers and sailors.

Under the moonlight, I navigated the steep pathway, aiming for the dark crimson sails I spotted above the squat, square ships bearing the Vodina crest. A four-headed sea serpent.

Gods, I hated snakes. One-headed or four.

Based on what Lord Sarros had said before the unfortunate incident of his head being severed, a small crew had traveled with Lord Claus—three additional Lords.

The briny scent of the sea filled the air and dampened my skin as I reached level ground and entered one of the alleys between the dark, quiet buildings. The soles of my boots made no sound against the cracked stone. I prowled toward the edge of a building catty-corner to the Vodina ship, the edges of the gown's hem fluttering soundlessly around me. Years of intensive training with Sir Holland had ensured that my steps were light, my movements precise. The near-silence in the way I could move was one of the reasons some of the oldest servants feared I wasn't truly flesh and blood but some kind of wraith. Sometimes, it felt like I…I was nothing more than a faint trace of a specter—not fully formed.

Tonight was one of those nights.

A dozen feet from the docks, I stopped and waited. Sailors and workers crossed before the mouth of the alley, some hurrying about and others already stumbling. I slipped my hand through the thigh-high slit in the gown, curling my fingers around the handle of my dagger. The iron warmed to my touch, becoming a part of me. I felt the edge of the blade just above its sheath. Shadowstone. The shadowstone dagger was rare in the mortal realm.

A door down the street opened. Raucous laughter staggered out, followed by high-pitched giggles. I stared straight ahead, motionless in the shadows as I thought of my mother—my *family*. They'd probably already moved to the banquet hall, where they would share food and conversation, pretending as if the Lord of the Vodina Isles hadn't just returned their Advisor to them minus his body. Pretending that this wasn't another sign that the kingdom was on the brink of failure. I had never, not once, experienced supper with them. Not even before I'd failed. It hadn't bothered me before. Not often, at least, because I had been *Chosen*. I'd had a purpose.

I have no need of a Consort.

Things had been hard after that. But when I turned eighteen? I was once more veiled and wrapped in that gauzy shroud of a gown and brought to the Shadow Temple as they summoned the Primal of Death.

He hadn't shown.

Things were even harder when I turned nineteen. And then, six months ago, when I turned twenty and found myself once more seated on the throne in that damn veil and gown for the third time? They'd summoned him again, and still, he didn't come. Everything changed then. I hadn't known what *hard* was until then.

Before, they always sent my meals to my room—breakfast, a small lunch, and then dinner. After the first summoning, that changed. They skipped deliveries. Less food was sent. But by the last summoning, they sent nothing at all to my chambers. I had to raid the kitchens during the short window of time where any food worth consuming could be found. But I could deal with that, as I could the lack of other necessities and new clothing to replace well-worn items. Many within Lasania had even less. The worst part was the fact that my mother had hardly spoken to me over the last three years. She barely looked at me, except on nights like this when she wanted to send a message. Weeks passed without me catching even a single glimpse of her, and while she had always been remote, I'd still spent time with her. She would check in on our training and even share a lunch with me every so often. Then there was Tavius, who now behaved with the knowledge that there was little if no consequences for his actions. The hours when I wasn't training with Sir Holland—who believed the Primal would still come for me because I had never told anyone what he'd said, not even my stepsister, Ezra—and I was alone without anyone to spend time with or be close to, were long and passed slowly.

But tonight, she had looked at me. She had spoken to me. And *this* was what she wanted.

A bitter taste pooled in the back of my mouth as a familiar form appeared at the edge of the alley. I recognized the cut of the dark crimson tunic and the shine of his fair hair in the moonlight.

The beat of my heart was steady and slow as I lowered the hood, stepping out of the shadows and into the lamplight. "Lord Claus," I called.

He stopped, turning to the mouth of the alley. His head tilted, and I didn't know if I felt relief or pain or nothing at all as he said, "Handmaiden?"

"Yes."

"Hell," he drawled, stepping into the alley. "Did the bitch Queen change her mind?" Each step toward me was cocksure, unhurried and at ease. "Or did I catch your fancy?" He adjusted himself. "And make up your own mind?"

I waited until he was several feet from me, far enough away from the street. Then again, in this area of Carsodonia, one could scream, and no one would blink an eye. "Something like that."

"Something?" Air whistled between his teeth as his gaze once more fixed south of my face on the swells of my breasts above the gauzy bodice. "I'm betting you know a lot about some things, don't you?"

I wasn't even sure what that meant, and I truly didn't care. "The Queen was quite displeased with your answer."

"I'm sure she was." His thick chuckle faded. Finally looking at my face, he stopped in front of me. "I hope you didn't come all the way down here and wait for me just to tell me that."

"No. I came to deliver a message."

"Is that message under here?" Lord Claus asked, curling a finger in the slit of my gown. "I bet it's nice and warm and…" He pulled on the thin material, revealing my thigh sheath.

"The message is neither tight nor wet nor whatever other coarse word was about to come out of your mouth." I withdrew the dagger.

His gaze shot to mine, his eyes widening briefly with shock. "You've got to be joking."

"The only joke here is that you thought you'd live to see the night through." I paused. "And that you so eagerly stepped into a trap."

Anger crowded out the shock, mottling and twisting his features. Men and their fragile egos. They were so easy to manipulate.

Lord Claus swung a meaty fist at me, just like I knew he would, and I dipped under his arm, rising swiftly behind him. I kicked out, planting my foot in the center of his back. He staggered forward, grunting as he caught himself. Withdrawing his sword, he swept out with it in a wide arc, forcing me to dance back. That was one of the benefits of a larger weapon like a sword. It forced the opponent to keep back and on their toes, risking life and limb to get close. But it was heavier, and only a few could wield one gracefully.

Lord Claus wasn't one of them.

Neither was I.

"You know what I'm going to do?" He stalked forward.

"Let me guess. I'm sure it's something disgusting having to do with your cock and then your sword."

He made a misstep.

"Knew it." I rushed under his attack, aiming low and kicking out, catching him in the midsection. The impact knocked him back a step, but he was quick to regain his footing, swinging out with an elbow that would've landed if I hadn't ducked. He spun, thrusting out with the sword as I whirled to my left. The blade embedded deeply into the wall. Tiny plumes of stone dust exploded into the air, and I turned back, gripping his arm.

He pulled on the sword as I twisted around, slamming my elbow in the general vicinity of his face. Lord Claus cursed as his head jerked back. He tore the sword free, spinning toward me. Blood ran from his nose. He charged me but feinted to the right, twisting and lifting the sword high.

I lurched forward, grabbed his wealth of hair, and pulled hard, yanking him back sharply. The movement caught him off guard, and he lost his balance and started to go down. There was a reason I kept my hair braided and tucked under the cowl of my hood.

Grabbing his sword arm with my free hand, I slammed my elbow down on his wrist. I swept his legs out from under him, and he released the sword with a gasp.

Breathe in.

The sword fell with a heavy thump against the ground, and I brought the shadowstone dagger down. The blade was lightweight, but it was double-edged, each side sharp. *Hold.* The nothingness inside me began to crack, allowing the brief, choking heaviness of before to settle in my throat once more. *I'm a monster* whispered through my head.

"You stupid cu—"

Breathe out. I forced myself to move then. I struck fast, jerking his head up as I stabbed the dagger down. The end of the blade pierced the back of his neck, severing the spine and thus the connection to the brain.

Lord Claus jerked once, and that was it. There was no more sound. Not even a gasp. An internal decapitation was quick, not nearly as gruesome, and *almost* painless.

Exhaling raggedly, I eased the dagger free and gently lowered his too-loose head to the alley floor.

I rose, wiped the blade clean on the side of my gown, and then sheathed it. Turning, I spotted Claus's fallen sword. Warmth gathered in my hands, the heat of my gift pressing against my skin. I clenched my fist, willing the warmth away. Stepping over the Vodina Isle Lord, I picked up the sword and got to work sending the message that would make my mother proud.

All I thought about while hopping down from the ship onto the docks was my lake nestled deep in the Dark Elms.

I was decidedly…*sticky* as I severed the rope anchoring the Vodina ship to shore. The current was always strong in the Stroud Sea. Within minutes, the vessel was already drifting away. It would take days, maybe weeks, but the Vodina Isles Lords would return home.

Just not whole.

Stepping back from the glistening waters, I inhaled deeply. I smelled of blood and pungent, White Horse smoke—an addictive powder derived from an onyx-hued wildflower found in the meadows of the Vodina Isles and often ferried in by merchants. The Lords had been indulging in the smoke, and the scent was probably the source of the dull ache setting up residency in and around my temples. The headaches had been infrequent, starting in the last year, but had become more common. I was beginning to wonder if they would eventually become like those my mother suffered from, causing her to retreat to her private quarters for hours and sometimes even days at a time. Seemed fitting that one of the rare things we had in common would be pain.

At least the dark fabric of my gown hid the worst of my evening's activities, but red spotted my arms and hands, already beginning to dry. Looking back at the drifting ship, I pitied the person who boarded that vessel.

I'd taken a step from the docks when a rough shout ended in a deep groan, and a peal of husky laughter drew my gaze to one of the nearby ships. The outline of two figures was visible in the glow of the streetlamps. One was nearly bent all the way over the railing of the ship, and the other was pressed tightly to their back. Based on how they moved, they were as close as two people could get.

My gaze flicked to where silhouettes leaned across the front of a den across the street. I wasn't the only one watching.

Goodness.

In many parts of Carsodonia, people would be aghast by the behavior of those on the deck. But here in Lower Town, anyone could be as openly improper as they desired. It wasn't the only place debauchery was welcomed.

One side of my lips tugged up, but the smile quickly faded as a bitter, piercing ache went through my chest. The emptiness opened, and I looked down at myself, a little disgusted at the sight of the dried blood on my arms. I didn't have to go to the lake. In reality, I didn't have to do anything now that I'd done what my mother wanted. I was mostly…free. That was one of the small blessings of failing. I was no longer cloistered away, forbidden to travel beyond Wayfair grounds or the Dark Elms. Another blessing was the knowledge that my *purity* was no longer a commodity, a part of the beautifully crafted package. An innocent with a seductress's touch. My lip curled once more. No one else knew that the Primal of Death would not be coming for me, but I did. And there had been no reason for me to guard what shouldn't even be valued.

My gaze flicked back to the couple on the ship. A man had the other pinned to the railing, moving fiercely, his hips plunging with rather…impressive force. Based on the sounds, rather pleasurably.

My thoughts immediately wandered to The Luxe.

Sir Holland had once bemoaned my lack of interaction with my parents, claiming it made me prone to great acts of impulsivity and recklessness over the last three years. And he said this, not even knowing half of my most ill-advised life choices. I didn't know if lack of attention from my mother and stepfather was of any consequence, but I couldn't exactly argue with the knight's perception.

I was impulsive.

I was also very curious.

Which was why it had taken me nearly two out of the past three years to work up the nerve to explore things forbidden to me as the Maiden. To experience what I'd read about in those improper books stored on the shelves of the city Atheneum, too high up for little fingers and curious minds to reach. To find a way to stop from always feeling so hollow.

"Oh, gods," a sharp cry of release echoed from the ship's deck.

The Jade had bathing rooms where I could wash away the blood. The Jade had many things to offer, even to me.

Mind made up, I lifted my hood and quickly crossed the street and headed for the Golden Bridge. In the last three years, I had discovered countless shortcuts, and that was the quickest way to cross the Nye River that separated the Garden District from other less fortunate quarters like Croft's Cross. Where only one to two families occupied freshly painted manors and grand townhomes, and the inhabitants spent coin on luxe material, shared food and drink in rose-filled courtyards, and easily pretended that Lasania wasn't dying. On the other side of the Nye River, people couldn't forget for a minute that the kingdom was doomed, where the only taste of an easier life was for those who crossed the Nye to work in the grand homes there.

Thinking of the bath and other activities awaiting me, I hurried along the narrow alleys and roads and finally made the steep walk up the hill, catching sight of the bridge. Gas streetlamps lined the Golden Bridge, casting a buttery glow across the jacaranda trees running along the riverbank. Before I crossed the river, I entered one of the many shadowy pathways that connected the many corners of the District.

Vines heavy with purple and white sweet pea blossoms covered the sides and tops of the arbors, spreading from one to another and another, forming long tunnels. Only the thinnest bit of moonlight led the way.

I didn't let my mind wander. I refused to think about any of the Lords. If I did, I'd have to think about the nine that'd come before them, which would lead me back to the night I'd failed. And then I'd have to think about how no one would ever be as close to me as the two on the ship had been if they knew who I once was and what I had now become. I only allowed myself to think about washing away the blood and the scent of smoke. Of stealing some time where I could forget and become someone else.

A shrill cry stopped me in my tracks. I wasn't sure how far I'd traveled, but that was nothing like the cries that had come from the deck of the ship.

Wheeling toward the source of the sound, I found the closest exit and hurried out from under the vine tunnels onto an eerily quiet street. Scanning the darkened buildings, I saw the lit stone bridge that joined the two sides of the Garden District and knew exactly where I was.

The Luxe.

The narrow lane didn't come by that moniker because of the stately townhomes. It was the things secreted away in the lush gardens. The establishments with black doors and shutters that promised…well, all different types of splendor and, ironically, exactly where I'd been heading.

I wouldn't have expected The Luxe to be so sedate at this time of night. The gardens were almost always full of people. Tiny bumps prickled my skin as I walked down the stone sidewalk, staying close to the hedges that obscured the gardens.

A man suddenly darted out onto the path several feet ahead of me. I jerked back a step. All I could make out in the glow of the streetlamp was that he wore light-colored breeches, and his white shirt was untucked. He shot past me, seemingly unaware that I was there. I twisted at the waist, watching him disappear into the night.

The sound came again, this time shorter and hoarser. Slowly, I turned around and crept forward, passing a townhome where curtains billowed out from windows, stirred by the warm breeze. My hand drifted inside the slit of my gown to my dagger.

"Do it," the raspy voice broke the silence. "I will never—"

A flash of bright, silvery light spilled out onto the sidewalk and into the empty lane as I reached the corner of the townhome. What in the…?

Telling myself that I needed to mind my business, I did the exact opposite and peered around the side of the building.

My lips parted, but I made no sound. Only because I knew better. But I wished I had minded my business.

In the courtyard of the darkened townhome next door, a man was on his knees, his arms outstretched, and his body bent backward at an angle that wasn't natural. The tendons in his neck stood out in stark relief, and his skin…it looked lit from within. A whiteish light filled the veins of his face, the inside of his throat, and ran down into his chest and stomach.

Standing before him was a…it was a *goddess*. Under the moonlight, her pale blue gown was nearly as translucent as my wedding gown. The dress gathered low over the swells of her breasts and was cinched tightly at the waist and hips, ending in a pool of shimmering fabric around her feet. A glittering sapphire brooch pinned the diaphanous material over one shoulder. Her skin was the color of smooth ivory. Her hair glossy and jet-black.

Spotting a god or goddess in the capital wasn't exactly a shock. They often found their way into the mortal realm, usually out of what I imagined was extreme boredom or the need to carry out some business on behalf of the Primal they served—who rarely, if ever, crossed over.

From what I'd been taught about Iliseeum, their hierarchy was similar to that of the mortal one. Instead of kingdoms, each Primal ruled over a Court, and in place of noble titles, they had gods who answered to their Courts. Ten Primals held Court in Iliseeum. Ten that ruled over everything that lay between the skies and the seas, from love to birth, war and peace, life, and…yes, even death.

But what shocked me was that this goddess had her hand on the man's forehead. She was the source of the white light inside his veins.

The man's mouth stretched open, but no sound came from his throat. Only silvery-white light. It poured from his mouth and eyes, crackling and spitting as it shot up into the sky, stretching higher than the townhome.

Dear gods, it was eather, the very essence of the gods and the Primals. I'd never seen one use it like this, nor did I think it would ever be necessary to kill a mortal in this way. It simply wasn't needed.

The goddess lowered her hand, and the eather vanished, casting the courtyard once more into shadows and fractured moonlight. The man…he didn't make a sound as he fell forward. The goddess stepped out of his way, letting him fall upon the grass face-first as she looked down at her hand, her full lips curling in distaste.

I knew the man was dead. I knew the eather had done that, even if I hadn't known it was possible to use eather in such a manner. Warmth gathered under my skin, and it took everything in me to push the urge down.

The goddess's head swung toward the open door of the townhome. A god walked out, his skin the same pearlescent shade, though his hair was nearly as long as hers, falling down his back like liquid night. He carried something in his hand as he walked down the short set of steps, something small and pale, lifeless and…

Horror turned my skin to ice, even in the heat of Carsodonia's summer. The god carried a…a swaddled babe by its feet. Nausea rose so swiftly, it clogged my throat.

I needed to turn around and truly start minding my business. I did not need the goddess or god to notice me. I had nothing to do with the nightmare happening here. I didn't need to see more than I already had.

The god *tossed* the babe so it landed beside the male mortal at the edge of the goddess's shimmering gown.

None of this concerned me. None of what the gods chose to do concerned *any* mortal. We all knew that while the gods could be benevolent and giving, many could be cruel, and they could be vicious when offended. Every mortal was taught that from birth. The mortal man could've done something to earn their wrath, but that was a *baby*—an innocent that the god had tossed like a piece of trash.

Still, the last thing I should be doing was curling my fingers around the hilt of my shadowstone dagger—a blade that could very well kill a god. But the horror had given way to scalding fury. I was no longer empty and hollow. I was full, brimming with dark rage. I doubted I would be able to take out both of them, but I was confident that I could get *him* before I finally came face to face once more with the Primal of Death. No part of me doubted that my life would end tonight.

And another tiny, hidden part of me, one born the moment my mother's slap had stung my cheek, had stopped *caring* if I lived or died.

I stepped out from around the building—

The only warning was the stir of air around me—a breeze that smelled of something clean and citrusy.

A hand clamped down on my mouth, and a strange jolt went through me at the exact moment an arm folded around me, pinning my arms to my sides. The shock of the contact—the jolt of someone touching me, *touching* my skin with theirs—cost me the split second I had to break the hold. I was jerked back against the hard wall of a chest.

"I wouldn't make a sound if I were you."

Chapter 2

The warning came from a male voice, spoken barely above a whisper directly into my ear as he lifted me off my feet. Shock blasted through me. He carried me back from the courtyard with stunning ease, as if I were nothing more than a small child. And I was not small, not in height nor weight, but the male was also extraordinarily fast. In one heartbeat, he'd taken me into one of the nearby vine tunnels.

"I'm not sure what you planned to do back there," the male spoke again. Alarm rang through me as clear and loud as the bells that rang every morning from the Sun Temple. "But I can assure you, it would've ended disastrously for you."

The moment he let me go, things would end *disastrously* for him.

My heart thumped heavily, and I tried to wiggle free. His hold around my waist only tightened as he stepped farther into the tunnel where only thin streaks of moonlight slipped between the thick trailing plants, and the bushy, sweetly scented blossoms. Stretching my fingers, I reached for the hilt of my dagger as I twisted my head to the side, attempting to dislodge his hand. I was unsuccessful in both endeavors.

Panic-laced frustration burned through me. I wasn't used to being handled like this outside of training or fighting. Not even during my time at The Jade. The sensations of his hand over my mouth, his fingers resting against my cheek, and being held so tightly—being held *at all*—was nearly as overwhelming as the realization that I was *trapped.*

I curled my legs up and kicked out into nothing but air. I did it again and again, swinging my legs back and forward until the muscles in my stomach protested.

"And whatever you're planning to do now…" he continued, standing completely still—my movements hadn't rocked him even an inch. He almost sounded *bored.* "Also won't end well for you."

Breathing heavily against his hand, I allowed my body to go limp so I could *think.* The man was strong, able to hold my dead weight with ease. I wasn't going to break free by struggling like a wild animal.

Be smart, Sera. Think. I focused on the feel of him, trying to gauge his height. The chest pressed against my back was broad and hard…and cold. As was the hand against my mouth. It reminded me of how my skin felt after entering the lake. I shifted, drawing a leg up to run my booted foot down his leg to find where his knee was.

"On second thought…" His voice was full of smoke, a decadent drawl as I drew my foot up the side of his leg. There was something odd about his voice. It had a shadowy lilt that struck a chord of familiarity— "I am thoroughly interested in exactly what you're attempting to do."

My eyes narrowed as fury eroded the panic. I found the curve of his knee and then jerked my leg up to gain enough space to deliver a brutal—

He chuckled darkly, sidestepping my kick. "No, thank you."

The smothered sound I made against his palm was one born of pure, unfettered rage.

That midnight laugh came again, quieter, but I felt it along every inch of my back and hips. "You're a feisty little thing, aren't you?"

Feisty? Little? *Thing*?

I was neither little nor a *thing*, but I *was* feeling all kinds of feisty.

"Also, a bit ungrateful," he added, his cool breath against my cheek. *My cheek.* Air stilled in my throat. My hood had slipped back in my struggle, not nearly covering as much of my face as it normally would. "They would've killed you before you had a chance to do whatever ill-advised idea sprang into your head. I saved your life, and you're trying to *kick* me?"

My hands balled into fists as I twisted my head again. He suddenly stiffened against me, his body crackling with tension.

"Is that all, Madis?" a voice reached us from outside the tunnel, distant and feminine.

"Yes, Cressa," came the answer, spoken in a deep voice laden with power.

It was the god and goddess. I stilled completely against my captor.

"For now." Annoyance dripped from those two words spoken by this Cressa.

"We must be close," Madis answered.

There was a beat of silence, and then Cressa said, "Taric, you know what to do with them."

"Of course," a second male answered.

"Since we're here, we might as well enjoy ourselves," Madis remarked. Enjoy themselves? After he'd just slaughtered a babe?

"Whatever," the goddess muttered, and then there was quiet.

Three of them. *Taric. Madis. Cressa.* I repeated those names over and over as silence fell around us. I wasn't familiar with them and I had no idea what Court they belonged to, but I would not forget their names.

The male that held me shifted his stance, and then his breath touched my cheek once more. "If I remove my hand, you promise you won't do something silly like scream?"

I nodded against his chest. Screaming was never on my priority list.

He hesitated. "I have a feeling I'm going to regret this," he said with a sigh that caused me to grit my teeth. "But I guess I'll add this to the ever-growing list of things I end up regretting."

His hand lifted from my mouth, but it didn't stray far, sliding down so that his fingers curled around my chin. I dragged in deep breaths as I tried to ignore the sensation of his chilled flesh against mine. I waited for him to release me.

He didn't.

"You were going to go after those gods," he stated after a moment. "What were you thinking?"

That was a good question since mortals were forbidden from interfering in the actions of gods. To do so was considered an insult against the Primal they served. But I had an answer. "They slaughtered a babe."

He was quiet for a moment. "That is none of your concern."

I tensed at his words. "The slaughter of an innocent child should be of everyone's concern."

"You'd think," he replied, and I frowned. "But it is not. You knew what they were when you saw them. You know what you should've done."

I did, and I didn't care. "Do you also believe we're supposed to leave the bodies there?"

"I doubt they left them," he answered.

Whenever gods killed a mortal, they left the bodies behind, usually to serve as a warning. If they didn't, where did they take them? And why? Why had they done this? Could anyone else have been in that home?

I straightened my head. His hand followed. "Are you going to let me go?" I demanded in a quiet voice.

"I don't know," he answered. "I'm not sure I'm ready for whatever it is that you're about to do."

I stared at the mass of dark vines above me. "Let me go."

"So you can run back out there and get yourself killed?" he countered.

"That's none of *your* concern."

"You're right." A pause. "And you're also wrong. But since saving your life is *still* interfering with my evening plans, I want to make sure my generous and benevolent actions are worth what I lost by coming to your aid."

I couldn't believe what I was hearing. "I did not ask for your help."

"But you have it nonetheless."

"Let me go, and you can get back to your oh-so-important evening plans that apparently do not involve having the common decency to care about senseless murders," I retorted.

"There are a couple of things you need to understand," he drawled, his thumb sliding along my jaw, causing me to stiffen at the unexpected and unfamiliar caress. "You have no idea what my evening plans *were*, but yes, they *were* very important. Nor do you know what I do and do not care about."

My face scrunched. "Thanks for sharing?"

"But you are right about one thing," he went on as if I hadn't spoken. "There isn't a decent bone in the entirety of my body. So, no, I do not have this thing you call *common decency*."

"Well, that's…something to be proud of."

"I am," he agreed. "But I will pretend to be decent right now and let you go. However, if you attempt to run back out there, I will catch you. You will not be faster than me, and the whole thing will just annoy me."

His devotion to stopping me—a complete stranger—from getting myself killed actually seemed like a rather decent thing to do. But I wasn't going to point that out. "Have I given you any indication that I care about annoying you?" I retorted.

"I have a feeling you don't. But I'm hoping you discovered whatever smidgen of common sense exists inside you and have decided to use it."

My entire body prickled with anger. "That was rude."

"Be that as it may, do you understand?" he asked.

"And if I say no? Will you stand here and hold me all night?" I spat.

"Since my plans are now shot, I do have some spare time on my hands."

"You have got to be kidding," I snarled.

"Actually, no."

Every part of my being ached with the desire to punch him. Hard. "I understand."

"Good. To be honest, my arms were getting tired."

Wait. Was he insinuating that I was—?

He released me, and gods, he was *tall.* There had to be a good foot between the ground and my feet based on how hard I landed. I stumbled forward, and his hands clasped around my arms, steadying me. Another *decent* act I was not even remotely grateful for.

Tearing myself free, I whirled toward him as I reached for my dagger.

"Now you've got to be kidding me." The male sighed, snapping forward.

He was as fast as a strike of lightning, catching my wrist before I could even free my blade. I gasped. Dressed in all black, he was nothing more than a thick shadow. He yanked me toward his chest as he spun us, forcing me back. Within a few too-quick heartbeats, he had me trapped again, this time between the vine-covered wall and his body.

"Dammit." I leaned back, lifting my right leg—

"Can we not do this?" He shifted, simultaneously wedging a thigh between mine and catching my other wrist, bringing my hands together.

I fought, using every ounce of strength I had as he lifted my hands, stretching my arms above my head and then pinning my wrists to the wall. Flowers broke free, raining down on us. I drew up my other leg. I just needed to get space—

"I'll take that as a no." He leaned in then, pressing his body to mine.

I froze. Air lodged in my throat. There didn't seem to be a part of me that wasn't in contact with him. My legs. Hips. Stomach. Breasts. I could feel him, his hips against my stomach, his stomach and lower part of his chest against my breasts—his skin through his clothing, cool as the first touch of autumn. My senses were a chaotic mess as I forced air into my lungs—a breath that was fresh and citrusy. I couldn't even smell the sweet peas beyond his scent. No one—not even Sir Holland or anyone I fought who knew what I was—got this close to me.

I hadn't seen his other hand move, but I felt it slide behind my head, becoming an immovable wedge between me and the wall. "There's something I need you to understand." His whisper filled with tendrils of darkness again. "While I'm not suggesting you *don't* attempt to fight me—you do whatever you feel you need to—you should know that you will not win. Ever."

There was a finality to his words that sent a tremor through my captured hands. I tipped my head back and looked up…and up. He was well over a foot taller than me, maybe even as tall as the Primal of Death was. A shiver of unease prickled the nape of my neck. Most of his face was cast in shadow, and all I could see was the hard line of his jaw. When his head tilted into a slice of moonlight, I saw him.

This man was…he was absolutely, without a doubt, the most *stunning* man I'd ever seen. And I'd seen some gorgeous men. Some from here within Lasania, and others from kingdoms that stretched into the east. Some had finer, more symmetrical features than the one holding me to the wall, but none were put together so perfectly, so…sensually as this man's. Even in the moonlight, his skin was a lustrous, golden-brown color, reminding me of wheat. His cheekbones were high and broad, his nose straight as a blade, and his mouth…it was full and wide. He had the kind of face an artist would love to shape with clay or capture with charcoal. But there was also a coldness to his features. As if the Primals themselves had crafted the lines and planes and forgot to add the warmth of humanity.

I looked up to his eyes.

Silver.

Eyes that were an incredible, luminous shade of silver, bright as the moon itself. Beautiful. That was all I could think at first, and then…I saw the light behind his pupils, the wispy tendrils of *eather*.

"You're a *god*," I whispered.

He said nothing while instinct fired through me, urging me to either submit or run—and to do either of those two things fast. It was a warning, a reckoning that screamed I wasn't even *inches* away from one of the most dangerous predators in any realm.

But I…I couldn't get over how he looked no more than a handful of years older than me, somewhere between Ezra's and Tavius's ages. That most likely wasn't the case. He could be centuries older. But other than the night I was to be married, I'd never been this close to a being from Iliseeum before. It unnerved me how young he appeared.

It struck me then that I'd tried to kick a god—multiple times. I'd tried to *stab* a god.

And he…he hadn't struck me down.

He hadn't even hurt me. All he'd done was stop me from harming myself. And, well, now he was holding me here. Still, he could've done much, much worse.

Could that mean that he was from the Shadowlands Court and answered to the Primal of Death? My stomach tumbled. I had no idea if any of the gods that served the Primal of Death knew about me since any deal struck between a mortal and a god was known only to those two, but this deal had been different. It was quite possible that every god within the Shadowlands knew that the Primal had a Consort he hadn't claimed, even though he'd bartered for one.

Thick, wavy hair fell against this god's cheeks as he dipped his head. His gaze snared mine, and I couldn't look away—not even if the Primal of Death himself appeared beside us. Not when the wisps of eather swirled through the silver of his eyes.

My throat tightened, but it was a surreal feeling to have someone look upon my face so intently. After seventeen years of wearing the Veil of the Chosen, I wasn't used to it. Being so seen left me feeling…vulnerable, which was why I opted to keep my face hidden beneath a hood whenever I wasn't around my mother, who now preferred that my face be shown as if it were a reminder of my failure. As silly and nonsensical as it was, a sense of wonder bubbled up.

"Fuck," he murmured.

A tripping motion went through my chest. Did he know who I was? If so, how was that possible? I'd been kept so hidden. Not even the Shadow Priests had ever seen my face while knowing who I was. "What?"

His gaze flicked over my features so intensely that each and every freckle across my nose and cheek started to tingle. His eyes closed briefly, and as close as we were to each other, I could see just how thick the fringe of his lashes was as they swept back up. "Every mortal knows better than to interfere with a god."

I swallowed hard, feeling all the building wonder collapse. "I do know. But—"

"They killed an innocent," he cut me off and glanced up toward the entrance of the vine tunnel. "You still know better."

My fingers curled helplessly in his grasp. I knew I shouldn't talk back. I should thank him for his aid—help I didn't ask for—and then put as much distance between us as possible. But that wasn't what I did. It was like I had no control over my mouth. And maybe that was the recklessness that Sir Holland bemoaned every chance he got. Maybe it was that small part of me that had stopped caring. "Shouldn't you be more concerned about the fact that they killed an innocent child than what I was about to do?" I demanded. "Or do you not care because you're a god?"

Those eyes burned even brighter. Dread blossomed in the pit of my stomach, and a trickle of fear entered my blood. Mortals did not talk back to a god. I also knew that. "Those three will pay for what they've done. You can be assured of that."

A chill erupted over my skin, despite him not acknowledging my ill-advised behavior. He spoke as if he had the power and authority to carry that out. As if he *wanted* to see to it personally.

His attention snapped in the direction of the lane again, and then his gaze met mine. "They're coming," he warned.

Before I could say a word, he lowered my arms and let go. There wasn't time to make use of the freedom. The god grasped my hips and lifted me off my feet, sliding a hand down the *bare* length of my left thigh. He hooked my left leg around his waist. A ripple of shock whipped through me. What in the—?

"Wrap your other leg around me," he commanded quietly against the side of my head. "You do not want them to see you."

I didn't know if it was his ominous tone or how unbalanced his hold and touch had left me, but I obeyed. Curling my right leg around his waist, I gripped the front of his shirt, suspecting that *he* didn't want to be seen by them, either. "If you try anything…" I warned.

His head dipped, and I sucked in a startled breath as I felt his lips curve into a smile against my cheek. They were as cool as the rest of him. "You'll do what?" he whispered. "Go for that weapon on your thigh again?"

"Yes."

"Even though you know you wouldn't be fast enough to deliver a blow."

My grip on his shirt tightened. "*Yes*."

He chuckled softly, and I felt it from my hips to my breasts. "Shh."

Had he just *shushed* me? My entire body went as tight as a bowstring. The bridge of his nose coasted over the curve of my cheek, and I went taut for an entirely different reason. His lips were near mine, brushing just the corner of my mouth. A riot of sensations rocketed through me, a wild mix of disbelief, anger, and something like the *anticipation* I felt when I entered The Jade. I couldn't understand that. This wasn't the same. I didn't know this male. It didn't matter that many mortals would eagerly exchange places with me as we were often drawn to gods like night-blooming roses were to the moon. But one such as he was dangerous. He was a predator, no matter how beautiful or benevolent he was.

But it was so rare that anyone got this close to me and allowed their skin to encounter mine. To touch me. Those who did had been strangers, too. Except when they touched me, I wasn't really me. I was as nameless as they often were when I let them pull me into shadowy alcoves or behind closed doors and into rooms where things weren't meant to last. Where I wore a veil even though my face was bare.

But I felt like *me* in this moment. More than I had in years.

"Kiss me," he ordered.

My temper flared. I hated being told what to do. And if I were being honest, that had started long ago. Maybe that was one of the reasons I'd been rejected. But his *demand* made sense. It would appear quite odd for us to just stand here like this, doing nothing but glaring at each other.

So, I kissed him.

A god.

The contact of my mouth against his caused my stomach to pitch like it did when I came too close to the edges of the Cliffs of Sorrow. His lips *were* cool, but they were somehow soft yet firm, a strangely enticing juxtaposition as they moved against mine. It was the only thing about him that moved. His mouth. The hand on my left thigh and the one on my hip remained still. He was motionless, and I didn't know why I did what I did next. Could've been that *impulsivity*. Could've been my irritation over being in this situation. Could've been how *still* he was. And if I were being completely honest with myself, it could've been the possibility that he was from the Shadowlands and served the

Primal who'd stolen every chance I had to save my kingdom. All those reasons were probably wrong, but I didn't care.

I caught his lower lip between my teeth and bit down. Not hard enough to draw blood, but his entire body jerked, and then he wasn't still any longer.

The god pushed in as his head tilted, deepening the kiss. Nothing about his mouth was soft then. He parted my lips with a fierce stroke of his tongue, and a tight shudder rolled through me at the sharp graze against my lower lip. His teeth. *Fangs.* Oh, gods, I'd somehow forgotten about that. Fear lit my veins because I knew how sharp they were. I knew what a god could do with them. But something else entered my blood, a wicked and decadent, heady thrill as I flicked my tongue over his. He tasted of something woodsy and smoky—like whiskey. A sound came from him, deep within his throat, and it sent my heart to pounding.

The hand on my thigh curled, his fingers pressing into my skin, becoming an icy brand that somehow scorched my flesh. A wild shiver shimmered through me as his hand left my hip and worked its way between the wall and the back of my head. His fingers curled into my hair, surely loosening the pins keeping my braid in place. I really didn't care as he drew my head back, as he…kissed me like he wouldn't allow a single part of my mouth to go unexplored. As if he'd been waiting for ages to do this. I knew that was a silly, whimsical thought, but I kissed him back, utterly forgetting why we were doing this, and only vaguely aware of the sound of footsteps and the deep laughter of an intruder—of the god.

Were all kisses from a god as dangerously intoxicating as this one? That too-faint *smidgen* of common sense told me I should be worried. What if the Primal did come for me? What if he changed his mind, and I had kissed one of his gods? I should care, but instead I kissed the god even harder because I refused to think about that damn Primal. I let myself exist in the moment.

This felt chaotic, like when I slipped under the surface of the lake and stayed until my lungs burned, and my heart raced, just to see how far I could push myself.

And I felt that now—that need to see how far I could push this. I slid my hands up his shirt, over his chest. The edges of his hair brushed my knuckles. I sank my fingers into the silky strands and pulled him closer. I tipped my hips against his lower stomach. The hand on my thigh slid up and around, over the curve of my ass. The thin undergarment was no barrier against the press of his hand.

He squeezed the flesh there, wringing a gasp from me as he slid his tongue over mine. He drew my lower lip between his teeth and nipped. I cried out at the elicit shock of pleasure and the pain thrumming through my body. His tongue flicked over my lip, soothing the biting sting.

Then his mouth was gone. His forehead rested against mine, and for a handful of seconds, there was nothing but silence between us. Nothing but my pounding heart and his shallow breaths as his hand slid back to my hip. Another moment passed, and then he slowly lowered me to my feet. I forced my fingers to open, to let go of his hair. My hands fell to his chest once more.

Under my palm, his heart beat as fast as mine.

I opened my eyes as the seconds ticked by. He remained there, his forehead against mine, one of his hands still a shield between my head and the wall.

"You," he murmured, his voice sultry and thick. "You were quite convincing."

"So were you," I said, a bit breathlessly.

"I know. I'm very skilled at pretending."

Pretending? *Pretending* to do what? Enjoy himself? Kissing me? My eyes narrowed as I shoved him away.

He stepped back, laughing softly as he ran a hand over his head, dragging his hair back from his face.

I stepped away from the wall, turning my attention to the darkened pathway, but I saw nothing in the filtered moonlight. I lifted a finger to my still-throbbing lips, then withdrew it and looked down to see a spot of darkness on the tip of my finger. He'd…

He'd drawn blood.

My head snapped up. "You—"

The god stepped in, folding his hand around my wrist. He lifted my arm, and before I could even wonder what he was about, his mouth closed over my finger, and he sucked. I felt the hard pull in a most shameful way—all the way to my core in a rush of hot, damp heat.

Good gods…

Slowly, he drew his mouth from my finger as his gaze flicked up, catching mine. "My apologies. I should've elaborated. I'm very good at pretending to enjoy things I do not, but I was not pretending when I had your tongue in my mouth."

I stood there as he released my wrist, at an utter loss for what to say for several seconds. "It…it's very inappropriate to take my blood,"—I heard myself saying—"when I don't even know your name."

"That was the only inappropriate thing about what just occurred?"

"Well, no. There was a whole lot of inappropriate in there."

He chuckled again, the sound rich like dark chocolate. I eyed him. Maybe I was wrong about who he served, or at the very least, he had no knowledge of who I truly was. If he did, I doubted he would've kissed me. I started to ask if he knew who I was but stopped, realizing I had to be careful in case he didn't.

"Why did you stop me from going after those gods?" I asked, curling my hand—and the finger that had been in his mouth.

His brows pinched. "Do I need a reason other than stopping someone from getting themselves killed?"

"Normally, I would say no. But you're a god, and you said there wasn't a decent bone in your body."

He faced me. "Just because I'm not mortal doesn't mean I run around murdering people or allowing them to get themselves killed."

I sent a pointed look in the direction of the tunnel entrance.

His chin dipped, his features sharpening in the silvery light. "I am not them," he said, low and deadly soft.

Hairs along the nape of my neck rose, and I fought the urge to take a step back. "I guess I'm lucky?"

His gaze flickered over me. "I'm not sure how lucky you are."

My back stiffened. What in the hell was that supposed to mean?

"And perhaps I do have one decent bone in my body," he added with a shrug.

I stared at him, and it took a moment for me to refocus on what was important, which wasn't the quantity of decent bones. "The god that walked past… He couldn't sense you?"

He shook his head. "No."

This god had to be very powerful. I'd read that only the strongest could hide their presence from others—very much like a Primal. I had a feeling that my early suspicions were correct. He hadn't only been seeking to hide me but also himself.

He started to turn from me. "You should go home."

"Are you?" I retorted, annoyed by how quickly and easily he dismissed me.

He shot me an incredulous look. Mortals didn't ask questions of the gods—especially impolitely. Tension crept into my muscles as I braced myself for anger or condemnation.

Instead, a slow grin tugged at his lips. Standing under the fractured rays of moonlight, I saw that the curve of his lips softened his features, almost warmed them. "No."

He didn't elaborate, and that was fine. I didn't need to know. It was far past time for me to remove myself from this god's presence before I became even more annoyed.

Or worse yet, did something else impulsive.

Besides, I had plans—ones that had changed from earlier.

"Well, this was…interesting." I stepped around him and started for the entryway. I could practically feel his stare boring into my back. "Have a good night."

"Are you going home?"

"No."

"Where are you going?"

I didn't answer. God or not, it was none of his business, and I wouldn't linger just for him to attempt to send me home again. Still, it felt…odd walking away from him. It was strange how *wrong* it felt, and that wrongness made no sense. He was a god. I was a failed Maiden. He'd stopped me from doing something rash. We'd kissed out of necessity, and it had been *pleasant*. Okay. It had been more than that, and I feared I'd inevitably spend my life comparing every future kiss to this one, but none of that explained the bizarre feeling I had that I shouldn't be walking away from him.

But I did.

I walked away from the god, leaving him in the shadowy tunnel, and I didn't look back. Not once.

Chapter 3

Once clear of the tunnel and bathed in the light of the streetlamp, I yanked up my hood and forced myself to keep walking, even though the strange sensation of wrongness lingered. I really didn't have the mental space to even begin understanding why I felt this way. As I hung a right, I figured that was something I could dwell on later while trying to fall asleep.

I drew in a deep breath. Nearing the edge of the townhome, I realized I no longer smelled of the White Horse or blood but of sweet pea and the god's fresh, citrusy scent.

Swallowing a groan as the courtyard of the townhome came into view, I prepared myself in case they hadn't taken the bodies. I allowed that veil of emptiness to return, for me to go to a place where nothing could scare me, could hurt me.

But in the pale shine of the moon, I saw that the courtyard was empty.

Skin pimpling, I passed through the open gateway and headed down the stone walkway, a patch of ground snagging my gaze. I stopped. The area where the mortal man had knelt was scorched as if a fire had been lit there. No blood. No clothing. Nothing but burnt grass.

"You going in there?"

I spun at the sound of the god's voice, hand halting above the hilt of my dagger. "Gods," I spat, heart racing as he stood there, the hood of his black, sleeveless tunic up, creating a shadow over his face. I hadn't even heard him follow me.

"I apologize," he said, slightly bowing his head. I saw then that he wore a silver band around his right biceps. "For startling you."

My eyes narrowed. He didn't sound sorry at all. To be honest, he sounded *amused*. That annoyed me, but what irritated me more was the soft leap I felt in my chest, followed by the buzz of warmth and *rightness*.

Maybe it was my near-empty stomach causing the sensation. That made more sense.

He strode forward, and again, his height struck me. It made me feel *dainty*, and I didn't like that. His hooded head turned toward the area I'd been staring at. "When Cressa used the eather and it touched the ground, this is what happened," he said, bending down to run his palm over the grass. Sooty ash darkened his hand as he looked up at the open doorway of the townhouse. "You were going inside."

"I was."

"Why?"

I folded my arms. "I wanted to see if I could find any reason for why they did that."

"As do I." The god rose, wiping his hand on his dark breeches.

"You don't know?" I studied him, understanding dawning. This god hadn't just happened along. He'd most likely already been in the passageway before I even walked past it, or he'd at least been nearby. "You were watching them, weren't you?"

"I *was* following them." He drew out the word. "Before I decided to not let you get yourself killed—which you still haven't thanked me for."

I ignored that last part. "Why were you following them?"

"I saw them moving about in the mortal realm and wanted to see what they were up to."

I wasn't sure if he was being honest. It seemed like an awfully big coincidence for him to have chosen to follow them the night they killed a mortal male and a babe.

His head turned to me. "I imagine if I advise you to go home, you will do the exact opposite once more."

"I imagine you won't like my response if you advise such a thing once again," I returned.

A soft chuckle came from inside the shadowy hood. "I don't know about that. I actually might," he said. My brows knitted when he started forward. "We might as well investigate together."

Together.

Such a common word, but it too felt strange.

The god was already at the steps of the townhome. For someone so tall and large to be so silent had to be the result of some godly magic. Avoiding the charred area on the grass, I quickly joined him.

Neither of us spoke as we entered the silent home. There was a door on either side of the small entryway and a set of stairs leading to the second floor. The god went left, into what appeared to be a sitting room, and I headed straight, climbing the stairs. Only the creaks of my steps broke the eerie silence of the home. A gas lamp burned faintly at the top of the stairs, situated on a narrow table. There were two bedchambers, one outfitted with a single bed, a desk, and a wardrobe. Upon closer inspection, I found breeches folded and shirts hung, the size that would fit someone of the mortal male's stature. There was nothing in the small bathing chamber of note. I backed out and made my way to the bedchamber at the end of the hall. I nudged open the door. Another lamp burned beside a tidied bed. The crib sitting at the foot of it turned my stomach.

That veil I imagined wearing wasn't as in place as I believed it to have been.

Slowly, I entered the room. A tiny blanket lay in the crib. I reached in, feeling the soft fabric. I'd never thought about having children. As the Maiden, it wasn't even a *desire* that could take shape as I grew and got older. It was never part of the plan because even if I had been successful and managed to make the Primal of Death fall in love with me, creation of a child wasn't possible between a mortal and a Primal.

But a babe was truly innocent and relied on everyone around it, including the gods, to keep it safe. Killing one was unforgivable. The back of my eyes burned. If I had a child, or if any descendant of mine had been harmed, I would burn through both realms just so I could flay the skin from the body of the one who'd hurt them.

Breathe in. I held my breath until the churning in my stomach stopped. Until I felt nothing. Once I did, I exhaled long and slow and turned away from the crib and the tiny blanket inside.

My gaze skipped over a deep green divan. Someone had draped an ivory-hued silk wrapper over the back. I went to the wardrobe and opened the doors. Gowns hung neatly beside brightly colored tunics. Undergarments were folded and placed on the shelves among other garments, but there was more than enough room for the clothing that had been in the wardrobe next door.

Could someone else be in this house? Maybe the mother? Or had she not been home? "Where is the—?"

"Downstairs."

"Gods," I gasped, nearly coming out of my skin as I whirled to where the god stood, leaning against the doorjamb, arms crossed over his broad chest, the hood of his tunic still up. "How are you so quiet?"

Better yet, how long had he been standing there?

"Skill," he said.

"Perhaps you should alert someone to your arrival," I snapped.

"Perhaps."

I glared at him, even though he couldn't see my face.

"If you're looking for the owner of those gowns, I imagine that is who I found downstairs near the entry to the kitchen," he offered. "Well, I found a charred section of floor and a lone slipper, anyway."

I turned back to the wardrobe. "I don't think the man I saw and the woman shared a room here," I said, gesturing at the wardrobe. An idea formed. "Is there a study?"

"There appeared to be one, to the right of the foyer."

"Did you find anything?" I brushed past him, wholly aware of how he unfolded his arms and turned, following in that silent way of his.

"I only gave it a cursory glance," he said as I reached the top of the stairs. "I wanted to make sure the home was empty first." He paused. "Unlike some. And by *some*, I mean you."

I rolled my eyes as the steps groaned under my feet. The god followed, close enough behind me that my back tingled, yet his steps made no noise—while I sounded like a herd of cattle coming down the stairs.

"What would you have done if you'd discovered the home wasn't empty?" he asked as we reached the first floor.

"I would've celebrated, knowing that at least someone survived," I told him, walking to the study. Moonlight filtered in through the window, casting light over the small chamber.

"Would you?"

I glanced over my shoulder as I rounded the desk. The god had gone off to the side, checking out the mostly empty shelving units built into the walls. "Would you not have?" I looked down at the desk. The surface was cleared with the exception of a small lamp.

"I would think surviving while your child and someone you shared your home with are both killed would be a hard life to celebrate," he said, pulling open the center drawer. Nothing but quills and closed ink jars.

I closed it and moved to the one on the right, a deeper one. "I guess you're right. She would be in the Vale," I said, speaking about the territory within the Shadowlands where those who had earned peace upon death spent an eternity in paradise.

"If that is where they went," he murmured, stopping to pluck a small wooden box off a shelf.

My heart skipped. Did he think they could've gone to the Abyss, where all beings with a soul paid for evil deeds they committed while alive—both god and mortal? There was no way the babe had gone there. But the adults? Well, they could've done any number of things during their lives to earn themselves several lifetimes of horror.

I thought of the Vodina Isles Lords. A horror I would likely become acquainted with when my time came.

I shook my head, closing the drawer and moving on to the bottom, finding a thick, leather-bound ledger. I pulled it out, placing it on the desk. Quickly untying the cord, I opened the cover to find scribblings on pages and several pieces of loose, folded parchment. What I'd been searching for was the second piece of paper I unfolded.

I turned on the lamp and quickly scanned the document. It was an entailment of the townhome between the Crown and a Miss Galen Kazin, daughter of Hermes and Junia Kazin and Mister Magus Kazin, son of Hermes and Junia Kazin.

"Find something?"

Unsurprisingly, the god had drifted closer without being heard. "It's an entailment of the property. They were brother and sister. That is if that was who lived here." Which also meant that if Galen Kazin was the child's mother, she was also unwed. Among the working classes, that wasn't exactly rare, nor was it considered shameful. But to afford a home within the Garden District, one had to be descended from nobility or have found wealth through business. It was less common to find unwed mothers here. "I wonder where the father is."

"Who's to say the man outside wasn't the father? Maybe it wasn't the brother." He paused. "Or, he could've been both."

My lip curled. Even if that were the case, it was an unlikely reason for why the gods had killed them and the babe. Based on the stories I'd read about the gods and Primals, I doubted they would even bat an eyelash at that.

There was nothing else to be found in the study to give any indication as to why the gods had killed them. Though I wasn't exactly sure what I could've found that would have answered that. A journal chronicling their misdeeds?

"You're frustrated."

I lifted my gaze to where the god stood at the window overlooking the courtyard, his back to me. "Is it that obvious?"

"It's not like this was fruitless. We know that they were likely siblings and that one was an unwed mother. We have the parents' names."

"True." But what did that even tell us? I closed the ledger, retying the cord. "I have a question."

"Do you?"

I nodded. "It might seem like an offensive thing to ask."

The god had glided forward. That was exactly how he moved—as if his booted feet didn't touch the floor. He stopped on the other side of the desk. "I have a feeling that won't stop you."

I almost grinned again. "Why are you curious about the gods killing mortals? And I don't mean to insinuate that you don't care. Although you did say you weren't decent—"

"With the exception of the one bone," he interjected, and it sounded like he smiled.

"Yes, with that exception."

He was quiet for a long moment, and I could feel his stare, even though I couldn't see it. "Let me ask you the same question. Why do you care? Did you know them?"

I crossed my arms once more. "Why do I care? Besides the fact that they killed a babe?"

He nodded.

"I didn't know them." Blowing out a breath, I looked around the study, seeing books that would likely never be read again, and knick-knacks whose value would no longer be appreciated. "When a god kills a mortal, it's because of some offense," I started. That was the tricky thing about the gods. They decided what warranted consequence, what was an offense, what was punishable, and what the punishment would be. "And you all like to make an…example out of such things."

His head inclined. "Some do."

"The act is to send a message to others. What the offense was is clearly known," I continued. "Gods don't kill in the middle of the night, take the body, and leave nothing behind. It's almost as if they didn't want this to be known. And *that* is, well, not normal."

"You'd be correct." He drew a finger along the edge of the desk as he walked, the silent slide of his fingertip catching my attention. "That is why I am so interested. This isn't the first time they've killed like this."

I dragged my gaze from his hand. "It isn't?"

He shook his head. "In the last month, they've killed at least four others like this. They took some of the bodies with them, and a rare few were left behind. But with not a single clue as to why."

I racked my brain to see if I remembered hearing anything about any mysterious disappearances or strange deaths, but I hadn't.

"Now we're at seven mortals." He drew his finger up the glass globe of the lamp. "Most were in their second and third decades of life. Two females. Four males. And the babe. As far as I know, they have never killed one as young as the child tonight. The only thing they had in common was that they were all from Lasania," he said, curling his finger around the beaded chain. With a click, he extinguished the lamp, returning the chamber to the moonlight. "One of them was someone most would consider…a friend."

I hadn't expected that. It wasn't that gods couldn't make friends with mortals. Some had even fallen in love with them. Not many, though. Most had simply fallen into lust, but friendships *could* be formed.

"You're surprised," he noted.

I frowned, wondering exactly what had revealed that. "I guess it surprises me that gods can be bothered by the death of a mortal when they will outlive us no matter what. I know that's wrong," I quickly added. "A murdered friend who happens to be mortal is still a…friend."

"Yes."

And it had to be hard to lose one. I didn't have many friends. Well, come to think of it, if I didn't count Ezra and Sir Holland, then I didn't have *any* friends. Still, I imagined losing a friend would be a lot like losing a part of yourself. I felt the emptiness begin to leave me with an aching pierce to my chest. I didn't try to bring it back. There was no reason to at this moment. "I'm sorry about your friend."

In the blink of an eye, he'd rounded the desk and was only a handful of feet from me. The urge to step back hit me at the same moment the desire to step forward did. I remained where I was, refusing to do either.

"As am I," he said after a moment.

I searched the shadows gathered inside his hood, unable to make out even a single feature. "But you…you knew exactly what they were doing. That's why you followed them. Why didn't you stop them?"

"They got here before me." That finger of his had returned to the desk, trailing along the corner. "By the time I found them, it was already too late. I had planned to capture at least one of them. You know, to *chat*. But, alas, my plans changed."

My heart turned over heavily as I craned my neck to look up at him. "As I said before, I didn't ask you to step in." I glanced at his hand, at the long finger gliding over the smooth surface of the desk. "You *chose* to change your plans."

"I guess I did." He dipped his head, and I wondered exactly how much of my features he could see now. A shivery awareness danced over my skin. I wondered if he would— "To be honest, I find myself quite annoyed with that decision. If I had allowed you to continue on your merry way, it would've most certainly ended with your death, but I would've accomplished what I set out to do."

I wasn't quite sure how to respond to that. "Like I said, I guess I'm lucky."

"And as I said before," he replied, his idle touch of the desk replaced by a tight grip, one that bleached his knuckles white. I unfolded my arms, senses alert as my pulse ticked up. "Are you really?"

The same reaction swept through me. I stiffened as the keen awareness vanished. A long gap of silence reigned, wherein he lifted a hand and lowered his hood. When his face had been hidden, I'd felt the intensity of his stare. Now, I saw it.

"I know you're curious about why those gods did what they did, but when you walk from this house, you need to leave this alone. It doesn't involve you."

His demand dug into every wrong cord inside me. What little control I had over my life, I *owned*. Tension crept into my neck as I held his stare. "Only I get to determine what does and doesn't involve me. What I do and do not do is of no concern to anyone. Not even a god."

"Do you really believe that?" he asked in that same too-soft voice, the kind that stretched my nerves.

"Yes." Slowly, I inched my hand toward my dagger. He'd shown no ill will toward me, but I wasn't taking any chances.

"You'd be wrong."

My fingers brushed the hilt of my dagger. "Maybe I am, but that doesn't change the fact that you have no say about what I do."

"You'd also be wrong about that," he replied.

I was totally wrong. In reality, no one superseded a god. Not even Royalty. The authority of mortal Crowns was more for show than anything else. The true power lay with the Primals and their gods. And all Primals, all gods, answered to the King of Gods. The Primal of Life.

But that didn't mean I had to like it, nor the predatory way he looked at me. "If you're trying to intimidate or scare me into obeying you, you can stop. It's not working. I don't scare."

"You should be afraid of many things."

"I'm afraid of nothing, and that includes you."

In one heartbeat, he was standing several feet from me. In the next, he towered over me, and his fingers were curled around my chin. The shock of how fast he'd moved paled in comparison to the jolt of static that followed and erupted across my skin at the contact of his hand. It was stronger. Sharper now.

His flesh was so very cold as he tilted back my head. He didn't dig his fingers in, nor was his hold tight. It was just…*there*, cold and yet burning like an icy brand.

"How about now?" he asked. "Are you afraid?"

Though his grip wasn't firm, I found it difficult to swallow as my heart fluttered like a trapped bird. "No," I forced out. "Just mostly annoyed."

A beat of silence passed, and then, "You lie."

I did. Kind of. A god had his hand on me. How could I not be afraid? But strangely and inexplicably, I wasn't *terrified*. Maybe it was the anger. Perhaps it was the shock of what I had seen tonight, the unnerving feel of his touch, or the fact that if he wanted to harm me, he would've done it by now a dozen times over. Maybe it was the part of me that didn't care about consequences.

"A little," I admitted and then moved. Fast. Unsheathing the dagger, I brought it to his throat. "Are you afraid?"

Only his eyes moved, flicking to the hilt of the dagger. "Shadowstone? Unique weapon for a mortal to have. How did you come upon such a weapon?"

It wasn't like I could tell the truth. That it had been located by an ancestor who'd gain the knowledge of what a shadowstone dagger could do to a god and even a Primal once weakened. So, I lied. "It belonged to my stepbrother."

The god arched a dark brow.

"I sort of borrowed it."

"Borrowed it?"

"For the last couple of years," I added.

"Sounds like you stole it."

I said nothing.

He stared down at me. "Do you know why such a dagger is rare in the mortal realm?"

"I do," I admitted, even though I knew it would've been wiser to pretend ignorance. But the need to show him that I wasn't a helpless mortal who could be bullied was far stronger than wisdom.

"So, you know that the stone is quite toxic to a mortal's flesh?" he said, and of course I knew that. If it came into contact with a mortal's blood, it would slowly kill them even if the wound didn't get them. "And do you know what will happen if you attempt to use that blade against me?"

"Do you?" I stated, heart thumping. The incandescent white glow pulsed behind his pupils and seeped into the silver in wispy, radiant tendrils. It reminded me of how the eather had spilled and spit into the air around the Primal of Death.

"I do. I bet you do also. But you'd still try." His gaze flicked down to where I had the dagger pressed against his skin. "Is it strange that knowing that makes me think of how your tongue felt in my mouth?"

My entire body flashed hot even as I frowned. "Yes, a little—"

The god moved so quickly, I couldn't even track his movements. He gripped my wrist and twisted, spinning me around. Within a heartbeat, he had the dagger pinned to my stomach. His other hand hadn't even moved from my throat.

"That was unfair," I gasped.

"And you, *liessa*, are very brave." His thumb moved, sweeping over the curve of my jaw. "But, sometimes, one can be too brave." The dusky silkiness of his words wrapped around me. "To the point it borders on foolishness. And you know what I've found about the foolishly brave? There's a reason they often rush to greet death instead of having the wisdom to run from it. What is your reason?" he asked. "What drowns out that fear and pushes you to run so eagerly toward death?"

His question threw me. Sent my pulse racing. Was that what I was doing? Rushing eagerly toward death? I almost wanted to laugh, but I thought about that not-so-hidden part of me that…just didn't care. That overrode restraint and sound judgement. "I…I don't know."

"No?" The word rippled from him.

"When I get nervous, I ramble. And when I feel threatened or am told what to do, I get angry," I whispered. "I've been told on more than one occasion that my mouth would get me into trouble one day and that I should take heed."

"I see you took that advice to heart," he replied. "Always meeting a threat with anger isn't the wisest of choices."

"Like now?"

The god said nothing as he continued holding me against his chest, his thumb slowly sweeping back and forth, back and forth. With his strength, he wouldn't even need to use the eather. All it would take would be a sharp twist of his wrist.

It was then that I realized I might have come to the end of whatever goodwill this god had regarding me.

My mouth dried, and the dread of what was sure to come settled heavily in my chest. I was teetering on the edge of death. "You might as well get on with it."

"Get on with what, exactly?"

"Killing me," I said, the words like wool on my tongue.

His head lowered a bit. When he next spoke, his breath coasted over my cheek. "Killing you?"

"Yes." My skin felt inexplicably tight.

He drew back his head far enough that I could see that he had one eyebrow raised. "Killing you hasn't even crossed my mind."

"Really?"

"Really."

Surprise flickered through me. "Why not?"

He was silent for a moment. "Are you seriously asking me why I haven't thought about killing you?"

"You're a god," I pointed out, unsure if he was being truthful or just toying with me.

"And that is reason enough?"

"It's not? I threatened you. I pulled a dagger on you."

"More than once," he corrected.

"And I've been rude."

"Very."

"No one speaks to a god or behaves toward one in such a way."

"They typically do not," he agreed. "Either way, I suppose I'm not in a murderous mood tonight."

I search his tone for a hint of deception as I stared at the window. "If you're not going to kill me, then you should probably let go of me."

"Will you try to stab me?"

"I…hope not."

"You *hope*?"

"If you try to tell me what to do or grab me again, I am likely to lose that hope," I told him.

A quiet laugh rumbled from him—through me. "At least, you're honest."

"At least," I murmured, trying not to notice the cold pressure of him at my back. The feel of him. It didn't scare me. It didn't even disturb me, which made me wonder exactly what was wrong with me. Because I was fighting the muscles in my back and neck that wanted to relax into him.

His hand slipped away from my chin, and I immediately whirled. He stepped back and, in the blink of an eye, was on the other side of the table.

"Be careful," he said, lifting his hood and sending his features into the darkness. "I'll be watching."

Chapter 4

I inhaled slowly and evenly in the darkness. Tension built in my muscles. "Now," came the order.

Spinning around, I threw the blade, and a soft thud answered a heartbeat later. Eager to see exactly where the blade had landed, I started to reach for the blindfold when I felt the cold press of steel under my throat. I froze.

"Now what?" came the low voice.

"I cry and beg for my life?" I suggested.

A quiet laugh answered. "That would only work if someone wasn't intent on killing you."

"Shame," I murmured.

Then I moved.

Grabbing the wrist of the hand that held the blade, I twisted the arm away from me as I stepped in. A sharp gasp brought a savage smile to my lips. I pressed my fingers into the tendons, *right* in that spot. The entire arm spasmed as the fingers opened on reflex, and the hilt of the short sword dropped into my hand. I dipped low and kicked out, planting my booted foot into a leg. A heavy body hit the floor with a grunt.

I leveled the sword on the prone body as I reached up and tugged the blindfold down. "Was that a sufficient response?"

Sir Braylon Holland was sprawled across the stone floor of the west tower. "Quite."

I smirked, tossing the thick braid of hair over my shoulder.

Groaning under his breath, Sir Holland rolled to his feet. Born at least two decades before me, he appeared much younger since there wasn't a single crease in his deep brown skin. I'd once heard him tell one of his guards who'd asked if he'd summoned a god in exchange for everlasting youth, that his secret was to drink a fifth of whiskey each night.

Pretty sure he'd be dead if he drank that much.

"But your aim is lacking," he said, dusting off his black breeches. Absent of the obnoxious gold and plum uniform of the Royal Guard, he looked like any other guard. I'd never seen him in the finery. "And in need of much improvement."

Frowning, I turned to where the dummy was propped against the wall. The sad thing had seen better days. Cotton and straw leaked from numerous stab wounds. Its linen shirt had been replaced many times over the years. I'd stolen this one from Tavius's room, and it hung in shreds from wooden shoulders. The burlap head, stuffed with more straw and rags, flopped sadly to one side.

Sunlight streamed in from the narrow window, glinting off the handle of the iron dagger protruding from the dummy's chest. "How is my aim off?" I demanded, wiping a hand across my sweat-slick brow. The summer…it was steadily becoming unbearable. Last week, an elderly couple had been found in their tiny apartment in Croft's Cross, dead from heatstroke. They weren't the first, and I feared they wouldn't be the last. "You said to aim for the chest. I hit the chest."

"I told you to aim for the heart. Are hearts typically on the right side of the body, Sera?"

My lips pursed. "Do we really think someone would survive taking a blade to either side of the chest? Because I can tell you that, no, they would not."

The look he shot me could only be described as unimpressed as he took the sword from my hand and started for the dummy. It was a look I was unfortunately quite accustomed to.

He gripped the dagger and pulled it free. "They wouldn't recover from such a wound, but it wouldn't be a quick death nor an honorable one, and it would bring dishonor to you."

"Why should I care about giving an honorable death to someone who just tried to kill me?" I asked, thinking that was an incredibly valid question.

"Several reasons, Sera. Do I need to list them for you?"

"No."

"Too bad. I like hearing myself list things," he replied, and I groaned. "You, my dear, live a dangerous life."

"Not by choice," I muttered under my breath.

One eyebrow rose sardonically. "You are not protected like Princess Ezmeria," he stated as he crossed to the wall opposite the small window, where numerous weapons were stored. He placed the sword next to heavier, longer ones. "No Royal Guards are assigned to watch over your chambers or keep an eye on you as you run wild throughout the capital."

"I do not *run wild* throughout the capital."

The look he sent me this time said that he knew better. "Many of the people may not realize who you are," he went on as if I hadn't spoken. "But that doesn't mean there aren't some out there who have heard rumors of your existence and have figured out that you are no handmaiden but carry the Mierel blood in your veins," he continued. "All it takes is for one of them to tell someone who thinks they can use you as a means to achieve what they want."

My jaw clenched. There had been two in the past three years that'd somehow learned that I was, in fact, a Princess and attempted to kidnap me. That hadn't worked out well for them, but their blood wasn't on my hands.

It was on Tavius's, who I strongly believed had been behind the rumor.

"Not only that, it's only a matter of time before the Vodina Isles Crown learns of their Lords. They will attempt a siege." He faced me. "You will just be another body they cut through to get to the Crown."

I was already just another body around here. One that was mostly ignored. But whatever…

"And then there is the heir," Sir Holland stated flatly. "Who is still extremely angry over what happened in the stables last week."

"Yeah, well, I'm still upset with him for whipping that horse because of his foolishness and lack of skill," I retorted. "Every time I see him, I want to punch him again."

"While his behavior towards that animal was abominable, blackening the Heir of Lasania's eye and then threatening to use the whip in the same manner as he did was not the wisest choice."

"But it *was* the most satisfactory," I said, grinning.

He ignored that. "The Prince should've already ascended the throne by now. If it weren't for Princess Kayleigh becoming *ill* and having to return to Irelone, he likely would have." He looked over his shoulder at me, his hickory-hued eyes boring into mine as I quickly wiped the grin from my face. "Something I'm sure you had nothing to do with."

"Princess Kayleigh *is* very ill and had to return home to be cared for. Tavius could've chosen another as his bride. However, he's too lazy to ascend the throne and have, you know, *responsibilities* beyond being a drunken, lecherous pig. So, he's going to delay marriage for as long as possible."

"And I suppose Princess Kayleigh's sickness had nothing to do with the potion you acquired that made her skin pale and her stomach unsteady?"

I kept my face perfectly blank. "I have no idea what you speak of."

"You're a terrible liar."

Lies, a shadowy voice echoed in my thoughts. I desperately ignored it. Like I had for the last two weeks, since the night I stood in the study of the townhome. "How do you even know about that?"

"I know more than you think I do, Sera."

My stomach tumbled a bit. Was he talking about when I actually *did* run a bit wild through the capital? Namely at The Luxe? Gods, I hoped not. Sir Holland wasn't exactly a fatherly figure, but still, the idea of him knowing about the time I spent there made me want to vomit a little.

I couldn't even consider that, so I pushed it from my thoughts. "I can handle Tavius."

"Barely," he replied, and I stiffened. "And only because you're faster than he is. One day, he'll get lucky. You won't be fast enough." Sir Holland's features softened. "I don't bring this up to be cruel, but until you're gone from here, he's a threat."

I knew he wasn't being cruel. Sir Holland was never that. He was just stating a fact. But there was only one way I would ever leave Lasania, and that would be when I died. I sighed heavily. "What does any of that have to do with an honorable or quick death?"

"Well, besides the fact that a dying mortal can still wield a weapon, an enemy is rarely one by choice," he told me. "They usually become such due to other people's choices, or they become enemies because of situations they had little control over. I would think you, of all people, would be more empathetic to that."

I knew he wasn't talking about the Vodina Isles Lords, but those who became desperate due to situations so out of their control, they found themselves doing things they'd never consider. Mortals who became someone else's nightmare because it was the only way they could survive.

Shame scalded the back of my neck as I shifted uncomfortably on my feet.

Sir Holland's gaze flickered over my face. "What is going on with you, Sera? You've been off the last couple of days. What's wrong?"

"What's wrong...?" I trailed off. There were many things wrong, starting with why Sir Holland still met with me daily to train. It wasn't just to keep me prepared in case I needed to defend myself or if the Queen decided my skill could be used to deliver a personal blow.

Sir Holland behaved as if I were still integral to the survival of Lasania. That the Primal of Death would come for me. I still didn't have the heart to tell him what the Primal had said to me. I thought… I thought he needed to believe there was hope, because nothing had stopped the Rot from spreading. The only way we knew to do that was to kill the Primal.

And the Rot was getting worse. There had been a few showers in the last month, but nothing of substance. Before that, the storms had brought chunks of ice, crushing and sheering vegetation as it slammed to the ground. People were concerned the cornfields would yield only half what they did last season.

How much longer could Lasania continue on like this?

It was the Kazin siblings that had been murdered. That small babe, and the lack of answers surrounding why they had been killed.

I had gone back to their neighborhood the following day to ask around about the Kazin family. I'd learned that their parents had passed a year before. No one had anything bad to say about them or the siblings. Galen had been described as comely and shy, someone who was often seen strolling the nearby garden's early in the mornings with her babe. And no one had been sure who the child's father was, but it was believed to be some ne'er-do-well who'd abandoned her after discovering that she was pregnant. Magus was said to be a flirt but loyal and friendly. Come to find out, he had been a guard for Carsodonia. Not as high-ranking as a Royal Guard or Royal Knight, but a defender of the city. I wondered if I'd seen him before. If I passed him in the halls of Wayfair. He was one of thousands, a name with no face. It was also the knowledge that four other mortals had also been killed.

I'll be watching.

An icy shiver danced across the nape of my neck. It was also *him.*

The god whose name I didn't know. It had taken a good week for me to fully accept that I had, in fact, threatened a god. *And* kissed one. Had *enjoyed* being kissed by him. But what I couldn't figure out was the lingering memory of *rightness* when I'd been around him. A feeling that still made no sense, but I couldn't help but wonder if he watched as I moved about the streets of Carsodonia. And some incredibly idiotic, reckless, and disturbed part of me…anticipated crossing paths with him again. I wanted to know why he'd kissed me. There'd been other ways to hide and disguise ourselves, like moving farther away from the other gods for starters.

My focus shifted to the closed door. "I don't know. I'm just in a weird mood."

Sir Holland approached, handing the dagger to me. "You sure that's all?"

I nodded.

"I don't believe you."

"Sir Holland—"

"I don't," he insisted. "Do you know why we still practice every day?"

My grip tightened on the dagger as everything I wanted to say started to bubble up in me. "Honest? I don't know why we do this."

His brows flew up. "That was a rhetorical question, Sera."

"Well, it shouldn't be," I shot back. "What is the point?"

Shock splashed across his face. "The point? The lives—"

"Of everyone in Lasania depend on me ending the Rot," I interrupted. "I know that. I've lived that since birth. And it's all I can think about every time I see the Rot spreading through farm after farm. Every day that it doesn't rain, and the sun continues scorching crops, and every time I think about what winter might bring, I think of all those lives." I inhaled sharply but didn't hold it as he'd taught me. There was no space for air. "I think about it every time someone takes one of our ships or there are rumors of another siege. All I think about when I'm trying to sleep or eat or am doing *anything* is how I was the Maiden and found unworthy by the Primal of Death."

"You're not unworthy. You're not a curse or anything like that. You carry the ember of life in you. You carry *hope* within you. You carry the possibility of a *future*," he said. "You don't know what the Primal of Death thinks."

"How could he not think that?" I shot back.

Sir Holland shook his head. "What is happening with the Rot is not your fault."

I almost laughed at the absurdity. Some people believed the Primals were angry, and the Rot was a sign of their wrath. That had led to the Temples filling with worshippers, and blame being cast on everything from failed marriages to false icons. They were close to the truth without realizing that others believed the fault should be placed on the Crown. That nothing had been done to plan for worsening weather and soil. And they too were correct. The Crown had placed all their eggs in one basket, and that basket had been me. Now, the Crown had begun stockpiling goods that could be dried or canned, and had decreed that hardier crops be planted. They'd attempted to establish alliances, and while none had ended as poorly as the one with the Vodina Isles had, no other kingdom wanted to be saddled with one that couldn't feed its residents.

I could count on one hand how many people knew that Lasania was doomed. The agreement King Roderick had struck had come with a time limit. I hadn't only been promised to a Primal. My birth was a sign that the deal had run its course. And even if the Primal of Death had taken me, Lasania would continue on its path to destruction.

I ran a finger across the blade. A god could be killed if their brain or heart were destroyed by shadowstone. And paralyzed by it if the blade were left in their body. But a Primal was different. Destroying their heart and/or brain would only injure them, not kill them. It would weaken them but not enough to make them truly vulnerable to shadowstone.

But they *could* be killed.

By love.

Make him fall in love, become his weakness, and end him.

That was what I'd spent my entire life preparing to do. I had become skilled with the dagger, sword, and bow, and I could protect myself if it came to hand-to-hand combat. I had been instructed in how to behave in a manner believed to be appealing to the Primal once he claimed me, and the Mistresses of the Jade had taught me that the most dangerous weapon wasn't a violent one. I'd been ready to make him fall in love with me. To become his weakness and then kill him.

It was the only way to save Lasania.

Any deal made between a god or Primal and a mortal ended in the favor of whoever had been granted the boon upon the death of the god or Primal who answered the summons. In our case, it meant that all the things that had happened to restore Lasania two hundred years ago would return and remain until the end of time. That was the piece of information my family had discovered in the years it'd taken for me to be born.

But he hadn't claimed me, so that knowledge had proven useless so far. Somehow, I…I had messed up. He'd looked at me, and maybe he saw what was in me. What I tried to hide.

I thought about what my old nursemaid, Odetta, had told me when I asked her if she thought my mother was proud to have a Maiden as a daughter.

She had gripped my chin with gnarled, cold fingers and said, *"Child, the Fates know you were touched by life and death, creating something that should not be. How could she be anything but afraid?"*

I shouldn't have even asked that question, but I was a child, and I…I had just wanted to know whether my mother was proud.

And Odetta had been the wrong person to ask. Gods love her, but she was as blunt as the back of a knife—and cranky. Always had been. But she had never treated me differently than she had anyone else.

What she'd said really hadn't made much sense then, but I sometimes wondered if she had been talking about my *gift*. Had the Primal of Death somehow sensed that? Did it even matter now?

I'd failed.

"How could it not be my fault?" I demanded and then twisted toward the dummy before throwing the dagger.

The blade struck its chest, right where the heart would be located.

Sir Holland stared at the dummy. "See? You know where the heart is. Why didn't you do that before?"

I twisted toward him. "I had a blindfold on before."

"So?"

"So?" I repeated. "Why am I even practicing with a blindfold? Does someone expect me to go blind sometime soon?"

"I would hope not," he replied dryly. "The exercise helps you hone your other senses. You know that, and you know what else you should know?"

"Whatever it is, I'm sure you're going to tell me." I angrily tossed the braid back over my shoulder.

"It's not your fault," he repeated.

A knot formed in the back of my throat at his tone. It was the same gentleness he'd used when I was seven, crying until my head ached because I had been forced to remain behind while everyone else left for the country estate. The same compassion he'd shown when I'd been eleven and sprained my ankle after landing on it wrong, and when I was fifteen and nearly gutted when I hadn't deflected his attack in time. The kindness had been there when I was first sent to the Mistresses of the Jade in the months before my seventeenth birthday and didn't want to go. Sir Holland and my stepsister Ezra were the only two people who treated me as if I were an actual person and not a cure—a fix that didn't work.

I forced air around the burning knot. "Yeah, well, someone needs to tell the Queen that."

"Your mother is…" Sir Holland shoved a hand over his closely cropped hair. "She is a hard woman. She and I don't agree on a lot of things when it comes to you. I think you know that. But history is repeating itself, and she is watching her people suffer."

"Then maybe she should summon a god and ask for the suffering to stop," I suggested.

"You don't mean that."

I opened my mouth but then sighed. Of course, I didn't. It wasn't often that any were desperate or foolish enough to find their way to one of the Temples, but it did happen. I'd heard the stories.

Orlano, a cook in the castle, had once spoken about a childhood neighbor of his who had called upon a god, desiring the hand of the daughter of a landowner who'd refused to entertain his offer of marriage.

The god had granted exactly what he'd asked for.

The hand of the landowner's daughter.

My stomach churned as I walked over to the dummy. What kind of god would do that?

What kind would kill a babe?

"Do you think you're unworthy?" Sir Holland asked quietly.

Shaken by the question, I stared ahead but saw none of the burlap sack. "The Primal of Death had asked for a Consort in return for granting Roderick's request. He came and left without me—without what he asked for. And he hasn't come back since." I looked at him. "So, what do you think?"

"Maybe he thought you weren't ready."

"Ready for what? How exactly could he determine if a Consort was ready?"

He shook his head. "Maybe he wanted you to be older. Not everyone believes someone is mature enough or *ready* enough to marry at seventeen or eighteen—"

"Or nineteen? Twenty? Everyone is pretty much married or on their way to being married by nineteen," I stated.

"Tavius isn't married. Neither is Princess Ezmeria. Or me," he pointed out.

"Tavius isn't married because Princess Kayleigh got sick and he's too lazy to ascend the throne and have, you know, responsibilities beyond being a drunken, lecherous pig. So, he's going to delay marriage for as long as possible. And Ezra has other plans. You..." I frowned. "Why *aren't* you married?"

Sir Holland shrugged. "Just haven't felt like doing it." He watched me for a moment. "I think he will come for you," he said. "That's why I still train with you. I haven't given up hope, Princess."

I barked out a laugh. "Don't call me that."

"Call you what?"

"Princess," I muttered. "I'm not a Princess."

"Really?" Crossing his arms, he returned to his normal stance when he wasn't either attempting to knock me on my ass or wound me with all kinds of sharp, stabby things. "Then what are you?"

What am I?

I looked down at my hands. That was a good question. I may be a Royal by blood, but I had only been recognized as such three times in my life. I certainly wasn't treated as one. My whole life had been focused on me becoming a... "An assassin?"

"A warrior," he corrected.

"Bait?"

His expression was as bland as the leftover bread I'd managed to grab that morning from the kitchen. "You are not bait. You are a trap."

And maybe I had become nothing more than a flesh-and-blood weapon.

What else could I be? *What layers exist under that?* I wondered as I toyed with the blindfold dangling around my throat. There was no time for hobbies or entertainment. No skill set developed beyond handling a dagger or a bow and how to live with grace. I considered no one a close confidant—not even Ezra or Sir Holland. Growing up, I had only been allowed a nursemaid. Not even a lady's maid out of fear they would have some sort of terrible influence on me. Not that I needed a companion at all times. But the company would've been nice. All that I had that didn't involve *this* was my lake, and I wasn't sure if that really counted for anything since it was, well...a lake.

I blew out an aggravated breath. I didn't like to think about this—

any of this. I didn't like to think at all, to be honest. Because when I did, it made me feel like I was a real person. And when I couldn't stop the thoughts from coming, I dwelled on that small seedling of relief I'd felt when the Primal had rejected me. Then I drowned in that shame and selfishness. Those times, I made use of the sleeping drafts the Healers had brewed for my mother. Once, while Sir Holland had been dealing with something related to the Royal Guard and Ezra had been in the country visiting a friend, I'd slept for nearly two days. No one had even checked on me. And when I awakened, I had stared at the vial, thinking it would be all too easy to drink it all. My palms became clammy like they did any time I thought about that, and I wiped them on my tights. I didn't like to think about that day either—about how that vial had become a different type of ghost than the ones that haunted the Dark Elms, refusing to enter the Shadowlands.

"Come," Sir Holland said, pulling me from my thoughts. "Put the blindfold back on and continue until you hit the target."

Sighing, I reached for the cloth and tugged it back up. Sir Holland retied the binding so it stayed in place. I allowed my world to turn dark because what else did I have to do? Where did I have to be?

He turned me to the dummy, and then I sensed him step back. As I firmed my grip, I thought about what he'd said. *A warrior.* He could be right, but I was also one more thing.

A martyr.

Because whether the Primal came for me, regardless of if I succeeded if he did, the end result would be the same.

I wouldn't survive.

Feeling a dull headache coming on, I entered the narrow stairwell after finishing with Sir Holland. Sunlight struggled to penetrate the darkness as I navigated the sometimes-slippery steps to the floor below. Crossing to Wayfair's east wing, that hall was far dimmer. I walked to the last, little room at the end of the quiet hall. The door was ajar, and I pressed it open.

Candlelight flickered from a table by the narrow bed, casting a soft glow across the small form on the mattress. I tiptoed into the room and made my way to the stool beside the bed. I winced as the wood creaked under my weight, but the form on the bed didn't stir.

Odetta had been sleeping a lot lately, each time seeming to slip deeper and deeper. She had already been aging when I came into this world, and now…now, her time was coming to a close. Sooner rather than later, she would leave this realm and pass into the Shadowlands, where she would spend eternity in the Vale.

A different kind of heaviness settled into me as my gaze touched the silvery strands of hair still so incredibly thick, and then moved to the bent, spotted hands resting atop a blanket that would've been too thick for anyone else given the warm breeze entering the window and stirring the blades of the ceiling fan. I fixed the edge of the blanket at her side.

When Odetta learned that the Primal hadn't taken me, she had looked at me with rheumy eyes and said, *"Death wants nothing to do with life. None of you can be surprised."*

I hadn't exactly understood what she'd meant then. I hardly ever did, but her response hadn't come as a shock. Odetta had never coddled me. She had never been particularly loving, either, but she was more of a mother than the one I had. And soon, she would be gone. Even now, she was so still

Too still.

My breath caught as I stared at her frail chest. I couldn't detect any movement. My heart hammered. Her skin was pale, but I didn't think it had taken on that waxy sheen of death.

"Odetta?" My voice sounded rough to my ears.

There was no response. I rose, speaking her name once more as panic blossomed in my chest. Had she…had she passed?

I'm not ready.

I reached for her hand, stopping before my skin touched hers. I sucked in a shuddering breath. I wasn't ready for her to be gone. Not tonight. Not tomorrow. Heat rushed to my hand as my fingers hovered inches above hers—

"*Don't,*" Odetta croaked. "Don't you dare."

My gaze flew to her face. Her eyes were open, just thin slits, but enough to see that the once-vibrant blue had dulled. "I wasn't doing anything."

"I may already have one foot in the Vale, but I haven't lost my mind." Her breath was faint and shallow. "Or my vision."

I glanced down at my hand, hovering so close to her skin. I jerked it to my chest, my heart still pounding. "I think you're seeing things, Odetta."

A dry, cracked laugh parted her lips. "*Seraphena*," she said, startling me. Only she ever used my full name. "Look at me."

Shoving my hands between my knees, I looked at her, never knowing a time when her face was free of the heavy lines of age. "What?"

"Do not play coy with me, girl. I know what you were about," she rasped. Denial rose, but she was having none of it. "What have I told you? All these years? Have you forgotten? What have I told you?" she repeated.

Feeling as if I were a small child perched on a stool, I shifted uncomfortably. "To never do that again."

"And what do you think would've happened if you'd done that? You were lucky when you were a child, girl. You won't get lucky again. You'd bring the wrath of the Primal onto yourself."

I nodded, even though I had gotten lucky more than once since I was a child and had picked up Butters. Not once had my…gift captured the attention of the Primal of Death. And I…

I didn't know what I had been about to do.

Shaken, I slid my hands from between my knees and looked at them. They looked normal now. Just like everything about me did. I exhaled raggedly. "I thought you were gone—"

"And I will be gone, Seraphena. Soon," Odetta predicted, drawing my gaze once more to hers. Was it my imagination, or did she look even smaller under that blanket? Thinner. "I have lived long enough. I'm ready."

I bit my lip as it started to tremble and nodded.

Those eyes might be dull, but they still held the power to hold mine.

"I know," I said, clasping my hands and keeping them firmly in my lap.

She eyed me through half-open lids. "Is there a reason you're in here, other than to disturb me?"

"I wanted to check on you." And that was true, but I did have another reason. A question. One that had been preying on my mind for a while. "And I wanted to ask you something if you're up for it."

"I'm not doing anything but lying here, waiting for you to leave," she groused.

I cracked a grin at that, but it quickly faded as my stomach started jumping and twisting. "You said something a long time ago, and I wanted to know what you meant—what it meant." The breath I took was shallow. "You said I was touched by death and life. What does that mean? To be touched by both."

Odetta coughed out a raspy laugh. "After all these years, *now* you're going to ask?"

I nodded.

"There a reason you're asking now?"

"Not really." I shrugged. "It's just something I've always wondered about."

"And you thought you'd ask before I kicked the bucket?"

I frowned. "No—" White, bushy brows crept up on her forehead. I sighed. "Okay. Maybe."

Her laugh was dry and raspy, but her eyes brightened with a sharpness that erased much of the dullness. "I hate to disappoint you, child, but that's not a question I can answer. It's what the Fates claimed upon your birth. Only the Fates can tell you what that means."

Chapter 5

Stifling a yawn the following morning, I entered the quiet, candlelit room through the door often used by servants. My steps were a bit sluggish as I crossed the stillness of the Queen's sitting room. Between the annoying headache that hadn't gone away until this morning, and trying to figure out Odetta's vague non-answer to my question, I hadn't slept well the night before.

I didn't even know why I tried to understand what Odetta had meant. That wasn't the first time she'd spoken in what reminded me of a riddle. And to be honest, half of the time, I truly believed she was simply embellishing whatever she was saying. Like the Fates—the Arae—claiming that both life and death had touched me upon my birth. How would Odetta even know that? She wouldn't.

Shaking my head, I passed the plush ivory settees, my steps silent against the thick carpet. I made my way to the back of the long, narrow chamber on the second floor, where two candelabras burned. I'd never known a time when those candles hadn't been lit.

In the still, rose-scented chamber, I looked up at the painting of King Lamont Mierel and took the time to really soak in his image, knowing my mother would be at brunch at this time. It was safe to look upon him now.

My father.

There was a tightness in my chest, a pressure that I thought could be grief, but I wasn't sure how I could mourn someone I'd never met.

He'd died shortly after my birth, having leapt from Wayfair's east tower. No one had ever said why. No one ever spoke of it. But I often wondered if my birth—the reminder of what his forefather had done—had driven him to it.

I swallowed as I took in the image of him captured in such detail it was as if he stood before me in white and plum robes, the golden crown of leaves resting upon hair the color of the richest red wine.

His hair fell in loose waves to his shoulders while my hair was, well, a mess of tight and loose curls…and knots that tangled their way down to my hips. Our brows were shaped the same, arching in a manner that gave me the appearance that I was questioning or judging something. The curve of our mouths was identical, but somehow his had been captured with the corners tilted upward in a soft smile, while according to the Queen on more than one occasion, I looked *sullen*. He had a smattering of freckles along the bridge of his nose, but it looked like someone had dipped a brush in brown paint and flicked tiny brown spots all over my face. His eyes were a forest green like mine, but it was how those eyes had been painted that always got to me.

There was no light in his stare, no glimmer of life or hidden mirth to match the curve of his mouth. His eyes were *haunted*, and I wasn't sure how an artist could capture such emotion with oils, but clearly, they had.

Looking into those eyes was hard.

Looking at him at all was difficult. He had more masculine, far more refined features than I did, but we shared so much that I wondered long before I'd failed if that was one of the reasons my mother had struggled to gaze upon me for any length of time. Because I knew she'd loved him. That a large part of her still did, even if she had found space to hold tender feelings for King Ernald. That was why those candles were never extinguished. It was why King Ernald never entered this sitting room and why when the painful headaches struck my mother, she retreated to here instead of to the chambers she shared with her husband. It was why she often spent hours in here, alone with this painting of Lamont.

I often wondered if they were mates of the heart—if there was even such a thing that was written about in poems and songs. Two halves of a whole. It was said that the touch between one was full of energy and that their souls would recognize one another. It was even said that they could walk in the dreams of another, and that the loss of one wasn't something repairable.

If mates of the heart were something more than legend, then I believed that was what my mother and father had been to one another.

A heaviness settled in my chest, cold and aching. Sometimes, I also wondered if my mother blamed me for his death. Maybe if he'd fathered a son. If he had, would he still be alive? Instead, he was gone, and I didn't care what the Priests of the Primal of Life may believe or claim. He had to be in the Vale, finding whatever peace he hadn't been able to attain in life.

In the center of the aching coldness was a spark of heat—anger. That was another reason it was so hard to look upon him. I didn't want to be angry because it seemed wrong to feel that, but he'd left me before I even had a chance to know him.

The doors to the sitting room suddenly creaked, causing my stomach to drop. I spun, knowing there was no way I could make it to the servants' door in time. Any hope that it would be one of my mother's Ladies vanished at the sound of her voice. A storm of emotions whipped through me. Dread over how she'd respond to finding me here. Hope that she wouldn't take issue with my presence. Bitterness that warned I was foolish to hold onto such hope. I locked up as the Queen of Lasania swept inside, a force of flowing lilac skirts and sparkling gems. Behind her, Lady Kala and a seamstress stood, the latter clutching a gown.

I couldn't help but stare at my mother. I hadn't seen her since the night the Vodina Isles Lords had rejected the offer of allegiance. Did she look different? The creases at the corners of her eyes appeared deeper. She looked slimmer, and I wondered if it was the gown or if she struggled with her appetite. If she were ill…

"Thank you so much for finishing the gown—" My mother drew up short, the yellow-jeweled comb pinning her curls in place glittering in the lamplight. Her gaze landed on me, widening slightly and then narrowing. My shoulders straightened as I braced myself. "What are you doing in here?" she demanded.

I opened my mouth, but any ability to form words left me as she stalked forward, leaving Lady Kala and the seamstress by the door.

She stopped several feet from me, her chest rising sharply. Tension bracketed the Queen's lips as she turned away from me. "I'm sorry, Andreia," she said, speaking to the seamstress. *Andreia.* I thought I'd recognized her. Joanis was her last name. She had a clothing shop in Stonehill frequented by many of the noblemen and women. "I know your time is very valuable. I wasn't aware that my handmaiden would be here."

Handmaiden.

Lady Kala's gaze dropped to the floor as the seamstress shook her head. "It is fine, Your Grace. I will just go ahead and get set up."

My focus shifted from my mother to the seamstress. Andreia had dark shadows under her eyes, and stray brown hairs escaped the neat bun at her neck. I was willing to bet she had spent many long nights finishing the froth of ivory silk and pearls she carried. A muscle ticked at the corner of my mouth as I thought of how many coins that gown must've cost. Andreia's services didn't come cheap. Meanwhile, thousands—if not more—were starving.

But my mother needed a new gown that could feed dozens of families or the entire orphanage for months—if not longer.

"I'm not sure why you're in here," the Queen advised under her breath, having drifted closer to me in that often-eerie, silent way of hers while I watched the seamstress hang the gown from a hook on the wall. "But quite honestly, at this moment, I do not care."

I looked at her, not even bothering to search for any glint of warmth in her features. That brief glimmer of hope was already long gone. "I did not expect you to be here."

"For some reason, I feel as if that is a lie, and you're here just to be a disturbance." The creases at the corners of her eyes were far more noticeable now as she too, watched Andreia root around in the bag she'd brought with her. "After all, I am sure the seamstress is currently questioning why a handmaiden would be dressed as a stable hand while in one of my private quarters. This possible catastrophe has your name written all over it, having willed it into being."

I stared at her, stuck between disbelief and amusement. "If I had the ability to will things into being, it would not be this."

"No, I suppose you're right," she remarked in a flat, icy tone I'd never heard her use with anyone else. "You would use that gift for something far more harmful."

My skin flamed hot as the insinuation struck a chord. There was no doubt in my mind that she was horrified by what I'd become. I really couldn't blame her. The knowledge that her firstborn child murdered people on the regular had to haunt her. Except it was far too often upon her request.

I told myself not to respond. There was no point. But I rarely heeded that voice of reason. "I'm only capable of what is expected of me."

"And yet, you stand here beside me, having failed what was expected of you," she replied quietly. "While our people continue to starve and die."

The skin along the back of my neck prickled as I forced my voice low. "You care for the people?"

The Queen watched Andreia in silence for several seconds. "They are all I ever think about."

A low, harsh laugh fought its way out of me, and she looked at me then, but I didn't think she saw me. "What is so funny?" she asked.

"You," I whispered, and the skin under her right eye twitched. "If you care for the starving people, then why didn't you take the coin spent on yet another gown and give it to those who need it?"

Her shoulders stiffened. "I wouldn't need to keep up appearances and spend coin on *yet* another gown if you had fulfilled your duty, now, would I? No more Rot. No starvation."

Her words fell upon me as if they were made of the numerous sharp pins that jutted from the ball of material Andreia had placed on a nearby table.

"Instead, I am called the Beggar Queen by kingdoms that once prayed for an alliance with Lasania." My mother cast her gaze to mine. "So, please, do go and find another area of this vast property to haunt."

"Then I suppose I will go roam the woods and join those spirits there," I muttered.

Queen Calliphe's mouth tightened until her lips were bloodless. "If that is what you'd prefer."

The apathy of her tone—the utter dismissiveness—was worse than if she had smacked me in the face. Anger stung my eyes, took root deep inside me, loosening my tongue as it had so many times before. I wasn't always like this. I'd spent the better part of my life doing exactly what I was told, rarely refusing any request or order. I'd been quiet, whispering through the halls of Wayfair, so focused on capturing the attention—and maybe even the affection—of the Queen. But that had stopped three years ago. I'd stopped holding my tongue. Stopped trying. Stopped caring.

Maybe that was the answer to what that damn god had asked. Why I ran so eagerly toward death.

"You know, if begging for alliances is such a step down for you, you could always do what the Golden King did," I pointed out, keeping my voice barely above a whisper. "Then you can continue standing by while everyone else cleans up whatever mess there may be."

Her gaze snapped back to mine. "One day, that mouth of yours is going to get you in the kind of trouble you won't be able to talk your way out of."

"Wouldn't that make you happy?" I challenged, aware of how Lady Kala and the seamstress were dutifully attempting to ignore us.

Her gaze iced over. "Leave," she ordered. "Now."

Brimming with anger and a heavier, suffocating emotion I refused to acknowledge, I dipped into an overly elaborate curtsy. My mother's nostrils flared as she stared at me. "Your wish is my command, Your Grace," I said, rising and crossing the room.

"Close the door behind you so there are no more inconsequential interruptions," Queen Calliphe stated.

Closing my eyes, I shut the door without slamming it—a feat that took every bit of willpower I had as I reminded myself that her words could no longer reach me soon. In the hall, I drew in a long, deep breath and held it. Held it until my lungs burned, and my eyes started to water. Until tiny white bursts of light appeared behind my lids. Only then did I exhale. It was the only thing that stopped me from grabbing the door handle and slamming it over and over.

Only when I was confident that I could trust my actions did I open my eyes. Two Royal Guards stood across from my mother's chambers.

Gods, they looked…absurd in their uniforms, like puffed-up peacocks.

The two men stared straight ahead, their expressions bland despite the fact that I'd just stood in front of them for several moments, eyes closed while holding my breath. I supposed that wouldn't even register on the scale of odd things they'd witnessed me do.

The stinging in my eyes and the burn in my throat were still there as I started walking, rubbing the back of my left shoulder where the crescent-shaped birthmark tingled. It had to be the numerous sconces lighting the hall. It had nothing to do with my mother. There was no way she could have any effect on me. Not when she wore her disappointment in me like a second skin.

The balmy night air tugged at the hem of my surcoat, tossing it about my knees as I cut through the overflowing Primal Gardens that took up several acres around the outer wall. I then crossed the castle bridge, passing several jewel-adorned carriages heading in and out of Wayfair as water rushed underneath. Lifting the hood of the coat, I skirted the narrow district known as Eastfall, where one of the two Royal Citadels stood, as well as the dormitories where the guards trained and lived. The other Royal Citadel, the largest, was located on the outskirts of Carsodonia, facing the Willow Plains, and was where most of Lasania's armies trained.

I had no real destination in mind as I continued past the many vine tunnels of The Luxe, lifting my gaze to the right, not wanting to see what I would but unable to stop myself.

The Shadow Temple sat in the foothills of the Cliffs of Sorrow, behind a thick stone wall that encircled the entire structure. It didn't matter how many times my steps took me near the Temple I couldn't get used to the imposing beauty of the twisting spires that stretched nearly as high as the cliffs, the slender turrets, and sleek, pitch-black walls made of polished shadowstone. It seemed to lure the stars from the sky at night, capturing them in the obsidian stone. The entire Temple glittered as if a hundred candles had been lit and placed throughout.

There was no suppressing the shudder when I looked away and forced myself to keep walking. I tried not to go near the Shadow Temple. Four times in the past three years was more than enough. The last thing I needed to do tonight was dwell on what could've caused the Primal of Death to change his mind.

An antsy, nervous energy had crept into me after I'd checked in on a sleeping, too-still Odetta. The thought of facing a long night of watching shadows creep across the ceiling had driven me from Wayfair.

I didn't want to be alone, but I also didn't want to be around anyone.

So, I walked like I did on nights when the buzz of energy made sleep impossible—nights that were becoming more and more common over the last several months. The scent of rain hung heavy in the air. It was still early enough that the hum of conversation and the clink of fancy glasses filled candlelit courtyards. The sidewalks were a sea of gowns and shirts far too heavy for the heat. I didn't blend in with them as I kept walking. I moved unseen, a ghost among the living. Or at least that was how it felt as I traveled over a second, far-less-grand bridge that connected the banks of the Nye River. A fine mist had begun to fall, dampening my skin. I entered the hilly quarter known as Stonehill. The mist eased some of the heat, but I hoped the thick clouds rolling in from the water were a harbinger of much-needed heavier rains.

The Temple of Phanos, the Primal of the Sky, Sea, Earth, and Wind, sat at the crest of Stonehill, its thick columns hazy in the drizzle. That's where I was heading, I realized.

I liked it up there. It wasn't nearly as high as the Cliffs of Sorrow, but I could look out over the entire capital from the Temple steps.

People still milled about, crowding the slender streets and steep hills, even though most of the shops had closed for the night. I stared up at the torch-lit house numbers, narrow one-story homes with canopied rooftop pavilions—

Warmth poured into my chest without warning, pressing against my skin. My steps faltered on the obnoxiously steep hill. The tingling warmth cascaded down my arms. I sucked in a sharp breath as my heart banged against my ribs.

That feeling…

I knew what it meant—what I reacted to.

Death.

Very recent death.

Forcing air in and out of my lungs in slow, even breaths, I turned in a circle and then started walking up the hill again. As I forced the warmth away, tamped it down, I still charged forward. It was as if I had no control. The…gift inside me drove me forward, even though I knew I would do nothing once I found the source. Still, I kept going.

Less than a block ahead, I saw *him.*

The god with long hair the color of the night sky. He strode down the opposite side of the street, his bare arms colorless in the moonlight.

Madis.

That was his name.

Stepping back into a narrow alley, I pressed against the still-sun-warm stucco of a home. I reached into the folds of my surcoat, folding my fingers around the hilt of my dagger. And I bit the inside of my cheek as I watched the god, seeing in my mind the small babe he'd tossed like a piece of trash.

Madis crossed under a streetlamp, stopping as a dog barked nearby, and then he turned halfway, facing the other side of the street. His head cocked to the side. The dog had ceased barking, but it was like…he'd heard something else. I started to pull the dagger free.

What are you doing?

The voice that whispered in my thoughts was a mixture of mine and the silver-eyed god's. I could strike Madis. I was sure of it. But then what? Surely, a mortal killing a god would not go unnoticed. The fury I felt at what he'd done to the child tipped me toward not caring about the *then-what?* part.

What drowns out that fear and pushes you to run so eagerly toward death?

The silver-eyed god's words haunted me as I stood there, and it cost me. Madis had started walking toward the shadowy pathways between the homes, moving fast. I cursed under my breath and pushed away from the wall. The hilt of the dagger dug into my palm, and I followed him. I stopped once I reached the sidewalk, my gaze shooting in the direction he'd come from as I thought of the tingling warmth that had now faded.

I had a sinking suspicion the feeling was related to him.

"Fuck," I muttered, glancing at the dark walkway and then back.

I started walking again, stopping near the end of the street. A faint bit of warmth returned as I turned to a building. No courtyard. The front door sat right off the sidewalk. Soft candlelight flickered behind the latticed windows along the side of the squat, stucco house. The white canopies on the roof were drawn, offering the pavilion a level of privacy.

A gas lamp sconce sat below the house number and a sign that read: *Joanis Designs.*

Icy air rushed down my spine. It couldn't be the seamstress that had brought the frothy silk and pearl gown to my mother. That seemed too much of a coincidence—that I would be here for no reason, and that the god Madis would've harmed her.

I moved before I could stop myself and turned the handle of the front door. Unlocked. I resisted the urge to kick it open, even though that would make me feel better. Instead, I *sedately* inched it inside.

The smell of *burnt flesh* hit me as soon as I walked into the small foyer, the food I had eaten earlier souring in my stomach. I brushed past leafy potted plants in a den. Large spools of fabric and garment mannequins sat in the shadows. I held tight to the dagger and crept forward, entering a narrow, dark corridor where another door sat ajar. I knew the layout of these types of cottages. The chambers were stacked one after the other, with the kitchen typically at the back of the home, farthest from the living areas. The bedchambers would be in the middle, and the sitting rooms up front, where I'd seen the candlelight from the windows along the side of the home.

Quietly, I inched open the door that separated the den used for business from the rest of her home. My gaze skipped over the empty, light-colored chairs and settee and the lit gas lamp I hadn't seen from the street that sat on a tea table. A glass had been toppled, spilling red liquid across the oak table and a half-closed book. On the floor, a slender pale foot peeked out from the front of the settee. I went farther in, inhaling sharply. There was another scent here. One that was fresher than the godsforsaken charred smell. It was familiar, but I couldn't place it as I rounded the settee.

Dear gods.

Lying on her back was what remained of Miss Andreia Joanis. Her arms were placed over a bodice of pale lilac chiton as if someone had folded them. One leg was curled, the knee pressing into the leg of the tea table. Dark veins stained the skin of her arms, neck, and cheeks. Her mouth was open as if she were screaming, and the flesh—it was singed and charred. As was the area around her…

She had no eyes.

They had been burned out, the skin around them charred in a strange pattern, reminding me of…wings.

The soft stir of air behind me was the only warning I had. Instinct took over, screaming that if someone were still in this home and had moved upon me that quietly, it didn't bode well. I turned, sweeping out with my arm—

A cool hand closed over my wrist as I twisted, thrusting up sharply with my right hand—my dagger. The blade met resistance, and the shadowstone, so sharp and deadly, pierced the skin, sank far—sank deep into *his* chest at the very same second the jolt of energy danced across my flesh, and I realized who had grabbed me.

Who I had just stabbed in the chest.

In the heart.

Oh, gods.

I lifted my gaze from where my hand and the dagger's hilt were flush with a chest adorned in black, to eyes…

Wide eyes streaked with swirling wisps of eather.

Eyes of the silver-eyed god.

Chapter 6

My heart stuttered and then sped up. Air lodged in my throat as I watched him slowly lower his gaze to his chest—to the dagger I'd shoved deep into him. Shock turned my entire body numb. I didn't even feel his hand still wrapped around my left wrist. I didn't feel anything but disbelief and pounding, sheer terror.

Shadowstone could kill a god if they were stabbed in the heart, and my aim had only been off by a fraction of an inch—if that. In the back of my mind, I knew he'd survive this, but it had to *hurt*.

Quicksilver eyes lifted to mine once more. The wispy tendrils of eather whipped through his irises, and I knew he would kill me. There was no way he wouldn't. Pressure clamped down on my chest as he let go of my wrist and slowly took a step back, freeing himself. Slick blood coated the blade, dark and *shimmery* in the lamplight—nothing like mortal blood. I stared at my dagger, bracing myself as I took several steps back.

"Yet again, you entered a home without taking a moment to see if you were truly alone," the god said, and my gaze flew to his. The eather swirled even more wildly in his eyes. "That was incredibly reckless. Don't ever do that again."

My lips parted on a harsh exhale. "I…I just stabbed you in the chest, and *that* is what you have to say?"

"No. I was getting to that." Tilting his head to the side, dark hair slid across his cheek. "You stabbed me."

"I did." I took another step back, throat now too dry to swallow.

"In the chest," he tacked on. The front of his tunic was torn, but there was no stain of blood. Nothing. If it weren't for the smear on the blade, I wouldn't have believed I had actually done it. "*Almost* in my heart."

A tremble ran through my hands. "Well, it seems it had very little impact on you." Which was terrifying on a whole other level.

"It stung," he growled, head straightening. "Deeply."

"Sorry?"

His chin lowered. "You are not sorry."

I actually was. Sort of. "You grabbed me."

"Do you stab everyone who grabs you?"

"Yes!" I exclaimed. "Especially when I'm in a home with a dead body and someone grabs me from behind without any warning!"

"I'm not ready to talk about why you're even in this home with a dead body," he stated, and I frowned. "But first, you don't sound sorry."

"I was—*am*—but I wouldn't have stabbed you if you hadn't grabbed me."

"Are you seriously blaming *me*?" Disbelief rang in his tone.

"You grabbed me," I repeated. "Without warning—"

"Perhaps you should look before stabbing?" the god argued. "Or has that never occurred to you?"

"Has it ever occurred to you to announce your presence so you don't get stabbed?" I shot back.

The god moved fast. I had no chance to do anything. He was suddenly in front of me, gripping the dagger *blade*-first. He yanked it from my hand. A second later, silver-white energy crackled over his knuckles. The light flared and pulsed, swallowing the blade and the hilt. The shadowstone and the iron handle crumbled under his grip.

My mouth dropped open.

He opened his hand, and the lamplight caught the ashes of what remained of my dagger as they fell to the floor.

"You destroyed my dagger!" I exclaimed.

"I did," he parroted my words.

Stunned, all I could do was stand there for several moments. I couldn't even think about the years my family had kept that dagger safe, waiting for me. "How dare you!?"

"How dare I? Do you think that maybe I don't want to be stabbed again with it?"

"You wouldn't have to worry about that if you simply said hello!" I shouted.

"But what if I just happened to startle you?" he challenged. "You'd likely stab me even then."

I balled my hands into fists. "Now, I really want to stab you again."

"With what?" His chin lowered once more, eyes a swirling storm. "Your bare fingers? I'm half-tempted to allow you to try."

I inhaled sharply at the almost teasing tone. He was amused by this. But he had destroyed my favorite dagger. Whatever flimsy hold I had on my restraint had been severed. "Maybe I'll get my hands on another shadowstone blade. And instead of going for your heart, I'll aim for your throat? Can a god survive without their head? I'm eager to find out."

He arched a brow. "I think you actually mean that."

I smiled widely then—the same kind of expression I'd given my mother earlier. "Perhaps."

Shock briefly flickered across his face, widening those churning eyes. "You actually dare to threaten me? Even now?"

"It's not a threat," I said. "It's a promise."

He drew back. Immediately, I recognized that I may have let my temper get the better of me, forgetting exactly *what* he was.

A ripple of energy rolled across the chamber, licking my skin. The feel of it was icy-hot, leaving a wake of goosebumps behind as it rattled the paintings on the walls.

I could barely force air into my lungs, but I held my ground instead of caving to the instinct to run—to bolt from the house and this being with incomprehensible power, never looking back. Shaking, I lifted my chin. "I'm supposed to be impressed by that?"

The god became very still as the light pulsed intensely. Every muscle in my body locked up. Maybe my mother had been eerily prophetic about my mouth?

He laughed, low and throaty. I didn't see him lift his hand but I did feel the cold press of a finger against my cheek. My heart faltered as I tried to prepare myself for the pain of the eather burning me from the inside, just like it had with the Kazin siblings and the poor woman on the floor here.

But no pain came.

All I felt was the rough pads of his fingers trailing over my cheek, stopping just at the corner of my lips. "What truly scares you, *liessa*?" he asked, and I thought…I thought I heard a hint of approval in his voice. "If I do not?"

Liessa. That was the second time he'd called me that and I wanted to know what the word meant. Now didn't seem the most opportune time to ask such a question.

"I…I am afraid," I admitted because…who wouldn't be?

The intense, silvery light faded from his eyes. "Only on a superficial level. Not the kind of fear that shapes a mortal, changes who they are and guides what choices they make," he said, his thumb sliding over my chin, brushing the underside of my lip. His touch was solid, an icy brand that sent a wave of apprehension and…something stronger through me. Something that felt like *finally*, like that same sense of *rightness* I'd felt before. Obviously, something was very wrong with me. Because that didn't make sense. "You may feel terror, but you're not terrified. And there is a kingdom's worth of difference between the two."

"How…how would you know?" I asked, my heart hammering as his fingers splayed across my jaw and cheek. I didn't know if my heart beat so fast because he was touching me, or because he did it so gently. His hand grazed the curve of my neck, and I wondered if he could feel how fast my pulse thrummed. "Are you a God of Thoughts and Emotions?"

He let out another raspy, rough laugh as his fingers slipped under my hood, moving beneath the braid hanging at the nape of my neck. "You," he said, his thumb moving in a slow swipe over the side of my throat. There was something about the way he said that. "You are trouble."

I bit the inside of my cheek as another wave of shivers pulsated through me, settling in very indecent places, and leaving me to question how unwise I actually was.

Which, I had a feeling, was very.

Because the sharp swirl of tingles tightening my skin was utterly insane. He didn't even look mortal right now.

"Not really," I whispered.

"Lies."

I searched the hard, brutally striking lines of his features. "You…you aren't angry with me?"

"I'm definitely perturbed," he replied, and I could think of dozens of better adjectives to describe the state of my rage if someone had *almost* stabbed me in the heart. "As I said, it stung. For a moment."

Only for a moment?

"I have a feeling your next question will be if I'm sure I'm not going to kill you," he continued, and I'd be lying if I said I hadn't been thinking that. "I won't say it didn't cross my mind when I felt the blade pierce my skin." His thumb made another slow pass over my pulse.

"What stopped you?"

"Many things." His head tilted slightly, and I felt cool breath coast over the curve of my chin. "Though I find myself questioning my sanity, considering you then proceeded to threaten me again immediately."

I stayed quiet, listening to instinct for once.

"Color me surprised," he said, lips curving upward. "I expected you to have some sort of retort."

"I'm trying to employ common sense and remain somewhat quiet."

"How is that working out for you?"

"Not very well, to be honest."

The god laughed quietly, and then his fingers left me. "Why are you here?"

The swift change in him and the subject left me reeling for a minute, and I almost sank against the wall as he turned to the body. Why was I here? My gaze flicked to where the woman lay. Oh, yes, murder. Gods. "I was walking…" I folded my arms across my waist, knowing I couldn't tell him the complete truth. "I saw that god from earlier leave this house and thought I should check it out."

"You saw him leave but did not see me enter?" he questioned.

Dammit. "No."

He looked over his shoulder at me. "Why would you think you should check it out?"

I stiffened. "Why not? Shouldn't people be concerned when they see murderous gods leaving mortals' residences?"

An eyebrow rose. "Shouldn't mortals be more concerned about their safety?"

I snapped my mouth shut.

The god turned away, and without his piercing gaze on me, I took a moment to really look at him. He was dressed like the last time I'd seen him: dark breeches, hooded tunic, sleeveless and black. Gods, he was even taller than I remembered. There were also leather straps across his chest and upper back, securing some kind of sword to his back. The hilt was tipped down and to the side for easy access. I didn't remember seeing him with one when I encountered him before.

Why would a god need a sword when they had the power of eather at their fingertips?

I shifted my weight. "She was killed like the Kazin siblings, wasn't she? That's why you're here."

"I was alerted to one of them entering the mortal realm," he said, edging around the body of Miss Joanis. So, someone was aware of him tracking the responsible gods. "I got here as fast as I could. Madis was lazy this time. Leaving her here. I was looking for some evidence of who she was when you arrived, let yourself in, and failed to check the rest of the home."

My eyes narrowed. "You mean when you failed to announce your presence?"

He looked over his shoulder at me. "Come now, do you believe someone who harbored ill will towards you would've announced their presence?"

"No. I believe that someone who doesn't, would," I replied. "All others would end up with a dagger in their chest." The corners of my lips turned down. "That is if I had a dagger."

"Perhaps you would still have a dagger if you didn't go around stabbing people."

I actually still had one. Tucked in my boot. Not a shadowstone blade, but a slender iron one. However, that was beside the point. "I don't go around stabbing people." Usually. "And you owe me a shadowstone dagger."

"Do I?"

I nodded. "You do."

"By the way, how did your stepbrother come upon such a weapon?"

It took me a moment to remember the lie I'd told him. "Someone gave it to him for a birthday. I don't know who or why. My stepbrother has never expressed interest in weapons."

"You do realize that it's forbidden for mortals to hold shadowstone daggers."

I did, but I lifted a shoulder in a shrug.

One side of his lips tipped up, and then he looked away. "Did you let go of what you saw at the Kazins' home like I asked?"

My spine stiffened. "I don't recall that you asked. More like demanded. But, no, I did not."

"I know."

"Were you watching?"

Molten silver eyes connected with mine. "Perhaps."

"That's…creepy."

One broad shoulder lifted. "I told you I would. I figured I should keep an eye on you. Make sure you didn't get into any *more* trouble."

"I don't need you to do that."

"I didn't say you did." He inclined his head as he eyed me.

"Then what are you saying?"

"I wanted to," he said, and he sounded surprised by the admission.

I opened my mouth and then closed it. How…how was I supposed to respond to that?

"What did you find out?" he asked after a moment.

It took some effort to gather my thoughts. "If you were watching, you should know."

That faint grin reappeared. "I imagine you discovered that no one had anything bad to say about those mortals."

"In other words, you already know I didn't find out much," I admitted. "Has…have there been any more deaths? Besides this one?"

He shook his head. "Do you know her?"

"I…I know *of* her. She's a seamstress. Andreia Joanis." I inched forward. "She's very talented. In high demand. Or was." I cringed a little. "I actually saw her earlier."

His gaze sharpened on me. "You did?"

I nodded, looking at the body. "Yeah. It was only for a few minutes. She was bringing a gown to my mother," I told him, thinking that piece of information didn't matter. "What a strange coincidence, right?"

"Right," he murmured.

When I looked up at him, I saw he watched me in that intense way that felt as if he could see everything I wasn't saying. "Did you find anything that could indicate why Madis did this?"

The god shook his head. "Nothing."

"But you believe that she died for the same reason as the others?"

"I do." He dragged a hand over his head, shoving his hair out of his face.

I started to speak but stopped.

"Why do I sense you want to ask something?"

The frown returned. "You're a god. How do you not know what the other gods are up to?"

"Just because someone is a god doesn't mean they have some sort of inherent knowledge of the comings and goings of other gods, or the reasons behind their actions," he answered. "Neither would a Primal."

"That wasn't exactly what I was suggesting," I pointed out. "I meant that since you seem pretty—"

"Thank you."

I shot him a bland look. "Since you seem pretty powerful, couldn't you demand to know what they're doing?"

"That's not how it works." He leaned forward. "There are things that gods and Primals can and cannot do.

Curiosity sparked through me. "Are you telling me that not even a Primal can do as they please?"

"I didn't say that." His head tilted down. "A Primal can do whatever they want."

I threw up my hands. "If that's not the most contradictory statement I've heard in my entire life, I don't know what is."

"What I'm saying is that a Primal or a god can do whatever they please," he said. "But every cause has an effect. There are always consequences for every action, even if they don't impact me directly."

Well, that was an incredibly vague explanation that kind of made sense. I looked at the seamstress. Something occurred to me. When a mortal passed, it was believed that the body must be burned so the soul could be released to enter the Shadowlands. I wasn't sure that what had happened to the Kazin siblings counted as a burial burning. "Those who die like the Kazins…do their souls make it to the Shadowlands?"

The god was quiet for a long moment. "No. They…they simply cease to exist."

"Oh, my gods." I pressed my hand to my mouth.

His eyes lifted to mine. "It is a cruel fate, even one greater than being sentenced to the Abyss. There, at least you are *something*."

"I…I can't even process what it would be like to simply stop being." I shuddered, hoping he didn't notice. "That is…"

"Something only the vilest should face," he finished for me.

I nodded as I took in the sitting room, the bright blue and pale pink throw pillows, the small stone statues of sea creatures rumored to live off the coast of Iliseeum, and all the tiny knick-knacks that were little parts of Andreia Joanis's life. Pieces of who she was and who she would never be again.

I cleared my throat, desperately searching for something else to think about. "What Court do you belong to?"

He raised a brow again.

"I mean, are you from the Shadowlands?"

The god studied me for a moment and then nodded. I tensed, although I wasn't surprised. He continued to watch me. "There's something else you want to ask."

There was. I wanted to know if he knew who I was. If that was why our paths had crossed twice now in such a strange way. He may not know about the deal but he could know that I was the would-be Consort of the Primal he served. But if he didn't know, it would be a risk. This god could tell the Primal that I had been in possession of a shadowstone dagger and hadn't been afraid to use it.

So, I landed on something else I'd always been curious about—something I would've asked the Primal himself if I'd had the chance. Being from the Shadowlands, there was a good chance he might know. "Are all souls judged upon death?"

"There isn't enough time in a day to do that," he said. "When someone dies and enters the Shadowlands, they are once more given physical form. Most will pass through the Pillars of Asphodel, which will guide them to where the soul must go. Guards there ensure that happens."

"You said *most*. What about the others?"

"Some special cases must be judged in person." His gaze bore into mine. "Those who need to be seen to determine what their fate may be."

"How?" I crept closer to him.

"After death, the soul is exposed. Raw. No flesh to mask their deeds," he explained. "The worthiness can be read after death."

"And…what about a soul now? I mean, when someone is alive."

He shook his head. "Some may know things just from looking upon a mortal or another god, but the core of one's soul is not one of them."

I halted when I caught his faint citrusy scent. "What things?"

A small grin appeared. "So very curious," he murmured, his gaze coasting over my face, seeming to linger on my mouth. A warmth entered my veins, one that seemed wholly inappropriate since I now knew for sure which Court he served. But he looked at me as if he were fascinated by the shape of my mouth.

As if he might want to taste my lips again.

A shivery wave of anticipation swept through me, and I knew if he did, I wouldn't stop him. It would be a bad choice on my part. Maybe even on his. But I often made bad decisions.

The god's gaze cut away, and I didn't know if I felt disappointment or relief. He dragged his teeth over his bottom lip. The hint of fangs became apparent. It was definitely disappointment I felt.

An odd feeling pressed against the center of my chest without warning, where the warmth often gathered in response to death. The heaviness unfurled through me, feeling like a coarse, suffocating blanket. I drew in a shallow breath, frowning at the sudden, strange scent of lilacs. Stale lilacs. It reminded me of something I couldn't place at that moment as I felt myself turn back to the body without consciously willing myself to do so.

Wait.

I took a step closer. "Did you move her legs?"

"Why would I do that?"

Unease slithered through my veins. "When I came in, one of her legs was bent at the knee, pressing against the table. Both are straight now."

"I didn't move her," he replied as my gaze lifted to her face. The charred skin shaped like wings across her cheeks and forehead seemed to have faded a little. "Maybe you—"

The rattle of a breath being drawn and the crackle of lungs expanding silenced the god. My gaze flew to her chest just as the bodice of her gown rose. I froze in disbelief.

"What…?" the god muttered.

Andreia Joanis sat up, that gaping mouth opening even farther, the singed lips peeling back to reveal four long canines—two along the top of her mouth and two along the bottom. Fangs.

"The *fuck*?" the god finished.

"That's not…normal, right?" I whispered.

"Which part? The fangs, or the fact that she's dead and still sitting up?"

Andreia's head tilted toward the god, seeming to look at him with eyes that were no longer there.

"I don't think she's dead," I said. "Any longer."

"No," the god growled, causing my skin to pimple. "She is still dead."

"You sure—?" I swallowed a gasp as the seamstress's head snapped in my direction. "She's staring at me, I think. I can't be sure. She doesn't have eyes." Out of instinct, I reached for my thigh, only to come up empty. I started to turn to the god. "I would really like to have my dagger—"

A hissing sound came from Andreia, the kind of noise no mortal should be able to make. It rose and deepened, turning into a piercing snarl that raised every single hair on my body.

Andreia rocketed to her feet, the movement so inexplicably fast that I jerked back out of reflex. Fingers curled, she launched forward—

The god was just as unbelievably fast, stepping in front of me as he withdrew a short sword. The blade glimmered like polished onyx in the candlelight. Shadowstone. He stepped forward, planting a boot in her midsection. The seamstress flew backward over the tea table.

She fell onto the floor, quickly rolling into a crouch. Popping back up, she came at us again. I started to reach for the blade in my boot when the god met her attack, thrusting the shadowstone sword deep into her chest.

The seamstress's body spasmed as she reached out, trying to grab hold of the god. Tiny, spiderweb-like fissures appeared along her hands and then raced up her arms, spreading over her throat and then across her cheeks.

Jerking the shadowstone sword free, the god stepped to the side, his focus intent on the seamstress. Those fissures deepened into cracks as her legs collapsed under her. She went down hard, folded into herself.

I stood there, mouth hanging open. Patches of her body seemed to sink in as if she were nothing more than a dried-out husk. "What…what did I just see?"

"I have no idea." The god tentatively stepped forward, nudging Andreia's foot. The skin and bone turned to ash, quickly followed by the rest of her body.

Within a span of several heartbeats, nothing remained of the seamstress but her gown and a dusting of ash.

I blinked. "That was…different."

The god looked at me. "Yeah, it was."

"And you…you have no idea what just happened? Like that's never happened before?"

Steel-hued eyes met mine. "I have never heard of something like that happening before."

Being a god from the Shadowlands, I imagined he would know about mortals coming back from the dead. "What do you think was wrong with her? I mean, why did she act that way?"

"I don't know." He sheathed his sword. "But I don't think Madis simply killed her. He did…something. What, I have no idea." A muscle ticked along his jaw. "I would not repeat what you've seen here."

I nodded. As if anyone would believe me if I did.

"I must go," he said, glancing back at the ash-covered gown and then to me. "You should, too, *liessa*."

I didn't want to spend another second in this house, but a hundred different questions exploded in my head. The absolute least important one of all was what came out of my mouth. "What does *liessa* mean?"

The god didn't answer for what felt like a small eternity. "It has different meanings to different people." The eather pulsed in his eyes, swirling once more through the silver. "But all of them mean something beautiful and powerful."

Chapter 7

A day later, I was yet again squirreled away in the east tower and blindfolded.

Sliding the iron blade between my fingers, I drew in a long, measured breath as I tried not to think about how the god had destroyed my dagger the night before. Luckily, I never practiced with it. I didn't even want to know how Sir Holland would respond to learning that I'd lost such a weapon.

Or to the news that I'd stabbed a god in the chest with it.

I didn't think Sir Holland would react all that calmly.

Looking back, I could understand why the god had destroyed the dagger. I *had* stabbed him. But I was still furious. It was over a century old, and if I had any hope of fulfilling my duty—if I were ever given a chance—I needed a shadowstone blade.

I also tried not to think about what I had seen—what had happened to Andreia. The image of her sitting up and launching herself to her feet like some sort of wild animal had lived in my head, rent-free all night long. I had no idea what could've been done to her, but I hoped the god figured it out.

Something beautiful and powerful.

His words still caught me off guard. But in my defense, he had called me a name that meant something beautiful and powerful, even after I'd stabbed him. That seemed even more unexplainable than whatever had happened to the seamstress.

Liessa. I couldn't believe I asked that instead of a hundred other more important questions. Starting with asking what his name was.

"Now," Sir Holland ordered.

Spinning, I threw the blade, exhaling at the sound of the smack it made striking the dummy's chest. This went on for a godsforsaken amount of time until I could no longer *not* speak about what I had seen the day before.

After throwing the blade, I tugged down the blindfold. "Can I ask you something?"

"Of course," he replied, starting toward the dummy.

"Have you ever heard of a…?" It took me a moment to figure out how to ask what I wanted without giving too much away. "A dead person coming back to life?"

Sir Holland stopped and turned around. "That…that was not the kind of question I was expecting."

"I know." I toyed with the hem of my airy cotton shirt.

He frowned. "What would make you even ask something like that?"

I forced a shrug. "I just heard someone talking about it when I was out. They claimed to have seen someone come back to life with fangs like a god but…different. They had fangs on the upper and lower teeth."

His brows lifted. "I've never heard of anything like that. If whoever said that was speaking the truth, then it sounds like an…abomination."

"Yeah," I murmured.

He studied me. "Where did you hear this?"

Before I could come up with a believable lie, a knock sounded on the tower door. Sir Holland retrieved the blade from the dummy. He looked over his shoulder at me as he walked toward the door. I shrugged. "Who is it?" he called, slipping the blade behind his back.

"It's me," came a hushed voice. "Ezra. I'm looking for Sera." There was a pause while Sir Holland rested his forehead against the door. "I know she's in there. And I know that you know that I know she's in there."

A grin tugged at my lips, but it faded quickly. There was only one reason I could think of that would've drawn Ezra to the tower to find me. My gaze drifted briefly to the many stab wounds that punctured the dummy's chest, and I thought of all the *harmful* things I'd done in the last three years.

Sir Holland shot me a scowl. "You never should've told her where you train." He sliced the blade through the air. "She could've been followed here."

"It wasn't intentional," I said, wondering who in the castle didn't already suspect who I was and could've followed her.

"Truly?" Sir Holland demanded.

"Just so you know, I can hear you," Ezra's muffled voice came through the door. "And Sera speaks the truth. I simply stalked her through the castle one morning. And since I'm not unobservant, I figured out that this is where she spends a decent part of her days."

"Like you didn't know you were being followed," he muttered.

I lifted a shoulder. Of course, I knew she had been following me, but since Ezra had remained kind towards me after I failed, I really hadn't attempted to throw her off my trail. And it wasn't like she didn't know I trained. Sir Holland was just being dramatic.

"I haven't been followed," Ezra announced from the other side of the door. "But I can only imagine that the longer I stand here talking to a door, the more attention I will draw."

"Let her in, please," I said. "She would only come here if she had to."

"As if I have a choice." He threw the lock and opened the door.

Princess Ezmeria stood at the top of the narrow stairwell, her light brown hair swept back in a bun at the nape of her neck. Even though it was sweltering in the tower and most likely no better outside, she wore a black, pinstriped short waistcoat over an ivory and cream gown made of the same lightweight cotton. Ezra always seemed immune to the heat and humidity.

"Thank you." She smiled as she nodded at an exasperated Sir Holland. Her features were similar to Tavius's, but her brown eyes held a keen sharpness, and her jaw had a stubborn hardness that Tavius lacked. "It is good to see you, Sir Holland."

Sir Holland pinned her with a look of utter impassivity. "It is good to see you, Your Grace."

"What do you need?" I asked as I took the iron blade from Sir Holland, sheathing it.

"Many things," she replied. "One of those chocolate scones Orlano makes when he's in a good mood would be lovely. Along with cooled tea. A good book that isn't misery fiction, which begs the question—why do the curators of the city Atheneum think any of us wants to read things that only depress us?" she asked, rocking back on her heeled slippers as Sir Holland rubbed at his brow. "I'm also in need of an end to this drought—oh, and peace among the kingdoms." Ezra smiled widely as she slid an amused glance at Sir Holland. "But right now, the Ladies of Mercy and I are in need of your assistance, Sera."

Sir Holland lowered his hand, frowning as he looked at me. "What would the Ladies at the orphanage need from you?"

"Her ability to *borrow* excess food from the kitchens without anyone noticing," Ezra answered smoothly. "With the influx of recently parentless children, their cupboards are rather bare."

I stiffened just a fraction. Suspicion clouded Sir Holland's features. My ability to do just as Ezra claimed had come in handy quite frequently. I often took whatever leftover food I could scrounge from the kitchens to the Cliffs of Sorrow, where the old fortress had been converted into the largest orphanage in Carsodonia. Still, even as big as it was, the orphanage hemorrhaged with those orphaned by death or abandoned by parents who could not or would no longer care for them. But Ezra had never once come to me for that. I turned to him. "I will see you tomorrow morning?"

His eyes had narrowed, but he nodded. I didn't linger to give him time to start asking questions.

"Have a good day, Sir Holland," Ezra said as she stepped aside, allowing me to exit the tower.

Dust danced in the streaks of sunlight seeping through the arrow slits in the walls of the tower as we made our way down to the third floor, where my bedchambers were located among the row of empty chambers. We didn't speak until we stepped into the narrow hall. Ezra turned to me, keeping her voice low, even though it was unlikely that anyone was around to overhear us. "You should probably change your clothing." Her gaze flickered over the loose tunic I wore. "Something a little more…suitable for where we must travel."

I cocked my head to the side. "Exactly what am I assisting you with?"

"Well…" Ezra dipped her chin toward mine, standing close but not close enough to touch me. I pretended not to notice how she made sure her skin didn't come into contact with mine. "I received a letter from Lady Sunders regarding a child—a young girl named Ellie—that just came under her guardianship, courtesy of one of the Mistresses of the Jade."

I frowned in surprise. "What was a young girl doing with the Mistresses?" The only reason Jade had even been willing to discuss the things involved in the act of seduction with me was because she believed I was far older than sixteen. Even then, with the veil obscuring my features, I saw that she had been suspicious, even though others were married at that age. "That is not like them—"

"It's not. One of the women who works for them found the poor girl in an alley. She had a blackened eye among numerous other injuries, as well as being undernourished. Ellie's healing," Ezra quickly added. "Lady Sunders says that the child's mother died many years ago, and her father had lost his source of income. She believes the child's father was once a laborer at one of the farms that fell to the Rot."

"I'm sorry to hear that," I murmured because it felt like I needed to say something, even though there was nothing to be said.

"I wouldn't feel too sorry for the father. It appears that he enjoyed spending his money on liquor more than food, long before he lost his job as a harvester." Ezra's lips tightened. "Lady Sunders got the impression that the mother's death may not have been a natural one, but the kind aided by the father's heavy fists."

"Lovely," I muttered.

"It gets worse," she said, and I wasn't sure how. "At some point, the father entered the business of selling intimate moments—"

"The sex trade?" I clarified for her.

"Yes, that is one way of saying it when the person is actually *willing* to trade time with their intimate parts for coin, protection, shelter…or whatever. But he was the type to *make* others willing," she corrected. And, yes, she was right. It did get worse. "Which is also why the Mistresses of the Jade are very displeased with this man. As you know, they are not fans of those types of peddlers."

No, the courtesans were not fans of anyone being forced into the trade they'd entered into willingly.

"The girl who was given over to Lady Sunders has a younger brother, who is still with the father. The boy is in a very precarious situation, being forced to commit all manner of thievery to keep his father's cups full. She fears he's being made to agree to other unspeakable things in exchange for food and shelter—as was the daughter."

I inhaled sharply, disturbed but sadly not surprised. Both Ezra and I had seen this before. Hardship could exploit the worst in people as they struggled to survive, forcing them to do things they'd never consider. But then there were those who always had that darkness in them, the ones who were predators long before they faced adversity.

"Lady Sunders inquired to see if my *friend* who has a certain set of *talents*," she said, glancing pointedly at where the blade was sheathed, "would be able to assist in extracting the child."

In other words, the kind of skills that Sir Holland had spent years honing for a completely different reason. "And why would that require me to wear something more *enticing*?"

"The father? His name is Nor. Lady Sunders believes it's short for Norbert."

"*Norbert*?" I repeated, blinking. "Okay."

"Anyway, Nor does his business out of Croft's Cross," she explained. Croft's Cross was one of the districts that the Nye River separated from the Garden District. Near the water, that quarter of Carsodonia was full of homes stacked upon one another with little space between them. The warehouses, pubs, gambling dens, and other establishments nowhere near as resplendent as those found in the Garden. Most who called Croft's Cross home were good people just trying to live. However, there were also people like Nor, who could infect Croft's Cross as easily as the Rot did to the land.

"He's been keeping his son close since he can't get his hands on his daughter," she went on. "The only way to get into that building is if he thinks you're looking for a certain type of employment."

"Great," I muttered.

"I would do it myself, but—"

"No. No, you will not," I said. Ezra had a brilliant mind, but she had no knowledge of how to defend herself. Not only that, she was an actual Princess, even if she was often involved in things one didn't typically find a Princess engaged in. "Give me a few moments."

Ezra nodded, and I turned, starting for my bedchamber. "Oh, and do wear something you aren't worried about getting…bloody."

I stopped, looking over my shoulder. "There is no reason for me to get blood on any of my clothing. I'm going in to get a child. That is all."

She smiled faintly as her brows rose. "Sure. That is all that will happen."

Chapter 8

The plain, black carriage bounced along the uneven cobblestones. That's how I knew we'd entered Croft's Cross.

Sitting across from me, Ezra frowned over her shoulder at the driver's seat where *Lady* Marisol Faber sat, cloaked and unrecognizable. I imagined she must be suffocating in the godsforsaken heat.

Waving a hand in front of my face, I knew I was. I wanted to unhook the lightweight, hooded cape and throw it aside. Tendrils of hair had plastered themselves to the back of my neck.

I had no idea how long Marisol had been assisting Ezra in her many endeavors to aid those most endangered in Carsodonia. They had been friends since Ezra's father married my mother, and she came to live here. But I hadn't become involved in what they were doing until three years ago. I'd only discovered what Ezra was doing when I saw her at the old fortress while leaving behind a bushel of potatoes Orlano had left out for me to do with as I pleased. When we spotted one another, we pretended as if we had no idea who the other was. Later that night, I'd waited for Ezra to return from her walk in the gardens. It was then that I learned why she spent so much time beyond Wayfair grounds.

I looked over at my stepsister, studying her. There wasn't even a sheen of sweat on her features. Unreal.

"How are you not hot?" I asked.

She pulled her attention from the window. "I think it's

comfortable," she said, her brows pinching as her gaze dropped. "Your gown is…well, it should do the job."

I didn't need to look down to know that she was staring at the delicate, white lace of the low and very, *very* tight bodice of the sage-colored gown. If my chest managed to remain in my gown throughout this adventure, it would be no small miracle. "I think this used to belong to Lady Kala." Which also explained why my boots were clearly visible since the hem only reached my calves. "There weren't many options."

"Ah, yes. I suppose there aren't." The skin puckered between her brows as she looked back out the window. A moment passed. "Do you need gowns?" she asked, looking back at me. "I have some that would surely be of more comfort to wear."

I stiffened, feeling my cheeks start to burn. "No, that won't be necessary."

"Are you sure?" She leaned forward. "My gowns will not put you at risk of bursting the seams across the chest."

"I have other gowns—nicer ones than this," I told her, which wasn't exactly a lie. "This was the only one I thought would be enticing."

Ezra sat back. "I think the enticing part is the limited amount of time you have before your breasts break free."

I snorted.

Her smile was brief. The look that settled on her face made me more uncomfortable than her offer of the gowns. It wasn't one of pity but of sadness, and she looked as if she were about to speak but couldn't find the words. Ezra always had words, a plethora of them, but she never spoke of the curse. The question rose to the tip of my tongue. I wanted to ask if she still believed that the Primal of Death would come for me, but I stopped myself. Her answer wouldn't soothe me when I knew the truth.

Instead, I asked, "How did you sneak away without any Royal Guards following?"

One side of her lips curled up. "I have my ways."

I started to ask about said ways when the carriage slowed. I glanced out the window. A mass of people hurried along the crowded street, heading toward the small shops and into dark, winding alleys under rickety metal staircases attached to narrow buildings that rose several stories. Many of them, faded to a dull yellow and drab brown, were packed side by side. Somehow, the proprietors managed to cram twenty or more rooms into those buildings without electricity, and in some instances, plumbing. It was irresponsible to allow anyone to live in these so-called apartments, but the people and their families would be on the streets without them. However, it wasn't like there were no other options.

"The land that has been ruined by the Rot… It can still be built upon, can it not?" I asked. Ezra nodded. "I don't understand why new homes aren't being built on those farms. Small ones, but at least places where you don't have to risk your life climbing stairs that could give out from under you at any moment."

"But what of the farmers once the Rot is dealt with?" she countered.

Well, I had asked my answer, hadn't I? If she believed the Rot would vanish, then she must be holding onto some kernel of hope that I would be able to fulfill my duty. "What if it doesn't?" I asked.

Ezra knew what I meant. "Mari's father is determined to discover the cause. You and I both know he won't, but his mind is brilliant. If anyone can figure out a natural way to end this, it will be Lord Faber."

I hoped she was right, and not just to alleviate some of the guilt I felt. "Could the farmers not become proprietors then? Gaining their income from leasing the homes?"

"They could." Her nose wrinkled. "But there is the question of where the materials to build the homes would come from."

And there was the flaw in my idea. The rock deposits in the Elysium Peaks used to build much of the buildings were mined and paid for by business owners or landowners. The stone had a cost, as did the labor it took to build the homes. The Crown should pay for it, but the Crown's coffers were not as abundant as they once were since they paid for more and more food and goods from other kingdoms.

And yet, there was somehow still enough for a new gown for the Queen.

"The home Nor is in has red shutters over the windows. I believe it's to our right," Ezra said as the carriage jerked to a halt. "He is on the first floor—the entirety of the first floor. His *offices* are right inside."

I nodded, reaching for the carriage door. "Do you know the son's name?"

Ezra looked down as she pulled the rolled letter from the sleeve of her coat, unfurling it. "His name is…Nate." Her gaze met mine. "Far less confusing than Nor."

"Agreed." I lifted the hood of the cape. While it was unlikely there would be much involved in this event, the paleness of my hair was noticeable, and I would rather not take the chance of someone recognizing me in case things, well, ended poorly. "Stay here."

"Of course." She paused. "Be careful."

"Always," I murmured, cracking the door open wide enough for the noise of the street to seep in and for me to slip through. Refusing to think about whatever liquid I stepped in since it couldn't be what fell from the sky, I walked to the front of the carriage. "Marisol?" I whispered. The hooded head turned in my direction. The Lady knew exactly who I was, but like Ezra, her treatment of me whenever I saw her was the same as it had been before the curse. We weren't close by any means, but she wasn't cruel, and she didn't behave as if she were afraid of me. "Make sure she stays in this carriage."

She glanced up at the already-full streets. "I will drive around to prevent her from doing something idiotic."

"Perfect." I turned, stepping onto the cracked stone sidewalk and into the throng of people.

Knowing better than to breathe too deeply or to linger in any one spot, I waited only until the carriage pulled away from the curb before heading right, giving the pigeons having a party in the filth a wide berth. I moved among men and women returning from work or heading to it. Some wore capes like mine to shield their faces from the sun or to keep from being recognized. They were the ones I kept an eye on. Others stumbled out of pubs, their blouses and tunics stained with beer and who knew what else. Vendors shouted from nearly every building, selling questionable oysters, flat muffins, and cherries on sticks. I kept my arms to my sides, ignoring the lingering stares and the lewd, drunken comments from males leaning against the front of buildings.

Croft's Cross was one of the only places in all of Carsodonia where neither the Sun Temple—sometimes referred to as the Temple of Life—nor the Shadow Temple was visible. It was almost as if the district were outside their reach of authority, where life and death couldn't be managed by any Primal.

"The Crown doesn't care that we're losing our jobs, homes, families, and futures!" A woman's voice rose above the noise of the crowd. "They go to sleep with full bellies while we starve! We're dying, and they're doing nothing about the Rot!"

I searched out the source of the words. Up ahead, where Ezra's carriage had disappeared into the sea of similar transports and wagons, the road split into a vee. In the center was one of the smaller places of worship in Carsodonia. The Temple of Keella, the Goddess of Rebirth, was a squat, round structure of white limestone and granite. Children raced barefoot around the colonnade, darting in and out of columns. I moved closer, able to see that the woman was dressed in white, standing in the middle of the wide Temple steps as she shouted to the small cluster of people gathered before her.

"The age of the Golden King has passed, and the end of rebirth is near," she yelled. Nods and shouts of agreement answered her. "We know that. The Crown knows that!" She scanned the crowd and lifted her head, looking past them—looking beyond the street to me. I stopped, my breath hitching in my throat. "No Mierel sits upon that throne," she said. Chills broke out over my skin as I stared at the dark-haired woman. "Not now. Not ever again."

Someone bumped into my shoulder, startling me. I tore my gaze from the woman as the person muttered under their breath. Blinking, I forced myself to start walking. I looked over at the Temple. The woman was focused on the group in front of her, speaking now about the gods and how they would not continue to ignore the people's struggle. There was no way she could've even seen me on the sidewalk or knew who I was—not even without the hood.

Still, unease tiptoed through me, and it was a struggle to push thoughts of the woman aside as I passed an alley where several women hung clothing on lines strung between two buildings. A block down from the Temple of Keella, I spotted a tall building that'd once been a shade of ivory but was now stained to a dusty gray color. Red shutters covered the windows. Then, I was able to set aside the woman on the Temple steps.

I picked up my pace, edging around an elderly man whose lopsided gait wasn't improved by the wooden cane he heavily leaned upon. And my steps slowed. A man stood under the arched stoop of the apartments. Instinctually, I knew it was Nor. It could've been the way he leaned against the stained stone, one side of his mouth curled in a smirk as he eyed those on the sidewalk. It might've been the tankard he held in a large hand, his knuckles split open and an angry shade of crimson. Perhaps it was the untucked, vivid blue shirt that he'd left open at the neck to form a deep vee that revealed the hair on his chest.

Or it could've been the fair-haired woman who stood beside him. It wasn't the low-cut gown or the black corset cinched impossibly tight beneath her breasts, nor was it the slits in the skirt of the gown that exposed the garter that encircled her upper thigh like a ring of blood. It was the swollen bottom lip and the blackened eye poorly concealed with paint.

The woman's gaze flicked to me. Her eyes were empty, but she stiffened as I neared.

"Excuse me?" I called out.

Nor's head slowly swung in my direction as he lifted the tankard to his mouth, his dark hair slicked back from a face that could've been handsome at one time. His complexion now looked ruddy, his features too sharp. His bloodshot gaze crawled over me, even though he couldn't see much under the cape and hood. "Yeah?"

"I'm here to see a man named Nor." I kept my voice low and soft, unsure as I slipped into the role of someone else.

He took another swig from his cup. Liquid glistened on his lips and the several days' worth of stubble under his chin. "Why ya lookin' to see the man?" He chuckled smugly as if he'd said something clever.

I spared the woman a glance. She twitched nervously beside him as she stared at the street. "I…I was told that he could help me find employment."

"Were ya, now?" Nor lowered his cup, eyes narrowing. "Who told ya that, girlie?"

"The man at the pub, just down the street." I glanced over my shoulder and then stepped onto the stoop. I reached up, lifting the hood. "When I asked if he was hiring or knew of anyone, he said you might be."

Nor let out a low whistle as he eyed my features. "I'm always hirin', girlie, but I ain't lookin' for pretty things like you to sweep floors and serve drinks. Am I, Molly-girl?"

The woman beside him shook her head. "No."

His head shot in her direction. "No, *what*?"

Molly's already pale skin lightened even further. "No, sir."

"Yeah, that's a good girlie." Nor reached over, pinching her. He laughed when she squeaked, and the anger in my blood grew to a song.

"I know," I said, reaching up to toy with the button on my cape. The movement parted the folds, exposing the upper part of my gown. "I know what kind of work." I moved my fingers to the laces. "I was hoping we could speak in private and reach an agreement."

"An agreement?" Nor's interest returned to me, his dark eyes lit. "Gods be good to ya, girlie." His gaze followed my fingers over the swells above the lace as if they were leading him to his next full tankard. "Like I said, I'm always hirin', but I don't hire just any girlie."

I seriously doubted that.

He pushed off the wall hips-first, dragging a hand through his oily hair. "I got to make sure ya be worth hirin'."

"Of course." I smiled at him.

"Gods be good to me, then," he murmured, licking his lower lip. Coins jangled from the pouch secured to his hip as he turned. "Then step into my private office so we can reach an agreement."

Molly turned, her misshapen lips opening as if she wished to speak. Those flat eyes met mine, and she gave a slight shake of her head. All I could do was smile at her as I stepped into the alcove. She clamped her mouth shut, wincing, and then refocused on the street as Nor pushed the door open with one meaty hand.

A hand I had no doubt had left those bruises on Molly's face.

Nor held the door open for me, bowing and extending an arm. Liquid sloshed over the rim of his tankard, splashing onto the already sticky wood floors. I stepped inside. The smell of sweat and the heavy, sweet smell of White Horse smoke lingered in the air of the candlelit chamber. I looked around quickly, gaze slipping over settees draped with dark cloth. Several pipes lay atop a coffee table cluttered with empty cups. White powder dusted nearly the entire surface. Surprisingly, there was a desk. Flames flickered weakly from the gas lamp sitting on the corner, a spark or two from slips of parchment…and more cups.

The door closed behind me. The turn of the lock was a soft click. My eyes lifted from the desk.

"Boy," Nor barked. "I know ya in here."

The child rose from behind the desk like one of the spirits in the Dark Elms, silent and pale. He *was* young. Couldn't be more than five or six. His dark hair fell against sunken cheeks. The only color there was the purplish-blue bruise along the curve of his soft jaw. His wide, round eyes were nearly as empty as Molly's had been.

My fingers dug into the lace, tearing it.

"There ya are." Nor staggered past me, placing his cup on the parchment. "Get ya self busy somewhere else," he ordered. "I got business to deal in."

The little boy scurried around the desk, heading for the door without looking once in my direction. If he went outside—

"Not there, boy. Ya know better." Nor snapped his fingers and pointed to a narrow, dark hall. "Get to bed while there's one empty, and don't go runnin' off like ya did last time."

The child wheeled around with surprising speed, disappearing into the hall. A door clapped shut. I truly hoped the child stayed there, but I wouldn't blame him if he didn't. Which meant, I didn't have a lot of time to get to him.

"Godsdamn kids," Nor muttered. "Ya got any?"

"No."

"Didn't think so. I got two of 'em. Or did." He laughed as he dragged what sounded like a chair across the floor.

"Did?" I questioned.

"Yeah, my girlie went and got herself into some trouble, I imagine. Probably that damn mouth of hers. She never learned how to use it right. Just like her mother didn't know." Another laugh, thick and wet. "How old are ya?"

I turned to Nor, brushing the cape so the halves rested over my shoulders. "Does it matter?"

His eyes fixed on the only *enticing* part about the gown. "Nah, girlie. It don't." Nor sat down in the chair, spreading his legs. "Ya lookin' fresh. I bettin' you were some Lord's fancy little plaything. He get tired of ya?"

"I was." Ducking my chin, I smiled coyly. "But his wife…"

He snickered. "Ya ain't gotta worry about no wives 'round here." Eyeing me, his hand slid below his waist. "Ya sure are a pretty girlie."

I stood still, no longer acting like someone else but becoming *nothing*. No one. Not something beautiful and powerful. It was like donning that veil as he spewed vulgarity and decay. I wasn't me. I became this thing that had been groomed into a submissive, moldable creature. One that could be shaped into whatever the Primal of Death desired, what he might fall in love with. A servant. A wife. A warm, soft body. A killer. And this disgusting excuse for a man looked at me as if he could sculpt me into one of his *girlies*.

"Don't be nervous." Nor patted his knee. "I work out the best agreements when I got a pretty girlie in my lap."

"I'm not nervous." I wasn't. I felt absolutely nothing but disgust and anger, and those feelings didn't even run deep enough to speed up my heart rate or pulse. I think I only felt them because I believed I should feel something when I knew how this would end.

I went to him, making a mental note to scrub the soles of my boots as I climbed onto his lap, slowly lowering myself onto him.

"Damn." His hand clasped my hip and squeezed hard. I twitched, not at the discomfort but at the contact. It was nothing like those long nights when I sought to chase away the loneliness. It was nothing like when that god had touched me. "Ya ain't nervous."

"No."

"I think I'll like ya, girlie." Nor lifted his other hand, leaning his head back against the chair. Those broken knuckles grazed my cheek before reaching around to grasp the braid I had twisted into a bun. A fiery sting traveled across my scalp as he jerked my head back. I closed my eyes, not fighting his hold. "Now, girlie…"

If he called me girlie one more time…

"Ya got to show me why I should let ya give it to me," he said, his breath hot against the length of my neck. "Instead of just takin' it from ya and keepin' ya all for myself until I get tired of ya. Then I'll let ya make some coin off that pretty face. Maybe I'll just do that anyway, so you better be impressin' me."

My eyes opened as I placed my hand on his shoulder. Fighting the burn of hair pulled too tight, I lowered my chin until his dark, rheumy eyes met mine. His face was even more flushed, with lust or maybe anger. I didn't think this man could tell the difference between the two. "I will impress you."

"Confident, are ya?" He licked his lips again. "I like that, girlie."

I smiled.

Stretching so that *enticing* area was all he could focus on, I shifted my hips forward, drawing my right leg up. I didn't think about the sound he made, what I felt under me, or how he smelled as I reached into the shaft of my boot with my free hand. All I needed to do was knock him out, which wouldn't be difficult. I fully recognized I'd allowed it to get to this point. I could've incapacitated him the moment I knew where the child was, but I hadn't, and I supposed that was very telling. I also supposed that I should be worried about that as my fingers curled around the hilt of the slender iron blade, and it pressed against my unmarked palm. But this male was a user and an abuser. I was willing to bet he was worse, and that Lady Sunders' impressions were spot on about his wife. I knew this man reaching for the flap of his breeches was like the gods who'd killed those mortals. I slid the blade from my boot.

"Ya gonna get down to business?" Nor asked, and I felt a wet tongue slide against the skin of my throat—something I would absolutely never think of again. "Or am I gonna have to show ya how to do it?"

On second thought, I doubted I would worry about my actions.

I leaned back, and he let go of my hair. "I'm ready to get down to business."

His beady gaze was still fixated on the swells of my breasts. "Then get to it."

I got to it.

Sweeping my arm in a wide arc, I watched his eyes go wide with shock. The sharpened edge of the blade sliced deep across his throat as I jumped away from the spray of hot blood. I was fast, but I still felt it mist my chest.

Dammit.

Nor lurched to his feet, stumbling and clasping his ruined throat. Red spilled over his hands and between his fingers. His mouth opened, but nothing but a gurgle came out. Those cold, panicked eyes latched onto mine as he staggered forward, reaching out with a blood-smeared hand. I carefully stepped to the side. A heartbeat later, his body hit the dirtied floor with a fleshy thud and a jangle.

Mindful of the spreading pool of blood, I gathered my skirts and crouched. Spasms ran through him. I wiped my blade clean upon his shirt and then resheathed it in my boot. "May the Primal of Death take no mercy upon your soul." I started to rise and then stopped. I reached to his left hip, gripping the bag of coins. I snapped the pouch free. "Thank you for this."

Standing, I stared down at him for a few seconds as I wished away the warmth gathering in my hands, the instinctive reaction to death. I stared at his still form, ignoring the unwanted knowledge that I could undo this.

I wouldn't.

I wouldn't even if I could allow myself to.

Turning away, I walked around the desk and entered the hall. There were only two chambers. One door had been left ajar. It was packed wall-to-wall with cots covered by dirtied linens. I turned to the other door. "Nate?" I called out quietly. "Are you in there?"

There was no answer but I did hear the soft smack of feet against the floor.

"I'm here to take you to your sister." I buttoned my cape. "Ellie's at the Cliffs with a lovely lady who has been taking care of her."

A beat of silence passed, and then a small voice stated, "Ellie ain't her full name. It's short for her given name. What's her given name?"

Hell.

I shook my head, partly relieved that the child wasn't all that trusting. Ellie. What could Ellie be short for? Elizabeth? Ethel? Elena? "Eleanor?" I guessed, squeezing my eyes closed.

There was a long gap of silence and then, "Is Ellie really okay?"

I opened one eye. Maybe the gods were good to me. "Yes. She is. And I want to take you to her, but we have to leave."

"What…what about Papa?"

Biting my lip, I looked over my shoulder to the room his *papa* currently bled out in. I turned back to the door. "Your papa had to…take a nap." *A nap?* I cringed.

"He'll be mad when he wakes and can't find me," Nate whispered through the door. "He'll give me another shiner or worse."

Yeah, well, he wasn't going to be giving anyone a shiner ever again. "He won't come after you. I promise. The Ladies of Mercy will keep you safe from him. Just like they're keeping your sister safe."

I heard nothing from the other side of the door, and there was a good chance I would have to kick it in. I didn't want to traumatize the child any further, but… I stepped back.

The door cracked open, and a waifish face appeared. "I wanna see my sister."

Relief swept through me. I smiled down at the child—a real smile, not one I'd been taught. I offered him a hand. "Then let's go see your sister."

Nibbling on his lip, his gaze darted back and forth between my hand and face. He came to some sort of decision and placed his hand in mine. The contact of his warm skin jarred me, but I forced myself to get over it and curled my hand around his.

I led him out of the hall and walked straight past the front chamber, not allowing him to look toward the desk. I unlocked the door and ushered him out onto the stoop.

Molly was still there, fidgeting with the laces of her corset. She turned, raising her eyebrows as she glanced between the young boy and me. Her sunken eyes lifted to mine.

I pressed the bag of coins into her hand. "I wouldn't linger outside this door for very long," I whispered as Nate tugged on my arm. "You understand?"

Molly's eyes darted to the closed door behind me. "I…I understand." Her slim fingers curled around the pouch.

"Good." I stepped out from under the alcove into the too-bright sunlight and didn't look back.

Not once as I led the boy away.

"I see I was correct." Ezra noted the moment I sat across from her in the carriage after depositing the boy beside Marisol.

"About what?"

Ezra flicked a finger toward my chest. I looked down, seeing dark spots sprinkled across the freckles there. I sighed.

"Did you kill that man?"

Smoothing out the skirts of the gown, I crossed my ankles. "I believe he slipped and fell upon my blade."

"Was it his throat that fell upon your blade?"

"Odd, right?"

"Odd, indeed." Ezra tilted her head to the side as she stared blankly at me. "That happens quite often around you."

"Unfortunately." I arched a brow at my stepsister. "Men with careless fists should be more mindful of where they step."

A faint smile appeared on Ezra's face. "You know, you do frighten me a little."

I turned to the carriage window as we rolled down the sunny street. "I know."

Chapter 9

Fractured sunlight streamed through the thickly branched elms as I walked through the forest toward the lake. What I had done to Nor threatened to haunt each step. I felt nothing with just a little bit of…*something.*

Something I didn't like.

Something I didn't want to think about.

I pictured the smile of relief on Nate's face, how toothy and contagious it had been when he saw his sister waiting for him at the orphanage along the Cliffs of Sorrow. I tried to use that to replace the image of his father's shocked, wide eyes. I thought of the joyous rush the boy made toward his sister. I watched through the carriage window instead of dwelling on the utter lack of remorse I felt for ending a man's life.

Or I tried to, at least. My stomach gave another sharp twist as I passed the musky-scented wildflowers growing into thick bushes at the base of the elms. *What is wrong with you?* My voice echoed in my thoughts, over and over. Something had to be, right? My palms dampened, and I carefully made my way over the branches that had fallen, and the sharp rocks hidden under the foliage—hidden just like the wake of death I was leaving behind.

Something beautiful and powerful…

I didn't feel like either of those things.

Two mortals had come for me since the night I'd failed, having learned my identity and thinking to use it to gain whatever they wanted. There were three more, including Nor, that had met death at the end of my blade. None of them were good people. They were all as unworthy as I was. Abusers. Murderers. Rapists. Death would've found them eventually. Five had died by my hand on the orders of my mother, and they didn't include the Vodina Isles Lords. Fourteen. I had ended fourteen lives.

What is wrong with you?

My stomach churned again, and I blew out a ragged breath. Barely any sunlight penetrated this deep into the forest, and it was slightly cooler here, but my skin was sticky like those wood floors in that chamber. Tacky with sweat and blood. I was half tempted to pull the cape and gown off now. I could. I knew no one else would enter these woods. Everyone was afraid of the Dark Elms—even Sir Holland. But I kept my clothing on because walking in a slip or nude through the woods just seemed odd, even for me—

A sudden rustling of bushes stopped me mid-step. The sound…it had come from behind me. Spinning, I scanned the trees. There weren't just spirits in the Dark Elms. Bears and large cave cats called the forest home, too. As did barrats, which grew to ungodly sizes, wild boars, and

A shock of brown and red burst out from the foliage ahead, startling me. I stumbled and then jerked back against the trunk of the nearest elm, heart dropping at the flash of russet fur breaking through the trees. For a moment, I couldn't believe what I was seeing.

It was a *kiyou wolf*.

They were the largest breed of wolves in all the kingdoms. I'd often heard their calls in the woods, and sometimes even from within the castle. But I'd only seen one up close; when I was half the size I was now. The white wolf.

Every single muscle in my body locked. I didn't dare make a sound or breathe too deeply. Kiyou wolves were notoriously fierce, as wild as they were beautiful, and not exactly friendly. If someone got too close to them, they usually paid dearly for it, and I prayed it didn't see me. That it wasn't hungry. Because I hadn't even reached for my blade. There was no way I could kill a wolf. A rat the size of a wild boar? Yes. That I could stab all day and night.

The wolf rushed over a moss-blanketed boulder, its hefty paws kicking up loose soil and small rocks. It took several shocking leaps past where I stood, seemingly unaware of me. I still didn't move as it went to jump again. My breath caught when it stumbled. The wolf's legs simply crumpled beneath it, and it went down onto its side with a heavy thud.

Then I saw what had caused the creature to collapse.

My heart sank at the sight. An arrow protruded from where its chest rose and fell in ragged, too-shallow breaths. Its fur wasn't a reddish-brown. That was blood. A lot of blood.

The wolf tried to gain its footing, but it couldn't get its legs under itself. I glanced in the direction it had come. Wayfair. The wolf must've gotten too close to the edges of the forest and had been spotted by one of the archers stationed on the inner curtain wall. Anger twisted the knot of sorrow weighing heavily in my chest. Why would they shoot such a creature when they were safely perched high above? And even if the wolf had been stalking someone, I still didn't see the need. They could've made a noise or struck the ground near the wolf. They didn't need to do this.

My gaze swept back to the wolf. *Please be all right. Please be all right.* I repeated the words over and over, even though I knew that the poor animal wasn't okay. Still, the childish hope was a powerful one.

The wolf stopped trying to stand, its breathing becoming labored and more uneven as I peeled away from the tree. I winced as a twig snapped under my weight, but the wolf barely stirred or noticed. Barely breathed.

I was truly experiencing a temporary lapse in sanity while creeping forward. The animal was wounded, but even a dying creature could lash out and do damage. And it was definitely dying. The whites of the wolf's eyes were too stark. Its brown eyes didn't track my movements. The chest didn't move. The kiyou wolf was still.

Too still.

Just like that terrible man's chest had been when I tore the pouch of coins free. Just like Odetta's chest was every time I checked in on her.

I tipped forward, staring at the animal. Blood trickled from its open mouth as tears pricked my eyes. I didn't cry. Hadn't since the night I'd failed. But I had a soft spot for animals—well, except for barrats. Animals didn't judge. They didn't care about worthiness. They didn't *choose* to use or hurt another. They simply *lived* and expected to either be left alone or loved. That was all.

I was kneeling at the wolf's side before I even realized I'd moved, reaching for the animal. I halted before my skin touched fur, sucking in a shuddering breath. My mother's words from long ago echoed through my thoughts. *Do not ever do that again. Do you understand me? Never do that again.* I looked around, seeing nothing in the darkened woods. I knew I was alone. I was always alone in these woods.

My heart hammered as I thrust my mother's voice from my mind and gripped the arrow's shaft. No one would know. My hands warmed again, like they had when Nor's heart had beat its last, but this time, I didn't ignore it or will the feeling away. I welcomed it. I called it forward.

"I'm sorry," I whispered, yanking the arrow free. The sound it made turned my stomach, as did the iron-rich scent in the air.

The wolf showed no reaction as blood slowly leaked out, a sure sign that the heart had stopped beating. I didn't hesitate even a moment longer.

I did what I'd done in the barn when I was six years old and realized that Butters, our old barn cat, had died. It was the same thing I'd done only a few times since I learned what I could do.

I sank my hand into the blood-soaked fur. The center of my chest thrummed, and the dizzying rush flooded my veins to spread across my skin. Heat flowed down my arms, reminding me of the feeling of standing too close to an open flame, and slid over and between my fingers.

I simply *wished* for the wolf to live.

That was what I'd done with Butters as I held the cat in my arms. It's what I'd done those few times before. Whatever wound or injury that had taken them simply vanished. It all seemed unbelievable, but that was my *gift*. It allowed me to sense that a death had just occurred—like it had done with Andreia.

It also brought the dead back to life, but not like what had been done to the seamstress.

Thank the Primals and gods for that.

My heart beat once, twice, and then three times. The kiyou wolf's chest rose suddenly under my hand. I jerked back, falling on my rear.

The heat throbbed and then faded away from my hands as the kiyou wolf scrambled to its feet, its eyes rolling wildly until they landed on me. I went still once more, both hands in the air as the wolf stared, ears pinned back. It took a wobbly step toward me.

Please don't bite my hand off. Please don't bite my hand off. I really needed my hand for lots of things—like eating, dressing, handling weapons…

The wolf's ears perked as it sniffed the hand free of its blood. Fear punched through me. Oh, gods, it was going to bite my hand, and I'd have no one to blame but—

The wolf licked the center of my palm and then turned, running off on steady legs before quickly disappearing into the gathering shadows between the elms. I didn't move for a full minute.

"You're welcome," I whispered, all but sinking into a puddle of relief on the ground.

Heart racing, I looked down at my hands. The blood that smeared my palm was dark against my skin. I wiped away what I could in the cool grass beside me.

I'd never used my gift on an animal I hadn't seen pass, and I had never used it on a mortal, even though I'd come close with Odetta. If she hadn't been alive…

I would've broken my rule.

I believed all living beings had souls. Animals were one thing, and mortals were completely different. To bring back a mortal felt unthinkable. It was…it seemed like a line that couldn't be uncrossed, and there was too much power in that—in the choice to intervene or not. That was the kind of power and choice I didn't want.

No one knew how I'd gained such a gift or why I'd been marked for death before I was even born. It made no sense that I would carry an ability that linked me to the Primal of Life—to Kolis. Had he somehow learned of the deal and imparted me with the gift? Was that what Odetta had meant when she claimed the Arae had said that I was touched by both life and death? He was the King of Gods, after all. I imagined there was very little he *didn't* know.

I lifted my palms once more. I hadn't known when I entered the barn with Ezra that Tavius had followed us. When he saw what I'd done, he'd run straight for the Queen, who had been afraid that using such a gift would anger the Primal of Death.

Maybe she was right.

Perhaps that was why the Primal of Death had decided that he no longer needed a Consort. After all, I carried the ability to steal souls away from him.

There seemed to be many reasons…

I thought of when Sir Holland had sat me down after the incident with Butters and explained that I hadn't done anything wrong by bringing Butters back. That it wasn't something to fear. He had helped me, at six years old, to understand why I had to be careful.

"*What you can do is a gift, a wonderful one that is a part of who you are,*" he'd said, kneeling so we were at eye level. "*But it could become dangerous for you if others were to learn that you could possibly bring back their loved ones. It could anger the gods and Primals, for you to decide who should return to life and who should not. It is a gift given by the King of Gods, one that should be held close to your heart and only ever used when you're ready to become who you were destined to be. Until then, you are not a Primal. Play as one, and the Primals might think you are.*"

Sir Holland had been the only one to ever refer to it as a gift.

And what he had said made sense. Well, the part about it being a potential danger. People would do all manner of things to bring back their loved ones. Who knew how many went to the Sun Temples, asking for just that? But it was never granted.

Now, the part about me using the gift only when I was ready to be who I was destined to become didn't exactly make much sense. I imagined he'd been talking about once I fulfilled my duty. I had no idea.

Closing my eyes, I let my hands fall to my lap as a heady warmth filled my chest. I'd felt that before when I used the gift. I hadn't done it often. Just a few times on a stray dog struck by a carriage and a wounded rabbit. Nothing as large as a kiyou wolf.

The warmth invading my blood was stronger this time, and I figured it had to do with the size of the wolf. The feeling reminded me of how a swallow of whiskey seemed to blossom in the chest and then spread to the belly. The tension in my shoulders and neck eased.

It was a strange feeling, knowing that I had taken a life and then gave one back in the span of a few hours.

My thoughts drifted to that tiny babe. If I'd had a chance, would I have attempted to use my gift then? Would I have broken my rule?

Yes.

I would have.

I didn't know how long I sat there as night fell around me, but it was the distant, mournful wail of a spirit that pulled me from my thoughts. Tiny goosebumps pimpled my skin as I squinted into the deep shadows between the trees. Grateful that the keening sound hadn't come from the direction of my lake, I rose. As long as the spirits left me alone, they didn't bother me. I started walking, hoping the wolf didn't come close to the wall again. The likelihood that I'd be around next time wasn't high.

Traveling deeper into the woods, I pulled the pins free of my hair and unraveled my braid, letting the heavy length fall over my shoulders and down my back. Eventually, through the cluster of narrow elms ahead, I saw the glittering surface of my lake. At night, the clear water seemed to catch the stars, reflecting their light.

Carefully navigating the moss-covered boulders, I slipped through the cluster of trees and let out a soft sigh as grass gave way to loam under my feet and I saw the lake.

The body of water was large, fed by the fresh springs birthed somewhere deep in the Elysium Peaks. To my left, only a dozen or so feet away, water tumbled out of the cliffs in a heavy sheet. But farther out, where it was too deep for me to travel, the water appeared unearthly still. The dark beauty of these woods and this lake had always felt enchanted to me. Peaceful. Here, with only the whistle of the wind between the trees and the rushing water of the falls, I felt like I was *home.*

I couldn't explain it. I knew it sounded ridiculous to feel at home on a bank of a lake, but I was more comfortable here than I'd ever been within the walls of Wayfair or on the streets of Carsodonia.

Bright moonlight spilled across the lake and the bulky chunks of limestone dotting the shore. Placing the pins on one of the rocks, I slid the blade from my boot and set it beside the hairpins. Quickly, I peeled off the blood-spotted gown, letting it fall. I shimmied out of my slip and undergarment, removing my boots, and wondering if I could somehow make it to my rooms in just my slip without being seen. The thought of donning the sticky clothing that smelled of White Horse smoke made my nose wrinkle. It was unlikely that I would be able to go unnoticed by the Royal Guards standing watch at the entrances, especially after what'd happened tonight. The King and Queen would surely learn of my scandalous arrival. My smile kicked up a notch at the thought of the horror that would fill my mother's face.

That alone made it almost worth risking discovery.

The too-long length of my hair brushed the curve of my waist and fell forward over my breasts as I placed the slip next to the pins and the dagger. I really needed to cut my hair. It was becoming a pain when it came to detangling the numerous knots that formed at the first breath of air.

Shoving the curls out of my face, I padded forward. I knew the exact location of the rocky bank that had become an earthen set of steps, anticipation a heady trill in my blood.

I found the step in the moonlight. The first touch of chilled water was always a shock, sending a jolt through my system. Like the utter idiot I often proved myself to be, I'd once jumped into the lake during a particular hot day and nearly drown when my lungs and body seized on me.

I would never do *that* again.

Slowly making my way onto the flat floor of the glimmering pool, I bit down on my lip. Water steadily lapped up my calves and spread out from me in small, rippling waves, which were swept away in the soft current. My breath caught when the water reached my thighs and again when it kissed far more delicate skin. I kept going, exhaling softly as my body adjusted to the temperature with each step. By the time it teased the tips of my breasts, tension had already begun to seep from my muscles.

Taking a deep breath, I let myself fall. Cool water rushed the still-heated skin of my face and lifted the strands of my hair as I slipped under the surface. I stayed there, keeping my eyes squeezed shut, scrubbing at my hands and then my face before breaking the surface. And I stayed even longer, letting the water wash more than the stale stench and sweat away. Only when my lungs began to burn did I rise, breaking the surface. Smoothing away the hair plastered to my cheeks, I cautiously crept forward.

The water was a little over waist-deep where I was, but there were dips that came out of nowhere and seemed bottomless, so I was careful. I had no fear of water, but I couldn't swim, and I had no idea what the depth of the middle of the lake was nor the area near the waterfall. I wanted so badly to explore there, but I could only get within ten feet of it before the water started to rise above my head.

Sighing, I tipped my head back and let my eyes drift closed. Maybe it was the sound of the rushing water or the isolation of the lake, but my mind was always blissfully blank here. I didn't think about everything I'd done or my mother. I didn't think about the Rot and how many more bellies it would rob of food. I didn't think about how I'd had a chance to stop it and failed. I didn't think about the man whose life I'd ended today, any that had come before him, or what had happened to the Kazins or Andreia Joanis. I didn't wonder what would happen once Tavius took the throne. I didn't think of the damn god with silver eyes, whose skin was cold but made my chest feel warm.

I just existed in the cool water, neither here nor there or anywhere, and it felt like a…release. Freedom. Lulled and maybe even a little enchanted, the strange, prickly sense of awareness was a sudden shock.

Water clung to my lashes as my eyes snapped open. Goosebumps pimpled my skin as I sank lower until the water reached my shoulders. I reached for my dagger, but my fingers brushed bare skin.

Dammit.

I'd left the iron blade on the rock, and that was most unfortunate because I knew what that feeling was. It was wholly recognizable, even if hard to explain, and it sent my pulse skittering.

I wasn't alone.

I was being *watched*.

Chapter 10

I didn't understand the inherent sense that alerted me to the fact that I wasn't alone, but I knew to trust it.

Remaining crouched in the water, I scanned the dark banks around me and then quickly looked over my shoulder. I saw nothing, but that didn't mean someone wasn't there. The moonlight didn't penetrate the deeper shadows clinging to large swaths of the shore and farther back among the trees to the cliffs.

No one ever came here, but the feeling continued, pressing against my bare shoulders. I knew it wasn't my imagination. Someone was here, watching me, but for how long? The last couple of minutes? Or from the moment I undressed and *slowly* walked into the lake, naked as the day I was born? Anger flooded my system so fiercely, I was surprised the water didn't start to boil around me.

Someone, getting over their fear of the woods, must have followed me. That same instinct warned me that wasn't a good sign.

Muscles tensed as I called out, "I know you're there. Show yourself."

The only answer I received was the rush of water. I heard no night birds singing to one another nor the constant low hum of insects. I hadn't since I entered the woods. A chill swept over me as my throat tightened. "Show yourself now!"

Silence.

My gaze skipped over the waterfall and snapped back to the sheet of falling water, turned white in the drenching moonlight. There was a deeper shadow behind the waterfall, a thickness that didn't seem right.

And that tall *shape* was moving forward, coming through the fall of water. My stomach dipped like it did when I goaded a horse into running too fast.

A moment later, a deep and smooth voice came from within the waterfall. "Since you asked so nicely."

That voice…

The shape became far too clear in the moonlight. Broad shoulders shattered the water, and then I saw him as he stepped out into the pool of moonlight.

I stopped breathing. My heart may have stopped beating.

The god.

Nothing about him seemed real. He stood there with the water pounding off the rocks behind him. More tiny bumps spread across my flesh as I stared at him in shock.

"Here I am," he said. "Now, what?"

His question yanked me out of my stunned silence. "What are you doing here?"

Water stirred around him when he broke the surface and slicked back his hair, the spray lapping at the defined lines of his chest. I snapped my gaze to his face. He appeared to be studying me. "What does it look like?"

His blasé answer struck that reckless part of me. It didn't matter that the pretend kiss in the vine tunnels had become very real, or that he hadn't struck out at me when I stabbed him in the chest—something most would be furious about—or end up dead over. It didn't matter that he was a powerful god that had continuously crept into my thoughts since I'd last seen him. He had been *watching* me when I'd been at my most vulnerable. "It looks like you shouldn't be here."

His head tilted slightly, and a lock of dark hair slipped over the hard line of his jaw. "And why would I not be allowed to?"

"Because it's private property." Why did I feel like we'd already established this?

"Is it?" Amusement crept into his tone. "I was unaware of any land prohibited to a god."

"I imagine that there are many areas that would be off-limits to anyone, including a god."

"What if I told you there aren't?"

My stomach dipped. "I would be thoroughly irritated to learn that."

A low chuckle rumbled from him. "So fearless."

Common sense indicated that I should be experiencing some level of fear, but all I felt was anger. "None of that answers what you're doing here."

"I suppose it doesn't." He lifted an arm again, the one with the silver band, to brush back another strand of hair that had slipped against his jaw. "I was around, and since it was extremely warm, I thought I'd take a swim and cool off."

Anger crowded out any tendrils of fear and potential wisdom. "And prey upon young women?"

"Prey upon young women?" There was a hint of incredulity in his tone. "What young women have I preyed upon this eve?"

"The one who is standing before you."

"The one who is naked, standing before me?"

"Thank you for the unnecessary reminder. But, yes, the one you followed to the lake."

"Followed?"

"Is there an echo here?" I demanded.

"I'm sorry—"

"You don't sound sorry," I snapped.

There was a soft, barely audible chuckle. "Let me rephrase. I don't know how I followed you to this lake to prey upon you when I was here first. Trust me—"

"Not going to happen."

A cloud slipped over the moon as his chin dropped again, casting his face in shadows. "*Trust me* when I say I was not expecting you to be here."

In the back of my mind, where reason still existed, I knew he spoke the truth. I hadn't been under the water long enough for even a god to undress, then enter the lake and the waterfall without me noticing. He must have been here first. But, frankly, I didn't care.

This was *my* lake.

"I was minding my own business," he said. "Taking a few moments to enjoy this beautiful night."

"In a lake you do not belong in," I muttered, not caring if no place was truly off-limits to a god.

"I swam underwater and ended up beyond the waterfall. It's quite beautiful there, by the way," he continued unrepentantly. "Can you, for one moment, imagine my surprise when a few seconds later, a young, very demanding mortal appeared out of the darkness and started removing her clothing? What was I supposed to do?"

Fire swept across my face. "Not watch me?"

"I wasn't." A pause. "At least, not intentionally."

"Not intentionally?" I repeated in disbelief. "As if that makes it less inappropriate."

That half-grin appeared again. "You do have a point there, but as it *was* unintentional, I would wager to say it is far less inappropriate than it would have been if it *had* been intentional."

"No." I shook my head. "No, it is not."

"Anyway," he stressed the word with such a highbrow air, my mother would've been impressed. "I was quite shocked, as this was not what I had been expecting."

"Shocked or not, you could've announced yourself." I couldn't believe I had to explain this. "I don't know what would be expected in Iliseeum, but here, that would've been the polite, less inappropriate thing to do."

"True, but it all happened very fast. From the point of your arrival and, sadly, brief reveal of many, *many* unmentionable places, to when you decided to enjoy the lake. It was only a matter of seconds," he said. "But I'm glad we're now in agreement over my actions being less inappropriate. I will sleep better tonight."

"What? We are not in agreement. I—" Wait. *Sadly brief reveal of unmentionable places*? My eyes narrowed. "You still could've said something so I wasn't just standing there—"

"Like a goddess made of silver and moonbeams, rising from the depths of the darkest lake?" he finished.

I snapped my mouth shut. Like a…a goddess? Made of silver and moonbeams? That sounded incredibly… I didn't even know what that sounded like or why my stomach was whooshing again. What he said was ridiculous because he knew actual goddesses.

"I considered announcing my presence just so you knew, especially after last night. The Fates know I don't want to be stabbed again."

I so wanted to stab him again.

"But then I thought it would only lead to unnecessary embarrassment for all involved," he went on, snapping me out of my momentary stupor. "I figured you would be on your way, none the wiser, and this awkward—albeit very interesting—meeting never had to occur. I didn't think you would realize I was here."

"No matter what your intentions were, you should've said

something." I started to stand straight and then remembered that wasn't the wisest idea. "I mean no offense in what I'm about to say—"

"I'm sure you mean absolutely no offense," he purred. "Just like you meant no offense when you stabbed me."

I ignored the rumble of his voice *and* the reminder of what I'd done. "But you should leave."

"There you go, being so very demanding. Meanwhile, you ignore what I've demanded of you." His head tilted back, and a slice of moonlight kissed one cheek. "It's very different."

My pulse skittered. "What? A mortal who doesn't cower before you or beg for a favor?"

"Some beg for quite a bit more than a favor." His voice was like smoke, a shadowy caress. And that voice…it stoked that same odd feeling of warmth and familiarity. "But you're not the type to cower. I doubt you're the type to beg."

"I'm not," I told him.

"That's a shame."

"Maybe for you."

"Maybe," he agreed and then drifted forward.

"What are you doing?" I demanded, tensing.

He stopped, close enough for me to see an arched brow. "If I'm to leave as you so kindly *demanded*, I will have to walk forward."

My jaw was beginning to hurt from how tightly I held it. "You can't leave from any of the other banks?"

"I'm afraid that the lake is far too deep in those areas for that. And there is the issue of a cliff to one side."

I stared at him. "You're a god. Can't you do something…godly?" I sputtered. "Like will yourself from the lake?"

"Will myself from a lake?" he repeated slowly, the half-grin making another appearance. "That's not how that works." The moon eased free of the clouds, bathing him once more in pearlescent light. "Should I stay, or should I go?"

I glared at him. "Go."

"As you wish, my lady." He bowed his head slightly and then proceeded forward.

I watched him closely. The water dipped below his chest, revealing the ridges of the lean muscles of his stomach. I knew I should look away. Continuing to stare *there* meant I was being equally inappropriate. But his body was…it was very interesting, and I was curious because, well…

I didn't have a good, appropriate reason for looking.

I knew how strong he was, so the fact that his body represented his strength came as no surprise. Despite the coolness of the water, the warmth in my skin steadily spread as those…thick lines on the insides of his hips became visible, a deep black that followed the indentations there, traveling down and over toward his—

"Oh, my gods!" I shrieked. "Stop!"

He halted a mere breath from the water revealing far, *far* too much. "Yes?" he inquired.

"You're naked," I informed him.

A heartbeat of silence passed. "Are you now just realizing that?"

"No!"

"Then you have to realize I will continue to be naked until I retrieve the clothing you apparently didn't notice in *your* haste to undress."

The breath I inhaled scorched my lungs.

"If it makes you uncomfortable, I suggest closing your eyes or keeping them off *my* unmentionables." He paused. "Unless you would like for me to stay?"

"I don't want you to stay."

"Why do I think that's a lie?"

"It's not."

"That's another lie."

I twitched at the near-decadent drawl of his tone and managed to keep my eyes on his face as he proceeded forward. Kind of. My gaze dropped again, but to those strange black lines. He was close enough that I could see that they did indeed creep along the side of his body. But they weren't solid. Instead, some smaller marks or shapes followed the pattern of a line. Did they continue onto his back? Curiosity blazed through me now. What were the shapes?

Don't ask. Keep your mouth closed. Don't ask. Don't—

"Is that ink?" I blurted out, hating myself for asking and for continuing to speak. "The kind needled into the skin?"

He stopped. "It is…something like that."

I didn't know if gods and Primals had a different process when it came to tattoos. "Did it hurt?"

"Only till it didn't," he replied, and my gaze lifted. There was a slight curve to his lips—just the faintest of smiles. But like before, it had a startling effect, warming the coldness of his features. "You're familiar with tattoos?"

I nodded. "I've seen them on some of the sailors. Mostly on their backs and arms."

Another lock of hair slipped forward over his cheek this time. "You've seen the bare backs of many sailors?"

Not that many, but that was none of his business. "So what if I have?"

"So what, indeed?" The faint smile remained. "It just makes all of this far more…interesting."

I tensed to the point it almost became painful. "I don't see how."

"I could explain," he offered.

"Not necessary."

"You sure?"

"Yes."

"I have time."

"I don't. Just go," I repeated, my frustration with him, the day, and with the fact that he was here in my lake, and that this place would *never* be the same again, rising to the surface. "But do not come any closer to me. If you do, you will not like what happens."

The god became very still then, so much so that I wasn't sure if he even breathed. And the water… I swore the water around him stopped its lazy rippling. My heartbeat stuttered.

"I won't?" he queried softly.

Tiny hairs began to rise all over my body. "No."

"What will you do, my lady?" Moonlight kissed the apple of his cheekbone as he tilted his head once more. "You have no shadowstone dagger to threaten me with."

"I don't need a dagger," I said, my voice thready. "And I'm not a lady."

His head straightened. "No, I imagine not, considering you're nude in a lake with an unfamiliar man, whose lip you bit upon meeting, and have seen the bare backs of many sailors. I was only being polite."

My lip curled at the presumed insult. I knew I should let it go. Keep my mouth shut, but I didn't. I hadn't in three years, and my inability to do so had grown and festered into an incurable disease. The kind that provoked further, dangerous recklessness. "What I am is a *Princess* who is nude in a lake with an unfamiliar man and has seen the bare backs of men," I told him, speaking the forbidden. "And you, with each passing moment, are getting closer to no longer having the ability to see anyone's unmentionable places ever again."

For a long moment, he stared at me, his features unreadable. My heart began to pound with trepidation—

The god laughed. Tipped his head back and actually *laughed*, long and deep. And his laugh was…well, it was a nice sound. Deep and husky.

It was also highly infuriating.

"I'm not sure what you find so funny," I bit out.

"You," he answered between laughs.

"Me?"

"Yes." He lowered his head, his stare piercing even though I couldn't see his eyes. "You amuse me."

If there were some kind of switch deep inside me that controlled my anger and impulses, he'd found it with unerring accuracy over and over.

And then repeatedly flipped it each time I crossed paths when him.

I was a lot of things, but I was *not* the source of anyone's amusement. Not even a god's.

Fury pulsing through my blood, I rose to my full height. "I doubt you will find me so amusing when you're gasping for the last of your breaths."

He became still again, and…good gods, the water coursing down his chest *froze*. The droplets ceased.

"I'm already gasping," he whispered, his voice rougher, deeper.

Confusion rippled along the flood of rage. Did he have some sort of breathing ailment? Could gods have health issues? If so, I doubted these cold waters would be good for his lungs. Not that I remotely cared for the condition of his lungs. Nor did I even know why I was wondering about their condition.

A warm breeze lifted the strands of my wet hair and slipped over the chilled skin of my bare shoulders and my…

Oh.

The water only reached my waist here.

"In case you're wondering,"—his voice was a kiss against my skin—"this is me *intentionally* staring."

I started to lower, seeking the shield of the water, but I stopped myself. I would not shrink or cower to anyone or anything. "Pervert."

"Guilty."

"Keep staring," I growled. "And I will claw out those eyes with my fingers if need be."

He barked out another short laugh, this one tinged with surprise. "Still no fear, *Your Grace*?"

I bristled at the way he used the Royal title as if it were something silly and irrelevant. All the more frustrating was the fact that he was perhaps the first person to ever refer to me as such.

"I'm still not afraid of you," I replied, briefly glancing down. There was only a minor bit of relief when I saw several pale strands of hair plastered to my chest. They didn't hide nearly enough, but it was better than nothing.

"Well, I'm a little afraid of you," he said, and he was somehow closer without seeming to have moved. He wasn't even a foot from me now, and an icy heat radiated from him, pressing against my flesh. His closeness heightened the sensitivity of every inch of skin. "You want to claw my eyes out."

Hearing him say what I'd threatened sounded ridiculous. "You and I both know it would be impossible for me to claw your eyes out."

"And yet, based on my limited interactions with you, I know you'd try, even when you know you'd fail."

I couldn't exactly argue against that. "Well, if you're that concerned about the possibility of me attempting to do that, you should be careful of where your eyes wander."

"I'm being extra-careful as incredibly hard as that is, given the…abundant allure of being less careful."

"I'm sure you say that to all the ladies you accost."

"Only the ones I would be tempted to allow to try and claw my eyes out."

"That…that makes no sense." Drawing in a too-short breath, I stepped back through the water, folding an arm over my chest.

He watched me, but his stare was nothing like Nor's. There was curiosity there. "It's amazing to witness."

"What is?"

"These moments when you suddenly remember what I am. Is this another attempt to use common sense?"

I lifted my chin a notch. "Unfortunately."

"Is it not going well again?"

"Not exactly."

He chuckled, and the sound…well, it was as nice as his laugh. I wished it weren't because it made me want to hear it again, and that seemed like a silly need. "Why do you think you need to remain quiet now?"

I spared a glance at the shore. "I'm likely to say something that would make you forget that one decent bone in your body."

He drew his lower lip between his teeth, and for some inane reason, my full attention was drawn to that. "I don't think that's the kind of mood you have to worry about putting me in."

"What kind of—?" I cut myself off as what he said sank in. There was a sharp curl low in my stomach that I didn't like at all—for a multitude of reasons.

"I know. That was…inappropriate of me."

"Very," I muttered, thinking my response was just as inappropriate, all things considered.

"You're unexpectedly outspoken."

"I'm not sure how you can be expectant of anything as we don't really know each other."

"I think I know enough," he responded.

"I don't even know your name," I pointed out.

"Some call me Ash."

"Ash?" I repeated, and he nodded. Something about that was familiar. "Is it short for something?"

"It is short for many things." His head suddenly snapped toward the shore. A moment passed. "By the way, I would think you would've learned from our last interaction. I don't make a habit of punishing mortals for speaking their minds." He shot a glance in my direction. "Mostly."

Threatening to claw out his eyes and actually stabbing him in the chest weren't examples of speaking my mind, but I wisely didn't share that thought.

"And I didn't accost you. I may be a lot of things…" He strode forward with the warning. "But I am not *that*."

I opened my mouth, but all words left me when he neared the shallower end of the lake. I stared. Gods help me, I couldn't take my eyes away from him as he climbed the earthen steps to the shore. It wasn't his rear that snagged my attention. Though I did see that. I shouldn't have, and I should've turned away right then because that made me a hypocrite of the highest order—being inappropriate went both ways. But I didn't. What I did see of his ass was…well, it was as well-formed as everything else I shouldn't have seen.

But it was the ink sprawling across the entire length of his back from the upper swells of his rear all the way to the edges of his hair that I couldn't look away from. In the center of his back was a circular, twisted swirl that grew larger, lashing out to form the thick tendrils I'd seen reaching around his waist to flow along the insides of his hips.

There wasn't nearly enough light for me to make out what made up the swirling design, but I had never seen any sailor with a tattoo like his. Again, my curiosity stirred. "What kind of tattoo is that?"

"One that is inked into the skin." He started to turn toward me, and I quickly averted my eyes. "You should get dressed. I won't look. I promise."

I peeked at him, finding that he'd turned away from the lake and held what appeared to be a pair of black breeches that I truly had not seen upon my arrival. My gaze shot to my pile of clothing. I couldn't stand here forever and question him.

I charged through the water, my eyes trained on his shoulders as he bent. Reaching the damp shore, I grabbed my slip and pulled it over my head. It only reached an inch or two past my thighs, but it was the quickest option, and the last thing I wanted to do was force my breasts into the bodice of the damn gown in front of him.

I picked up my sheathed blade—

"I do hope you aren't planning something foolish with that blade."

I turned to him, my irritation spiking when I saw that he still had his back to me. Obviously, he wasn't worried at all about what I would do with it.

"I haven't been the one issuing threats, so I would hope not." He faced me then, a smirk fixed on those well-formed lips. He stood there, the flap of his breeches undone, still wearing no shirt. I was positive he could've finished dressing. His fingers made quick work of the flap of his breeches. "You should unsheathe that blade."

My brows lifted at the unexpected request. "Do you want me to use this one on you, too?"

He laughed again. "Are you always this violent?"

"No."

"I'm not sure I believe that. But, no, I do not want you to use it on me," he replied. "We're not alone."

Leafy branches rattled, shook by a sudden burst of high wind. I tightened my grip on the dagger as I looked up. The limbs had stilled, but there was a sound, a low moan that came from deep within the woods.

Ash bent once more, retrieving a scabbard. Gripping the silver hilt, he withdrew the short sword I'd seen him use before.

Seeing it reminded me of what I'd thought when he first used it. "Why do you carry a sword?"

He looked over at me. "Why wouldn't I?"

"You're a god. Do you really need a sword?"

Ash eyed me. "There is all manner of things that I can do and try," he said. Something about his tone and the intensity in his stare made my skin even warmer. "Things I'm sure you'd find as equally interesting as I find your bravery."

I sucked in an edgy breath as his words made me think of those damn books in the Atheneum. The *illustrated* ones.

"But just because I can do something, doesn't mean I should," he finished, snapping me out of my wayward thoughts.

My gaze shifted to the shadowy tree line and then back to him. A god with limitations? Interesting.

"We are about to have company," he said, and I blinked. "I don't believe they will be nearly as entertaining as you surely find me."

"I don't find you entertaining," I muttered, and that was a foolish lie the god didn't even bother challenging. Who wouldn't be entertained by a god or Primal, even one as annoying as he? "These woods are haunted. What we heard could just be spirits."

"You sure about that?"

"Yes. They like to moan and make all manner of obnoxious noises." I sent him a frown. "Shouldn't you know that, being that you're from the Shadowlands?"

Ash stared into the woods. "These are not spirits."

"No one enters these woods," I reasoned. "It has to be a spirit."

"I entered these woods," he pointed out.

"But you're a god."

"And what makes you think that what is coming is of your mortal realm?"

I halted, my stomach hollowing.

"I have a question for you. Are your spirits flesh and bone? The ones that haunt these woods?"

My gaze flicked up. All I saw was the darkness among the elms. "No." I turned to him. "Of course, not."

Ash lifted the sword, pointing the blade toward the trees. "Then what would you call these things?"

"What things?" I leaned forward, squinting. There were only shadows, but then I saw something drifting out of the darkness between the elms, a figure cloaked in black. A nightmare.

Chapter 11

They *almost* looked mortal, but if they were once that, they weren't anymore.

Their skin held the waxy pallor of death, scalps bare of hair, eyes endless black pits, and mouths…they were all wrong. Their mouths were stretched too far across the cheeks as if someone had carved out a wider smile for them. And that mouth appeared *sewn* shut like the Shadow Priests.

I unsheathed the blade. "What are they?" I whispered, quickly counting six of them.

"Definitely not wayward spirits."

Slowly, I looked over at him. "No, really?"

One side of his lips curved up. "They're known as Gyrms," he answered. "This type? They're called Hunters."

This type? There were more of these things? I had never heard of such a creature. "Why would they be here?"

"They must be looking for something."

"Like what?" I asked.

Ash spared me a glance. "That is a very good question."

My heart thumped erratically against my ribs as the Hunters stood there, staring at us—or at least that was what I thought. I couldn't be sure with those holes for eyes. My stomach churned as the urge to run seized me.

But I hadn't run from *anything* since I was a child, and I wouldn't start now.

An unearthly moan filled the air once more, and the trees shuddered in response. The Hunters moved in unison, sweeping forward in a vee.

Ash struck before I had a chance to respond, thrusting his sword through the back of one and into the chest of another, striking down two with one blow. The creatures made no sound, their bodies only spasming.

"Gods," I rasped.

He looked over his shoulder as he pulled the sword free. "Impressed?"

"No," I lied, jerking back a step when the two recently impaled creatures collapsed into themselves. It was like they'd been drained of all moisture with a snap of a finger. They shriveled in a matter of seconds and then shattered into nothing but a fine dusting of ash that was gone before it hit the ground.

"You should go home." Ash moved forward, sword at his side. "This doesn't concern you."

The remaining creatures continued forward, hands reaching around to their backs. They unsheathed swords with shadowstone blades.

Ash moved with the fluid grace of a warrior, with a skill I doubted most mortals could acquire with years of training. He spun, sweeping his sword in a wide arc, slicing through the neck of one of the creatures.

There was no spray of red, no iron-rich scent clogging the air. There was only the smell of…stale lilacs. The scent reminded me of something. Not that poor seamstress, but—

One of the creatures swung its sword, and Ash twisted, meeting the blow. The blades clanged with a force that must have shaken them both.

Ash laughed as he stared the Hunter down. "Nice. But you should've known you'd have to try harder." He pushed the creature back, but the thing quickly regained its footing and charged at the same moment another lurched forward.

I should actually listen to him this time, but I couldn't just stand there or leave him to be stabbed in the back. These Hunters had shadowstone blades. If their aim was slightly better than mine had been, they could kill him.

My bare feet glided over the damp grass as I shot forward, shifting the dagger in my hand without much conscious thought. The Hunter took aim, preparing to plunge his sword deep into Ash's back. Having no idea if iron would work on such a creature, I slammed the hilt of the blade into the back of its skull. The crack of iron meeting bone twisted my stomach as the creature stumbled backward, lowering the sword.

But it did not fall like expected. And I'd hit him hard enough to put the thing to sleep for the night—or the week. Dumbfounded, I watched it turn to face me. Its head cocked to the side, and a low moaning sound reached me, coming from the thing's throat and sealed mouth.

It stalked toward me.

"Dammit," I whispered, jumping back as it swung out with the sword.

"Did I not tell you to go home?" Ash bit out. "That this does not concern you?"

"You did." I ducked under the creature's arm.

"I have it handled." Ash cleaved through the midsection of another Hunter. "Obviously."

"Then I guess I should've allowed him to stab you in the back?" I grabbed the creature's sword arm and twisted, spinning him away from me. "A thank you would've been sufficient."

"I would've said thank you." Ash wheeled around, shoving his sword deep into another creature's chest. The scent of stale lilacs smacked me in the face. "If there was a reason to do so."

"You sound ungrateful."

"Well, you would know what ungrateful sounds like," Ash shot back. "Wouldn't you?"

Another Hunter came at me, weapon lowered. I kicked out, catching him in the stomach as I eyed the sword he held.

"On second thought, thank you for doing that," he said, and I glanced over at him. My breath caught at the inexplicable and somewhat idiotic tug in my stomach and then lower when I saw the heated intensity in his stare.

There was *definitely* something very, *very* wrong with me.

"Please continue to fight in just a…well, whatever you call that very flimsy piece of clothing," he offered. "Is it distracting? Yes. But in the best possible way."

"Pervert," I snarled, snapping forward as the creature lifted its sword.

Ash spun toward me. "What in the hell are you—?"

I slammed the dagger blade into the Hunter's wrist. Immediately, the creature's hand spasmed open, releasing the sword. It fell to the ground, and I quickly dipped down to retrieve it. Straightening, I looked over, holding the sword in one hand and the dagger in the other. I smiled widely at him.

He bit out a short laugh. "Well then, carry on." He turned to the other creature. "Sever their heads or destroy their hearts. It's the only way to put them down."

"Good to know." I started toward the creature. The gaping wound on the Hunter's wrist had already begun to close as the creature…smiled. Or at least tried to. The stitched gash of a mouth lifted as if it were about to grin—

The stitches split, and its mouth tore open. Thick, ropey tendrils spilled out of the gaping hole—

Serpents.

Oh, gods. Horror locked up every muscle in my body and sent my heart pounding. Snakes were the one thing that truly terrified me, nearly to the point of loss of rational thought. I couldn't help it. And serpents inside a *mouth*? That was a whole new nightmare.

The serpents wiggled and hissed, stretching out from the Hunter's mouth as he lurched forward. There was no time to back away to avoid whatever gruesome injury this thing could inflict, or worse yet, be touched by one of the serpents. If that happened, I'd surely die. My heart would fail, right here.

Lifting the sword, I thrust the blade deep into the Hunter's chest. The creature jerked back, the serpents going limp before he began to shrivel, shrinking and collapsing into himself until nothing remained in that space.

"Are you okay?" Ash demanded, stalking toward me. "Did any of those serpents bite you?"

The sword I held collapsed into ash, startling me. "No. None of them bit me."

"Are you okay?" he repeated, stopping.

I nodded.

"Are you sure about that?" Ash asked, and I dragged my gaze from the ground to look over at him. Something about his features had softened. "You don't appear all that okay."

"I—" Something smooth and dry touched my foot. I looked down, spotting the long, narrow body *slithering* through the grass. "Snake!" I shrieked, my blood turning to ice as I pointed at the ground.

"Snake!"

"I can see it." Ash lifted his sword. "Get away from it. The bite will be toxic."

I couldn't get away from it quick enough.

Throwing myself back, my foot came down on a slick patch of exposed rock, and my leg slid right out from under me. I went down fast, too stunned to stop my fall—

A crack of sudden, blinding pain reverberated across the back of my skull, and then there was simply nothing.

I took a small breath and then a deeper one. A tantalizing, fresh, citrusy scent teased me.

Ash.

I blinked open my eyes.

His features were fuzzy at first, but slowly, the striking lines and angles became clearer. His face was above mine, thick strands of hair hanging forward, resting against his cheeks. I focused on the indentation in his chin, seeing now that it was definitely not a natural occurrence. What could leave a scar on a god? My gaze shifted to his mouth, to the very well-formed lips. He was…

"You're beautiful," I whispered.

His eyes widened slightly, and then thick lashes swept down halfway. "Thank you."

A slew of words detailing exactly how beautiful I thought he was formed on the tip of my tongue as the haze cleared from my thoughts…

Had I seriously just told him that he was beautiful? I had.

Gods.

The Mistresses of the Jade had said that men enjoyed flattery, but I didn't think my artless gushing was what they'd meant. Not that I needed to seduce this god. I would have to pretend that it'd never happened. I looked over his shoulder to the star-blanketed sky. We were still by the lake, and I was lying on the grass. Kind of. My head was elevated, resting on his *thigh*. Everything but my heart stilled. That started galloping like a wild horse.

"I have to admit, though," he said, drawing my eyes back to him, "I'm worried you hit your head harder than I believed. That was the first nice thing you've said to me."

"Maybe I did damage something." It almost felt that way because a part of me still couldn't believe that he was actually here. "Where's my blade?"

"Right beside you, to your right and within arm's reach."

I turned my head. I could make out the shape of the dark gray blade in the grass. I started to sit up.

He placed his hand on my shoulder, beside the thin strap of the slip, and a soft whirl of energy rippled down my arm. "You should lay still for a few more moments," he said. "You weren't out long, but if you did do some damage, you're going to be toppling right back over if you move too quickly."

What he advised made sense. I'd once taken a nasty hit to the head during training and had been knocked out. Healer Dirks had recommended the same thing. That's why I didn't move.

It had absolutely nothing to do with how all parts of me focused on the weight of his hand and the coolness of his skin. His fingers were the only bit that touched the bare skin of my shoulder, but it felt like…*more.* And that was silly. But sometimes I wondered if I were truly worthy of touch.

My brows knitted. "Why are you still here?"

"You were injured."

"So?"

His expression changed then, his gaze sharpening and lips thinning. "You really must not think very highly of me if you think I would just leave you here."

It wasn't only because he was a god—well, that did surprise me a little—but I could count on one hand how many people would've remained. I shifted a bit, uncomfortable with that truth.

A moment passed. "How are you feeling? Does your head hurt, or do you feel sick at all?"

"No. There's just a slight ache, that's all." I shifted my gaze from his. "I can't believe I…I knocked myself out."

"Well, I don't think you did it all alone. The serpent played a role in it."

I shuddered, closing my eyes. "I hate snakes."

"I never would've guessed that," he remarked dryly. "Did they do something terrible to you in the past? Other than keeping the pest population at bay?"

My eyes snapped open at the teasing edge to his tone. "They *slither*."

"That's all?"

"No. They slither, and they're fast, even though they have no limbs. You never know they're there until you almost step on them." I was on a roll now. "And their eyes… They're beady and cold. Serpents are not to be trusted."

One side of his lips lifted. "I'm sure they feel the same way about you."

"Good. Then they should stay away."

That half-grin remained. "Though these types of snakes were far from normal."

The image of the Hunter resurfaced, and acid bubbled in my stomach. "I…I've never seen anything like that."

"Most haven't."

I thought about the scent of stale lilacs. "Is that what happened to Andreia? Did she become a…*Gyrm*?"

"No," he answered. "I still don't know what happened to her."

"But they were once mortal, right?" I had so many questions. "How did they end up like that? Why the serpents? Why were their mouths stitched like the Priests?"

"There are two types of Gyrms. These were mortals who had summoned a god. In exchange for whatever need or desire they had, they offered themselves for eternal servitude. Once they died, that was what they became."

I swallowed, my stomach churning. Would a mortal still have offered themselves if they knew that the end result would be that? I supposed it all depended on how desperately they sought whatever they needed. "Why the stitched mouths? The eyes?"

"Supposedly, it's done so they are loyal to only the god or Primal they are in service to."

"Are the Priests Gyrms, then?" I asked. If they were no longer truly alive, it explained how they survived with their mouths sewn closed. It also explained their innate creepiness.

He nodded.

"The Primals stitch the Priests lips shut?"

The skin around his mouth tightened. "What happens to them when they die was established a very, very long time ago. It has become an expected act."

Expected or not, it seemed unnaturally cruel to do such a thing.

"And the serpents…" he spoke again, drawing me from my thoughts. "That is what replaced their insides."

I honestly couldn't speak for several moments. "I have no idea what to even say to that."

"There is nothing to be said." Ash relaxed against the rock as he stared beyond me to the lake.

My eyes widened. "I don't even know if I want to know this, but do the Priests in the Temples have snakes in them?"

His lips twitched as if he were fighting a grin. "I have to agree with you probably not wanting to know the answer to that."

"Oh, gods." I groaned, shuddering. "You said there are two types of Gyrms?"

"Those who offered eternal servitude in return are typically known as Hunters and Seekers. Their purpose is usually to locate and retrieve things. There are other classes of Gyrms, dozens really, but those are the main ones." Ash's fingers moved over my collarbone in a slow, idle circle, startling me. "Then there are those who enter servitude as a way to atone for their sins in lieu of being sentenced to the Abyss."

"So, for them, it is not eternal?" I asked as my focus shifted to his touch. The pad of his thumb was rough, and I imagined it was callused from years of handling a sword, as mine were already becoming. Though, as a god, I wondered how often he had to wield a sword. He could've used eather earlier to end whatever had become of Andreia, but he'd opted for a blade.

"No. For them it is for a set amount of time. They are usually known as Sentinels, who are, in a way, soldiers. The Priests fall into that group. They are more…mortal than the first group in the sense that they have their own thoughts."

"What happens if they turn to ash like the Hunters did?"

"For those who are atoning for their sins, it depends on how long they've been in service. They may return to the Primal or god they serve, or choose to go to the Abyss. The Hunters? They return to the Abyss."

My gaze lifted to his face. He was still staring out at the lake. Was he aware of what he was doing? Touching me so casually?

I couldn't even think of when I was last touched in such a way. Those I spent time with at The Luxe didn't touch like this, and they wanted me. Maybe he was unaware of it, but I wasn't, and if even a single flicker of hope resided inside me regarding fulfillment of my duty, I needed to put some distance between us.

But I didn't move.

I remained there with my head on his thigh, letting his thumb trace the lazy circle. The touch utterly transfixed me. I enjoyed it.

And why couldn't I? I was no longer the Maiden. I'd decided already in the last three years that I was allowed to enjoy everything I had been forbidden.

I cleared my throat. "You…you said the Hunters were most likely looking for something?"

"That is the only reason Hunters would be in the mortal realm." He was quiet for a moment. "They could be looking for me."

I thought that over. "Why would they be looking for you?"

His gaze touched mine. "I have plenty of enemies."

My pulse kicked. "What have you done?"

"Why must I have done something?" he countered. "Maybe I've drawn the ire of others for refusing their demands or because I involved myself in their business. It's a bit judgmental to assume that I did something wrong."

My brows knitted, and I thought of what those gods he'd been following did. "I hate to admit this, but you do have a point."

"Did it pain you greatly to admit that?"

"Yes," I admitted. His gaze left mine, but his thumb still moved. How could he not realize what he was doing? He had to know, right? The digit was attached to his body. I opened my mouth—

"You're about to ask if it has something to do with those gods I was following." A wry humor filled his tone.

I frowned. "No."

He glanced down at me again, raising a brow.

I rolled my eyes with a sigh. "Okay. I was. Is it because you are trying to find out why they are killing mortals?"

His laugh was soft. "It could be, but it's not often that I'm in the mortal realm for any length of time, *liessa*," he said, and my heart skipped in my chest in response to the nickname. "That alone would provoke the interest of others, and their interest is something I find greatly annoying. But I have refused and not allowed many things. I'm not sure I could pick just one. When the Hunters don't immediately return to them, they will know that they did, indeed, find me."

"It would seem rather reckless for the gods to spend their time seeking to provoke one another."

"You'd be surprised," he muttered.

I was.

His gaze flicked back to mine. "You do realize that you're not a god, and you've risked doing more than just irritating me."

My lips pursed as I looked across the lake. "Well,"—I drew out the word—"I have a bad habit of making poor decisions."

Ash laughed, and it was a deep one—one that taunted the corners of my lips. I ignored it.

"Does it bother you?" Ash asked.

"What?" I inquired, unsure of what he was referencing.

His eyes met mine. "Me touching you."

Well, that answered my unasked question. He knew exactly what his fingers were doing. "I…" I didn't mind it at all. The touch felt wonderfully grounding, as if I were a part of something or someone. I didn't realize that I was smiling until I noticed that Ash's lips had parted, and he was staring at me again in that heavy way that centered in my stomach. "It doesn't bother me. It's a…novel feeling."

"Novel feeling?" The half-grin returned. "A touch like this?" His fingers moved then, not just his thumb. He drew them up over my arm, curling them toward his palm, and a soft wake of shivers followed. "Is different to you?"

"It is."

His stare changed, a slightly perplexed pinch to his brow forming. It occurred to me that someone casually touching one's arm probably wasn't a unique feeling to most.

The burn of embarrassment increased as my gaze flicked to the sky. "I mean, it's all right. I don't mind it."

Ash didn't respond, but his thumb continued, this time slowly sweeping up and down. The feel of his skin against mine was different, and it had nothing to do with him being a god.

As I lay there, trying to forget the awkwardness, I couldn't help but wonder how old he was. From what I understood, Primals and gods aged like mortals until they reached eighteen to twenty years, and then their aging slowed to a crawl. Ash looked no older than Ezra or Tavius, the latter having just turned twenty-two. Gods tended to be on the younger side compared to Primals. "How old are you?"

He had returned to staring at the lake. "Older than I look, and probably younger than you think."

My brows furrowed. "That's not much of an answer."

"I know."

"And?"

"Does it matter?" Ash countered. "Whether I'm a century old or a thousand years? I've still outlived anyone you know. My lifespan would still be incomprehensible to you or any mortal."

Well, I guessed he was, in a way, right again. How many years he'd lived didn't really matter when he would still appear only a few years older than me a hundred or more years from now.

I didn't know what would've happened if I had become the Primal's Consort. Would my aging have stopped thanks to some sort of Primal magic? I'd never really considered it because it hadn't mattered when I would've died. It only mattered whether or not I succeeded at my duty.

I shifted my thoughts, not wanting to think about any of that. Not right now.

He looked down at me with eyes a swirling shade of quicksilver as his chin lowered. "What if I told you a secret?"

"A secret?"

He nodded. "The kind you could never repeat."

"The kind you'd have to kill me if I did?"

One side of his lips curved up. "The kind I would be very, very disappointed if you repeated."

The slowly churning wisps of eather in his eyes held my gaze. "Even though common sense tells me it's best that I don't know what this secret is, I am far too curious now."

A low chuckle rumbled from him as his thumb swept over the curve of my shoulder. "What is written in your histories about the gods, Primals, and Iliseeum is not always accurate. Some Primals' age would shock you."

"Because they're so old?"

"Because they're so young in comparison," he corrected. "The Primals you know of now didn't always hold those positions of power."

"They didn't?" I whispered.

Ash shook his head. "Some gods have even walked both realms far longer than the Primals."

If I weren't already lying down, I would've fallen over. What he said sounded unbelievable. And he was right. I had no idea how old the Primal of Death was. He, like Kolis, the Primal of Life, had never been depicted in paintings.

"I have so many questions," I admitted.

"I can only imagine." His gaze flickered over my face. "But I'm sure the questions you have cannot be answered now."

Not *now*? As in there'd be a later? A rush of anticipation surged through me before I could stop it.

There was never a later to look forward to.

The pleasant warmth his touch had created cooled, and I suddenly needed space. I sat up, and this time, he didn't stop me. His hand slipped from my arm, leaving a wake of awareness behind. I reached around, gingerly prodding at the back of my head. I didn't feel any cuts, so that was good, and it wasn't exactly sore either.

I glanced down at myself and nearly choked on my breath. Where the pale ivory slip had met my damp skin, the already near-translucent material had become even sheerer. I could see the halo of the rosier skin of my breasts, and the cold-water-hardened…

"You sure you're fine?"

"Yes." Hoping he couldn't see the blush I could feel spreading over my cheeks, I glanced at him. He was leaning against the rock that had taken me out, legs stretched out in front of him, crossed loosely at the ankles. Still shirtless. Did he not have a shirt with him?

Ash's eyes were shadowed as he watched me. "Did killing the creature bother you?"

"It didn't." I had no idea how we were even having this discussion. What made him think that it had bothered me?

"Just in case it *did* bother you," he said, "they weren't mortal."

"I know that." I tugged on the edge of my slip—it had ridden up my thigh as I moved. "But just because something isn't mortal doesn't make it okay to kill," I added, realizing how rich that was coming from my mouth.

"As admirable as that proclamation is, you misunderstand." He cocked an arm back on the boulder, and the roll and stretch of lean muscle was…well, distracting. "Or you've forgotten what I said. The Hunters were no longer alive."

"I remember what you said, but they were *something*. They walked, and they breathed—"

"They do not breathe," he interrupted, gaze flashing to mine. His eyes looked like pools of moonlight. "They do not eat or drink. They do not sleep or dream. They are the dead given form to serve whatever need the god has."

I shuddered a little at that description. "Maybe you simply have little regard for killing," I said, acknowledging to myself the hypocrisy of what I was saying, considering how many lives I'd ended in the last three years.

"Killing is not something one should have little regard for," he replied. "It should always affect you, no matter how many times you do it. It should always leave a mark. And if it doesn't, then I would have grave concerns about that individual."

I wanted to be relieved to hear that. Someone—mortal, god, or Primal—who could kill with hardly any thought was terrifying.

Which was why Ezra was a little afraid of me.

But I did give it thought…after the fact. Sometimes.

"So, you've killed a lot?" I asked.

He arched a brow. "That seems like an incredibly personal and somewhat inappropriate assumption and question."

"Yeah, well, spying on my *unmentionables* is an incredibly personal and inappropriate act, so my question or assumption can't be of greater offense."

That softer curve returned to his lips. "I was not spying on you, and I'm willing to bet that you know that by now. However, you were staring at me. Quite openly, I might add, as I walked out of the lake."

The skin of my throat flamed. "I was not."

"You lie so prettily," he murmured, and gods help me, it was a lie.

I sat back, crossing my arms. "Why are you even here? You could've left once you realized I was okay."

"I could've left, but like I said before, it would be incredibly rude to leave someone unconscious on the ground," he returned.

"Well, aren't I lucky that you're a polite pervert?"

Ash laughed, low and smoky. "Why haven't *you* left, *liessa*?"

Chapter 12

Well.

Dammit.

I exhaled noisily. "Good question."

"Or a pointless question."

"How so?"

He tipped closer, and that scent of his—the fresh, citrusy one, wrapped its way around me. "Because we both know why we remained right where we are. I interest you. You interest me. So, here we remain."

Denials rose, but even I had the foresight to know how weak they would sound if I attempted to give voice to them.

What *was* I doing here? With him?

My stomach tumbled as my gaze dropped to his mouth, and I quickly looked away. Staying here had nothing to do with his mouth for godssake. My heart skipped anyway. I was here because when would I ever get to speak so openly with a god who was rather mild-tempered? When did I get to talk so openly with anyone? Any other conversation was always shadowed by how I'd failed the kingdom.

But he was a *god*. And even if he wasn't, I couldn't say I knew him all that well. I was barely dressed, and Ash made me wary. Because right now, I could easily see myself doing something incredibly impulsive and reckless enough to blow up in my face.

I peeked at Ash. He'd drawn that bottom lip of his between his teeth as he watched me. My heart started thumping, and all I could think was that today had been so very…weird.

"Why are you interested enough to stay?" I asked.

Dark eyebrows rose. "Why wouldn't I be?"

"Why would a mortal be of interest to someone from Iliseeum?"

He tilted his head. "I am beginning to think you don't know much about us."

I shrugged.

A breeze picked up a strand of his hair, tossing it across his face. "We find mortals to be very interesting beings—the way you all choose to live, the rules you create to govern and sometimes limit yourselves. How fiercely you all live—love and hate. Mortals are uniquely interesting to us." He lifted a shoulder. "And you? You interest me because there seems to be little time between what occurs in your head and what comes out of your mouth. And there seems to be little regard for the consequences."

My brows knitted. "I'm not sure if that's a compliment."

He chuckled. "It is."

"I'm going to have to take your word for that."

That soft half-smile made another appearance, and that was all he said for a little while. "You asked earlier if I killed a lot," he said, surprising me. "Only when I had to. Has it been a lot? I'm sure to some it has been. To others? Probably not something they'd blink an eye at, but I haven't enjoyed any." His voice was heavy. "Not a single one."

Even though his answer caught me off guard, it was clear this was something he didn't like to talk about. I shifted, pressing my knees together. "I'm sorry."

"An apology?"

"I…I shouldn't have asked that question in the first place. It's not any of my business."

Ash stared at me.

"What?"

"You are entirely contradictory," he said. His gaze met mine and then flicked away. Several long moments passed. The silence wasn't uncomfortable, and maybe that was because I was used to the quiet. "I remember the first time I had to kill someone. I remember how the sword felt in my hand—how it felt as if it weighed double. I can still see the look on his face. I will never forget what he said. 'Do it.' Those were his words. Do it."

I squeezed my knees together even tighter.

"No death has been easy, but that one?" His hand opened and closed as if he were trying to work feeling back into his fingers. "That one will always leave the deepest mark. He was a friend."

I pressed my palm to my chest. "You…you killed your friend?"

"I didn't have a choice." He stared at the lake. "That's not an excuse or justification. It was just something that had to be done."

I couldn't understand how he could do that, and I needed to. "Why would it need to be done? What would've happened if you hadn't?"

A muscle throbbed along his jaw. "Dozens, if not more, would've died if I hadn't taken his life."

"Oh," I whispered, feeling a little sick to my stomach. Had his friend been hurting people, forcing his intervention? If so, then I could understand that. *Do it.* Had his friend known that he needed to be stopped? I didn't ask if that was the case. I wanted to. The question practically burned my tongue, but it didn't feel right. And it didn't feel right knowing that he'd been forced to do that and had also lost another friend to those three gods. "Then I'm sorry you had to do that."

Ash's head jerked toward mine, his stare searching. "I…" He fell quiet for several breaths. "Thank you."

"You're welcome." I gathered my damp hair and began twisting it, wishing I could share something so intimate, but I didn't know how to do that. How to make myself comfortable enough to do so. The only other thing that came to mind and unfortunately spilled from my lips was utterly ridiculous. "I hate gowns."

There was a beat of silence. "What?"

Perhaps I needed to have *my* lips sewn shut. "I just find gowns to be…cumbersome." And I also hated for my thighs to rub together, but that was *not* something I would discuss with him.

He watched me. Being the focus of those steely eyes was unnerving. "I imagine they would be."

I nodded, face feeling too warm as I stared at the gently rolling waters of the lake. I knew I shouldn't say anything, especially to a god who served a Primal, but what I'd done was something I never talked about. Not even with Sir Holland. And I hadn't realized until that moment how much weight those unsaid words carried.

But I couldn't voice them. They revealed too much. They were too much of a burden.

Staring at the lake, I sought to change the subject. "Have you found out anything more about why those gods are killing mortals?"

"Unfortunately, not. The three gods have been hard to track." He sighed. "And I can only pry so much without drawing unwanted attention. If I do, then I won't discover why they're doing this."

"Your friend, the one Cressa and the others killed?" I asked. "What was his name?"

"Lathan," he answered. "You would've liked him, I think. He never listened to me either."

A small grin tugged on my lips but faded quickly. "Was his body left or was he…?"

"His body was left, soul intact. He didn't become whatever it was that woman became last night."

"Oh," I whispered, watching the light of the moon ripple over the black waters. "It doesn't make his death any easier, I'm sure, but at least he wasn't destroyed."

Ash was quiet for a long moment. "You know what you remind me of?"

I looked over at him again, and his gaze snared mine. Warmth hit my skin once more, seeping into my veins. There was no sting of embarrassment. This was different, a more languid and sultry type of heat. "I'm half afraid to ask."

He was silent for a moment. "There was this flower that once grew in the Shadowlands."

Every part of my being zeroed in on him. Where he lived… He was talking about Iliseeum. One of the things I was looking forward to as the Consort was the chance to see the realm. I couldn't listen harder if I tried.

"The petals were the color of blood in the moonlight and remained folded in on themselves until someone approached. When they opened, they appeared incredibly delicate, as if they would shatter in the softest wind, but they grew wild and fiercely, any place there was even a hint of soil. They even grew between the cracks of stone, and they were incredibly unpredictable."

Did I really remind him of a delicate, beautiful flower? I wasn't sure what part of me could be considered delicate. A fingernail? "How are flowers unpredictable?"

"Because these were quite temperamental."

A laugh burst out of me. The wisps of white pulsed behind his pupil once more, churning slowly. His gaze shifted back to the lake. "Is that the part that makes you think of them?"

"Possibly."

"I'm curious to learn how a flower is temperamental, especially such a delicate one."

"The thing is, they only appeared delicate." He was closer now, having lowered his arm from the rock. "In truth, they were quite resilient and deadly."

"Deadly?"

He nodded. "When they opened, it revealed the center. And in that center were several spiky needles that carried a rather poisonous toxin. Depending on their mood, they released them. One needle could take down a god for a week."

"Sounds like an amazing flower." And slightly horrifying. "I'm not sure if it's a compliment to know that I remind you of a murderous plant."

"If you'd ever seen them, you would know that it is."

I smiled, flattered despite it all, and imagined that it must not take much to flatter me.

"I have a question for you now," he said.

"Ask away."

"Why are you here by a lake? I imagine a Princess has access to a large tub filled with steaming hot water."

I stiffened, having forgotten that, in my anger, I had revealed that I was a Princess. "I like it here. It's…"

"Calming?" he finished for me, and I nodded. "With the exception of the Hunters," he added. "How often do you come here?"

"As much as I can," I admitted, studying his profile. It was all so strange. Him. Me. Us. This conversation. How at ease I felt around him. Everything.

"Do you never worry that anyone could happen upon you?"

I shook my head. "You are the first person I've ever seen in these woods—well, the first god. And not counting the spirits, but they never come close to the lake."

"And no one knows what you do out here?"

"I imagine some of the guards know I've been in the lake since they see me return with wet hair."

His brows knitted. "I find it hard to believe that none of them has ever followed you."

"I told you, people are afraid of these woods."

"And what I know of mortal men is that many of them will overcome any number of fears the moment they realize a beautiful female can easily be caught in a compromising position. Especially a Princess."

"Beautiful?" I laughed again, shaking my head.

He cut me a look. "Please don't expect me to believe that you're unaware of your beauty. You do not strike me as the coy type, and I've been rather impressed by you so far."

"That's not what I'm saying. But thanks, I will be able to sleep soundly knowing that you're impressed by me," I retorted.

"Well, I wasn't exactly impressed when I told you to go home and you remained."

I stared at him.

"But then you kicked the Hunter, and I was…well, I felt something, all right."

My eyes narrowed.

"I can't say I was impressed when you appeared as if you were about to embrace the Hunter," he went on. "But then you disarmed it. That was impressive—"

"You can stop now."

"You sure?" The teasing grin had returned.

"Yes," I stated. "I'm not sure why I'm still sitting here talking to you."

"Perhaps you feel indebted to me since I watched over you while you were unconscious."

"I was unconscious for a few moments. It's not like you stood guard for endless hours."

"I am quite important. Those moments felt like hours."

"I do not like you," I said.

His eyes shifted to mine, and that curve of his lips remained. "But you see, you do. That's why you're still here and no longer threatening to claw my eyes out."

I snapped my mouth shut.

Ash winked.

"The clawing of the eyes could still happen," I warned him.

"I don't think so." He bit down on that lower lip of his again, the act snagging my gaze once more. "Besides the fact that you know you won't succeed, you said I was beautiful, and clawing my eyes out would ruin that, wouldn't it?"

My cheeks heated, but I wasn't sure if it was the reminder of what I'd said or the glisten on his lower lip. "I did suffer an injury to my head right before I said that."

His laugh was barely above a breath.

Twisting my hair once more, I focused on the ripples spreading across the lake. It had to be late, and I knew I should head back, but I was reluctant to return to life away from the lake. "What are the Shadowlands like?"

"A lot like these woods," he said. When I looked over at him, he was looking at the moonlight-dappled trees.

"Really?"

"You're surprised," he said, and I was.

"I just didn't think the Shadowlands would be beautiful."

"The Shadowlands consists of three separate places," he replied, and I jumped a little as I felt his fingers brush mine. That shiver of static danced across my knuckles as my head jerked in his direction. He gently disentangled my fingers from my hair. "May I?"

Seeming to lose the ability to speak, I simply nodded, even though I wasn't entirely sure what he was asking permission for. I was silent as he tugged on a strand of my hair, stretching it until the curl became straight.

"There is the Abyss, which is what everyone thinks of when they picture the Shadowlands—fiery pits and endless torment," he said, staring at the strand of my hair. "But there is also the Vale, and that is paradise for those worthy."

"What is the Vale like?"

His gaze lifted to mine, searching. A moment passed. "That, I cannot tell you."

"Oh." Disappointed, I lowered my gaze to the long fingers that held my hand.

"What awaits in the Vale cannot be shared with anyone, mortal or god. Not even Primals can enter the Vale," he added. "But the rest of the Shadowlands is like an entryway—a village before the city. It is beautiful in its own way, but it was once one of the most magnificent regions in all of Iliseeum."

Once was? "What happened to it?"

"Death," he stated flatly.

A chill swept over me. "What is the rest of Iliseeum like?"

"The skies are a color of blue you would never see in this realm, the waters clear, and the grass lush and vibrant," he told me. "Except for when it's night, the hours of darkness are brief in Dalos."

My breath caught. *Dalos.*

The City of the Gods, where the Primal of Life—Kolis—and his

Court resided. "Is it true that the buildings reach the clouds there?"

"Many surpass them," he answered, and for a moment, I tried to imagine what that must look like.

And failed.

I fell quiet as I watched him toy with the strand of my hair, sort of awestruck that a god was sitting beside me, playing with my hair, teasing me.

"Shouldn't you be home by now, safely and respectfully tucked away in your bed?" he asked.

"Probably."

His gaze flickered over my face. "Then others must be looking for you."

I laughed as I dragged my gaze from his. "They're not."

"Truly?" Doubt clouded his voice. "Because they believe you are already where you're supposed to be?"

I nodded. "I'm very skilled at coming and going without notice."

"Why does that not surprise me?"

I cracked a grin.

"Is that a smile?" He leaned over, eyeing me far too intently to be serious. "It is. You've graced me with three of them now. Be still my heart."

Shaking my head, I rolled my eyes. "It must not take much to still your heart."

"Apparently, it takes a mortal Princess," he said. "One who roams haunted woods in the dead of night and swims gloriously naked in a lake."

I chose to ignore the gloriously naked part. "Is it common for gods to sit and chat with mortals after spying upon them?"

He made that sound again, that deep and shadowy chuckle as he drew his thumb over my hair. I swore I felt that touch down my spine. "Primals and gods do all sorts of things with mortals after unintentionally crossing paths with them."

My mind took what experience I had with "*all sorts of things*" and happily played around in the gutter with it.

His gaze flicked up from my hair, eyes a molten silver. "Especially with those we've had the pleasure of glimpsing all those *unmentionable* places."

"Can we pretend as if that didn't happen?"

His grin spread. "Are you really pretending that it didn't?"

No. "Yes."

Ash's shoulders lifted in silent laughter.

"Are others as…?" I trailed off.

"What?"

It was hard to think of the right word. "Are others as kind as you?"

"Kind?" His head tilted. "I am not kind, *liessa*."

The way he said *liessa*. It was *indecent*. "You have reacted far kinder to things most would've reacted to cruelly and without hesitation."

"You mean when you stabbed me?" Ash clarified. "In the chest?"

I sighed. "Yes. Among other things. Are you going to say you only have one kind bone to go along with that one decent bone?"

"I would say that I have one decent, kind bone in my body when it comes to you, *liessa*."

There was a snag in my breath. "Why?"

Silvery eyes met mine once again, the wisps of eather still. "I don't know." He let out a short, surprised laugh, his brows furrowing. "I don't need to. Nothing would change from this moment, no matter if I left you upon waking or if I lingered longer. I don't know. And that is an…interesting experience."

What he said didn't offend me because I wouldn't have believed him if he had an entire list of reasons he was this strange with me. He was a god. Whether he lived hundreds of years or even longer, everything I knew could be contained in his palm. He was pure power given physical form, and there had to be countless beings in Iliseeum that were far more, well…*everything* than me. There were mortals far more intriguing and worthy of that one kind, decent bone in his body. And I didn't mean that as a blow against myself. It was just the truth. I was unique because of what my forefather had done and that I had been born in a shroud and given a gift somehow and for some reason. Not because of anything I'd done with my life. The only understandable part was that he didn't understand why we sat here.

"But there is something I do know."

Curiosity rose. "What?"

"I want to kiss you, even though there is no reason for me to other than I want it." The heated intensity of his stare held mine. "I would even go as far as to say I *need* to."

A wild flutter started in my chest and quickly spread, much like that deadly flower of his that I reminded him of.

Did I want to kiss him?

I thought of when we'd kissed the night I'd first encountered the three gods, and the sharp, swift curl low in my stomach told me that, yes, I did. I was attracted to him on a visceral level that hadn't been overshadowed by how infuriating he could be from one moment to the next, or the fact that he was a god—one who served the Primal of Death. Both of those things should extinguish any attraction I felt, especially the latter, but I couldn't deny that he was the source of the flashes of warmth that had nothing to do with embarrassment.

Nothing seemed real right now. Not from the moment I'd healed the kiyou wolf to this very second. It was as if I'd entered a different world, one where I didn't have to become someone else. One where I was *wanted* instead of scorned, *desired* instead of disliked. A world where I was just me and not the failed Maiden or would-be Consort.

I knew I shouldn't. Just like I probably shouldn't have worked up the nerve to enter The Jade and experience physical pleasure on my terms and just for me. I had no idea what the Primal would think if he ever came for me and realized that I was truly no longer the Maiden—if he would even know. I also knew there was a higher risk involved with Ash because he wasn't a god from another Court.

But I wanted to *feel*. I wanted to be *someone*. I wanted to be kissed again. By him

And I wouldn't let who I was supposed to be, who I ended up becoming, or any thought of the Primal of Death stop me from allowing myself to *want*.

My pulse pounded dizzyingly fast. "Then kiss me."

Chapter 13

The smile that spread across Ash's face wasn't slight or faint. It was wide and full of heated sensuality. I caught a brief glimpse of his teeth, two slightly elongated, sharp…*fangs*.

Now that I could really see them, I knew they weren't the size of a finger like Tavius had once claimed, but I knew they could tear into my skin with shocking ease, nonetheless. The sight of them was yet another reminder of what Ash was. They brought forth a shivery mixture of fear and shameful excitement.

He moved then, erasing the distance between us. Every cell of my body tensed in a breathless sort of anticipation as that woodsy, citrus scent surrounded me.

"I don't think I ever wanted to hear the word *yes* more than I do now," he said, the bridge of his nose brushing mine. The shiver coursing through me had nothing to do with the cool touch of his skin. "Ever."

Then his lips met mine, and the first touch was just that. A *touch*. But it was still a shock to my entire system, just like the moment I first entered the water. His lips were cool against mine, and the press of them was soft like satin over steel. He tilted his head slightly, and then I wasn't thinking about his lips.

I wasn't thinking at all.

The pressure of the kiss increased, and he tugged at my bottom lip with those sharp fangs. I gasped, my entire body shuddering.

His breathy laugh touched my lips. "I like that sound. A lot."

"I liked that," I whispered. "A lot."

"But that, *liessa*, was barely a kiss."

My blood thrummed as his hand settled around the nape of my neck. *Liessa. Something beautiful and powerful…* I felt like that now.

His mouth touched mine once more, and this kiss…it was nothing like the gentle touch of before. It was harder, and the feel of the tip of his tongue against the seam of my lips sent my heart racing. I opened for him, and the kiss wasn't only deep. The flick of his tongue against mine was an exploration that tasted of honey and ice, and he kissed as if the same, almost frenzied curiosity that drove me also rode him. To know what it was like to feel wanted, desired, cherished. To just *feel.* I knew that was ridiculous. I didn't think gods had that same curiosity, but the rawness of his kiss went beyond that need to know, as his hand threaded through my hair and his other flattened against my cheek. The kiss *became* all those things. I'd had no idea that a kiss could be like this.

Needing to feel more, I moved my hands to his shoulders. He shuddered at my touch. His skin was cool, and I didn't know how he could feel that way when I was a sparking fire. I tugged on him, wanting him closer, only slightly concerned that I wasn't apprehensive about that desire. A distant, still-operating part of my mind knew I should be more worried because I was feeling wonderfully impulsive and gloriously reckless.

But he was closer, and that was all I wanted to be concerned with. His large body urged mine down, and there wasn't even a flicker of hesitation before my back met the grass. The weight of his upper body and the coolness of his bare skin bleeding through the thin slip as his chest pressed against mine was a heady, decadent shock to my senses.

The rumbling sound that came from him danced over my skin, my breasts, and then lower still. He seemed to be as affected, and that left me reeling in a dizzying way, knowing that he—*a god*—could react so strongly.

Hands trembling slightly, I ran my fingers through his hair and then across his skin where the tattoo stretched to the nape of his neck. He slid his hand out from my hair as mine traveled over the corded muscles lining his spine. His fingers grazed the length of my arm, from the top of my hand all the way to my shoulder and then down again. His palm glided against the side of my breast and then to my waist. A soft sound left me as my back arched, one I'd only ever heard in the shadowy areas of the garden or in the heavily curtained rooms of The

Jade.

His hand stilled on my hip, his touch becoming heavier there as his mouth left mine. "Was that kiss satisfactory?"

My eyes fluttered open, colliding with his. "It will do."

He laughed, low and throaty. "You're hard to impress, aren't you?"

"Not really," I said, even though I was thoroughly impressed.

"Ouch." His hand tightened on my hip. "Then I suppose I'll have to change that."

This…the teasing was unfamiliar and exciting. Like when I discovered a new passageway in the Garden District, but way, way better. I liked it. A lot. It called to something inside me, something easy and free. "I suppose you do."

But it was me who did.

My mouth reclaimed his, and the way our lips met was fierce and demanding, igniting a riot of wild, breathless sensations inside me that I eagerly fell and spiraled into. I was wonderfully lost in them—in him. The feel of his cool lips. The touch of his tongue against mine, and that unexpected nip of his fangs. His honey taste, and his lush scent. And I knew these were the kinds of kisses I'd read about in those books. The ones I'd never experienced at The Jade when I sought to ease the restless energy in me. Because I could do this for hours and never grow tired. I knew this because I wanted *more.* His hand on my hip squeezed and then skidded lower. A wicked twist of anticipation curled low and deep inside me.

Ash's hand drifted to the edge of the slip, and then the rough skin of his palm skimmed my bare leg. In that moment, I didn't think I'd ever been gladder that I wasn't wearing pants.

His lips moved against mine as he drew his hand up the length of my leg, under the slip. I reacted without much thought, curling my leg in a silent request for him to keep exploring. Every part of my body went taut as his palm skimmed my bare upper thigh. An ache settled in a very *unmentionable* place, the one his hand was only inches from.

But he stilled.

Ash ended the kiss, breathing unevenly like me, and that shook me. A god was just as affected as I was. "This will…" He swallowed, looking down between us. "Gods…"

Every part of me focused on where the tips of his fingers brushed the lower curve of my rear. I looked down, following his gaze. The loose bodice of my slip had inched down, exposing just the hardened tips of my breasts. His gaze fell to where the hem of my slip had bunched around his forearm, dragged above my hips. The contrast of our skin, even in the moonlight, was a surprisingly intimate sight. As were the shadowy areas now exposed to the balmy night air—and to him.

Trembling, I glanced up at him. His features had sharpened, becoming stark. And there was this need and *hunger* to his parted lips. I could see a hint of those fangs, and another shudder ran through me. I wondered if I should attempt to shield myself from his gaze—if he expected that from me. But if he did, he would be disappointed. I wanted him to look upon me like he wanted to devour me.

And I thought I might actually want to be devoured.

I could feel the heated intensity of his stare as he lifted his gaze. He lowered his head, his mouth claiming mine. His kiss was demanding, tugging on my lower lip with his sharp fangs. I yielded to him, opening. The kiss deepened, and his tongue slid over mine, his mouth capturing my breathless moan. The taste of him, his smell…all of him invaded me, my senses, burning me. An aching, pulsing need centered in my core, so close to where his hand remained on my leg. His thumb moved along the crease of my thigh, sending a throbbing pulse through me as his mouth left mine, trailing down the side of my neck. He lingered over my pulse, his tongue a hot, wet slide against the flesh. His head tilted, and I felt the sharp, unexpected drag of his fangs.

My entire body arched as his name escaped on a soft exhale, "*Ash*."

Mind thick with desire, it took a moment for me to register that he'd stilled. My eyes opened. "Is…is something wrong?"

He gave a small shake of his head. "No. It's just that I…" He kissed the spot he'd nipped at. "I have never heard my name spoken like that. It's a strange feeling."

I skimmed my fingers down his arms, wondering how that could even be possible. "Is it a bad feeling?"

"No. It's not," he said, sounding surprised by his admission. I wasn't sure what to think of that.

But then I was completely lost again as his lips began to move once more, trailing tiny, hot kisses down the line of my throat and over my collarbone. He moved lower and lower until his chin grazed the swell of my breast. My fingers dug into the taut skin of his arms as his cool breath danced over the turgid nub of flesh.

"You know what?" he asked.

"What?" I stared at the top of his dark head, my heart pounding.

"You can call me whatever you like."

A light laugh spilled out of me. "I'm not sure you really mean that."

"I do." His head shifted, and his lashes swept up. Swirling silver eyes locked onto mine. "*Anything*."

I couldn't look away. His gaze held mine as his mouth closed over my breast, drawing the sensitive skin into the recesses of his mouth. I gasped at the shock of the coldness against the heat of my flesh. Another throbbing pulse darted through me as his hair fell forward, sliding over my skin.

He eased off, leaving me breathless. He kissed the space between my breasts. "Wouldn't want this other one to get lonely."

I grinned as my head fell back against the damp grass. "Is that the one kind, decent bone in your body rearing its head?"

"Perhaps." His tongue swirled on the nipple of my other breast. He drew the tingling peak into his mouth, dragging the edge of a fang across it. Another sharp cry left me. "But," he said, sliding his tongue over the stinging flesh, "I think it's all the wicked, indecent bones in my body guiding my thoughtfulness."

I bit my lip as his mouth closed over the skin there once more. The feel of him…it was quite wicked, and then his thumb moved along my inner thigh in slow, maddening circles again, coming so, so close to where a steady ache of need thrummed. I waited and waited, wondering if he would *touch* me. Hoping that he would. I needed him to, but that thumb, those fingers of his, drifted closer and then away, closer and then away, all while his mouth, lips, and teeth teased my breasts.

Need, wonder, and the intense fire he lit within me flooded every part of me with liquid heat. My patience, never my strong suit, failed.

I slid my hand down the corded muscles of his arm to where his hand remained on my thigh. His wandering thumb stilled, and his fingers splayed wide, grazing the dampness gathering between my thighs. My fingers ran over his.

His head lifted, and my eyes opened to find him staring down at me in a stark, hungry way that sent another wave of shivers through me. "What do you want from me, *liessa*?"

Something beautiful and powerful…

That's what I wanted.

His lips parted, revealing the tips of his fangs. "Show me."

Eyes locked with his and heart thumping, I slid his hand from my thigh to where I throbbed. My hips jerked at the cool touch against my hot, damp skin.

Radiant wisps of eather lashed through the silver of his eyes. "*Show me*," he repeated, voice rough as he skimmed one finger along my center. "Show me what you like, and I will give it to you."

I could barely breathe as I molded my hand to his. Never in my life had I done something like this. But it felt…so natural. So right. And yet so enticingly scandalous. I moved his thumb with mine, drawing those circles around the bundle of nerves. What air I managed to breathe snagged.

"Is that all?" he asked, his voice a dark, sinful drawl. He moved his thumb under mine. "Or is there more you need, *liessa*? More you like. Show me."

It was as if his voice carried a compulsion, one I had to obey. But I was in complete control as I pressed one of his long fingers against my softness, into the heat and wetness. I gasped at the feel of his cool finger parting my flesh before sinking slowly into me.

Ash's gaze left mine then, falling to where our hands were joined. His chest rose sharply as he watched me—as he watched *us* as we moved his finger, working it deeper and deeper. And still he watched as I lifted my hips, moving against his fingers and his hand. He didn't look away. He didn't even blink when I pressed in another of his fingers, piercing my flesh with it. I didn't think he breathed. I thought maybe we both stopped as his fingers filled me, stretching my flesh until I felt a bite of discomfort followed by a ripple of acute pleasure.

"You feel…" He inhaled sharply, drawing those fingers out before tracking the rise of my hips with those churning eyes. "So warm. So soft and hot. Wet." He shuddered, his voice thickening as he thrust his fingers while mine simply clung to his wrist. "You feel like silk and sunshine. Beautiful." He dragged his teeth over his lower lip, and I thought… I thought his fangs seemed longer, sharper as my back arched over the grass, and I ground against his hand. Something about watching him, watching us, was shocking. It sent my stomach dipping and tumbling. Stretched my nerves until they felt as if they'd snap. "That's it, *liessa*, fuck my hand."

His words scorched my skin, burning through every part of me. My head kicked back, and my eyes fell closed. Blood pounded as my hips rocked and twisted against him. Tension built and coiled tighter and tighter.

He moved over me, chest to chest as his mouth closed over mine once more. The way he kissed was just as wild as the sensations building inside me. My other hand sank into his hair as I did just as he'd demanded with wild abandon. All I could hear was the sound of our kisses and the wet thrust of his fingers. All I could feel was him and the tight tension settling deep in my core, curling and curling. My body went as taut as a bowstring, and then everything unraveled.

His mouth caught the cry of release as pleasure unfurled in wracking spasms, lashing out and flooding pleasure into every nerve, vein, and limb. It was shocking, the waves and waves of pure feeling.

Only when my hand fell away from his wrist did he slowly ease his fingers from me, his mouth from mine. "Beautiful," he whispered against my swollen lips, and my eyes fluttered open.

"I…" Words failed me when he lifted those two very wicked, glistening fingers. His luminous eyes held mine as he drew them into his mouth. My body arched as if his mouth sucked on my flesh, not his.

I had never seen anything so shameless in my life.

He grinned around his fingers, slowly drawing them from his mouth. "You taste like the sun."

My heart skipped. "What…what does the sun taste like?"

That curve of his lips was wicked. "Like you."

His mouth returned to mine. It could've been his words, the taste of myself on his lips, or how I could still feel his fingers inside me. It could've been all of those things. Whatever it was, it fueled the need to give him what he'd given me. To share that pleasure. I slipped my hand between us, finding his thick, hard length straining against the soft cloth of his breeches. Another ripple of tight pleasure radiated out through me at the feel of him. His entire body jerked, much like mine upon his first touch.

Ash made that dark, luscious sound again as he reached between us, folding his hand over mine. He pressed against my palm, shuddering. "This…this will become more than kissing and touching."

"Will it?" I'd never heard my voice sound so velvety before. I'd never quite felt my heart beat throughout my body like it did now, as another whirl of anticipation swirled. "I want to do what you've done for me."

His jaw flexed as I cupped him through his breeches. "You have no idea how badly I want that."

"I want that, too," I whispered in the space between our mouths.

"It's not your palm I want wrapped around my cock right now. It's *you* I want. Tight and wet and warm," he breathed, and a deep shiver rolled through me as my grip on him firmed. He groaned. "And if you keep touching me like that, that's what's going to happen. I'm going to get inside you, and it won't be my fingers you'll be fucking." He lowered his head again, brushing his lips over mine. "I think you know that."

I did.

Oh, gods, I totally did.

I swallowed, my hand unsteady as I slid it down over the hard plane of his chest. A hundred thoughts swirled, a battle between impulsivity and caution, recklessness, and wisdom. We'd already gone too far. A part of him had been *inside* me. He knew what I tasted like. There were countless reasons for why I should heed the latter, and only a few for the former. But those were louder, more incessant.

I didn't want this, whatever it was, to end quite yet. I didn't want to return to reality, where I knew I would never feel *this* again. This abundant wildness. This connection to my body. To his. The realness. No dying hope of fulfilling my duty; of taking something like this—something beautiful and powerful—and using it to kill. No need to be anyone but myself.

So, I shut down the caution and wisdom. "I know what will happen."

His lips curled into a smile against mine. "You're a Princess."

"So? You're a god."

Ash laughed then, the sound a thick and heavy smoke in my veins. "And you shouldn't be debauched on the floor of a forest."

"And what if I wasn't a Princess?" I countered, sliding my hand away from him. "Would it be acceptable to commence with said debauching then?"

Another low laugh teased my lips as his hand grazed the curve of my thigh. "No one should be debauched on the floor of a forest. Especially when they will surely feel the hot bite of regret later."

"How do you know I would feel regret?"

"You will." His lips touched the corner of mine.

It occurred to me then that he had to be referring to the consequence that often occurred from a good debauching. A child. I relaxed, relieved that he had the foresight to even think of such things when the thought truly hadn't even entered my mind. A child born of a mortal and god was extremely rare, so much so that I'd never met one. "That can be prevented," I whispered, referencing an herb I knew women could take, either before or after, that inhibited such things. "It's a—"

"I know what it is," he interrupted. "Surprisingly, that is not what I was talking about."

I frowned. "Then what exactly *do* you think I would regret? Or do you think that I don't know my own wants and needs?"

"You strike me as a person who knows *exactly* what they want and need," he returned. "But this is not wise."

"Then what are you doing?" I demanded, pushing lightly on his chest.

"Attempting to not commence with said debauching." His hand slid around to my rear, where his fingers pressed into my flesh.

A throbbing pulse of awareness shuttled through me. "In…in case you're not aware, you have an odd way of not engaging in debauchery."

"I know," he replied. "Probably because I don't have much experience with everything debauching entails."

Surprise flickered through me. I opened my mouth to ask if he meant what I thought he did—because surely, as a god, he couldn't—but his lips found mine once more. And kisses…*his* kisses were very distracting. His lips moved against mine in a slow, drugging way as if he were sipping from my lips. It felt like hours, even though I knew it was only minutes. Not nearly long enough, and then those kisses slowed even more, gentling. There were no more unexpected pricks of his fangs, and with each sweep of his lips and flick of his tongue, I knew we would go no further than this.

And despite how I'd challenged him and his somewhat annoying and surprising restraint, this…this coming to an end *was* okay. It was the wise thing because forgetting the way he kissed, the pleasure he'd given me, and how I felt now would be hard enough. Anything more would be impossible.

His lips tugged slowly on mine, leaving me in a pleasant haze as his head lifted. I opened my eyes, finding him scanning the elms.

It took a moment for concern to reach me. "Do you hear something?"

"Nothing like before." He looked at me as he slid his hand down my leg and then away. "If I stayed, I think I'd find myself obsessed with trying to count just how many freckles you have."

What he said…it tugged at my heart, and I inhaled sharply. I did *not* need to feel that.

"But I need to go."

Forcing my grip on his shoulders to loosen and unsure of how my hands had even gotten there, I nodded.

"I should've left already," he added. "I didn't expect to linger tonight."

I ignored the burn of disappointment I felt in the pit of my stomach. "I think tonight was…entirely unexpected."

"I can agree with that," he replied and touched my cheek. The act surprised me. Catching a curl, he tugged it straight and then slowly wrapped it around his finger. He stared at the strand of hair, smoothing his thumb over it. "Will you be heading home now to a bed far more comfortable than a forest floor?"

I nodded.

But he didn't move from atop me, his weight still pleasant in an intoxicating sort of way. While he appeared momentarily engrossed in my hair, I took the opportunity. Seized it, actually. I swept my gaze over his brow and the proud line of his nose, the angular height of his cheekbones, and those shockingly soft lips. I took in the cut of his jaw and the faint scar in his chin. I committed those details to memory as I had the feel of his flesh against mine and how my lips still tingled from the touch of his.

I blew out a soft breath. "If you're to leave, you will need to let go of my hair."

"True," he murmured, easing his finger from the twist. He didn't let the hair fall. Instead, he swept it back behind my ear with a gentleness I decided I also could *not* remember.

He dipped his head then, kissing the center of my forehead, and *that* was another thing I would make sure to forget. Then, Ash rose with the same grace he had when he'd faced those creatures.

I sat up quickly, making sure the slip covered all the unmentionables as best as it could. I kept stealing glances, my gaze wandering low to where I swore I could still see the hard ridge of his arousal. He was silent, then donned his shirt. Moonlight glinted off the silver band around his biceps as he set about pulling on his boots. The last thing he picked up was the scabbard and sword.

Ash faced me then, and his stare… I could feel it as if it were a physical touch along my cheek, on my breasts, and then down the length of a bare leg. A heat followed that stare, one I had a sinking suspicion would taunt me during sleepless nights.

He looked out into the woods again. "Don't wait too long to return," he advised.

My brows rose as I tamped down whatever antagonistic thing surely sharpened my tongue. I didn't know if his order came from a place of assumed authority or one of concern, and neither was something I was accustomed to. It wasn't often that anyone told me what to do outside of being shooed away, especially these last three years.

He stepped toward me and then stopped, his hair falling to rest against his cheek and his jaw, brushing his shoulder. "I…" He seemed to struggle with how to continue.

"It was nice talking with you," I said, speaking the honest to gods truth. Ash went completely silent and still, and my cheeks heated. "Even though you did spy upon me," I added quickly. "Most inappropriately."

A faint smile appeared. No hint of teeth, but his features warmed. "It was nice talking to you. Truly," he said, and my silly heart skipped around in my chest. "Be careful."

"You, too," I managed.

Ash remained there for a moment before turning, his steps barely making a sound as he walked away. My smile faded a little as I watched him go until I could no longer see him in the dense shadows. There was a strange ache in my chest. A sense of loss that had nothing to do with where the kisses had or hadn't led, nor even the absence of contact. It felt like meeting a friend and then immediately losing them. That was what it really felt like. What we'd talked about seemed like things one only shared with friends. The other stuff…well, I didn't think friends shared *that*.

But it was a loss of some sort because I didn't think I would see him again. That if he still watched, I would be as unaware as I'd been before. That maybe he realized that this had already gone too far. I thought this because he'd never asked for a name.

I was still a stranger to him.

I shook my head and rose to my feet, finding my gown in the moonlight. Pulling it on, I heard a sound that had been strangely absent.

The *birds*.

They called out to one another, singing their songs as life stirred once more in the woods.

Chapter 14

"There was a riot last night in Croft's Cross. It started as a protest against the Crown and what little was being done to stop the Rot, but the guards turned it into a riot by the way they responded." Sitting at the foot of my bed, Ezra dragged a hand down her face. She'd shown a little bit after breakfast was served, looking as if she had gotten even less sleep than I had. Shadows smudged the skin under her eyes. "Six were killed. Far less than anticipated—as terrible as that sounds. But many were injured. Fire destroyed a few homes and businesses. Some claiming that the guards set them."

"I hadn't heard." Absently twisting my hair into a thick rope, I sank farther into the faded emerald cushions of the chair placed before the window. The view overlooked the Dark Elms, a place that seemed like a different world now. "Let me guess, the guards were acting on the Crown's orders?"

"They were," she noted, falling silent as she looked around my bedchamber. Her gaze drifted over the narrow wardrobe, the only other piece of furniture other than the chair I sat in, the bed, and the chest at the footboard. Books formed leaning towers against the wall since there were no shelves to display them. I had no trinkets or serving trollies, paintings of Maia, the Primal of Love, Beauty, and Fertility. Or Keella. Or lush settees providing ample seating. It was nothing like her or Tavius's chambers. It used to get to me—the differences—even when I was the Maiden. Now, I was just used to it.

"But it's not like they have no sense of autonomy or control over their actions," Ezra continued. "There were other ways they could've handled the issue."

This wasn't the first protest to turn violent. Mostly, it was the response that always escalated the issue. Sometimes, it was the people, but I couldn't fault them when it was clear they felt that peaceful demonstrations weren't capturing the Crown's attention, and when too many of their family members and friends were jobless and starving.

"The guards could've handled it differently." I watched the tops of the elms sway. Somewhere beyond those trees, the lake waited. My stomach twisted. Even thinking of it felt different now, and I wasn't sure if that foretold something good or bad or nothing at all. "But I don't think they care enough to try to deescalate the situation, and they probably did set the fire as a form of punishment or to somehow make the protestors appear as if they were in the wrong."

"Unfortunately, I have to agree." She paused. "I'm surprised you weren't already aware of what happened or not in the thick of things."

There was a strange catch in the next breath I took, and I twisted my hair even tighter. Two luminous silver eyes formed in my mind. I felt another twisting motion, this time lower in my belly. How could I explain what I'd been doing last night? Or even speak about it when my mind immediately made its way to how Ash's skin had felt against mine. How his lips had felt, his fingers…

Show me.

I cleared my throat. "I was at the lake and lost track of time," I offered up the lame half-lie. If I told her anything about last night, even the less-intimate details, she'd understandably have questions. I would, but I…I just didn't want to talk about Ash or anything he'd shared with me. Everything felt too unreal. As if I started talking about it, tiny holes would appear, fracturing the whole memory.

I let go of my hair. "Did the Crown or its heir ever go out and check on their people last night? Try to assuage them? Listen to their concerns?"

Ezra's laugh was dry. "Is that a serious question?" She shook her head as she fiddled with the lace along the collar of her pale blue gown. "Tavius was holed up in his room. Still is, having taken breakfast there. And the King plans to address the people at some point, to assure them that everything that can be, is being done."

"How very timely of him."

Ezra snorted.

I let my cheek rest against the back of the chair and studied my stepsister, focusing on the shadows under her eyes. Without her saying as much, I knew she'd been out there last night with the people, helping however she could. Just like she went out there, day after day. "You should be the heir," I told her. "You would be a far better ruler than Tavius."

She raised her brows. "That's because anyone would be a better ruler than Tavius."

"True," I said softly. "But you would be a better ruler because you actually care about the people."

Ezra smiled a little. "You care."

How could I not, when the things happening to the people had been my destiny to stop? I bit back a sigh. "You know what will happen as the Rot continues to spread. How do you think Tavius will handle that?"

The curve of her lips faded. "We can only hope that day doesn't come soon, or that he marries someone far more…" She frowned as she searched for the right word.

A kinder word than what came out of my mouth. "Far more intelligent? Compassionate? Empathetic? Brave? Caring—?"

"Yes, all of those things." She laughed as her gaze swept over me. "Are you all right?"

"Yeah?" My brows furrowed. "Why do you ask?"

"I don't know." She continued staring. "You just seem…off. Call it familial intuition."

Familial? Sometimes, I forgot that we were family. I resisted the urge to squirm in my chair. "I think your familial intuition is a bit rusty."

"Maybe." She sat back, the curve returning to her lips, but the smile didn't reach her eyes. "I was going to head to Croft's Cross to see how the repairs were going on some of the damaged businesses and homes, and then check in with the Healers to see if they needed assistance dealing with the injured. Care to join me?"

The fact that she'd asked warmed me. "Thank you," I said, unfolding my legs from the chair. "But I was going to see if there were any leftovers in the kitchen and check in on the Coupers. I know both Penn and Amarys have been trying to find work since their lands are completely wasted now."

Ezra nodded slowly. "You know what I think?" she asked. "You are the Queen the people of Lasania need."

I laughed deeply and loudly, even though her voice had been as solemn as ever. That was something that could never and would never happen. I was still chuckling over that after Ezra left and I donned a plain brown skirt and a white blouse made of a thin cotton lawn. I could tell the heat would be brutal today, and even I didn't want to be wearing pants. Quickly braiding my hair, I sheathed a small knife with a wicked, serrated blade inside my boot and the iron blade to my thigh, then made my way to the west tower. The morning sun struggled to penetrate the tower as I navigated the sometimes-slippery steps to the floors below. I stepped out into one of the less-traveled halls. It had become a habit to move about in the empty corridors. There was less chance of becoming the focal point of curious stares from new servants who were not yet sure of who I was, and easier to avoid the way older servants who behaved as they'd been taught—to act as if they didn't even see me. As if I truly were nothing more than a lost spirit.

The lingering scent of fried meat permeated the air as I entered the kitchens. Servants fluttered between the workstations, either cleaning or prepping for later today. I veered to my right, toward the mountain of a man who was hacking away at a slab of beef as if it had delivered a vicious insult to him and the entirety of his bloodline.

Which meant, he barely tolerated me.

"Do you have anything for me?" I asked.

"Nothin' that would be fit for even the hungriest of mouths," Orlano replied gruffly, not even pausing in his swing.

I glanced around, eyes narrowing on the baskets of potatoes and greens stacked near the bushels of apples. "You sure about that?"

"All of what I know you be eyein' is for tonight. Some fancy guests are expected." His cleaver came down with a wet whack. "So no runnin' off with any of that. Those needy mouths will have to fend for themselves."

"They do fend for themselves," I grumbled, wondering what guests were coming. It took me a moment to remember that there was an upcoming Rite. "And they're still needy."

"Ain't my problem." He wiped a hand across the front of his apron. "Ain't your problem."

"You sure about that?" I winced as the strips of beef he tossed into a bowl landed with a wet smack. "Maybe it's the King and Queen's problem."

His cleaver froze mid-air as he turned his head toward me. His dark eyes narrowed under graying brows. "Don't you be sayin' stuff like that around me when even these damn pots and pans have eyes and ears. Not like I'm not disposable."

I could never tell if Orlano suspected who I was, but sometimes, like now, I thought he just might know that I was the failed Chosen *and* the Princess. "King Ernald loves your pastries and how you cook the roast," I told him. "You are probably the least disposable person in this entire castle, including the Queen."

Pride filled his eyes, even though he huffed. "Go on and get outta here. I need those gals back there peelin' apples instead of starin' at you and prayin'."

The corners of my lips turned down as I looked over to the bushels. Two younger servants in white blouses starched to the point where they could stand on their own, watched the cook and me nervously. The peelers in their hands were motionless, unlike their lips. Huh. They really did look like they were praying. The gods only knew what kind of rumor they'd heard that had led to this.

"All right." I pushed off the counter.

"There's some bruised apples and potatoes that are close to goin' bad by the ovens." Orlano returned to the hunk of meat. "You can have 'em."

"You're the best, you know that?" I said. "Thank you."

His face flamed red. "Get outta here."

Laughing under my breath, I scooted around him. I quickly transferred the food into one burlap sack and then made my way toward the large, rounded doorways. I made sure to hurry past the bushels and the two servants.

My steps slowed as I looked over at them. "Be careful how hard you pray. A god or a Primal just might answer."

One of them dropped their peeler.

"Girl!" Orlano shouted.

Sending the two females a wink, I got my butt out of the kitchen before Orlano tossed me out of it. The good mood didn't last long when I made my way out into the early morning sun and saw the activity at the stables.

Damn.

Nobles from districts outside of Carsodonia *had* already begun arriving for the Rite, their carriages a sea of familial shields. The last thing the Crown needed to be doing was feeding families from all over the kingdom who had no problem feeding themselves.

This wouldn't go over well with the people.

All the food that would be prepared over the next several days could go to those who needed it. But then the Crown wouldn't be able to keep up the pretense of stability—one that was cracking and showing signs of breaking. No number of fancy gowns or elaborate feasts could hide that.

I climbed the dusty hill, the sack of apples and potatoes an unnaturally heavy burden in my arms, even though there was less than half left. The lack of sleep made each step feel like twenty, but still, despite *everything*, I grinned a little as the large oaks lining the dirt road blocked the glare of the morning sun.

Last night felt surreal, like a fevered dream, which seemed more plausible than spending a few hours beside the lake, speaking with a Shadowlands god—being *touched* by one. Pleasured by one.

Sweat dotted my brow as I reached up, tugging the hood of my blouse farther to shield my face from the sun. *Ash.* Warmth pooled low in my stomach. Thinking about his kisses, his touch, did very little to cool my already overheated skin, but it was far better than dwelling on the state of the kingdom or any of the other numerous things I could do nothing to change. Doing that only made me feel useless and guilty. But those kisses, the way he touched me, and what he said? They made me feel exhilarated and wanton and a dozen other different, maddening things. And there wasn't even a hint of regret. I'd enjoyed myself…*thoroughly*, and I'd unexpectedly created a wealth of memories that would stay with me for however long.

There *was* a twinge of sadness, though, because it was over. And with each passing day that came, I knew those memories wouldn't be as vivid and clear. They would become just like a faded dream. But I didn't let it take hold. If I did, it would taint the memories, and I refused to allow that to happen. There were too few good ones as it was.

What Ash had said about not having a lot of experience when it came to debauchery returned for me to obsess over, which I'd already done a decent amount of. Could he have really been insinuating that he didn't have a lot or any experience when it came to intimacy? That seemed impossible. He was a god who was probably, at the very least, several hundred years old. And he seemed awfully good at kissing and touching for someone who didn't. But…

He *had* asked me to show him what I wanted—what I liked. And I had.

Did it matter if I had lain with more than he had? Or if he had been with none at all? No. It just made me curious about him—his past and what he did when he wasn't hunting gods or apparently keeping an eye on me. Had he never found someone he was attracted to? Or at least attracted enough to be with? Someone he had fallen in lust or even love with? And if so, how could I be the first? There had to be others who were more…well, more *everything*. Starting with, like, every single goddess.

Except Cressa.

Thoughts of Ash quickly faded to the background as the sun bathed me in its light, and I saw what awaited.

The Rot had spread.

My steps slowed as I looked over the trees to my right, and my stomach sank. The limbs of the jacaranda trees had once been heavy with trumpet-shaped purple blossoms. Now, they blanketed the ground, the blooms brown, their edges curled. Limbs bare, there was no mistaking the strange grayness of the Rot that now clung to the tree's branches and trunk like moss.

The farmers had tried what they believed King Roderick had done. They'd spent day and night, weeks and months, digging and scraping, but the Rot was deep. And under it, a hard, rocky type of soil absent of the nutrients needed to grow crops.

A coldness drenched my chest as I stared at the Rot. The spread was definitely occurring faster. Even if the Primal of Death did come for me now, I wasn't sure I could even make him fall in love with me in time.

Lasania didn't have years.

I walked over, toeing aside a dead blossom with my boot until I saw what I already knew I'd see. The dirt itself had spoiled, turning gray.

"Gods," I whispered, staring at the ruined ground. *Breathe in.* The breath I took snagged as the scent of the Rot reached me. It wasn't an unpleasant smell, exactly. It reminded me of…

Of stale lilacs.

Just how the Hunters had smelled. The same scent that had filled the air before Andreia Joanis sat up, dead but still moving.

It wasn't my imagination. The Rot smelled the same.

I looked back at the city. Through the remaining trees, the Shadow Temple glittered darkly in the sunlight. Toward the center, the Sun Temple shone brightly. Both were almost painful to look upon. Farther back, Wayfair Castle rose high on the hill, and beyond the ivory towers, the Stroud Sea shimmered a deep blue. How long until the Rot reached the farms I'd passed and the city beyond? What would happen if it reached the Dark Elms and then the sea?

When I came upon the Massey farm, I saw that only an acre of untainted land remained behind the stone home and the now-empty stables. Worse yet, the gray of the Rot was dangerously close to the leafy heads of cabbage not yet ready to be picked.

Holding my sack to my chest, I resisted the urge to run past the Massey home, to put distance between myself and the catastrophe waiting to happen. There was no point, though. My destination was far worse than this.

The creak of hinges drew my gaze to the home. Mrs. Massey stepped outside, a woven basket in hand. The moment she spotted me, she waved.

Shifting my load to one arm, I returned the gesture, riddled with guilt. Mrs. Massey had no idea that I could've stopped the devastation to her farm. If she did, I doubted she'd come outside to greet me. She would probably attempt to beat me over the head with that basket.

"Good morning," I called out.

"Morning." She drifted down the cracked stone of the walkway. The dirt clinging to the knees of her pants told me that she'd already been working what was left of the farm as Mr. Massey likely went to town. People like these were often up before anyone else and to bed after everyone else.

Tavius often referred to them as the lower class. Only someone not fit to rule would think of the backbone of the kingdom as such, but the heir was, well…an ass. Tavius held little respect for those who put the food on his plate, and I wouldn't be surprised if the feelings were mutual. And if they weren't already, it was only a matter of time before they shared the same opinion.

"What brings you out here?" Mrs. Massey asked. "Did the Crown send you?"

She assumed I worked in the castle, believing the Crown offered the food I brought. I never gave her any indication to think otherwise. "I wanted to check in on the Coupers. I wasn't sure if they knew about what'd happened last night in Croft's Cross. With the damages to some of the buildings, I'm sure extra hands will be needed for repairs."

Mrs. Massey nodded. "Such a terrible thing." She rested the basket on a rounded hip as her gaze shifted in the direction of the city. "But I suppose the upcoming Rite will bring…some joy."

I nodded. "I'm sure it will."

"You know, I've never been to a Rite. Have you?"

"Haven't had the opportunity," I told her. It would be risky for me to show up there, especially when the Crown would be in attendance. But I was curious about all that occurred. "I'm sure it's boring."

The skin on her sun-darkened face creased as Mrs. Massey laughed. "You shouldn't say that."

I grinned, but my humor faded as my gaze skipped over the gray fields. "It's spread since the last time I was here."

"It has." She brushed away a wayward curl that'd escaped the lace of the white cap she wore. "It seems to be moving faster. We'll probably have to harvest before any of its ready. That's our only option at this point since the blockade that Williamson built out of wood didn't stop it like we'd hoped." She gave a small shake of her head, and then a wan smile appeared. "I'm just glad our son found work on the ships. It gets to Williamson, you know? That his son won't be following in his footsteps like Williamson did with his father before him. But there's no future here."

I held my sack tighter as my chest squeezed, wishing I knew what to say—wishing there *was* something to say.

Wishing I had been found worthy.

"I'm sorry." Mrs. Massey laughed nervously, clearing her throat. "None of that is your concern."

"No, it's all right," I told her. "There's no need to apologize."

She exhaled roughly as she stared at her ruined farm. "You said you were visiting the Coupers?"

I nodded, glancing at what now felt like a sad sack of food. I'd already stopped at three other homes before coming here. "Do you need anything? I have apples and potatoes. There isn't much, but—"

"Thank you. That is a kind offer and much appreciated," she said, but her spine had gone straight, and her mouth tightened.

Shifting my weight from foot to foot, I realized that I might have offended her with such an offer. Many of the working class were proud people, not used to nor desiring what they sometimes saw as handouts. "I didn't mean to insinuate that you were in need."

"I know." The press of her mouth softened a bit. "And I won't be too proud to accept such generosity once that day comes. Fortunately, we are not there yet. The Coupers can benefit far more than we can. They haven't been able to grow a single crop in far too long, no potato or bean."

I glanced ahead to where the short, rolling hill shielded the Couper home from view. "Do you think Penn has already found another source of income?"

"Amarys was telling me the other day that they've both tried," she said, her gaze fixed in the same direction. "But with the harvesters fleeing to other farms and the shops in the city, nothing has been available. I think they decided to wait it out. Hopefully, it's not too late for Penn to see if some of the businesses need aid."

There was a chance for Penn to find temporary work—for some good to come out of what'd happened in Croft's Cross last night. I wanted to ask what the Masseys would do once their property became like the Coupers'. Would they hang onto their lands, believing that it would once again become fertile? Or would they leave the home and acres farmed by their families for centuries? The Masseys were older than the Coupers, but age wasn't the issue. Other sources of income weren't plentiful.

Something had to be done now, curse or not. This wasn't the first time I'd thought that. It wasn't even the hundredth.

Turning back to Mrs. Massey, I said my goodbyes and started toward the Coupers'. The potatoes and apples wouldn't last them long, but it was something, and I was positive that I would have more than I could carry tomorrow. So much of the food being prepped now would go untouched by the guests.

The dead trees had long since fallen and had been cleared away, but it was still a shock to reach the hill and see nothing but what looked like a fine layer of ash.

By the time the Couper home came into view, I'd expected to hear their daughter's girlish laughter and their son's happy shrieks, both too young to fully understand what was happening around them. The only sound was the dead grass crunching under my boots. As I grew closer to the home, I saw that the front door was cracked open.

I walked onto the stoop. "Penn?" I called out and nudged the door open with my hip. "Amarys?"

There was no answer.

Maybe they were out back in the barn. They did have a handful of chickens left, at least they had when I was here a few weeks ago. They could also be in the city. Maybe Penn had already thought to go to the shipping companies. Figuring I could leave the apples and potatoes in their kitchen, I pushed open the door the rest of the way.

The smell hit me right off.

It wasn't the scent of Rot that sent my heart racing. This was thicker and turned my stomach, reminding me of meat left out to spoil.

My gaze swept the kitchen. Candles sat on the otherwise bare table, burned to the quick. The gas lanterns on the hearth mantel had long since gone out. The living area, a collection of chairs and worn settees, was also empty. Little balls and cloth dolls were neatly piled in a basket by the short hallway that led to the bedrooms.

I stared at the doorway, my fingers digging into the scratchy burlap.

Don't. Don't. Don't.

My steps were slow as if I walked through water but they still carried me forward, even as the voice in my head whispered and then shouted for me to stop. Tiny bumps pimpled my skin as I entered the hall, and the smell…it choked me.

Don't. Don't. Don't.

The door to my right was closed, but the one to the left wasn't. There was a buzzing sound, a low hum that I should've recognized but couldn't in the moment. I looked into the room.

What was left of the bag of apples and potatoes slipped from my suddenly numb fingers. I didn't even hear it hit the floor.

The buzzing was from *hundreds* of flies. The smell was from…

The Coupers lay on the bed together. Penn and his wife, Amarys. Between them were their children. Donovan and…and little Mattie. Beside Penn was an empty vial, the kind the Healers often used to mix medicines in. I imagined they'd shared the bed like this many times in the past, reading stories to their children or just enjoying their time together.

But they weren't sleeping. I knew that. I knew the only life in that room was the godsforsaken flies. I knew that other than the insects, life hadn't been in this house for quite some time. And that was why my gift hadn't alerted me to what I was about to find. There was nothing I nor anyone else, mortal or god, could do at this point. It was far too late.

They were dead.

Chapter 15

I was shaking as I stalked through the main hall of Wayfair, passing the Royal banners and the gold-plated sconces that burned even with all the daylight streaming in through the many windows. Servants came and went in a continuous stream as they scurried from the kitchens to the Great Hall. They carried vases of night-blooming roses that were currently closed, pressed table linens, and glasses scrubbed spotless. As I walked, I *couldn't* believe how the entire floor of Wayfair Castle smelled of roasted meat and baking desserts, while the Coupers lay dead in their bed, the evidence of what Penn and Amarys believed was their only option resting in that empty vial. They'd chosen a quicker death over a longer, drawn out one. Meanwhile, there was enough food being prepared right now to have fed them for a month.

I wanted to tear down the banners and the sconces, rip the cloth and shatter glass. Fisting my dusty skirts, I climbed the wide, polished limestone stairs to the second floor, where I knew I'd find my stepfather. The greeting rooms on the lower level, lining the banquet room, were only used when meeting guests. I'd already checked there, and both rooms had been empty.

Reaching the landing, I headed into the castle's west wing. As soon as the hall came into view, I saw several men outside my stepfather's private rooms. The Royal Guards stood in their ridiculous uniforms, staring straight ahead, their hands resting on the hilts of swords I doubted they'd ever lifted in battle.

None of them looked in my direction as I approached. "I need to see the King."

The Royal Guard who blocked the door didn't even blink as he continued to stare straight ahead. He made no move to step aside.

My patience had left me the moment I saw what had become of the Couper family. I stepped closer to the guard, close enough that I saw the tendons of his jaw clench. "You either step aside, or I will knock you aside."

That got the older man's attention. His gaze flicked to me, the lines at the corners of his eyes deepening.

"And please feel free to doubt that I would carry through on that threat. Because I would love nothing more than to prove just how wrong you are," I promised.

Pink seeped into the man's face as his knuckles bleached white from how tightly he held the sword.

I cocked my head to the side, arching a brow. If he even dared to lift that fist an inch, I would break every godsdamn bone in his hand or die trying.

"Step aside, Pike," another Royal Guard ordered.

Pike looked as if he would rather shove his entire face into a pot of boiling water, but he stepped aside. He didn't reach for the door as he would've done for anyone else. The blatant disrespect wasn't surprising, but I couldn't care less as I gripped the heavy, gold handle and pushed the door open.

The rich sent of pipe tobacco surrounded me the moment I stepped into the sunlight-drenched chamber. Rays of light reflected off the handblown glass figurines lining the shelves. Some were of the gods and Primals. Others were animals, buildings, carriages, and trees. The King had collected them for as long as I could remember. I found him sitting behind the heavy iron desk at one end of the circular chamber.

King Ernald's back was to the windows and balcony he'd stood on the night before. He had always been larger than life to me, broad of chest and tall, quick to laugh and smile. He wasn't as ageless as my mother, though. The brown hair at his temples was beginning to gray, and the lines at the corners of his eyes and across his forehead were deepening.

Right now, there was nothing large about him.

Surprise shuttled across the King of Lasania's face as he looked at the door. It was brief. His features soon smoothed out into the mask of impassivity he always wore when I was present. Those laughs and smiles always faded once he knew I was near.

Deep down, I think he feared me, even before I had been found unworthy.

My stepfather wasn't alone. I realized that the moment I stepped into the office and saw the back of my stepbrother's head. He was seated on the settee in the center of the room, idly picking through a bowl of dates.

The room was otherwise empty.

"Sera." The King's tone was flat. "What are you doing here?"

No warmth or fondness. His question was a demand, not a request. In the past, that'd stung. After I was found unworthy, I felt nothing. Today, however, it sent a hot flash of rage through me. If he didn't know why I was here, that meant he had no idea that I'd spent the last several hours watching the first guards I'd come across bury the Coupers.

"The Coupers are dead," I announced.

"Who?" my stepbrother asked.

My back stiffened. "Farmers whose lands were infected by the Rot."

"You mean the Rot you failed to stop," Tavius corrected, lifting a date.

I ignored him. "Do you at least know who they are?"

"I know who they were," my stepfather said, placing his pipe on a crystal tray. "I was notified of their passing no more than an hour ago. It's most unfortunate."

"It is more than unfortunate."

"You're right," he agreed, and my eyes narrowed because I had enough sense to know better. "What they decided to do is tragic. Those children—"

"What they felt they *had* to do, you mean." I crossed my arms to stop myself from picking up one of his precious figurines and throwing it. "What is tragic, is that they felt they had no other option."

My stepfather frowned and shifted forward in his seat. "There are always other choices."

"There should be, but when you're watching your children—" My breath caught, and it burned through my lungs as little Mattie's giggles echoed in my ears. "I don't agree with what they did, but they were pushed to their breaking point."

"If things were so bad for them, why didn't they simply seek other employment?" Tavius tossed out as if he were the first to have thought of such a thing. "That would've been a far better choice."

"What employment would they have been able to find?" I demanded. "Do you think a person can just walk into any shop or company or onto a ship and find a job? Especially when they spent their entire lives perfecting one trade?"

"Then perhaps they should've learned another trade the moment *your* failure ruined *their* land," he suggested.

"How many trades have *you* decided to learn and mastered to the point you could then demand a job?" I challenged.

Tavius didn't answer.

Exactly. The only skill he'd mastered was how to be an expert ass.

"I believe what your stepbrother is attempting to say is the same as I have," the King reasoned, placing his hands flat on the desk. "There are always choices. They chose wrong."

"You make it sound as if they had no reason. They were already dying. Starving to death!"

"And they chose to take their lives and those of their children instead of doing everything possible to feed them!" The King rose from his chair in a rush of plum-adorned black silk. "What would you have had me do that could have possibly altered that outcome? I have no control over the Rot. I cannot heal the land. You know that."

I couldn't believe he would even ask that question. "You could've fed them. Made sure they had food until they could grow their crops again or find employment."

"And is he supposed to do that for every family that can no longer work their land?" Tavius asked.

Hands balling into fists, I turned to where he sat. There wasn't a speck of dirt on the leather boot propped on the hard surface of the ottoman. He tilted his head in my direction, not a single curl spilling over his forehead. The blackened eye I'd given him had faded far too quickly. His features were perfectly pieced together. Yet all those handsome attributes were somehow wrong on Tavius's face. "Yes," I answered. "And not just the farmers. You should know that as the heir to the throne."

His lips, already thin, pressed tightly together.

"It's the harvesters who rely on the fields to feed their children. It's the shop owners who struggle each week to buy food because the prices have increased." I stared at him. "Do you even know why the prices have gone up?"

The tautness eased from his face. "I know why. You." He smiled, popping a date into his mouth. I doubted that he did. "Tell me, *sister.* How do you think we could provide for every family?"

Disgust curdled my stomach. "We could ration. We could give them some of the food here, starting with the dates in that bowl."

Tavius smirked and then bit down on another piece of fruit.

I turned back to the King. "There is more than enough food here, within these very walls, to feed a hundred families for a month."

"And then what?" my stepfather asked, lifting his hands, palms up. "What do we do after a month, Sera?"

"It's not like we'd run out of food. There are other farms—"

"That are already being pushed to their limits to make up for the lands that can no longer produce," he cut in. "Where would we draw the line? Deciding who we feed and who we do not. As you said, it's not only the farmers. It's the harvesters and more. But there are others who either cannot or will not fend for themselves. Those who will come with their hands out and their mouths open. If we attempted to feed them, we'd all starve."

I took a deep breath that did nothing to calm my temper. "I sincerely doubt anyone would choose not to fend for themselves and starve."

The King huffed out a laugh as he sat. "You'd be surprised," he said, picking up a ruby-encrusted chalice.

"There has to be something we can do," I tried again.

"Well, I have an idea," Tavius announced, and I didn't even bother to look at him. "This rationing thing you speak of? We could start by taking the food spent on the most useless within these walls."

"Oh, let me guess… You're talking about me." I looked over my shoulder at him. He arched a brow. "At least, I realize just how useless I am." I smiled as his disappeared. "Unlike some in this room."

The smug look vanished completely from his face, wiped away by the heat of anger. "How dare you speak to me like that?"

"There's nothing daring about speaking the truth," I retorted.

Tavius rose swiftly, and I faced him. "You know what the problem is with you?"

"You?" I offered, not even caring how childish it sounded.

His eyes thinned into slits. "Me? The irony would be funny if it wasn't so pathetic. The problem is you. It's always been you."

"Tavius," his father warned.

My stepbrother took a step toward me. "You failed that family. They're dead because of you. Not me."

I stiffened as his words cut through me, but I didn't let it show as I met his stare. "Then more are going to die because of my failure unless the Crown does something. What are you going to do once you take the throne? Continue letting *your* people die while you sit in the castle eating dates?"

"Oh." His laugh was harsh and grating. "I cannot wait till I take the throne."

I snorted. "Seriously? Taking the throne would actually require you to do something other than sit around all day and drink all night."

His nostrils flared. "One of these days, Sera. I swear."

Something dark and oily opened inside the center of my chest, much like where the warmth from my gift usually sprang to life. This feeling was slick and cold, snaking through me as I stared at my stepbrother. "What? Are you suggesting you're going to do something? You? Have you forgotten that black eye?" I smiled as his eyes narrowed. "I can easily remind you, if so."

He took a step forward. "You little bi—"

"That's enough, Tavius." My stepfather's voice boomed, startling me enough that I jumped. "*Enough*," he growled when my stepbrother started speaking once more. "Leave us, Tavius. Now."

Stunned that my stepfather wasn't sending me from the room, I wasn't paying attention when Tavius pivoted back to the table. "Here, my dear *sister*." He picked up the bowl of dates. "You can ration this among the needy." He flung the bowl at me.

Dates flew through the air. The hard ceramic cracked into the arm I lifted instead of my face. A flare of pain ran up the bone. I sucked in a sharp breath as the bowl fell to the floor, cracking upon the marble tiles.

Arm burning, I started toward him. "You son of—"

"That is enough! Both of you!" The King slammed his hands on the desk. And a moment later, the doors swung open. The two Royal Guards entered, hands on their swords. "Sera, you stay right where you are. Do not take one single step toward your stepbrother. That is an order. Disobey it, and you will spend the rest of the week in your chambers. I promise that."

Rage flashed through me like wildfire, stinging my eyes. I forced myself to stand down, even though I wanted to pick up that shattered bowl and beat Tavius over the head with it. But the King would carry through on his threat. He'd lock me in my rooms, and I…I would lose myself if he did that.

"And you, my son," my stepfather continued. Tavius stopped, eyes widening at the thunder in the King's voice. "I do not want to see you for the remainder of the day. If I do, it will not be a bowl you suddenly find in your face. Do you understand me?"

Tavius nodded curtly and then turned without another word, brushing past the Royal Guards. The King motioned at them, and they crept out of the room, quietly closing the door behind them.

Silence enveloped us.

And then, "Are you okay?"

His softly spoken question left me a bit bewildered as I looked down. My throbbing arm was already a bright shade of red. It would bruise. "I'm fine." I looked at the broken bowl. "I'd be better if you hadn't stopped me."

"I'm sure you would be, but if I hadn't, you'd have likely seriously injured him."

I turned around slowly.

The King picked up his chalice and downed the contents in one gulp. "You'd make short work of your stepbrother."

What he said shouldn't feel like a compliment, but his words wrapped around me like a warm blanket, nonetheless.

"He will never do that again," he added, dragging his hand over his head, and clasping the back of his neck. "That type of behavior isn't like him. He has a temper, yes. But he normally wouldn't do that. He's worried."

I wasn't so sure about that. Tavius always had a cruel streak, and my mother and stepfather were either blind to it or chose not to see it. "What does he have to worry about?"

"The same thing that plagues you," he answered. "He just doesn't express it as vocally as you do."

No part of me believed that Tavius worried about the people unable to feed themselves. If anything, he worried about how it would affect him one day.

"I'm sorry you had to see what you did this morning," he continued. Once more, I was struck silent in surprise. "I know you found them." He leaned back, resting his hand on the arm of the chair. "No one should have to bear witness to that."

I blinked, and it took me a moment to work past more unanticipated words. "Maybe not," I cleared my throat. "But I…I think some *do* need to see to truly understand how bad it's getting."

"I know how bad it is, Sera. And that is without seeing it." His gaze met mine.

I took a step toward his desk, hands clasped together. "Something has to be done."

"It will."

"What?" I asked, suspecting that he believed I still played a role in stopping it.

His gaze flicked to one of his many shelves and the glass trinkets on it. "We just need time." Weariness clung to the King's tone when he sat back in his chair. So did heaviness. "We only need to wait, and the Rot will be fixed. It will all be fixed in time."

Leaving my stepfather's office, I had the same feeling I had when a bad nightmare lingered hours after waking, and I had to remind myself that whatever horror had found me while I slept wasn't real.

It was an anxious sort of feeling. As I left the stairs and made my way to the banquet hall, I kept my head down, ignoring the many servants and how they ignored me. I didn't know what the King thought would change. There needed to be action. Not patience. Not reckless hope.

Entering the banquet hall, I rubbed at my sore arm. I needed to change and then find Sir Holland. I was sure to be late for our training. I didn't know if—

"*Please.*"

I stopped mid-step and turned, scanning the space. The long, wide chamber was empty, and the alcoves leading to the meeting rooms appeared empty, as well. I looked up to the second-floor mezzanine. No one stood at the stone railing.

"Please," came the whisper again, from my left. I turned to the candlelit alcove and the closed inside door. "Please. Someone…"

Stepping into the shadowy area, I pressed a hand against the door handle and held my breath as if that would help me hear better. For a too-long second, I didn't hear anything.

"Please," the soft cry came again. "Help me."

Someone was in trouble. The worst kind of thoughts entered my mind. When these rooms weren't in use, no one checked them. All manner of terrible things could happen in them. I thought of some of the Royal Guards and the younger, pretty servants. My blood heated with anger as I turned the knob. In the back of my mind, I thought it was strange that the door opened so easily. Heinous deeds were usually carried out behind locked doors. Still, someone could've fallen while cleaning one of the obnoxious chandeliers that hung from the ceiling of every chamber. One of the servants had suffered an agonizingly slow death that way a few years ago.

Stepping into the chamber lit only by a few scattered sconces, my gaze landed on the dark-haired girl kneeling beside the low table, centered between two long settees. "Are you okay?" I asked, hurrying forward.

The girl looked up, and recognition flared. It was one of the young women from the kitchens who'd been praying. She didn't answer.

"Are you all right?" I asked again, starting to kneel when I noticed there was nary a wrinkle in her starched, white blouse. She was pale, her light blue eyes wide, but not a single strand of hair had fallen free from the bun secured at the nape of her neck, nor was her lace cap askew.

The servant's eyes darted over my shoulder to something behind me.

Every muscle in my body tensed as I heard the thud of boots, softened by the plush carpet. The door closed…

Then I heard it lock.

The girl's gaze shifted back to mine, and her lips trembled. "I'm sorry," she whispered.

Godsdamn it, this was a trap.

Chapter 16

The back of my neck prickled. I turned my head slightly to the left, seeing two pairs of legs in dark breeches by the door. I should've known better than to blindly rush into any room, even in Wayfair.

Hadn't I learned that lesson a time or a dozen over the last three years?

"I didn't have a choice," the servant whispered. "Truly, I—"

"That's enough," a male voice snapped, and the servant immediately fell quiet.

His voice had come from my right. Either the one I saw by the door had moved, or there were two in the room. Irritation buzzed through my veins as I slipped my right hand into my boot. I was not having a very good day, and that really sucked after such a wonderful few hours by the lake. The poor Coupers were dead. My arm still throbbed. Sir Holland would be annoyed because I was sure to miss training now, and the one nice skirt I had that didn't make me want to tear it off was about to be ruined.

After all, I knew how this would end.

With me bloody.

And someone dead.

"I know what you're thinking," I said, rising slowly and unsheathing the knife from my boot. It was small enough that when I held it pressed to my palm with my thumb and kept my hand open, it appeared as if I held nothing. I looked slightly to my left again, and the pair of legs was still there. "You've heard some rumor. That I'm cursed. That if you kill me, you'll end the Rot. That's not how it works. Or, you've heard something about who I am and think you can use me to gain whatever it is you need. That's not going to happen, either."

"We aren't thinking about anything," the man to my left replied. "Other than about the coin that will fill our pockets. Enough not to ask questions."

That was…different.

I shifted the knife slightly, turning the slender blade between my fingers. *Killing is not something one should have little regard for.* Ash was right. I forced myself to breathe in slowly and then hold it as I looked over my shoulder to my right once more in response to the whisper of steel being drawn. I saw black, and my stomach lurched. Black breeches. Well-muscled arms. A glimpse of purple brocade over a wide chest.

They were *guards.*

An unsettled skip came from my chest, but I couldn't let it take hold. I shut down my thoughts and feelings and became the thing that had stood in Nor's *office.* That empty, moldable creature. A blank canvas primed to become whatever the Primal of Death desired or be used in whatever way my mother saw fit. I sometimes wondered how the Primal would've painted me, but as the handle of the small knife now slipped between my fingers, I was still blank. Exhaling a long and slow breath, I turned to my right. But that wasn't where I aimed. I cocked back my arm and let the knife fly.

I knew it struck true when I heard the ragged gasp, and the servant let out a startled cry. There was no time to see if Sir Holland's blindfolded training had paid off as the other guard charged me, sword drawn.

He was young. Couldn't be much older than I was, and I thought about the *marks* Ash had said every death left behind.

I kicked out, planting my booted foot in the center of the guard's chest. My skirt slid over my leg as he stumbled back. Reaching down, I gave the room a quick scan as I unsheathed the iron blade. I'd been wrong about how many were in the room. There were three, and they were all young.

Well, probably only two in a few seconds.

Sir Holland would be disappointed.

My aim hadn't been spot-on. The knife had caught the guard in the throat. Crimson streamed down his arms and darkened his tunic. He staggered forward, falling against the settee. The servant scrambled backward as the other guard rushed me.

He swept out with his sword, and I dipped under his arm, popping up directly in the path of the third guard. He jabbed out with a shorter blade. Cursing under my breath, I grasped the guard's sword arm. I spun, dragging him along with me. Letting go, I slammed my elbow into his back. The act jarred the already sore bone and flesh, causing me to suck in a sharp breath as I pushed hard. The guard's shout ended abruptly in a gasping breath.

I whirled around to see that his partner's blade had impaled the guard.

"Shit," the guard growled, shoving the other to the side. The man went down on one knee and then fell face forward, slamming into the low table. The vase of lilies crashed. Water spilled as delicate white petals hit the carpet.

"That wasn't me," I said, backing up. The girl had retreated to the wall and…appeared to be praying once again. "That was all you."

He shifted his blade to his other hand. "More coin for my pockets, I suppose."

The remaining guard shot forward. He was fast, blocking my stab. He spun out before I could strike again. My gaze flicked to the locked door. There was no way I would make it there and unlock it in time.

"Who paid you?" I asked.

He circled me slowly, eyes narrowed. "Doesn't matter."

Maybe it didn't. I already had my suspicions. I spun, slicing out with the blade. The guard brought his fist down on my arm, right on the bruise. I yelped. The shock of pain rippled through me. My hand opened on reflex. The dagger fell, hitting the carpet without a sound.

The guard laughed under his breath. "For a moment there, I actually started to worry."

"Yeah, well, don't stop yet." Twisting at the waist, I grabbed the first thing I could get my hands on.

Turned out to be an embroidered pillow.

"What are you going to do with that?" he asked. "Smother me?"

"Perhaps." I winged the surprisingly heavy pillow directly at his face.

He jerked back. "What the—?"

I spun, kicking out and up, catching the pillow and his face with my boot. He grunted, staggering several steps back. I snagged my blade from where it had fallen and snapped up. I grasped the hand that held his dagger and pushed down as I thrust the iron through the pillow.

The man howled as red-tinged feathers puffed into the air and dropped his sword as he reached for me. I jerked the blade free, desperately ignoring the soft, wet sound of suction and his shrill screams.

I slammed the blade into his chest again, over his heart. The dagger pierced the heavy brocade and the bones there, sinking through his body as if it were nothing but spun sugar.

His screams cut off.

Tugging the blade free, I stepped aside as the guard's legs went out from under him. He fell to the side, twitching. A pool of crimson swept across the ivory carpet, joining the other deep red stain.

"Gods," I uttered, glancing up to where the female servant stood against the wall. "The carpet will definitely require more than a spot clean, won't it?"

Wide-eyed, she slowly shook her head. Her lips moved for several moments without sound. "I didn't want to do this. They caught me outside. Told me they needed my help." Words spilled out of her between ragged sobs. "I didn't know what for until they led me in here. I thought they were going to—"

"Do you know who was supposed to pay them?" I cut her off.

"N-no," she said, shaking her head. "I swear to you. I have no idea." Tears filled her eyes. "I don't really even know who you are. I thought you were a handmaiden."

I swallowed a sigh as I looked down at the three guards, not letting myself take in their faces—to see if I recognized any of them and allow them to leave a *mark* behind. Who could've gotten to them that had the kind of coin needed to convince someone to kill someone else who was either employed or protected by the Crown?

There was only one who would do it, knowing there'd be no repercussions.

Tavius.

My stomach tumbled. Could he truly be behind this? I pressed my lips together. Was I seriously asking myself that? Of course, he would, but could he have pulled something like this together in the short time between when he left his father's office and now? Or had it been planned? His taunts came back to me, and my grip tightened on the dagger. Did he even have the kind of coin he would need or be willing to fork it over?

A loud thud sounded near the door. I turned just as a male voice announced from the other side, "Let me try."

Before I could even walk forward and unlock the door, I saw the knob turn and *keep* turning. Metal creaked and then cracked as gears gave way.

Dear gods…

I took a step back as the door swung open, and several Royal Guards filed into the chamber. They drew up short, but it was the male who stood in the doorway that snagged my focus.

I'd never seen him before.

I'd never seen *anything* like him before.

He was tall and…golden all over. His mane of hair. His skin. The elaborate…facial paint. A shimmery gold swept up over his brows and down his cheeks, a design that resembled wings. But his eyes…they were such a pale shade of blue they nearly blended with the faint aura of eather behind the pupils.

I knew then that he was a god, but that wasn't what left me unsettled. The facial paint reminded me of the charred skin on the seamstress's face.

That pale gaze drifted over to where I stood, still breathing heavily, and landed on the bodies behind me, ending where the servant girl was still pressed to the wall as if she were trying to become one with it. I slipped the hand holding the dagger behind me.

The god grinned.

My mother appeared behind him, her face paling to match the ivory and cream of her gown. I suddenly wished that *I* could become one with the wall.

"I found them like this," I lied, glancing at the servant. "Right?"

She nodded emphatically, and I turned back to them. The god's pale gaze burned into mine, the wisps of eather in his eyes far fainter than Ash's. What was a god even doing here in the castle? I swallowed, wanting to take a step back as he continued staring at me.

The god's smile grew. "What a terrible thing to discover."

I glanced at my mother. Not for one second did I think she believed what I claimed, but she wouldn't say anything. Not in front of a god.

The Queen's expression smoothed out. "Yes," she said, her chest rising sharply. "What a terrible thing, indeed."

"You really think Tavius had something to do with the attack?" Ezra asked, her voice low as we hung freshly washed linens on nylon lines in the courtyard of Healer Dirks' home the following afternoon.

I'd taken Ezra up on her earlier offer to help those injured in the protests. Well, I sort of overheard her giving directions to the carriage driver and followed her to the very edge of the Garden District today, where the most severely injured from the protests were being treated. But it was clear that Dirks needed as much help as possible. Nearly a dozen cots and pallets lined the front chamber of his residence, containing those who had been hurt. Wounds needed to be cleaned. Linens washed before they aided in infection. The injured coaxed into eating or drinking. Healer Dirks hadn't said a word to me beyond pointing to the baskets of linens that needed to be hung to dry. I could never tell if the older man knew who I was. He hadn't asked questions over the years when Sir Holland brought me to him to treat the injuries I'd received while training. If he suspected anything, he never said a word. Ezra had eventually joined me. It was the first chance we had to speak about what had occurred yesterday.

"I do think he's responsible." I glanced to where several Royal Guards stood positioned at the iron gateway to the courtyard as I grabbed one of the damp sheets from the basket. "Who else would've had the coin?" Flipping the sheet over the line, I pulled it straight. "Or the courage to risk recruiting the guards?"

"Not that I'm trying to defend my brother, but even I don't think he's idiotic enough to kill the one thing that can stop the Rot," Ezra pointed out.

"You're giving him far more credit than I can, then." I tugged the hood of my blouse farther down, more so to shield the glare of the sun than to hide my identity.

"And the girl?" Ezra asked, bending to pick up the last linen. She shook it out, and the astringent scent tickled my nose. "You really think she had nothing to do with it?"

"I don't know." I caught the other end of the sheet and helped her spread it over the line. "She was scared, but I don't know if that was because I was in the room or because she had been forced into it."

Ezra swept one of the linens to the side as she stepped through, joining me. "Either way, someone should relocate her out of Wayfair just in case."

"Where would she go?" I asked. "If you say something about her, she will most likely lose her job."

"And if she played a role in this attack, should she continue working in the same household that you live in?" she challenged as she straightened the tiny white bow on the bodice of her robin's egg blue gown.

"But if she didn't, then she's out of a job." I picked up the basket. "Not only would we be punishing a victim, she would likely blame me and the curse, and that is the last thing I need."

Ezra sighed. "You're right, but you should at least say something to Sir Holland. He could probably look into her background and see if she may be a continued threat." Her brow wrinkled; her gaze moving between the Royal Guards and me. "I'm just not sure that Tavius played a role in this. And you know I do not say that because I believe he's not capable of such a thing. Tavius hardly has spare coin," Ezra explained. "I know this because he's always trying to borrow from me. He spends whatever he has on Miss Anneka."

"Miss Anneka?" I frowned, holding the wicker basket to my chest as I turned toward the Shadow Temple, where it loomed at the base of the Cliffs of Sorrow. The shadowstone spires reflected the sunlight as if it repelled life itself.

"She is a recently widowed merchant's wife," she explained, lifting her brows. "They have been having a rather sordid affair. I'm surprised you didn't know about it."

"I really try not to think about Tavius and block out anything about him," I told her, wondering if it were possible that this widow had given Tavius the money. I sighed. "I can't believe all of that had to happen right as the Queen was coming in from the gardens. She was not entirely pleased."

"She spent a good portion of supper last night bemoaning the ruined carpet," Ezra said, and I rolled my eyes. "Apparently, it had been imported from somewhere east and, according to her, was 'utterly irreplaceable.'"

Apparently, my life wasn't.

My mother hadn't said a word to me after I left the room. She hadn't checked on me to make sure I wasn't injured like Sir Holland had. Neither had the King.

"What happened to your arm?" Ezra demanded, her eyes narrowing. "Did that occur when you fought off the guards?"

"Not entirely, though I'm sure that didn't help. It's courtesy of *Prince* Tavius," I replied and then told her what had happened.

Her jaw hardened as she stared at my arm. "You know, I have always had a hard time believing that people are inherently evil," she said, lifting her gaze to mine. "Even after everything I've seen while helping those in the city. Misdeeds are either done by choice or by circumstance. Never by nature. But, sometimes, I look at my brother and think that maybe he is evil. Perhaps he was simply born that way."

"Well," I murmured, "I can't say that I would disagree with you on that. I just wish more realized it."

"As do I." Ezra stepped in close enough that if either of us moved, her bare arm would touch mine. "By the way, the god you saw with the Queen yesterday?" she said, and I immediately thought of the gold-painted face mask. "I overheard her speaking with my father after supper about him. His name is Callum." Her chin dipped. "He's from the Court of Dalos."

My stomach flipped. "He's from The Primal of Life's Court?"

She nodded. "I imagine it has something to do with the upcoming Rite."

That made sense, but I couldn't remember a god from the Court of Dalos ever coming to the castle before.

We started to make our way through the winding path that cut through the numerous raised planters full of medicinal herbs. "Let's see what else we can help Healer Dirks with," Ezra said, and I nodded. "Then I must head home. Father has requested to speak with Lord Faber. I'm not sure why, but Mari was finagled into joining her father, and I was somehow included in the conversation."

Wondering what the King wanted to speak with Lord Faber about, I followed Ezra toward the curtained doors.

"Hey."

I looked over my shoulder toward the voice as Ezra stopped in front of me. I looked past the Royal Guards and beyond the courtyard to where…

A fair-haired male stood by Ezra's carriage, rubbing the muzzle of one of the horses. He was tall and slender, his features sharp—his eyes, cheeks, and jaw. He wore a black, sleeveless tunic trimmed in silver brocade, and polished, dark boots that reached his knees. There was something…off about the way he casually stood there. It raised the hair along the back of my neck. It took me a moment to realize that the sun's glare didn't appear to touch him—that he and only he stood in the shadows.

My heart started thumping heavily as I turned to Ezra, to see her trying to peer around me. "I'll be right back."

"Who is that?" she asked as the Royal Guards eyed the male with what I suspected was the same unease I felt.

"Not sure. If I find out, I'll tell you later." I bit back a smile as she sent me an impatient look. "I promise."

"You'd better," she muttered and then snapped the skirt of her gown with how quickly she turned.

Senses alert, I kept my right hand close to where I had the blade sheathed to my thigh. As I passed the Royal Guards, my steps slowed near the stranger who had returned to petting the horse.

"Who are you?" I asked.

His head turned toward me, and I saw his eyes. They were a deep amber color, and I was close enough to see the glow of eather behind his pupils.

The stranger was a god.

Out of reflex, I placed my hand over my heart and started to lower to a knee in a gesture of respect reserved only for a god or Primal. Something I just then realized I'd never done for Ash. "Your Highness."

"Please don't do that," he requested, and I froze for a heartbeat and then straightened. "My name is Ector."

I opened my mouth—

"I don't care what your name is," he interrupted, and I snapped my mouth shut. I *was* going to say hello. "You're probably wondering why I'm here."

I was.

"If so, we have that in common," he continued, tilting his head. Several locks of blond curls slid over his forehead. "I'm also wondering that, but I know better than to ask questions and to simply do as I'm told."

My brows lifted in confusion.

Ector gave the horse one last scratch and then turned fully toward me. I saw then that he held something in his other hand. A narrow, wooden box made of pale birch. "I was ordered to give you this."

I stared at the box. "By whom?"

"I think you missed the part about knowing better than to ask questions. You *should* know better." He offered the box. "Take it."

I took the box, only because…what else was I supposed to do? Glancing down at it, I turned it slowly in my hands and then looked up. The god called Ector had already walked off toward the street.

Okay, then.

Curious and a bit wary, I stepped into the shadows of the building next door. I would be lying if I said that I wasn't a little afraid of what could be in a box given to me by some random god. I found the seam of the lid and lifted it.

I gasped as a tremor of shock rippled through me. The box wobbled in my hand. I steadied myself, unable to believe what I was looking at.

Nestled against cream velvet was a dagger. Not just any dagger, though.

The corners of my lips tipped up, and a smile stretched across my face as I freed the blade from its soft nest. The dagger was…it was a magnificent creation. A piece of art. The hilt was made of some kind of smooth, white, surprisingly lightweight material. Perhaps stone of some sort? The pommel of the hilt was carved into the shape of a crescent moon. I gripped the hilt and pulled the dagger free. The dagger…gods, it was delicate yet strong.

Beautiful and powerful.

The blade itself was at least seven inches long and shaped like a thin hourglass—deadly sharp on both sides. Someone had etched an elaborate design into the dagger—a spiked tail on the blade, and the muscular, scaled body and head of a dragon carved into the hilt, its powerful jaws open and breathing fire.

The dagger was made of shadowstone.

The polished black blade blurred. I blinked away the sudden wetness and swallowed, but the messy knot still clogged my throat. The emotion had nothing to do with the shadowstone. It didn't even have to do with who I knew must have given it to me. It was just

I'd never been gifted anything in my life.

Not on the Rites when gifts were often exchanged among family and friends. Not on my birthday.

But I had been given a gift now—a beautiful, useful, and wholly unexpected one. And it had been a *god* who'd given it to me.

Ash.

Chapter 17

Odetta passed into the Vale in the early morning hours of the following day.

I'd only learned this because when I went to check on her before training with Sir Holland, I had discovered a servant in her chamber, stripping the linens from the bed.

And I knew what had happened before I even spoke—before I asked where she was. The sudden tightening in my chest and the knot in my throat told me that the moment Odetta had warned was approaching had come and gone.

I hadn't gone to the tower. Instead, I'd traveled to Stonehill, where I knew she had family who still lived, arriving just as the services began. I wondered if that was why I often found myself in this district and spent time at the Temple of Phanos—if I thought of Odetta as family, and that was why it drew me.

I stayed near the back of the small cluster of mourners, surprised when I felt the presence of others coming to stand beside me. It was Sir Holland and Ezra. Neither said anything as the pyre Odetta had been laid upon was raised, the slender linen-wrapped body coming into view. They stood quietly beside me, their presence lessening some of the pressure in my chest.

I didn't cry as torches were carried forward and placed on the oil-soaked wood. Not because I couldn't, but because I knew that Odetta wouldn't have wanted me to. She'd told me that I had to be ready. So, I was as ready as I could ever be as the flames slowly crawled over the wood, stirred by the salty breeze coming off the sea until I could no longer see the pale linens behind the fire.

I turned and left then, knowing that nothing of the cranky woman was left in this realm. She had entered the Shadowlands, passing through the Pillars of Asphodel that Ash had spoken about. I walked the coast, confident that Odetta had been welcomed into the Vale and was likely already complaining about something.

I woke the morning before the Rite with a throbbing headache that didn't go away, no matter how much water I forced myself to drink throughout the morning.

Training was sheer torture as the headache managed to spread into an ache that settled in my jaw and brought queasiness to my stomach. The stifling heat of the tower room didn't help.

Sir Holland circled me, sweat glistening off the dark skin of his forehead. I tracked him wearily. He lunged at me, and I should've easily blocked his kick, but my movements were slow. His bare foot connected with my shin. A pained breath punched out of my lungs as I hobbled back on one leg.

"You okay?" Sir Holland demanded.

"Yeah." I bent over, rubbing my shin.

"You sure?" He came to my side, dragging the back of his hand over his forehead. "You've been sloppy all afternoon."

"I feel sloppy," I muttered, straightening.

Concern pinched Sir Holland's face as his gaze swept over me. "You look a little pale." He planted his hands on his waist. "What's going on? Is it Odetta?"

I shook my head as sadness flickered through me. It had been two days since Odetta had passed, and I'd caught myself heading to her floor to check in on her at least a dozen times before realizing there was no reason to do so. "I just have a bad headache, and my stomach feels a bit off."

"Does your jaw hurt?"

I frowned. "How do you know?"

"Because you're rubbing your face," he pointed out.

Oh, I totally was. I stopped doing that. "My jaw hurts a little," I admitted. "Maybe I caught something, or a tooth has gone bad."

"Maybe," he murmured, and my frown increased. "Go ahead and take the rest of the day off. Get some rest."

Normally, I would've protested and trained through whatever discomfort I felt, but all I wanted to do was sit down. Or lay down. "I think I'll do that."

Sir Holland nodded, and after giving him an awkward wave goodbye, I turned for the door. He spoke out. "I'll bring something up for you that I think will help."

"I don't want a sleeping potion," I told him, reaching the door.

"It won't be that."

The throbbing and gnawing ache in the pit of my stomach had intensified by the time I made it back to my chambers. I barely managed to peel off my clothing and change into an old men's shirt that had been left behind in the laundry. As oversized as it was, the hem reached my knees. It wasn't as light as my night rail, but it was all I had the effort for.

A knock sounded on my bedchamber door a little while later. It was Sir Holland, and as promised, he carried a tankard and a pouch.

"What is this?" I asked as he handed the items to me, and I looked down at the steaming, dark liquid.

"A little bit of chasteberry, chamomile, fennel, willow, and peppermint," he said, lingering at the doorway. "It'll help."

I sniffed the liquid, brows lifting as I sat at the foot of my bed. The scent was sweet, minty, and earthy. "It smells…unique."

"That it does. But you need to drink all of it, and you should drink it fast. Okay? You don't want the potion to cool any more than it already has."

I nodded, taking a long drink. It didn't taste bad but wasn't particularly easy to swallow either.

Sir Holland sat on the edge of the bed, his gaze fixed on the sunlight drifting through the small window. "You know what I was thinking about? The conversation we had a while back when I asked you what you were."

"Yeah." My brow scrunched. "You said I was a warrior."

Smiling faintly, he nodded. "I did. I've been thinking about that. About who you remind me of."

I was half afraid to hear this. "Who?"

"Sotoria."

It took me a moment to remember who that was. "The girl so frightened by a god that she fell to her death from the Cliffs of Sorrow?" I wasn't sure if Sotoria was more myth than reality, but I was kind of offended. "What about me makes you think I'd run off the side of a cliff?"

"Sotoria wasn't weak, Sera. Her being frightened by the god was only a part of her story."

"Wasn't the other part her being dead?"

Wry amusement settled into his features. "The young maiden's story didn't end with her death. You see, the one who ultimately caused her death believed that he was in love with her."

"Correct me if I'm wrong," I said, relieved to feel the ache in my head already lessening, "but he only saw her picking flowers. He didn't speak to her or anything. So, how did he believe that he was in love with her?"

Sir Holland shrugged. "He saw her and fell in love."

I rolled my eyes.

"That is what he believed, but it was more like he fell into obsession."

"You mean after he spoke to her?"

He shook his head.

I let out a choked laugh. "I'm sorry. I don't even know how you can become obsessed with someone by only seeing them *pick flowers*. I mean, love at first sight? I could maybe believe in that, but only if they'd actually spoken." I frowned, rethinking that. "And even then, I would say they probably fell into lust. Not love."

He grinned, stretching out a leg. "Well, he was obsessed with bringing her back and being with her."

My breath caught. I had never heard this part of the legend. "Did he?"

"He was warned that it wouldn't be right. That her soul had crossed into the Vale and that she was at peace. But he…he found a way."

"Gods." I closed my eyes, both saddened and horrified. If she were real, her life had already been taken from her. To learn that her peace had also been stripped away sickened me. It was an unconscionable violation.

"Sotoria rose and wasn't grateful for such an act. She was frightened and unhappy. The one responsible couldn't understand why she was so morose. Nothing he did made her better or made her love him." Several moments passed. "No one knows exactly how long Sotoria lived her second life, but she ended up dying. Some say she purposefully starved to death, but others say she began to *live* again, to fight against her captor despite how powerful he was. She was strong, Sera. She was the kind of warrior that fought back through the grief of losing her life at such a young age. Through the loss of peace and control, no matter how badly the odds were stacked against her. That's why you remind me of her."

"Oh," I whispered, finishing the last of the tea. "Well, that's nice," I said, hoping Sotoria's story was just some old legend.

"Finished?"

"I am."

"Good. It may make you a little drowsy, but nothing like a sleeping potion," he explained, rising. "There's extra in the pouch in case you need more. Just make sure you steep the herbs in boiling water for about twenty minutes."

"Thank you," I said, finding the words strange to speak.

"No problem." He started for the door and then stopped. "Everything will be okay, Sera. Get some rest."

As soon as he left, I did what he'd said to do. I closed my eyes. The drumming in my entire head and the churning had almost completely gone away, and as Sir Holland had warned, the potion did make me tired—or at least relaxed enough to drift off.

I wasn't sure exactly when I had fallen asleep, but quite some time later, there was no ache—not in my temples nor in my jaw—and my stomach felt steady enough for me to put on pants and scrounge up something to eat.

How Sir Holland had come across such a potion, I didn't know. But it was a miracle, and I just might hug the man when next I saw him.

With food in my belly, I felt mostly normal. I entered the bathing chamber to brush my teeth and bent over the small basin to rinse out my mouth. As I placed the pitcher on the narrow shelf above the basin, I looked down.

"What the…?" I whispered, staring at the streaks of red among the foamy paste.

Blood.

I knew very little about the Chosen, whether this one was male or female, but either curiosity or restlessness had drawn me to the Sun Temple on the afternoon of the Rite.

Nobles, wealthy merchants, and landowners already filled the Sun Temple, but dressed as I was in the pale blush gown that I wore on the rare occasion my mother wanted me seen, I was recognized as one of the Queen's handmaidens. I moved easily among the crowd as the people climbed the wide steps. Like the entire courtyard, the Temple was constructed of crushed diamond and limestone. Sunlight poured off the walls and spires, reflecting off the specks of diamond. Two large torches jutted out from the pillars at the top of the steps. Silvery-white flames flickered gently in the hot breeze. The hairs on the back of my neck rose as I pressed on, weaving in and out of the masses to enter the main hall of the Sun Temple. The corridor was long and narrow, full of closed doors, and I could imagine the whisper of robes behind them. A shudder worked its way through me as I thought about what Ash had said about what filled the Priests' insides.

Gods, that was the last thing I needed to think about. As I came to the entrance to the cella, the main chamber of the Temple, sunlight streamed in through the glass ceiling, streaking the ivory and gold floors. The hair continued to rise on the nape of my neck and under the gauzy hood of my gown as I entered the cella. They'd only lit a few dozen or so of the hundreds of candelabras staggered along the walls. It wasn't often that I entered the Sun Temple or any Temple for that matter, but the cella had a unique energy, one that coated the very air I breathed and often crackled over my skin, reminding me of the jolt of energy I had felt when my skin came into contact with Ash's.

The pews and benches were already packed, and as I made my way to one of the pillared alcoves, I lowered my hood. To keep it up in the Sun Temple would not only be seen as an act of great disrespect, but it would also draw far too much attention.

I stopped near the golden sheen of a column, my gaze tracking to the dais. White peonies had been scattered across the floor and at the foot of a throne constructed from the same crushed diamonds and limestone used to build the Temple. The back of the throne had been carved into the shape of a sun, absorbing the powerful rays streaming in from the ceiling. Two Sun Priests stood on either side of the throne, their white robes pristine. They appeared just as gaunt as the Shadow Priests as they stared out into the crowd.

Dragging my gaze from them, I searched the front pews for the glimmer of crowns, quickly finding the Queen and King. They were seated up front and to the right of the dais. My lip curled as the many tiny pearls on my mother's gown glittered in the sunlight.

I supposed she was lucky that the gown had been finished when it was.

Crossing my arms, I shifted my attention to where Ezra sat stiffly beside her brother. She didn't even look like she breathed. I imagined it took nearly everything in her to remain there. Tavius sat in the kind of sprawl only a man could accomplish, his legs spread wide, taking up at least two spaces worth of room.

What an asshole.

I looked for Sir Holland among the Royal Guards that waited in the alcove closer to the family, but I didn't see him.

My skin felt uncomfortably warm as I flicked a look out over the crowd, wondering if any of the people here knew what'd happened to the Coupers—what had surely happened to other families, and was currently happening as they sat in the pews, most likely thinking of the feasts and fine wine they'd celebrate with later. Did they even care?

My jaw ticked. Maybe I wasn't being fair. Many of them did care. Wealth and nobility didn't automatically make a person apathetic to the needs of others. I knew for a fact that Lady Rosalynn, who stared up at the dais now, often sent food for the children under the care of the Ladies of Mercy. Lord Malvon Faber, Marisol's father, had opened his home on more than one occasion to shelter others when fire or rain damaged their homes. Lord Caryl Gavlen, who sat behind the Crown with his daughter, still paid the harvesters even though they hadn't been able to work the same amount of land.

Many of those in attendance cared, probably even more than I knew, but all it took was a handful of others to not. All it took was a soon-to-be King more concerned with hunting for pleasure and chasing skirts than feeding his people, for all of the others' good work to come undone.

The shimmer of pearls in Ezra's hair caught my attention. I stared at the tiny, round gems. They were pretty, but I didn't wear jewelry other than the gold chains that had once held my veil in place. No one had ever given me a piece—not a ring, necklace, hairpin, or bauble. I'd never purchased any for myself with whatever coins I'd found in my travels throughout the city, either. I never sought to own jewelry because I didn't think it was meant for me. That sounded silly, but when Ezra or Mother wore such sparkly, beautiful things, they felt meant for them. Just as they did for nearly every female and many of the males in attendance tonight.

My mother's head turned toward Ezra in response to something she'd said. The Queen smiled, and the breath I took was too thin. It was a beautiful smile, and I couldn't remember her *ever* directing one like that at me.

She smiled at Ezra that way, but not me. Not her daughter.

I swallowed in hopes of easing the lump that had filled my throat, and all I succeeded in doing was nearly choking myself. My mother laughed, and I felt it in every bone. I had never made her laugh. Why would I? I was the failed Maiden, and Ezra was a Princess.

Gods, I was actually…jealous. After all these years. How could that even be possible? I wanted to laugh, but for the briefest of moments, I wanted to be Ezra.

I wanted to be the one sitting there, worthy of the family that surrounded me. Well, all but Tavius, but Ezra *counted.* And I wanted that.

The strangest thought entered my mind—something I had stopped wondering many years ago. How different would my life be if my forefather hadn't agreed to such an outrageous price? If I hadn't been born in a shroud, a Maiden promised to the Primal of Death. Would birthdays have been celebrated with cakes and candies? Would my first gift have been a doll or some lovely trinket? Would there be warm embraces and evenings spent gossiping in the tearoom? Would I sit beside my mother at Rites? Possibly even by my father?

Would my mother then be proud of me instead of disappointed? Instead of disturbed by what I'd become?

Those questions floated away from me as the thick, white curtains bearing the golden symbols of the sun behind the throne stirred and then parted. My grip on myself tightened as a Sun Priest led the Chosen out. This one was male, dressed in loose, white pants and a vest. The Veil of the Chosen obscured all but his jaw and mouth. His skin had been painted gold, reminding me of Callum.

Conversation lowered to a whisper as the Chosen was placed on the throne. A crown of peonies and some other fragile flower was then added to the veil. The Sun Priest moved to stand behind the throne, and then three more Priests lowered to their knees.

Flames sparked to life from the remaining unlit candles as an awareness pressed down on me. I recognized the feeling. It was similar to what I had felt at the lake. I was being watched.

Tensing, I glanced at the front pews, and my stomach sank as my gaze collided with Tavius's. His lips twisted into a smirk, and I resisted the desire to give him the middle finger, something I imagined would be viewed as highly inappropriate in the Temple of Life.

I watched Tavius lean forward, his head dipping to my mother's. Her pale, silk-covered shoulders stiffened. *Bastard.* I tensed as the Queen turned her head. I wanted to step back into the shadows, but there was no place to go. My jaw locked as I felt her stare land on me.

I would never hear the end of this.

I knew I shouldn't have come, and if I lingered, it would only make the Queen angrier. I started to turn when a gust of warm air whipped through the chamber, stirring the flames. I halted as a hush went through the crowd. That wind carried a scent—

Energy charged the air, crackling across my skin and those around me. My gaze shot to the center aisle as the space there appeared to warp and vibrate. Knowing what was coming, I looked up to the raised dais, to where the male sat, his hands folded, ankles still crossed. There was a tremendous smile on his face. He wasn't nervous about his Ascension. He beamed, his body rigid with anticipation as all that Primal energy ramped up. A crack of thunder echoed through the golden cella, and outside, cheers rose. Flames roared from the hundreds of candles, stretching toward the glass ceiling as the realm split open with a rumble. Wispy eather poured out, slipping onto the floor of crushed diamond and limestone. A mass of pulsing silver light appeared in the aisle, whirling and throbbing around the shape of a tall male.

All around me, bodies moved, dropping to one knee as they pressed a hand against their chests. As the winding, spinning tendrils of silver light dimmed, I jerked into motion, lowering myself to my knee as I lifted my hand to my chest, as well.

I stared at the center of the aisle as all others did. It was the first time I'd seen Kolis, the Primal of Life. He was golden-haired and skinned, much like the god, Callum. He was tall and broad of shoulder. His clothing was white and sparked with embers of gold. My attention snagged on the golden band encircling one heavy biceps.

The Chosen rose from the ceremonial throne and lowered onto his knee, his shrouded head bowed. Kolis was a blur of white, gold, and spitting tendrils of eather as he ascended the dais, the force ruffling the edges of the Chosen's veil. His large body blocked my view of the Chosen as he lifted the veil, exposing the Chosen's face only to him.

I didn't know if he spoke to the Chosen. I didn't know if anyone else's heart was beating as fast as mine, or if they felt the Primal energy bearing down on their necks like I did, making it almost impossible to keep my head lifted. If it made them feel churning nausea as Kolis straightened to his full height once more and spoke in a voice that made my insides tremble. "You, Chosen, are worthy."

Hands slammed down on the Temple floor all around me. The thunderous pounding echoed from those crowding the streets outside the Sun Temple and all through Carsodonia. But I flinched, unable to move my hand. *Worthy*. That word curdled my insides as the Primal turned to the audience. My chest seized, and the Temple seemed to shudder under the force of hundreds of beating palms. The Primal's face…

It was too bright and too painful to look upon for any length of time, for the time it would take to decipher much of his features. He slowly scanned the pews and beyond into the alcoves. His gaze stopped, along with my heart, as my eyes began to water and burn. My skin pimpled, and the breath I took lodged in my throat.

The Primal of Life stared directly into the alcove I knelt in, and I could no longer keep my eyes open. Wetness gathered against my lashes as they lowered, but I still felt his stare, as hot as the sun itself—as warm as the gift throbbing in my chest.

By nightfall the day of the Rite, a faint ache had started in my jaw again. Nothing like before, but restlessness still invaded me. I moved aimlessly through the Primal Gardens, not feeling up to traveling beyond Wayfair, even though the Great Hall was chock-full of nobles and others celebrating the Rite. I had managed to avoid my mother, an act that would be harder once the guests left. Then, she was sure to summon me.

I sighed, my mind drifting back to the Sun Temple and the Primal of Life. A shiver crawled along the nape of my neck as I stopped in front of the night-blooming roses near the entrance to the gardens. They trailed across the ground and over the large basin of the water fountain. Kolis's attention focused on me had to be my imagination. The alcove I'd knelt in had been packed with people, but I thought of my gift and its source. It must have come from him.

A high, piercing whistle snapped my head up and around, toward the harbor. A shower of white sparks erupted high in the sky over the bay of the Stroud Sea. Another high-pitched scream of fireworks went up, this time exploding in dazzling, red sparks.

Drawn to the fireworks, I left the Primal Gardens and stepped under the breezeway. The bluffs would be the perfect viewing spot. Maybe afterward, I would visit the lake. I hadn't returned since the night Ash had been there. I didn't know if that was because I feared the lake would no longer feel—

"*Sera*," came the soft whisper.

I stopped, turning to my left. "Ezra? What are you doing out here instead of…?" Words died on my tongue as I got a good look at my stepsister in the dim lamplight of the breezeway. Her features were pale and drawn, and…

My stomach dropped as my gaze swept over the splotches of dark red that stained her bodice. There were even reddish-brown spots on the green of her gown. "Are you hurt? Did someone harm you?" Everything in me went still and empty. I would do terrible, horrible things to anyone who dared to touch her. "Who do I need to hurt?"

Ezra didn't even blink at my demand. "I'm fine. I'm not injured. The blood isn't mine, but I…I need your help."

A little bit of relief seeped into me as I stared at her. "Whose blood are you covered in?" I asked, searching her gaze in the soft glow of the gas lanterns. My eyes narrowed. "Do you need help burying a body?"

"Good gods, I hope you're joking."

I wasn't.

"Though, you are who I would come to if I needed help burying a body," she amended. "I feel as if you would be adeptly skilled at such an endeavor, and I know you would take that secret to your grave."

Well, that didn't feel like a glowing attribute one should be proud of. But what she said was no lie.

"But that is neither here nor there. I do need your help, Sera.

Quite desperately." She clasped her hands together. "Something terrible has happened, and you're the only person who can help."

For an entirely different reason, the churning surged back to life as I spared the breezeway a glance. It was empty. For now. "Ezra—"

"It's Mari. You remember her, right? She—"

"Yes, I remember your *childhood* friend who you are *still* friends with and who I just saw earlier today at the Temple," I interrupted, wondering if Ezra had lied and she had injured her head. "What happened to her?"

"Another child needed our help. It wasn't supposed to be dangerous. The girl had been living on the streets by the Three Stones—you know the place?"

"Yes." My gaze searched hers. The pub was in Lower Town. "What happened there?"

"It's all very confusing. We were supposed to retrieve her, and with everyone celebrating the Rite, tonight was our best chance. That was all." Ezra spoke in a low, hushed voice as she started walking, giving me no other option but to follow her. She led me out from the breezeway and into the neatly manicured courtyard, toward the stables as another firework exploded over the sea, casting a blue shadow across her features. "And we found her immediately. She was in a bit of a bedraggled state, dirty and unkempt," she rambled on, a trait we shared when nervous, even if we didn't share a drop of blood. "And so very scared, Sera."

"What happened?" I repeated.

"I don't really know. It all seemed to happen in a matter of seconds," she said as we rounded the corner, and the stables came into view, lit by numerous oil lanterns. Immediately, my gaze focused on the unmarked carriage Ezra used for such purposes. It was parked a bit off from the entrance to the stables, mostly in the shadows of the interior wall. Tiny bumps erupted on my skin, despite the warmth of the air.

My steps slowed, but Ezra walked faster. "Some kind of argument broke out between a few men in the bar, and it carried outside. Someone threw a tankard, and it frightened the little girl. She ran back toward the den, to this—this alley she'd been living in and—" Ezra sucked in a sharp breath as we neared the silent carriage. She reached for the door as white embers lit the sky beyond the wall.

All thoughts of escaping and the ship vanished. Dim light from an oil lamp spilled out from the carriage as Ezra opened the door. "The men started fighting outside, and Mari was caught in the middle of it when she ran after the girl. I think they believed she was another male. Her cloak was up, you see?" Ezra climbed in, holding the door open for me. "She got knocked down and hit her head on either one of the buildings or the road. I don't know, but…"

The first thing I saw were slender legs encased in black breeches, bent at the knees, and hands limp in a lap. Then a beige blouse untucked and wrinkled beneath a sleeveless tunic, stained with blood at the shoulders and collar. I lifted my gaze to Mari's face. Blood smeared the rich brown of her forehead. Eyes I remembered being a sharp black were halfway closed. Her lips were parted as if she were inhaling.

But no breath entered the lungs of the woman propped on the bench, slumped against the wall of the carriage.

I looked at Ezra as she crouched, picking up a bloodied rag. "She's dead," I told her.

"I know." Ezra looked over at me. "I think she—" She drew in another too-short breath. "I was bringing her here for the Healer, but she…she passed right before I found you. She hasn't been dead long."

I stiffened. "Ezra—"

Her eyes met mine. "She doesn't have to stay dead, Sera."

Chapter 18

"I haven't forgotten what you did when we were children," Ezra said, her chest rising and falling rapidly. "When that ugly cat of yours—"

"His name was Butters," I cut in. "And he wasn't ugly."

Her brows lifted. "He looked like he crawled out of the depths of the Shadowlands."

"There is no need to disparage Butters' memory like that. He was just…" The tabby cat formed in my mind, complete with a half missing ear and patchy fur. "He was just different."

"Different or not, you brought *Butters* back to life when he got into that poison. You touched him, and that cat sprang to life."

"Only to die less than an hour later."

"But that wasn't because of you," Ezra reminded me. "His second death had nothing to do with that."

But hadn't it?

I tried not to think of that night, of what'd happened when Tavius had gone to my mother to tell her what he'd seen me do. The Queen had promptly lost her ever-loving mind. Granted, I was sure discovering that your child had brought life back to a dead barn cat would be quite unsettling, but enough that she had ordered the cat to be captured and…?

Squeezing my eyes shut, I reopened them as Ezra said, "You can help her."

I slowly shook my head. Marisol had always been kind to me. She was a good person. "Butters was a cat—"

"Have you done it since?" Ezra challenged. "Have you given life back to some poor creature since then? I'm sure you have, so don't lie. You've always had a soft spot for animals. There's no way you haven't."

I thought of the kiyou wolf.

"Have you tried it on a person?" Ezra asked.

Immediately, Odetta replaced the wolf. That was what I'd been about to do when she opened her eyes, but I'd been panicked then. I hadn't been thinking. I was thinking now.

"Ezra…" I loathed the mere idea of refusing her. She was family. The real kind that went beyond shared parents and even blood. On more than one occasion, she'd been there to shield me from Tavius's barbed remarks when I'd been the Maiden and couldn't talk back. It was always Ezra who stayed close to my side during the rare moments when we all gathered—like last night—so I didn't look as awkward as I felt. She saw me as someone and not a *thing*. But bringing back a dead person?

"I haven't tried it with a mortal," I said.

"But you can at least try now, Sera. Please? There is no harm in trying," she said. "If it doesn't work, then I know…I'll at least know we tried everything. And if it does? You will have used this gift you have to help someone deserving." She carefully dabbed at the blood on Marisol's neck. "And if it works, I'll make sure she doesn't realize how injured she was. No one but you and I have to know the truth."

Pressure clamped down on my chest as I stared at Marisol. The chalky gray pallor of death hadn't yet set in. The animals I'd brought back had all been normal afterward, living until fate or old age took them once more. But people had to be different.

"Please," Ezra begged, and my heart squeezed. "Please help Mari. I can't… You don't understand." Her voice cracked as she focused on Mari. "I just can't lose her."

The breath I drew hitched in my throat as I glanced between them. Things began to fall into place. The two had been close, from childhood and into adulthood. Marisol remained unmarried, and Ezra had shown no interest beyond courtesy in any of the numerous suitors who'd called upon her. I thought I might've just figured out why.

"Do you love her, Ezra?" I whispered.

My stepsister's gaze lifted to mine, but there was no hesitation. "Yes. I love her very much."

Love.

I wondered what it felt like to care for someone so deeply and completely that you would be willing to do anything for them. I'd barely felt anything beyond passing curiosity and lust, and the gods knew I'd tried to feel more—to want more and seize it. But nothing like that had ever sparked for those I met in the Garden District.

I had no idea how it felt to have that kind of love inside you. Was it as exhilarating as I believed it to be, or was it terrifying? Both? I knew it had to be miraculous. And I knew I couldn't let Ezra lose that.

Cursing under my breath, I leaned forward. "I have no idea if this will work."

"I know." Her eyes met mine. "I wouldn't ask this of you, but—"

"You love her, and you would do anything for her." I knelt before Marisol's legs, unable to believe that I was actually doing this.

"Yes," she rasped.

I reached out, placing my hand on Marisol's. Her skin already felt different due to the lack of pumping blood. I ignored the feeling as I curled my fingers around hers and did what I'd done before. It required no real concentration or technique. Warmth poured into my hands, causing them to tingle. Moving my eyes to Mari's face, I simply *wished* that she was alive.

But there was no sign of life from Marisol.

I stretched up, placing my other hand on her cheek. *Live.* She should live. Like Ezra, she was actually helping the people of Lasania. She was good. *Live.*

Something happened then as another firework exploded in the distance. With my touch.

I gasped. Or maybe it was Ezra. It could've been both of us at the sight of the faint whitish glow seeping out from *under* my skin and along the edges of my fingers.

"I don't remember that happening with Butters," Ezra whispered.

"It…it didn't." I watched with wide eyes as the silvery glow throbbed, sluicing over Marisol's skin. The light…it was eather. The thing that had to fuel my gift. I had just never seen it coming from me before.

But still, nothing happened.

Sorrow for Ezra and Marisol started to creep into me, and the warmth dimmed in my hands, along with the faint radiance. "I'm sorry, Ezra, but—"

Marisol's fingers twitched against mine. Then her hand jerked. Her entire arm spasmed.

"It worked," Ezra uttered hoarsely and then said louder, "Did it work?"

My gaze shot back to Marisol's face. I swore the warm undertones had already returned to her skin, but it was hard to tell in the lamplight. I didn't dare speak, and in the farthest corners of my mind, I thought of the seamstress. What if she came back like that?

I probably should've thought of that beforehand.

Marisol's eyelashes fluttered as her chest rose in a deep, sucking breath that ended in a hacking cough that rattled her entire body. I saw her teeth then. No fangs, thank the gods.

It'd worked.

Good gods, it'd actually worked.

Letting go of her fingers, I leaned back as I looked down at my hands. I lost my balance, falling onto my butt as Ezra clasped Marisol's shoulder.

It'd *worked.*

A sudden breath of cold air touched the damp skin of my neck, causing my head to jerk up. A shiver crawled its way down my spine. I slipped my hand under my hair and clasped the back of my neck, feeling nothing but skin.

"Take a couple of deep breaths." Ezra glanced at me, eyes shining before she shifted her focus back to Marisol. "How do you feel?"

"A little woozy. My head aches like it's been trampled by horses." Marisol frowned, turning toward Ezra. "But, otherwise, I feel fine. A bit confused, but did…did we retrieve the girl? Is she okay—?"

Ezra clasped Marisol's cheeks and kissed her, silencing whatever she was about to say. And it was no friendly peck.

I guessed that cleared up any doubts about their relationship I might've had because it was the kind of kiss I'd read about in those books—the kind I had shared with Ash.

When they parted, there was a dazed sort of smile on Marisol's face. "I have a…a strange feeling that I might've done something incredibly unwise."

Ezra laughed hoarsely. "You? Do something unwise? Not this time." She smoothed her thumbs over Marisol's cheeks. "You were knocked aside. You hit your head."

"I did?" She pressed a palm to her temple. "I don't even remember falling." She lowered her hand. "Sera?" A slight frown pinched her brow. "What are you doing here?"

"Ezra thought you died," I said. "So, she brought you here so I could help bury you."

"What?" she mumbled, looking at Ezra.

My stepsister laughed, idly rubbing Marisol's palm between hers. "She's being silly. I was bringing you to the family Healer when I ran into her. Right, Sera?"

"Right." My hands were trembling, so I hid them under my legs. "But you're okay, so I should go."

"Okay." Marisol smiled faintly at me. "Thank you for not burying me alive."

I blinked as I rose to my feet. "You're welcome."

"You look nice, by the way," Marisol said, looking up at me. "Beautiful, really. The surcoat. The color suits you."

"Thank you," I whispered, having forgotten that I had changed into that earlier. Turning, I dipped out the door of the carriage as white fireworks exploded.

Ezra followed in the flashes of the light. "I'll be right back."

"Not planning to go anywhere." Marisol leaned back as she looked down at herself. "Gods, I'm filthy. What did I hit my head on? A pile of mud…?"

I hopped down and walked a few feet before stopping, the hem of the surcoat swishing around my knees. A jittery sort of warm energy filled me as Ezra stepped out, closing the door behind her.

"I really didn't think it would work," I began.

Crossing the distance between us, Ezra went to touch me but halted. "I want to hug you, but the blood—it will ruin your surcoat." That was a sentence I never expected to hear from Ezra. "And it really is flattering on you." She took a deep gulp of air. "Thank you. Gods, Sera, thank you. I don't know how I can ever repay you."

"You don't need to repay me—well, you could by ensuring that she never finds out the truth." I had no idea what Marisol would think if she knew. Would she be grateful? Or would she be confused? Scared, even? Angry?

"I will make sure she never knows," she swore, and a moment passed. "You have no idea, do you?"

"No idea about what?"

"That what you just did is nothing short of a blessing." She appeared as if she wished to shake me. "*You're* a blessing, Sera. No matter what anyone says or believes, you are a blessing. You always have been. You need to know that."

Feeling my cheeks warm, I started messing with the buttons on the lightweight coat. "My hands are special sometimes. That's all."

"It's not your hands. It's not even your gift, and that is what it is. A gift. Not a failure. You're not a failure."

I drew in a shuddering breath that did nothing to ease the sudden burn in the back of my throat. I kept toying with the button. What she said…

I didn't think she could understand how much those words meant to me. And I didn't think I could acknowledge it because doing so meant acknowledging how much all the other words *hurt*.

"Sera," Ezra whispered.

I cleared my throat. "You should probably get her checked out by the Healer. Maybe not tonight," I said, quickly changing the subject. "In case there are still some signs of how serious her injury was. But she should be looked over."

"I'll make sure she is."

I nodded and then peeked up at her. "Does your father or the Queen know about her? About you two?"

Ezra coughed out a laugh. "Absolutely not. If they did, the wedding would be planned before there was even an engagement."

My lips twitched as I unfolded my arms. "And would that be so bad? You love her."

"And I…I think she loves me." She dipped her chin, a half-grin forming. "But it's still new. I mean, we've known each other our entire lives, but it's not like either of us knew what we meant to each other the whole time. Or, at least, realized it. I don't want the Crown involving themselves in it."

"That's understandable." I rubbed the back of my neck. "You should get back in there."

"I will." She hesitated. "Why don't you join us? While we're getting cleaned up, I can have food sent to my chambers."

"Thanks, but I think I'm going to head to bed soon." I saw her throat work on a swallow. "You should get back in there with Marisol."

Nodding, she started to turn but then stopped. She crossed the short distance between us and folded her arms around me.

I stiffened at first, shocked. She was touching me. She was *hugging* me, and I didn't know how to respond to that for several seconds. My senses were overloaded as I lifted my arms and wrapped them around her, returning the gesture stiffly. The hug felt awkward and strange…but then it felt like something *wonderful*.

Ezra embraced me—squeezed me tightly—and then let go. "I love you, Sera."

Overwhelmed, I watched her step back and smile shakily. I stood there as she turned and made her way back to the carriage. I didn't breathe until she was inside.

I swallowed thickly, briefly closing my eyes. "I love you, too," I whispered.

Turning slowly, I hurried across the courtyard, away from my stepsister and the carriage—away from the first time someone had *hugged* me. And away from the cold kiss I felt against the nape of my neck, the dread that was steadily replacing all that warmth, settling like a stone in the center of my chest and warning me that I had crossed a line.

I had done as Odetta had warned.

Played like a Primal.

Chapter 19

It had worked.

I couldn't…I couldn't even begin to process what I'd done. I'd brought a mortal back to *life*. I wasn't sure if I'd just never believed my gift would work on a mortal or if it was because I'd never believed I would do it. And the silvery glow? That was completely new. Did it happen because I had used my gift on a mortal? I wasn't sure. I lay in bed for hours, unable to shut down my thoughts enough to fall asleep, even though the cold press against the nape of my neck had long since faded.

No one would ever know but Ezra. Marisol would never learn the truth, and Odetta's warning would not come to fruition.

Everything was fine.

Nothing had changed. Marisol's soul hadn't entered the Shadowlands yet, so it wasn't like *he*—the Primal of Death—would even know. I'd only done it this once, and I would never do it again, so I needed to stop dwelling on it.

The night sky had already begun to give way to the gray of dawn by the time I finally drifted off to sleep. I tossed and turned on the narrow bed, the thin night rail itchy in the stale heat of my room, the pillow too flat and then too full. I dreamt of wolves and serpents chasing me. I dreamt of chasing a dark-haired man who wouldn't look at me no matter how many times I called out to him. And each time I woke, I swore I heard Odetta's voice in my ear.

I wasn't sure what finally drew me from my fitful sleep, but when I opened my eyes, my head wasn't even on the pillow, and the glare of the late-morning sun was bright. I blinked rapidly, surprised that I had managed to sleep this late. I hadn't planned on that, but I was relieved that the ache in my temples had receded as I rolled onto my back.

Tavius leaned against the closed door of my bedchamber, arms crossed over his chest.

I stared at him for what felt like an eternity, not quite sure if I was really seeing him. There was no logical reason for him to be in here. None at all. I had to be having a nightmare.

"Nice of you to finally wake," Tavius said.

I snapped out of my stupor, jackknifing upright. "What in the hell are you doing in my bedchamber?"

"Do I need a reason? I'm the Prince. I can go wherever I please," he replied and then laughed as if he had said something funny.

I studied him as I dropped one bare foot to the stone floor. His hair was uncombed, face flushed under the shadow of his unshaven jaw. The white shirt he wore was untucked and wrinkled. So were the loose white pants. He looked as if he hadn't yet gone to bed. My gaze returned to his face. His eyes were *bright*.

"Are you drunk?" I asked. "Is that how you lost your way to your rooms?"

"I know exactly where I am." Tavius unfolded his arms and pushed away from the door. "You and I need to have a chat."

The remnants of sleep vanished in an instant. My gaze flicked over him once more, searching for signs of a weapon. I saw none. "There is nothing that you and I need to talk about," I said, inching my hand across the thin mattress toward the underside of my pillow where, during the last three years, I'd started keeping my dagger as I slept. "Unless you're here to express remorse for being the cause of three young guards' deaths."

He frowned at me. "I have no idea what you're talking about."

"Are you really going to pretend that you had nothing to do with those guards who attacked me?" I lowered my other foot to the floor as I shifted toward the head of the bed.

"Oh, you're talking about them."

"Yes, the guards you hired to risk their lives for coin you do not have."

He sneered. "You think far too highly of yourself if you believe I'd waste even one coin on anything that has to do with you."

"If that was supposed to be an insult, you need to do better," I snapped back, slipping my fingers under the pillow.

"It's just the truth, little sister."

"Do not call me *sister*," I hissed. "*That* is an insult."

He sucked in a breath, his nostrils flaring as he jerked his head back. "You will speak to me with respect."

I coughed out a harsh laugh. "No. I will not. What I *will* do, is give you a chance to leave this room with your flesh and ego intact."

A muscle throbbed in his temple, and I braced myself for an explosion of anger. Instead, he laughed softly, and unease unfurled. "You're so mouthy now, *sister*. I must admit, I preferred the meek and submissive version of you."

"Is that so?" Under the pillow, I spread my fingers out and…and found *nothing*. I glanced at the pillow, my stomach dropping.

"What is it, sister?" Tavius queried, and my gaze shot to him. He reached around to his back. "Missing something?"

Disbelief thundered as he pulled the shadowstone dagger from behind him. The unease took root deep in my chest. "How did you get that?"

"You were sleeping. You didn't even feel me slide it out from under the pillow," he replied. "What a tacky place to keep such a weapon." He grinned. "It would've been safer under the mattress."

How…how long had he been in my bedchamber? Bile crept up my throat as I pulled my hand out from under the pillow and gripped the edge of the mattress. There was no way Tavius could've been quiet or stealthy enough to do that. I had been sleeping far more deeply than I realized. I forced myself to take a long, slow breath. He may have my dagger, but that was all he had. "What do you want to talk about, Tavius?" I asked, gauging the distance between us to be about six feet.

"So defiant," he whispered, the flush of his cheeks heightening. He slammed the dagger into the wardrobe without warning, causing me to jump. The white handle reverberated from the impact. I hated that he'd caught me off guard. I really hated how that smirk deepened.

I bet he was rather proud of what he'd done with the dagger. And I would also be willing to bet that he was too much of an arrogant fool to realize that he'd given up the only chance he had of protecting himself—as paltry an opportunity as that would've been. "You're going to want to leave my bedchamber," I warned, flattening my feet on the floor.

"And you're going to want to change that attitude of yours,

especially after what happened."

What happened?

"Is this because I attended the Rite?" Muscles in my legs tensed as I stood. "Am I really to be punished for such a horrid offense?"

"That was one hell of a stunt you pulled, daring to show your face. But…" He swallowed as his gaze lowered again. The night rail barely reached my knees. His perversion distracted him.

And it would cost him.

I shot forward, not for him but for the dagger. It seemed like the smart choice if not the choice I wanted. Instinct demanded that I go at him and lay him out, but I also knew that whatever harm I inflicted upon him would be paid back tenfold. That was why I chose the dagger, thinking I could threaten him into leaving.

And that choice cost me.

Tavius moved faster than I anticipated. In a stuttered heartbeat, I realized I'd underestimated him. He crashed into me, holding my arms to my sides. "I don't think so," he said.

He twisted us so sharply, my legs went out from under me. He pushed hard, forcing both of us forward. I kicked out, but there was nothing but empty space. He turned again, and the sparse bedchamber whirled wildly. I caught a glimpse of the bed before he dropped me, belly-first onto the mattress.

It provided little softness. The impact knocked the air out of my lungs and sent a jolt of dull pain across my midsection. I started to flip over, but he came down on top of me, pinning my legs and torso under the weight of his body, and my arms under the pressure of us both.

I was trapped.

"You may be trained, but at the end of the day, you're still just a weak female." He pushed me down. "Who is finally going to fucking listen to me."

I was trapped.

"Get off me!" I screamed into the mattress.

His elbow pressed into the back of my head, forcing my face into the bedding. I breathed, only to inhale the sheet covering the bed. Panic exploded like a wild beast as I struggled, gaining nothing more than an inch. I screamed into the mattress, the sound captured and muffled. My heart pounded. I couldn't get enough air. Not even when I managed to turn my head to the side enough that I was no longer inhaling the sheet. I still couldn't get air into my lungs.

"You will start respecting me now. Want to know why?" His foul breath, full of stale ale and liquor, blasted my cheek. "Ask me, *sister*. Ask me why."

"Why?" I spat, gasping as his elbow pressed into the space below my neck, sending a blast of pain down my spine. Fury roared through me, crashing into the building panic. I couldn't get enough air in, and the weight of him, the feel of him was unbearable. I screamed again, and he shoved his forearm into the back of my head, pressing my face back into the mattress. My heart clawed at my chest. Dear gods, I was going to kill him. I was going to dig out his eyes with my bare fingers and then slice off his hands, his—

He put his mouth to my ear. "Because I am now King."

My heart thudded with disbelief.

"Yeah," he breathed, grabbing a fistful of hair. He lifted my head, and I dragged in mouthfuls of air. "You heard me right. I am King."

"How? Your father—"

"He died in the middle of the night. In his sleep." He yanked my head back. Fiery pain erupted over my scalp, and pressure pushed down on my spine as he held my head and neck at an unnatural angle. "The Healers say it was an ailment of the heart."

I couldn't believe what I was hearing. None of it made sense. But if he spoke the truth…? How was Ezra? How was my mother?

"So, I've ascended the throne, even with all my drinking and chasing skirts. What do you think about that?"

What did I think about that? "Fate must have a sense of humor," I forced out.

"Stupid cunt." Spittle hit the side of my cheek as he continued to pull. Good gods, he was going to snap my neck. "I don't think you understand what this means for you. My father let you do whatever you wanted, even though you failed us. Let you speak to people however you wanted. Speak to me like you do. Not anymore."

"Is your ego that fragile?" I spat.

Tavius shoved my face back into the mattress. Whatever relief came from the pressure being gone from my neck and spine was replaced by smothering panic. My struggles renewed as I managed to get a thin breath of air. "But things are going to change. You won't have protection any longer. Nor do you have the aid of your knight."

I stopped moving. I stopped fighting as his words sank in through the panic.

His fingers tightened around my hair. "Sir Holland has been reassigned as of this morning. He was on the ship that left for the

Vodina Isles. He will personally oversee a treaty of peace between our kingdom and theirs."

My throat seized. Sir…Sir Holland had been sent to Vodina? After what had been done to their Lords—after what *I'd* done? That was a death sentence. That is if Tavius spoke the truth. I couldn't imagine that Sir Holland would've left without finding me. He would've made time. Unless he hadn't been given a chance. A heavy knot settled in my chest. "Is he alive?" I rasped out.

"As of now, he should be," Tavius answered, and I wasn't sure if I could believe him. But could I allow myself to doubt his truth? "But you? I think you're going to wish you were on your way to Vodina with him."

The back of my eyes burned as I desperately tried to rein in my emotions. King Ernald was dead. I'd never been all that close to the man, but I'd known him for my entire life. And Ezra? My mother? Sir Holland? What about the people of Lasania? This couldn't be happening.

"I'm not like my father," he said. "Nor am I like your mother. I don't, for one second, believe that the Primal will come for you. He saw what a worthless thing you are. He rejected you. You won't save the kingdom."

His words cut into my skin. "And you will?"

"Yes."

I almost laughed. "How?"

"You'll see soon enough," he promised. "But first, there's something you need to understand. I can do whatever I want to you right now. There isn't one damn soul who would step in and stop me or, let's be honest, care enough to do so." He tilted my head to the side again. "Not so mouthy now, are you?" Tavius laughed. "Yeah, it's time to rethink that attitude of yours."

"Why? Why do you hate me?" I asked, even as I told myself I didn't care. "You were like this from day one."

"Why?" Tavius laughed. "Are you that obtuse?"

I was surprised he knew what the word meant. "I guess so."

"You were the Maiden, fated to belong to the Primal of Death," he said. "You failed at that, but that doesn't change who you really are, *Princess* Seraphena, the last of the Mierel bloodline."

My heart stuttered as understanding seeped into me, along with a hefty dose of disbelief. "You…you're worried I will try to stake a claim to the throne."

"You could," he whispered. "Many wouldn't believe you. I doubt you'd have the support of even your own mother. But enough people would be willing to believe you—believe anyone who claimed to be a Mierel."

All these years, I'd assumed that Tavius had little to no desire to take the Crown. Never once had I even considered that my right to the throne drove his hateful behavior. I'd been wrong—so wrong.

"I have a question, sister? What do you want me to do right now?"

Die.

Die a long, slow, and painful death.

"You want me to get off you?" he taunted. "Then say it."

I said nothing.

He dug his fingers into my hair and jerked my head so sharply, pain shot down my spine. "Say it with respect, Sera."

Every part of my being rebelled, but I forced my jaws open. I forced the words to the tip of my tongue. "Get off me, Tavius."

"No. That's not it. You know it."

I hated him. Gods, I *hated* him. "Please."

He tsked under his breath, clearly enjoying this. "It's, '*Will you please get off me,* King *Tavius*?'"

Opening my eyes, I focused on the rays of light streaming in through the small window. "You are not my King, nor will you ever be."

Tavius stilled above me and then released his grip, suddenly rolling off me. I quickly shifted to my back, breathing heavily.

Tavius smiled as he backed away. "Gods, I hoped you'd answer that way. Do you know what you just did?"

I glared at him, my jaw aching.

"You made a treasonous statement." That fevered glow returning to his eyes, Tavius gripped the handle of my dagger, tearing it free. A chunk of wood flew into the air. He slipped the dagger into his belt and barked out one word. "*Guards.*"

I shot to my feet as the door swung open, and two Royal Guards stalked in. But it wasn't them that sent a cold bolt of dread down my spine. It was the one who remained in the hallway. It was Pike—the Royal Guard who'd stood outside my…my stepfather's office the day I'd found the Coupers. It was what was in his hands.

A bow.

Aimed straight at my chest.

Everything in me slowed as I stared at the sharp edge of the arrow, held steady in Pike's hands.

"Fight them, and I think you know exactly what will happen," Tavius said.

I couldn't look away from the sharp point.

I was fast, but not faster than an arrow. The eager look on Pike's face told me that he really hoped that I fought. The smile on Tavius's face said the same.

And it was in that moment that I realized that whatever Tavius planned, now or later, there was a good chance he didn't expect me to survive. And there was also a high probability that he wanted me to beg, cry, or plead.

I wouldn't give them that. I wouldn't fight them. They would not get any of that from me. My back straightened as I inhaled slowly and deeply. I would not give them *anything.*

Things had slowed inside me but felt as if they'd sped up outside of me. The two guards gripped my arms with gloved hands, walking me from the chamber. Tavius spoke to the Royal Guard who waited at the end of the hall, speaking too quietly for me to hear. The guard turned, quickly jogging off ahead of us as I was forced down to the main floor and led through the hall the servants used.

The faces of those we passed were a blur. I didn't know if they looked our way, how much they saw, or what they thought as the guards walked me into the Great Hall, passing between columns adorned in gold scrollwork as we entered the grandest chamber in Wayfair. Banners taller than many of the homes within Carsodonia hung from the dome-shaped glass ceiling to the floors, the golden Royal Crest glittering in the light from the numerous gas lamps and candle sconces. A secondary wall of pillars circled the main floor, creating a somewhat private alcove. They too were adorned with golden designs, and that scrollwork continued across the marble and limestone floor, down the wide steps of the alcove, and then forward like veins of gold, stretching all the way to the raised dais where the King's and Queen's diamond and citrine-jeweled thrones sat.

They were empty now, but one was draped in white fabric. Black petals had been strewn about the cloth, a ceremonial act representing the King's passing.

The massive circular chamber was still in a state of disarray from the prior night's celebrations. Servants came to a complete standstill as we entered—dozens of them.

"Everyone out," Tavius barked. "Now."

No one hesitated. They scurried from the Hall in a flurry of starched white tunics and blouses. My gaze collided with one. *Her.* The young girl who'd been in the room where the guards had been lying in wait. Her blue eyes were wide as she quickly looked away, casting her gaze to the floor.

Tavius strode down the wide steps onto the main floor, and my gaze traveled to what he walked toward. The statue of the Primal of Life. Breathtaking detail had been given to Primal Kolis. The heavy-soled caligae and armored plating shielding his legs looked real, as did the knee-length tunic and the chainmail covering his chest and torso, all carved from the palest marble. He held a spear in one hand and a shield in the other. The warrior. The protector. The King of the Primals, gods, and mortals. Even the bones in his hands and the curl to his hair had been captured in astonishing detail. But his face was nothing but smooth stone.

The lack of features always unnerved me, just as it did whenever I saw the rare renderings of the Primal of Death.

Tavius looked up at the statue. "This would work." He turned to me, that smirk fixed upon his lips. "A rather fitting place for you, I think."

Breathe in. I had no idea what he was up to or what my punishment would be as the Royal Guards forced me down the steps. Spilled liquid dampened the soles of my feet. *Hold.* White petals crumbled under my steps. I glanced up at Kolis's stone, feature-less face, fighting the tremble starting in my legs. I forced my muscles to lock as footsteps entered the Hall from behind. *Breathe out.*

"Ah, perfect timing." Tavius clapped his hands together. "Bind her and put her on her knees."

Breathe in. I felt the edge of the arrow poking me in the back. I went down stiffly to my knees, at the feet of the Primal King. The Royal Guards brought my wrists together, and the guard who had been waiting outside my chamber at the end of the hall was suddenly beside me, wrapping one end of a rope around my wrists. I showed no reaction to the tight pull against my skin as he jerked the bindings around the statue's arm, forcing my arms above my head. *Hold.* My lungs burned as the guards backed away. The breath I'd dragged in hadn't been deep enough. I exhaled a thin stream of air. *What was happening? What was—?* Tavius moved out of my line of sight. I cranked my head to the side to see what he was doing—

Air cracked with a thin whistle, turning my skin to ice. No. No, he wouldn't. My heart started racing as I pulled at the bonds, my stomach twisting. I knew that sound. I'd heard it when I walked into the barn that night as he'd whipped his horse for throwing him. There was no—

"You've always reminded me of a wild horse. Too stubborn. Too temperamental. Too proud despite your numerous failures," Tavius drawled, drawing closer. I heard him dragging the leather lash over his palm. "There's only one way to get a steed to respect its master. You have to break it." Tavius knelt beside me. Nothing about his eyes was warm. There was nothing humane. "Just like you should've been broken the night you failed the entire kingdom. But you'll learn today."

I stared at him, my heart slowing. I wasn't there. I didn't feel the cool tile under my knees or the too-tight, rough rope around my wrists. I donned the veil. I retreated into myself, but I didn't fade to nothing. I wasn't an empty vessel. The canvas wasn't blank. Something dark and tremendous sparked inside me, like a violent strike against flint. An icy fire was birthed in the center of my chest. It poured through my body, filling all those hollow places. My blood hummed, and the center of my chest throbbed. I tasted shadow and death in the back of my throat as that icy fire burned through me. I lifted my eyes to Tavius's, the corners of my lips curling up.

I heard words pass my lips, sentences full of smoke. "I'm going to kill you." I barely recognized the voice as mine. "I will slice the hands from your body and then carve your heart from your chest before setting it on fire. I will watch you burn."

Tavius's pupils expanded. "You…you stupid bitch."

I laughed. I didn't even know where the laugh had come from, but it felt ancient and endless. And it wasn't mine. I thought Tavius heard it. For a second, I swore I saw fear in his eyes. Doubt. For just a second, and then his lips curled into a sneer.

"You won't be doing anything, sister. I doubt you'll be able to even speak your name by the time I'm through with you. You'll be broken," he swore. "You will respect me."

"Never," I whispered and then looked away, focusing on the stone hand holding the hilt of the spear.

Seconds ticked by as Tavius remained kneeling beside me, his chest rising and falling rapidly. I stayed in that faraway place where nothing but icy fire filled my insides, leaving no room for dread or fear or anything else. When Tavius rose, I felt nothing but the kiss of promised retribution. When he walked behind me, I held my chin high. When he roughly tossed my braid over my shoulder, exposing my back,

I didn't move. When the air cracked again, I didn't flinch.

The snapping pain streaked across my back, from my shoulders to my waist, sudden and intense. A harsh breath punched out of me. That was the only sound in the Great Hall. The Royal Guards remained silent. Tavius didn't even speak. I forced myself to breathe through the pain.

The whistle of the whip was the only warning. I braced myself, but there was no way to prepare. No breathing exercise to ease what was to come. Fiery pain erupted as my entire body jerked forward and then fell back as far as the ropes would allow. I shuddered, telling myself that I could handle this. Tavius wasn't strong enough to break skin.

He was the weak one.

The night rail slipped down my arms, gaping in the front as I slowly rightened myself. As soon as I could, I would carry out my promise. I would cut off his hands and feed that whip to him until he choked on it. I would carve out his heart and then watch him burn.

"Look at you." There was a thickness to Tavius's voice. He snapped the whip off the tile, and my entire body flinched. He laughed. "Still so defiant, but it's an act. You're afraid. Weak. Would you like me to stop? You know what to say."

I turned my head to the side, seeing him through the strands of hair that had slipped free. He was standing behind me. "Tavius," I said between gritted teeth. "*Please*…kindly go *fuck yourself*."

Someone inhaled sharply—one of the Royal Guards. I heard boots shuffling, but Tavius laughed again, cursing me. I could make out him lifting the whip, and I closed my eyes.

"What in the gods' name are you doing, Tavius?" My mother's voice suddenly rang out through the Great Hall. My eyes flew open to see them both garbed in the white of mourning. She gasped. "Dear gods—"

"Have you lost your senses?" Ezra. That was her. The flare of stinging pain along my back faded as I saw her standing next to my mother. "My gods, what is wrong with you?"

"First off, neither of you two addressed me appropriately. But given the shock of the last several hours, I will let it slide," Tavius stated calmly, unbothered by their reaction. "As for what I'm doing, it is what should've been done—" He staggered to the side, eyes widening as he stared at the floor. "What the…?"

Ezra had come to a stop on the steps. A blur of plum and gold poured in through the open doors of the Great Hall as Royal Guards arrived, and under me, the petals vibrated as the floor *trembled*. Thin fissures formed in the tile and ran across the carved caligae enclosing Kolis's feet. I watched as the tiny splinters traveled up the stone legs. Confused, I lifted my head. What in the world…?

A blast of thunder shook the entire Great Hall. Someone cried out. Delicate flutes left behind on trays and tables exploded. Chairs toppled. Tables shattered. Plaster fell from the columns and walls as cracks raced up pillars and screamed across the ceiling's glass dome.

A gust of icy wind whipped through the Great Hall, and the air…the air charged with power. The hairs all along my body rose as a faint mist seeped out from the fissures in the floor.

Eather.

Tavius took a step back as the space between us began to *vibrate*. Air crackled and hissed, emanating silvery-white sparks that swirled and lashed through the space just as the whip had. Then the very realm *tore* open.

And darkness tinged in silver spilled out from the tear, splashing on the floor and rising in a thick, dark, swirling mist. In the throbbing mass, a tall form could be seen as thick tendrils curled through the air, spreading across the floor, forming a pillar of night and then another, completely obscuring all others in the Hall. In each column of churning shadows, a form took shape. As the shadows—all of them that filled the Hall—retracted as if drawn back to *him*.

I knew who stood in the center without even seeing his face or any features inside the pulsing mass of midnight that stretched up and outward in the shape of massive wings that blocked the sun's light.

Death had finally returned.

Chapter 20

There were only ten beings in either realm that were powerful enough to tear open the realms.

A Primal.

But as the shadows stopped the maddening spinning, and the shape of wings became nothing more than a hazy outline, I saw who stood in the center, and it made no sense.

Because it was him. The Shadowlands god.

Ash.

He looked over his shoulder at me, the striking planes of his features a brutal set of harsh lines. I stared at him, my heart thumping. His skin…it had thinned, taking on a silvery-white glow. The breath I took lodged in my throat.

Oh, gods…

The silver of his irises seeped throughout his entire eyes until they were iridescent. They crackled with power—the kind that could unravel entire realms with just a lift of a finger. A web of veins appeared on his cheeks, spreading across his throat and down his arms under the silver band on his right biceps then traveling along the swirling shadows that had gathered under his skin. He was…he was like the brightest star and the deepest night sky given mortal form. And he was utterly beautiful in this form, wholly terrifying.

The buzz of incredulity filled me, throwing me straight into denial because it couldn't be.

It couldn't have been *him* this entire time.

"Who…who are you?" Tavius rasped.

Slowly, *his* head turned to where my stepbrother stood. "I am known as the Asher," he said, and I shuddered. *Is it short for something,* I'd asked when he told me his name. *It is short for many things.* "The One who is Blessed. I am the Guardian of Souls and *the* Primal God of Common Men and Endings." His voice traveled through the Great Hall, and absolute silence answered. I could barely force air through my lungs. "I am Nyktos, ruler of the Shadowlands, the Primal of *Death*."

The whip slipped from Tavius's hand, falling to the cracked marble tile.

Ezra and my mother were the first to react, dropping to their knees as they placed their hands over their hearts. The Royal Guards who'd entered behind them followed suit. Tavius and the other guards were as frozen as I was.

Nyktos looked to his right, to who I slowly realized was the god who'd given me the shadowstone dagger. Ector nodded curtly before turning to me.

As the Primal returned his attention to those before him, Ector knelt beside me. Distaste filled his deep amber eyes. "Animals," he muttered.

"That's an insult to animals," came another voice, and I looked up to see the god who had stood to the Primal's left. The deep black skin of his jaw was hard as he glanced at my back. "There is no blood."

"He didn't break the skin," I heard myself whisper. "He's not skilled enough with a whip for that."

His eyes, the color of polished onyx, flicked to mine. Eather glowed behind the barely visible pupils as a slow grin started to appear. "Apparently, not."

"Saion?" Ector carefully touched my shoulders. "Can you get rid of the ropes?"

"Gladly." The god curled his fingers around the bindings. Immediately, the edges of the rope frayed under Saion's hand. A faint charge of electricity danced around my wrists, and then the rope broke apart, falling to the floor as ash. I started to topple forward, but Ector kept me upright.

A sharp sensation of pinpricks rushed down my arms as they fell to my sides, the blood returning to them. "Is this…is this real?"

"Unfortunately," Ector muttered.

Saion snorted as his hands replaced the other god's.

"Unfortunately?" He eased me down, so I was sitting, but his hands remained, causing another jolt of energy to rush over my skin. "I'm about to get my daily dose of entertainment."

Ector sighed as he rose. "There's something wrong with you."

"There's something wrong with all of us."

"This won't end well."

"When does it ever?" Saion asked.

"Who?" the Primal snarled, jerking my attention to where he stood. Fury radiated from him, and I had…I had never heard him sound like that. "Who took part in this?"

"Them," a soft, shaking voice answered—the same frightened voice that had lured me into that room to be attacked.

I found her by the doors on one knee, her head barely lifted. "I saw them in the hall with her, Your Highness. Three of them were with the Prince, and the fourth joined with…" She shook. "I went to get Her Grace."

The Primal's chin lifted to where the three Royal Guards stood with Pike, who still held the bow. A guard spoke in a trembling voice. "I thought he was just going to scare her. I didn't know—"

The Primal turned his head to the male, and that was all. He *looked* at him. Whatever the Royal Guard had been about to say in his defense ended in a choked gasp. The man stumbled forward, the blood draining rapidly from his face. His head kicked back as his lips peeled over his teeth in a scream that was never given life. I jerked as tiny cracks appeared in the man's pale, waxy flesh—deep, bloodless splits opening across his cheeks, down his throat, and over his hands.

The Royal Guard shattered, broke apart like fragile glassware, into a fine dusting of ash and then…nothing. Nothing remained of him, not even the clothing he wore or the weapons he bore.

My wide eyes shot to the Primal. That kind of power…it was inconceivable. Terrifying and impressive.

"Here we go," Ector murmured.

My gods, *that* was what *he* was capable of. And I had stabbed him? I'd actually threatened him. Multiple times. The strangest thought occurred to me as one of the other Royal Guards turned to run and only made it a step before he froze mid-flight, his arms whipping out, stiff at his sides. Why in the hell did the Primal ever use a sword if he could do *that*? A grossly inappropriate laugh crawled up my throat as the guard's mouth dropped open in a silent scream. Cracks appeared across his cheeks as he rose off the floor. He…he *crumbled* slowly, from the top of his head to his boots, collapsing in a stream of dust.

Ector glanced down at me, raising a brow.

"Sorry," I mumbled. It had to be the pain in my back that ebbed and then surged. The shock. *Everything.*

The third guard fell to his knees, begging. He too shattered into nothing.

"He seems angry," Ector spoke over my head.

"You…well, he's been moody lately," Saion replied, and I felt another laugh taking form. "Let him have his fun."

"I'm not going out like that." Pike—the utterly idiotic man—lifted the bow and fired.

The Primal twisted, moving so fast it was nothing more than a blur. He caught the arrow just before it made contact with his chest. "

"Now that was a bold move," Saion commented. "A really bad one, but bold."

"You fired an arrow at me? Are you for real?" The Primal tossed the arrow aside. "No, you don't have to go out like that."

"Oh, man," Ector added with another sigh.

The Primal was suddenly in front of Pike. I hadn't even seen him move.

Taking hold of Pike's arm, he twisted sharply. Bone cracked. The bow fell, clattering off the tile as the Primal gripped the man around the throat. "There are many ways you can be taken out. Thousands. And I'm well acquainted with all of them," he said. "Your options are endless. Some painless. Some quick. This way won't be either."

The Primal's head snapped forward. There was a brief flash of fangs, and my stomach hollowed. He tore into Pike's throat, ending the man's short, abrupt scream of terror. Wrenching his head back, the Primal forced the man's jaw open as he spat a mouthful of Pike's own blood into his mouth. My stomach churned with nausea as I planted a hand on the tile. The Primal shoved Pike aside. The mortal fell to the floor, twitching and grasping at the jagged tear in his throat. I couldn't look away. Not even when he stopped moving and his blood-coated hands slipped away from his neck.

Ector's head cocked to the side. "You call *that* moody?"

"Well…" Saion trailed off.

The Primal then turned to Tavius. "You." Ice fell from the word." He looked down, his blood-smeared lips curling into a smirk. The breeches along the inside of Tavius's leg had darkened. "So afraid you pissed yourself. Do you regret your actions?"

Tavius said nothing. I didn't think he could. All he could do was nod jerkily.

"You should've thought about that before you picked up that whip," the Primal growled. "And touched what is mine."

What is mine?

Another laugh tickled the back of my throat. *Now* he claimed me?

A rush of air stirred around me. I blinked. That was the amount of time that had passed. The spot where Tavius once stood was empty. My brows lowered. A second later, my mother screamed. I turned, barely feeling the pull against the tender skin of my back.

The Primal had Tavius pinned to the statue of Kolis, several feet off the floor, the whip wrapped around his throat. The Primal's skin was more silvery than dusky now, thinner, and those shadows became even more apparent. "I would ask what kind of mortal you are, but it is evident that you're a pathetic pile of shit shaped into that of a man."

Tavius's face turned a mottled red and purple as he sputtered, digging at the whip around his throat.

The Primal's chin dipped as his head cocked. With his other hand, he reached for Tavius's waist and jerked his hand back. He held the dagger he'd gifted me. "*This*," Nyktos growled, hooking the blade into one of the leather straps that crossed his chest, "does not belong to you."

"No! Please! He's my stepson." My mother rushed forward, stumbling over the hem of her gown. "I don't know what got into him. He would never do this. Please. I beg of you—"

"Beg and pray all you want. It matters not to me." The Primal's voice turned guttural as the shadow wings swept high, stirring the air once more. "He has proven what little significance and value he has to this realm."

"Don't do this," my mother cried, holding out her hands. I squeezed my eyes shut. Not wanting to hear her beg for him… "Please."

"He's a monster. He's always been a monster." Ezra's steady voice cut through the room, and I opened my eyes. She hadn't risen from where she knelt. "Our…our father knew that. Everyone knows that. He is, as you said, of little significance."

"But he is the future King," my mother said as Tavius's eyes bulged, and veins protruded from his temple. "He will never do something like this again. I can promise you that."

I stared at my mother, my chest rising and falling rapidly as she continued pleading for his life. That icy fire returned, washing away the shock and the disbelief. It dulled the pain in my shoulders and upper back. It dulled *everything*. I pulled away from Saion and pushed to my feet. I stood on surprisingly steady legs, my gaze never leaving my mother, even though she had not looked at me.

"Let him go," I said. "Please."

"You would beg for his life?" The Primal's voice was barely recognizable. The limestone of the statue cracked behind Tavius. "He hurt you. He forced you onto your knees and whipped you."

"I don't beg for his life," I said, that throbbing icy hotness taking root in my chest as I turned to the Primal.

A long moment passed, and then the Primal looked down at me. His eyes… The silver was radiant, almost blinding, the wisps of eather nearly obscuring the pupils. The glow seeped out of his eyes, crackling and spitting. Power charged the air, and behind him—all around him—a darkness continued to gather, pulling from all the nooks and shadowy areas of the Great Hall. Shadows also moved *under* his skin.

"As you wish, *liessa*." The Primal dropped my stepbrother. He fell forward onto his knees, and then rolled to his side as he tore the whip free of his throat, tossing it aside as he wheezed. The whip slid across the petals and cracked flooring, coming to a stop before me.

I looked down at it. "Thank you."

"Do not thank me for that," he bit out. The shadows collapsed back into the Primal's skin and were released to the hidden corners of the room. The luminous glow was the last thing to fade. His eyes met mine. "Do not allow this to leave a mark." He then turned back to Tavius, kneeling beside him. "You will not die by my hands, but I will have your soul for an eternity to do with as I see fit. And I have a lot of ideas." He winked as he patted the mortal's cheek. "Something to look forward to. For both of us."

Saion laughed under his breath. "He's giving like that."

"Thank you," my mother whispered. "Thank you for your—"

"Shut the fuck up," Nyktos snarled as he stepped over Tavius's trembling body.

My mother did just that, and I turned to her. Finally, *finally* she looked at me. Her eyes were wide, red, and swollen, and I felt *nothing* as I faced the Primal. He shifted an arm to the side, revealing the hilt of a sword strapped to his lower back as Tavius righted himself, leaning against the statue of Kolis. The redness had eased from his face as he tilted his head back. The mark the whip had left behind on his throat was clearly visible.

Grasping the hilt of the Primal's sword, I pulled it free. Ector stepped to the side. The shadowstone was heavier than I was accustomed to, but it was a welcome weight in my hands as I turned to my stepbrother. Tavius looked up at me.

"What did I promise you?" I asked.

His watery eyes widened with realization. He threw up an arm as if he could somehow ward off what was to come.

I swung the shadowstone sword down, across his right forearm. The blade met no resistance, cleaving smoothly through tissue and bone. Tavius howled a sound I'd never heard a mortal make before as he scrambled against the statue, blood spraying and spurting. Someone screamed. Probably my mother as I brought the sword down on his left arm, just below the shoulder. His shrieks rang across the glass ceiling.

I thrust the sword through Tavius's right chest in a most dishonorable manner, impaling him to the statue of the Primal of Life. He flailed and jerked, wide eyes rolling as blood sprayed the length of my night rail. I stepped toward him.

"I think that's enough," the Primal said.

"No, it's not." I picked up the whip and snapped forward, grasping Tavius's blood-and-sweat-soaked hair. I jerked his head back. Wide, panicked eyes met mine as I shoved the handle of the whip into his mouth, pushing it down as hard as I could.

"Okay." Saion cleared his throat. "Got to admit, I was not expecting that."

The light was quick to go out of Tavius's eyes then. The icy heat in my chest throbbed in response, but I let go of his head before my gift could undo all my hard work. I stepped back, wiping his blood on my night rail. Blood now trickled from his ragged wounds.

I didn't carve out his heart or set him on fire, but what I had done…it would do, and it would not leave a mark.

Taking another step back, I looked around the room. My mother had stopped screaming. The faces were a blur as I looked at Ezra. "Take the throne," I said hoarsely, and she stiffened. "You are next in line."

Ezra shook her head. "The throne belongs to—"

"The throne belongs to you," I cut her off.

Her gaze darted to the presence behind me and then to where my mother had collapsed in a pool of white skirts, one hand clutching her chest as she looked at me—as she saw what I was, what she had helped to mold.

A monster just like Tavius, only of a different sort.

I turned to the Primal, to the other who had helped to shape me into this thing, and slowly lifted my gaze to his face. He stared down at me, his expression unreadable as Tavius's blood seeped across the floor, cool against my bare feet.

A roar replaced the nothingness as I stood there, staring up at him.

The Primal of Death.

My would-be husband.

Nyktos.

The very key to stopping the slow, painful destruction of my kingdom.

Suddenly, that feeling of familiarity made sense. I had heard his voice before.

I have no need of a Consort.

The Primal inhaled sharply as emotions rolled through me, wave after wave, crashing into a rising tide of so many feelings that I choked on them—the disbelief, the hope, the dread, and the anger. So much *anger.*

"*You*," I croaked.

"Get everyone out of here," the Primal ordered. "Get everyone out of here, including yourselves."

The gods hesitated. "Are you sure?" Ector asked.

"*Go*." The Primal didn't take his eyes off me.

I heard the gods walking away, heard them rounding up those still alive—heard Saion asking, "You have whiskey? I'm in the mood for whiskey."

A shudder worked its way through me as the Primal continued staring down at me. Did he…did he now just realize who I was? Three years had passed since he'd last seen me. A lot had changed in that time. Whatever softness of youth had lingered in my features had faded. I was a little taller and fuller, a little harder, but I wasn't unrecognizable. Apparently, I was just *forgettable* while my entire life had only ever been about him. And because of him, the last three years of my life had been…well, they had been *nothing* but pain, disappointment, and unfulfilled duty.

Every part of my being centered on him as my chest continued to rise and fall rapidly.

His head tilted again, the slash of dark brows lowering. Reddish-brown hair slid against his cheek, and something…something deep inside me began to rattle and crack open. I tasted rage, a hot and acidic *rage* so potent and consuming, my throat burned with it.

I lost whatever control I normally had. I launched myself at him, swinging my closed fist straight for the Primal's face.

His eyes widened with a flicker of surprise and that second *almost* cost him. My knuckles grazed his jaw as he stepped to the side. He twisted at the waist, his hand snapping out. Catching my wrist, he spun me around. The columns of the Great Hall whirled as my bare feet slipped in the blood. In a stuttered heartbeat, my back was pressed to his chest, and an arm pinned me to him around my waist.

"That was not the reaction I expected now," he said from behind me. "Obviously."

An inhuman sound crawled out of my throat, a growl of fury as I winged my free arm back, fingers reaching for his hair. It was such an unbecoming move, but I didn't care.

"Oh, no you don't." He caught my other wrist, pressing both my arms to my waist as he crossed his arms over my chest.

Ignoring the protest of the raw skin across my shoulders, I drew up my foot and slammed it down. He shifted out of the way as he lifted me enough that my foot didn't make contact with the hard floor.

He turned us so we faced away from the statue and Tavius. "You seem angry with me."

"You think?" I threw my weight back against him, hoping to upset his footing.

He didn't move. "I see I was correct about you striking me as the type to fight even if you knew you wouldn't succeed." His chin brushed the top of my head. "It's exhausting always being right."

I threw my head back with a shriek. Pain lanced my skull as I connected with some part of his face.

"*Fates*," he grunted, and a savage smile tore at my mouth. His hold on me tightened as he dropped his chin, pressing his cool cheek against mine. Within the span of a too-short breath, he effectively pinned my head between his and his chest. "Are you done yet?"

"No," I seethed, fingers splaying uselessly. Frustration scorched my skin, stroked against the icy heat in my chest, as did the knowledge that even with years of training, he had still easily rendered me absolutely harmless.

"I think you are." His cool breath touched my cheek.

"I don't care what you think," I spat, trying to pull free, but it was useless, and it was starting to *hurt*. I didn't gain an inch. I pulled both legs up, but that did nothing. He didn't budge.

He sighed. "Or I suppose you could just keep doing this until you tire yourself out."

Planting both feet on the floor, I pushed as hard as I could against him. The Primal still didn't move, but he did tense.

"I would suggest you stop doing that," he advised, his voice deeper, rougher. "Not only are you going to further irritate the wounds along your back, but I don't believe your actions are inciting the type of reaction you're aiming for."

It took a couple of moments for the firestorm in my blood to ease enough for me to make sense of his words…and for some inkling of rationality to seep in. *Breathe in.* I stared at the cracks in the white and gold columns, dragging in a deep breath. My chest rose, pressing against his arms. *Hold.* Slowly, my senses returned. My cheek tingled from the contact with his. The night rail was barely a barrier. The length of my back and hips prickled from the feel of his flesh against mine. The coarse hairs of his arms tickled the sensitive skin of my chest through the sagging bodice. My pulse thrummed erratically as I stared forward, unable to understand the riot of sensations. The skin-to-skin contact was a lot.

I squeezed my eyes shut. *Breathe out.* Had I seriously tried to attack the Primal of Death?

I didn't want to think about that. I couldn't think about what surely awaited me after what I'd done to the would-be King of Lasania. All I could focus on was that I was here now with him, the object of over a decade's worth of training and grooming. A strange sort of laugh worked its way up my throat, but it found silence against my sealed lips. Because no matter what had happened in this Great Hall, no matter who took the throne now, I still had a duty to Lasania.

I was supposed to be seducing Nyktos, not dismembering people in front of him and trying to kill him. Not until I'd made him fall in love with me. In my anger and disbelief, I'd apparently lost sight of a very important step there.

The reality of the situation once again settled over me as the anger slowly returned to the simmer of the last three years…and maybe even longer than that.

Nyktos.

A name known but never spoken out of fear of gaining his attention or inciting his wrath. A name I'd never even allowed myself to think.

But he was finally here. How many times over the last three years had I wished for just such a chance to fulfill my duty? Countless. He was finally here. This could be it.

Could've been the chance.

I wasn't sure how one could seduce another into falling in love with them after stabbing them in the chest.

But I knew what he'd meant when he said that my actions were inciting a reaction I didn't intend. I'd been around enough men in my life to understand what he was saying…and to feel now what I had been too furious to register when I pushed back against him earlier. The thick, hard length of him had pressed against my lower back. He had been aroused.

He *still* was.

My mind was quick to push past everything, seizing on the knowledge that this was *something* to work with. Perhaps there was still a chance—a small one. Physical intimacy was only part of a seduction. It was everything else that would be damn near impossible now—forging a friendship, learning what he liked and disliked so I could mold myself into what he wanted, gaining his trust and then his heart.

My stomach churned. *Molding myself into what he wanted.* When I was younger, there had been a time that I hadn't questioned any part of my duty or what it entailed. I was young then and wanted nothing more than to save my kingdom.

Now, every part of me chaffed at the idea of becoming someone else to gain the love of another. If that was what it took to make someone fall in love, then I didn't think I wanted anything to do with it.

But this wasn't about me. It never had been. This was about the Nates and the Ellies and everyone else who would continue to suffer. I needed to remember that.

"Did you forget to breathe?" the Primal asked softly.

Possibly.

I exhaled raggedly as I opened my eyes, my lungs burning and white spots blinking in and out of my vision. I needed to think. He'd come for me. That had to mean something.

He shifted his stance behind me, the slight movement sending a shiver of awareness through me.

There was no way I could think with him holding me so closely. "Let me go."

"I don't think so."

I bit back a retort that surely would not help me. "Please?"

A deep chuckle rumbled out of him and through me. My eyes widened at the sensation. "You saying please makes me warier of letting you go."

My hands opened and closed. "You're a Primal. I can't hurt you."

"Do you think I'm incapable of feeling pain because I'm a Primal?" His cheek dragged against mine, sending a shiver across my skin. "If so, your assumption would be incorrect."

My gaze dropped to the floor. "I wouldn't be able to seriously hurt you."

"True." He didn't relax his hold. "But I don't for one second believe that piece of knowledge would stop you from trying yet again."

It wouldn't. Except attempting to harm him again wouldn't further my duty one bit. "I'm not going to do anything. I promise."

"That sounds about as likely as a cave cat not clawing through the skin of the hand that attempts to pet it."

I inhaled sharply and then jerked at the sensation of those coarse hairs against my breasts. "Are you afraid of me, then?"

"A little."

I let out a rough, biting laugh. "Nyktos? The Primal of Death, afraid of a mortal girl?"

His breath teased my jaw. "I am not foolish enough to underestimate a mortal, female or not. Especially after what I just saw you do," he said. "And don't call me that."

I frowned. "Nyktos? That's your name."

"I am not that to you."

I wasn't sure if I was supposed to be offended by that or not, but whatever. Calling him Ash was far easier than using the name that meant death.

My gaze skipped over the floor to where his arms were folded across my chest. His skin tone was several shades deeper than mine in the sunlight, and smooth under the dusting of hair. "You don't have scales for flesh."

"What?"

Tavius's taunt still echoed in my thoughts as I closed my eyes, and I felt my control slip once more, letting out something other than anger. It was a rawness that came in a rush. "You rejected me."

His hold loosened.

"And worse yet, you didn't even realize who I was, did you?" I said, not faking the hoarseness in my voice. I wished that was an act.

A wake of tingles erupted as Nyktos' arms slid away from me. Warm air rolled over my back and shoulders. "I always knew who you were."

My eyes flew open, and I turned to face him. "You did?"

Quicksilver eyes fixed on mine. "I knew who you were when I stopped you from getting yourself killed when you went after those gods."

He…he'd known and hadn't said anything? He knew and appeared surprised by my anger?

"You knew who I was *then* and said nothing? You knew the night we found that body and didn't say a word? And the night at the lake?" A tremor worked its way through me. "You knew *then* and didn't tell me what the name Ash was short for?"

He bit his lower lip as he glanced at the still-impaled body. "I have a feeling if I answer that question honestly, you will be inclined to go back on your promise."

"I'm already halfway there," I snapped before I could stop myself. I stepped forward, lowering my voice. "*You* made a deal. *You* didn't fulfill it, *Ash*."

His jaw locked as his gaze returned to mine. "Why do you think I'm here now?"

Chapter 21

Why do you think I'm here now?

I opened my mouth, but no words came out. The floor felt like it was trembling under me again. It took several moments for me to fully register what he'd said. What it could mean. "You…you are here to fulfill the deal?"

"What other choice do we have?" Ash stated. "I cannot leave you here, not after this." He extended his arm to Tavius's slumped body. "Princess or Consort, you murdered an heir apparent King."

I blinked. "You were getting ready to kill him."

"I was." He looked back at me. "But I am a Primal. Your mortal laws regarding killing pieces of shit men do not apply to me. You wanted his death." His silver eyes brightened. "I do not doubt for one second that you earned it."

I had. Many times over. But… "You're only fulfilling the deal so I don't face the executioner's block?"

"Is that now just occurring to you?" His brows furrowed as incredulity crept into his tone. "Wait. It is. Do you not value your life at all?"

I didn't even bother answering that.

Barely leashed anger simmered beneath his skin. "You killed him believing that I would leave you to face the consequences?"

"I'm sorry, but why would I believe anything else? You refused to hold up the end of the deal you made."

"You have no idea what you're talking about."

A harsh laugh burst from me. "I know exactly what I'm talking about. I was ready to uphold the end of the bargain my forefather made. It was you who failed to do so. But it is the—" I stopped myself before I revealed my knowledge that the deal he'd made came with a time limit. If he realized that I knew that, he could discover that I knew even more. I forced the next words out. "It is I who paid for it."

That muscle in his jaw ticked. "How exactly have you paid for it, *Princess*?" he challenged, and my spine stiffened. "You were given back your life, were you not? Your freedom to choose what to do and not do with it. Something I already know you value very highly."

I gaped at him, heart skipping and then speeding up. "Do you really need to ask that question?"

His head jerked stiffly toward Tavius's body and then slowly turned back to me. The eather whirled in his eyes. "How have you paid?"

There was no way in the entire vast kingdom I would speak to him of how my life had been. That I would ever peel back my skin like that and expose all those raw nerves. Maybe I already had based on the way he eyed me as if he were trying to pry his way into my thoughts.

"What led to *this*?" He took a measured step forward. "What did they do to you?"

His question pierced the chaotic storm of emotions. The sticky embarrassment that always accompanied thoughts of my family surged through me, and *that* was a blessing. It was familiar. Grounding. I latched onto it, finding Sir Holland's instructions. I went through the steps until I no longer felt coated in shame, no longer felt as if I were about to suffocate.

"Impressive," Ash murmured.

I stared at him. "What is?"

"You."

My lip curled. Empty flattery was the last thing I needed. "You were…you were never going to come for me." I already knew this, but having it confirmed was an entirely different thing. "Were you?"

"What I said three years ago has not changed," he replied flatly. "What has is the situation. I will fulfill the deal now and take you as my Consort."

My brows flew up. "You couldn't sound less enthused if you tried."

Ash said nothing.

It shouldn't matter. All that did was that he was taking me as his Consort. That gave me a real opening. A chance. It gave the kingdom a real chance, but my mouth…gods, I had no control over it, and this was *insulting*. "And what if I don't want to be your Consort?"

"It doesn't matter what either of us wants now, *liessa*. This is the hand we've been dealt," he said. "And we must go with it. I will not leave you here to be executed."

I drew back in disbelief. "Am I supposed to be grateful for that?"

Ash smirked. "I wouldn't dare ask for your gratitude. Not when this was inevitable. It was bound to happen one way or another."

"Because you caused this!" I nearly shrieked. "You made the deal—"

"And I am here to honor it!" Ash shouted, startling me. His eyes were like pure chunks of ice. "There is no other choice. Not for you. Not now. Even if you managed to escape punishment for what happened here, I staked my claim on you in front of others. That will spread, eventually reaching the attention of the gods and other Primals. They will become curious about you. They may even believe you hold some sort of sway over me. They will use you, and whatever ways you have paid these past three years will pale in comparison to what they will do."

I have plenty of enemies.

I clearly remembered him saying that. So many questions rose. I wanted to know more about these enemies—what exactly made them opponents. I wanted to know why they would want to sway him—what they hoped to gain from the Primal of Death. I really wanted to know who was bold enough to attempt to incite his anger. I had a lot of questions, but none of that mattered.

Neither did his reasons for deciding to finally fulfill the deal. I had insulted Tavius's fragile ego, but mine was no better.

It could be pity or empathy, lust or a situation out of his control. The *why* behind it didn't matter. The only thing that did was Lasania. I looked away from him, my gaze briefly falling on Tavius. I closed my eyes. What was I doing standing here arguing with him? That surely wouldn't aid me in earning his affections and saving Lasania.

A sharp twist went through my chest. *End him.* I couldn't stop it. The memory of how I felt sitting beside him at the lake resurfaced. The way he made me smile—made me laugh. How easy it had been to talk to him. The twisting motion intensified, settling in my throat. I thrust all of that aside and made myself see the Coupers, all of them, lying side by side in bed together. I held onto that image as I exhaled roughly, opening my eyes.

Ash was watching me. Neither of us said anything for a long moment and then he spoke. "Choice ends today. And for that, I am sorry."

I curved my arms around my waist, unsettled for a multitude of reasons. He genuinely sounded sorry, and I didn't understand. We were in this situation because of the deal he made.

Everything I had to do and would have to do was because of what he chose.

I watched him extend a hand toward me, and the urge to take flight hit me hard. "I…I want to say goodbye to my family."

"No," he refused. "We leave now."

Stubbornness dug in. "Why can't I say goodbye?"

His cold stare held mine. "Because if I see the woman who may be your mother again, I am likely to kill her for pleading for that shit's life."

I sucked in a surprised breath. There was no mistaking the truth of his words. He *would* kill her, and a dark, savage part of me wanted to see it.

There was something so very wrong with me.

"Will my family know that I am with you?" I asked.

Ash nodded. "They will be advised."

Unfolding my arms, my hand trembled as I placed it in his. A static charge danced between our palms as his hand closed firmly around mine.

Air lodged in my throat as a white mist seeped over the floor, heavy enough to obscure the cracks in the tile. The mist churned the edges of my night rail. Ash stepped into me, and the tendrils thickened. His thighs brushed mine, and the scent of citrus lingered on my breath.

His gaze caught and held mine as the tips of his fingers touched my cheek. The mist grew, slipping over my legs, my hips. As much as I tried to fight it, panic cut through me as it glided over our hands, the feel of it cool and silky.

"This may sting a little," he said, the silver of his eyes beginning to swirl, to mix with the mist—with the power. "For that, I'm also sorry."

There was no chance to ask what he meant or to struggle. The mist swallowed us, and a sharp, burning sting swept from the tips of my toes to the springy curls that had slipped free. Silvery-white light flashed before my eyes and behind them, and then I was falling.

I came aware, all my senses firing at once. I was astride a horse, seated sidesaddle, and the entire side of my body was nestled against the hard, cool length of Ash. My cheek rested on his shoulder, and every breath tasted of citrus and fresh mountain air. For a moment, I could almost pretend that this was a normal embrace. That the strong arm around my waist holding me so carefully and tightly was because I was wanted. Cherished.

But I was never good at pretending.

I started to sit straight.

"Careful." Ash's voice was like smoke in my ear, his arm tightening around my waist. "It's a long fall from Odin."

My gaze lowered, and I felt my stomach drop. The sable-black steed was several feet taller than any horse I'd ever seen. A fall would surely break bones or worse. I shifted, frowning when something soft glided over my once bare arms. A black cloak had been draped over me.

"Saion found the cloak," Ash answered my unspoken question. "Not sure where he got it, and I decided that neither of us probably wanted to know. But he figured you'd be more comfortable with it."

Curling numb fingers around the edges of the soft cloak, I lifted my gaze to the heavy canopy of tree limbs I'd recognize anywhere.

"We're in the Dark Elms," I said, throat and mouth feeling as if they were full of tufts of wool.

"We are." His breath stirred the top of my head. "I expected you would be asleep for far longer. You shouldn't have awakened until we were in the Shadowlands."

I looked at him then, his features cast in shadows as we passed under the canopy of branches. "What did you do?"

"The mist? It's eather. Basically an extension of our being and will. It can have a certain effect on mortals if we allow it. In your case, making you sleep," he explained. "I didn't want to draw any more unnecessary attention."

"What kind of effect does the mist have on others?"

"It can kill them within seconds if that is our will."

Swallowing hard, I realized that I was holding myself stiff and straight as a board. I thought of Ezra, Marisol, and Sir Holland—wherever he may be. "You said that other gods could learn of you coming for me. Will my family be okay?"

"They should be," he answered. "Once you are introduced as my Consort, only the most foolish of gods would go after your family, as they would become an extension of mine."

That wasn't exactly reassuring. *Breathe in.* Ezra was smart. So was my mother.

"Saion or Ector will warn them though, or already have," he added. "And there are…certain steps that will be taken just in case. Wards they will be left behind."

"Wards?"

"Spells fueled by Primal magic that will block gods from entering their homes." He shifted slightly, and a moment passed. "I will make sure they are safe, even if I don't feel they deserve it."

My gaze cut to his as a feeling of gratitude swelled. I didn't want to feel that. "Ezra—my stepsister. She's good. She deserves it."

"I'll have to take your word for that."

In the silence that fell between us, the many questions I had rose again as I stared at the Dark Elms. "How did you know what was happening?" I asked, feeling my cheeks warm. "How did you know to come?" *Why did you finally come?* I didn't ask that because I didn't need to know.

He didn't answer for a long moment. "I knew you had been hurt."

My brows puckered as I glanced back at him. "How?" Then it struck me. "The deal?"

"Partly."

A prickly sensation swept over me when he didn't elaborate. "Partly?"

"The deal linked us on a basic level. I knew when you were born. If you were ever seriously injured or close to death, I would know."

"That's…kind of creepy."

"Then you're sure to find the next part even more so," he told me.

"Can't wait to hear it," I muttered.

A hint of a smile appeared as he glanced down at me. "Your blood."

"My blood?"

He nodded. "I tasted your blood, *liessa.* It wasn't intentional, but it has come in handy."

It took me a moment to remember the night in the vine tunnel when he'd nipped my lip. "My blood lets you feel my emotions when I'm not around you?"

There was a tightening in his expression. "Only if they're extreme. And what you felt was extreme."

Uneasy, I turned back around. Had it been the pain? Or the panic from when I was held down? Or had it been that ancient, icy-hot thing inside me? I didn't like knowing that he had felt any of that. I also didn't like this stupid sidesaddle position. Leaning back, I lifted my right leg and swung it over to the other side of Odin. The act caused an ache in my shoulders and upper back, reminding me that the skin was very tender there. Ash's arm tightened as I squirmed my way until I was facing forward.

"Comfortable?" he asked, the one word thick and heavy.

"Yes," I snapped.

He chuckled.

I gripped the saddle's pommel to keep myself from turning around and doing something reckless. Say, punching a Primal who had turned a mortal to *dust* with a single look for example. "Why are we in the woods?"

"You cannot travel where we're going through an opening in the realms," he answered, and I became aware of where his hand now rested on my hip. His thumb…it moved like it had the night by the lake, in slow, idle circles.

"Doing so would rip a mortal apart," he continued, and that managed to shift my focus from his thumb. "We will have to enter another way."

The only sound when the Primal fell silent was Odin's hooves upon the ground. No birdsong. Just like the night at the lake when there had been no signs of life. It was as if the animals had sensed what I hadn't realized. That death was among them.

After what I had seen, I didn't think I could forget that again. But that damn thumb of his was still drawing small circles, over and over. Even through the cloak and night rail, I felt the coolness of his skin. I didn't understand why his skin was so cold or how his touch could still make *my* skin feel so warm. Hot, even. "Why is your skin so cold?"

"What do you think death feels like, *liessa*?"

My heart lurched as I stared ahead. This wasn't the god Ash, who had teased and touched me by the lake. This was the Primal of Death, who had set all of this in motion along with the Golden King. I couldn't forget that.

"You are surprisingly…amiable at the moment," Ash observed.

I glanced back at him. "It probably won't last."

Another faint smile appeared. "I didn't think it would." He guided the horse around an outcropping of boulders. "You're still angry with me."

It would be wise to lie. To tell him that all was forgiven. That was what I had been taught. To be submissive. Never challenging. Become what he desired. Vocalizing my anger wouldn't help, but my thoughts were far too scattered to formulate a plan, let alone behave as if I weren't furious that he hadn't told me who he really was and that he never planned to fulfill the deal. That I wasn't confused as to why he'd even intervened today.

"Why?" I demanded. "Why didn't you tell me who you really were at the lake? Why did you lie?"

"I didn't lie." His gaze cut to me. "Some do call me Ash. Not once did I say I was a god or deny that I was a Primal. That was your assumption."

"A lie by omission is still a lie," I argued, fully aware of the fact that my anger was utterly hypocritical since I was also omitting a whole hell of a lot. Like, for example, what I planned to do.

Ash said nothing.

And that didn't help. "We talked. We *shared* things about ourselves." A bit of warmth crept into my face. "There was time. You should've told me before I—"

"Before you told me to kiss you?" His breath touched my cheek, startling me.

"That was not what I was going to say." I was totally going to say that.

The rumble of his low laugh came then. "If you realized who I was, would you still have been so…interested?"

My head snapped in his direction, and I sucked in air as I felt his cool breath dance across my lips. Our faces were so close, our mouths lined up in a way where if either of us moved half an inch, they would meet.

I would've been more interested, but for all the wrong reasons. Or the right ones. Whatever. My gaze flicked to his mouth. A heightened, heated edginess swept over me. His thumb moved at my hip, and warmth spread there. That warmth and electric edginess had felt *right* before—welcomed and full of anticipation. Of heated, sensual promise.

And it still did, but I didn't think that it should, knowing what I could and would do with it—how I planned to use it.

I turned my head away, my chest and stomach twisting. For some reason, I thought of the first night I'd been taken to the Shadow Temple. When I had soaked in that scented bath for hours and then had the hair removed from places I never even considered before. It was almost as if what I had been expected to do hadn't become a reality until that very moment. Not even the time spent with the Mistresses of the Jade had truly prepared me for the fact that weakening the Primal called for a level of seduction. And it had only been after the hair had been stripped, and the balm applied to soothe the sting that it had struck me that I would have to be naked with the Primal of Death. No horrendous wedding gown. No tunic or tights. Not even a dagger. There would be no shields, and that…that had terrified me. In the time since, whenever I allowed myself to be someone, anyone else while in The Luxe, I was never completely nude. And maybe being so exposed still terrified me. But I had been nude with him in the lake. And outside of it? I might as well have been.

In the entire time spent preparing for this very moment, the time when he claimed me, I'd never once considered that I might actually enjoy the seduction. I hadn't believed the Mistresses when they'd said that I could. Not because I didn't think I would find pleasure in such intimacy, but because I didn't believe I could find pleasure seducing the Primal that I needed to kill.

The heat in my veins now told me that I most likely would. And that had to be wrong. Twisted, even. Monstrous. But this was partly his doing. He'd made this deal. He'd known that it came with an expiration date. He'd shown no sign of compassion toward the mortals who were now suffering because of it. Pressure clamped down on me again just as the twinkling surface of the lake appeared between the trees, and the sound of rushing water greeted us.

I sat straighter. "Why are we at my lake?"

"Your lake?" He laughed again, still low but longer this time. "Interesting that you feel a sense of…ownership to this lake. Is it because of how it made you feel?" Odin carried us past the last stand of trees. "How did you describe it? Calming?" There was a pause. "Perhaps at home?"

I clamped my mouth shut and said nothing as we neared the shore.

His grip tightened on Odin's reins. "You do know what covers the floor of this lake."

"Shadowstone," I whispered, my stomach beginning to tumble.

"This is the only place in the mortal realm where you'll find shadowstone. There's a reason for that." His chest brushed my shoulder and arm, and I tensed. "There's a reason mortals fear these woods. Why spirits haunt them."

My gaze swept over the water pouring from the rocks and the ripples cascading across the lake.

"Perhaps there's even a reason you never feared them." His breath was against my cheek again, and the beat of my heart skipped and then sped up. "Why you felt so *calm* here."

"What are you saying?" I whispered.

"There are ways to travel to Iliseeum. One is to travel east—far east until we cross not only the Skotos Mountains but even farther to where mortals believe the world simply ceases." He shifted Odin's reins into my numb hands. "That would take far too long. There are quicker ways, through what one would consider gateways. Only those from Iliseeum know how to find and reveal them. Use them. Each gateway can take one into a certain part of Iliseeum. Your lake is a gateway to the Shadowlands."

To him.

A shiver erupted over my skin as I stared at the dark waters.

Ash lifted his hand, and everything stopped. Froze. The water spilling over the rocks halted, suspended in the air. The ripples ceased, and my heart could have, too.

My hands slipped from the pommel as the lake…split in half, peeling back and exposing the flat, glossy shadowstone bottom. In the moonlight, a fissure appeared in the stone. Wisps of silvery-white mist seeped from the crack, and without a sound, a wide and deep rift appeared.

I'd been in this lake hundreds of times throughout my life, splashing and playing as a child, hiding and forgetting. This lake, the water and the land around it, *had* felt like home. And the whole time, *this* was what existed under the surface. This was what *my* lake was.

Ash's fingers brushed mine as he nudged Odin forward. The horse followed, whinnying softly.

"You're right, you know? There was time at the lake to make sure you knew who I really was. I should have told you." His arm curled at my waist, and he tugged me back. I didn't fight him. I pressed against him, my heart careening.

A white haze swirled around Odin's legs as he took us into the misty rapture. Another shudder rocked me. I didn't know if it was the descent or the Primal's words. "But you spoke with no fear. You acted fearlessly. Each time I saw you," he continued. "You interested me, and I hadn't expected that. I didn't want that. But at that lake, you were just Seraphena," he said, and my breath snagged at the sound of my name spilling from his lips. It was the first time he'd said it. "And I was just Ash. There was no deal. No perceived obligations. You stayed simply because you wanted to. I stayed only because I wanted to. You let me touch you because that was what you wanted, not because you felt as if you had to. Maybe I should've told you, but I was…enjoying myself with you. I wasn't ready for that to end."

And then he took me into the Shadowlands.

Chapter 22

What Ash admitted, the truth of what he said, was swept into air that was neither warm nor freezing. Into the complete and total darkness that swallowed us.

Lightheaded and dizzy, I feared I would never see again. I reached down as I strained against the unyielding wall that was Ash's chest. It caused the rawness along my back to ache as I clasped his arm. I couldn't see. I couldn't see anything—

A tiny pinprick of light appeared above, then another and another until hundreds of thousands of specks of light cascaded over the sky.

Stars.

They were stars, but not like the ones in the mortal realm. They were more vivid and radiant, casting a silvery glow that was far more powerful than the moon. I scanned the skies, searching and searching.

"Where is the moon?" I asked hoarsely.

"There is no moon," Ash answered. "It is not night."

My brows snapped together as I took in the sky that very much resembled night. "Is it day?"

"It is neither day nor night." The arm around my waist loosened. "It just is."

I didn't understand as Odin traveled forward, each step clanging off cobblestone. I looked down, spying fingers of mist trailing softly over the road. I returned my stare to the sky. The longer I looked at it, the more I realized it didn't resemble a night sky. Yes, there were stars, and they were brighter than anything I'd seen, but the sky was more…shadowy than black. Darker than the stormiest, most overcast day in the mortal realm. It reminded me of the moments before dawn, when the sun rose behind the moon and beat back the darkness, turning the world a shade of iron.

"Is there no sun?" I asked, wetting my lips.

"Not in the Shadowlands."

Barely able to comprehend that I was actually in the Shadowlands, I wasn't sure what to do with the knowledge of there being no sun or moon. "Then how do you know when to sleep?"

"You sleep when you're tired."

He stated this as if sleeping were that simple. "What about the rest of Iliseeum?"

"The rest of Iliseeum appears as it should," he answered flatly.

I wanted to ask why and what that meant, but the barren landscape changed. Tall trees appeared, and as we traveled, they grew closer and closer to the road. Bare, twisted trees that were nothing more than skeletons. Several large, rocky hills loomed ahead, spaced around the road we traveled on.

Uncertainty beat at me, along with all those messy emotions I couldn't describe. But so did curiosity. The part of me that had always yearned to know what Iliseeum looked like stirred. I started to lean forward but stopped and forced my body to relax against his.

Putting space between was the exact opposite of what one did when they wanted to seduce another. I looked down at the arm held firmly around me. And despite how cool his skin was, the feel of him was…pleasant.

A deep, chuffing sound jerked my head up. One of the hills *shuddered* and rose. That was no hill ahead of us. My mouth dropped open. Wings swept out and then up into the starry sky. The ground around us trembled, scattering what was left of the mist as something thick and spiked swept across the road. My gaze followed the sidewinding *tail* to the creature that was at least twice Odin's size.

Black and gray under the starlight, it stood on four muscular legs as it shook its great body, sending a fine layer of dirt into the air. Spikes traveled from the tail and along the thick scales of its back, some as small as my fist, others the size of several hands in length. The creature twisted sharply, faster than I would've ever anticipated something that size to move, turning its long, graceful neck in our direction.

Air thinned with each breath. I choked on a scream that never made it past my throat as a massive talon landed in the center of the road, claws wide and sharp. A moment later, the frilled head was directly in front of us—a head nearly half the size of Odin's body.

I fell back against Ash, staring at it—at the flat, broad nose and wide jaw, the pointed horns that sat upon its head like a crown, and eyes that were such a vibrant shade of red, they contrasted sharply with the pitch-black, thin, vertical pupil.

I knew what I was staring at. I'd read about them in dusty, heavy tomes. I knew what purpose they served. They were the guardians of Iliseeum. I knew they were real, but I couldn't believe I was actually seeing one—couldn't believe I was face to face with a *dragon.*

A very large dragon with gray and black scales and many, many teeth. It leaned in even closer, its nostrils flaring as it appeared to sniff the air—sniff *us.*

"It's okay," Ash told me, and I realized I was once again clutching his arm. "Nektas won't harm you. He's just curious."

Just curious?

I flinched as the dragon's hot breath lifted the hair around my face.

Nektas let out a soft purring sound as he tilted his head even closer and then lowered it so it was only inches above Odin's mane.

"I think he wants you to pet him," Ash said.

"What?" I whispered.

"It's his way of knowing you mean him no harm," he explained, and I wondered exactly how in the two realms I could ever be a threat to this creature. "And him allowing it is how he shows you that he won't hurt you."

"I believe you—him." I swallowed.

The dragon made that low trilling sound again.

"Where's all that bravery?" Ash asked.

"My bravery ends when I'm faced with something that can swallow me whole."

Nektas puffed out a hot breath as he cocked his head.

"He's hurt that you would think he'd do such a thing," Ash observed. "Besides, I don't think he can swallow you whole."

My mouth dried as I continued staring at the beast. He was beautiful and terrifying, and I didn't know if any mortal alive today had seen one. I swallowed again, slowly easing my grip on Ash's arm. My breath caught in my throat as I reached out.

If he bit my hand off, I would be so very disappointed.

Nektas vibrated with sound once more. The very tips of my

fingers touched his flesh. I pressed lightly, surprised to find that his bumpy scales felt like smooth leather. I petted his nose rather awkwardly. The dragon made a chuffing sound again, this time sounding very much like a laugh.

Pulling his head back, Nektas's gaze focused over my shoulder and then he turned. The ground trembled as he pushed off his hind legs. Air whipped around us as powerful, clawed wings swept back. He lifted into the sky with a shocking surge, rising fast.

"See?" Ash held Odin's reins tightly. "He will not harm you."

I touched a dragon.

That was all I could think.

"You can lower your hand now." Amusement danced in his tone.

Blinking, I pulled my hand to my chest. "It's a dragon," I murmured.

"*He's* a draken," he corrected as Nektas flew ahead. "They are all draken."

They? Draken? The remaining hills weren't hills, either. They shuddered and lifted their diamond-shaped heads to the sky, tracking Nektas. Wings unfurled against the ground, stirring dirt and dust as they rose, stretching their necks. They were smaller than Nektas, their scales a shimmering onyx in the starlight, but no less powerful as they pushed off their hind legs and launched into the sky.

"You…you have four…draken protecting you?" I asked, my stomach sinking. It wasn't like I'd forgotten who the Primals' guards were. But seeing it was a shock.

Ash nudged Odin forward. "I do."

I watched the three others join Nektas, their wings sweeping gracefully through the sky. "And they have names?"

"Orphine, Ehthawn, and Crolee," he answered. "Orphine and Ehthawn are twins. I believe Crolee is their distant cousin."

"You call them draken?" I asked. "How is that any different from a dragon?"

"Very different."

I waited. "Please tell me you're going to explain further."

"I am. Just thinking of a way to make it less confusing," he said, that thumb of his beginning to move again. "Dragons were very old creatures. Very powerful. Some believe they even existed in both realms long before gods and mortals did."

"I…I didn't know that."

"You wouldn't," he said. "A long time ago, a very powerful Primal befriended the dragons, despite being unable to communicate with them. He wanted to learn their stories, their histories, and being quite young at the time, he was rather…impulsive in his actions. He knew one way he could talk to them was to give them a godly form—a dual life. One where they could shift between that of a dragon and a godly form."

This young Primal he spoke of had to be Kolis. That was the only Primal who could create any form of life. "They can…they can look like you and me?"

"For the most part," he confirmed. I really wanted to know what he meant by that. "Those who chose to take the dual life were called draken."

"Are there any dragons left? Ones that don't shift?"

"Sadly, no. Dragons and draken live for an extraordinarily long time, but their ancestors went extinct quite some time ago." His thumb moved in that slow, idle circle again. "They weren't the only ones this young Primal gave a dual life to."

I thought of the creatures I'd once heard of that lived in the sea off the coast of Iliseeum. I had so many additional questions, but they fell to the wayside as I saw what the draken were flying towards.

A torch-lit wall appeared below, tall as the inner wall of Wayfair, but the castle I had grown up in paled in comparison to what sat atop a gently rolling hill. A massive, sprawling structure that was as wide as it was tall. Turrets and towers stretched high into the sky, and the entire palace was star-kissed, glittering as if a thousand lamps had been lit. It reminded me of the Shadow Temple but was far larger.

A heavily wooded area pressed against the back of the palace walls and beyond them, as far as I could see, were specks of light too numerous to count. A city—there was a *city*.

My pulse galloped as we rode down the hill. Tiny balls of dread and anticipation formed in my stomach as we drew close to the gated wall. I was stuck in a chasm of apprehension and something akin to curiosity but stronger.

"That is…that is your home?" The air seemed thinner, and I wasn't sure if it was my imagination or not as I saw the draken circling the palace.

"It is known as the House of Haides. The wall surrounding it is called the Rise," he told me. "It encompasses both Haides and the city of Lethe, up to the Black Bay."

Ahead, the trees still encased the road, but more of the wall became visible, as did the gate. There was something on the wall—several somethings I couldn't make out. We rounded a slight bend in the road. The wall also appeared to be made of shadowstone, the surface not nearly as glossy or smooth. Instead of reflecting the starlight, it seemed to swallow any and all light, which was what made those shapes so difficult to discern until the massive, iron gate silently began to open.

My gaze crept over the wall, over the shapes, and I started to feel lightheaded. The shapes on the wall were that of a cross. My breathing was too shallow, even though my chest heaved with each breath.

They were *people*.

People stripped bare and impaled on the wall with some sort of stakes through their hands and chests. Their heads hung limply, and the stench of death filled the air.

Bile climbed my throat as my grip tightened on the pommel. "Why?" I whispered. "Why are those people on the wall?"

"They are gods," Ash answered, his voice flat and as cold as the waters of the lake. "And they serve as a reminder for all."

"Of what?"

"That life for any being is as fragile as the flame of a candle—easily extinguished and stamped out."

Two of the draken circling the palace descended on either side of the gate, stirring up a gust of wind. They landed on the Rise. Neither the shuddering impact nor the deep, rumbling sound they made penetrated the horror of what I'd seen on the Rise.

I sat in stunned silence as I saw men—men *and* women in black and gray armor—along the Rise, stop and bow deeply as Ash rode past. But I barely saw them. Barely saw the numerous balconies and spiraling outdoor staircases that seemed to connect every floor of the palace to the ground.

Ash had gods impaled to his wall.

The cruelty and inhumanity of that and his words left me numb and confused as we entered the brightly lit stables. For someone who'd once said that every death should leave a mark, his actions told a different story.

A man approached from one of the stables, bowing before taking Odin's reins. If he spoke, I didn't hear him. If he looked up at us, I didn't see it.

I felt like I might be sick.

I didn't protest when Ash dismounted first and lifted his hands to help me down. I barely felt the touch of his hand on my lower back or the soft straw under my feet as he led me outside and toward a side entrance to the castle, tucked behind a staircase.

The windowless door opened to reveal a man with golden-red hair and the same rich, wheatish skin tone. He looked at me with dark brown eyes—eyes that carried a silvery glow behind the pupils. A god. Those luminous eyes shifted to Ash and then back at me. "I have so many questions."

"I'm sure you do," Ash answered dryly, looking down at me. "This is Rhain. He's one of my guards. Like Ector and Saion."

I forced my lips to move as I looked up into Rhain's dark eyes. "I'm—"

"I know who you are," Rhain said, startling me. He raised a brow at Ash. "Which is why I have so many questions. But I know. They have to wait." He paused as Ash guided me into a shadowy interior stairwell. "Theon and Lailah are inside," the god added quietly as he followed us.

Ash sighed. "Of course." He stopped in the narrow space, facing me. "I'd hoped there'd be time before anyone realized you were here. Very few people have…known of you. The ones you're about to meet, don't. And I'm sure they will have questions, too."

"Most definitely," Rhain agreed.

"Questions that will mostly go unanswered," Ash stressed, shooting the god a look. "You will be introduced as my Consort, and that is all. Okay?"

Any other time, I would have asked many questions. Instead, I nodded. My hands were trembling slightly as Ash reached around me and pushed open a second door.

The unexpected, intense light caused me to take a step back. I blinked until my eyes adjusted. The light was as bright as sunshine, and for a moment, I thought it had been Ash glowing again with power. But it wasn't.

I looked up at a glittering chandelier of cascading glass candles hanging in the center of an entryway. There was no flame. The candles glowed a bright yellow, nonetheless, as did the sconces on black pillars that stretched upward onto the second floor.

"It's Primal energy," Ash explained, seeing what I stared at. "It powers the lighting throughout the palace and Lethe."

Speechless, I dragged my eyes from the lights. A curved staircase sat on each side of the space, facing one another. Their railings and steps were carved from shadowstone. Beyond the staircases and through a wide, sharply pointed archway was an expansive room.

"Come." Ash nudged me forward, and I took a tiny step when two people drifted out from the room and walked under the arch.

What I saw stopped me from moving another step and had me really considering if I had, perhaps, unintentionally smoked the White Horse.

A tall male and female stood before me, dressed in the same clothing style as Ash, except their silver-brocaded tunics were long-sleeved. The male wore his hair in neat, braided rows along his scalp, and the female's was braided straight back and cascaded beyond her shoulders. They were of the same height and shared the same rich black complexion and wide-set, golden eyes. Their features were nearly identical. The male's brow was broader, and the cheekbones on the female were more angular, but it was clear they were twins. I'd never seen twins before—not even fraternal twins—but it wasn't them I stared at.

There was…a purplish-black, winged creature about the height of a medium-sized dog beside them, flapping its leathery wings as it nudged the female's hand with its head.

They stopped when they saw me.

I knew my mouth was hanging open. I couldn't close it because there was a tiny draken standing between them.

"Hello." The female drew the word out as her widened eyes flicked to Ash. "Your Highness?"

Ash's hand remained on my lower back. "Theon. Lailah. This is Sera. She is a guest."

"I sort of figured she was a guest," Theon remarked. "Or at least I hoped you didn't decide to start following the family tradition of kidnapping mortal girls."

Wait. *What*?

Ash's jaw hardened. "Unlike some, nothing about that is appealing to me."

"Is she a *special* friend?" Lailah asked.

"Actually, yes. She is…" He seemed to take a deep breath and prepare himself. "She is to be my Consort."

The two stared at us.

Several long moments stretched while the small draken's head swung side to side.

"I have a question," Lailah announced as she scratched the draken under the chin. The creature let out a trilling purr. "Well, I have several questions, starting with why does *your* Consort look like she was thrown from the mortal realm into ours?"

Did I look *that* unkempt? I glanced down at myself. The hem of my cloak ended at my calves, exposing blood-stained feet. Through the halves of the cloak, the night rail hung limply. I didn't even want to know what my hair looked like or what might cover my face.

"I didn't throw her into this realm," Ash grumbled. "There was an incident before we arrived here."

"What kind of incident?" Rhain asked from where he leaned against one of the pillars.

"One that is no longer an issue."

Interest sparked in Lailah's eyes. "Do tell."

"Maybe later," Ash answered.

Her brother now raised a hand. "I have questions, too."

"And I don't care," Ash replied. Rhain coughed under his breath. "Do you two have nothing to do? If not, I am sure there is plenty you could be doing."

"Actually, we were about to take little Reaver-Butt here out for some airtime." Lailah grinned as the draken let out a squawk of agreement.

"The draken's name is Reaver-Butt?" I blurted.

Lailah laughed softly as she sent me a quick smile. "His name is Reaver," she said, and he hopped on his hind legs. "But I like to add the *butt* part. He seems to enjoy it, too."

"Oh," I whispered, fingers itching to reach out and pet the small draken. At this size, it was nowhere near as frightening as Nektas.

"Then why don't you two get on with that?" Ash suggested.

Grinning, Theon bowed his head. "As you wish." His sister joined him, strolling forward. As he neared me, the god bowed once more and spoke, lowering his voice. "Blink twice if you have been kidnapped."

Lailah grinned and sent Ash a long, sideways look. "Or just blink."

I *almost* blinked because it was clear they were teasing Ash—a Primal who had gods strung up on the walls outside his palace.

"Go," Ash ordered, and I turned as they moved on, my attention focused on the small draken teetering on Lailah's shoulder.

"That's a baby draken," I said.

Ash looked down at me. "Draken don't hatch the size of Nektas, and Reaver would be highly annoyed if he heard you refer to him as a baby."

"I would hope not, considering that would be one hell of a large egg," I retorted. "I just…" I trailed off, shaking my head and folding my arms over my waist. I felt like my head was going to explode.

"Seeing any draken, large or small, must be a shock," Rhain commented, and I peeked over at him. His golden-red hair was a flame against the darkness of the pillar. "I imagine it will continue to be a shock for some time."

I nodded tentatively. "I think it will be."

The god smiled faintly.

Ash shifted so he halfway blocked Rhain. "Why are you still here?" he demanded of the god.

"I figured since Saion wasn't here, I would undertake the honor of annoying you," he replied, his tone flat.

The Primal let out a low rumble of warning. My breath caught. Rhain had to know about the gods on the Rise, as did the twins. Would any of them really want to annoy Ash?

"I actually have a valid reason for hanging around. I need to talk with you." Rhain pushed off the pillar as I peeked around Ash. His face was set in taut, drawn lines. "It's important."

And, obviously, it was also something he didn't want to speak about in front of me.

Which was annoying.

Ash nodded and looked down at me, about to speak, but he narrowed his eyes. He moved quickly, folding his hand over my biceps. I jerked at the contact. He turned my arm slightly. "What caused this bruise? I meant to ask about it earlier."

"What?"

"This bruise. It's an older one," he stated, and I looked at my arm. *Tavius.* Gods. I'd forgotten about him and the bowl of dates. "How did this happen?"

"I walked into something." I tugged on my hand.

"You don't strike me as the type to walk into things."

"How would you know?" I demanded, pulling on my arm again.

Ash lowered his chin. "Because you've appeared very sure-footed and precise in your movements."

"That doesn't mean I don't have moments of clumsiness."

"Really?" He held on for a moment longer but then let go.

I folded my arm back to my waist. "Really."

"This is entertaining," Rhain commented.

Ignoring the god, Ash's piercing stare remained fixed on me. "You must have walked into it pretty hard to create that bruise."

"Must have," I muttered, nervously taking in the large entryway. There were no statues, no banners or paintings. The walls were as bare as the floor, cold and desolate.

And this was to be my…home? For how long?

As long as it took.

A bone-deep weariness settled into me, and I became aware of the ache in my temples, which seemed to match the steady throbbing in my shoulders and back. I had no idea if my legs had felt this weak for a while, or if that was something new. It took everything in me to remain standing.

"Hey." Ash's fingers pressed under my chin, startling me.

"What?"

"I asked if you were hungry." His gaze searched mine intently. "You must not have heard me."

Was I hungry? I wasn't sure. I shook my head.

His regard was so singularly focused on me that I wondered if he could see beyond the surface. "How is your back feeling?"

"Okay."

He continued staring and then nodded as he hooked a finger around a wayward curl that had fallen forward before carefully tucking it back. The tender act reminded me of the lake, and I didn't understand how his touch could be so gentle when he impaled gods on the Rise.

Ash tilted his head back and then turned to the archway. "Aios?"

I turned as a woman stepped out from beyond the archway. I blinked, yet again feeling as if I were hallucinating. She was…good gods, she was *beautiful.* Her face was heart-shaped, eyes a bright citrine with thick lashes, plump lips, and high and full cheeks. She crossed into the entryway, smoothing several strands of vibrant red hair back behind an ear before clasping her hands over the midsection of a long-sleeved, gray gown cinched at the waist with a silver chain.

Aios stopped before us, bowing slightly. "Yes?"

"Can you please show Sera to her room and make sure she has

food sent to her and a bath readied?" Ash asked.

The desire to tell him that he didn't need to speak for me died on the tip of my tongue. He'd said "please" to who I assumed was a god. But maybe she was a household servant of some sort. To many, the use of the word seemed like a common courtesy, but growing up around nobles and the wealthy, I knew that too few ever spoke it. And I honestly didn't expect it to come from the lips of someone who had impaled gods on his wall as a horrific warning.

Then again, I would never have expected such a sight from Ash.

"Of course. I'll be happy to." Aios turned to me. She blinked rapidly and then her expression cleared. "Yes. Definitely a bath."

My lips pursed, but before I could say a word, she hooked an arm through mine. The same strange jolt of energy nearly overshadowed the ease with which she touched me.

Aios's brows lifted as her gaze flew to the Primal. "Nyktos…"

"I know," he said, and he sounded weary. I glanced at Ash, wanting to hear what he *knew*, but he spoke first. "I'll return to you in a little bit. You can trust Aios."

I didn't trust any of them, but I nodded. The sooner I was alone to think, the better. Surely, this ache in my temples would fade by then. Ash remained there for a moment, his eyes deepening to the shade of a thundercloud. He turned stiffly, joining Rhain. They headed beyond the archway.

"Come," Aios insisted softly, leading me toward the staircase.

The stone of the steps was cool under my feet as we climbed and then headed to our left.

"The room has been readied for you. Well, it's been ready for quite some time and dusted frequently just in case. I think you will find it most pleasing," she said, and my head jerked to hers. She appeared as if she were my age, but I knew that could be incredibly misleading. "It has its own adjoining bathing chamber and balcony. It's quite a handsome room."

Several things occurred to me at once. "How did you know I was coming?"

Aios's gaze flicked away from me. "Well, I didn't know for sure. I just knew there was a chance."

For her to have expected me, she must have some knowledge of the history. "You knew about the deal?"

"I did," she said, smiling brightly as she ushered me beyond a second flight of stairs.

"Can you tell me how long you knew there was a chance?"

"A couple of years," she announced as if that meant nothing, but it said a whole hell of a lot.

We continued to the fourth floor. From there, she steered me toward a wide hall lit by sconces with frosted glass globes. The walls were otherwise bare.

We passed a set of black-painted double doors with some kind of silver, swirling design etched into the center. Aios stopped at the next set of double doors, ones that were identical to the only other set I could see in the entire hall.

"Are there no other rooms on this floor beside the one we passed?" I asked as she fished a key from the pocket of her gown.

"There is only one room in the other wing, but most guests stay on the third or second floors." She unlocked the door, and I glanced over my shoulder at the doors down the hall.

"What about the staff—you?"

A look of confusion briefly pinched her striking features. "I am not staff."

"I'm sorry." I could feel my face reddening. "I just assumed—"

"It's okay. Anyone would assume that. There is no staff."

"Well, now I'm confused," I admitted.

A faint smile appeared. "There are those of us who help out because we choose to. We've sort of…forced our assistance upon Nyktos," she said, and it was a little jarring to hear her use his real name. "Otherwise, Haides would be a mess, and he would probably never eat."

I could only stare.

"Anyway, I tend to be around during the day." She laughed. "I know. It doesn't look like day outside, but you'll see that the skies do tend to darken as the hours pass."

"Wait." I needed to make sense of this. "You help, acting as household staff by choice, but you're not paid?"

"We don't need to be paid. Nyktos provides for those who see to Haides' functionality. Actually," she said, her brow pinching, "everyone you will come across here and in Lethe are well provided for, even if they do have more official responsibilities."

"Well provided for?" I repeated those words as if they were a language I didn't understand.

"Shelter. Food," she said, lips parting as if she wished to add more to the list but then changed her mind. Her smile turned a bit brittle.

"But to answer your other question, no one else lives here."

"Not even the god downstairs? Rhain?"

"No, he has a home in Lethe."

"What about the men and women near the wall—I mean, the Rise? The draken?"

"The guards? They have their own quarters—a dormitory of sorts between here and Lethe," she explained, gripping the handle. "The draken also have homes."

Only Ash lived in this enormous palace? Normally, the core staff and a set of guards resided within a residence. "Why does no one else live here?"

Aios's smile finally faded away. "It wouldn't be safe for them to do so."

Chapter 23

Icy fingers trailed down my spine. "What do you mean by it wouldn't be safe?"

"Well, Nyktos wouldn't want—" Aios's eyes widened as she twisted toward me. "I'm sorry. I just realized how that sounded." She laughed, but there was a nervous quality to it. "You see, all manner of people need to speak with His Highness, and some of them can be a bit…unpredictable. Of course, you are completely safe here."

"Really?" I said doubtfully.

She nodded emphatically. "Yes. It's just that Nyktos likes his privacy, and it's…it's better this way." Turning back to the door, she pushed one side open and then motioned me inside before disappearing into the darkness.

I didn't believe for one second that she had misspoken, but I took a tentative step inside as light appeared from another stunning, glass chandelier hanging from the center of a *massive* space.

A couch, a settee, and two armchairs in what appeared to be a lush, cream velvet were on one side of the room. A small, circular, low-to-the-floor table sat in the middle of the sitting area. Behind it, near curtained doors, was a table with two high-back chairs and a clear vase full of some kind of blue and gray stones. A chaise was positioned in front of an enormous fireplace, and it looked as if it were made of the finest, luxurious material dyed to a shade of ivory. A plush rug sat under the chaise. There was even a basket full of rolled blankets.

I turned slowly, my heart dropping upon seeing a four-poster, canopied bed that would've made Ezra's appear fit for a child. The room had a large wardrobe against the wall by a window. There were three more sets of double doors: one beyond the sitting area, a set near the table, and another past the bed.

"This is my room?" I asked.

Aios nodded as she walked toward the nightstand. She twisted a switch on a lamp. "Yes. Is it not suitable? If not, I'm sure—"

"No, it's fine. It's more than fine." It was unbelievable. My mother's private quarters weren't even this size.

"Perfect." She breezed past the bed. "You'll see a switch on the wall by the doors. That controls the ceiling light. The rest of the lights can be turned on and off by just twisting the switch. Your bathing chamber is here. Come. Have a look."

I followed her in a daze. Aios flicked another of those wall switches. Light flooded the space, and I thought I might faint.

My bathing chamber at Wayfair had the barest necessities—a toilet, sink, and a small copper tub barely big enough for me to sit in. That was it. This was…extraordinary.

The claw-foot tub was large enough for two fully grown adults to stretch their legs and arms. There was not one but two standing mirrors, one on the other side of the tub, and another beside the vanity. The space was spotless and smelled like lemons.

"What do you think? Is it suitable?"

Shaking my head, I turned back to the main room. Ten of my old bedchambers could fit in this space, and there'd still be room leftover. For some inane reason, the back of my throat burned. "This is more than suitable."

"Good." Aios swept out of the bathing chamber, stopping beside me. Her head tilted. "Are you all right?"

"Yeah. Yes." I cleared my throat.

She hesitated for a moment and then glided toward the doors near the table. "Through here, you can access the balcony. It's rather large, and there is a seating area outside. I would suggest keeping the doors closed when you rest. The temperature doesn't change a lot, but colder winds do come in from the mountains sometimes."

Mountains?

"Would you like a fire started?" she asked.

"No-no, thank you."

"If you change your mind at any point, all you need to do is pull on the rope by the door, and someone will answer." Aios tied back the curtains on the bed, revealing several furs and a small heap of pillows. "What would you like to eat? Two cooks come by daily. Arik and Valrie are both amazing. There's nothing too small or too large for them."

"I…I don't know," I admitted, for once having no idea what I wanted to eat.

A small smile returned. "How about I have them whip you up a small plate of soup and bread?"

"That sounds okay."

"Perfect. I will have hot water brought up for you, and…" She pressed a forefinger to her lips. "Is it safe to assume that you didn't bring any clothing with you?"

"It's safe to assume that." I toyed with the fold of the cloak.

"Well, that won't do. I'll see what I can scrounge up for you."

"Thank you."

"Is there anything else you need at the moment?"

I started to say no. "Wait. Where do those doors lead?" I pointed at the ones behind the sitting area.

"To the chambers next door," she answered. "To Nyktos' rooms."

My heart leapt somewhere unconnected to my body. "His rooms are adjoined with mine?"

"They are."

That made sense. I *was* his Consort.

Aios lingered near the door, one hand toying with the chain of her necklace. "I don't know the circumstances that led to your arrival, but what I do know is that I trust no one in either realm more than Nyktos, nor would I feel safer anywhere else," she said, and her gaze met mine. Her eyes were *haunted* in a way that reminded me of the woman who had been standing outside with Nor. "I just thought you should know that."

I watched her slip from the room. I didn't know how long I stood there. It could have been a minute or five. When I started walking toward the curtained doors, I wasn't even sure why.

Tugging aside the wispy white drapes, I pushed open the glass doors and stepped out. The space was large. A wide, deep-seated chair sat near the railing, along with a daybed. There were no winding staircases, no way down from here except for a long fall. But the balcony was connected to the one next door.

To Ash's bedchamber. There was a similar chair on his, and I wondered if he ever sat out here.

I wondered why he'd put me in the room next to his.

A cool breeze lifted the pale strands of my hair as I crept between the lounges. Goosebumps spread across my flesh. I stared up and out, placing my hands on the railing. The stone was smooth and cold under my palms and I saw the twinkling lights of the city, and beyond, the distant rocky domes and cliffs encased in mist…or clouds. Were there even clouds here? I looked down and gasped.

Color.

I saw *color.*

Beyond the washed-out courtyard, there were trees. Hundreds of them. Thousands of them grew between the palace and the glittering lights of Lethe, and they were nothing like the ones I had seen on the road into the Shadowlands. Their trunks were gray, as were the twisted, sweeping branches, but their limbs weren't bare. These were full of heart-shaped leaves.

Leaves the color of blood.

Aios returned rather quickly with food and the first article of clothing she had managed to obtain. It was a belted robe made of chenille or some other soft material I'd never owned before. She hung that on one of the hooks inside the bathing chamber.

Turned out, I *was* hungry, managing to devour the soup and several chunks of the toasted, garlicky, and buttery bread before the man I'd seen in the stables arrived with several pails of steaming-hot water. He introduced himself as Baines, and he hadn't gotten close enough for me to see his eyes, but I assumed that he too was a god. Several pitchers of water sat on the floor while Aios dropped some sort of frothing salt into the tub that smelled of lemon and sugar.

Once more alone, I made my way into the bathing chamber. Aios had turned off the overhead light, leaving only the sconces on. The soft glow was more than enough to see myself in one of the standing mirrors.

No wonder Lailah had asked if I had been thrown into this realm.

Specks of dried blood dotted my face, mixing with the freckles. Both stood out starkly on my pale skin. There were also streaks of red in my hair, half of which had escaped its braid and now hung in tangles. My eyes appeared too wide. The green too bright. I looked feverish.

Or terrified.

I didn't know if I felt that. If I felt anything as I let the cloak fall to the floor. My lip curled at the sight of my night rail. It was more red than white. There would be no salvaging it. I carefully pulled it over my head, wincing at the movement. Dropping the ruined garment, I scooped the braid and the loose strands of my hair over my shoulder as I turned halfway in the mirror.

"Gods," I hissed at the ropey, raised streaks across my upper back. They were an angry shade of pinkish-red. Blood had beaded along one of the stripes.

I really wished I could've carved Tavius's heart out.

The utter lack of remorse I felt for what I'd done to my stepbrother should've concerned me as I stepped into the tub, but it didn't. I'd do it again because not even the near-scalding water could erase the suffocating memory of his breath against my cheek.

I eased into the deep tub, air hissing between my teeth as the lemony-scented water touched the edges of the wounds the whip had left behind. Closing my eyes and clenching my jaw, I slowly lifted my fingers from the sides of the tub and began unwinding the braid. Picking up the bar of soap, I began scrubbing at my skin and then did my best to reach the raised welts on my back as my thoughts tiptoed their way through the events of the last two days. Using my gift to bring Marisol back seemed like it'd happened a lifetime ago. I still couldn't believe that King Ernald was dead. The man had been healthy as far as I knew. I hoped Ezra was okay, and I hoped she listened to me. And my mother? She would remain Queen unless Ezra married. But she was probably relieved. I was sure that Ezra was, too, knowing there was a chance for the Rot to be stopped. And I…I wished I had my dagger. Ash had taken it. Would he give it back? So caught up in my thoughts, I didn't realize that anyone had entered the bedchamber until I heard the steps outside the bathing room door.

Weaponless, I twisted just enough to see who had intruded as I reached for the sides of the tub. My heart thumped heavily at the sight of who stood there.

The Primal.

He said nothing as he stared, his silvery eyes unnaturally bright as he looked at my back. His chest rose with a sharp breath. "I cannot wait to pay that bastard a visit in the Abyss."

Air slowly left my lungs, and I placed the soap in the small caddy on a nearby bench, letting my hands fall into the water. "Is that where he is?"

"Yes."

"Good."

His head tilted to the side, and a long moment passed. "I didn't mean to interrupt. I thought you'd be finished with your bath."

I forced myself to relax. "You're not interrupting."

"I'm not?" His brows rose.

"No."

"You're bathing," he replied. "Are you not worried about me spying upon your…*unmentionables*?"

A dry laugh left me. "You saw far more at the lake than you can see now."

"True." His lashes lowered halfway as he drew his bottom lip between his teeth. "I brought something for your back that should help with the wounds." There was a pause as he lifted a hand to reveal that he held a jar containing some kind of white cream. "This will ease whatever pain they may be causing and ensure they don't scar."

"Thank you," I murmured, the words sounding strange on my tongue. I didn't say them often. I didn't have a reason to say them often.

Ash said nothing, but he didn't move from where he stood. He didn't look away, and I wasn't sure if it was the water or his regard that made me feel overheated. Finally, he spoke. "I can help you with the ointment once you've finished your bath."

I tilted, letting the strands of my hair fall forward to float on the surface of the water. There hadn't been nearly enough time to decide how I would go about fulfilling my duty, but I had enough sense to recognize the interest in Ash's stare. The why behind the fact that he lingered instead of leaving. "I need to wash my hair, and then I'll be done."

"Do you need help?"

His offer surprised me. The word *no* rose so quickly, I almost spoke it. I nodded instead.

Ash pushed away from the doorway, placing the jar on a shelf just inside the bathing chamber. He came forward, lowering to his knees behind the tub. Brushing his hair behind an ear, his gaze flicked up from my back to my face. "How bad does it hurt?"

I swallowed. "Not that much."

"You lie so prettily," he murmured. "So easily."

Facing forward, I drew in a deep breath. "It could've been worse."

"We will have to disagree on that." The tips of his fingers brushed the curve of my arm, sending a tight shiver of energy over my skin. He gathered my hair, pulling the strands away from my shoulders. "Tip your head back."

Glancing down at the soapy water, my breath caught. The tips of my breasts were clearly visible, and as close as he was, as tall as he would be even on his knees, I knew they were also visible to him.

The Primal of Death.

Who was about to wash my hair.

"Sera?" he said softly, his breath against the top of my head.

Another shiver curled its way through me at the sound of my name. I tipped my head back, thoughts racing too fast to really make much sense of them.

Ash picked up one of the pitchers, slowly pouring the water over the lengths of my hair. "I have some questions for you."

"I too have questions." My heart was beating too fast again as I sat there, struck by the instinct carved into me that demanded that I seize this moment and use it to my benefit. The other half simply had no idea what to do. A part of me was utterly bewildered by this act, transfixed by it. No one had ever done this. Not since I was a child, and Odetta had washed my hair.

"I'm sure you do." His hand curled around the nape of my neck, supporting my head. "I'll start first. What has your life been like these last three years?"

His question caused me to squirm. "The kind of life any Princess lives."

"I do not believe that for one second. You are quite confident with a dagger and sword for a Princess."

"I thought we already established that you don't know many Princesses," I retorted.

"I know enough to know that most wouldn't fight a Hunter without fear or even know how to. Someone trained you," he said, wetting the strands on the back of my head.

"I was trained," I admitted, knowing that if I lied, it would be even more obvious that I had something to hide.

"With what weapons?"

"All of them."

"Why?"

"My family wanted to make sure that I could defend myself."

"You didn't have Royal Guards to do that?" he asked. "Tip your head back a little bit farther."

"No one wants to rely on guards. They wanted to make sure I stayed alive to fulfill the deal." To keep my balance, I lifted my arms and rested them on the sides of the tub. My back arched as I tilted my head back more.

"Perfect. That's…perfect," he said, his voice rougher as water cascaded over the rest of my hair. "Who trained you?"

"A knight." Every part of my body became aware of the water slipping farther down my breasts to lap at my ribcage. "It's my turn to ask a question."

"Go ahead." Ash shifted forward, the coolness of his body pressing against my back. The rosy-pink skin at the tips of my breasts tingled.

This did not feel like those times Odetta had washed my hair. At all. My eyes drifted shut. "Did you really believe that I had simply gone about my life and forgot the deal?"

"That's what I hoped." Ash sat the pitcher aside to pick up one of the bottles from the caddy.

Irritation spiked. "Did it never occur to you that I hadn't, considering you were summoned three more times?" I asked.

"What do you mean?"

The confusion in his voice made it even harder to rein in my temper. "You were summoned three times since the…" Realization flickered through me. I started to face him.

"Don't move," he ordered.

I halted, not because he'd commanded it but because that roughness had returned to his voice. Opening my eyes, I turned my head just enough to see the heat of his gaze scorching the skin of my chest. My pulse skittered as I fought to gather my thoughts. "The Shadow Priests didn't summon you?"

"Why would they? They knew my decision just as you did. If you came back, they would've either ignored the request or humored you by pretending to summon me." He began working the soap through my hair. "But why would you or your family even attempt to summon me again?"

A prickly sensation blistered my skin as I realized I'd exposed a rather shameful secret with my questions. "I…I didn't tell anyone what you said to me that night."

The Primal was silent.

"I was surprised and disappointed." I managed a partial truth. "And…and too embarrassed to tell them you rejected me."

"It wasn't personal."

"Really?" I sucked in a laugh.

"It wasn't." He was careful not to tug on my scalp as he continued working the vanilla-scented cleanser through the strands. "You have beautiful hair. It's like spun moonlight. Stunning."

"I think I will cut it all off."

Ash chuckled. "You would, wouldn't you?"

I didn't respond, my eyes drifting closed as his fingers massaged the strands and my scalp. Somehow, the touch eased the muscles in my neck. "You're good at this. Do you often wash others' hair?"

"This would be my first."

"Mine, too," I admitted in a whisper, and I felt his hands still for a moment before returning to his gentle scrubbing. In the pleasant haze of his ministrations, something he said tugged at my memories. My suspicions of his experience resurfaced, but so did what he'd said about his age—about how he was younger than I would expect.

"There are some things we need to discuss once you're settled," he said before I could ask about his age. "But there's something I want to make clear. You didn't do anything wrong to cause me not to fulfill the deal."

I opened my eyes. "Because you changed your mind and simply had no need of a Consort?"

"Especially not one who stabs me," he remarked.

I frowned at the hint of teasing in his voice. "Are you going to bring that up continuously?"

"Every chance I get."

"Great," I muttered, rolling my eyes despite the rising curiosity. "Now I wish I'd stabbed you harder."

"That's rude."

"Some would consider leaving your Consort to be abandoned on a throne for three years rude," I retorted. "But what do I know?"

Ash laughed, the sound low and smoky.

My eyes narrowed. "I'm not sure what I said that could be funny to you."

"You didn't say anything funny." He eased his fingers from my hair. "It's just that you are very…outspoken. And I find that—"

"If you say '*amusing*'…" I warned.

"Interesting," he answered. "I find you interesting." His head tilted, causing several strands of hair to fall over his cheek. "And unexpected. You're not as I remember."

"You weren't around me long enough to know who I was or what I'm like," I said.

"What I felt when I saw you seated on that throne in that dress told me enough."

I stiffened. "I hated that dress with every fiber of my being."

"I know," he said. "Close your eyes. I'm going to rinse your hair."

I did as he asked as the pitcher scraped against the stone floor. "What do you mean, you know? And what exactly about me sitting on that throne and in that dress told you anything about me?"

"It told me that you appeared willing to be packaged and presented to a stranger," he said as he began rinsing the soap from my hair. "It told me that you seemed eager to be given away, even though you likely had no say in it. No choice."

I inhaled swiftly, hating that what he said was exactly how I appeared. "You could've looked upon me and seen someone brave enough to fulfil a deal I never had a say in."

"I saw that, too." He lifted the strands of my hair, rinsing them clean of soap. "I knew you were brave. I knew you must be honorable."

My stomach churned. Honorable. What honor lay in what I must do? There was…and there wasn't.

"But that was not what I felt when I looked upon you," he continued. "What I sensed, what I tasted in the back of my throat, was the bitterness of fear. The tanginess of anguish and hopelessness. And the saltiness of determination and resolve. That was what I felt when I saw you. A girl who was barely a woman, forced to fulfil a promise she never agreed to. I knew you did not want to be there."

The accuracy of his words rattled every part of me, including that place that had been relieved when he refused. But there was no way he could've known that. "You could tell all of that from looking at me for a handful of moments?" I forced out a laugh. "Come on."

"Yes." His fingers wove through the strands, working at the soap. "I felt all of that."

"You have no idea what I was feeling—"

"Actually, I do. I know exactly what you were feeling then and what you're feeling now. Your anger is hot and acidic, but your disbelief is cool and tarty, reminding me of iced lemon. There is something else," he said as my heart stuttered, and my eyes opened. "Not fear. I can't quite place it, but I can *taste* it. I can taste your emotions. Not all Primals can do it, but I have always been able to, as all who carried my mother's blood in them could."

Chapter 24

My hands slipped from the tub to the cooling water as my heart thundered. "Really?" I whispered.

"Yes."

I sucked in several breaths. "You can tell what I'm feeling?"

"Right now, it's just disbelief."

"That…" I was glad I was sitting down. "That seems like a really intrusive ability."

"It is," he agreed, placing the pitcher aside. He didn't move. Neither did I. "That's why I rarely intentionally use it. But, sometimes, a mortal or even a god feels something so strongly, I cannot prevent myself from feeling what they do. That is what happened when I looked at you. Your emotions reached me before I could block them. I knew that as willing as you appeared, you were not."

What did you do, Sera?

My mother's panicked cry echoed. I closed my eyes as harsh realization swept through me. Sir Holland was wrong. My mother had been right. That insidious voice inside me had been right. It *had* been my fault.

Pressure constricted my chest and throat as I shook my head. No. That wasn't true, either. It wasn't only my fault. I opened my eyes. "I was…scared. I was to marry the Primal of Death," I said, my voice hoarse. "I was anxious. Of course, I felt hopeless. I felt like I had no control. But I was there. I was *still* there." None of that was a lie. "I knew what was expected of me, and I was willing to fulfill it. You were not."

He was quiet, but I felt his gaze on me—on my back. "No, I wasn't. I had no need of a Consort forced to marry me. And whether or not you were willing to carry through doesn't change the fact that it wasn't your choice. It never was."

"It *is* my choice to honor the deal," I argued.

"Truly?" he challenged. "Your family would've allowed you to refuse to take part in the deal? To refuse a Primal? Are you saying that you were in a position to refuse? One where the expectation hadn't been drilled into you since birth? There was never any consent in your choice."

Gods, he was right. I knew that. I had always known that. I hadn't expected him, of all people, to acknowledge or care about that, though, especially since it had been the deal *he'd* made. But that didn't change anything. Not what the deal did for the kingdom, not what my birth signaled, or what I must do.

I opened my mouth and then closed it as a different type of emotion reared its head. Respect. For him. For the being I needed to kill to save my kingdom, and for the Primal who had unintentionally become the source of my misery. How could I *not* respect him for being unwilling to take part in something I truly had no real choice in?

Confusion also followed because had he not considered any of this when he first set the terms? He could have set any price. He'd chosen this.

Another thought occurred to me, and my head jerked up so fast, it tugged on the skin of my upper back. "Are you reading my emotions now?"

"No," he answered. "And that is the truth. I know to keep my…walls up around you."

I wasn't sure if he was suggesting that I was highly emotional. Regardless, I was grateful he had his… "What do you mean by *walls*?"

"It's like the Rise around Haides and the lands but in here." He tapped a finger on the side of my head. "You build them mentally. They are shields of sorts."

"That sounds…difficult."

"It took a very long time to learn how to do it."

"There's something I don't understand," I said after a moment. "Why did you even ask for a Consort? When you made the deal, you could've asked for anything."

"The answer you seek is a very complicated one."

"Are you suggesting that I'm not clever enough to understand?"

"I'm suggesting it's a conversation that should take place when you're fully clothed."

"And you don't run the risk of me attempting to drown you?" I snapped.

Ash chuckled as he wrung the excess water from my hair. "That, too." Using one of the pins I'd removed, he twisted the length of my hair, pinning it so the ends didn't fall back into the tub. "I hope my services this evening lived up to whatever expectations you may have had."

Immediately, my mind flashed to a different sort of *service*, and I wanted to punch myself. Hard. "They were passable."

My response got another laugh from him. "If you're done," he said, rising. "I can put the balm on your wounds."

I was still dumbfounded by his ability to read emotions—still irritated by his refusal to answer why he had asked for a Consort. But I gripped the edges of the tub. Water splashed as I rose and turned to where he stood.

His chest was so still, I wasn't sure he breathed, but the white, luminous wisps in his molten silver eyes churned wildly. The intensity of his stare scalded.

Attraction. Desire. He was definitely attracted to me. He wanted me. I reminded myself that was something I could definitely work with. "I'm wet."

"Fuck," he rasped, his gaze tracking the droplets of water as they coursed over my breasts, the curve of my stomach, and headed lower still, between my thighs.

My skin tingled everywhere his gaze followed. "Can you help me with that?"

The tips of his fangs became visible as his lips parted. "Trouble," he murmured thickly. "You are trouble, *liessa*."

Something beautiful and powerful…

I couldn't help but feel that way as I stood there. "A towel," I said, chasing away some lingering drops of water just below my navel with my hand. "I was hoping you could hand me that towel."

One side of his lips tipped up as his stare followed my hand. "Yeah." He reached out without taking his eyes off me and grabbed a towel from the shelf. "I can help you."

Heart thrumming once more, I stepped out of the tub. I tipped my head back as he approached. Ash said nothing as I reached for the towel.

"No," he said, his chin lowering. "You asked for my help."

Wordless, I remained standing as he drew the towel along my left arm and then my right, fully aware that he was staring down at me. Heaviness filled my breasts as he dragged the towel over my stomach, where my hand had been, and then over my hip. My skin felt as it had when I'd sunk into the steaming tub, except this heat invaded my blood and pooled.

"I'm not sure you will appreciate what I'm about to say. I wouldn't blame you if you didn't," he said. "At least now, I know what you feel when I touch you." He smoothed the towel up my stomach and between my breasts. The hair on his arm grazed the insides of my breasts, causing me to gasp. "That sound you make? It's not forced."

It wasn't.

The tips of his fangs dragged over his lower lip as he moved the towel over the aching peaks. I jerked at the sharp swirl of pleasure I felt. "You don't let me do this because it is your duty. What is expected of you." He moved around me, swiping the towel over my back, careful to avoid the welts. "You allow me to touch you because you enjoy it."

And that was true. It shouldn't be. I shouldn't enjoy any of this. I should remain removed from this part of my duty. Calculating. But there was no denying the tight tremor of *anticipation* coiling its way through me. There was no denying that I desperately wanted to *feel.* Like I had at the lake when I was just Sera, and he was simply Ash—just like he'd said earlier. "Are you reading my emotions?"

"I don't need to." The soft towel rasped over my lower back. "I can tell by the flush on your skin and how it…hardens in the most interesting places. The hitch of your breath, and the way your pulse quickens."

"My pulse?" I whispered, legs strangely weak.

"Yes." His cool breath danced over my bare shoulder. "I can feel that. It's something that even a god can feel. It is a…predatory trait."

I shivered in response to his words and where the towel now roamed, following the curve of my backside. My skin practically vibrated as that curl of anticipation coiled tighter, this time below my navel and then again even lower.

"You want my touch." He guided the towel down my legs and then back up between them. His breath now touched my lower back. My eyes closed, but my mind provided the image of what I could not see—the Primal of Death kneeling behind me. "And that want?" His towel-covered hand slipped between my thighs, gliding over the throbbing flesh between them. Another ragged sound left me as his hand moved back and forth, gently rubbing. "It has nothing to do with any deal."

It really didn't.

"And what…what does that—?" I gasped as the cool skin of his arm brushed my heated, not even remotely *dry* flesh. "What does that change? You said you still have no need of a Consort."

"I don't." He moved that damnable towel away from me, sliding it over my side and then between the crease of skin at the hip. He rose as the towel slipped between my thighs once more. I shuddered at the feel of the cold skin of his forearm pressing against my lower stomach. He moved the towel in soft, short circles. "But that doesn't mean I am not interested in certain aspects of this union." The cool tips of his fingers grazed my arm as he stepped closer to me, near enough that I felt his breeches-clad thighs against the backs of mine. "Just like that doesn't mean you're not interested in those very same aspects."

The utter arrogance in his confident assumption irked me—and emboldened me. "There is very little about those aspects I find all that interesting."

"You don't?" The towel-covered hand continued moving slowly, tauntingly.

"No." My hips jerked and then started to move, following his lead. *His lead.* Gods, it should concern me how quickly I'd lost control of this seduction. It would. But later.

"I think you lie again," he murmured, a hint of a smile in his tone. "You're as interested as you were when you begged me to kiss you at the lake."

"Your memory is faulty. I gave you permission to kiss me."

His fingers grazed the side of my breast as he moved his hand up and down my arm while moving the towel between my legs. "Or demanded that I kiss you."

"Either way, that is not begging."

"Semantics," he murmured.

"It's not." I widened my stance, giving him better access.

"Really?"

"Really." My eyes drifted open, and I looked down, past the puckered peaks of my breasts to where he had the towel snagged around the wrist of his hand.

"Lying so prettily, yet again."

"I'm not lying. You're just overconfident—" I gasped as he dropped the towel, and the cool length of his fingers replaced the soft material, pressing against my bundle of nerves. "Gods," I breathed, immediately swamped by a riot of sensations as the tension curled so tightly, I felt breathless.

"No," he murmured, his thumb swirling against that sensitive nub. "You are not interested at all in those certain aspects." He sank a finger inside, parting the flesh.

I cried out, grasping his arm. I hadn't forgotten the shocking contradiction of his coldness against my heat, but no memory did it justice. I shook.

"I remember how you showed me the way you like it. I play that over and over in my head. I could write a fucking tome on it by now." His thumb continued moving. "When I'm fisting my cock, I remember how you held my hand against you at the lake."

"Oh, gods," I gasped. "Do you…do you really?"

"More times than I should admit." His finger pumped in and out of me, bringing me closer and closer to the edge.

Suddenly, all that curling tension unfurled as fast and unexpectedly as a streak of lightning. It came on hard and fast and shockingly. If he hadn't folded his other arm around my waist, there was a good chance the pounding waves of release would've taken my legs out from under me.

Ash's fingers slowed, and only when my hips stopped twitching did he ease his hand from me. Several long moments passed as he simply held me there, our bodies only touching from the waist down. Neither of us spoke, and I had no idea what he was thinking, but as my body cooled, I realized that my attempt to seduce him had failed spectacularly. I had been the one seduced.

I sat on the bed, facing the closed balcony doors as the top of the robe I held closed pooled at my elbows.

Ash walked forward, unscrewing the lid on the jar he'd brought with him. "This will probably feel cold against your skin at first," he said, sitting behind me. "And then it will have a numbing effect."

I nodded, feeling off-kilter from what had transpired in the bathing chamber. He'd walked away before I even had a chance to regain control of the situation, the sign of his arousal a thick, hard ridge pressing against his breeches as he unhooked the robe and handed it to me. His restraint when it came to his pleasure was quite impressive.

The touch of his fingers brushing some of the curls that had fallen free from their twist aside steered my mind to the present. A spicy and astringent scent reached me. "What is this ointment made of?"

"Yarrow, arnica, and a few things native to Iliseeum," he told me. I sucked in a sharp breath as the salve touched one of the wounds. "Sorry."

"It's okay." I lowered my chin. "It doesn't hurt. It's just cold."

His hand moved, spreading the balm over my skin. He didn't have to do this. He hadn't needed to wash my hair. Both acts were kind but didn't match what he'd done to those gods on the Rise.

Which hadn't stopped me from enjoying his touch. Gods. I *should* feel ashamed, but I didn't. Maybe because my conscious mind recognized that I was destined to do far worse things.

For some reason, as I sat there rather obediently, I remembered what I'd wanted to ask while in the bathing chamber. "How old are you? Really?"

"I thought we already established that my actual age doesn't matter," he said, parroting my words back.

"It didn't when I didn't know who you were."

"I'm still the same person who sat beside you at the lake." His balm-covered fingers slid up my shoulders. "You know that, right?"

Was he? "How would I know that?"

"You should," he answered as the coolness of the ointment started to fade, replaced by the numbness he'd promised.

"We may not be complete strangers, but do we really know each other?" I reasoned. "You talked as if killing should always affect a person, leave a mark that never fades. But you have—" I pressed my lips together. "I don't know you at all."

"You know more than most."

"I doubt that."

"I've never spoken about the first person I killed. Not with anyone but you," he said, his hand leaving my back. I heard the lid turning on the jar. "No one knows it was someone close to me." He took hold of the collar of the robe, lifting it to cover my back and shoulders.

"Nothing I told you at the lake was a lie."

"If everything you said was true, then why do you have gods impaled on your wall?" I demanded, tightening the sash around my waist as I twisted to face him. There was absolutely no pain from the movement. "How can killing leave a mark when you do things like that?"

"You think…?" The white aura behind his pupil bled into the silver. It was a beautiful effect and a slightly terrifying one. "You think I did that to them?"

"When I asked you why, you said they served as a reminder that life is fragile, even for a god."

Disbelief flickered across his features. "How did those words incriminate me?" His expression smoothed out quickly. "Yes, they serve as a warning, but not one I issued."

I stared at him, stunned. Could he be telling the truth? I wasn't sure what he'd gain from lying about it. "If it wasn't you, then who did it?"

The swirling in his eyes abated as he reached out and picked up one of the curls that had fallen over my shoulder. "I am not the only Primal god, *liessa*."

"Who did that, then? Who would be willing to anger the Primal of Death?"

"You have no problem attempting to anger or argue with me."

"I'm not arguing with you now."

One eyebrow rose. "I feel as if every conversation we have verges on an argument when it comes to you."

"It was you who started arguing with me." I watched him. Lashes lowered, he appeared absurdly focused on separating the mass of curls.

One side of his lips curved up as he drew one of the curls straight. "You're arguing with me now."

I threw up my arms. "That's because you're saying—never mind."

Ash released the strand of hair, his faint grin fading as his gaze met mine. "What do you know about the politics of Iliseeum?"

His question threw me. "Not much," I admitted. "I know that Primals rule the Courts, and that gods answer to them."

"Each Court is a territory within Iliseeum with more than enough land for each Primal and their gods to carry out their time as they see fit. And each Primal has more than enough power to do whatever they would like." He rose from the bed and went to the table. There was a decanter there that hadn't been there before, along with two glasses.

"But no matter how powerful any one being is, there are always some who want more power. Where what they have is not enough."

A chill swept down my spine as he pulled the stopper from the decanter. He poured the amber liquid into two short glasses. "And for them, they like to push other Primals. See how far they can go. How much they can push before the other lashes out. In a way, it can be a source of entertainment for them." He carried the glasses over. "Whiskey?"

I took the glass he handed me. "Are you saying that another Primal did that because they were bored?"

"No. That was not done out of boredom." He turned from me, taking a long drink. "That was done to see how far they could push me. Quite a few Primals enjoy…pushing me."

The smoky flavor of the whiskey went down surprisingly smooth. "I know I'm about to sound repetitive, but I cannot understand why anyone would do that. You're the Primal—"

"Of Death. I'm powerful. One of the most powerful. I can kill quicker than most. I can deliver lasting punishment that goes beyond death. I'm feared by mortals, gods, and the Primals, even those who *push*." Ash faced me as he took another drink. "And the reason some push has to do with that question you seem rather obsessed with. Well, one of *two* questions you have asked multiple times. The one with the very complicated answer best not answered while one is bathing."

It took me a moment. "Why you didn't fulfill the deal?"

He nodded. "It's because I did not make the deal."

Shock seized me as I slowly lowered the glass to the bed beside me. "What?"

"It wasn't me. I was not the Primal of Death then." A tightness settled into his features. "My father was. He made the deal with Roderick Mierel. It was he who demanded the first female of the bloodline as a Consort."

Chapter 25

All I could do was stare at Ash as what he said echoed over and over in my head. Denial immediately rose because of what it meant. I wanted to latch onto that denial, but Ash had said at the lake that not all Primals had been the first.

I'd just never thought he was referring to the Primal of Death.

My thoughts whirled. "Your…your father was the Primal of Death? He made the deal?"

"He did." Ash stared down at his nearly empty glass. "My father was many things."

Was.

"And he died?"

"It is not often that a Primal dies. The loss of a being so powerful can create a ripple effect that can even be felt in the mortal realm. Could even set in motion an event that has the potential to unravel the fabric that binds our realms together." He swished the remaining liquid in his glass. "The only way to prevent that from occurring is having their power—their eather—transferred to another who can withstand it." His hand stilled. "That is what happened when my father died. All that was his transferred to me. The Shadowlands. The Court. His responsibilities."

"And me?" I asked hoarsely.

"And the deal he made with Roderick Mierel."

I exhaled roughly as the strangest burst of emotions blasted through me. There was definitely relief because if that deal hadn't transferred to Ash, there would be no way to stop the Rot. But then I realized that if it hadn't transferred, the deal would've been severed in favor of Lasania at the time of the Primal's death. It hadn't. Obviously, it had moved to Ash. And what I felt wasn't relief. It was an emotion I didn't want to acknowledge—and couldn't.

He hooked one leg over the other. "Drink, *liessa*. You look like you need it."

I needed an entire bottle of whiskey to get through this conversation, but I took a healthy swallow. I was surprised that I actually did it. Something occurred to me as I placed the glass on the table. "You said there were Primals younger than some of the gods. You were talking about you, weren't you?" When he nodded, my grip tightened. "Were you…were you even alive when he made the deal?" Immediately, I wished I hadn't asked because if he hadn't been, and he now had to die for something his father did…it made it all the worse.

"I had just gone through the Culling—a certain point in our lives where our body begins to go into maturity, slowing our aging and intensifying our eather. I was…" His lips pursed. "Probably a year or so younger than you are now."

Hearing that he had at least been alive didn't make it better at all. He'd been my age. What he'd said in the Great Hall came back to me. *Choice ends today, and for that, I am sorry.* Gods. It wasn't just the loss of my choice but his, too. He hadn't chosen this. I felt like I would be sick.

His head tilted. "You're surprised?"

I tensed. "Are you reading my emotions?"

"A bit of your shock got through my walls, but they're up." His gaze met mine. "I swear."

I believed him because staying out of my emotions would be a *kind and decent* thing to do.

I took another drink. "Of course, I'm surprised. By a lot. You're really not as old as I thought you were."

A dark eyebrow rose. "Is there a difference between two hundred years and two thousand to a mortal?"

Had he not asked the same while we'd been at the lake? "Yes. As bizarre as that may sound, there is a difference. Two hundred years is a long time, but two thousand is unfathomable."

Ash didn't respond to that, which allowed me time to try and make sense of all of this—of why his father would do this. "Your mother…?"

That eyebrow climbed more. "You say that as if you're not sure that I had one."

"I figured you did."

"Good. I was afraid for a moment that you might believe I was hatched from an egg."

"I really don't know how to respond to that," I muttered. "Were your parents not together?"

"They were."

I opened my mouth, then closed it before trying again. "And did they…like each other?"

His chin lowered. "They loved each other very much, from what I recall."

"Then I'm sure you understand why I'm even more confused that your father would've asked for a *Consort* when he already had one."

"He no longer had one when he made that deal," Ash corrected quietly. "My mother…she died during the birthing."

My lips parted as sorrow rose within me—sadness I didn't want to feel for him. I tried to shut it down, but I couldn't. It sat on my chest like a boulder.

"Don't apologize." He stretched his neck from side to side. "I don't tell you this to make you feel sorry for me."

"I know," I said, clearing my throat. I resisted the urge to ask how they'd died. I wanted to know, but instinct told me the more I knew about their deaths, the harder it would be for me to do what I must. "This is why you never collected on the deal."

"You never consented to it."

The ball of tension inside my chest tightened even further when it should've loosened. As did the knowledge that he hadn't been the one to make the deal that had made me what I was today. A killer. A deal that had taken away every choice I could make. A deal that had set my life on a path that would ultimately end with the loss of my life.

But, gods, I wished he had. Because I could hold onto that. I could convince myself that he was getting what was coming to him. I could justify my actions.

"You didn't consent, either," I stated flatly, looking up at him.

He watched me in that intense way of his. His gaze flicked away. "No, I did not."

I looked down at my drink, no longer feeling as if I would be sick. Instead, I felt like I wanted to cry. And, gods, when had I cried last?

"Do you know why your father asked for a Consort?"

"I have asked that question myself a thousand times." Ash laughed, but there was no humor to the sound. "I have no idea why he did it. Why he would ask for a mortal as a Consort. He died loving my mother. It made no sense."

It really didn't, which made all of this so much more frustrating. "Why didn't you come to me at any point and tell me this?" I asked. It wouldn't have changed anything, but maybe it could have? Perhaps we could have found another way.

"I considered it—more than once—but the less contact I had with you, the better. That is why Lathan often watched over you."

Watched over me? "The one who was killed?"

"He was a…trusted guard," he said, and I caught that he did not refer to him as a friend then. "He knew about the deal my father made, and he knew I had no intention of fulfilling it. But that didn't mean that others wouldn't learn that a mortal had been promised as my Consort. Either because of your family speaking about the deal, or because you were marked at birth, born in a shroud because of the deal."

My breath caught as a shiver danced along the nape of my neck.

"And that mark, while unseen by mortals and most, can be felt at times. That would make some curious about you." Ash drew his booted foot off the table. "It was Lathan who noticed the gods' activity in Lasania— the ones we saw that night."

"The ones that killed the Kazin siblings and the child? Andreia?"

"There was some concern that they may have felt this mark and were searching for it."

My stomach hollowed. "You think they died because of me? Because they were looking for me?"

"At first, possibly." He tapped his fingers on his knee. "But who they killed never really made sense or fit a pattern, other than the possibility that they all might've had a god perched somewhere on their family trees. That's the only thing I could figure out. They weren't true godlings, but they could've been descendants of a god."

"Godlings?" I repeated, brows pinching.

"The offspring of a mortal and a god," he explained. "If a godling then has a child with a mortal, that child would carry some mark upon them, too, but they would not be a godling."

I understood then. Children could be born of a mortal and a god but it was rare—or at least that was what I'd believed. "I haven't heard them called that before."

"It is a term we use. Some of them will have certain godly abilities, depending on how powerful the parentage is. Most godlings live in Iliseeum," he continued, his lips pursed. "Only the seamstress was someone you seemed to have had any contact with. And as far as we know, what was done to her wasn't done to the others."

There was a little relief there. I didn't want their blood on my hands. There was already enough. "The Kazin siblings? Magus? Apparently, he was a guard, but I don't know if I ever saw him or if he was even stationed at Wayfair."

A thoughtful look crept into Ash's face. "Still, if you did not know him nor the seamstress well, I don't see how their deaths are related to you."

I didn't either. But it also seemed…too close to me. "Have you found out anything more related to what was done to Andreia?"

"Nothing. No one has heard of such a thing, even a mortal with the possibility of a god somewhere in their family line. And, yes, I find the lack of information to be beyond frustrating."

It must not be often that a Primal couldn't figure something out. Another thought rose. "Was Lathan mortal?"

The breath Ash let out was long. "He was a godling. I should've corrected your assumption."

But would it have been necessary? Godling or mortal, a life was a life. "How did he die?"

"He tried to stop them." His features were unreadable as he stared out the balcony doors. "He was overpowered and outnumbered. He knew better, but he did it anyway." Ash finished his drink. "Either way, I didn't come to you because I didn't want to risk revealing you to those who would seek to use you."

"Your enemies?" I asked. "Do those gods serve the Court of a Primal who likes to push you?"

"They do."

"But why would any Primal or god believe that what happens to me would sway you?"

"Why wouldn't they? They would not have known my intentions regarding you, especially if they had no knowledge of the deal my father made." His gaze cut to me. "They would have no reason not to believe you were important to me."

He was right.

I realized in that moment that I'd spent a lifetime believing that the Primal of Death was a cold, apathetic being because of what he represented. I'd been wrong. Ash wasn't either of those things. He knew that each death left a mark. He understood the power of choice. I even thought of what Aios had said. That there had to be a reason she felt safe with him and trusted him. Ash cared, and I was willing to bet there was more than one decent bone in his body.

And none of that helped.

At all.

My duty was bigger than me—than what I felt. But it hadn't been him who'd forced that duty upon me.

"Thank you," I whispered, and the words still felt strange on my lips. They hurt a little this time.

His gaze returned to me. "For what?"

I let out a short laugh. "For having that one decent bone in your body."

A faint smiled appeared. "Are you hungry? I know the cooks sent up some soup, but I can have more of whatever you want made."

I wished he'd refuse me food. "I'm fine." I dragged my finger over the beveled edges of the glass. Another question rose from the endless cyclone of them. "Are there any…consequences for you?" A surprising, unwanted and wholly hypocritical dose of concern blossomed within me. "I mean, from what I understand of the deals, they require fulfillment from all parties involved."

"There are no consequences, Sera."

I eyed him. He'd answered without hesitation. Maybe even too quickly, but that wasn't a concern of mine. At all. "How long had Lathan been keeping an eye on me?"

"It wasn't until the last three years, when you were more…active," he told me. "Does it make you angry to know that?"

It was really weird to know that someone had been keeping an eye on me without my knowledge. Of course, I didn't like it, but it wasn't that simple. "I'm not sure," I admitted. "I don't know if I should feel angry or not." However, it did make me think of all the weird and dumb things Lathan could have witnessed. But it made sense that there would've been no need to keep an eye on me before the night of my seventeenth birthday. Before then, I'd only ever left Wayfair to travel into the Dark Elms outside of a few, rare occasions. "Why did you have him do that? You didn't know me. You didn't make the deal. You have no obligation to me."

"That's a good question." Ash's thundercloud-hued eyes drilled into mine. "Maybe if I hadn't, I wouldn't have been there that night to stop you from attacking those gods. They would've killed you. And, perhaps, that would've been a better fate for you."

Ice drenched my skin as he continued holding my stare. Air thinned in my chest.

"Because now here we are. You're in the Shadowlands. And soon, you will be known as the Consort," Ash said. "My enemies will become yours."

Sleep came surprisingly easy after Ash left, leaving me with even more questions. I expected to do nothing but lay in bed and dwell on everything he'd shared, but either I was exhausted, or I simply wanted to escape everything I'd discovered. I slept deeply, and it felt like a long time before I woke. I had no idea how many hours had passed. The sky was the same shade of gray, still full of stars, but a dull twinge had taken up residence in my upper shoulders. When I checked them in the standing mirror, the wounds appeared significantly less red and swollen. Whatever was in that balm Ash had used was a miracle.

Cinching the sash on my robe, I walked to the balcony doors and opened them. The gray sky was full of stars and no clouds as I walked to the railing overlooking the canopy of blood-colored leaves and the twinkling lights of the city beyond.

I'd learned so much that my thoughts raced from one thing to the next, but they kept coming back around.

Ash hadn't made the deal.

Sucking in a sharp breath, I closed my eyes as I gripped the railing. It had been his father, for reasons known only to him. A great bit of unease still festered in the pit of my stomach. It wasn't right that Ash should pay with his life for what his father had done. It wasn't right that I would also pay with mine.

Nothing about this was fair.

The smooth stone pressed into my palms as I continued to squeeze the railing. Nothing had changed, though. It couldn't. The Rot had to be stopped, and Ash…he was the Primal of Death, the one who now held the deal. I had to fulfill my duty. If I didn't, Lasania would fall. People would continue dying. There would be more families like the Coupers, no matter who took the Crown.

Was one life more important than tens of thousands? Millions? Even if it was a Primal? But what would happen if I managed to succeed? If he fell in love with me, and I became his weakness, what kind of wrath would his death force upon the realms? How many lives would be lost until another Primal took his spot?

A Primal that didn't have a kind and decent bone in their body. Who didn't think highly of freedom and consent. A Primal who didn't interfere when others took delight in violence. Who didn't care about murdered descendants that carried some small trace of godly blood within them.

"Gods," I whispered, stomach twisting. How could I…how could I do this? How could I hide this mess of emotion from him, stop it from piercing whatever walls he had built around himself?

How could I not?

The people of Lasania were more important than my distaste of what I must do. They were more important than Ash. Than me.

Opening my eyes, I jerked back from the railing as movement from the courtyard below snagged my attention. I scanned the ground, breath catching as I recognized Ash's tall, broad form. Even from a distance, I knew it was him. A breeze moved across the courtyard, tossing the loose strands of his hair around his shoulders. His strides were long and sure as he walked alone, heading toward the cluster of the dark red trees.

What was he doing?

A knock on the door drew me from my thoughts. Knowing it wasn't Ash, habit had me reaching for my thigh, but there was no dagger there. No real weapon at all. I went to the door, only to discover that it was Aios.

She flowed into the room with clothing draped over her arm. "Glad you're awake," she said. "We were starting to worry. You've been asleep for a day."

A day?

I blinked as a younger man entered behind her, bowing his head in my direction before placing a covered dish and a glass on the table. The aroma of food reached me, stirring my nearly empty stomach. He kept his head down, and most of his face was hidden behind a sheet of blond hair. Aios made a beeline for the wardrobe, throwing it open as I watched him turn to leave, noticing that he favored his right leg over his left. It wasn't until he was closing the door behind him that he looked up, and I saw that his eyes were brown and there was no glow of eather in them.

"I wasn't sure what you'd like to eat," Aios said. "So, I had a little bit of everything made. Please eat before it gets cold."

Somewhat in a daze, I roamed over to the table and lifted the cloche to reveal a mound of fluffy eggs, a few strips of bacon, a biscuit, and a small bowl of fruit. I stared at the food for several moments, unable to remember the last time I'd had warm eggs. I sat slowly, my gaze falling to the glass of orange juice. For some reason, the back of my throat burned. I closed my eyes, wrangling my emotions. It was just warm eggs and bacon. That was all. When I was positive that I had control of myself, I opened my eyes and slowly picked up the fork. I tasted the eggs and nearly moaned. Cheese. There was melted cheese in them. I nearly devoured the entire mound in less than a minute.

"You'll be happy to know that I was able to find some clothing for you," Aios said as she hung the items inside the wardrobe.

Forcing myself to slow down, I looked over my shoulder at her. I thought of the glow in her eyes. "You're a goddess, right?"

Aios faced me with a quizzical lift to her brows. "On most days."

I cracked a grin. "And the young man that was just here. Is he a…a godling?"

She shook her head as she turned back to the wardrobe, hanging what appeared to be a gray sweater. "Have you ever met a godling?"

"Not that I know of," I admitted, thinking of Andreia. "I don't know much about them."

"What would you like to know?" she said, turning from the wardrobe.

"Everything."

Aios laughed softly, the sound warm and airy. "Finish eating, and I'll tell you."

For once, I didn't mind being told what to do. I broke apart the toasted, buttery biscuit as Aios said, "Most godlings are mortal. They carry no essence of the gods in them. Therefore, they live and die just like any other mortal."

I thought of how Ash had said that most godlings lived in Iliseeum. "Do they typically reside in the mortal realm?"

"Some do. Others choose to live in Iliseeum. But for those who carry the eather in their blood, it's usually because their mother or father was a powerful god. That eather is passed down to them."

Was that the case for the Kazin siblings? One of them, or maybe even the babe, had enough eather in them to make them a godling? The babe with the missing *father*? Or did they just have a trace? Either way, why would the gods kill them?

"For the first eighteen to twenty years of life, they live relatively mortal lives," she continued, snapping my attention back to her. "They may not even know that they carry the blood of the gods in them. But they soon will."

"The Culling?" I guessed, picking up a slice of bacon.

She nodded. "Yes. They will begin to go through the Culling. That is when some learn that they are not completely mortal."

My brows lifted. "That would be one hell of a way to find out."

"That it would be." Her head tilted, sending several long locks of red hair cascading over a shoulder. "But for most, they don't survive the change. You see, their bodies are still mortal. And as the Culling sets in, and the eather in them begins to multiply and grow, infiltrating every part of them, their bodies can't facilitate such a process. They die."

"That..." I shook my head as I dropped the slice of bacon back onto the plate. "The eather sounds like a weed growing out of control in their bodies."

Aios let out a surprised laugh. "I suppose that is one way to look at it. Or maybe, for some, a beautiful garden. Those who survive the Culling will then age much, much slower than mortals. Basically, for every three or so decades a mortal lives, it is equivalent to one year for a godling."

What mortal lived to a hundred? Odetta had to have been close. "That sounds like immortality to me."

"Godlings can live for thousands of years if they're careful. They are susceptible to very few illnesses. But they're not as impervious to injuries as the gods and Primals are," she explained. "For that reason, most godlings who survive the Culling live in Iliseeum."

That made sense. A five-hundred-year-old person who looked as if they were twenty would definitely draw attention. That was also probably why we believed that the children of mortals and gods—godlings—were rare. A thought struck me, causing my stomach to twist. "Can Primals and mortals have children?"

She shook her head. "A Primal is an entirely different being in that way."

I took a drink of the juice to hide my relief. It could take months...or even years to fulfill my duty. I didn't want to bring a child into this only to leave them orphaned like Ash had been.

Like, in some ways, I had been.

My hand trembled slightly as I placed the glass down. "So how do some survive, while others don't?"

"It all depends on whether a god assisted the godling," she said, reaching up to toy with the chain around her neck. "That is the only way a godling survives."

"And how would a god assist them?"

She grinned, a mischievous sort of look filling her golden eyes. "You may find such information to be quite scandalous."

"Doubtful," I murmured.

Aios laughed again. "Well, all right, then." The hem of her flared sweater swished around her knees as she drifted closer. "They need to feed from a god."

I leaned forward. "I assume you do not mean the type of food I just consumed?"

"No." Her grin spread as she lifted a finger to her rosy lips. She tapped a fingernail off one delicate fang. "They do not grow these, but they will need blood. Quite a bit of it at first. And then, every so often once the Culling is complete."

"Do all gods need to feed?" I asked. "Like that?"

She sat on the chair opposite me. "Yes."

My stomach tumbled a bit. I'd obviously known that they could…bite, but I hadn't known it was something they had to do.

A bit of her smile faded. "Does that bother you?"

"No," I said quickly. "I mean, the idea of drinking blood makes me a little nauseous."

"As it would for most who are not like us."

But I…I also remembered the scrape of Ash's fangs against my skin. I felt myself flush. "Do you all feed off mortals?"

Aios arched a brow as she watched me. "We can. It does the same for us as feeding off a god would."

My gaze flicked back to Aios's beautiful face. Who did Ash feed from? "Are Primals the same?"

"They do not need to feed unless they've experienced some sort of weakening." Her fingers returned to the chain. "Which isn't often."

"Oh," I murmured, not exactly thrilled with the buzz of relief I felt. Something occurred to me. "Does anything happen to the mortal when a Primal or god feeds off them?"

"No. Not if we're careful. Obviously, a mortal may feel the effects of the feeding more than any of us would, and if we were to take too much, then…well, it would be a tragedy if they were not third sons or daughters." Her lips tensed. "It's forbidden to Ascend them—to save them."

Curiosity trickled through me. "Why?"

Tension bracketed her mouth. "They would become what we call demis—a being with godlike power that was never meant to carry such a gift…and burden. They are something else."

I frowned, thinking that wasn't much of an answer.

"But to answer your original question," she continued, changing the subject, "the young man who was in here? His name is Paxton, and he's completely mortal."

So many *more* questions flooded me. Surprise flickered through me. "What is a mortal doing here?"

"Many mortals live in Iliseeum," she told me, and it was clear that she thought that was common knowledge.

"Are they all…lovers?" I fiddled with the sash on the robe, thinking Paxton appeared far too young for that.

"Some have befriended a god or became their lover." She lifted a shoulder. "Others have talents that appealed to one of the gods. For many of them, coming to Iliseeum was an opportunity to start over. Their paths are all different."

An opportunity to start over. My heart skipped. Wouldn't that be nice? I glanced down at my plate. There was no starting over, no other paths. There never had been.

"May I ask you something?" Aios asked, and I looked up, nodding. "Did you know?" She had come closer, her voice lower. "About the deal, before he came for you?"

"I did."

"Still, that must've been a lot to deal with." Aios clasped her hands together. "To know you had been promised to a Primal."

"It was, but I learned a while ago that if you can't deal with something, you *find* a way to do so," I said. "You have to."

A far-off look crept into Aios's features as she nodded slowly. "Yes, you have to." She cleared her throat, rising abruptly and making her way to the wardrobe. "By the way, I was able to find two gowns that I believe will fit. But Nyktos mentioned that you preferred pants over gowns."

I rose slowly and tentatively walked forward. He'd thought enough to mention that to Aios?

"I couldn't get my hands on any tights, but these breeches should fit you." Aios tugged on a pair of fawn-colored pants and then on a black pair she'd hung. "I hope these are sufficient."

"Actually, I prefer them over tights. They're thicker and have pockets."

She nodded, flipping through the items she'd hung. "You have some long-sleeved blouses, vests, and sweaters. They're a bit plain," she said, running a hand over something silky and pale. "There are two nightgowns here for you and some basic undergarments. I imagine you'll soon have many more items to choose from." Turning to me, she once again folded her hands. "Is there anything else you need?"

I opened my mouth, reluctant to let her leave. I'd spent the vast majority of my life alone and left to my own devices. But this room was huge, and nothing about it was familiar. I shook my head.

Aios had just started for the door when I stopped her. "I do have one more question."

"Yes?"

"Are you from the Shadowlands Court?" I asked.

She shook her head. "I once belonged to the Court of Kithreia."

It took me a moment to recall what I had been taught about the different Courts. "Maia," I said, surprising myself that I remembered the name of the Primal of Love, Beauty, and Fertility's Court. "You served the Primal Maia?"

"At one time."

Curiosity hummed through me. I had not known of any gods leaving the Primal they had been born to serve. "How did you end up here?"

Her shoulders tightened. "As I said before, it was the only place I knew would be safe."

Left unsettled, I didn't stop her as she left. While I found relief in the knowledge that she felt safe here, how secure could it be when those who liked to *push* the Primal of Death had strung those gods to the wall?

That was roughly about the time I realized that Ash hadn't told me who had done that to the gods.

I turned back to the wardrobe. The undergarments were nothing more than scraps of lace I imagined most would find indecent. I flipped past the gowns, finding a narrow leather strap beside the remaining clothing. I grabbed a sweater and breeches, changing into them.

After I found a comb and spent an ungodly amount of time working out the numerous knots in my hair, I braided it, remembering what Ash had said. Hair that looked like spun moonlight.

That was such a silly thing to say.

Returning to the bedchamber, I found myself staring at the chamber door.

Was I locked in my room?

Oh, gods, if they'd imprisoned me, I would—I didn't even know what I would do, but it would probably involve finding the closest blunt object and knocking Ash over the head with it.

My heart hammered as I went to the door, bare feet whispering over the cool stone. I placed my hand on the brass knob. I took a deep breath and turned.

It wasn't locked.

Relief shuddered through me, and I opened the door—

I gasped. A light-haired and fair-skinned god stood in the middle of the hall, facing my room. He was dressed as before, in black adorned with silver scrollwork across the chest, a short sword strapped to his side.

"Ector," I squeaked. "Hi."

"Hello."

"Can I help you with something?"

He shook his head, remaining exactly where he stood, feet planted in the center of the hall like an unmovable tree.

Wait…

I inhaled sharply. "I doubt you're standing there because you have nothing better to do, correct?"

"I have many, many better things I could be doing," he replied.

"And yet, you're standing guard outside my chamber?"

"Sure appears that way."

Anger simmered, threatening to boil over. What good did an unlocked door do when *he* placed a guard outside my room? "You're here to make sure I don't leave my chambers."

"I'm here for your safety," Ector corrected. "I've also heard you tend to wander off into dangerous areas."

"I don't have a habit of roaming."

"I'm sorry. Maybe I misheard and it's that you have a habit of entering places without making sure they're secure."

"Oh, well, now I *know* you spoke to Ash."

"Ash?" Ector repeated. His brows rose. "I didn't know you two were on that kind of name basis."

And he wasn't? *I am not that to you.* That was what Ash had said when I'd called him Nyktos.

I blew out an aggravated breath. It didn't matter. "If I wanted to leave my room right now, would you stop me?"

"At the moment, yes."

"Why?"

"Because if something were to happen to you, I imagine *Nyktos* would probably be displeased."

"Probably?"

Ector shrugged.

"What about later?" I demanded.

"That will be different, and we would have to see."

"Have to see?" I laughed harshly. Unbelievable. "Where is he?"

"He's busy at the moment."

"And I imagine he can't be interrupted?"

Ector nodded.

"So, what am I supposed to do?" I asked. "Stay in my room until he isn't busy?"

"I'm not entirely sure what you're supposed to do." Amber eyes met mine. "And to be honest, I don't think even *he* knows what to do with you."

Chapter 26

The following morning, I jerked upright in bed, wrinkled and dazed as a woman strolled into my bedchamber after knocking once.

"Brought you something to eat," she announced, stalking past the bed in a rapid clip, her short, honey-brown hair snapping at her rounded, reddish-brown chin.

I blinked slowly, still half asleep. The long, flowing sleeves of her white blouse slid up her arms as she placed a covered dish and a pitcher on the table, revealing a slender, black-bladed dagger affixed to her forearm. That wasn't the only one. She had another strapped to her breeches-clad thigh. I tensed as the cobwebs of sleep vanished at the sight of the weapons. "Who are you?" I demanded.

"Davina is my name. Most call me Dav." She whipped around. "And I suppose I should call you *meyaah Liessa*."

My lips parted as goosebumps spread across my scalp. It wasn't her words that drew the reaction. It was her *eyes*.

A shade of vibrant blue that rivaled the Stroud Sea stood out in stark contrast to her black, vertical pupils.

Pupils that reminded me of the draken I'd seen on the road on our way into the Shadowlands, but his eyes had been red.

She stared unblinkingly at me. "Are you all right?"

"Are you a draken?" I blurted.

One eyebrow rose. "That was kind of a rude question. But, yes, I am."

At first, the only thing that entered my mind was how in the world someone roughly my height and slimmer than me could *transform* into something the size of the draken I'd seen. Then again, I couldn't imagine her shifting into something even the size of Reaver, which was much smaller. But still.

Then I realized I was still gaping at her. Heat crept into my face. "I'm sorry. It was rude of me to ask that. I just…" I didn't really have a response.

She nodded, and I wasn't sure if that was in acceptance of my apology or not.

My gaze dropped to the dagger at her thigh. "What does…*meyaah Liessa* mean?"

That eyebrow seemed to climb even higher. "It means *my Queen*."

My entire body jolted. "Your Queen?"

"Yes," she drew out the word. "You are the Consort, are you not? That would make you like a queen."

I understood that, though it seemed weird to even acknowledge. But Ash… Another jolt ran through me. Ash had said *liessa* meant many things, all something beautiful and powerful.

A Queen would be powerful.

A Consort *was*.

"Are you sure you're okay?" Dav asked.

"I think so." Giving a small shake of my head, I shoved the covers aside. "Where is—?" I started to call him Ash but then remembered Ector's reaction. "Where is the Primal?" I hadn't seen him since I'd caught a glimpse of him entering those strangely colored woods.

"Busy."

My spine stiffened. "Still?"

"Still."

I told myself to take a deep breath and to remain calm. I did not know this woman. She was also a draken, and most likely not someone I wanted to anger. So, I forced my voice to remain level. "What is he busy with?"

For a moment, I thought she wouldn't be any more detailed than Ector, but then she said, "He was in the Red Woods, dealing with Shades."

Dying Woods? Shades? "I have a distinct feeling that you probably won't appreciate the fact that I have more questions," I started, and a faint trace of humor crept into her otherwise stoic features. "But what is the Dying Woods, and what are Shades?"

She studied me for a long moment. "The Dying Woods are the…dying woods. Dead trees. Dead grass." She paused. "Dead everything."

My lips thinned, even though I supposed I'd walked right into that one. "Then perhaps they should be called the Dead Woods."

That glint of humor moved in her blue eyes. "I have said that myself many times."

Relaxing a fraction, the robe fell around my legs as I stood. "And the Shades?"

"Souls who have entered the Shadowlands but refuse to cross through the Pillars of Asphodel to face judgement for the deeds committed while alive. They can't return to the mortal realm. They can't enter the Vale. So, they remain trapped in the Dying Woods. They become…lost, wanting to live but unable to gain that life.

"Oh," I whispered, swallowing. "That sounds terrible."

"It is," she answered. "Especially since they are driven mad by unending hunger and thirst. They tend to get a bit bitey."

My brows shot up. Bitey?

"Normally, they don't cause that many problems, but sometimes, they find their way out of the Dying Woods and into Lethe," she explained. "Then, Nyktos must round them up. Fun times had by all."

"Fun times," I repeated.

"Now, if you'll excuse me, I have much to do." Dav started for the door. "None of which involves answering questions. No offense meant." She stopped at the door and bowed. "Good day, *meyaah Liessa*."

Dav left the room, closing the doors behind her.

"Wow," I murmured, my gaze drifting to the table. A short laugh left me. Despite the general unfriendliness of the draken, I kind of liked her.

Hours passed with no sign of Ash. It was Ector who brought a light lunch and then supper. He didn't linger, flat-out ignoring my questions. Just as he had each time I opened the door and found him standing in the hallway.

Night had fallen once more, and when I stepped out onto the balcony and looked up, the sky had turned a deeper shade of iron, the stars and the lights from the city beyond brighter. The leaves from the woods below had become a deep crimson, almost a red-black.

I'd gone to bed slightly annoyed two nights ago, and more than slightly last night. When I woke again this morning, no less than thirty minutes ago, to find Ector standing outside yet again, I went from irritated to *furious.*

The god, on the other hand, had given me a rather jaunty wave.

Only a tiny part of me wondered exactly what Ector had done to earn his spot standing outside my door. He had to be going stir-crazy. I knew I was. The only thing that kept me somewhat sane and stopped me from breaking random things in the too quiet, too large room was the pacing—the pacing and the plotting.

Okay. *Plotting* wasn't the best word for what I'd been doing. But plotting the many different blunt objects I could use to strike Ash over the head as I paced, filled me with a disturbing amount of satisfaction. None of those fantasies would do anything to aid in my seduction of the Primal, but how in the hell could I even begin to make him fall in love with me when he kept me locked in my chambers?

Then there were the glimpses of the young draken they called Reaver. Every so often, I caught sight of him in the courtyard, usually with Aios or one of the unknown guards, hopping on the ground and attempting to take flight with his thin wings. I watched from the shadows of the balcony, utterly enthralled.

A knock on the door whipped me around. I rushed forward, throwing it open. And came to a sudden halt. The god who stood in the threshold was neither Ash nor Ector.

"Hi there." The god bowed deeply. "I don't know if you remember me—"

"Saion," I said. "You were there, in the Great Hall."

"I was. How are you feeling?" he asked rather politely. "I hope better than I last saw you."

He'd last seen me shoving a whip down someone's throat. "Much better," I answered truthfully. The marks the whip had left behind were no longer raised welts but faint red streaks that no longer ached.

"Glad to hear that." The smooth brown skin of his head glinted richly in the hallway light. "Would you like breakfast?"

"I would like to leave this room."

"The offer for breakfast, if you accept, would require you to leave." He stepped back into the hall and to the side. "Yes, or no?"

There was a moment of hesitation. I didn't know Saion, but I did know that I had to get out of this chamber before I started tying bedsheets together and attempting to scale the building from the balcony.

"Yes."

"Perfect." Saion waited until I was in the hall and then closed the door. "Please. Follow me."

Wary, I did as he requested, wishing I had any weapon at this point as I followed him, continuously scanning my surroundings. We made our way down the wide hall and toward the staircase. Saion didn't speak, and never one good with small talk, I was more than fine with the silence.

A jittery energy descended as we reached the first level. The brightly lit entryway was empty. I glanced at the double, windowless, wooden doors painted black.

"I hope you're not planning to make a run for it," Saion observed.

My head whipped in his direction. "I wasn't."

"Good. I'm feeling a bit too lazy to chase you down," he said, the corners of his lips turning up. The smile was charming and as perfect as the rest of his features, but the sharpness in his gaze left me doubting the sincerity of that smile. He motioned for me to follow him through the archway. "And Nyktos would be quite irritated with me if he learned you'd managed to evade me on my watch."

Why would he think I'd run off? "If he is so worried about me running off, then perhaps he should be the one watching over me."

"Interestingly enough, I said the same thing."

"Really?" I asked doubtfully, taking in the space beyond the sharply pointed archway. There were doors on either side, but the walls were black and bare. The only thing in the space was a white pedestal in the center of the room, but nothing sat on it.

"Really."

I glanced at him. "How did he take that?"

The smile was easier now, but no less charming as we entered another hall. "He grumbled something about feeding me to Nektas."

My eyes widened. I hoped he was joking. "What…what do draken eat?"

"Not me, that's for sure," he replied. "And this was said in front of Nektas, who claimed to have no interest in eating me, thank the gods."

The hall split into two, going in opposite directions. Ahead, two doors were spaced so far apart, each room could belong in a different home. But it was what rested in the center, between the two doors, that caught my attention. My steps slowed. Two thick, black pillars framed a short hall that opened into a circular chamber lit by hundreds of candles. Reminded of the Shadow Temple, a shiver curled down my spine as we drew closer. The golden candlelight broke apart the shadows in the chamber, casting a glow of fire over the massive blocks of shadowstone seated upon a dais. It was the throne. *Thrones*, actually. Two of them sat side by side, their backs carved into large and widespread wings that touched at the tips.

The Primal's and Consort's thrones.

They were hauntingly beautiful.

I looked up to see that the ceiling was open to the sky. No glass. Nothing. Did it never rain here?

Saion stalked toward the chamber to the left of the throne room, and it was a bit of a struggle to pull my gaze from the thrones. He opened the door. "After you."

A whole host of spices and aromas filled the chamber as I continued in, my gaze touching on everything all at once. The walls were bare except for some candle sconces. No Primal magic there. Their flames cast a soft glow off the smooth ebony walls. A table sat in the center of the circular room, as large as the one in the banquet room in Wayfair. A dozen or so candles of varying heights glowed from the middle of the table, but I saw a silvery gleam cast across the covered dishes and glasses.

I looked up, my breath catching. The dome-shaped ceiling was made of glass, and it was the stars above that shone on the table. My lips parted.

"Beautiful."

Gasping, I whirled around. Ash stood only a few feet from me. He wore all black, the tunic devoid of any embellishments. His hair was down, softening the sharpness of his cheekbones and the hardness of his jaw.

Startled by his sudden appearance, I bumped into one of the winged-back chairs. "It is," I whispered. There was no way I could deny the eerie beauty of the cavernous chamber. "This room is very beautiful."

A tight-lipped smile appeared as his gaze, so much like the starlight, swept over me. "I hadn't even noticed the room."

It took me a moment to realize what he meant. I glanced down at myself in surprise. I wore no gown, instead opting for the long-sleeved blouse and vest, much like Dav had been wearing. I glanced up at him, a rush of conflicting emotions rolling through me as his stare lingered on the laces of the vest, the cut of the blouse, and then strayed over the tight fit of the breeches. I was annoyed for a multitude of reasons, starting with being trapped in my chambers, and ending with his blatant perusal. But there was a different emotion—something smokier and warm—as we stood there in silence, seeming to just soak each other in. Ash had drifted closer, the heated intensity in his gaze sending a shivery wave of awareness and anticipation—

I jumped at the sound of the door clicking shut. Only then did I realize that Saion had left us. I snapped out of whatever spell I had fallen into. "Did you have your lackey lock the door, or was that unnecessary since you are here?"

"I do hope you don't call Saion that to his face," Ash replied smoothly. "I'll get little peace if you do."

"Have I given you the impression that I would care if things were peaceful for you or not?" I snapped. The moment those words left my mouth, I cursed myself. I shouldn't show my irritation. I should let it go. Be malleable. Understanding. Whatever. Any of those things would help me.

"You're angry with me."

"Are you surprised? You kept me in my chambers as if I were your prisoner."

"Keeping you in your chambers was a necessary evil."

I took a deep breath. It did no good. "There is nothing *necessary* about becoming your captive."

His eyes turned to steel. "You are not my captive."

"That's not what it felt like."

"If you think being kept in your chambers for a day or two is equal to being a prisoner, then you have no idea what being held against your will feels like," he replied coolly.

"And you do?"

His skin thinned, features honing to an edge. "I am well acquainted with what that feels like."

My mouth clamped shut. I hadn't expected that.

Ash's expression smoothed as he broke eye contact with me. "The food is growing cold." He strode forward, pulling out the chair to the right. "Have a seat," he said. "Please."

I peeled away from the chair and took the seat he offered, replaying what he'd said over and over. Had he been held captive? Even though he was young compared to others, he was still powerful.

Who could've done that?

Ash moved to my side and reached over my shoulder, beginning to lift the lids while I refused to allow myself to acknowledge how nice he smelled. An array of food was revealed under each lid. Bacon. Sausage. Eggs. Bread. Fruits. "Water? Tea? Lemonade?" he offered, extending his hand toward a cluster of pitchers. "Whiskey?"

"Lemonade," I answered absently. I watched him pour the juice into a glass and then set about placing a little bit of everything on a plate—bacon, the sausage, the eggs, the fruit, and two rolls. Then he placed that plate in front of me.

The Primal of Death was serving me. Apparently, he believed I needed to eat for five. A nearly hysterical giggle climbed up my throat, but I squelched it as he poured himself what appeared to be whiskey and took the seat at the head of the table to my immediate left. The positioning surprised me. My mother and stepfather had sat at opposite ends of the table. The seat to the right of a King or, in some cases, the Queen, was usually reserved for an Advisor or other position of authority.

He reached over, picking up something that had been folded in a cloth. My breath snagged as he unwrapped it, revealing a sheathed shadowstone dagger—the one he'd gifted me with.

"I forgot to give you this when I saw you last." He handed it over. "The sheath and strap are adjustable. It should fit."

I stared at the dagger, my heart thundering. He was handing me a weapon that I could use to end his life. The blade he'd given to me.

Doing everything in my power to ignore the pressure clamping down on my chest, I reached over and took it. The brush of our skin sent a soft wave of energy over my fingers. Hands trembling slightly, I lifted my right leg and slid the strap around my thigh, securing the sheath.

"Thank you," I whispered, the words tasting like soot on my tongue.

There was no response for several long moments, and then Ash said, "I hadn't planned on leaving you alone in your room for so long. That wasn't intentional."

My gaze shot to his. "Then what did you intend?"

"Not to make you feel as if you were my prisoner. You're not my captive. You never will be my captive." His gaze shifted to his glass. "Something came up."

He sounded genuine. "And you didn't trust me to have free rein of the palace?"

Ash arched a brow. "Is that a serious question?" I pressed my lips together, and I thought he might smile, but he said, "Making sure you were safe in one place while I was occupied was all I could come up with at the moment. Either way, I wanted to…" He cleared his throat. "I wanted to apologize for upsetting you."

My brows lifted. "That apology sounded like it pained you."

"It did."

I narrowed my eyes.

His gaze slid back to mine. "I am sorry, Seraphena."

The way he said my name, my full name… He made it sound like a sin. I looked away so quickly, several curls slid over my shoulders and fell against my cheek. I'd left my hair down, figuring it could help since he seemed to enjoy it. "I don't like being locked in. Kept somewhere, hidden and—" *Forgotten.* Hidden and forgotten. "I just don't like it."

"I heard," he finally said, and I exhaled softly. "According to Ector, you were quite vocal in expressing your dislike."

"Don't do it again." The word *please* went unspoken, but I could feel it in every bone. Wait… "You can read my emotions, but can you read my mind?"

His brows lifted. "Thank the Fates, I cannot read your thoughts."

Relief crashed through me—*thank the Fates?* I eyed him, letting that comment slide. "You said your ability to read emotions came from your mother's bloodline?"

"Yes," he said, picking up his glass. "Her family descended from the Court of Lotho—the Primal Embris' Court."

Interest sparked. "What was your mother's name?"

"Mycella."

"That's pretty."

"It was."

My gaze lowered to my plate. "It has to be hard not having known your mother. I didn't know my father, so…" I pressed my lips together. "Do you get to visit her?" I asked, assuming that she'd passed onto the Vale.

"No."

I peeked over at him, thinking of my father. "Is there some kind of rule against that? Visiting loved ones who've passed on?"

"As the Primal of Death, I risk destroying the mortal's soul if they're in my presence for any extended period of time, at least for those who have passed through judgement. That is a balance to prevent the Primal of Death from creating his or her version of life. There is no exact rule against it for gods or other mortals, but it wouldn't be wise. Visiting loved ones who have moved on can cause both the one living and the one who has passed to become stuck—to want what neither can have, whether that be to continue seeing their loved one or to return to the living. It can even cause them to leave the Vale, and that does not end well."

I thought of the spirits in the Dark Elms. Those who had refused to enter the Shadowlands altogether. They never sounded happy. Just sad and lost. Would those who left the Vale become the Shades that Dav had spoken of? Either way, I wouldn't want that for the father I'd never met. I wouldn't want that for anyone.

Except Tavius.

I'd be fine with him finding that fate.

Ash leaned forward. I hadn't heard him move. I didn't see him move. It was as if I'd sensed that he'd moved closer, and that made no sense. But when I looked over at him, I'd been right. He lifted a hand, curling his fingers around the strands of hair that had fallen forward. He brushed them back over my shoulder. "The food is getting cold."

I nodded as he sat back. I didn't even know why. Feeling foolish, I watched him place nearly the same amount on his plate but he went far heavier on the bacon.

"So, you eat food?" I asked, my thoughts reluctantly traveling to the conversation I'd had with Aios.

His gaze flicked up. "Yes," he said, drawing out the word. "I can't survive on consuming the souls of the damned alone."

I stared at him.

"I was kidding." His lips twitched. "About the eating souls part."

"I hope so," I murmured. "I didn't know if Primals needed to eat or…" I forced a shrug.

"We can go quite some time without food, far longer than a mortal." He took a sip of whiskey. "But we would eventually become weak. And if we continue to weaken, we can become…something else."

"What does that mean?"

His eyes met mine once more. "Eat, and I'll tell you."

I raised a brow. "Is this bribery?"

He lifted a shoulder as he helped himself to a piece of sausage. "Call it whatever you like, as long as it works."

Being coerced into anything, even eating when I was, in fact, hungry, didn't top my list of favorite things. Be that as it may, I helped myself to a forkful of eggs because curiosity was always far more potent. "Happy?" I asked around a mouthful.

One side of his lips curved. A piece of egg may have fallen from my mouth and quite possibly plopped onto my plate.

All the training I'd gone through was a waste. I was terrible at seduction.

But he smiled fully then, and I was surprised that more food didn't fall from my mouth. The smile, the way it lit up his features and turned his eyes quicksilver, was breathtaking every time I saw it.

Ash chuckled. "Very."

"Great."

Grinning, he chewed a piece of sausage. "We can be weakened," he said after swallowing, and my hand trembled. "Hunger. Injury," he continued. "Among other things."

I took a quick drink of the lemonade, having a very good idea of what the *among other things* was. "Then?"

"And then, when we become weak from something like starvation or hunger, we can become something more…primitive. Something *primal*." He swallowed his food. "Whatever semblance of humanity we have? That veneer slips away, and what we are underneath becomes the only thing we can be." Those thundercloud eyes held mine. "You don't want to be around any of us if that happens."

A chill skated down my spine. "That happens only to Primals?"

Thick lashes swept down, and Ash shook his head. "A Primal was once a god, *liessa*. A god of powerful bloodlines, but a god, nonetheless. What happens to a Primal can happen quicker with a god."

"Oh," I whispered, barely tasting the sweet and salty bacon. "But then you could *feed*, right? That would stop that from happening."

"They could."

Something about the way he said that caught my attention. "*You* could."

"I could," he confirmed, placing his fork beside his plate. "But I do not feed."

I frowned. "Ever?"

"Not anymore."

Confusion rose. "But what about when you're weakened?"

His eyes lifted to mine. "I make sure that does not happen."

What about when I'd stabbed him? Had that not weakened him at all? And why didn't he feed? Neither of us spoke for quite some time, appearing to be focused on feeding ourselves.

When I wiped my fingers clean on the napkin, I couldn't hold back any longer. "Were you a prisoner before?"

There was no response from Ash. His gaze was fixed ahead as he drew his thumb over the rim of his glass. "I have been many things."

I twisted the napkin in my hands. "That's not much of an answer."

Ash turned his eyes toward me. "No, it's not."

Pushing down my frustration, I placed my fork beside my plate before I did something irrational with it. I wanted to know exactly what he'd meant, and it wasn't just a sense of morbid curiosity. I understood that other Primals pushed one another's limits, but how could one be held captive?

And I wanted to be wrong. Wanted that not to be what he'd meant. Thinking of him—of *anyone*—as a captive without due cause turned my stomach and made me empathize with him. And I couldn't do that. "Wouldn't this be easier if we actually got to know each other? Or would you rather we remain basic strangers?"

"I do not prefer for us to remain strangers. To be quite blunt, Sera, I would prefer that we were once again as close as we were at the lake." His eyes met and held mine as the breath I'd inhaled went nowhere. Heat crept into my veins as he dragged the edges of his fangs over his lower lip. I wanted that, too. Because of my duty, of course. "I want that very much, but some things are not up for discussion, Seraphena. That is one of them."

I looked away, my shoulders tensing as I started to press him. I tamped down that desire, though. Not only because knowing more about him could prove…well, dangerous to my duty, but also because there were things I believed weren't up for discussion. My mother. Tavius. The night I'd drunk the sleeping draft. The truth of what it had been like for me at home. I could understand that some things were just too hard to talk about.

A soft mewling sound drew my attention. I leaned forward as a small, greenish-brown, oval-shaped head appeared over the edge of the table.

My mouth dropped as I stared at the tiny draken as it stretched its long, slender neck and yawned.

Ash looked over with a raised eyebrow. "Huh. I didn't even know she was in here."

I dropped my napkin. "What is her name?"

"Jadis. But she has recently taken a liking to being called Jade,"

Ash told me as the draken flapped a wing onto the table and scanned the many dishes. "I'm surprised it took her this long. Usually, she wakes at the first scent of food."

The female draken squawked as she placed her front claws on the table. They were tiny but already sharp enough that they rapped off the wood. Her wings were thin and nearly translucent, and I swore her eyes doubled in size as she got an eyeful of the remaining food.

"How old is she?"

"She turned four a few weeks ago. She's the youngest. Reaver—the one that was with Lailah the other day—is ten years old," he said, and she hauled herself onto the table. He sighed. "Jadis, you know better than to be on the table."

The little draken swung her head toward the Primal and made a soft trilling sound.

A smile appeared on Ash's face. "Off."

My eyes widened as the draken stomped its back foot and emitted a sharp cry.

"Off the table, Jadis," Ash repeated with patient fondness.

The draken made a sighing sound and hopped down. Spike-tipped wings appeared over the edge of the table as she made quite the disgruntled-sounding yap.

Ash chuckled. "Come here, you little brat."

Jumping down from the chair, Jadis's claws tapped on the stone. Ash bent to the side, extending an arm. "She can't fly yet," he said as Jadis hopped onto his arm and then into his lap. She trilled, eyes glued to the plate of bacon. "She's still got a few more months before she can hold her weight for any amount of time. Reaver is just learning to fly."

I watched him reach over and pick up a slice of bacon. "Can you understand them in this form?"

"I've been around them enough to understand them when they're like this," he explained as Jadis munched away happily. "For the first six months of their lives, they are in their mortal forms, and then they shift for the first time. They typically remain in draken form for the first several years. That's not to say you won't see them in their mortal forms, but I've been told it is more comfortable for them to be this way. They mature just like a god or a Primal does—like a mortal for the first eighteen or so years of their life. But during that time, they hit a rapid growth spurt in their draken form. Within a few years, they'll be nearly Odin's size, and by the age of maturity, the size of Nektas."

It was hard to imagine the little thing now eating bacon growing to the size of the massive draken that had greeted us upon entering the Shadowlands. I thought of Davina. "How do they shift from something that's the size of a mortal to Nektas's size?" My brows pinched. "Unless he is an incredibly large male in that form, too?"

"He is about the same size as I am," he said. That was large but nothing like the draken. "You would think it would be painful, but I've been told it's like stripping off too-tight clothing."

There had to be Primal magic involved. "How long do they live?"

"A very, very long time."

"As long as the gods?"

"For some, yes." He glanced over at me. "Reproducing is quite complicated, or so I'm told. One could go several centuries without a fledgling being born."

Several centuries.

I sat back, swallowing heavily.

"That's enough." Ash moved the plate away when she made a grab for it. "Nektas will burn me alive if he finds out I've been feeding you bacon."

"Is Nektas her father?"

"Yes." His tone thickened as Jadis lifted her head and looked back at him. "Her mother died two years ago."

My chest constricted. It made my heart ache to think of something so small being motherless.

Jadis lowered her head and vibrant, cobalt eyes met mine. She hummed, lifting her wings.

"She wants to come to you," Ash told me. "Are you okay with that?"

I nodded quickly, and Ash lowered her to the floor. She was fast, reaching my side and rising onto her hind legs. "What do I do?"

"Just extend your arm. She'll grab on without using her claws. Luckily, she's past that stage," he added with a mutter.

Yikes.

I did what Ash had instructed, and Jadis grabbed onto my arm without hesitation. The press of her paws was cool as she climbed up my arm and then hopped into my lap.

The draken stared at me.

I stared at her.

She made a bleating sound as she swished her tail over my leg.

"You can pet her. She's not a serpent," Ash said softly, and when I looked over at him, two of his fingers shielded a corner of his mouth.

Clearly, he hadn't forgotten my reaction to those snakes. "She likes the underside of her jaw rubbed."

Hoping she didn't view my finger as something as tasty as the bacon, I curled the side of my finger under her jaw. Her scales were bumpy where I imagined the frills would eventually grow around her neck. She immediately tucked her wings back and closed her eyes.

I grinned, a bit awed by the creature. "I still can't believe I've seen draken—that I'm touching one," I admitted, my grin spreading as she tilted her head. "I read about them in the books chronicling the history of the realms and had seen drawings of them. They were always written as dragons and not draken, but I don't think many believed the dragons truly existed. I don't even know if I did, to be honest."

"It's probably best that way," Ash commented. "I do not think either would live very long in the mortal realm, neither draken nor mortal."

I nodded as Jadis's neck vibrated against my finger. Mortals tended to destroy things they'd never seen before or were afraid of. "I have a question that feels sort of inappropriate to ask in front of her."

Ash laughed quietly. "I cannot wait to hear this."

I wished he wouldn't laugh. I liked the sound far too much. "Do they eat…?" I pointed at myself with my free hand.

He was smiling again, and that was another thing I wished he wouldn't do. "They're hunters by nature, so they eat almost anything—including mortals and gods."

"Great," I murmured.

"You shouldn't worry about that. You'd have to really make a draken mad for it to want to eat you. We're not nearly as tasty as we probably think we are. Too many bones and not enough meat, apparently."

"That's good, then." I smiled as Jadis pressed her little head against my finger. "How do they act as your guards?"

Ash was quiet for several moments. "They know when a Primal they have become close to has been wounded. They can feel it. They will defend those Primals in certain situations."

"Like what kinds of situations?"

He finished off his whiskey. "Any that doesn't involve other Primals. They are forbidden to attack another Primal."

"Did…did Nektas know what I did before, in the mortal realm, when you walked up on me without announcing your presence?"

"You mean, when you stabbed me in the chest?" He grinned.

"I don't know why you're smiling."

His eyes had changed. They weren't doing that swirling thing again, but they'd lightened to a shade of pewter. "Your unwillingness to say what you did gives me a little hope that I won't have to fear another attack."

"I wouldn't get too comfortable with that belief," I muttered. All at once, I wished I actually thought before I spoke—for many reasons.

He laughed, though, and his response equally amused me. I also felt something a lot like shame. "To answer your question, yes. Nektas knew something had happened," he told me, and my heart skipped against my ribs. "He sensed that I wasn't seriously injured, though."

"I stabbed you—" Jadis nudged my hand because it had stopped moving. I returned to rubbing her.

"It was barely a flesh wound."

"Barely a flesh wound?" I sputtered, offended.

"If you *had* managed to seriously injure me, Nektas would've come for me."

"Even into the mortal realm?"

"Even there."

Thank the gods I hadn't seriously injured the Primal. If so, I'd be nothing but a pile of ashes. "How would he have felt it?"

"He's bonded to me." Ash paused. "All who reside here are bonded to me. Just as the draken in the other Courts are bonded to those Primals."

I swallowed thickly at the further confirmation that I would not survive this. "I really need to get a better grip on my anger."

Ash laughed. "I don't know about that. Your anger is…"

"If you say amusing, I'm already going to fail at getting a handle on my anger."

His answering smile evoked a whole other emotion, one I really hoped he couldn't sense at the moment. "I was going to say interesting."

"I'm not sure that's any better." I continued scratching Jadis under the jaw, pushing the bubbling unease aside. "I didn't know about the bonding part."

"Of course, not. Mortals have no need of that knowledge." A couple of moments passed. "Not as scary as her father, is she?"

"No." She was still happily vibrating. "She's adorable."

"I'll remember you said that when she's Nektas's size."

His teasing words sent my heart racing. She was several years away from Nektas's size. And if I succeeded in my plans, neither of us would be here to see that.

"I assume you're done with your breakfast?" Ash spoke, drawing me from my thoughts. I nodded. "Good. You and I need to talk, and I prefer to do that away from any potentially breakable items you may or may not want to throw."

Chapter 27

Ash had taken Jadis as we stood, which was a good thing since I apparently wasn't going to like anything he was about to say to me.

The small draken had immediately thrown herself over one of his shoulders, front and hind legs sprawled and wings lowered. I had to stop looking at her because she looked totally ridiculous and utterly adorable.

Saion was waiting for us in the hall. "Here," Ash said to him and reached up, plucking Jadis off his shoulder. "We disturbed her morning nap, so she's in need of another."

The god's forehead wrinkled as he took the limp draken. "And what am I supposed to do with her?" He held the draken the way I imagined one would hold a child that'd soiled itself.

Jadis squawked at him.

"Rock her to sleep," Ash suggested, and I blinked. "She likes that."

Saion stared at the Primal. "Rock her? To sleep? Seriously?"

"That's what I do." Ash shrugged. I was also gaping at him now. "It always works for me. If you don't, she'll resist falling asleep. Then she'll get cranky, and you don't want that. She's been able to cough up sparks and some flames lately."

"Great," Saion muttered, draping the draken over one arm.

"Have fun." Ash nodded at me to follow him, and it took me a moment to get my legs moving.

Glancing over my shoulder as we walked down the hall to our

right, I saw Saion swinging his arms back and forth. "I don't think he knows what rocking something to sleep means."

Ash looked and laughed under his breath. "She'll let him know soon enough."

I dragged my gaze from what had to be one of the weirdest things I'd ever seen in my life.

"I thought this would be a good time to discuss your future here," he said as we walked past the throne room.

"That sounds ominous."

"Does it?"

"Yes." I sighed. "Has anyone ever told you that you have a knack for decorating?"

"I'm a minimalist."

That was an understatement.

I wondered what his private quarters looked like. Probably just the necessities. A nightstand. Wardrobe. Enormous bed. It felt like it went beyond minimalism, though. There were no paintings or sculptures, no banners or any other signs of life. The walls were as cold and hard as he was, so maybe that was just him.

Unnerved, I didn't realize that Ash had stopped until I walked straight into his back. I gasped. "Sorry—"

Ash jerked, air hissing between his teeth. That *sound*. My gaze flew to his face. Tension bracketed his mouth—his eyes had darkened to a steel gray, and the white aura had brightened behind his pupils. Instinct urged that I take a step back because the sound he'd made reminded me of a wounded animal. Was he hurt?

I reached for him out of a different kind of instinct, like I had when I'd come upon the kiyou wolf. Immediately, I thought of the Shades. "Are you okay?"

"Don't," he snapped.

I froze, my hand inches from him. Heat stung my cheeks as I pulled my hand back. The sting of embarrassment went deeper, sharpening into a bitter slice of rejection. It was a silly feeling. I told myself that. I didn't care if he suddenly had no interest in my touch. I just needed him to want it, and there was a world of difference there.

"I'm fine." His jaw flexed as he turned his head to the side. "I should've known you wouldn't be more aware of your surroundings."

"And I would've expected you to be less jumpy," I retorted. "I can already tell it was wise of you to remove me from the dining hall. And very unwise to give me back my dagger."

He arched a brow. "Why? Should I suddenly be worried about a sharp instrument being plunged into my chest?"

"Among other things," I muttered.

His head tilted. I saw it as it happened, then—his eyes changing. It wasn't so much the color as it was the shadows gathering behind them. They retracted until they became the color of a thundercloud. "I have to admit, I'm interested in the *among other things* part of your statement."

A shivery wave of irritation and heat rippled through me, stirring that reckless, impulsive side of me that should have everything to do with my duty but instead felt as if it had very little to do with it. I met his stare as I stepped into him, close enough that I felt the chill of his body. "Well, you have no chance of ever finding out what those things are if you jump away from contact with me."

A tendril of eather flickered across those eyes. His lashes then lowered to half-mast. "Now, I'm very interested."

"Doubtful."

Ash had become still again, like he had in the lake and when I'd risen from the tub. Nothing about him moved. Not even his chest. "You don't think I am?" he asked quietly.

My skin tingled with a heightened sense of awareness. The urge to step back hit me again. It was the way he stared at me, like a predator that had sighted its prey. I knew I should keep my mouth shut, but the burn of his words still scalded my skin, and my mouth had an entirely different idea of what to do. "I think you're a lot of talk. You seem to have no real interest in anything beyond touching me, no matter what you claim you do with your hand and—"

Ash moved as quick as a strike of lightning, blocking my path. "I want to make one thing clear."

My eyes flew to his. The wisps of eather had seeped out into the irises. He took a step toward me. This time, I moved back.

One side of his lips curled up as his chin lowered. "Actually, I *need* to make one thing clear."

"Okay?" I swallowed as he stalked forward. I didn't realize I'd continued to move away from him until my back pressed into the cold stone of the bare wall behind me.

Lifting an arm, Ash placed his hand beside my head. He leaned in close enough that the air I breathed tasted of citrus. "My interest in you is the furthest thing from just talk."

A tremor of energy coursed through me as the tips of his fingers grazed my cheek. My tongue became tied. He was so incredibly tall that when he stood this close, there was only him and nothing beyond.

"My *interest* in you is a very real, very potent need." His fingers skimmed the curve of my jaw and then the line of my throat. They stopped over my wildly beating pulse. "It's almost as if it's become its own thing. A tangible entity. I find myself thinking about it at the most inconvenient moments," he said, his breath dancing over my lips. Against my better judgement, anticipation sank into my muscles, tightening them. "I find myself recalling the taste of you on my fingers a little too frequently."

I sucked in a heady breath as tiny shivers hit every part of me. My palms flattened against the wall.

"I try not to," he continued, tilting his head as his voice lowered to barely above a whisper. "Things are already complicated enough between us, aren't they?"

I said nothing, just remained there, heart thrumming and waiting.

"But when I'm around you, the last thing I want is to be uncomplicated." Ash's lips coasted over my cheek, dragging a ragged gasp from me as they neared my ear. "Or in control. Or *decent*," he said, and I shuddered at the decadent, wet flick of his tongue across my skin. "What I want is your taste on my tongue again. What I want is to be so deep inside you that I forget my own fucking name." His sharp teeth closed around my earlobe. My entire body jerked, and nothing about it was forced. "And I don't even need to read your emotions to know how much you want that, too."

A shameless ache settled in me, and I didn't even bother trying to muster up the idea of not enjoying this—him and his touch.

"So, keep that in mind the next time you doubt the realness of my interest," he warned. "Because I won't have you up against a wall. I will have you on your back, under me, and *neither* of us will remember our fucking names." He pressed a kiss to my pounding pulse. "Are we clear, *liessa*?"

It took effort for me to find my voice. "Yes."

"Good. Glad we're on the same page," Ash drawled and then stepped back. "Now, I thought I should also give you a quick tour."

I remained against the wall, knees feeling oddly weak as my pulse pounded.

The curve of Ash's lips was smug. "That is, if you're up to it."

I stiffened, my eyes flashing to his. His smile had deepened. Forgetting myself, I pushed off the wall. "I do not like you."

"It's better that way," he said as he turned from me. I frowned at his back. "Most of the chambers on this floor aren't in use." He strode forward, and I was left to follow him. "The kitchens are at the end of this hall, and at the end of the other is the Great Hall. That, like most of the chambers, is not in use."

I finally managed to pull myself together. "What about your offices?"

"They are located through there." Ash gestured at a set of doors inside a shadowy alcove. "And it's just an office."

Interest sparked as Ash continued forward. "Does it just contain a desk and a few chairs?"

He looked over his shoulder at me. "Are you prophetic?"

I snorted.

A faint smile returned as he focused ahead. "It has what it needs."

A desk and chairs were all that was needed. But if he were anything like a mortal ruler, I knew a lot of his time was likely spent in such chambers. I thought of the glass figurines lining my stepfather's office walls. Or had. Were they still there, or had Mother removed them?

Ash continued on to another alcove and opened the double doors. "This is the library."

A light turned on as Ash walked inside the large chamber, casting a buttery glow across the rows and rows of books lining the walls. They went from the floor to the ceiling, the top shelves only accessible by a rolling ladder that traveled across some sort of track along the top shelves. In the center of the room I saw the only hint of real color I'd seen so far in the palace. Two long couches were situated across from each other, each the color of deep crimson. There appeared to be two portraits above several lit candles along the back wall, but they were too far away for me to make out any detail.

"That is a lot of books." I drifted to the left. Many of the spines were covered in a fine layer of dust.

"Most belonged to my father. Some my mother." Ash had moved to the center of the room, watching me as I made my way around the shelves. "There's not a lot of…stimulating reading material. Most are ledgers, but toward the back, there are a few novels I believe my mother collected." There was a pause. "Do you like to read?"

I nodded, glancing over at him. He stood with his hands clasped behind his back. "Do you?"

"When I was younger, yes."

"But not now?" I pulled my gaze away from him. Some of the

spines had language on them that I couldn't even begin to decipher.

"The escape that reading once provided has sadly faded," he said, and I turned to him, about to ask what he sought to escape, when he spoke again. "You may help yourself to the library whenever you'd like."

I nodded, eyeing him. "I'm not sure what part of that made you believe I would throw sharp objects at you."

That half-smile returned. "It's this part. You're free to move about the palace and its grounds as you wish, but there are conditions."

"Rules?" I clarified.

"Agreements," he amended.

"I do not know how you can call them agreements when I haven't agreed to anything," I pointed out.

"True. I suppose I hope they will become that."

"And if I don't agree?"

"Then I guess they will be rules that you won't enjoy."

My eyes narrowed. "What are these *conditions*?"

"The first *hopeful* agreement is that you're free to go anyplace within the palace and on the grounds, as I said, but you are not to enter the Red Woods without me with you."

That surprised me. "I would've assumed you would tell me not to enter the Dying Woods because of the Shades."

An eyebrow rose. "I see someone has been talking."

I shrugged.

He clasped his hands behind his back. "Sometimes, Shades find their way into the Red Woods. It is not often," he explained.

I was glad to hear that since there appeared to be no wall between the Red Woods and the palace. "So, why can I only enter them with you? Does your presence keep the Shades away?"

"Unfortunately, no."

Once again, I thought about his reaction when I'd walked into his back. "Were you injured when you were wrangling them? I've heard they can bite."

"Someone *really* has been talking," he remarked. "They do bite, and they do claw."

A shiver crawled down my spine. "Can their bites pierce your skin?"

"My skin is not impenetrable, as you know."

I rolled my eyes. "It was a shadowstone dagger."

"Sharp objects, whether they be teeth or daggers, can pierce my skin and the skin of a god."

"Is that what happened to your back?" I drifted closer.

He didn't answer for a long moment. "It was."

"And why hasn't it healed?"

"You have a lot of questions."

"So?"

A faint smile appeared. "Do we have an agreement?" Ash countered.

"You haven't told me why I cannot enter them without you."

His eyes met mine. "Because you'd likely die if you did."

"Oh." I blinked. "What else is in—?"

"The second agreement is that you can enter the city if you wish," he went on, and I snapped my mouth shut. "But only after I have introduced you as my Consort. And if you have an escort."

"I have more questions."

Ash's stare was bland. "Of course, you do."

"Why must I wait until I am introduced as your Consort?"

"All mortals who call the Shadowlands and Lethe their home have my protection. But even the protection of a Primal can only go so far. Gods from other Courts can and do enter Lethe. As my Consort, any god or Primal would be extremely foolish to mess with you. Even those who like to push," he explained. "But until then, you will only be seen as another mortal."

I did not remotely like the sound of that. "Because mortals are at the bottom of the pecking order?"

"You know the answer to that."

My lips thinned. "Nice."

A muscle ticked in his jaw. "And I hope you know that I also don't believe that—not as some do."

I did and I wished I didn't because if he truly viewed mortals as beneath him, it would make what I had to do easier. "Why, as a grown woman who has been introduced as your Consort, would I need an escort?" I questioned.

"Why, as a grown woman, would you enter residences without making sure they were empty first?" he countered.

My hands curled into fists. "You bring that up as if it were some sort of habit."

"Is it not?"

"No."

The look he sent me said that he greatly doubted that. "Whether or not that is a dangerous, reckless habit of yours, you are not familiar with the city or its inhabitants, and they are not familiar with you. And while most Primals and gods know better than to harm a Consort, some simply do not follow the rules or have common decency."

"Is it a rule? To not harm a Consort?"

He nodded. "It is."

"And has that rule been broken?"

"Only once," he answered. I started to ask who, but he continued. "The next agreement—"

"There's more?" I snapped.

"Oh, yes, there are more," he replied.

I glared at him. "You have got to be kidding me."

"There are times when I may have…visitors. Guests who I would not want to be around you," he said. "Those times can be unexpected."

My jaw began to ache from how tightly I clenched it.

"But when they occur, you are to return to your chambers and remain there until one of my guards or I retrieve you."

I stiffened. None of his rules should bother me. My mother would insist that this was one of the moments that called for complete submission. And, surely, if I simply went along with these rules, it would aid me in my duty. But my skin tightened in a way that wasn't at all pleasant. I'd spent a lifetime living behind a veil, even when I was no longer required to wear one. Hidden away, seemingly ashamed of. Forgotten.

"Why does this make you…sad?" Ash asked.

My head snapped toward him as I whispered, "What?"

His chin had tilted again. "You feel sad."

"I feel annoyed—"

"Yes, that, too. But you also feel—"

"I don't." My stomach dipped. "You're not reading my emotions, are you?" When he said nothing, anger shot through me like an arrow. "I thought you said you don't do that."

"I try not to. But, apparently, my guard was down, and what you felt was like a…" He appeared to search for a word as I silently screamed. "I couldn't block it out."

The breath I sucked in was shrill. I didn't want him knowing that what he said had made me sad. I didn't want anyone to know that. "There are more rules?"

"Not exactly a rule," he said after a long moment. "But we must discuss your coronation as Consort."

My stomach tumbled a bit. I didn't know why it made me nervous, but it did. "When will that take place?"

"In a fortnight."

Two weeks. Gods. I swallowed as I crossed my arms over my waist. "And what does that entail?"

"It will be like a celebration," he said. "High-ranking gods will come from other Courts. Possibly even Primals. You will be crowned before them." His gaze flickered over me. "I will have a seamstress from Lethe come to fit you for an appropriate gown."

I tensed. "It'd better look nothing like that wedding gown."

"I have no intention of displaying you to the entirety of my Court and all others within Iliseeum," he replied, and there was no denying the relief I felt. "And she will also be able to outfit you with a wardrobe."

Nodding, my thoughts raced forward. "Will I…?" I took a deep breath and then exhaled slowly. "Will I be Ascended like the Chosen are upon being found worthy?"

Shadows rippled just beneath his skin. It happened so fast that I thought I'd imagined it. "What do you know about the act of Ascension, *liessa*?"

I lifted my shoulder. "Not much beyond the Primal of Life granting the Chosen eternal life."

His features tightened and then smoothed out. "And how do you think one Ascends?"

"I don't know," I admitted. "The secret of the act is highly guarded."

Faint wisps of eather seeped into his eyes. "The act of Ascension requires a mortal's blood to be drained from their body and replaced by that of a Primal or god. It is not always a successful transition," he said, and I thought of what I had learned of the godlings and their Culling. "But those who are Chosen are born in a shroud. They already carry some mark—some essence of the gods—in their blood. It allows them to complete the Ascension if it were to occur."

My gaze immediately went to his mouth. What did a mortal become once Ascended? I knew they did not become a god, but that wasn't my most important question. "Will my Ascension take place then?"

The eather in his eyes flared intensely. "You will not be Ascended. You will remain mortal."

Surprise rolled through me as I looked up at him. Even though I knew that it didn't matter whether or not I Ascended. I didn't plan for either of us to be around long enough to even begin comprehending something akin to immortality. But he didn't know that. "How can you have a mortal Consort? Has there ever been one?" I asked. If so, it had never been documented.

"There has never been a mortal Consort. But this was never your choice. It wasn't mine, either," he stated, and the twinge of rejection was so utterly ridiculous, I wanted to smack myself. "And I would never force someone into a near eternity of *this.*"

Of this.

He spat those words as if he spoke of the Abyss. For a moment, I didn't understand, but there was so much I didn't know about Iliseeum and their politics—the gods and Primals that pushed the limits of others, and what exactly that often entailed beyond what I'd seen on the way into the palace.

And it was yet another thing that didn't matter. I didn't need him to be open to the idea of Ascending me. I just needed him to love me.

Nervous, I lifted my gaze to his. "Are there any more rules, Your Highness?"

A half-grin appeared, stroking my temper. "Why do I find you referring to me as such arousing?"

"Because you're an arrogant, controlling misogynist?" I suggested before I could stop myself.

Ash laughed, and I swore the corners of my vision started to turn red. "I am arrogant and can be somewhat controlling, but I feel no hatred for women, no more need to control them than I would a man."

I stared at him blandly. "Are there any more rules?" I repeated.

"You're angry—and no, I'm not reading your thoughts. It's obvious."

"Yes, I'm angry." I turned from him, once more walking the length of the shelves. "What you call agreements are rules, and I don't like rules."

"I never would've guessed that," he remarked.

"I don't like that you think you can establish rules as if you have the..." Common sense finally seeped in, urging me into silence.

Ash arched a brow. "The what, *liessa*? Like I have what? The authority? Is that what you were going to say? And did you stop yourself because you realized I have exactly that?"

I pressed my lips together. That wasn't why, but it also probably should've been.

"I do have the authority. Over you. Over everyone here and every mortal in and outside of this realm, but that is not why I have these conditions," he said as I came to the end of the shelves, near the portraits. "They are in place to help keep you safe."

"I don't need that kind of help," I said, my gaze lifting to the portraits. One was a man. The other a woman.

"One of the bravest things to do is to accept the aid of others."

"Do you do that?" I asked, staring at the woman. She was beautiful. Deep red-wine hair, almost the same as Aios's, framed an oval-shaped face, the skin painted a rosy pink. Her brows were strong, her silver-eyed gaze piercing. The cheekbones were high, and her mouth was full. "Do you often accept the aid of others?"

"Not as often as I should." His voice was closer.

"Then maybe you don't know if that is brave or not." My attention shifted to the male, and even though I suspected I already knew who these people were, I still wasn't prepared for how much he looked like the Primal standing behind me. Hair shoulder-length and black—a bit darker than Ash's hair—he had the same bronzed tone of skin as Ash. The same features, really. Strong jaw and broad cheekbones. Straight nose and wide mouth. It was like looking at an older, less defined version of Ash, courtesy of the woman's softer features. "These are your parents, aren't they?"

"Yes." He was directly behind me now. "That is my father. His name was Eythos," he said, and I silently repeated the name. "And that is my mother." He came to stand beside me, and a long moment passed. "I remember my father. His voice. The memories of it have faded over the years, but I can still see him in my mind. This is how I know what my mother looked like."

Fighting the burn in the back of my throat, I folded my arms over my waist once more. "It's hard to see her…in your mind, isn't it? When you're not standing directly in front of this painting."

"Yes."

I could feel his gaze on me. "There is a portrait of my father in my mother's private chambers. The only one that still remains. It's strange because all the other Kings' portraits line the banquet hall." I took a deep breath, hoping to ease the burn in my throat. "I think it…pained my mother too much to see him. She loved him. Was *in* love with him. When he died, I think…I think he took part of her with him."

"I imagine it did." Ash was quiet for a moment. "Love is an unnecessary and dangerous risk."

Heart turning over heavily, I looked at him. "You really think that?" I thought of Ezra and Marisol and what came out of my mouth was the truth—just not *our* truth. "I think love is beautiful."

"I know that." Ash stared up at his parents. "My mother died because she loved my father, struck dead while I was still in her womb."

Every part of me froze upon hearing his words. Even my heart.

"That is why I am called the Blessed One. No one knows how I survived that kind of birth," he said, and pressure clamped down on my chest. "Love caused their deaths long before either had taken their final breaths. Before my father even met my mother. Love is a beautiful weapon, often wielded as a means to control another. It shouldn't be a weakness, but that is what it becomes. And those most innocent always pay for it. I've never seen anything good come from love."

"You. You came from love."

"And do you truly believe I am something good? You have no knowledge of the things I've done. The things that are done to others because of me." Ash turned his head to me. His eyes were a steely, sheltered shade of iron. "My father loved my mother more than anything in these realms. More than he should have. And still, he could not keep her safe. That is why I have these conditions. These *rules* as you like to call them. It's not about me attempting to exert authority over you or control you. It's about trying to do what my father failed at. It's about making sure you do not meet the same fate as my mother."

Chapter 28

Later that night, after I'd taken a quiet supper in my chambers alone, I picked up a soft throw blanket and went out onto the balcony.

Wrapping the blanket around my shoulders, I stood beside the railing. The whole day had been a blur of me turning over what Ash had said about his parents—about love.

I exhaled shakily as I stared out over the gray courtyard. His mother had been killed while he'd still been in her womb. I couldn't…

A knot returned to my throat. It took no leap of logic for me to consider that the one time the rules regarding Consorts had been broken, it had meant the death of his mother.

Her murder.

Grief rose, pressing down on my chest as I stared at the slowly darkening leaves of the Red Woods. Who had killed his mother? Was it the same person who'd killed his father? And was that how his father had become weak enough to be killed? Because he loved his wife more than anything in the realms? It had to be another Primal who'd done that. Which one, I couldn't be sure. I only knew what had been written about them by their Priests and mortals, and what little information there was on them wasn't enough to formulate any opinion.

Was that why his father had asked for a Consort? But if his wife had already been killed, why would he then seek a mortal bride, one who would be even more vulnerable?

Or one that he never had to fear falling in love with?

But that didn't make sense either because his love for his wife had already done its damage. Her being alive or dead would not change that.

It didn't make sense. There had to be a reason his father had done this, but did the reason matter?

No, whispered the voice that sounded like a mix of my mother's and mine.

What did make sense was the very real possibility that Ash was…that he was incapable of love because of what had happened to his parents. No part of me doubted he believed every single word he'd said about love, and that was sad.

And terrifying.

Because if he couldn't allow himself to love, what could I do to change that? Hell, I couldn't even stop myself from being antagonistic for more than a handful of minutes.

I never should've been the first daughter born after the deal had been made. Anyone or anything would be far better suited for this task than me. Possibly even a barrat.

A keen sense of desperation invaded me as I sat on the edge of the daybed, facing the Red Woods. The leaves had turned to a deep shade of reddish-black, a signal that night had fallen. As I sat there, I allowed myself to think about what I had done the night before Ash had come for me. Before everything had happened with Tavius.

I'd helped Marisol because I loved Ezra. Obviously, not the same kind of love shared between Ash's parents, but love…it truly made one do foolish things. How would Ash respond to my gift, to the knowledge that I could stop a soul from crossing over to the Shadowlands, returning them healthy and whole to their bodies?

As the Primal of Death, I doubted he would be overjoyed to learn of it—

Movement from the courtyard drew me from my thoughts. Once more, I recognized Ash's tall form. Like the last time, he was alone as he disappeared into the crimson-tinted darkness of the Red Woods.

Three days later, the dull ache had returned, settling in my temples. Along with the faint traces of blood when I brushed my teeth. The pain was nothing like the day Sir Holland had given me the tea he'd brewed, but as I stood in the deep shadows of the throne room, surrounded by the Primal's guards, I worried that it would worsen. I couldn't remember the herbs that had been in that pouch Sir Holland had left for me.

Shifting from one foot to the other, my gaze traveled across the raised, shadowstone dais to the Primal sitting in one of the thrones. My body tightened upon seeing him. Dressed in black with the iron-hued brocade around the raised collar and a line of the richly woven fabric swirling in a thin, diagonal line across his chest, he looked as if he'd been conjured from the shadows of a star-kissed hour of night. He eyed a man striding down the center of the chamber toward the dais. He wore no crown as he held court, meeting with those from Lethe. No grand banners had been raised behind the thrones. There was no ceremonial grandeur. The guards lining the alcove wore no livery or finery, but they were armed to the teeth. Each had a short sword strapped to their hip and a longer sword sheathed down their backs, the hilts pointed downward and slanted to the side for easy access. Across their chests hung daggers with wicked curves. All of the blades were shadowstone.

"Do you normally fidget this much?" a voice whispered to my right.

I stilled, ceasing my endless shifting as I glanced at Saion. He stared ahead. "Maybe?" I said in a low voice.

"I told you we should not have allowed her in here," Ector commented from my left.

Behind me, Rhain chuckled. "Are you worried Daddy Nyktos will be upset with you for allowing her in here and send you to bed without your supper?"

I lifted my brows. *Daddy Nyktos?*

"It will not be me who he will be irritated with," Ector commented, watching the man as closely as Saion was. "It will be you two, as I was the only one to raise objections to this."

"Are we not a team?" Saion asked. "If one of us goes down, we all go down together."

Ector smirked. "I am part of no such team."

"Traitor," Rhain murmured.

I rolled my eyes. "No one can even see me. I doubt he even knows

I'm here."

Saion looked down at me, one eyebrow raised. He, like the other two gods, were just as armed as the guards before us. "There is not a single part of Nyktos that doesn't know exactly where you are."

A chill of apprehension swept through me as, at that very moment, the Primal on the throne turned his head in the direction of the darkened alcove. I could practically feel his stare piercing straight through the line of guards who stood outside the alcove. I held my breath until his focus left me.

I had a feeling I would be in trouble for this later, even though I didn't think I was breaking any rules. Holding court wasn't the same as having an unexpected guest. At least, that was my reasoning as I watched the man stop before the Primal and bow deeply. I hadn't known Ash would be holding court today. In my defense, I had thought Ash and his guards were once more disappearing into a chamber that was located behind the dais, something I'd caught him doing several times in the last three days.

Which made me extremely curious about what went on in that chamber. What was discussed.

I'd been roaming aimlessly through the silent and otherwise empty palace, as I had been doing for the last *three days* when I saw him entering the throne room with several of the guards yet again and decided to follow. I'd made it about two steps into the chamber before Saion appeared out of nowhere and blocked me. I'd half expected him to turn me away, but he didn't.

And so, here I was, the longest I'd been in Ash's presence since the library. There had been no shared suppers or breakfasts. No surprise visits. He'd joined me briefly the day before when I stood under one of the outdoor stairwells watching Aios and Reaver. He'd stopped long enough to ask how I was and then left. A few minutes later, I'd seen him riding through the gates on Odin with several of the guards.

Needless to say, I was not only restless, I was also irritated and a hundred other emotions. But mostly, I was frustrated. How was I supposed to seduce him when I never saw him?

Of course, each night, I stared at those damn doors joining our rooms. On more than one occasion, I had stood in front of them, debating whether to knock. Every time I did, I thought about what he'd said about love and retreated to my bed.

I didn't think about why.

Instead, I thought about what an absolute failure this was turning out to be.

The dark-haired man rose from his knee to stand straight. "Your Highness," he said.

"Hamid," Ash replied, and a sudden gust of wind whirled through the chamber, stirring the candles' flames.

My gaze flicked to the open ceiling to see a draken flying overhead. They'd been circling the entire time as people came before the Primal to speak about incoming shipments, arrivals from other Courts, and arguments between tenants. It was all surprisingly mundane.

Except for the draken.

"What can I do for you today?" Ash asked.

"There's…there's nothing that I need of you, Your Highness." Hamid clasped his hands together as he glanced nervously up at the Primal.

"Is he mortal?" I asked.

"He is." Ector inclined his head. "How did you know?"

I shrugged. It was hard to explain, but the man didn't have the almost inherent sense of confidence or arrogance the gods and Primals seemed to have in how they moved.

"There's just something that I have grown concerned with," Hamid continued, looking up through a sheet of dark hair. "And while I hope it turns out to be nothing, I'm afraid that it may not."

"What is it?" Ash's fingers tapped on the arm of the throne.

"There is a young woman who is new to Lethe. Her name is Gemma—"

"Yes." Ash's fingers stilled. "I know who you mean. What about her?"

"I've seen her each day for the last month. She comes into the bakery. Always asks for a slice of chocolate torte with strawberries," Hamid explained, and for a moment, I imagined the deliciousness of such a treat. "Very quiet girl. Very polite. Doesn't make a lot of eye contact, but I imagine—well, that doesn't matter." He inhaled deeply. "I haven't seen her in a bit. Asked around. No one has."

Ash had gone completely still on the throne, as did the gods around me. "When was the last time you saw her?"

"Four days ago, Your Highness."

"Have you noticed anyone with her, at any time? Or seen anyone who may have taken an interest in her?" Ash asked.

The mortal shook his head. "I have not."

"I will have it looked into." Ash sent a quick glance to the alcoves. "Thank you for bringing this to my attention."

Saion immediately stepped away from me. He looked over his shoulder at Rhain and then to me, "If you'll excuse me?"

Before I could say a word, both he and Rhain left the alcove, stalking toward the entryway to the chamber. I turned to Ector with a frown. "Who is this Gemma?"

The line of Ector's jaw was hard. "No one."

I didn't think for one second she was no one. Not to incite that kind of reaction from Ash. My interest was more than just piqued as I watched Hamid leave the chamber and Theon enter.

I hadn't seen the god since the day I'd arrived. The easy grin and teasing air were gone as he strode quickly toward the dais. Like the other gods, he had a short sword strapped to his hip, and a long sword across his back. He went to the dais as Ash leaned forward. Whatever Theon said, he spoke too quietly for me to hear, but I knew that something was happening because Ash sent another quick look in the direction of the alcove.

"Stay here," Ector ordered before walking off.

Antsy, I watched him part the line of guards and take the steps of the dais. Wind stirred the flames once more as another draken flew overhead, calling out in a shrill, staggered sound. Tiny bumps spread across my flesh as Ector bent his head to Ash's. The god looked at Theon and then nodded. He pivoted quickly as Ash rose from the throne. I started to step forward as Ector hopped down from the dais and returned to my side.

"Come," he said, reaching for me but stopping short of touching me. "We must go."

Some things never changed it seemed. My frown deepened. "What is going on?"

"Nothing."

No part of me wanted to follow, but I felt the sudden tension in the air. One that warned me I should obey.

I went, noting that Ector walked to my left, forcing me between him and the wall. The moment we were out in the hall, I stopped. "What is going on, and don't say nothing? Something is."

"There has been an unexpected…arrival." The fair-haired god's lip curled. "His Highness stated that you're aware of what to do when there are guests."

I squeezed my hands into fists. "I am."

"Perfect." He led me down the wide corridor. "Would you like to return to your chamber?"

"Not really."

He raised a brow. "Then your only other option..." He stopped, stepping into the alcove and opening a set of doors. "Is the library."

I stared into the dimly lit space. The room was slightly better than my bedchamber, even though there was a heavy, haunting quality to it—a sadness that clung to the walls and coated the tomes lining the shelves, just as the fine layer of dust did, seeping into the floors and the air. My gaze fell on the candlelit portraits at the back of the chamber. Was it Ash who lit the candles each day, replacing them when they burned to the quick? Did he come in here often, so that his memory of his father remained fresh? So that he had a face to place with his mother's name?

I stepped inside, surrounded by the scent of books and frankincense, and welcomed by the sadness. I faced Ector. "Am I supposed to stay in here until I'm allowed to return to roaming aimlessly?"

"Pretty much. I doubt she will have any interest in a library," he replied, and I went completely and utterly still. "Someone will let you know when you're free to resume roaming around aimlessly."

My heart was suddenly pounding. *She*. "Who…who is the guest?"

"A friend of Nyktos'," he replied flatly, and it didn't sound like this was someone Ector was fond of. Then again, I didn't think Ector was too fond of me. His luminous eyes met mine. "Remember what you agreed to."

"I remember."

Ector eyed me as he slowly closed the library doors. The moment I heard them snick into place, I went to them and waited.

Who was *she*?

Better yet, who was she that Ash didn't want me around? A sour sensation pooled in my stomach, one that couldn't be jealousy. More like…indignant anger. For someone who claimed to think of how I *tasted* at the most inappropriate times, he sure hadn't shown any *interest* over the last three days. Nor had he shown any interest in receiving pleasure, something males generally always wanted. Could it be because he'd been finding pleasure elsewhere despite the impression I'd gotten regarding his experience?

The last thing I needed was competition when it wasn't like I could win his heart with my sparkling personality. My options were limited.

And not only that, I was to be his Consort. If he were going to be *interested* in others, he could at least do it elsewhere.

Cracking open the door, I peered out into the hall, half surprised not to find Ector standing there. I didn't waste a second. I quietly closed the doors behind me and crept out into the hall. I only made it to the area of Ash's office when I heard voices.

"You've been particularly difficult to obtain an audience with lately." A velvet-wrapped voice filled the hall.

"Have I been?" came Ash's response.

I cursed under my breath, quickly scanning the hall. I darted into an alcove and pressed my back against the cool stone wall.

"You have," the woman replied. "I was beginning to take it personally."

"Nothing personal, Veses. I've just been busy."

Veses? The Primal of Rites and Prosperity? My throat dried as I leaned toward the thin slit of a gap between the thick pillar and the wall. She was heavily celebrated during the weeks leading up to the Rite, in rituals only known to the Chosen. Many prayed to her for good luck but doing so came with risks. Veses could be vengeful, dishing out misfortune to those she found unworthy of blessings.

"Too busy for me?" Veses asked, a sharpness edging into the softness of her tone. Was she one of the Primals that pushed Ash?

"Even you," Ash said.

"Now, I'm a little offended." That sharpness had become a blade, just as they entered my narrow line of sight. "I'm sure it's unintentional."

Ash moved into view first. He was unarmed, as he had been in the throne room. But considering what he was capable of, I didn't know if that meant he didn't view this Veses as a threat or not. "You should know by now that I never cause unintended offense."

The Primal laughed, and I gritted my teeth at the honey-coated sound. A second later, she stepped into the narrow opening. If Ash was midnight personified, she was sunlight manifested.

Golden-blonde hair cascaded over slim shoulders in thick, perfectly coiled ringlets, reaching an impossibly narrow waist cinched by a gown a shade or so paler than her hair. The gossamer fabric clung to a lithe body. I glanced down at the breeches I wore, thinking that one of my legs was probably the size of both of hers.

I looked back up as she turned to Ash, and I wished I'd continued staring at my leg as none of the many paintings and renderings I'd seen of her had done her justice. Her creamy complexion was smooth and pink, clear of freckles. The line of her nose and the shape of her brow were delicate, as if she had been constructed of the same handblown glass as the figurines that had lined my stepfather's office. And her mouth was full, a perfect pout the shade of apricots. She was incredibly beautiful.

I didn't like this Primal.

I didn't like her, knowing damn well my reasons were…well, quite petty.

"No," Veses remarked, lifting a bare arm. She wore a similar silver band around her slender biceps. Her hand coasted up his arm. "You just offend intentionally."

"You know me all too well." Ash opened the door to his office.

Now, I *really* disliked her.

And him.

And everyone.

"Do I? If so, I wouldn't have been so blindsided by the rumor I heard." Her slender fingers reached the silver band around his upper arm.

For one of the incredibly rare moments in my life, I heeded caution and stayed where I was. She was a *Primal.* One that could bestow bad luck with a graze of her fingers. And the gods knew I already had enough of that in my life. Still, it took everything in me to remain hidden.

He looked at her. She was nearly his height, so they were almost eye to eye. "What is this rumor you heard?"

She toyed with the band while I wondered exactly how badly a shadowstone dagger to the chest would sting a Primal. "I heard that you have taken a Consort."

My lips parted as I pressed against the pillar.

A half-smile appeared and curved Ash's lips. "News does travel fast."

Veses' fingers stilled as she stared at him. A faint, silvery glow rippled over her skin. The delicate features hardened. "So, it's true?" she asked, and I didn't think she sounded happy at all.

"It is."

She didn't speak for a long moment. "That is…very intriguing."

"Is it?" His blasé tone irked me.

"Yes." Veses' smile was tight-lipped. "I'm sure I'm not the only one who will find that intriguing, Nyktos."

A muscle ticked in his jaw as she slid her hand from his arm and brushed it across him, stepping into the darkness of the office. Ash followed, hand still on one of the doors. He stopped in the doorway, turning…

He looked directly at the alcove.

Eyes widening, I jerked back against the wall. He knew I was here. What in the hell? Heart thumping, I waited until I heard the door close before I peeked between the pillar and the wall. The hall was empty.

A whole new wave of irritation surged through me as I stepped out from under the alcove. Ash had been so busy the last several days that I'd barely seen him, but he was making time for this Veses? Who was a Primal, but whatever.

I hurried past the library to the back stairs I'd discovered a few days ago and stalked out the side door near the kitchen, into the gray world of the Shadowlands. There was no breeze today. The air was stagnant, unchanging. I looked up, noting that there were no clouds. There were never clouds, but the stars were shining, blanketing the sky.

Crossing the courtyard, I looked up at the tall, imposing Rise. As I expected, there were no guards. I had never seen them on this side. Normally, they patrolled the western portion, the front, and the northern part of the Red Woods, which faced Lethe.

The gray grass crunched under my boots as I continued forward. I really had no idea where I was going. All I knew was that I couldn't spend another moment in the dusty, sad library, my chambers, or in the bare, empty palace where I felt as unseen as I did in Wayfair.

And that was silly. I only needed to be seen by Ash, but I was still a ghost. Nothing.

I hadn't realized how close I'd come to the Red Woods until I found myself mere feet from one of the blood leaves. My steps slowed as I took them in, curious. I'd never seen a leaf such a vibrant shade of red before. Nor iron-hued bark. What could have turned them this color? I walked forward, just a few feet into where I was forbidden to travel. I remembered Ash's warning, but how dangerous could they be when no gate or wall separated the woods from Haides?

I looked over my shoulder, seeing no sign of Ector. With Saion and Rhain checking on the missing woman in Lethe, there was no one who would run back and tell on me.

And it wasn't like I couldn't take care of myself while Ash was busy with Veses, doing the gods' only knew what.

A faint ache threatened to return to my temples as I reached up, touching a leaf on a low-hanging branch. The texture was smooth and soft, reminding me of velvet. I dragged my thumb over the supple leaf, my mind conjuring the image of Ash doing the same with a strand of my hair.

Was Ash as fascinated with Veses' hair as he so often appeared to be with mine? I imagined he would be. Her curls were thick and bouncy and didn't resemble a nest of tangles.

"I'm the worst," I muttered, rolling my eyes as I lowered my hand and drifted forward.

I shouldn't be surprised that he was expressing his interest in that office with Veses. I'd obviously been wrong in my perception of what he'd said about his experience. The way he'd kissed and touched me should've been enough evidence that he had quite a bit of skill—skill I was betting *Veses* also knew all too well. My lip curled—

A shrill shriek of pain stopped me dead in my tracks. I looked up as something winged and silver crashed through the red leaves, plummeting to the ground with a heavy thud. A *hawk*. It was a large, silver hawk. Another swooped down from above, veering off when it spotted me. I didn't even know these types of hawks were in Iliseeum, let alone the Shadowlands. I'd only ever caught rare glimpses of them circling the very tips of the Dark Elms.

With wide eyes, I watched the hawk try to lift a clearly broken wing. Red streaked its throat and belly as it flailed on the gray grass. It squawked pitifully, dark talons thrashing and digging into the soil.

What was it with wounded animals and me? How did I always—?

Warmth pulsed in my chest, sudden and intense. The tingling rush of eather flooding my veins followed, stunning me. It was very much like when I was around something that'd died, but this hawk…it was still alive.

Confused, I looked down at my hands as a faint aura appeared, the light flickering softly between my fingers and over my skin. It was just like when I touched Marisol.

But Marisol had been dead.

"What the hell?" I looked over at the hawk as my chest throbbed, and this…urge swept through me. A demand that hummed, driving me forward. I was kneeling beside the hawk before I realized what I was doing. The whites of its eyes were stark as its wild gaze rolled from the sky to me.

The hawk stilled. I knew it was still alive, even though I couldn't tell if it breathed. It was the *gift*. It knew. Somehow, I knew the hawk still lived, even though it didn't strike with talons that could easily tear into my flesh.

Static danced over my hands as the heat gathered in my palms. I didn't know what was happening, nor did I understand this powerful instinct, but it felt old. Ancient. Just like that dark and oily feeling had when I'd been forced to my knees in front of the statue of Kolis and stared at Tavius. It was undeniable, and there was nothing I could do but obey. I placed a hand on the exposed belly of the hawk, hoping that it remained still.

The hum flared intensely in my chest, and the light around my hands brightened for a heartbeat before the glow swept over the hawk and onto the soil, sparking and crackling as it seeped into and crawled across the ground.

I sucked in a stuttered breath as the hawk twitched, emitting a sharp cry. Panic crowded the edges of my mind. I couldn't see the hawk under the glow. What if I had done something wrong? What if I killed the bird? If I did, I would never touch another thing—

A coarse, heavy wing straightened and swept down, brushing over my hand. Startled, I jerked back my arm and fell on my ass. The aura receded, and the hawk…

It stood, tentatively lifting both wings. The hawk's wingspan was enormous, and I thought of the old stories Odetta had told me about these types of birds of prey. How they could pick up small animals and even children. I hadn't believed her.

Seeing one this close, I now did.

The hawk's head swiveled toward me. I ensured I made no sudden movements as it eyed me with flat, black eyes full of intelligence. The hawk chirped softly, a staggering call that reminded me of what the draken had done.

Then it took flight.

And I remained there, on my ass, absolutely dumbfounded. My touch… It healed? It had never done that before, but I also hadn't tried. My stunned gaze fell to my hands as that heady warmth trickled through me, easing the tension in my neck and shoulders. Was my gift changing? Evolving? I didn't think it had always been like that because I'd been around wounded animals and people before. I hadn't felt like this when Tavius had been whipping his horse and I intervened, but I could…*sense* that it still lived. Just like I could sense when something had passed. And what about Odetta? My gift had come alive while she had been sleeping. I had chalked it up to fear igniting it, but maybe I had been wrong. Perhaps my gift had been urging me to heal her? I lowered my hands to the grass, curling them—

The *grass.*

I looked down. The grass was gray like…like the Rot but soft. I inhaled deeply, recognizing the stale scent of lilacs. My gaze rose, traveling over the thin, wispy weeds that ran along the floor of the Red Woods. The memory of the trees I'd seen when I first entered the Shadowlands formed in my mind. The Dying Woods. Their branches had been gnarled and leafless, and the bark was also gray, a deeper shade of steel, just like these.

Just like those in Lasania infected by the Rot.

"Shit," I whispered.

How had I not noticed that until now? Was this the Rot? A possible consequence of the deal not being fulfilled? Or was this something else?

A twig snapped, and immediately, I knew it wasn't Ash or any of his guards. None of them would've made a sound. Another crack came, and the smell of stale flowers intensified.

My hand went to where the dagger was sheathed to my thigh as I pushed off the ground and turned around.

The space between the red-leafed trees didn't look right. I squinted. The shadows there…they were thicker, and they moved *forward* into the fractured beams of starlight. Dark pants. Waxy skin. Bare skulls and mouths stretched too wide yet stitched closed.

I recognized them immediately.

Hunters.

Chapter 29

My stomach lurched as I darted under a low-hanging, thickly leafed branch. I remained under the limb, hoping they hadn't seen me, and quickly counted. Five of them. Gods. I stayed completely still as they drifted forward in a vee formation.

What were they doing in the Shadowlands?

Ash had insinuated that they'd been in the mortal realm looking for him. Were they searching for him again? Obviously, they'd found him, but why would they be here?

I made sure I made no sound as I unsheathed the shadowstone dagger. I didn't want to draw their attention since I never wanted to see their mouths split open ever again.

Reminding myself that Ash had struck against them first, there was a good chance they would keep going even if they had seen me. Not even daring to take a too-deep breath, I watched them move closer. *Keep going. Just keep on creepily walking—*

The closest Hunter's head snapped in my direction. The others stopped in unison and turned toward me.

"Shit," I whispered, straightening. The Hunter who stopped first tilted its head. "Hi…?"

The other four cocked their heads.

"I'm just out for a…stroll," I continued, grip tightening on the branch. "That's all. You do whatever it is that you all are doing and—"

The first Hunter stepped forward, reaching for the hilt of the sword strapped across his back. Dammit.

I yanked the limb back and then let go. The branch snapped forward, smacking the Hunter in the face. Staggering back, the creature let out a muffled grunt. I didn't waste a second. Not after knowing what could come out of the thing's mouth. I recalled Ash's instructions. Head or heart. I went for the heart because I didn't want to be anywhere near that mouth. I darted out from under the branches. Or tried to. My foot snagged on something—an exposed root or rock.

"Dammit!" I stumbled, losing my balance. Throwing out my hand, I planted my palm against the Hunter's chest to steady myself. His skin felt cold and bloodless, like modeling clay. I shuddered. My touch seemed to affect the creature. His eyes flared wide, and a muffled moan reverberated from him. The others made that same sound as I slammed the dagger deep into the Hunter's chest. It jerked, making no sound this time. Yanking the dagger free, I turned to the others as the first began to shrivel, collapsing into a fine layer of dust that smelled of stale lilacs.

Four more Hunters. The odds didn't look great, but I didn't let panic take hold as I thrust the dagger into the next Hunter's chest. I whipped around, muscles tensing. None of the creatures reached for their swords now, but they did come at me, and a wild feeling swept through me as adrenaline surged, welcoming the *fight*. The expenditure of energy. Maybe even the killing. I didn't know.

But I smiled. "Come on."

Two advanced, and I shot between them. Twisting, I kicked out, catching one in the chest. The Hunter stumbled as I turned, shoving the dagger into its chest. A cold hand clamped down on my arm. Cringing at the feel of it, I spun sharply, stepping into the Hunter. Its surprisingly sharp fingernails cut into the skin of my arm, drawing blood. I hissed through the sting and slammed my elbow into its chin, knocking its head back. The creature let go, and I stabbed it through the chest extra hard.

As it exploded, I spared my arm a quick glance. Small welts rose from where it had scratched me, beading tiny drops of blood.

"Bastard," I spat.

A muffled shout spun me around in time to see something grab the Hunter by the legs, dragging it into the *ground.*

I staggered back, staring at where the Hunter had disappeared into the disturbed gray soil. What had just happened? What in the—?

Chunks of gray exploded from the ground, showering the air.

Several streaming geysers all at once, spewing dirt and grass. I threw up a hand as tiny rocks pelted my cheeks. Just as I lowered my arm, another section of the ground erupted, directly in front of me.

And what launched out of that hole would fuel nightmares to last a lifetime.

Jumping back, I stared at what definitely wasn't a Hunter. It looked like it *had* been mortal once as it crouched on the edge of the jagged fissure, staring up at me. *Had been* being the keywords. Its skin was washed-out, a chalky gray color except for the dark, almost-black smudges under its eyes. The cheeks were sunken, its lips bleached of all color. The once-white robes it wore were dusty and ragged, torn and hanging off bony shoulders and hips, revealing patches of bloodless skin underneath.

Was this a Shade?

If so, Davina and Ash had failed to mention that they were in the godsdamn *ground.*

Carefully backing up, I tightened my grip on the dagger as more of these things appeared, climbing out of the ground so unbelievably fast. Too fast for something that looked really, really dead. I saw four of them, and they all were crouched, staring up at me as their nostrils flared. They…*sniffed* the air. A low, guttural moan came from one of them. My gaze shifted as I continued putting more space between us. It was a woman. Patches of dark, stringy hair hung from her skull. She rose.

"Don't come any closer," I warned, and the woman stopped. My heart thumped heavily. If these were Shades, I wasn't sure if I was supposed to kill them. No one had mentioned what wrangling them up actually entailed.

She stared at me—all of them stared at me, no longer smelling the air. The grating, raspy sound came again from another, increasing into a high-pitched whine. Tiny bumps rose all over my skin. It sounded…*hungry.*

Her mouth dropped open, lips peeling back over fangs. No one had mentioned *fangs* either when they'd said that the Shades could be bitey. Why in the hell did they have fangs? Why had Andreia developed them in death? Did that happen to godlings?

And why in the whole wide world of fucks was I even thinking about any of that right now?

The moaning sound ended in a hiss, and that was right about the time I decided that this was not a fight I wanted to be involved in. I started to turn, only realizing then how far from the palace I'd traveled.

Ash would be angry.

But that wasn't my most immediate problem or concern. The creature charged forward, hands curled like claws, mouth stretched wide.

There was no time to run.

Stepping into her attack, I thrust the dagger into her chest. The recessed area gave way to the blade, and a dark, shimmery red substance that smelled of rot and decay splashed my hand. Blood. It was shimmering *blood.* Her legs crumpled. I gasped under the sudden dead weight of her body. Unprepared, I almost went down with her, barely managing to yank the blade free and keep my footing. She remained where she'd fallen, legs twisted under her body, mouth hanging open and eyes fixed upon nothing. I waited, but she didn't break apart into dust like the Hunters.

My head jerked up as another hissed, and my blood turned to ice. Four more of these things had appeared among the trees, coming from openings in the ground I hadn't even realized were there.

Ash would be very, very angry.

One ran forward, fangs bared as it swiped at me. I ducked under its arm and kicked out, catching it in the leg. A bone cracked, turning my stomach. I hadn't kicked *that* hard, but the lower part of the leg was broken, and it still came at me, dragging the misshapen leg behind it. I shot forward, shoving the dagger deep into its chest. The creature started to fall—

Weight crashed into me, taking me to the ground. I twisted onto my back. A ghastly face appeared inches above mine, fangs snapping. I slammed a hand into its chest, holding it off. I yanked on the dagger, a scream of frustration building in my throat when it didn't give.

Oh, gods, it was *stuck* in the creature that had fallen.

I pulled as hard as I could, my arm trembling under the pressure of the thing as it continued biting at the air. I knew if those fangs got anywhere near my skin, they'd tear my flesh open. Panic began seeping in as I wiggled, managing to get a leg under the creature. I shoved my knee into its midsection, lessening some of its weight on my arm. The dagger slid an inch. I tugged harder—

Cold, *skinless* fingers dug into my ankle and jerked hard. The dagger slipped free, but so did my hand on the creature's chest. Terror was a bitter taste in the back of my mouth as I swung the dagger, driving the blade into the side of its *head.* Dark, foul-smelling blood sprayed my face. I gagged, jerking the dagger free as the other creature hauled me across the ground, its fleshless fingers pressing into my calf, my thigh. I shifted, reaching for the creature as I saw the others bearing down on us. There wasn't enough time. Even if I killed one or two more, it wouldn't be enough. I knew this even as I brought the dagger down—

A rush of cold air and icy fury roared through the trees, sending the red leaves above into a frenzy. The creature who had my leg was suddenly yanked backward and up.

Ash.

I caught a glimpse of the hard lines of his face as he flung the creature aside, impaling it on a low branch.

Exhaling raggedly, I looked up.

"Don't," Ash cut me off as he spun around. "Not a single word."

I scrambled to my feet. "Excuse me?"

"In case you have trouble counting, that is two words." He caught another by the throat, but he didn't throw this one aside. He lifted it into the air, and that silvery-white aura flared to life, flowing down his arm. "I want you to be quiet."

I opened my mouth as the crackling, spitting energy spread from his hand to ripple over the creature. A network of veins lit under the thing's skin, burning white. It howled as it erupted in silver flames. I snapped my mouth shut, stumbling back a step against stiff hands. I jumped to the side as the burning creature and flames evaporated. "I want—"

"I want you to be silent," Ash repeated, slamming his hand onto another's face. The silvery energy washed over it, and the thing shrieked. He pushed it aside, and it spun, flailing and falling. "And I want you to think about what you just did."

I blinked. "Do you want me to find a corner to sit in, too?"

Ash's head snapped in my direction, and my stomach tumbled. His eyes were brighter than the stars. "Will that help you think better?" He snagged another creature by the shoulder, catching it without even looking at it. "If so, then by all means, find a corner."

"I am not a child," I shot back as the creature caught fire and screamed.

"Thank fuck." He stalked toward the one impaled on the tree.

"Then don't speak to me like I am."

Ash placed his hand against its head as it snapped at him. Eather poured over the creature, obliterating it.

Then he faced me. "I wouldn't have to if you didn't behave as one who couldn't follow through on their promises." The woods fell silent around us. "What did I tell you about these woods? Did you forget what I said would happen if you entered them?"

"Well, I didn't forget. I just…"

Ash stared at me expectedly, nostril's flared and eyes swirling.

"*You* go into them!" I reasoned. "I saw you come in here twice."

"You are not me, Sera." He took a step forward. "Do you know what is in these woods? In the very place I forbade you to travel into? That you agreed to stay out of? Do you know what exists in here that turns the leaves of the trees red?" he demanded, the radiance of his eyes receding.

I glanced at the bodies that remained. "Shades?"

He laughed harshly. "Those things were not Shades. You are standing in the Red Woods, where the blood of entombed gods soaks every root of every tree These are blood trees."

A chill swept over me as I resisted the urge to climb one of the red trees just to get away from the ground. "Why in the world do you have gods entombed in the ground?"

"Their entombment is punishment," he answered, and there was no way I could stop the rising tide of horror at the thought. His eyes narrowed. "Punishment most would consider far too lenient for the atrocities they committed."

I would have to take his word for that. "How did they get free? Does that happen often?"

"It shouldn't." Those eyes bored into me. "These haven't been down there all that long," he said, and I really didn't want to think of the others who'd been down there longer. "But all of them are as close to death as they can be without actually being dead. They are usually magically chained and shouldn't be able to break those kinds of bonds."

Gods were extremely powerful. I couldn't imagine what could be used to restrain them. "What are their bonds made of?"

"The bones of other gods and Primal magic," he answered, and my stomach turned. "They are placed atop the gods and used to bind the wrists and feet. If they fight it, the bones dig into their skin."

My gaze flicked to the leaves of the tree. "Is the punishment what causes their blood to turn the leaves?"

"In this case, yes."

I lifted my brows.

"Wherever a god or Primal is entombed, or where their blood spills, you will see a blood tree. It serves as either a memorial or a warning," he explained. "Either way, it is not land one should ever disturb."

"Good to know," I murmured. "But I didn't disturb the land."

"But you did," he stated, his eyes flaring bright once more. "You bled."

At first, I didn't understand, having forgotten the scratches. I glanced down at my arm. "Barely."

"That doesn't matter. A single drop would've roused those who are not so deeply entombed. They are drawn to anything alive, and you, *liessa*, are very much alive. If I hadn't come when I did, they would've devoured you whole."

Devoured me…whole? I shuddered, thinking it was probably a good idea I hadn't mentioned the Hunters. "I was fighting them off—"

"Barely," he cut me off. "They would've overpowered you. And all of this—" He sliced his hand through the air. "All that has been done to keep you safe would have been for *nothing*."

I sucked in a heady breath. "Need I remind you that I never asked for you to do anything to keep me *safe*?"

"There is no need to remind me of such, but dealing with you does remind me of that saying."

"I can't wait to hear this," I muttered, sheathing my dagger.

"The road to hell is paved with good intentions," he said. "Perhaps you've heard that?"

"Sounds like something you'd have embroidered on a pillow."

The look he shot me said he was unimpressed.

"What are you even doing out here?" I demanded. "I thought you were *busy* with an unexpected arrival."

"I am very busy with that guest. And yet, here I am, saving you," he replied. "Again."

I wasn't sure which part of that statement irked me the most. The part where he referred to Veses as a guest, or the fact that he had saved me. Again. "I really, really want to stab you again."

One side of his lips curled up. "Part of me would really like to see you try. However, I am busy keeping said guest distracted—"

"Distracted?" I laughed as my heart twisted and dropped at the same time. "How are you keeping your guest distracted in your office? With stimulating *conversation* and your ample *charm*?"

His smile turned as cold as his fury. "As I'm sure you remember, my charm is very ample."

My cheeks heated. "I've been trying to forget your overinflated charm."

"Was it not you who just referred to it as ample?" His eyes flashed a deep quicksilver.

The heat of anger and something far more potent scalded the back of my neck. "I was being *facetious*."

"Sure, you were."

"I was—"

"I don't have time for this." He looked over his shoulder, yelling, "Saion!"

The god appeared between the red-leafed trees, lips pursed and eyes wide. "Yes?" He drew out the word.

Oh my gods, had he been lurking there the whole time? And when did he return?

"Can you make sure she returns to the palace yards as quickly as possible without getting herself into any more trouble between here and there? And when you are done, please find Rhahar. We will need to check the tombs," Ash said, shooting me a long look of warning. "I would be greatly appreciative."

"Sounds like a simple enough task," the god replied.

Ash snorted. "It sounds that way, but I can assure you that it will not be."

Offended, I stepped forward. "If the woods are so dangerous, why is there no gate or wall to seal them off?"

The Primal looked over his shoulder. "Because most are intelligent enough not to enter the Red Woods once warned." His eyes narrowed. "The keyword being *most*."

"That was rude," I muttered.

"And what you did was foolish. So, here we are." Ash turned away and started walking before I could respond. He passed Saion, saying, "Good luck."

My mouth dropped open.

Saion's brows rose as he looked back at me. Neither of us moved until Ash had disappeared amid the trees. "Well…this is somewhat awkward."

I folded my arms over my chest.

"I really hope you don't make this difficult," he added. "I've had a rather long day as it is."

I felt a small, incredibly childish urge to run off and make his day much, much longer than it already was. But I had no desire to be on the grounds where gods were entombed. So, I stomped forward like the adult I was.

The god arched a brow, grinning. "Thank you."

I said nothing as I passed him. He easily fell into step beside me. He was silent for only a few blessed seconds. "How did you end up bleeding?"

"Not sure," I lied. "Must've cut it on the bark. Did you find the missing woman?" I asked, changing the subject.

"No. We didn't."

"Do you think something—whoa." A wave of dizziness swept through me.

Saion stopped. "Are you all right?"

"Yeah, I…" A fiery pain exploded inside me, knocking me backward. I stumbled as the searing burn traveled up my arm and across my chest, stunning in its intensity and suddenness. In a daze, I looked to my right and down, expecting to see an arrow jutting out from me, but I saw nothing but the three scratches down my forearm and the thin, black lines radiating from the marks and spreading across my skin.

"Shit," Saion exploded as I bumped into the tree. He gripped my hand, and I barely felt the strange jolt of energy from his touch. "What caused this mark? And don't you dare say it was a tree. A tree would not do that."

I tried to swallow, but my throat felt weirdly tight. "I…there were Hunters in the woods. Gyrms. One of them…" A strange, floral taste gathered in the back of my mouth. Tingles swept down my arms, my legs. "I…I don't feel right."

"Did one of them scratch you?" The eather behind his pupils pulsed. "Sera, were you scratched?" He lowered his head to my arm and *sniffed* at the wound.

"Why are…are you smelling me?" My legs went out from underneath me. Light burst behind my eyes as I heard Saion snarl, "*Fuck.*"

And then I fell into nothing.

Chapter 30

Waking was like fighting my way through thick fog. Brief glimpses of memories were hard to latch on to, and they flipped endlessly through the misty nothingness. A missing woman. A beautiful Primal in a pale-yellow gown and a wounded, silver hawk. Hunters and entombed, hungry gods. A Hunter had scratched me, and it…did something. I'd been dizzy. There had been sudden, intense pain, and then I'd passed out.

The fog cleared as I came to, slowly becoming aware of lying on my stomach and having something soft under my cheek. A different taste gathered in my mouth. Bitter yet sweet.

I inhaled sharply, muscles tensing as I shifted my weight to my forearms, preparing to push up—

"I wouldn't do that."

At the sound of the unfamiliar voice, my eyes flew open and locked on the man sitting at the side of the bed. He had long, black hair—almost as long as the god Madis—and streaked with faint lines of crimson. It lay over the shoulders of his loose shirt, untied at the neck. I couldn't peg his age. His features were broad and proud, only a hint of creasing at the corners of his eyes. He was all but sprawled in the chair, his long legs stretched out and crossed at the ankles, bare feet resting on the bed, and elbows propped on the arms of the chair, hands hanging loosely to the sides. I didn't think anyone could look more relaxed, but there was an unmistakable coiled tension thrumming beneath warm, copper skin as if he could spring into action without warning.

As I stared at him, I realized three things at once. I'd never seen this male before. I was completely and utterly *nude* under a sheet that had been draped over me with no recollection of how that had occurred or why. And his eyes…they weren't *right*. The irises were a shade of wine, his pupils were thin, vertical slits, much like…like Davina's. My heart kicked unsteadily against my chest.

He was a draken.

The man wasn't smiling or frowning. There was nothing soft about his features. He simply stared at me from where he sat. Tiny bumps broke out across my skin.

"The toxin in your body should be all cleared out by now," he said. "But if you wish to sit up, I would do so slowly just in case. If you pass out again, it will probably disturb Ash."

Ash.

This draken was the first person I'd ever heard refer to the Primal by his nickname. "Who…who are you?" I rasped, my throat hoarse and dry.

"We've met before."

My heart pounded even faster. "On…on the road when I first arrived?"

He nodded. "I'm Nektas."

My gaze swept over him once more. He was a large man. Probably even as tall as Ash, but I still couldn't imagine him shifting into the massive creature I'd seen on the road. I looked beyond him, past the polished column of the bed, where gauzy white curtains had been tied back. There were only shadowy shapes in the gloom of the room. "Where…where is Ash?"

"He is checking the tombs." Nektas tipped his head slightly, and a long sheet of black-and-red hair slid over his right arm. "According to him, I am here to make sure you do not wake up and immediately get yourself into trouble."

That sounded like something *he'd* say. "I don't get myself in trouble."

Nektas raised a brow. "Really?"

I chose to ignore that. "Do I want to know why I'm nude?"

"The toxin was seeping out of your pores. Your clothing was ruined, and you were covered in it." Ash didn't think you'd want to wake in such a state," he told me. "Aios removed your clothing and bathed you."

Well, that was a relief.

Kind of.

"What kind of toxin?"

"The kind that Gyrms carry in their insides. It spreads through their mouths and nails." He *still* hadn't blinked. "The black streaks on your arms were the first sign. By the time Saion brought you in, those marks covered your entire body. You're lucky you're alive."

My stomach dipped as my gaze shot to my forearm. There were no streaks other than the faint pink scratch marks.

I suddenly remembered what Ash had said about the serpents that had come out of the Hunters. Their bite was toxic. He'd failed to mention the Gyrms' nails were, as well. "How long have I've been asleep?"

"A day," he answered.

My heart thumped heavily once more. "Why am I not dead?"

"Ash had an antidote," he stated. "A potion once derived from a plant grown just outside of the Shadowlands near the Red River. The blister weed stops the spread of the toxin, causing the body to expel it. There is very little of the potion to be found. His choice to give it to you saved your life, which was a surprise."

I honestly had no idea what to say to that. "You think he should've let me die?"

A close-lipped smile appeared. "It would've served him better not to have given you the potion."

My gaze lifted to him. "Because he'd be free of the deal then?"

Nektas nodded, confirming that he was one of the few who knew about the deal. "He'd be free of you."

"Wow," I murmured.

"I mean no offense," he replied. "But he did not choose this deal."

I held his unflinching stare. "Neither did I."

"And yet, both of you are here." Nektas lifted his brows. "And he saved your life when it only made sense to let you pass."

There was a catch in my breath, making it difficult to follow Sir Holland's instructions. "He probably felt bad," I reasoned, unsure of why I was even speaking this aloud to the draken. "About the deal. He feels…obligated."

A tight-lipped smile appeared. "I don't think his decision had anything to do with that deal. I don't think any of his recent decisions have."

Aios arrived shortly after Nektas had left me in a state of confusion. He'd stepped out onto the balcony, and I held the sheet to my chest as she retrieved an ivory robe made of some soft fabric, my thoughts spinning from one thing to the next.

Everything that Ash had done—was doing—was because of the deal. No part of me didn't believe that Ash felt an obligation toward me—a sense of responsibility I hoped to exploit.

The bitter taste still lingered in my mouth as Aios brought the robe over to me. "How are you feeling?" she asked. Her face was paler than normal. Concern pinched her brow.

"Not like I've been poisoned," I admitted, tying the sash on the robe around my waist.

"I suppose that is a good thing." She grabbed several pillows, fluffing them and then propping them against the head of the bed. "I'll get you something to drink."

"You don't have to do that."

"I know." Aios drifted toward the table, pushing up the sleeves of her sweater. "There are a lot of things I don't have to do that I choose to do. This is one of them. Whiskey or water?"

I eased into the mound of pillows. "Whiskey. I could really use some whiskey."

A small smile appeared. Picking up a crystal decanter, she poured amber liquid into a small glass then brought the drink over to me. "If this doesn't upset your stomach, I imagine you'll be able to handle some food shortly."

I took a small sip of the smoky liquor, welcoming the bite as it traveled down my throat and blossomed in my chest. "Thank you."

Nektas strode in from the balcony. "He comes."

My hand trembled. The draken didn't need to clarify who for me to know it was Ash. A nervous sort of energy invaded my senses, and I took a longer drink of the whiskey, downing half the glass. Swallowing, I glanced up.

Nektas stared at me.

"Would you like me to refill that?" Aios asked, grinning.

"No. That would…probably not be wise."

"Why?" the draken asked.

"I'm more likely to do something that would fall under the whole getting-myself-in-trouble bit," I admitted. What came out of my mouth next had to be the liquor already loosening my tongue. "Is the other Primal still here?"

"No." The grin faded from Aios's face. "She is gone."

"For now," Nektas tacked on. "She'll be back."

"True," Aios murmured, glancing at the closed doors.

Neither of them gave me the impression that they were fans of Veses. Ector hadn't either. When the doors opened, their reactions to the mention of Veses fell to the wayside. My entire being focused on Ash when he entered the bedchamber, especially that little ball of fuzzy warmth in my chest. I swore it buzzed happily as his gaze locked with mine.

I was also sure it wasn't the whiskey that made up the little ball of warmth.

Aios and Nektas quickly made their way to the doors, but the draken stopped. "She's worried about her alcohol consumption provoking her, allowing her to get into trouble."

My jaw unlocked.

"Just thought you should be aware," Nektas finished.

"Always good to be prepared," the Primal murmured, and my eyes narrowed on him. A deep, raspy chuckle came from the draken as he closed the doors. Ash hadn't taken his gaze off me.

I eyed him over the rim of my glass as I took a *dainty* sip. "I feel as if I've been wrongly labeled as a troublemaker."

"Wrongly?" Ash approached the bed. He didn't sit in the chair. Instead, he sat on the edge of the bed beside me.

I nodded.

His gaze tracked slowly over my face. "How are you feeling? Minus the whiskey?"

"I feel…normal." I lowered the glass to my lap. "Nektas told me you gave me a potion."

"I did."

"I don't remember that."

"You were going in and out of consciousness. I used a compulsion," he said, and I inhaled sharply. "If I hadn't, you would've died. But I am sorry for forcing you to do that. It was necessary, but force is not something I like to use."

My gaze lifted to his, and a strange whirring sensation started in my chest that had nothing to do with the warmth or the whiskey. I thought of the friend he'd had to kill. "You're being completely honest about that."

"I am."

"Thank you," I murmured, thinking of what Nektas had said.

He watched me closely. "Thanking me is not necessary."

"I thought you'd appreciate a show of gratitude."

"Not when it involves your life." A tremor coursed through me, and I lifted the glass, taking another drink as Ash studied me. "Does nothing faze you?" he asked.

"What do you mean?"

"You almost died, and yet you seem unbothered by it."

"Maybe it's the whiskey."

"It's not."

My eyes narrowed. "Are you reading my emotions?"

"A little." His head cocked. "Only for a few seconds."

"You should stop doing that, even for a few seconds."

"I know."

I stared at him.

"I will." A faint, brief grin appeared. "How did you get so strong, *liessa*?"

Liessa. Did he call Veses that? I stopped myself from asking. "I don't know."

"You have to know."

Glancing down at my nearly empty glass, I shook my head. "I…I had to be."

"Why?"

I opened my mouth and then closed it. "I don't know. Anyway." I swallowed, changing the subject. "So…those entombed gods weren't the only things in the Red Woods."

"I figured that," he replied dryly. "Why didn't you tell me? I saw the scratches. I would've been able to do something before the toxin had a chance to invade your system."

Did that mean he wouldn't have gone back to Veses? "I thought you were already angry enough over the gods. Figured I could tell you later about the Hunters."

He did not look as if he agreed with that decision at all.

"If I had known their nails carried the toxin, I would've said something," I pointed out.

"If you hadn't been where you weren't supposed to be, it wouldn't have been an issue."

Well, he had a point there. "Just so you know, I tried to hide from them. They were heading toward the palace when they saw me." My gaze flicked up to him. "Why do you think they were here?"

"That's a good question. The Hunters rarely have reason to come into the Shadowlands." He studied me. "And you're sure that's the type of Gyrm you saw?"

I nodded as unease trickled through my system. What I'd done in the woods couldn't have drawn them, could it? They had shown the night in the Dark Elms, after I'd healed the kiyou wolf. But how would they have even known?

I took another drink. "You went to the tombs?"

"I did."

"Did you figure out how they got out of their chains?"

"Someone would've had to very carefully free them."

My eyes widened. "Who would do that?"

"My guards are good men and women. Loyal to me. More importantly, none would even want to attempt that, knowing that if the gods were able to find their way out, it would be a disaster," he explained. "Other gods would do it, just to see what would happen. One of them could've been attempting to free a certain prisoner and changed their mind, resealing the tomb." Ash paused. "If this hadn't happened today, there is a good chance those who had been freed would've swarmed whoever opened the tomb next."

"So you owe me a thank you?"

"I wouldn't go that far."

I didn't think so.

Feeling the heaviness of his stare upon me, I peeked over at him. Much like Nektas, he seemed at ease, but there was an undercurrent of dangerous tension. I thought of what I'd realized before the Hunters arrived and what he said about the Shadowlands while we were at the lake. "Why is everything so gray here—everything except the Red Woods? It wasn't always like this, right?"

"No, it wasn't," he confirmed. "But the Shadowlands…it's dying."

Pressure clamped my chest. "Is it because the deal hasn't been fulfilled?"

A frown pulled at his lips. "No."

Surprise flickered through me. Then was this not like the Rot? I didn't get a chance to ask.

"Why were you in those woods, Sera?" Ash asked. "I warned you about them. The portion that leads to the city is safe to travel, but that is all. You should've never been in them alone."

"I didn't mean to," I started and then sighed. "It wasn't intentional."

"You walked into the woods. How is that not intentional?"

I couldn't tell him about the hawk. "It wasn't like I purposely set out to do it."

"You didn't?" Ash challenged. "Because I have a feeling there is very little you do without purpose."

Irritation sparked. "I have a feeling you know very little about me if you think that is accurate," I said. "I'll have you know there is a whole lot I do without purpose."

"Well," he drawled, lips twitching. "That's reassuring."

"Whatever. I wouldn't have been out there if—" I stopped myself. "I was bored and tired of being stuck in this place."

"Stuck? You have all of this." He extended his hands. "You can go wherever you wish within the palace—"

"Except your office," I blurted, and there was nothing to blame but the damn whiskey for that. His eyes sharpened to a steel gray as I quickly added, "I don't know if you've spent a lot of time in the library, but it's not the most exciting place to be."

"And you think my office is?"

I snorted like a little piglet. "I'm sure it was recently," I said, lifting the glass, only to realize I'd finished it off.

"What is that supposed to mean?" he demanded as I started to lean toward the nightstand. He took the glass from me, setting it down.

I raised my brows. "Really? I'm sure your office has been *very* stimulating and charming."

Ash sat back, a low laugh parting his lips. "Holy shit."

"What?" I gripped the edge of the sheet where it pooled in my lap.

"You're jealous."

Heat climbed up my neck. "I'm sorry, but I did not hear you correctly."

He laughed again, but the sound ended too quickly as he leaned forward. "You're actually jealous. That is why you went into those damn woods."

"What? That is not why I went."

"Bullshit."

My eyes widened as anger mixed with embarrassment, and

unfortunately, whiskey. "You know what? Okay. Yes. I was jealous. You have been too busy to even speak to me for longer than five seconds over the last couple of days, leaving me alone, like always. To walk the courtyard by myself. Eat dinner by myself. Go to bed by myself. Wake up by myself. I'm really starting to wonder what I did in this life to deserve *always* being alone."

His eyes widened in surprise. Nothing that was coming out of my mouth needed to be shared. This wasn't an act. A ploy. It was the truth, and I couldn't stop myself. "The only time I see anyone is when one of your guards tries to inconspicuously follow me or someone brings me food."

Ash's jaw had loosened at some point, and I wasn't sure what it was in response to, nor was I even sure exactly what I was saying anymore. I was like a volcano erupting. "So, yes. I'm stuck here, yet again, alone while my *husband*-to-be is busy doing whatever with a Primal, who acted awfully familiar with you. So, sure, I was jealous. Does that make you happy? Amused? Either way, all of that is so beside the point, it's not even funny."

He stared at me. "Why would you think you deserved to be alone?"

Out of everything I said, *that* was what he focused on? "I don't know. You tell me. I have no idea. Maybe there's just something wrong with me. Maybe my personality is a huge turn-off," I said, starting to push away from the pillows. "I mean, I am troublesome and mouthy—"

"Whoa." Ash shifted, placing his hand on the other side of my leg. His upper body blocked me from moving unless I wanted to attempt to knock him aside. "Can you stay seated?"

"I don't want to stay seated. I *hate* being still. I need to move. I'm used to moving around, to doing something other than absolutely nothing," I snapped. "And I don't even want to be talking about this. I'm sure you don't either since you're so busy—"

"I'm not busy now."

"I don't care."

His eyes flared. "Then maybe you'd care to know that I don't enjoy even a single moment in Veses' presence."

"Really?" I coughed out a dry laugh that caused my back to ache. "She is beautiful."

"So? What does that matter when she's as poisonous as a pit viper? Not only do I not trust her, I do not like her. She is…" A muscle flexed in his jaw once more. "She is of the worst sort."

"Then why was she here?" *Why did you allow her to touch you?* Somehow, I managed not to ask that, thank the gods.

"You already know. She heard that I had taken a Consort, and she was curious."

"Why would she even care?"

"Why do you?"

I snapped my mouth shut.

The eather brightened behind his pupils, and he was quiet for a moment. "I didn't mean to make you feel…alone here. I didn't know if you needed space or not, and I told the others to give you time. That's on me." He was closer, his scent teasing me. "But I have been avoiding you."

I felt a sudden, sharp drop in my stomach. "Your confirmation of what I just said isn't exactly necessary."

"It's not because you're troublesome or mouthy. I actually find those traits to be oddly…alluring," he said.

"Who in their right mind would find that alluring?"

"That's another good question," Ash replied, and I started to frown. "But I've been avoiding you because when I'm around you for longer than a few minutes, my interest in you quickly overshadows any common sense. And that is a distraction—a complication—I cannot afford."

I felt a strange flip in my chest that I didn't understand. "Bullshit."

"Is that what you really think?"

"I don't know what I think, but I know words mean nothing." I met his stare, and I didn't know if it was my duty that fueled my words or something equally terrible. "So, as I said before, when it comes to your *interest*, you mostly talk, *Nyktos*. That's what I—"

Ash moved so fast, one of his hands was on my cheek and his lips were on mine before I could even take my next breath. There was nothing soft and sweet or slow about it as his fingers splayed across my face. His kiss branded me within seconds, and I responded without hesitation, without thought. I gripped the front of his tunic and I kissed him back just as fiercely.

He shuddered and then rose, bracing his weight on his other hand as he came over me. Our bodies didn't touch, but he kept me right there, propped against the mountain of pillows as my senses spun. His tongue rolled over mine, and a primitive sound rumbled from him as I followed suit.

He lifted his head, breathing heavily. "You know what the hardest part is, *liessa*? I don't even know why I'm fighting this need. You would have me, wouldn't you?"

"Yes," I whispered without a hint of shame or guilt. It was the truth, even if there was no deal, no duty to be carried out. And that should've terrified me.

"I would have you." His lips coasted over mine. A tremble coursed through me as the tips of his fingers trailed down the side of my throat and over my shoulder. "You would have me."

Those fingers followed the vee of the robe, gliding over the swell of my breast. "*Yes.*"

"Then why can't we?" His thumb swept over the pebbled nipple as he cupped my breast. "It doesn't have to complicate things. It would probably make this agreement between us easier," he mused as his hand slipped lower, away from my throbbing breast and down the slope of my belly. "Maybe then I wouldn't have to worry about you wandering off into the Red Woods."

"I didn't wander on purpose," I said, pulse thrumming.

"No. Just unintentionally." He nipped at my lips as his hand slid between the halves of the robe. The feel of his cool flesh against my lower stomach caused me to gasp. "Open your legs for me, *liessa*."

I obeyed.

"Will this be the only time you actually do what I ask without a fight?"

"Probably."

Ash's chuckle teased my lips, his cool fingers slipping between my thighs, wringing a gasp from me. "Fuck," he rasped, his lips brushing mine. "You are so gloriously wet." He dragged his finger through the wetness in slow, teasing strokes and then eased it into me. I moaned, tugging on his shirt. "And you make such glorious sounds. They are like a song."

My body quivered as his finger began to move. I started to move my hips, but his hand stilled. "Don't." He lifted his head, and waited until I opened my eyes. "Don't move, *liessa*." He eased his finger back in, as deep as it could go. "You may feel fine, but your body has been through a lot today."

"I don't think I can stay still." My blood thrummed as his thumb swept over the bundle of nerves.

"Then we stop." Ash's gaze locked onto mine, and he added another finger, stretching me. "You don't get to come on my fingers, and I don't get to taste you again. You don't want me to stop, do you?"

"No." I fisted his tunic.

"Then don't move."

Heart thundering, I watched him sit back. His gaze left mine and traveled slowly down, over the shallow rise and fall of my chest to where the robe had parted at my navel. He could see the most intimate part of me, and this was nothing like the moonlight-drenched bank of the lake, or even when he'd stood behind me in the bathing chamber. There was no hiding anything. Not that I wanted to. Not even because I was completely at his will and trying everything to stay still as he moved his fingers faster, swirling his thumb over the throbbing bundle of nerves. I watched him watching himself—his long, slick fingers thrusting between my spread thighs. I had never seen anything so…erotic in my entire life.

My body coiled tight as a breathy moan parted my lips. My hips jerked, and Ash clasped them, his fingers pressing into the flesh, holding me still. A quake hit me.

"That's it." His voice was almost guttural, a tone I'd never heard from him before. "I can feel you."

His avid focus scorched my skin, turning my blood to liquid fire. Every point of my body seemed to tighten all at once. His fingers pumped inside me, and I started to shake. He let out a hoarse groan as I came apart, lost in the ripples of pleasure as my head fell back once more. Bliss swept through me, easing the taut muscles and clearing my thoughts. I didn't become nothing, not in the way I was painfully familiar with. Not in the way that made me feel alone, unworthy and inhuman. *Me.* Whoever I was. But I was present, and the soft touch of Ash's lips against mine was a reminder of that.

I was still there as he eased his hand from me and lifted it. I caught a teasing glimpse of his fangs as he drew his fingers into his mouth. My entire body reacted at the sight, clenching.

A grin appeared as he lowered his hand and then his mouth, kissing me, this time softly, slowly. There was something *sweet* about the shallow, almost tentative kisses. They were also wicked because I tasted myself on his lips.

I continued to sink into the pillows, body boneless as his mouth left mine. He brushed a strand of hair back from my face. "Thirty-six."

My eyes fluttered open. "What?"

"Freckles," he said, his cheeks…pinker than usual. "You have thirty-six of them on your face."

That strange, whirring sensation surged through my chest. "You actually counted them?"

"I did." Ash rocked back. "I did the first day you were here. I counted them again to make sure I was correct. I was." He fixed the loosened tie of my robe. "I really hope there's no doubt left when it comes to my interest in you."

"There's not."

"Good."

And it was good. I should feel good. His attraction to me was very real. It was a step in the direction I needed to take. Still, unease bubbled.

His gaze lifted to mine, and the slow swirl of eather had an almost hypnotic effect. "I need to clean up and change."

My brows knitted, and I started to ask why when he rose and I saw that his breeches were darker at his hip and pelvis. The material appeared damp. Had he…found release? My eyes shot to his. I hadn't touched him. He hadn't even touched himself.

A lopsided grin appeared on his full lips. "As I said, I hope there's no doubt about my interest."

I was at a loss for words as he walked to the doors joining our chambers. Ash stopped and looked back at me. "I'll be back."

I said nothing when he turned the deadbolt and opened the door, disappearing into the darkness of his chambers. Dumbly, I watched him close the doors, thinking it was strange that a lock and a too-thin sheet of wood separated our chambers.

Closing my eyes, I sank into the pillows. I didn't think he'd come back, and right now, that was probably for the best. I didn't…feel right. It had to be the whiskey and whatever was in that potion.

The soft click of a door a few minutes later drew my eyes open. I looked over, any and all thoughts fizzling upon sight of Ash.

He had cleaned up and changed, wearing some sort of loose black pants and a white shirt, the sleeves rolled up, and the collar left open. His hair was damp and pushed back from the striking lines of his face.

And he had come back.

Like he'd said he would.

My heart started thundering, beating so fast.

Ash stopped at the edge of the bed. "I know you should rest. I know I should…let you be, but I…" His chest rose with a deep breath. "If it's okay with you, I would just like to be here with you. That's all. Just be here."

Throat dry and stomach dipping, I nodded. "That's okay with me."

He didn't move for what felt like an eternity, and it made me wonder if he had thought I would refuse him. But then he eased his long body onto the bed beside me. He was on his side, facing me, and I might've stopped breathing as his gaze met mine.

"You okay?" he asked after a few moments had passed.

"Yes," I rasped.

One eyebrow rose. "You sure?"

"Uh-huh."

He grinned. "You appear frozen."

"Do I?"

"Yes."

"I don't mean to." My cheeks warmed. "I just…I've never lain with someone before."

"Really?" Doubt crept into his voice. "I assumed you had."

"No—*wait*." My eyes widened. "You mean have sex? Yes. I've done that." I stiffened. "Does that bother you?"

"No." He laughed, letting one hand rest in the space between us. "Then what do you mean?"

"I mean I've never lain in bed with someone. Slept or rested beside them," I explained. "Ever."

"Neither have I." His eyes were a soft gray, the pulse of eather muted behind his pupils.

"Slept beside someone?"

"That. Or anything really. Not with Veses. Not with anyone. I've never *lain* with anyone before."

Even though I suspected he didn't have much experience based on what he'd said at the lake, shock still rippled through me. I would've thought he had *some* experience. "Why?" I asked and then immediately cringed. "I'm sorry. That's probably not any of my business—"

"I think it is," he said, and there was that damn, strange whirl again. He picked up the tail of my braid from where it had fallen on my arm. "I don't know. I just never really…let anything get to that point. It seemed too much of a risk to become close to anyone."

A sharp slice of sorrow cut through my chest, unwanted but there. It could be because of the other Primals, but I thought it had a lot more to do with what'd happened to his parents.

I thought of the gods on the wall.

I thought of how Nektas was the only one I'd heard call him Ash. I had no idea if that symbolized anything or not, but he'd said it was a risk to become close to *anyone.*

"You have friends," I said. "Ector? Rhain? Saion—"

He looked over at me as he drew his thumb over my braid. "They are loyal guards. I trust them."

I was willing to bet that even though he'd referred to Lathan as a friend, it was probably nothing more than a word to him—no actual meaning behind it. The back of my throat burned as I stared at the scar on his chin. His life seemed as lonely as mine.

And maybe that was why I asked what I did. A question I wasn't sure I wanted the answer to, even if I needed it. "Why are you taking that risk now?"

Thick lashes lifted, and steel-gray eyes pierced mine. "Because I can't seem to stop myself, even though I know better. Even though I know I'll probably end up hating myself for it. Even though you will probably end up hating me."

Chapter 31

"You can do it," Aios cheered, hands clasped together under her chin. "Just jump."

The purplish-black draken teetered on the edge of the boulder, his leathery wings arced high. I held my breath as Reaver jumped into the air, lifting his wings. Below the boulder, Jadis wiggled her green-and-brown body in an excited circle. Reaver dipped precariously, and both Aios and I stepped forward until he swooped above our heads with a trill of victory.

"Thank gods," I muttered, exhaling heavily as he rose and glided. I watched Reaver sweep through the air, half afraid that he would fall for no reason. "I don't think I've been more stressed in my entire life."

Aios laughed softly as she brushed a coppery strand of hair over a shoulder. "Same." She glanced over at me. "How are you feeling today?"

"I feel fine." Jadis chirped, rushing across the ground of the courtyard, kicking up gray dust as she followed Reaver. I glanced down at my arm. "The scratches are barely even noticeable."

"You're lucky to have received the antidote when you did," Aios noted, watching the draken. "A few more minutes, and it could've been too late."

I nodded absently, my thoughts immediately finding their way to my bedchamber and to Ash. The emotions that pinged through me ran the gamut. Everything from that strange whirring sensation to a deep-rooted feeling of unease. I'd fallen asleep beside him the night before. I didn't know exactly when it had happened. Silence had fallen between us as he continued toying with my braid. I wasn't sure how long he remained at my side. He'd been gone when I woke, but his scent lingered on the pillows and sheets. I thought perhaps he'd spent the entire night with me.

And that was a good sign—a great one.

I nibbled on my lower lip as I turned back to Aios and the draken. The goddess had shown that morning with breakfast—one that she ate with me in my chambers. Afterward, she'd asked if I wanted to join her on a walk. Somehow, we'd ended up out here with the draken, and I wondered if Ash had something to do with that. If he had told Aios that I didn't need space. I didn't ask because that seemed like a rather awkward conversation. Besides, I still couldn't believe I'd admitted to feeling as if I'd done something to deserve being alone.

Fucking whiskey.

Jadis took off across the courtyard, apparently attempting to gain enough speed to take flight, something she had already tried several times. Aios went after her as Reaver landed a bit roughly by the boulder. He watched me from several feet away, his eyes narrowed. There was a thoughtful look about him, an almost wary one. I extended a hand toward him as Jadis peeked at him from behind one of my legs. Reaver tilted his head to the side as he tucked his wings back.

"Not very trusting, are you?" I remarked, lowering my hand as my thoughts returned to yesterday.

I flicked my gaze back to Aios. She had snagged Jadis by the arm, guiding the stomping draken away from the too-high boulder. "Can I ask you a question?"

"Sure."

"It's about the Primal, Veses," I said, and Aios stiffened a bit as Reaver took flight again. "I got the impression that no one here likes her, and Ash said that she was the worst sort. Did she have anything to do with the gods on the wall?"

A breeze whirled through the courtyard, picking up and tossing the strands of her hair as she let go of Jadis's arm and straightened. "No, she did not as far as I know, but she is…not well regarded by many in the Shadowlands. She can be rather vindictive when angered or ignored." Aios laughed, but it was a tight sound. "Have you ever met someone who feels they are entitled to whatever they want? That is Veses. And that entitlement extends to people. Many gods or goddesses would enjoy being the object of her affections. And many do." She turned to me, tucking a strand of hair behind her ear. "But she will fixate on what she perceives she cannot have. And if she is unsuccessful in achieving that, she can be very resentful."

"And she wants Ash?" I surmised.

"Only because he has never shown her that type of attention," she answered. "To her, it's personal. Even though he's never shown interest in anyone until you."

Until you.

My stomach dipped at the exact moment my heart jumped. I ignored both reactions. "Has she hurt anyone because of his lack of interest in her?"

"I don't think so, but she can make things…difficult for him. While she may not be liked by many, she is well-connected." Her brow creased. "You know, I don't think she has always been like this. At least, that is what I've heard. When I was young, Mycella told me stories about Veses—about how giving and kind she was, bestowing good fortune on gods and mortals, even to those who had not prayed to her for such. She's very old. Far past the time for her to rest, so I don't know if her nature is partly due to living such a long life or what."

Two things really caught my attention. "Mycella? You mean Ash's mother?"

She nodded as a faint, sad smile crossed her features. "We were distantly related. Cousins, as mortals would say. One of her aunts or uncles was from the Court of Kithreia. I was very young when she was killed."

Was that why she felt safe here? Because of her relation to Ash? I glanced down as Jadis hopped onto one of my feet. "What do you mean by rest? Like go to sleep?"

"For some, yes. For others, it's more like retiring. You see, Primals can be endless, and that kind of lifespan is even unfathomable to most gods. Though there have been a few who've become so powerful that they too are endless. And that amount of time…it can rot the mind." Aios crossed her arms over her chest as she watched Reaver glide through the air. "To watch the world fall and be rebuilt around you, time after time. To see nothing new. To no longer be surprised and to become so accustomed to loss that even the idea of love is no longer a thrill."

A wave of tiny bumps erupted along my skin under the black tunic I wore, and I tried to think of what that must be like. To live for so long you'd seen everything.

"The longer a Primal or a god lives, the greater the risk of them becoming more eather than person. Some can handle the endless time better than others, but eventually, it impacts all of us. There are ways to avoid it. One is to enter a deep stasis—to sleep. But very few have ever done that," she said. "For those who do not wish to sleep, they can enter what we call Arcadia, a place very much like the Vale. A garden, so to speak. It allows for an Ascension of another and peace for the Primal."

"Is that…another realm?" I asked as Jadis stretched, placing one talon on my other foot. I had no idea what the young draken was doing.

She nodded. "But Veses can't do that. None of them can."

I started to ask why when she looked past me, at the palace. A smile returned to her somber features. "Bele."

Looking over my shoulder, I saw two figures crossing the courtyard, both dressed in black tunics with the fine silver stitching along the collar and across the chest.

The one I assumed was Bele was tall and lithe, her skin a light, golden brown, reminding me of the sparkling sand along the Stroud Sea. Hair the color of midnight lay over her shoulder in a thick braid. Her features were strikingly sharp, her eyes a shade of light, golden brown sparking with the glow of eather. She had a short sword strapped to one hip. I caught the curve of a bow visible over one shoulder.

Beside her was a man with rich, brown skin, his sleeveless tunic tailored to the broad width of his shoulders and chest. His dark hair was cropped close to his head. Something about his handsome features and the impassive set of his mouth was familiar.

Aios's smile increased as they approached. The male glanced in my direction while Bele stepped forward to give Aios a quick, tight hug.

"It's so good to see you," Aios said, stepping back and clasping Bele's arms. "You've been gone so long, I was starting to worry."

The dark-haired goddess laughed. "You should know better than to worry about me."

"I worry about all of you when you're gone." A bit of the joy faded from Aios's tone, giving me the impression that was true.

"Do I get a hug?" the man asked as Bele stepped back, his dark brown eyes aglow with eather.

"I just saw you this morning, Rhahar." Aios arched a brow, and I immediately recognized the name. He was one of the gods who'd checked the tombs with Ash. "But do you actually want one?"

"Not really."

Laughing, Aios sprang forward anyway, giving the god an equally tight hug. I didn't think the god could look more uncomfortable with his arms pinned straight to his sides, and I couldn't help but grin as Jadis finally hopped off my feet and ambled toward Bele.

"Hey Jadis-bug." Bele bent, rubbing the draken under her chin.

"Holy shit, is that Reaver flying?" Rhahar squinted, looking up at the faint star-strewn sky.

"Yes." Aios glanced over her shoulder as Reaver flew in circles along the edges of the Rise. "He finally got the hang of it today."

"You must be her," Bele stated. Pulling my eyes from Reaver, I looked at her. She studied me with open curiosity. "Our soon-to-be Consort."

There was a snag in my breath, but I nodded. "Apparently."

Bele's grin was brief as she placed her right hand over her chest and bowed at the waist. The gesture threw me off. None had done that before.

"You don't have to do that," I blurted out as she straightened. "I mean, I'm not really the Consort yet. You can call me Sera."

"Just because it's not official doesn't mean you are not due the respect of your position," Bele stated and then turned slowly to Rhahar.

Rhahar frowned at her. "What?"

She raised her brows as she pointed one glossy black-painted fingernail at me.

I stiffened, feeling warmth creep into my cheeks. "It's really not necessary—"

"Yes. It is," Bele interrupted, looking at me. "If we do not show you the respect of your position, then none of the other Courts will. And if they do not respect you, it is unlikely you'll survive the coronation, Consort to the Primal or not."

I opened my mouth, but I honestly hadn't a clue how to respond to that less-than-reassuring statement.

"You know, she has a point," Rhahar mused, eyeing me. "News of you has already traveled far and wide. Many are very curious…and confused as to why Ash would choose a mortal as a Consort."

I still had no idea what to say.

"Okay," Aios said with a sigh. "This first meeting couldn't be more awkward."

"But it's true. Some of the gods are taking bets on how long she'll live," Bele said.

I blinked slowly. "Really?"

She nodded as her gaze dropped to where the shadowstone dagger was strapped to my thigh. "But Rhahar tells me you're a fighter."

My attention shifted to him, and I caught sight of Jadis hopping after Reaver, nipping at his tail. I didn't think I'd ever seen something stranger…or more adorable.

"Heard about how you held your own with the entombed gods," he remarked. "She can fight."

"Good." Bele smiled, crossing her arms.

"Well," I said, shaking my head. "This coronation sounds as if it will be fun."

Rhahar's laugh was rough and dry. "It's definitely going to be something."

His laughter struck that chord of familiarity again. I looked at him closer. The proud set of his features and the curve of his eyes resembled… "Are you related to Saion?"

A faint grin appeared. "Saion is my cousin. That is, when I claim him," he answered, his dark eyes sharp. "By the way, he told me what you did with a whip."

My eyes widened.

Bele's head cocked to the side. "What did you do with a whip?" She looked at Aios. "Do you know?"

Aios shook her head.

"She shoved the handle of a whip down some asshole's throat," Rhahar answered, and Aios turned to me.

"Really?" Bele's eyes glimmered.

I shifted my weight. "Yeah, I sort of did that, but he deserved it."

The smile on Bele's face grew as Jadis gave a pitiful squawk due to Reaver once more swooping up into the air. There was something else in Bele's stare, though. Something I couldn't quite place. "Strange that a Consort would have such a violent streak."

I stiffened. "Do you know many Consorts?"

"I do."

"Mortal ones?"

She flashed me a tight grin. "No."

"So…" I cleared my throat. "Admittedly, I don't know a lot about Iliseeum and the innerworkings of the Courts, so should I be concerned about this coronation?"

Aios's lips pursed. "Well—"

A cry of warning jerked my attention back to the draken. Reaver was flapping wildly, attempting to lower himself. My stomach plummeted. Jadis teetered on the edge of the boulder, her nearly translucent wings lifting weakly as she tipped forward off the edge.

"*Gods*." I shot forward, managing to grasp her tail as I curled an arm under her belly. Heart thumping heavily, I held her to my chest as she chirped madly. "You can't fly yet," I told her, having no idea if she understood me or not. "You would've broken a wing."

Bele smacked a hand over her chest. "Oh, Fates, I about had a heart attack."

"A heart attack? I just saw my life flash before my eyes." Rhahar looked shaken as Reaver made an unsteady landing near the boulder. "Nektas would've had our necks. That's after charbroiling us."

My lip curled at the imagery that statement provided, and I bent to put the squirming draken on the ground. Reaver was right there, squawking away. I don't know what he was communicating to her, but it did *not* sound pretty. The moment I let her go, she barreled into the larger draken.

"I think that's enough outdoor fun times for you." Aios stalked after Jadis.

My heart was still thumping heavily when Bele said, "To answer your question about the coronation… Should you be concerned? The answer is yes," she advised, and I turned to her. "And if I may give you a piece of advice? No matter what happens, do not show fear."

The piece of advice Bele had imparted lingered with me as I stood in my bedchamber, wearing only a slip as a woman I'd never met circled me with a cloth tape in hand.

Her name was Erlina. She was mortal, and I thought perhaps in the third or so decade of her life. A seamstress from Lethe. And she was here to take my measurements. Not just for the coronation gown but also so I actually had a wardrobe that went beyond borrowed, scattered pieces.

"Will you lift your arm, Your Highness?" Erlina asked softly.

Recalling what Bele had said, I bit back the urge to tell her she didn't have to address me so formally. I planned on staying alive long enough to fulfill my duty, so I lifted my arm.

I watched her step onto a small stool she'd brought with her and stretch the tape along the length of my arm, the flowing sleeves of her vibrant blue blouse fluttering. Then she turned, scribbling the measurements on a thick, leather-bound journal.

My gaze flicked to the closed chamber doors, where I knew Ector most likely stood. He had brought me to my chambers, letting me know that the seamstress had arrived. I hadn't seen Ash yet, and when I asked where he was, I'd been told that he was at the Pillars.

Was he judging souls? If so, what did that even feel like, that kind of responsibility? Pressure. I imagined it was a lot like deciding to use my gift.

"Your other arm," Erlina instructed. When I raised an eyebrow, a small grin crept across her delicate, almost impish features. "Believe it or not, some people do have arms and legs that are not equal. It's rare, and usually due to some injury, but I figure it's best to check."

"Learn something new every day," I murmured.

"Same length." Erlina nodded as she quickly measured my arm. She moved onto my shoulders, which I already knew were probably far wider than most ladies. And definitely broader than hers. She was tiny. "Did you know that your foot is roughly the same length as your forearm?"

I blinked. "Seriously?"

She peeked up at me through a fringe of lashes. "Yes."

"Huh." I looked down at my forearm. "Now I want to test that."

"Most do when they first hear it." She hopped down from the stool and went to the journal. Her dark brown hair she had twisted into a high bun slipped a little as she turned to me. "I was told that you prefer pants over gowns."

A wave of surprise flickered through me that it appeared Ash had, yet again, remembered what I'd said. "I do. Did—?" I caught myself before I referred to the Primal as *Ash*. "Did Nyktos tell you that?"

"He did when he stopped by the shop last week," she answered, and my stomach tumbled. Last week. It felt like I'd been here longer, and yet it still felt like yesterday when I knelt in the carriage before Marisol. "I would've been here sooner, but I was really backed up on designs."

"It's okay," I assured her.

Another brief smile appeared. "I will work on the gown first, along with some blouses and vests for you as they are far quicker to tailor than pants." She started to put the journal down on the table when she halted. "Do you prefer breeches or tights? But before you answer, I am currently wearing tights." She plucked out the black material. "They are almost as thick as breeches and as durable, but far more comfortable and soft. Feel them for yourself."

I reached out, brushing my fingers across the surprisingly supple feel. "I would've thought they were breeches. The tights I'm accustomed to are far thinner."

"And questionably opaque," she added, and I nodded. "Which is why I spent an obscene amount of time going through fabrics to find something as efficient as breeches. You would think with all the tailors and seamstresses in all the kingdoms, they would've improved the functionality of tights. Not that there is anything wrong with breeches, but I, myself, prefer a waistband that doesn't leave marks in my skin."

I grinned. "Tights then."

"Perfect." She hopped onto the stool once more.

As she slid the tape beneath my arms to measure my chest, I once again thought of what Rhahar and Bele had shared. If word of Ash choosing a mortal as his Consort had spread to the other Courts, wouldn't the people of Lethe have heard?

And what did they think?

I told myself I didn't care because it wouldn't matter. I would be no true Consort. My responsibilities lay with Lasania. I was their Queen, even if I never wore the crown. But I asked anyway because I…well, I couldn't help myself.

"They have heard of you." Erlina left the stool to write the numbers down. "Of course, many are curious. I do not think anyone expected His Highness to take a mortal as his Consort."

"Understandable."

"But they are excited. *Thrilled* may be a better word. And honored," Erlina quickly added, a faint hint of pink staining her sandy, golden-brown cheeks. She held the book to her chest. "There are a lot of mortals in Lethe," she explained, surprising me yet again. "For His Highness to take a mortal feels like…an acknowledgment to many of us. Like even though he is a Primal, he sees us as his equals, and there…well, there are not many like him. Many cannot wait to officially meet you."

I felt a strange flip in my chest and nodded. I didn't want to think about Ash viewing mortals as his equals. Not because it seemed ridiculous but because I thought that it was true.

I cleared my throat. "And they're thrilled that he is marrying?"

"Of course." A wider smile raced across her features. "We want to see him living—see him happy."

My stomach plummeted fast as I stood there. "The people of the Shadowlands…they respect him?"

There was a pinch to the slash of her brows and then a flash of understanding. "It must be hard believing that we have grown quite fond of the Primal of Death. Before I came to the Shadowlands, I would've laughed at the idea of such a thing, but…" A shadow crossed her features as she ducked her chin, coming to stand beside me. "But there were a lot of things I didn't know then. Anyway, His Highness is loyal to us." Her deep brown eyes met mine. "And we are loyal to him."

Many questions rose in response to what she shared, as did the bubbling sense of unease that settled in the center of my chest. "Where…where I am from, not many respected the Crown. They didn't have reason to."

She drew the tape around my waist. "Where are you from?" I asked.

She shifted the tape to my hips. "Terra."

I didn't know much about Terra except that it consisted mostly of farmlands with not nearly as many cities as Lasania. "Have you lived here long?"

"I suppose it depends on what one considers *long*," she answered, moving away to capture the measurements. "I left the mortal realm when I was eighteen, but I did not come to the Shadowlands until I was closer to nineteen. I've been here ever since, so that would be...thirteen years."

"Where were you before you came here?"

She knelt, stretching the tape the length of my leg. "The Court of Dalos."

My eyes widened. "You were at the City of the Gods? With the Primal of Life? I didn't know there were mortals there—I mean, besides the Chosen."

"There aren't," she stated, stilling for a moment. "At least, not when I was there."

Confusion swirled through me as the cool tape pressed against the inside of my thigh. "Then how did you…?" I trailed off.

"I was Chosen."

I stared down at her, struck silent for a moment. "Was?"

Erlina nodded.

"And you're not anymore? You didn't Ascend?"

A twist of a tight smile appeared. "I did not Ascend, thank the gods."

My lips parted, and immediately, I thought of Ash's reaction when I mentioned the Chosen's Ascension. He hadn't shared something then, that much was clear. "I have so many questions."

She halted, looking up at me, her eyes wide. For a brief second, I thought I saw fear in her gaze. Terror. A long moment passed, and then she moved on to my other leg, measuring the inseam. She said nothing more as she finished up and only spoke again to ask what colors I preferred. Erlina left shortly after, hurrying from the chamber as if it were filled with spirits.

I slid my arms through the robe, absolutely bewildered by what she'd shared—what she obviously wouldn't elaborate on. I'd just finished tying the sash when a knock sounded on the bedchamber door. "Yes?" I called out.

The door opened to reveal Ash. That odd whooshing sensation swept through my chest again at the sight of him. He wore the dark clothing with the silver trim as he'd done while holding court. His reddish-brown hair was pulled back to the nape of his neck, giving the harsh beauty of his features a blade-sharp edge.

I hadn't seen him since I'd fallen asleep. Beside him. Was that why I felt a flush invading my skin?

Ash had halted just inside the door, his silver gaze fixed on me—on where my fingers were still twisted around the sash. I saw a quick swirl of eather in his eyes, and then he moved, closing the door behind him. "I saw that Erlina just left. I thought I'd check on you, see how things went."

Check on me?

Why would he do that? Or was that just something normal people did? I had no idea, and I also didn't know why him doing that made my chest feel funny. I snapped out of my stupor. "Everything went fine."

"Good."

I nodded.

Ash stood there, and so did I, neither of us speaking. In the back of my mind, I knew that this was the perfect opportunity to strengthen his attraction to me. I wore nothing but scraps of lace under the robe. I could loosen the tie, let it fall open. Asking about what Erlina had shared would do very little to further my cause.

But I wanted to understand how a Chosen had ended up in the Shadowlands. "Erlina was a Chosen."

The change in his features was swift and striking. His jaw hardened, and his lips thinned.

"She didn't tell me much beyond that," I said quickly, not wanting her to possibly get into trouble. "Why didn't she Ascend?"

Tension bracketed his mouth. "Is that what mortals believe still happens to the Chosen?"

I stiffened. "Yes. That's what we've been taught. That's what the Chosen spend their lives preparing for—their Rite and Ascension. They serve the gods for all time."

"They don't," Ash stated flatly. "What you know of the Rite and the Chosen is nothing but a lie." A muscle ticked along Ash's jaw. "The Rite you celebrate—the one you hold feasts and parties in honor of? You're celebrating what will ultimately be the death of most of them. It wasn't always that way. At one time, the Chosen were Ascended. They *did* serve the gods. But that is not what it is now, and it hasn't been for a very long time."

A coldness seeped into my skin. "I don't understand."

"No Chosen has been Ascended in several hundred years." Ash's eyes were the color of the Shadowlands sky. "From the moment a Chosen arrives in Iliseeum, they are treated as objects to be used and given away, toyed with and eventually broken."

Horror swept through me as I stared at him. A huge part of me simply dove into denial. I couldn't believe it.

I couldn't…gods, I couldn't comprehend that. Couldn't wrap my head around the fact that these men and women who'd spent their lives in the mortal realm, veiled and groomed to serve the gods in one form or another, were taken from the mortal realm only to be *killed*. The smile of the young male Chosen formed in my mind. It had been so wide. Real and *eager*.

And there had to be thousands of Chosen like him. *Thousands*.

"Why?" I whispered, my stomach roiling as I sat on the settee.

"Why not?"

I sucked in air that went nowhere. "That is not a good enough answer."

"I agree." His eyes swirled slowly.

"Then why are the Chosen taken if not to be Ascended so they may serve the Primal of Life and the gods?"

"I do not know why the Rite is still held," he said, and I wasn't sure I believed him. "But they do serve the gods, Sera. They serve at their whims. And many of those gods do what they want with the Chosen, because they can. Because for some of them, that is all they know. That's not an excuse. At all. But as long as mortals continue the Rite, more Chosen will meet the same fate."

Red-hot anger whipped through me, and I was on my feet before I even realized it. "Mortals continue the Rite because the gods ask that of us. Because we are told that the Chosen will serve the gods. You speak as if this is our fault. As if we have the ability to tell the gods—a Primal—no."

"I do not think that it's the mortals' fault," he corrected.

My hands opened and closed at my sides as I took a step back. I turned away from Ash before I did something reckless. Like pick up the low-to-the-ground table and throw it at him. I crossed the bedchamber, stopping at the balcony doors. Did Kolis not know this was happening? Or did he not care? I glanced down at my hands. I couldn't believe that he wouldn't care. He was the Primal of *Life*.

But how could he be unaware? He was the most powerful of all the Primals. The King of Gods.

"How is this allowed by the King of Gods?" I asked, the image of him in the Sun Temple forming. *You, Chosen, are worthy*. I shuddered.

"Why would you think it is disallowed? Simply because he's the Primal of Life?" A sharpness entered his tone. "You believe he cares?"

I turned to him. Nothing could be gleaned from his expression. "Yes. I would believe that."

An eyebrow rose. "Then you know even less about Primals than I believed."

My heart thumped in my chest. "Are you really suggesting that Kolis is okay with the Chosen being brutalized?"

His icy stare met mine. "I wouldn't dare suggest that your Primal of Life could be so cruel."

A wave of prickly anger swept through me. "Why would he allow that? Why would anyone do that?" I remembered what Aios had said. "It can't be because they lived so long that this is the only way they find pleasure or entertainment."

"I couldn't answer that question—to even begin to tell you that it is due to losing humanity or simply because they view mortals as something beneath them. I don't know what corrupts and festers the mind that ultimately allows that type of behavior to occur. I don't know how anyone finds pleasure in the pain and humiliation of others." Ash had drifted closer. "I almost wish you hadn't learned this. At least, not yet. Some things are better left unknown."

"For the ones not involved, maybe. But for the Chosen? Their families? They're taught that it is an honor. People *wish* they were Chosen, Ash. How is that right?"

"It's not."

"It has to be stopped," I said. "The Rite. The whole act of being Chosen. It has to be."

Something akin to pride filled his eyes, but it was gone so quickly, I couldn't be sure. "And how would you propose doing that? Do you think mortals would believe it if they were told the truth?"

"Probably not if it came from another mortal." I didn't even have to think about that. "But they'd believe a god. They'd believe a Primal."

"Do you think they'd believe the Primal of Death?"

I snapped my mouth shut.

"Even if another Primal came to them and showed them what really happened, there would be resistance. It is far easier to be lied to than it is to acknowledge that you have been lied to."

I stared at him, taking in the cold lines and angles of his face. There was truth in those words. A sad, harsh one. "What do you do about this?"

His eyes searched mine. "I don't stand by and do nothing, even if it may appear that way. That is how I prefer it." Wisps of eather crackled along his irises. "That is how I keep people like Erlina alive."

"You…you saved her? Brought her here?"

"I've only hidden her away. Like I've done for other Chosen. I try to get as many as I can without drawing attention," he said, darkness gathering under his skin.

Only hidden her away? As if that were nothing. But was it enough? The answer was no. Thousands had been Chosen over the years. But it was something.

"Is it still dangerous for them?" I asked. "Other gods enter Lethe. Could they be recognized?"

"There is always a risk that someone who recognizes them will see them. They know that." A muscle flexed in his jaw as his gaze shifted to the empty fireplace. "We've been mostly lucky."

"Mostly," I repeated softly, and I thought of the woman who'd gone missing and how reluctant Ector had been to speak about her. "Is the woman who went missing a Chosen? Gemma?"

His iron-hued eyes swept to mine. "She is."

"And she hasn't been found?"

"Not yet."

My heart turned over heavily. "Do you think her disappearance is related to a god possibly recognizing her as a Chosen?"

"I believe it is related in some way, whether she was recognized or saw a god she knew and chose to go missing."

Meaning it was possible that this Gemma had seen a god that would've recognized her, and was so afraid she'd panicked. "Where could she have gone?"

"To one side of Lethe is the bay. The Red Woods borders the southern side, and the Dying Woods surrounds the western and northern sides. I've had guards searching the woods, but if she went in there…"

He didn't need to finish. If Gemma had gone into the woods, it was unlikely that she survived. I still didn't believe a single drop of my blood had drawn those entombed gods aboveground. But even if she didn't raise them, there were still the Shades and possibly even Hunters. Chosen were trained in self-defense. Not as extensively as I was, but they knew how to wield a weapon. Still, I doubted it would be enough.

I could only imagine what Gemma had faced as a Chosen that had caused her to take that kind of risk. Anger and disgust sat heavy on my chest along with a hefty helping of denial. I shook my head. "A part of me doesn't want to believe any of this," I admitted. "I do, but it's just…"

Ash watched me closely as if he were trying to figure something out. "I don't know why any of this comes as a surprise to you."

I looked up at him. "How could it not?"

"Do you think mortals are the only ones capable of brutality? Of hurting others for no reason other than the fact they can? Manipulating and abusing others? The Primals and gods are capable of the same. Capable of much worse out of anger, boredom, or for entertainment and self-serving pleasure. Whatever your imagination can conjure will not even begin to encompass what we are capable of."

What *we* are capable of? I looked away, pressing my lips together. He'd included himself in that statement, but he was trying to save the Chosen. He wasn't capable of that. And I was here to kill him. What would happen to the Chosen then? Even if he were only able to save a small percentage of them.

Gods.

My chest seized. I couldn't think about them. I couldn't think about what *could* happen when I knew what *would* happen to the people of Lasania if I didn't see this through. I swallowed hard. "You said this happens to most of them. Other than the ones you've hidden away, have some survived?"

"From what I could learn from those who help move the Chosen and find them some semblance of safety, some of the Chosen have disappeared."

"What does that mean? They can't simply just disappear."

"But they do." He met my stare. "There are no signs that they've been killed, but many are never seen or heard from again. They are simply gone."

Chapter 32

From the moment I climbed into bed, I tossed and turned, falling asleep for only a few minutes before waking, finding myself staring at the doors to Ash's chambers.

What I'd learned today haunted me, no matter how much I tried to stop it. The truth of what happened to the Chosen. The knowledge that so many gods were capable of such cruelty. The likely possibility that Kolis, the greatest Primal of them all, was aware of it. All of it circled and circled, despite the fact that none of it could matter. "Only Lasania," I whispered to the quiet chamber.

I rolled onto my back, staring up at the shadowstone ceiling. But what if I succeeded? What if I stopped the Rot? What in the *fuck* was I saving Lasania from at the end of the day if the Primal of Life and the gods who served him took no issue with brutalizing the Chosen? The answer seemed simple. There were millions in Lasania, and only thousands of Chosen to be potentially taken. Did one sacrifice the few to save the many? I didn't know, but it wasn't like I didn't realize that Ash's demise would cause death as the Primal power was unleashed and found a new home. I didn't even know why I was thinking about this.

I groaned as I shifted onto my side. I wouldn't be here if I succeeded. I'd probably be destroyed—soul and all. The Chosen weren't my problem. The politics of Iliseeum weren't my problem.

Flipping onto my back and then side once more, frustration finally drove me from the bed. I tossed the cover aside, rising as I caught the ridiculously tiny sleeve of the nightgown Aios had placed in the wardrobe the first day. I tugged it up over my shoulder and padded barefoot across the stone floor. Grabbing the fur throw off the back of the chaise, I draped it over my shoulders, stepping out onto the balcony and into the silence of a Shadowlands' night. I went to the railing, holding the blanket close as a rare breeze lifted loose strands of hair, tossing them across my face. The dark crimson leaves of the Red Woods swayed beyond the courtyard. How many gods were entombed there? Another random question that would—

"Can't sleep either?"

I gasped, whirling toward the sound of Ash's voice. He sat on the daybed outside his balcony doors. The silvery sheen of the stars above sluiced over the arm resting on one bent knee and the broad, bare expanse of his chest. My heart thumped even harder while the strangest urge to dash back inside and throw myself under the covers hit me.

Somehow, I managed not to do that. "I didn't see you," I said finally and then flushed. Obviously. "No, I can't sleep." I inched away from the railing. "How long have you been out here?"

"An hour. Maybe longer."

"Is everything okay?" I asked.

He nodded. "In a way."

I took another small step forward. "What does *in a way* mean?"

"In a way that things are okay because I'm alive," he replied after a moment, and even though most of his features were cast in shadows, I felt the intensity of his gaze. "I can imagine why you're not able to sleep after what you learned today."

"My mind won't shut down."

"I know the feeling."

I watched him. "Do you think of the Chosen often?"

"Always." There was a long pause. "Are you sure you're okay?"

He'd asked that once during a quiet supper we'd shared. He was concerned about how I was handling what I'd learned about the Chosen. And I…well, it was unusual for me to be on the receiving end of that. "I am." I ran my foot along the smooth stone. "I may be prone to impulsivity as Sir Holland would say quite frequently, but I also have a rather practical mind."

"You do?"

I shot him a dark look. "What I'm trying to say is that I deal with things. What I learned today? I will deal with it."

He studied me from the shadows. "I know you will. That's what you do. Deal with whatever is thrown your way."

I lifted a shoulder.

He was quiet and then said, "Would you like to join me?"

A tripping sensation invaded my chest. "Sure."

"You don't sound too confident in that choice," he said, and I heard the smile in his voice.

"No, I am confident in my choice. I'm just…surprised," I admitted.

"Why?"

I shrugged once more as I got my legs moving, telling myself that this was a good surprise. Him wanting me to stay out here with him had to mean something. I sat beside him, staring ahead.

Ash was quiet for a couple of moments. "I wasn't avoiding you today. I was at the Pillars."

"I didn't think you were." I looked at him, tensing as I remembered something my mother had once taught me. *Men don't like to have to answer for their time not spent with you*, she'd said. And considering what I'd done the day before, I should've remembered that piece of advice I would've otherwise ignored in another situation. "I mean, you don't have to explain your whereabouts to me."

His fingers moved restlessly in front of his bent knee. "I feel like I do after last night."

Focusing on the tops of the trees beyond the wall, I resisted the urge to press my hand to my cheeks and see if they felt as hot as I thought they did.

"I feel like I also have to let you know that one of the reasons I can't sleep is because I kept looking at the damn doors to your bedchambers."

My gaze shot back to him.

"And then I lay there wondering why in the hell I placed your chambers beside mine. Sounded like a good idea," he said, and my stomach rolled. "Now, I'm not so sure. Because I spent far too much time thinking that all I had to do was walk a couple of feet and that chamber wouldn't be empty. You'd be there."

The tripping sensation turned into a falling one. "And that is a bad thing?"

"Undecided."

I laughed, looking away. "Well, I feel that I should let you know that I too was staring at those *damn* doors, and I'm only a few feet away and…"

"And what?" Shadows gathered in his voice.

"And I don't mind engaging in bad ideas," I told him.

Ash chuckled. "You wouldn't, would you?"

I grinned as I tugged the edges of the throw up to my chin. "I am particularly talented at engaging in bad ideas." I cleared my throat, searching for something to say. "I met Rhahar and Bele today."

"I know."

My brows lifted as I looked over my shoulder at him. "How?"

"I saw you briefly when I returned to check in with the guards. I was busy but still fully aware of where you were. Who you were with. When you left."

"Well… That sounds creepy."

"I also talked to Rhahar and Bele." He shifted forward enough that the starlight caressed his face. There was an amused tilt to his lips.

His lips were so expressive. "I also learned something interesting from them today."

"About the bets the gods of other Courts are taking?" Ash asked.

I sighed. "Yes."

"They shouldn't have told you that. Both Rhahar and Bele often speak before they think."

"Well, since I am well familiar with that, I can't hold it against them," I said. "Where has Bele been? Aios reacted as if she had been gone for a long time."

"She is a bit of a huntress. Of information. She has a knack for moving about unseen, so she is usually in other Courts, attempting to uncover information that may be useful."

"Useful for what?"

"You have a lot of questions."

"You have a lot of answers." I eyed him. "Is she someone who helps get the Chosen out of Dalos?"

"She is," he confirmed.

I mulled that over. "Do they know about the deal your father made?"

"They don't, but I am sure they suspect that not all is as it seems."

I nodded slowly. I imagined anyone who knew Ash would have questions about him randomly appearing with a mortal Consort. "How did things go at the Pillars? Were there souls you had to judge yourself?"

"There were, and things went both good and bad. It's never easy making that choice. Life is important, *liessa*, but what comes after is an eternity. I know many believe that things are black and white. That if you do this or that, you will be rewarded with paradise or punished." He lifted his hand, brushing back a strand of hair that had fallen against his cheek. "It's never simple. There are people who do terrible things, but that doesn't always mean they're terrible people."

I twisted toward him, drawing a leg up onto the daybed. "You can say that because you see the soul exposed after death. You would know."

"I do, but I still see the taint of whatever they did. It overshadows a lot of the good, but some exist in a shade of gray where they are not as easy to judge as the person who prays to the gods to end the lives of others would be."

My brows lifted. "People pray for that?"

"I have lost count of how many times someone has come to the Shadow Temple, summoning a god to cause death upon another. I…" He exhaled slowly. "There was a time that I would answer those summonses."

I stilled. Gods often answered summonses, but he must have been like his father.

"I would enter the Shadow Temple and hear the words mortals spoke. Listen to the favors they requested—the lives they wanted to end. I knew immediately that some were bad. Spoiled and rotten to the core," he told me. "They asked for death for profit or because of some petty slight. Their motives were a pestilence, one I knew I couldn't allow to spread. They didn't leave the Temple."

My fingers loosened on the blanket. I had a feeling I knew why they didn't leave.

"And then there were others." His fingers had stilled, but they were stiff. "Those who asked for the death of another because they sought relief from a brutal employer or an abusive father. Some who were pushed to their breaking points and saw no other option because there was none. Even if those people didn't harm another, the intent was still there. Should they be punished? Should they be treated differently? What of those who kill to protect themselves or another? They are not like the others, but their crimes are the same."

"How…how do you know what to do?"

"All I can do is look at their life as a whole. And each time I sentence a soul, I always wonder if it was the right choice. Was I punishing someone who didn't deserve it? Or was I letting someone off too easily? I ask that every time, even though I know I will never have an answer."

"I can't imagine making that choice," I admitted. "What did you do for the ones you answered? Those asking for the death of another because they were being hurt?"

"I did not make a deal with them. I do not ever make deals. But I did grant the favor they sought." A muscle clenched along his jaw as he stared ahead. "I found the person and ended it. I told myself I didn't enjoy it. That I was removing evil from the realm."

"But that wasn't true?" I asked. "You did, but not in a…perverse way. You enjoyed the justice. The knowledge that they could never hurt another person, and you were the one making sure of that."

His gaze slid to mine, and he nodded. "An odd thing for you to know."

The blanket slipped down my arms, gathering at my elbows. "Why did you end up stepping back?"

"Because the deaths stopped leaving a mark," he answered. "And I started to enjoy it, especially the moment they realized exactly who I was that either answered their summons or visited them in their home. The realization as it dawned in their eyes that not only would I take their life, but I would also have their souls for eternity. That's when I stopped—when I stepped back and let the gods answer the summonses. Rhahar normally does it now."

I sucked in a shaky breath. "How…how did you know it was getting to that point?"

He didn't say anything for a moment, but I felt his gaze on me. "It's not something you can put into words. It's something you just know."

Just something you know. I tugged the halves of the blanket together, words crowding my throat. "Are you reading my emotions now?"

"No," he answered. "Should I be?"

I shook my head, not even wanting to know what he would pick up off me. I wasn't even sure what I was feeling. "I've killed."

Ash said nothing, but I felt his stare on me.

"Mostly men. Not good ones." The words were rough against my throat. "Abusers. Users. Rapists. Murderers. I never set out to do it. Like I didn't wake up one day and decide to take someone's life. I helped my stepsister retrieve endangered children, and it would just…happen. Or sometimes my mother—"

"Your mother?" Those two words fell like icy rain between us.

I nodded. "She used me to send messages—the kind that wouldn't be considered an act of the Crown." I knew there was no reason to share any of this. I doubted it would help me, but it felt like a seal had been cracked open deep inside me, letting out words I'd never given life before. "I mean, it's not like I didn't have control of myself. I did. I know that I sometimes let it escalate to the point where I convinced myself it was necessary." I thought of Nor. "That it was self-defense. But to be honest, I wanted to end them. To hand out justice." A curl fell forward, lying against my cheek as I shrugged again. "The funny thing is, I wondered if you knew. Did you?"

"I didn't," he told me, and I wasn't sure if that made me feel better or worse. "Being the Primal of Death doesn't mean I know who takes a life and doesn't when they are alive. It doesn't work that way."

I nodded slowly. "Sometimes I wonder if something in me enabled me to do it. You know? Because not everyone can. My stepsister wouldn't be able to. I don't even think my mother could. And I wonder if that is because of the deal—how I was brought up. Or is there just something wrong with me that is all me—this ability to shut off my emotions and coldly take a life? Was it always in me?"

"What do you mean by *how you were brought up*?"

"Being trained to defend myself," I answered smoothly because that wasn't necessarily a lie. But it was a warning that I could be revealing too much. Still, more words rushed to the tip of my tongue. I couldn't even blame whiskey for it this time. "I don't know if I ever felt those marks you spoke of. Sometimes, I think I did, but then I would make myself not think about what I'd done. And it was easy to do that. Maybe too easy. I felt like…I felt a little like a monster."

The tips of his fingers grazed my cheek, sending a jolt of energy across my skin. Surprised, I lifted my chin as he gathered the curls, tucking them behind my ear. "You're not a monster."

Gods, if he only knew. "I've done some monstrous things that I…that I would do again." *That I will still do.* "Look at what I did to Tavius."

"That bastard deserved it." His eyes brightened. "And when his soul comes out of the pits, I will personally do far worse to him."

The surge of satisfaction I felt upon hearing that was probably another good indication that something was wrong with me. "What do you mean the pits?"

"The Pits of Endless Flames," he explained. "I made sure his soul was immediately sent there. He burns until I free him."

Oh.

Damn.

"But those monstrous things most likely saved the others' lives," he said, and my breath caught. Sir Holland had once said something similar after the first time my mother had me send a message.

I wanted to ask how he would judge my soul, but I figured that was something I was better off not knowing.

His fingers trailed down the curve of my cheek. "I know one thing, *liessa.* A monster wouldn't care if they were one."

I felt another snag in my breath. I'd never considered that before, and that cut through me. I wasn't even sure why, or why I hadn't thought of it because it was a simple enough idea. But I hadn't, and it wasn't like his words erased the deeds I'd committed. Ash was right. Mostly. His words, though, they chased away a little of the darkness that always lingered at the back of my thoughts. And when I drew in a breath, it felt as if it were the first deep one I'd taken in a long time. I wanted to thank him for that.

Without much thought or motivation, I let go of the blanket and moved, erasing the small distance between our mouths. I kissed him, and his lips parted immediately, letting me in. He tasted of smoky whiskey and the coldest hour of night. I felt him tremble as I placed a hand on his chest. I moved again, sliding my hands to his shoulders and climbing into his lap. The feel of his skin through the thin night rail was an icy-hot shock to my senses. He shuddered as he delved his hand into my hair. I leaned into him, guiding him so he was on his back. The Primal of Death went without hesitation, without question. I kissed him, letting myself get a little lost in the feel of his lips, the flavor of his mouth, and the press of the thick hardness against my belly, letting myself enjoy all the sensations. To just exist in how carefully he wove his fingers through my curls, the soft touch of his hand against my back, and the deep groan he let loose when I lifted my mouth from his. To just live in that sudden breath he took when I kissed his scar and then the skin under his chin.

I followed the line of his neck with my lips and tongue, pleased when his head fell back against the arm of the daybed. My lips brushed over the edges of the ink on his skin. I lifted my head. In the starlight and with as close as I was, I could finally make out what each of the marks inked onto his skin was. "They're drops," I said, running a finger over a few of them. I looked up at him. "What kind of drops?"

"Blood," he told me. "They represent drops of blood. But red ink won't stay in my skin. It takes a lot to scar a god's skin, let alone a Primal's. Salt has to be applied for even black to stay."

Air hissed between my teeth. "Ouch."

"It's not exactly a pleasant process."

I dipped my head, kissing a drop. "What do they mean?"

He was quiet for a long moment. "They represent someone whose life was lost by my hands, actions, or because of a decision I made or didn't."

I stilled, staring at the ink. "There have to be…hundreds of them. Maybe even *thousands*."

"They are a reminder that all life can easily be extinguished."

That reminder. My heart twisted as my throat thickened. "You are not responsible for what others do."

"You don't know that, *liessa*."

I shook my head. "The ones who committed those acts are responsible."

Ash said nothing, and I knew—I *knew* that those blood drops inked onto his skin weighed heavily on the side of the lives lost and not the ones he'd taken. I looked down at the swirl that traveled along his waist and dipped under the band of his pants. Did one of these represent Lathan, the friend killed by Cressa and the other two gods? Ash's parents? The gods who had been on the wall? The Chosen he couldn't save? There had to be dozens just on this one part of his body alone, and that kind of loss of life was…it was almost too painful a reminder without collapsing under the grief and what I knew had to be misplaced guilt. I wouldn't be standing if I carried this kind of weight.

Ash had to be the strongest being I knew.

Back bowing, I tasted the skin of his chest, traced the defined lines of his stomach. Every part of me was aware of how each kiss, every graze of my fingers that followed my mouth, drew a quicker breath from him, a tremor. I kept going, my lips dancing around his navel and lower as I slid down his body. The tips of my breasts brushed over his rigid length, causing his body to jerk, and mine to clench. I settled between his legs, nipping at his skin above his waistband. My fingers slid over his sides to his hips and then to the band of his pants.

"What are you up to?" Ash asked, his voice deeper and full of shadows.

"Nothing." I trailed a line of kisses, finding the ink that flowed over his hips.

His fingers drifted through my hair, gathering the strands back from my face. "This does not seem like nothing, *liessa*."

"I'm…exploring," I told him.

"Exactly what are you exploring?"

I lifted my head, and my breath caught. His entire body was taut with tension. The muscles of his stomach and chest, his neck and jaw. His skin had thinned, showing a hint of shadow underneath. His eyes were like stars as he stared down at me. "You," I whispered, heart thumping fast. "I can stop if that's what you want."

He cupped the back of my head. "That is the very last thing I want," he said, and I started to smile. "Don't do that."

"Do what?"

"Smile at me," he murmured, the silver in his eyes swirling.

"Why?"

"Because when you do that, there's utterly nothing I would not allow you to do to me."

I smiled fully then.

"Fuck." He groaned. A laugh left me—a light and airy sound that felt good even as his eyes narrowed on me. "Don't do that either."

My smile was bigger now. "Does that mean I can do anything?"

"Anything." Those churning eyes were fixed on me.

I bit my lip as I looked down at him, where even in the shadows, I saw him straining against the fabric of his breeches. "Anything?"

He nodded.

I rose to my knees.

"Don't move."

I halted. "I thought I could do anything."

"You can, but…I'm now just seeing what you're wearing."

"What's wrong with…?" Glancing down at myself, I trailed off. The glow of the stars turned the sheer material nearly transparent, revealing the darker hue of the peaks of my breasts, and the shadowy area between my thighs. "Oh."

"If you want to wear that gown whenever you'd like, I won't complain," he said thickly, and I started to grin again. "You're beautiful, Seraphena."

There was another clench in my chest, one that threatened to shatter this moment with reality—with responsibility. I didn't want to allow that.

I just wanted to exist in this moment, with this beautiful, strong, and *kind* being.

"Thank you," I whispered, sliding my hand from his stomach. I drew my fingers over the soft material of his pants and over his hard length. I folded my hand around him through the fabric, and his entire body jerked again. I looked up at him. His lips were parted just enough that the tips of his fangs were visible.

"So, the whole *I can do anything*? What if I want to…?" I smoothed my thumb along him, and my stomach hollowed at the feel of him. "What if I wanted to kiss you?" I ran my finger back up, smoothing it over the curved head. His breath was a song. "Here."

"*Fuck*," he repeated.

"Does that fall under anything?"

His chest rose and fell heavily. "That would be the first thing under anything.

"The first thing?"

"And the last. The second thing would be that nightgown and you wearing it whenever you like."

Laughing again, I stretched up and kissed him, enjoying the playfulness, the closeness that I had never really felt before when I was intimate with another. Maybe because this wasn't about stealing a few minutes of pleasure that stole thoughts. It wasn't even about my duty. This was about him and me. It was just about us, and it was…*fun*.

His hands skimmed my waist as I eased my hand under the band on his pants. I felt him shudder as my fingers brushed his cool, hard skin. Breathing in his groan, I curled my hand around him and trembled as I moved it along his length. His hips lifted under me, and I broke off the kiss, a twist of pleasure curling deep in my core as those ultra-bright eyes locked with mine. He didn't blink, not once, as I moved my hand over him. I didn't want to either, enthralled by the tension settling around his mouth, in his jaw, and how the wisps of eather whipped through his eyes. Pulse pounding, I worked my way down once more, trailing a hand over his chest and stomach, where the shadows had thickened under his skin, creating a fascinating marbled effect.

I reached his pants and tugged on the band. Ash lifted his hips enough for me to pull them down over his thighs. Only then did I look away and look at him. A tumbling sensation swept through my chest and my stomach in a sharp, enticing way. The skin was darker, and he seemed even thicker, harder under my palm as I drew my hand to the tip of the glistening head and then back down his entire length.

He was beautiful.

Strands of my hair fell over my shoulder and against my cheeks as

I lowered my head. I kissed him, just below the ridge, and his hips jerked. I pressed short, quick kisses along his length and then licked at his skin, my breath quickening to match his. The tips of his fingers brushed my cheek as my lips coasted over that apparently sensitive spot. I lifted my gaze as he caught my curls, brushing them back from my face. I didn't think he breathed. Our gazes locked, and I felt the corners of my lips curl up as I closed my mouth over the head of his cock.

Ash's entire body reacted. His hips lifted, back bowed, and one leg curled as I drew him into my mouth. "Fucking gods," he growled.

I took him as far as I could, swirling my tongue over his skin, letting my hand reach the rest of him. His salty taste was powerful. The way he danced along my tongue was an aphrodisiac. I sucked at his skin, on his cock, a little surprised by how much I was enjoying myself. Maybe it was this moment, and maybe it was the rough, raw sounds he made. Perhaps it was the way his hand kept tightening in my hair, tugging on the strands and then relaxing. Or how he struggled to keep the thrusts of his hips short and shallow. It could've been the way his hand shook. Both of his hands—the one in my hair and the one on the nape of my neck. Maybe it was just him. Just me. The sudden rush of power I felt that came with the knowledge that he was the Primal of Death and I made him *shake*.

"Sera," he ground out, hand firming on the back of my neck. "I'm not…I'm not going to last."

My skin flushed. I moved my hand faster, sucked harder, and his hand tangled in my hair again as his hips moved, pressing deeper against my palm. Against my tongue.

Ash wasn't just lifting his hips anymore. He lifted me and pulled. "Sera, *liessa*…"

I grazed my teeth over that sensitive spot, and instead of trying to pull my mouth from him again, he pressed down, his entire body arching under me. I felt his cock jerk against my palm as he drew a leg up again. He stiffened. The deep, throaty groan scorched my skin when he let go, throbbing and pulsing.

His muscles were slow to relax, and I followed his body's lead, easing off with my hand and mouth. I dropped a kiss to where the ink followed the inside of his hip and then lifted my head as I carefully pulled his pants back into place.

Ash was staring at me with those wild eyes. He didn't speak. Not a word as he pulled on me, tugging me from where I'd settled between his legs. He drew me up the entire length of his body, and before I could even guess what he was about, his lips closed over mine and he turned, shifting us so I was under him. And this was no soft kiss. It was deep and stunning, and I knew he didn't just taste me on his lips, he also tasted himself. The press of his lips and each sweep of his tongue was a declaration of gratitude. Of *worship.*

And I didn't feel like a monster then.

Chapter 33

I slowly became aware of a fresh, citrusy scent, the soft, warm weight of the fur blanket, and the coolness pressing in at different points. Sleep clung to my thoughts as I snuggled closer to the long, hard length of the body behind mine, and the firm arm under my cheek.

Ash.

I didn't dare move as I lay there, my senses clearing at once and focusing on the feel of him—the sensation of his flesh pressed against mine. He was wrapped tightly around me, not even an inch separating our bodies. I felt his chest rising and falling against my back with each steady breath he took. A heavy arm lay on my waist as if he sought to keep me there. That was a fanciful thought, one quickly lost in the sweet, hot feeling rippling through me. One of his thighs was tucked between mine, the soft material of his pants pressing against a very intimate part of me. My pulse picked up, as did a sense of wonder.

I had never been held like this for any length of time—not this closely, and not awake or in sleep. I knew I had fallen asleep before he had, which meant that he could've woken me. He could've carried me back into the bedchamber, or he could've left me outside. Instead, he'd pulled the blanket up and over me and slept beside me. Again. But he'd been kissing me until I could no longer keep my eyes open, and I'd never been kissed like that before, either. It was as if he had been unable to stop himself. Like he couldn't go even one heartbeat without his lips upon mine. I'd never felt so wanted or *needed.* And that had been how he'd kissed me, as if he needed to do so. He'd kissed me like…like Ezra had looked upon Marisol when she realized that Marisol would be okay.

It felt like something had shifted in the moments before sleep claimed us. Like something was growing between us, making it more than mutual lust. There was respect, and I thought a certain understanding. He may be a Primal, but we were oddly similar in certain ways, and it connected us in a way that the deal his father had brokered didn't.

Warmth poured into my chest, very much like it had when I used my gift but different and stronger. It was exhilarating and new and…

And it was *terrifying.*

Because it felt too warm, too real, and too *desired.* And I couldn't want this. I may deserve those moments of living and just existing, but I didn't deserve for those moments to last. Too much rode on me fulfilling my duty to let myself get swept up in being *wanted.* What I needed to do was more important than me. Than Ash.

Even if he did carry the reminder of so many lost lives on his skin.

A faint ache once again returned to the sides of my face as I lifted my lashes, my gaze falling to where his hand was fisted loosely in the blanket. I reached for him slowly, running my fingertips over the top of his hand, following the tendons and strong bones.

My fingers stilled as something moved—*wiggled* toward the end of the daybed, against my covered feet. I looked down, and my eyes widened. Curled into a little ball next to my feet was Jadis.

I blinked once and then twice, but the draken was still there, in her neat little ball with her wings tucked close to her body. "What in the world?" I whispered.

"She's been there for quite some time," a voice answered quietly.

A shock went through me. My eyes shot to the source of the voice, to the railing on the balcony. What I saw made me wonder if I was still asleep.

Barefoot and shirtless, Nektas crouched on the railing, which seemed impossible given how narrow it was. He appeared completely at ease as if he had no fear of slipping from the railing and falling to his death.

How did he even get up here? His position seemed like an odd choice for someone if they'd come from inside the palace.

"I've also been here for quite some time," he added, his voice low. My brows lifted. "I was looking for my daughter. Figured she'd be wherever he was. I didn't expect to find you with him."

I couldn't even formulate a response.

A shock of dark and red hair fell over his shoulder as he cocked his head to the side. Those eerily beautiful crimson eyes shifted beyond me. "I have never seen him sleep so deeply. Not even when he was just a babe. The slightest sound would wake him."

Surprise rippled through me as the hand under mine remained relaxed and still. "You knew him then?" I asked, completely unable to picture Ash as a babe.

"I knew his parents. I called them my friends, and I call Ash one of my own," he answered, head straightening. His gaze caught mine and held it. "I think I will call you one of my own."

I really had to be asleep. "Why?"

"Because you've given him peace."

Ash woke shortly after the draken *jumped* from the railing to the ground below. Like an adult, I feigned sleep when he eased his arm out from under me and sat up, lifting himself over me. He paused above me as I lay there. My heart started skipping as his fingertips grazed my cheek, brushing a few stray curls back. Then it stopped altogether when I felt the cool press of his lips against my temple.

That was *sweet*.

I didn't want him to be sweet.

I didn't want Nektas to claim me as his.

I didn't want to give Ash peace.

"*Liessa*." Sleep roughened his voice. "If you continue pretending to be asleep, Jadis will start nibbling on your toes."

My eyes snapped open. "Yikes."

His cool breath danced over my cheek as he chuckled. "I hate to disturb your pretend rest."

"I wasn't pretending." I looked up at him, and there was a…softness to his molten silver eyes. Another silly leap occurred in my chest.

"Such a liar," he teased. "I need to get ready for the day." I heard reluctance in his voice, something that made me wonder if he preferred to stay here. "I hold court again this morning, and I have a feeling you're not going to like hearing this," he continued as Jadis stretched by my feet. "You can't be there again."

He was right. I opened my mouth.

"You haven't been officially announced as my Consort," he said before I could speak. "It's too much of a risk until then."

"Do you expect me to stay in my locked chambers—?"

"Not locked in your chambers," he cut in. "Just in them until court is over. You won't have to remain hidden for much longer, *liessa*."

Hidden.

I struggled to tamp down the disappointment. I needed to agree. To make this easy for him. To make *me* easier for him. But I hated being *hidden* away. "And then after? Will you be at the Pillars? Or doing something else? Am I supposed to remain hidden then, too?" I asked, and Ash stiffened above me. "Or will it be okay for me to leave the chamber as long as one of your trusted guards is there to keep a close eye on me?"

He shifted, moving so he sat on my other side, his feet on the stone floor. Jadis lifted her head, yawning. "I know this arrangement isn't perfect."

"This *arrangement* can't continue, is what you mean," I said as the draken crawled over my legs onto the bed and then stretched, raising thin wings. "There will still be risks once I'm your Consort."

"The risks will be less then."

"And what if they're not? What if a Primal attempts to push you by pushing me?"

He looked over his shoulder at me. "Then we reevaluate."

"No." I sat up, holding his gaze as his brows lifted. "I've spent most of my life hiding. I know it makes sense for me to keep a low profile right now, but I can't do that forever. You decided to fulfill the deal because it was no longer safe for me in the mortal realm. But if I'm not safe here either, then what is the point of me being here, Ash?"

White pulsed behind his pupils. "You are *safer* here. Out there, in the mortal realm? Any god could find you. And now that the word is out that I have taken a mortal Consort, you won't have any protection in the mortal realm. Not only that, but you're likely to end up walking into another home without checking to see if it's empty."

I welcomed the burn of irritation as I narrowed my eyes. "I can protect myself."

"That won't be enough," he stated.

"So what? Then I die."

His eyes flashed. "Do you not value your life whatsoever, Sera?"

"I'm not saying that." I reached out, scratching Jadis under the chin as she plopped down by my hip.

"Then what are you saying?"

What was I saying? I watched Jadis close her eyes and stick her head up. "I don't know."

"Really?"

I pressed my lips together. "It's just that I…I know my death is inevitable—"

"You're mortal, Sera. But most mortals don't live as if their life is already forfeit."

But mine was.

It had been forfeited before I was even born.

The tension was thick as Ash, with Jadis hanging over one of his broad shoulders, and I parted ways. I didn't think it had anything to do with me not wanting to stay in my chambers but rather with the perceived lack of value I had for my life.

But how could I value it when it had never truly been mine?

Feeling so very tired, I shuffled into my bedchamber. I had ended up agreeing to Ash's request, something I should've simply done as soon as he made it.

I picked up my robe, slipping it on. Rubbing my aching jaw, I sat on the settee and tried to figure out why I had argued with Ash. I didn't like to be hidden away. I was so *tired* of that. And risk or not, I didn't plan to spend however long it took for me to carry out my duty hidden away despite the risks. But what had provoked me earlier was more than that.

It was how I had shared things with him that I had never spoken out loud before. And how his words had lifted some of the darkness from me. It was the ink on his skin and what it represented. It was how last night had *nothing* to do with my duty and a lot to do with what Nektas had shared. All of that had left me reeling, feeling off-kilter…

Feeling as if I had been presented with something I must do that felt impossible in ways I'd never considered before.

I eventually dragged myself into the bathing chamber and got ready. Since my head ached as it did, I left my hair down and went to the wardrobe. With most of my clothing being laundered, the only thing left was one of the gowns.

Forcing myself to feel grateful that I even had clean clothing to wear, I changed into a simple, long-sleeve day gown a pretty shade of deep, cobalt blue. Hiking up the skirt, I fastened the sheathed dagger to the side of my boot. I'd just finished tightening the stays on the almost too-tight bodice when a knock sounded on the door. Hoping my chest actually stayed in the gown, I found Ector standing in the hallway, his hand resting on the hilt of a sword.

"Are you tasked with standing guard outside my chambers again?"

Several fair strands of hair slid over his forehead as he tilted his head to the side. "If I lied, would you believe me?"

"No."

A brief smile appeared. "I thought you might like to walk the courtyard since I got the distinct impression that you do not like to stay in the bedchamber."

"Does this *distinct impression* include me complaining about having to stay in my bedchamber?" I asked.

"Possibly."

Every part of my being preferred to be outside instead of in my chamber, even with my aching head. "*His Highness* said that I must remain in my bedchamber."

Ector had lifted a brow at the *His Highness* part. "As long as we're not near the southern gates, you will not be seen."

"Okay." I stepped out into the hall, closing the door behind me.

Seeming to fight a smile, he nodded and extended an arm toward the end of the hall, where a less elaborate staircase was located that fed into one of the many side entrances of the palace. "After you."

I started forward, only taking a handful of steps before something occurred to me. I glanced over at the god, who had fallen into step beside me. "Did he tell you it was okay for me to go into the courtyard?"

There was no need to clarify who *he* was. "Possibly," Ector replied and opened the heavy door.

As we traveled the winding, narrow staircase, I refused to acknowledge the fact that Ash had been thinking of me, even though I knew he was highly irritated. We stepped out into the placid air near an unguarded section of the Red Woods. I really had no desire to go near that place again, so I veered to our left, toward the area where Reaver had been learning to fly. It was on the west wall close to the front gate, but we wouldn't be seen.

We walked along the Rise in silence for several minutes. High above us, a guard patrolled. "Are all the guards gods or…"

"They're a mixture of gods and mortals," he answered. "There are even a few godlings."

"How does one become a guard here?"

"It's by choice. They go through extensive training. Usually, they only need to worry about the Shades, but every so often, something else comes to the wall."

"Something else?"

Ector nodded as he stared ahead. His features were relaxed, but he constantly scanned the courtyard as if he expected an entombed god to erupt from the ground at any given moment.

The only thing that came rushing at us was a small draken who'd come running out of a nearby side door, followed by an exasperated Davina, and a much more sedate Reaver.

"Hey there." I knelt as Jadis blew past Ector and plopped her front talons on my bent knees. "What are you up to?"

"Driving me mad," Davina griped as Reaver came to rest beside Ector. "The moment she saw you two walk past one of the windows, she started having a fit."

Grinning, I rubbed under her chin and received a purr. "We're going to be out for a bit. I can watch her."

Reaver grumbled as his diamond-shaped head swiveled toward me.

"I can watch both of them," I amended. "As long as you," I said, looking down at Jadis, "promise not to jump off things."

The young draken chirped.

"Not going to look a gift horse in the mouth." Davina pivoted, her neat ponytail swishing as she stalked back toward the palace. "Have fun with that."

I glanced up at Ector as Jadis pinwheeled into Reaver. "I don't know if she likes me."

Ector laughed. "No one knows if Dav likes them or is five seconds away from setting them on fire."

"Good to know it's not personal," I murmured as we trailed after the draken. "Do they understand us when we speak to them? The draken?"

"They do. Well, Jadis sometimes has trouble… paying attention long enough…" He trailed off, frowning as Jadis snapped at her tail. "To listen."

I smiled as the female draken stopped suddenly and launched at Reaver's tail. "She kind of reminds me of a cross between a puppy and a toddler."

"Yeah, but neither a puppy nor a toddler can belch fire."

I cringed. "Good point."

As we walked on, my thoughts drifted to what I'd learned yesterday about the Chosen. "Did you know Gemma?" I asked.

Ector blinked as his gaze jerked in my direction. "That's a random question."

"I know." I clasped my hands together. "I was just thinking about her—about the Chosen. Ash told me the truth about them."

The god was quiet for a moment. "I'm sure that came as a shock."

"It did. A part of me has a hard time believing it."

"And the other part?"

"The other part wants to burn the whole thing to the ground," I said, looking up as a large shadow fell over us. A deep green draken glided through the air, letting out a deep, rumbling call that was answered moments later by another that flew higher. Feeling Ector's gaze on me, I looked over at him. "What?"

"Nothing." He walked on, keeping an eye on Reaver as the draken lifted into the air above Jadis. "To answer your question, I didn't know Gemma very well. She hadn't been in the Shadowlands long, only a few months."

So, she definitely could've been skittish. Sadness pressed on my chest as I sighed. "Are there ever any clouds here? Rain?"

Ector arched a brow at yet another incredibly random question. "No. It is always like this." His chin tipped up to the gray sky. "You'd think after all these years, I'd have gotten used to not seeing clouds and the sun. But I haven't."

Surprise flickered through me. "You're not from here?"

He shook his head. "But I've been here for so long, it's the only real home I can remember—well, except for the blue skies of Vathi."

"Vathi?" I scrunched my nose as I searched distant memories concerning the different locations in Iliseeum. "Is that…Attes's Court?"

"It's the Court for both the Primal of Accord and War and the Primal of Peace and Vengeance," he said, also referencing the Primal

Kyn. "I was only there for a century or two."

A short laugh left me. "Only a century or two?"

He grinned. "I'm far older than I look."

"Older than Ash?" I asked.

"By several hundred years."

"Wow," I murmured.

"I look good for my age, don't I?" A teasing glint filled his eyes.

I nodded. "Did you know his parents?"

"I did. I knew Eythos and Mycella pretty well."

Turning to him, I stopped under the shadow of an imposing tower as Jadis came to my side. She tugged on the skirt of my gown, pulling the material against her cheek. I truly had no idea what she was doing, but I decided to let her continue. "Nektas made it sound like he was also close to his parents."

"He was." Ector's gaze flicked to me. "When did he tell you that?"

"This morning." I watched Reaver land behind Ector.

"When you were with Nyktos?" He laughed softly as my eyes widened. "I saw you two this morning when I went to speak with him."

"Oh," I whispered, feeling my cheeks warm and having no idea why. I glanced toward the southern area of the Rise where a guard shouted an order to open the gate. Nektas and Ector both knew Ash's father and appeared close to the Primal, yet neither knew why his father had made the deal. "Did either of you think this kind of deal was something that Eythos would've made?"

Ector didn't answer for a long moment. "Eythos loved Mycella, even more so after she was killed. He would've never remarried, but…" A heavy sigh shuttled through him as he squinted. "To be honest, Eythos was very clever. He was always planning ahead. He had a reason."

But what could that reason be—one that made sense?

"You know," Ector said, glancing at me. "I also watched you." He winced as my brows flew up. "That sounds creepier than I intended. What I meant is that I would sometimes join Lathan when he kept an eye on you. That's how I knew what you looked like to find you when Ash gave me the dagger."

"I…I hadn't known that." I let out a long breath. "And I really don't know how to feel about that—about anyone watching me when I had no idea."

"Yeah." Ector idly scratched his jaw. "Well, I guess it doesn't help to know that we had good intentions."

"It does," I told him. "And it doesn't—"

A shout from the other side of the courtyard snapped us around. Another yell was heard. I stilled. "What's going on?"

"I don't know, but that's coming from the southern gate." Ector started forward and then cursed. "Can I trust you to stay here?"

"Sure."

His eyes narrowed. "I have a feeling I'm going to regret this, but stay here," he ordered. "I'll be right back."

I nodded dutifully as Reaver craned his neck in the direction of the commotion. "I will be right here."

With one last look of warning, Ector turned and jogged off, disappearing around one of the palace's swirling turrets.

Kneeling, I pulled Jadis off Reaver. "Sorry," I said, extending my other arm toward Reaver as she trilled sharply. "But you two are coming with me."

Reaver's head snapped back to mine, and his bright crimson eyes narrowed.

"I have a feeling you listen to orders about as well as I do," I said. "But I'm hoping you come along with me. I want to be nosy and see what's going on. Don't you?"

He glanced toward the southern front and then nodded as Jadis climbed my left arm. I rose, hoping she held on as I turned. Reaver got a bit of a running start and then lifted into the air, flying beside where Jadis had perched herself. With him there, Jadis calmed, stretching her neck to rest her little head beside Reaver's talons. We rounded the west side of the palace, and I kept close to the walls, passing several guards on the ground, who sent long looks in my direction. This was the first time I'd been around most of them as I'd only ever seen the bulk of them on the Rise. As far as I knew, none of them entered the palace.

Up ahead, the southern gates were closing. A group had gathered before them around a wagon, and I immediately found Ector in the crowd. He leaned into the back of the wagon. Beside him was Rhahar.

"We found her about a mile from Mount Rhee. Orphine spotted her," Rhahar said while I crept forward, peering between those gathered. A sharp swirl of tingles spread out from my chest, causing my breath to catch. The answering, throbbing warmth caused me to stop. There was a bundled shape in the back of the wagon.

Rhahar ran a hand over his closely cropped hair. "We were closer to her than the Healers. I had Orphine go for help, but…you can see for yourself. It doesn't look good."

Ector's shoulders stiffened as he reached into the wagon. "No. It doesn't." He leaned in, gathering the bundle in his arms. He turned, looking past me, and then his gaze shot back. "Of course, you didn't listen."

I started to answer, but then I saw the woman wrapped in a blanket—first, the thin, limp arm and then the delicate blood-smeared fingers and broken nails.

Good gods.

Bile climbed up my throat as the warmth in my chest pulsed once more. Her face was a mass of swollen, blood-streaked skin—flesh split open over the cheeks and forehead. The lips were torn, the nose pushed to an angle, obviously broken. "Who…who is that?"

"Gemma," Ector bit out through a clenched jaw.

I was frozen in sickening horror. Ector strode past me, a muscle flexing in his jaw as he crossed under one of the staircases. I turned to see Aios step out into the courtyard. She jerked to a stop, clasping a hand over her throat. "Is that…?" Her gaze shot to Rhahar. "Was it Shades?"

"Looks like it," Rhahar answered.

Aios snapped into motion. "I'll grab some towels and supplies. You're taking her to the side chamber?"

"Yes." Ector looked over his shoulder at Rhahar as Aios wheeled around, quickly darting back under another staircase. "Get Nyktos."

"On it." The god rushed off.

"Sera," Ector said as he passed me, heading toward the door two armored men held open. "You need to return to your chambers."

I should.

I definitely should, especially since that warmth was spreading across my chest, invading my blood much like it had when I spotted the wounded silver hawk, but stronger and more intense. Whatever instinct had been given life inside me along with this gift warned me that Gemma…this Chosen, was dying. I could feel my gift sparking. I needed to be as far away as possible.

But I followed Ector as we entered a narrow hall, Jadis's talons tightening on my shoulder, Reaver flying ahead. I followed because this wasn't fair. I didn't know this woman, but I knew that she had spent her life behind a veil, caged and groomed. And for what? To be handed over to gods who would abuse her? It wasn't *fair*.

A door opened, and a light came on, casting a harsh glow over walls where several bundles of herbs hung, drying. Ector laid Gemma on the table, his movements careful, but she groaned.

"Sorry," he said softly, easing his arm out from under her as he brushed away several strands of blood-soaked hair that could've been a strawberry color or lighter when clean. The blanket parted, and I sucked in a sharp breath, seeing that the front of her blouse was drenched with blood—from the ragged wounds along her throat, her chest…

Ector's head jerked up, his swirling silver eyes fixing on me. "You really shouldn't be in here."

I stepped back and Jadis chirped softly. I opened my mouth, but I couldn't find words as I stared at her. A keening sense of…purpose filled me as Reaver stood in the corner of the chamber, tucking his wings back.

"Good gods," a hoarse voice interrupted. I looked over to see the goddess Lailah entering through a different door, her black braids swept back in a knot. She took a step back, a grayish pallor settling into her rich brown skin. "Fucking Shades."

"Yeah," Ector growled as Lailah's brother appeared.

Theon stopped, his nostrils flaring as his features hardened, locking down…and the center of my chest exploded with heat, much like it did when—

I sucked in a sharp breath as my gaze swiveled back to Gemma. "She…she's dead."

"You don't know that," Ector shot back. "There is no—" His words cut off sharply as he looked down at her. His arms fell to the sides.

I was right. Even though nothing about her appeared to have changed, I knew in my bones that she had passed, just as I'd known that the hawk had only been injured. The warmth in my chest was a powerful hum, invading my blood. Jadis trilled, louder this time, her wings lifting and brushing the back of my neck and head. Reaver lifted his head, calling from his corner and drawing the twins' attention.

"What is going on with them?" Theon asked.

"I…I don't know." Slowly, Ector pulled his gaze from the draken to where Jadis did the same from my shoulder. "I've never seen them do this."

Rhain was the first to arrive from court, his curse lost in the draken's sound. The vibrating heat…it was striking against an…an *instinct.* One I'd never felt this powerfully before. My stomach dipped with unease as Jadis nudged her head against the back of mine. Reaver called to the female draken, and in the back of my mind, I wondered if they'd somehow sensed whatever was building inside me. If they could feel it.

Jadis started to climb down, and I had enough presence to stop her from jumping. I caught hold of her squirming body, lowering her to the floor. She rushed over to Reaver, pressing against his side and under one wing.

I had to do something. It would expose my gift, and I didn't know what kind of consequences that would bring. But I'd stood by and let her die when I could have stopped that. I could've healed her. I couldn't stand by now.

Rhain was speaking, saying something about Ash and Saion seemingly appeared out of nowhere, going to the table. He stared down at Gemma, shaking his head as I walked forward. I went to the table, feeling my senses opening and stretching. Closer to the woman, I could now see through the blood and mangled skin that she couldn't be much older than me.

"You…you're *glowing*," Ector rasped, and Saion's head jerked up. The twins turned to me.

A faint, silvery-white glow had seeped out from the sleeves of my gown to lap at my hands.

"What in the actual fuck?" Theon whispered.

I inhaled deeply—taking in the scent of lilacs. Freshly bloomed *lilacs*. And that smell…it was coming from me. Someone spoke, but I didn't know who or what they said. Couldn't hear them over the humming in my ears and the urge…this *calling* that sank deep into my muscles, overriding any thought. I was aware of Lailah and Theon stepping back, of Saion and Ector staring in stunned silence.

"*Sera*," Ash's voice cracked through the hum.

I looked up. He stood in the doorway, Rhahar behind him. The Primal's eyes were wide, a brilliant shade of silver, and the tendrils of eather swirling through the irises were bright—as luminous as the glow radiating from my hands.

He appeared frozen in disbelief like the others, rooted to where he stood as the humming warmth continued spreading through me.

My heart started to trip over itself. I couldn't pull it back—push it down or turn away as I'd been able to do in the past. "I can't stand by and do nothing," I whispered, even though he had no idea what I was talking about. He didn't know about this. I'd never told him. And maybe I should've, but it was too late now.

Reaver cried again, the sound staggered in the otherwise silent room. Ector swore under his breath as the silvery-white eather swirled around my fingers. Throat dry and pulse racing, I placed my trembling hand on Gemma's arm.

"Holy shit," Saion whispered as he bumped into the wall. Herbs swayed above him. "You feel that, right? We all *feel* this."

I didn't know what Saion was talking about. And I also didn't wish for anything. I didn't have the clarity to do so in the whirling storm that was my thoughts.

The shimmering light flowed from my fingers and settled over Gemma in a bright, intense wave. My breath caught as the eather seeped into her skin, filling her veins until they became visible, a spidery network coming alive along her too-pale flesh and across the bruised, torn skin.

"What the…?" Aios entered the room, holding a basin of water to her chest. She jerked to a halt, slowly lowering the bowl.

The silvery light flared as intensely as sunlight on a summer's day all along Gemma's skin. Her chest rose with a deep, shuddering breath that seemed to roll through her entire body. I lifted my hand. The glow throbbed and then softened, slowly fading until…

Underneath the blood, her skin had smoothed and stitched itself back together across cheeks now pink with color. The tear along her forehead had healed, leaving only a rosy line behind. The wound at her throat had sealed, leaving only a ridged scar of puncture marks. Gemma's eyes fluttered open. Brown. She looked straight at me, and then her eyes closed. Her chest now rose and fell slowly, her breathing deep as she slept, healed lips parted with another steady exhale.

"You," Ash whispered, his deep voice hoarse. I looked over at him, and I…I'd never seen him so stunned, so exposed. "You carry an ember of life."

Chapter 34

Ember of life.

You carry the ember of life in you, Sir Holland's voice whispered through me. *You carry hope within you. You carry the possibility of a future.*

Reaver called out again, making that strange, staggered sound, echoed by Jadis. From outside the palace, a deeper call answered in a chorus that rattled the herbs hanging from the walls.

The only one who appeared able to move was Aios. She came to the table, placing the basin on the surface. Glancing over at me, she checked Gemma's pulse. "She's definitely alive."

"That's it," Ash spoke, the shadows spinning dizzily under his skin. I looked over at him and saw only him. Saw the disbelief give way to wonder—wonder that turned into something powerful and bright, something like *hope*. My chest tightened until I wasn't sure how I breathed. "That's what he did."

"Fuck," Saion uttered, and I thought he might need to sit down.

"Did what?" Theon asked as I pressed a hand to my chest. "Who did what?"

Ash straightened to his full height. His gaze remained fixed on me. "No one speaks about what they saw in this room. No one. Gemma wasn't as wounded as previously believed. She will be told the same. Cross me on this, and I will spend an eternity ensuring that you regret that choice. Does everyone understand?"

His words lifted the shock from the room. One by one, each god showed that they clearly understood.

"Good." Ash still hadn't taken his eyes off me. "Theon? Lailah? Please take Gemma to one of the rooms on the second floor."

The twins moved forward to obey the Primal's request. Both sent cautious looks in my direction—looks tinged with wariness and marvel. I watched Theon carefully lift the sleeping Gemma into his arms.

Lailah grabbed the basin. "To clean her up," she said. "She's going to need it."

"Thank you," Ash said, his gaze still boring into me. A wave of tiny bumps spread across my skin. "Ector?"

The god cleared his throat. "Y-Yes?"

"Make sure the guards on the Rise are at all four corners and at the bay. Then make sure those at the Crossroads know to alert us at once if *anyone* arrives from another Court. Go now," Ash ordered, his focus still on me. "And go *fast*."

Alarm raced through me as Ector left at once. "Why…why are you doing that?"

Shadows continued gathering under Ash's skin as he *kept* staring at me. "I felt what you just did. All of us did."

"We all did, too," Nektas's voice startled me. I looked up to see him entering through the hall I'd come through. He was shirtless, his long crimson-streaked hair windblown. His flesh appeared…harder than before, the ridges of scales more defined. Had he just shifted?

I watched Jadis peel away from Reaver's side and rush toward her father. He bent and picked her up. "I don't understand."

"That was a ripple of power," Ash said, and my attention shifted back to him. I stepped back from the table, from where Gemma's blood pooled. "One hell of a ripple of power, *liessa*. One that will most likely be felt through all of Iliseeum by many gods and Primals. There is no doubt in my mind that others will come searching for the source."

My stomach twisted. "I…I didn't know it caused a ripple of power. I assume that's a bad thing?"

"Depends on who felt it." A predatory edge had settled into Ash's features. "It could be a very bad thing."

I opened my mouth and reached for my dagger. Through the gown, I pressed my hand against the hilt. "When will we know if it is a very bad thing?"

Ash had tracked my movements, and his smile held a cold savageness. "Soon." He took a step toward me. "That wasn't the first time you did that, was it?"

I locked up.

"*Liessa*," Ash all but purred, his chin dropping as he slowly rounded the table. I glanced quickly at the other gods and draken, but I doubted any of them would intervene. "I've felt that before. Over the years. Never that strongly, and I didn't know what it was. Couldn't even exactly pinpoint where it was coming from."

I stiffened. He…he'd felt it before?

"And I know for a damn fact that I wasn't the only one who felt it before," he said, shadows starting to gather and move under the table, drifting toward him. Out of the corner of my eye, I saw Nektas motion for Reaver to come to him. "The night at the lake, *liessa*. I felt it earlier that day. I felt it the night before I came for you." The area behind him began to thicken enough that I could no longer see Nektas. "And I felt it recently, the day you went into the Red Woods and the entombed gods broke ground."

My heart pounded fast.

"The Hunters…they came for you twice that I know of," Ash said, and I jolted. "Yes." He nodded. "That is what they must be searching for. And I bet that is what Cressa and the other two gods are also looking for."

"What?" My chest twisted. "You said it was—"

"That was what I thought until now." Ash was only a few feet from me, the shadows behind him taking the shape of wings. "Now, I know they were searching for the source of the ripple of power, and somehow the mortals got mixed up in it."

"Why? Why would they care? Why would they hurt them if they believed it had been them?"

"Because that kind of ripple should not be felt in the mortal realm." His swirling eyes met mine. "Or even in Iliseeum. If I had felt it in any other part of Iliseeum, any part that was closer to the mortal realm, it would've drawn me out, too. Because the kind of power I just felt now? Many would take that as a threat." He shook his head. "You are so incredibly lucky, *liessa*."

I didn't feel very lucky right then.

"Why did you not tell me about this?" When I said nothing, his head tilted. "Don't go quiet on me now, *liessa*." An achingly cold smile crossed his features. I gritted my teeth. "Where is all that foolish bravery of yours?"

"Maybe you're scaring her," Aios suggested from somewhere behind the pulsing shadow wings.

"No. Sera doesn't scare that easily." Ash stood in front of me, so close that I tasted citrus and fresh air when I breathed. I tipped my head back. "Sera knows very little of fear. Isn't that right, *liessa*?"

"Right," I managed to force out.

His skin thinned as his head dipped. Icy breath coasted over my cheek. "Then why didn't you tell me about this little talent of yours?"

"Because you're the Primal of Death," I snapped. "And I didn't think you'd appreciate knowing I'd stolen souls from you. That's the truth. So back off."

Someone made a choked sound, but Ash…gods, he laughed, and that sound was full of dark smoke. "So, you have brought someone back to life before."

"Only once—well, twice if I count this one. I only really used it on animals before. Never mortals. That was a rule I made," I rambled. "Until I broke it. That was the night before you came for me, but that was the only time. And the other day, there was an injured silver hawk. That's why I was so far in the Red Woods. I touched it, and its injuries healed. That was the first time that happened, and it was like…it was like I knew it was only injured and not dying. That was also a first. I didn't know it would even work. I'm not even sure how I ended up with this—this gift."

"I know how." His breath glanced off my lips, sending a strange mixture of nervousness and anticipation through me. "I know exactly who you got the ember of life from. The Primal of Life."

I figured that. "Kolis?"

There was a harsh sound in the chamber, very possibly a curse, and Ash laughed again, this time colder. "My father."

My entire being focused on him. "What?"

"My father was the true Primal of Life." Ash's cool fingers touched my cheek. "Until his brother stole it from him. His twin, Kolis."

Chapter 35

We moved to the chamber behind the thrones. It was a war room of sorts, numerous swords and daggers lining the walls. A long oval table was situated in the center, the wood covered in nicks and grooves, giving the impression that daggers had been slammed into the surface on more than one occasion. Probably by one of the gods sitting there at this moment. Ector had returned by the time we entered the chamber, bringing with him Bele, who was trying but failing not to be obvious about openly staring at me.

Rhain and Saion, along with Rhahar, weren't doing much better. All of them stared at me. Even Nektas, who stood in the corner. He hadn't come straight to the chamber. When he joined us, I saw why. Something nearly as much of a shock as learning that Ash's father had been the Primal of Life.

Cradled to Nektas's chest was a dark-haired girl, wearing a loose nightshirt and wrapped in a blanket. It was Jadis, who…who very much looked like a small, mortal child no older than five. One tiny, bare foot poked out from the blanket.

"Blanket," Nektas said, walking past me while carrying her. "She wanted her blanket."

All I could do was stare and wonder if that was why she had been pulling the edges of my gown against her face earlier.

When she looked like a draken.

Reaver remained in his draken form, alert and resting beside

Nektas.

Aios placed a glass of whiskey in front of me that I didn't touch. Slowly, I looked over at Ash. The shadows had receded from his skin, but he watched me with the same intensity as he had in the chamber, and since he'd returned from checking in on Gemma. She had been looked over by the Healer who'd arrived at some point when we were in the chamber. I had no idea what Ash had told him, to keep how severely Gemma had been injured hidden.

Drawing in a too-short breath, I looked over at Ash. My stomach was still twisting itself into knots. "So…Kolis is your uncle?" My voice sounded so very far away.

He nodded. "They were twins. Identical. One fated to represent life and the other death. My father, Eythos, the Primal of Life, and my uncle Kolis, the Primal of Death. They ruled together for eons as they were meant to."

A wave of goosebumps rippled over my skin as my arms fell to my sides. "What happened?"

"My uncle fell in love."

I hadn't expected him to say that. "I think there must be more to the story."

"There is always more to the story," Aios said, sitting beside Bele.

"It all started a very long time ago. Hundreds of years in the past, if not close to a thousand. Long before Lasania was even a kingdom." Ash sat in the chair beside me, at the head of the table. "I don't know if the relationship between my father and his brother was always strained or if there had been peace between them at one time. But there had always been this competitive side to them. To both of them. My father wasn't wholly innocent in that, but from what I've learned, there was an issue of jealousy. After all, my father was the Primal of Life, worshipped and loved by gods and mortals alike."

Nektas nodded. "He was a fair King, kind and generous, and curious by nature. It was him who gave the dragon a mortal form."

Wide-eyed, I turned to Ash, and my heart stopped.

There was a small, distant smile on the Primal's face. A beautiful and sad one. "He was fascinated with all life, especially the mortals. Even when he became the Primal of Death, he was in awe of everything they could accomplish in what, to Iliseeum, was an incredibly short period of time. He often interacted with them, as did many of the Primals back then. But Kolis, he was…respected and feared as the Primal of Death instead of welcomed as a necessary step in life—a doorway to the next stage."

Rhahar's brows pinched. "I always wondered if mortals wouldn't be so afraid of death if they viewed it differently—as not an end but a new beginning."

Maybe, I thought, swallowing. But death was the great unknown. No one knew how they would be judged or what truly awaited them. It was hard not to be afraid of that."

"When Kolis entered the mortal realm, those who saw him cowered and refused to look him in the eyes while mortals rushed to greet his twin. I imagined that got to him," Ash said, the faint smile turning into a wry grin, and I imagined that had to get to *him*. "On one of those trips into the mortal realm, Kolis saw a young mortal woman gathering flowers for her sister's wedding or something along those lines."

"Wait. Was her name Sotoria?" My thoughts spun. "The one that fell from what is now the Cliffs of Sorrow?"

"That would be her," Bele confirmed, and I was stunned yet again.

I shook my head. "No one really knew if the legend of Sotoria was even real."

"It is." Bele smiled faintly. "Kolis watched her, and supposedly fell in love right then and there."

I blinked once and then twice, glancing back at Ash as I recalled what Sir Holland had told me about Sotoria. He'd said that a god had frightened her. Could that part of the legend have gotten lost over the years?

"Either way, he was absolutely besotted with her," Ash said. "So much so that he stepped out from the shadows of the trees to speak to her. Back then, mortals knew what the Primal of Death looked like. His features were captured in paintings and sculptures. Sotoria knew who he was when he approached her."

Oh, gods… "I know what happened. He scared her, and she ran, falling to her death."

Saion raised dark brows. "Romantic, huh?"

I shuddered. "He brought her back, didn't he?"

"He did." Ash tilted his head. "How did you know?"

"It's a part of the legend—not a well-known part, and no one knew it was Kolis—but I…I hoped that part wasn't true."

"It is." Ash scratched at his jaw as he straightened. "Kolis was distraught and somehow heartbroken. He called for his brother, summoning Eythos into the mortal realm. He begged for Eythos to give Sotoria life, an act that Eythos could do—and had done in the past—but my father had rules that governed when he granted life," he explained, and I shifted on the chair, thinking of the rules I'd made that I hadn't followed. "One of them was that he would not take a soul from the Vale. You see, the tradition of burning the body to release the soul is a mortal one, an act more for the benefit of those left behind than those who have passed. The soul immediately leaves the body upon death."

"I didn't know that," I whispered.

"You wouldn't." He sighed. "For most mortals, those who don't refuse to leave the mortal realm like those in the Dark Elms, pass through the Pillars of Asphodel rather quickly. A lot linger for a little bit for one reason or another. Although Sotoria had died far too young and unexpectedly, she accepted her death. Her soul arrived in the Shadowlands, passed through the Pillars, and entered the Vale within minutes of her death. She did not linger."

I drew in a shaky breath. Had Marisol lingered? Gemma? I sank a little into the chair. "So…the soul isn't trapped at all? They don't have to wait?"

"Not most of them," he said, and I remembered the souls he'd said had required his judgement. "My father would not take a soul from the Vale. It was wrong. Forbidden by both him and Kolis. Eythos tried to remind his brother that he'd agreed never to do something like that. When that failed, my father reminded him that it wasn't fair to grant life and then refuse it to another of equal worth. But I suppose that was one of my father's flaws. He believed he could decide when a person was worthy. And maybe as the Primal of Life, he could. Maybe there was some sort of innate ability that allowed him to make that judgement and decide that Sotoria was not one of those chosen while another would be. I don't know what made him choose when and when not to use that power."

My heart turned over heavily. "That is why I never used my gift on a mortal until the first time." It was hard to continue, feeling his gaze on me—feeling all their stares. "I didn't want that kind of…power, the ability to make that choice. And I always felt that once I did, the knowledge that I could become that power any time I was presented with the choice to do it or not… Well, I don't know if it makes me weak or wrong, but I don't want to have that kind of power."

"That kind of power is a blessing, Sera. And it is a curse," Nektas said, drawing my gaze to his. "Acknowledging that is not a weakness. It has to be a strength, because most would not realize how quickly that power can turn on them."

"My father didn't," Ash said, and my gaze flicked up to him. "If he had never used his gift of life on a mortal, then Kolis may not have expected him to do it. But he did, and my father's refusal…it started all of this. Hundreds of years of pain and suffering for many innocents. Hundreds of years of my father regretting what he chose and chose not to do."

A chill skated down my spine. "What happened?"

"Nothing at first. My father believed that Kolis had accepted his decision. Eythos met my mother during that time. She became his Consort and life was…normal. But in reality, a clock was counting down. Kolis spent the next several years—decades—attempting to bring Sotoria back. He couldn't visit her, not without risking the destruction of her soul."

"But he found a way?"

"He did, in a way." Ash exhaled heavily.

"After all his years of searching, he realized that there was only one way," Rhain said, staring at the table. "Only the Primal of Life could give Sotoria back her life. So, he found a way to become that."

"How?" I breathed.

"I don't know," Ash admitted with a shake of his head. "None of us do. Only Kolis and my father know, and one will never speak of it, and the other is no longer here to tell."

"Kolis was successful," Ector said. "He managed to switch places with his twin, somehow exchanging destinies with him. Kolis became the Primal of Life, and Eythos became the Primal of Death."

"The act was…catastrophic." Nektas shifted Jadis slightly. "Killing hundreds of gods that served both Eythos and Kolis, and weakening many Primals—and even killing a few—forcing the next in line to rise from godhood into Primal power. Many of my brethren were also killed." Nektas's features turned harder as he dropped a quick kiss atop Jadis's head. "The mortal realm felt it in the form of earthquakes and tsunamis. Many areas were leveled. Large portions of land broke off, some forming islands while other cities sank into the oceans and seas. It was chaotic for quite some time, but Eythos knew immediately why his brother had done it. He'd warned Kolis not to bring Sotoria back. That she was at peace, in the next stage of her life. That it had been too long, and if he were to do what he planned, Sotoria would not come back as she was. It would be an unnatural act, an upset to the already unsteady balance of life and death."

I folded my arms over my waist. "Please tell me he didn't do it."

"He did," Nektas stated.

"Gods." I closed my eyes, saddened and horrified for Sotoria. Her life had already been taken from her, and to learn that her peace had also been stripped away sickened me. It was an unconscionable violation.

"Sotoria rose, and as my father had warned, she was not the same. Not evil or anything like that, but morose and horrified by what had been done," Ash continued quietly, repeating what Sir Holland had told me. "When she died again, my father…he did something to ensure that his brother could never reach her. Something only the Primal of Death can do. With the aid of the Primal, Keella, he marked her soul."

I tipped forward. "What does that mean?"

"They designated her soul for rebirth," Aios answered. "Meaning that Sotoria's soul never enters the Shadowlands and is continuously reborn upon death—over and over."

"I…" I shook my head. "Does that mean she's alive today? Does she remember her previous lives?"

"Her memories of her previous lives wouldn't be anything substantial if she had any at all, but Kolis continues to look for her. Because of what my father and Keella did by marking her soul, she would be reborn in a shroud. Kolis knows this. He still searches for her."

I sucked in a sharp breath. "Has he found her?"

"As far as I know, she has remained out of his reach." He looked away, jaw tensing. "I hope she has in each life."

I wanted to ask if he knew who she was, but her identity felt like another violation and a risk to her soul. It had already suffered enough. "So, what your father did for Sotoria was to keep her safe."

"What he did for Sotoria wasn't perfect. Some could argue that, in a way, it was even worse. But it was the only thing he could do to try to keep her safe."

"Was Kolis always like this?"

Ash glanced in Nektas's direction. "He's always had a reckless, wild edge to him. A sense of grandeur that he believed was owed to him," the draken said. "But there was a time when Kolis loved mortals and his gods. Then, he slowly changed. I don't think even his age can be blamed. His rot…it took him long before we lost him."

My mind felt like it would implode.

"Both my father and Keella have paid dearly for that over the years." Ash's gaze settled on me. "He didn't just grow to hate my father, he came to despise him and vowed to make him pay."

I tensed, trying to prepare myself for what I would learn next. It was almost hard to believe. To think of Kolis, who I had been raised to believe was without flaw, the gracious and benevolent King of Gods, as this selfish monster.

But now I knew why he did nothing to stop the abhorrent treatment of the Chosen.

"It was Kolis who killed my mother, striking her down while she was pregnant with me," Ash shared, tone flat. "He did it because he believed that it was only fair that my father lose his love just as he did. He destroyed my mother's soul, ushering in her final death."

I clapped my hand over my mouth in horror. There was this immediate desire to deny what he said. Not to allow myself to believe it. But that wouldn't be right. It would be unfair and wrong to force Ash to prove what I instinctively knew was true. Sorrow burned the back of my throat and stung my eyes. His parents being murdered was bad enough, but to know it had been done by someone who shared his blood? I thought I might be sick.

Ash swallowed thickly. "Like your mother, I believe that her death took a piece of my father with him."

I wanted to go to him. Touch him. Comfort him—something I wasn't sure I had ever felt the need to do before. I wouldn't even know how to do it, so I pressed my hand to my chest and remained seated. "I'm so, so sorry. I know that changes nothing. I know you don't want to hear that, but I…I wish I could somehow change that."

Stormy gray eyes met mine, and then he nodded.

I lowered my hand to my lap. "How have the other Primals allowed this? How did none of them other than Keella step in when he took your father's place? When he brought that poor girl back to life?"

"Kolis destroyed all record of the truth," Ector explained from the other end of the table. "Both in Iliseeum and in the mortal realm. It was then that the Primal of Death was no longer depicted. He went to great extremes to hide that he was not supposed to be the Primal of Life. Even when it became apparent that something was not right. That he was losing his ability to create life and maintain it."

"What do you mean?"

"The destiny was never his, just as the Primal of Death's was never my father's," Ash said. "I was born into it, my destiny reshaped. But

Kolis forced this onto himself and my father. What powers of life he gained were temporary. It took centuries for those powers to wane, and by that time, my father was dead, and Kolis had mastered…other powers. But there has been no Primal born since me. He cannot grant life. He cannot create it."

Something struck me. "Is that why no Chosen have Ascended?"

"Yep," Bele said with a nod. "But he can't stop the Rite, can he? That would raise too many damn questions. And so, the unstable balance has shifted even more."

"Toward what?" I asked.

"Death," Ash replied. Ice touched my skin. "Death of everything, eventually. Both here and in the mortal realm. It may take several mortal lifetimes for it to destroy the mortal realm completely, but it's already started. Two Primals of Death cannot rule, and that is what is happening. Because at Kolis's very core, that is what he is."

My gods.

"Only the Primals and a handful of gods know what Kolis did—what he truly is," Ash spoke again. "Most of the Primals are loyal to him, either out of apathy or because his actions Ascended them into Primal power. The others who think that what he did was unthinkable? They do not act out, either out of fear or an abundance of caution and intelligence."

"Intelligence?" Disbelief rose. "How about cowardice? They are Primals. He may be the King, but he is only one—

Ash inclined his head. "You don't understand, Sera. The powers he stole have weakened and become nearly nonexistent, but *he* has not weakened. He is the oldest Primal. The most powerful. He could kill any of us. And then what? A new god can't rise. Not without Life. That will impact the mortal realm. Your home. Nothing can be done." He leaned toward me. "At least, that's what I believed. My father never told me or anyone about why he made the deal. It's been a godsdamn mystery for over two hundred years. But he had a reason." His gaze flickered over my features. "He gave us a chance for something to be done."

I rocked back and then forward. "Like what? What can I do with just an ember of life besides bring back the dead?" I said, and then a strangled laugh left me. "And, yes, I know that sounds impressive and all—"

"Sounds?" Saion coughed out a laugh. "It is impressive."

"I-I know that, but how can that change anything? How can that undo what Kolis has done?"

Ash touched one of my hands, causing the familiar jolt. "What Kolis did can't be undone, but what my father did by placing what had to be his ember of life in you? Hidden away in a mortal bloodline this whole time? He made sure there was a chance for life."

"It's got to be more than that," Rhahar said, leaning against the back of his cousin's chair. "Most of us weren't alive when Eythos was King. Hell, some of us weren't even alive when Eythos lived."

Rhain and Bele lifted their hands.

"But I just don't think what he did only means that a Primal ember of life is still in existence." Rhahar shook his head. "It has to mean something else."

"Agreed." Saion eyed me.

"But what?" I looked around the room.

"That part is still a mystery." Ash's hand slid off mine as he leaned back. "What's going on in your head right now?"

I laughed, eyes widening slightly. "I don't think you really want to know."

"I do."

I saw Saion raise his brows in doubt. "Wait. This is your father's ember of life. Does that somehow make us…related?"

Ash barked out a laugh. "Good gods, no. It's not like that. It would be like taking someone's blood. That doesn't make you related to them."

"Oh, thank gods. 'Cause that would be…" I trailed off at the sight of the eager stares, hoping I would continue. I cleared my throat. "I just…I don't know. I can't think of what else this gift could mean. How it can help. Your father, was his soul destroyed, too?" I asked, thinking that if it hadn't been, it could be worth the risk of contacting him, even if Ash couldn't. Then it hit me. "If you could've, you would've had someone contact him already."

"His soul wasn't destroyed." Ash's skin had thinned as wisps of eather swirled in his eyes once more. "Kolis still retained some ember of death in him, just like my father retained some of his ember of life. Enough power for Kolis to capture and hold a soul. He has my father's soul."

"Gods," I uttered, my stomach churning with nausea. I briefly closed my eyes. "Is your…is your father aware in that state?"

"I don't believe so, but I don't know if that is what I tell myself just to make it easier to deal," he admitted. A moment passed, and the eather slowed in his eyes. His chest rose with a deep breath, and then he glanced over at Ector. "Now we know why the poppies came back."

"What?" I glanced between them.

Ash's gaze returned to me. "Remember the flower I told you about?"

"The temperamental plant that reminds you of me?" I remembered.

Rhain smothered a laugh behind his hand as Ash nodded. "It's not like the poppies in the mortal realm. Besides their very poisonous needles, they are more red than orange, and they grow far more abundantly in Iliseeum. Gods…" He drew his thumb along his lower lip. "They haven't grown here in hundreds of years, but a few days after your arrival, one blossomed in the Red Woods."

I remembered seeing him then, crossing the courtyard and entering the Red Woods alone. More than once, that had been what he was checking on. "But I didn't do anything."

"I don't think you had to do anything but be here," Nektas said, rubbing a hand along Jadis's back as she wiggled a bit in his arms. "Your presence is slowly bringing life back."

That sounded…utterly unbelievable, but something Ash had said earlier resurfaced. "You said the effects of there being no Primal of Life was already being felt in the mortal realm."

Ash nodded. "What you call the Rot? It's what happened in the Shadowlands. It's a consequence of there being no Primal of Life."

I stared at him as my heart felt as if it stopped in my chest. There was nothing—absolutely nothing—in my head at first. I couldn't have heard him right. Or I didn't understand. "The Rot is a byproduct of the deal your father made with Roderick Mierel expiring."

Ash's brows lowered as he rested an arm on the nicked table. "That has nothing to do with the deal, Sera."

Shock rippled through me, rocking me to my very core. "I don't understand. It started after I was born. It appeared then, and the weather started to change. The droughts and the ice that falls from the sky. The winters—"

"The deal *did* have an expiration date because what my father did to the climate wasn't natural. It couldn't continue that way forever." Ash's gaze searched mine. "But all that meant is that the climate would return to its original state—more seasonal conditions like in some areas of the mortal realm. Of course, I doubt it will ever get as cold as Irelone, not where Lasania is located, but nothing too severe."

My heart sped up. There was a buzzing in my ears. I barely heard Saion when he said, "The weather has been affected by what Kolis did. That's why the mortal realm is seeing more extreme weather like droughts and storms. It's a symptom of the destabilization of the balance."

"The deal has nothing to do with the Rot?" I whispered, and Ash shook his head. I…I wanted to deny what he was saying. Believe that this was some sort of trick.

"Did you think these two things were related?" Ash asked.

A tremor started in my legs. "We knew the deal expired with my birth. That's when the Rot showed. That's what we'd been told, generation after generation. That the deal would end, and things would return to as they were."

"And they did," Ash said. "The weather changed back to its original state years ago. But as Saion explained, it's been more extreme because of the destabilization. Every place in the mortal realm has seen strange weather patterns."

"This Rot showing when it did sounds like a coincidence," Rhain stated. "Or maybe it is tied to your birth and what Nyktos' father did. Maybe the emergence of the ember of life triggered something. Why it would cause the land to sour is beyond me."

Ash leaned toward me. "But it's not a part of the original deal my father made. What is happening in Lasania would've happened even if my father hadn't made the deal, and it will eventually spread throughout the entire mortal realm, just as it will spread in Iliseeum."

"Actually, you know what? I think Rhain was onto something. It might have to do with the deal," Aios said, and my head swung in her direction. Her gaze met mine. "But not in the way you might think."

"What are you thinking?" Ash asked, looking over at the goddess.

"Maybe this Rot—this consequence of what Kolis did—has taken so long to appear because the ember of life was alive in the Mierel bloodline over the years. I mean, the mortal realm is far more vulnerable to the actions of Primals. The fallout of there being no Primal of Life should've been felt long before this, right?" Aios glanced around the table. There were a few nods of agreement. "That ember of life was, in a way, protected in the bloodline. Still there, but…when you were born, the ember of life entered a mortal body—a vessel so to speak—that is vulnerable and carries an expiration date."

"You mean my death," I rasped.

Aios cringed. "Yes. Or maybe not," she added quickly when I

shuddered. "Maybe the ember of life is just weakened in a mortal body, no longer able to hold off the effects of what was done." She sat back with a faint shrug. "Or I could be completely wrong, and everyone should just ignore me."

"No. You may be onto something," Ash said thoughtfully, and I thought I might be sick as his attention shifted to me. A heartbeat passed while he studied me. "What's going on, Sera?"

I couldn't answer.

"This is more than just a surprise to you." Eather trickled into his irises. "You're feeling way too much for this to be confusion surrounding some sort of misinterpretation."

Misinterpretation? A wet-sounding laugh rattled out of me. I knew he must be picking up on my emotions, reading them, and at that moment, I couldn't even care. I didn't think even *he* could decipher exactly what I was feeling.

The tremors had made their way through my body, shaking out any chance of denial.

What everyone said made sense. The day in the Red Woods, I realized how similar the Shadowlands were to the Rot in Lasania—the gray, dead grass, the skeletons of twisted, bare limbs, and the scent of stale lilacs that permeated the ruined soil.

But that meant—oh, gods, that meant that if the deal wasn't responsible for the Rot, there was nothing I could do. Worse yet, it would spread throughout the entire mortal realm. And if Aios was right, it was because of my birth. Because this ember was now alive in a body that would eventually give out and die, taking the ember of life with it. The clock that had been counting down this entire time wasn't the deal coming to an end. It was *me* coming to an end.

I pressed a hand to my roiling stomach as I stood, no longer able to stay seated. I backed away from the table.

"Sera." Ash turned in the chair toward me. "What's going on?"

I shoved hair back from my face, tugging on the strands. I didn't see Ash. I didn't see anyone in that room. All I saw was the Coupers lying in that bed, side by side, flies swarming their bodies. And then I saw countless families like that. Hundreds of thousands. Millions. "I thought I could stop it," I whispered, the back of my throat burning. "That's what I spent my…my entire life on. I thought I could stop it. Everything I did. The loneliness. The *fucking* Veil of the Chosen. The training—the becoming *nothing*. The godsdamn grooming," I dragged my hands down my face. "It was *worth* it. I would save my people. It didn't matter what happened to me in the end—"

Ash was suddenly in front of me, the press of his hands cool against my cheeks. "Did you all think fulfilling the deal would somehow stop the Rot?"

Another strangled laugh left me. "No. We thought…"

Make him fall in love.

Become his weakness.

End him.

I shuddered as I felt it—that swift, acute sense of being able to truly *breathe.* Like I had felt when he hadn't taken me the first night I'd been presented to him. *Relief.* The reason was different this time. I didn't have to manipulate him. I didn't have to make him fall in love with me and then hurt him—kill him.

His face came into view, the sharp angles and the hollowness under his cheekbones. The rich, reddish-brown hair and striking, swirling eyes. The features of a Primal, who was nothing like I assumed or wanted to believe. Thoughtful and kind despite all he'd lost—despite all the pain he'd felt that would've changed most into something of a nightmare. A man that I…that I had begun to *enjoy.* To *care* for, even before I realized who he was and we'd sat side by side at the lake. A person who made me feel like *someone.* Like I wasn't a blank canvas, an empty vessel.

Someone who had only been born to kill.

I didn't have to do what I didn't want. And, oh gods, I didn't want to hurt him. I didn't want to even be capable of that. And I didn't have to be. The relief was so all-consuming, so potent, the rush of raw emotion threatened to swallow me. The only thing that stopped it was what had the night he hadn't claimed me.

The guilt.

The bitter, churning guilt.

Millions would still die, even if I didn't have to take his life. That was no blessing. No real reprieve.

"Sera," Ash whispered.

I lifted my gaze to his, my breath seizing in my chest as his thumb swept over my cheek, chasing away a tear. The whipping tendrils of eather in his ultra-bright eyes snared mine.

"I don't think she thought becoming your Consort would save her people." Bele's voice was a crack, reminding me that we weren't alone and shattering something deep in me as the wisps in Ash's eyes stilled. "I think she learned how to end a deal in favor of the summoner."

Ash said nothing as he stared at me. Someone cursed. I heard the scrape of chair legs over stone, and then I felt *it.* A tremor in Ash's hands, and the charge of energy suddenly pouring into the chamber, crackling over my skin. I saw *it.* The thinning of his skin and the shadows gathering underneath.

"You believed that the future of Lasania hinged on this deal—on you fulfilling it, but not as my Consort." His voice was so quiet, so soft it sent a chill over my skin. "Do you know how to end a deal in the favor of the summoner?"

Every part in me screamed that I should lie. A surprising dose of self-preservation kicked in. That was the smart thing to do, but I was so tired of lying. Of *hiding.* "I do."

Ash inhaled sharply. Shadows peeled away from the corners of the chamber and gathered around him—around us. "Is that why you kept going back to the Shadow Temple after I refused you? Is that why you wanted to fulfill the deal you never agreed to?"

Another fissure cut through my chest. "Yes."

Eather crackled from his eyes as light began streaking through the swirling shadows winding up his back. The breath I took formed a misty, puffy cloud in the space between us. "Your training. Your *grooming.*" The tips of his fangs became visible as his lips peeled back. "All of what you've done from the day you were born until this very moment was to become my weakness?"

Pressure clamped my chest. I couldn't answer. It was like all the air had been sucked out of the chamber, and what was left was too cold and thick to breathe. A burn started in my core, spreading to my throat as the eather-laced shadows took shape behind him, forming wings.

I was going to die.

I knew that then as I stared into those so-very-still, dead eyes. I couldn't even blame him for it. I stood before him because I'd planned on killing him. I'd always known my death would come at his hands or because I had ended his life.

"You," he said, his voice a whisper of night, his hand sliding over my jaw. His palm pressed against the side of my throat. He tilted my head back, and I was no longer looking up at Ash. This was a Primal. The Primal of Death. He was Nyktos to me now. "You had to know you would not have walked away from this, even if you had succeeded. You'd be dead the moment you pulled that fucking shadowstone blade from my chest.

"Ash," Nektas said, his voice close.

The Primal didn't move. He didn't blink as he stared down at me. "Does your life hold no value to you at all?"

I jolted.

"*Ash,*" Nektas repeated as Reaver made a soft sound.

The eather lashed through his eyes. The mass of shadows collapsed around him as he slowly lifted his hands from me. He stood there for a moment, his features far too stark, and then he took a step back.

Knees weak and heart racing, I sagged against the wall. "I… I'm—"

"Don't you fucking apologize," Nyktos snarled. "Don't you dare—"

A horn blew from somewhere outside, the blast echoing through the palace. Another sounded. I jerked away from the wall. "What is that?"

"A warning." Nyktos was already turning away from me. "We're under siege."

Chapter 36

"The ripple of power was felt." Bele was on her feet.

I peeled away from the wall as the rest of the gods rose. "Do you think it—do you think it's Kolis?"

No one looked at me. Only Nektas. "He would not come himself," he answered as Jadis lifted her head, yawning. "He would send others."

"If he did come for you, you would get what you so desperately seek for yourself." Nyktos looked over his shoulder. "Your death."

My chest twisted as the iciness of his words fell upon me. They stung. There was no denying that.

"Saion—go find out what you can. I will meet you by the stables. Rhahar. Bele. Go with him. Speak no word of what you've learned in here. None," Nyktos ordered. "Understood?"

The three gods obeyed, quickly leaving the room. None of them looked in my direction.

"I will take the younglings to safety." Nektas motioned for Reaver to join him. "Just in case I was right about who has come to our shores. We will join you as soon as they're safe."

Nyktos nodded, his back to me as Nektas went to the door. Jadis's head rested on her father's shoulder, and she gave me a sleepy wave as she passed. The little wave… I didn't know why, but it carved at my heart. The look her father sent me froze that knife in there.

I think I will call you one of my own.

I sucked in a shrill breath. I doubted Nektas felt that way now. Why would he? I came here, plotting to kill the Primal that he considered family.

Aios rose, sending a hasty look in my direction, "I'll go check on Gemma. Make sure the sirens haven't woken her and deal with that if they have."

"Thank you," Nyktos replied, taking one of the short swords from the wall. He secured it to his hip then grabbed a dagger next, sliding it into his boot. A long, sheathed sword went over his back, hilt downward.

"What are we going to do with her?"

My head jerked to Ector, who had asked the question. "I can help."

Slowly, Nyktos faced me as Rhain's brows flew up. There was nothing but endless coldness in his stare. I fought the urge to step away from him.

"I can." I forced my voice steady. "I'm trained with an arrow and sword."

He sneered. "Of course, you are."

I flinched as the sharp, slicing motion cut even deeper into my heart, leaving its own kind of mark. The burn returned to my throat, crowding my eyes as a burst of something bitter and hard swelled inside me. I couldn't take in air. The rawness clogged my throat. I couldn't allow it. I shut it down. Shut it all down. *Breathe in.* In my mind, I slipped on that veil. It was harder than all the times before, and it felt flimsy and sheer, in a way it never had. *Hold.* I became nothing but the blank canvas, an empty vessel that couldn't be hurt by words or actions outside of the ones I caused myself.

I exhaled. "Danger has come to the Shadowlands because of what I did. I will not stand back and do nothing when I can fight." I lifted my chin, meeting Nyktos' chilly stare. "I am no threat to any of your people."

His head tilted. "You are no threat to me."

I stiffened, but that was all. "I can help, but you do whatever you want. Lock me away or take me with you. Either way, you're wasting time."

Nyktos' chin dipped as he stared me down. "While the idea of locking you away holds much appeal at the moment, there is no time to ensure that you'd be secure and wouldn't escape. So, you're coming with me." In the span of a heartbeat, he was within a foot of me. I tensed, managing to hold my ground. "But if you do *anything* that jeopardizes any of my people, being locked away will be the least of the things you'll face."

I didn't miss the looks of disbelief that Rhain and Ector exchanged, nor did I doubt Nyktos for one second. "I don't want to harm any of them."

"No." His smile was a tight mockery. "Just me."

The veil slipped. "I didn't want to harm you either."

"Save it," he snapped, grabbing my hand. The jolt of energy was a warm buzz. His grip was firm but not painful as he led me from the room.

Nyktos tugged me past the thrones and off the dais. Ector and Rhain were right behind us. The darkened room was eerily quiet except for the clap of our boots. It was a struggle to keep up with his long-legged pace. All I focused on was keeping my mind from going back to the chamber and why he was now Nyktos to me. I couldn't think about it as we neared the foyer. Nyktos walked so fast, I missed the slight rise in the floor, the barely-there step between the open chamber and the foyer. I tripped—

Nyktos' hand tightened on mine, catching me and keeping me from tumbling face-first into the hard shadowstone.

"Thanks," I mumbled.

"Don't," he bit out.

I pressed my lips together as the veil slipped even more. His anger was no surprise. I couldn't and wouldn't blame him. It was my inability to remain in that nothingness that caused my chest to twist.

Saion stormed through the open doors, drawing to a halt as he spotted us. "Something's happening at the wall, along the bay." His gaze flicked to our joined hands, but he showed no reaction. "I'm not sure what yet. Rhahar is readying Odin. Bele has gone ahead."

"Do you know if there have been any injuries yet?" Nyktos asked, striding forward.

"One of the smaller ships capsized," Saion advised, a step behind us. Ahead, Rhahar led the massive, midnight steed toward where several horses already waited. "Rescue efforts were halted when one of those ships turned over."

"What in the world is in that bay that could capsize ships?" I asked.

"There shouldn't be anything," Nyktos shared, surprising me since I half expected no answer.

"The waters have been dead for years. Not many things can survive in them for long," Rhain added. "Not only that, the waters are pitch-black—"

"Which makes rescues even more difficult," Saion said. "If not impossible. Anyone, god or mortal, goes into those waters, they're not likely to come back out."

A chill swept over me as Nyktos took the reins from Rhahar. He turned to Ector. "I need you to grab me a hooded cloak and meet me at the gates to the bay."

Ector sent a glance in my direction, brows pinched. He looked as if he wanted to say something but reconsidered. "Of course." He turned, racing off toward one of the many side entrances hidden under the staircases.

"Have the other gates to the city been sealed?" Nyktos asked.

"In the process, from what one of the guards shared," Saion confirmed. "And they've started evacuating those along the bay, moving them inland."

I turned to Odin, unsure exactly how I was supposed to mount a horse of his size. I'd have to figure it out because I wasn't foolish enough to ask for my own mount. I reached for the strap on the saddle as Nyktos gripped my hips, lifting me with shocking ease.

I started to thank him but kept my mouth shut as I slid a leg over the saddle, seating myself.

"Is she really coming with us?" Rhain asked, hoisting himself onto the back of his horse.

"You want to stay back and make sure she remains wherever we put her?" Nyktos swung himself up behind me, and I clamped my jaw shut.

"No," Rhain answered.

"Then she comes with us." Nyktos reached around, tightening his hold on Odin's reins. "Hold on."

I firmed my grip on the pommel a second before Odin launched into a gallop that quickly picked up speed, kicking up dirt and stirring dust. Out of instinct, I tipped forward as Nyktos guided Odin around the side of Haides and along the Rise. Saion and Rhain fell in line beside us. We raced through a narrower gate, across hard-packed dirt that glittered with specks of embedded shadowstone. Bare-limbed, bent trees that reminded me of the dead ones I'd first seen upon entering the Shadowlands surrounded the road. Mist gathered and seeped around the gray trunks. Through the gnarled, heavy branches full of blood-tinted leaves, I caught glimpses of the Rise, where it began to climb so high, I couldn't see the tops of the ramparts. Sweeping towers appeared through the trees, spaced hundreds of feet apart before the Rise appeared to flow outward, farther away from the road until I could no longer see it.

Nyktos guided Odin sharply to the right, off the road. He leaned in, his chest pressing against my back. The feel of his cool body against mine threatened to short out my senses and my not-so-rigid control on myself. The contact was…gods, I couldn't let myself even think of that as we flew between the blood trees. White mist pooled and thickened, whipped into a frenzy. The mist—the eather—rose higher and higher, causing my heart to feel as if it too were being stirred into a frenzy.

"We're going to take a shortcut." His arm dropped to my waist, his grip tight. "You might want to close your eyes."

My eyes were wide open. "Why—?" I sucked in air as the trees disappeared ahead and the very ground itself seemed to fall into a misty abyss of *nothing*.

A scream lodged in my throat as Saion broke forward, riding low over a black steed almost as large as Odin. Saion and his horse *disappeared*. I started to press back against Nyktos—

Odin leapt into the mist.

For a moment, there was nothing but white mist and the feeling of…flying. I couldn't even take a breath in those seconds of weightlessness—

The impact of Odin landing knocked whatever air there was out of my lungs, throwing me back against the Primal's hard, unyielding body.

Nyktos held onto me as we rode at breakneck speed through the film of eather, Odin's hoofs thundering off rocks. I couldn't see anything. Nothing but mist. But if we were going to ride off the face of a mountain or whatever it was we descended, I wouldn't go out with my eyes closed.

Odin leapt once more, and then we were free of the thickest of the eather, rushing across patches of gray grass and hard dirt. It took me a moment to even know what I was seeing as Rhain and Rhahar joined us, remaining at our side. I saw who I believed was Saion, riding along the wall where the mist gathered in thinner, wispy pools.

I looked back at the mountain of mist to see dozens of guards on horseback, erupting from the wall of mist. Nyktos called out commands I couldn't hear over the thunder of hoofs.

A closed stone gate appeared ahead, and on the Rise, torches glowed from the height of the wall where I saw the distant forms of guards, all turned to what lay beyond the Rise.

Nyktos slowed Odin down, coming to a stop a distance from the group of guards. A guard broke free of the others. I squinted, recognizing Theon. One of the few gods who hadn't been present when my treachery became known. I doubted it would take long for him or his sister to hear. Or would the others obey Nyktos' command to not speak of what they'd witnessed?

"Something's in the water," Theon said, grabbing Odin's bridle, barely sparing a glance in my direction. "It came from the sea, whatever it is, cutting through one of our supply ships. Snapped the son of a bitch in two."

"Fuck," Nyktos growled, jumping from the horse. He turned immediately, extending his arms to me without a word. I took them, a bit stunned that even in his cold fury, he was still…thoughtful. "Any sign of what it is?"

"Not yet," Theon answered.

Nyktos took a step and then stiffened at the exact moment I felt a throbbing in the center of my chest, a warmth. Under the starlight, the shadows lifted from the thin mist running along the ground. His eyes closed as his features appeared to sharpen.

"Death," I whispered.

His head whipped toward me, eyes opening. "You feel it?"

I swallowed, nodding. "I feel death."

A muscle ticked along his jaw. "What you feel are souls separating from their bodies."

Theon swore under his breath, and I stared up at Nyktos, having not thought of the fact that as the Primal of Death he would be able to feel it. Feel death when it happened.

As I did.

Chilled, I turned to see Ector arriving, bearing down on us. He drew the horse to a stop, scattering the mist, and tossed a black cloak down to Nyktos. The Primal nodded his thanks and then turned to me, draping the soft material over my shoulders as guards raced up the rampart stairs.

"You will remain with Ector and Rhain," he said as Ector dismounted. He tugged the hood up over my head.

I glanced at them. They looked less than pleased by that, but I nodded.

"Stay with them," Nyktos ordered. I reached for the buttons on the cloak, but he was faster. His fingers made quick work of them, and his gaze met mine, still shockingly bright. "Remember my warning."

Theon frowned at the Primal's tone, but one sharp look from Rhain silenced him.

"I remember," I said.

Nyktos' gaze held mine for a moment longer, and then he looked at Rhain and Ector. "Make sure she stays alive." He returned to Odin's side, seating himself and turning toward the guards. I watched him ride forward, trails of shadows cutting through the mist as he leaned sideways in the saddle, snatching up a bow and quiver held up by another guard. Saion, Rhahar, and Theon followed. The gates opened, and he rode out. Only the two gods and another, who was hooded like me, broke free of the guards on horseback and followed.

"He'll…be okay, right?" I asked as Rhain came to my side, his reddish-gold hair windblown. "Going out there with just three gods? Will they be okay?"

"Do you really think I believe you are concerned?"

I looked over at him. "Will he be okay?"

"He's the Primal," the god answered. "What do you think?"

What I thought was that he lived and breathed. Therefore, he could be harmed. And gods could be killed.

"You shouldn't be here," Ector stated.

"But I am." I turned to the steps and started forward, affixing that mental veil once more. "What could be in the water?"

Ector brushed past me, reaching the steps first. He looked over his shoulder. "Do you believe in monsters?"

My stomach dipped. "Depends."

He smirked before he faced forward. I glanced back at Rhain, but he stared ahead. I followed at a quick clip, not allowing myself to think about exactly how high the steps were carrying us.

"Whatever you do," Rhain said as we neared the top, "please don't get yourself killed. I'm sure Nyktos wants the honor for himself."

"Wasn't planning on it," I told him.

"He's not going to kill her," Ector said from ahead. "Not when she carries the ember."

Rhain sighed behind me, and it struck me then that Ector was right. Nyktos wouldn't. Not until he figured out what it meant for me to carry the ember besides returning life to the dead. And if that were it? Would he kill me? Possibly sentence the mortal realm to a quicker death if Aios was right? Or keep me locked away, safe from those who meant me harm and those he believed I could harm?

My stomach took another tumble as I walked along the wide roof. In the distance, there was nothing but rocky hills and flat ground. I didn't see Nyktos or any of the guards. I followed the curve of the wall, my pace picking up as I looked both ways, seeing that we were now entering some part of the city—a district of low, squat buildings that reminded me of the warehouses in Carsodonia. I kept on, my gaze tracking the nondescript buildings until I finally saw the city within the Shadowlands for the first time.

My breath caught as I stared out. It was larger than I expected.

As far as the eye could see, starlight glistened off tiled roofs, most homes and businesses stacked one upon another with tight, winding alleys between them, reminding me very much of Croft's Cross. Specks of illumination from either candles or gas lamps shone along the streets and from windows. There were no Temples in the sprawling city, none that I could see, anyway, and there was a rather large portion that had been cut into the slope of a hill where buildings were staggered all the way down.

"How many people live here?" I asked as Ector strode ahead.

"Hundred thousand." Rhain edged around me. "Or close to it."

Good gods, I had no idea. Were they mostly gods or mortals? How many of them were Chosen—?

A sound like thunder came from the ground below. From the streets, shouts grew louder, mingling with screams. Pressure clamped down on my chest, and I moved to the nearest parapet, just as Rhain and Ector had. Placing my hands on the rough stone, I leaned out, squinting into the murky gloom.

A mass of people barreled through the narrow streets, some on foot and others on horseback or in carriages. Horror seized me as they pressed forward, pushing and falling, clamoring overtop one another as they ran—

"They're running from the area of the harbor," Ector shouted, peeling out of the parapet. "Shit. I thought the area was emptied."

"They were in the process of doing that." Rhain hurried along the wall, looking ahead. "What the fuck is in the water?"

I heard guards shouting orders, trying to calm the people and restore some semblance of order, but their yells were swallowed in the panic. The cries of pain were sharp, and I flinched as I backed away from the disaster unfolding below. People were getting hurt in that crush. They would die in their desperation to reach the safety of the castle grounds.

I forced myself to turn away and leave the parapet, the skirt of my gown whipping around my legs. I couldn't afford for this ember to seize control again. Guards scrambled along the eastern wall as I hurried behind Ector and Rhain, reaching the section that overlooked the bay. None of the other guards paid me any attention, either completely unaware or simply not caring, too fixated on what was happening down below. I walked out onto another parapet, passing unused shields, quivers, and curved bows. The stale wind reached inside the hood, lifting the strands of my hair and tossing them over my face as the glistening surface of the bay loomed ahead.

What I saw brought forth a decade-old memory of the day a ship carrying oil had run abroad, hitting another. Ezra and I had climbed out onto the bluffs to watch the men King Ernald had sent out to stop the spill. The ship sank, and the oil spilled into the waters, enraging Phanos, the Primal God of the Skies and Seas. He had erupted from the sea in a terrifying cyclone, his roar of fury creating a shockwave that caused our ears to bleed. Within seconds, he'd obliterated every ship in the port. Hundreds had died, either drowned, flung into the buildings below, or they simply ceased to exist, along with the dozens of ships.

The waters had been free of pollutants ever since.

But there was no Phanos in the water, as far as I knew. And still, what I saw stopped my heart. In the bay, a supply ship had been ripped in two, across the center, sinking beneath the surface of the violently churning waters.

Another ship rocked unsteadily as men struggled with the vessel's rigging, shouting at one another. Wooden dinghies, from those who must've gone out to help those on the fallen ship now floated overturned in the rough waters. I saw no person swimming or treading water, and I thought of what Nyktos and I had sensed at the gate.

Death.

Something was in that water. The guards lining the wall had their arrows nocked and pointed.

"Holy fuck." Rhain drew up short in front of me.

I saw them then as they broke the dark, glimmering surface of the bay.

My lips parted. Good gods, they were the size of horses, climbing up the sides of the ships, their heavily muscled bodies glistening like midnight oil. The ships docked in the harbor trembled as if they were saplings. Wood cracked and splintered under their grips. Their feet punched holes through the decks.

I had never seen one outside of sketches in the heavy tomes that dealt with Iliseeum, but I knew they were dakkais—a race of vicious, flesh-eating creatures, rumored to have been birthed from bottomless pits located somewhere in Iliseeum.

Featureless except for gaping mouths full of jagged teeth, they were rumored to be one of the most vicious creatures that existed in Iliseeum.

"Why are they here?" I looked over at Rhain.

"They are like trained bloodhounds, able to sense eather. They're drawn to it." The god's luminous gaze landed on me. "Whoever sent them, sent them here for you."

I turned back to the docks. A sickening horror settled in my stomach. The dakkias would reach the city in no time, and there was nothing between them and the homes on that hill, where many still desperately tried to gain higher ground. They came for me, and innocent people could die—

A flash of sudden, bright light streaked through the sky, blinding me. I stumbled back against stone as a whooping cry went up from the guards. They leapt onto the ledge of the wall, kneeling as they took aim with bows and arrows.

The shrill pitch of a scream spun me back to the harbor just in time to see an arrow strike a dakkai in the head. It fell back, exploding into *nothing,* just as the Hunters had. Another arrow struck a second dakkai as it reached the top of the bluff—*the bluff,* where there was no protection. The arrows were coming from there. I twisted, and my legs almost gave out on me.

Five massive black steeds erupted from the mist, their hooves shattering rock as they sped down the bluff. *Nyktos.* He and the other four rose onto the backs of their horses, kneeling in a crouch as they fired arrows at the dakkais. The one cloaked, who had joined them as they left the gates, stood completely upright, the force of the steep descent lifting the hood, revealing a thick braid the color of the darkest hour of night. It was a female who fired the next arrow, standing astride her horse.

"Fucking Bele," Rhain muttered with a grin as he leapt onto a nearby ledge, drawing an arrow tight. "Is there ever a time when she doesn't like to show off?"

That was Bele?

A volley of arrows was released, and I snapped into action. I grabbed a bow and an arrow from a nearby quiver, quickly nocking it like Sir Holland had taught me so many years ago.

As Nyktos broke to the front, I pulled the string back and took aim, firing an arrow. Several of the dakkais rushed the sailors who'd made it to the piers, apparently unaware that their ships were far safer. I released another arrow and then watched it cut through the night, smacking into the back of the dakkai's head. My lip curled as the thing shattered into nothing.

"Who?" I asked, nocking another arrow. I truly didn't understand what I was seeing. "Who do you think sent them?"

Rhain fired a second after me. He twisted, grabbing another arrow. "They're pets of the Court of Dalos."

My breath thinned. Kolis. I still hadn't processed what I'd learned about him. I fired, striking one of the beasts as it reached the bluff.

Several more dakkais took notice of the sailors, who scrambled to get back to their ship. A man screamed as one of the dakkais launched itself onto where he clung to the side of the boat. I let the arrow fly, striking the dakkai in the back before it could land on the sailor. The creature exploded as it fell back into the waters.

Quickly readying another arrow, I aimed and fired, over and over as a horde of the creatures swarmed the ship and the men as the horses reached the edge of the bluff. The one who rode out front rose even higher, snagging my attention as I nocked another arrow. Nyktos leapt from Odin, twisting in midair. He landed in a crouch, and for a moment, I let myself be a little impressed by that feat.

And a little envious.

"He's a showoff," I muttered and then pitched forward as Odin bore down on him, leaping into the air—

Nyktos raised a hand, closing it into a fist, and Odin…Odin became nothing more than a shadow—one that wrapped itself around Nyktos' arm, sinking into the skin around the silver band.

"What the hell?" I whispered, my eyes wide.

"That's the first time you've seen him do that?" Ector asked from where he stood on the other side of Rhain. "Neat party trick, huh?"

"How is that even possible?" I asked.

"Odin isn't your normal horse," Ector replied.

"No shit," I retorted.

Nyktos spun, catching my attention. The silver band glinted on his biceps as he caught a dakkai in one hand, lifting the enormous creature. He slammed the thing into the ground, planting a booted foot against its throat and reaching across his chest to unsheathe the short sword with a blade that glinted like onyx moonlight. He brought it down with a quick thrust, and the dakkai was no more.

Bele landed near him, striding forward, cloak lost somewhere. The stallion she'd ridden on raced away from the docks, joined by the other horses as they got out of the dakkais' path. Bele reached back, unhooking the arrow at her hip. Her long legs were encased in either breeches or tights, arms bare, but no bands adorned them. She was too far away for me to make out the details of her face. Nyktos must've said something to her because her laugh reached us on the wall, sounding like wind chimes. Guards stilled along the wall as she picked up speed, launching into the air and coming down on the dakkai with her fist—no, with some sort of weapon. The dakkai shattered, and she landed where it'd once stood.

"I think I'm in love," Ector said, and I felt like I might've fallen a little in love, too.

Rhain snorted.

A dakkai shot across the docks, launching into the air. Theon kicked out, knocking a dakkai back and thrusting his sword, shoving it deep into the creature's chest.

"Now I think I'm in love," Rhain murmured as Theon spun, slicing through the dakkai he'd kicked.

I loaded another arrow and spotted Nyktos once more. He planted a booted foot in a dakkai's chest, pushing the thing back with stunning strength and sending it skidding several feet. Saion took it down as he turned, thrusting his sword into another.

Bele seemed to be having a grand old time as she made quick work of the dakkais clamoring for the men on the ship—sailors who now stood transfixed. Letting go of the string, I watched long enough to know that the arrow had struck the head of one of the things before reaching for another arrow.

"There's more!" a guard down the wall shouted. "Coming inland."

Nyktos turned as several dakkais broke the surface of the bay, clamoring over one another as they spilled onto the docks, their claws snapping more sections of wood.

One of the dakkais rushed Nyktos from behind, and I shifted my aim, releasing the arrow. Just as the Primal spun, it struck true, taking out the dakkai.

Nyktos' head jerked up. With unnerving accuracy, he turned to where I stood.

My hand shook as I broke his stare and reached for another arrow. I doubted I'd get a thank you for that.

"Several just made it up," a guard shouted, racing down the wall. "They're heading for the gates."

"Go!" Nyktos ordered.

Bele took off running. She quickly disappeared around the corner of a building as shouts of alarm filled the air. I rose from the parapet to see dozens more swarm the docks, scrambling out from the bay like a tide of death.

"Good gods," Rhain rasped. "There are too many."

Heart thumping heavily, I snapped forward, taking aim. I struck one, and three more took its place. My wide gaze scanned the docks. I saw Nyktos shove a dakkai back as another crashed into his side. A shout lodged in my throat as he stumbled. I fired an arrow, striking the dakkai. "Why isn't he using his power? Why aren't any of them using the eather?"

"Dakkai can sense eather—they feed off it. It'll draw more to them," Rhain said, throwing an empty quiver aside. "They'd be fucking swarmed."

A harsh breath punched from my lungs as I looked at my nearly empty quiver.

"The wall!" a guard shouted. "On the wall!"

I looked down, and my stomach plummeted. A dozen or so dakkais were scaling the wall, punching their fists into the stone and breaking off enough of it to gain purchase on the otherwise smooth surface.

Dear gods…

They were moving fast, climbing several feet a second. Within a few too short heartbeats, they would crest the ledge and overwhelm us.

Chapter 37

Spinning toward the quiver, I grabbed an arrow. There was only a handful left, not nearly enough. I returned to the gap in the stone as I nocked the arrow and fired, catching one of the dakkai on the top of its slick, shiny head. It fell from the wall, shattering into nothing as another took its place. A too-close scream sent a blast of fear through me as I lined up an arrow and pulled the string taut. I quickly scanned for Nyktos. I saw him near the water's edge, surrounded—

Without warning, the sky and bay beyond the ledge blotted out. For a moment, I couldn't understand what'd happened. A stuttered heartbeat later, I saw a flash of jagged, white teeth the size of my finger and realized that the dakkais weren't exactly featureless. There were two thin slits where a nose would normally be. They flared wider as they sniffed at the air.

Sucking in a shallow breath, I released the string. The arrow pierced the dakkai's mouth, knocking it back. Another hoarse shout echoed around me as I twisted, chest throbbing with the ember of life. I grabbed an arrow, spinning around, fingers steady even though my heart thundered.

My hood slipped and I jerked, falling on my rear as a dakkai came over the wall, landing in the parapet. Tiny pieces of stone were jarred loose and pelted my face as it too sniffed at the air like a dog hunting a fox.

I would never think of a bloodhound the same again.

The creature swung out with a thickly muscled arm, crashing its fist into the bow. The weapon cracked in two. Panic sank its icy claws into my heart as I yanked up my skirt and unsheathed the dagger in my boot. Twisting, I thrust the dagger up, slamming the blade deep in the vicinity of the thing's chest with all my strength. The blade met resistance against its hard, shell-like skin, but the momentum of my swing brought the dagger home. Howling, it threw its head back as it shattered into a fine mist. Dampness hit my cheeks and arms, and the fine mist of whatever was left of the dakkai was soon swallowed by another creature launching itself over the wall, sniffing loudly. My heart stopped. Someone shouted as hot, stale breath blasted me in the face. An arrow pierced the dakkai's chest, knocking it back from the Rise's ledge.

Twisting onto my knees, I scrambled to my feet in time to see Rhain tossing the bow aside to pull his sword free. He thrust the blade through another dakkai that'd come over the Rise. I whirled at the sound of a grunt. Ector was pinned to the parapet wall, holding a creature back as it snapped at his throat. Grabbing the skirt of my gown, I leapt onto the short wall and shifted the dagger to my other hand so I held it by the blade. I cocked my arm back as I slid into the parapet behind Rhain and then threw the dagger. It struck the dakkai in the back, and a heartbeat later, my dagger fell to Ector's feet as the dakkai shattered.

Ector's head snapped up, his wide eyes landing on me. "Thank you."

Nodding, I snatched up the dagger and rose, turning to the ledge. The dakkais were still coming over the wall. Guards were strewn about, throats and stomachs torn into and blood pooling. The center of my chest warmed, the ember sensing the injuries, seeking out the deaths. Some of the fallen guards had to be gods. I swallowed thickly, forcing the ember back down.

Heart thumping, I turned as another dakkai climbed the wall. I shot forward, slamming the dagger home. The damp mist hit my arms as I peered over the wall. My chest lurched as dozens more swarmed the docks. I searched for Nyktos or the other gods that had been with him but was unable to find any of them in the swarm of slick, muscled bodies. There were only three of them against a horde of teeth and claws, and they could only use their blades?

"Fuck this," I muttered.

I backed away from the wall and then turned, scanning for the nearest stairs. Spotting them, I started toward the steep steps.

"Where are you going?" Ector demanded.

"Down there."

"You can't!" Rhain shouted.

"Try and stop me." I jerked back as a dakkai rushed out from the parapet. Cursing, I dipped low, slamming the dagger into the beast's side. I popped up as Rhain jumped over the parapet wall, stalking toward me. His expression made it clear that he would do exactly what I warned against. I spun around, determined to be faster than the god—

A low rumble echoed from the west, in the direction of the mist we'd rode through. My head jerked up as the sound turned into a thunderous growl that rattled the loose, broken stone.

"Fucking finally," muttered Ector.

Something dark and broad took shape in the distant wall of mist—*something* very large and winged. Tiny bumps broke out over my skin as another appeared in the mist and then another. Air thinned in my lungs as a bone-rattling snarl overtook the shouts and screams.

A massive gray and black draken broke free of the mist at a startling speed. *Nektas.* He flew over the wall, the tips of his wings grazing one of the towers as he let out a deafening roar. I whirled, tracking his flight while he swooped sharply, jaws cracking open. Silvery-white fire erupted from him in a crackling roar. A fiery stream slammed down on the beach and docks, burning through the creatures, obliterating them as Nektas glided out toward the bay. He flew up and turned, surging back as another silvery ball of flame lit up the dead waters—

"Get down!" Rhain grabbed my arm, pulling me to the top of the wall as something blotted out the stars above.

Stale, lilac-scented air swirled over us, pulling at the edges of my cloak. The entire Rise shook as a draken landed on the ledge of the parapet I'd been firing from. I lifted my head just as the onyx-hued draken stretched out its neck, breathing the silver fire down on the shadowstone wall, burning the climbing dakkais. Several feet down the wall, an identical draken made impact, shaking the wall once more. The twins? What were their names? Orphine and Ehthawn. A large ball of silvery flames erupted overhead, slamming down on the docks while a black-and-brown draken rocketed over the wall—

Rhain clasped the back of my head, forcing it down as the draken's horned tail swept over the Rise, sweeping dropped swords and bows off the edge. Another blast of silvery fire lit up the world.

"Good gods," I whispered.

"Yeah," Rhain drew out the word. "The draken aren't all that aware of their surroundings. Especially not Orphine."

Obviously.

Her brother Ehthawn kicked off the ledge, gliding down to the ground. Rhain's hand slipped away, and I took that as a sign that it was safe to rise. I stood and stumbled forward on shaky legs. Ector did the same a few parapets away. There were deep grooves in the stone of the ledge now where the draken's claws had dug in.

Silver fire lit the ground below as a draken fired on a cluster of dakkais. Nektas flew overhead, and I searched for anyone standing. I saw Theon first, near the charred docks. Then Saion and Rhahar farther up near the area of the bluffs. My thumping heart skipped. Where was—?

The rippling stream of fire faded, and I saw Nyktos then, stalking toward the wall, sword at his side. He had to hate me now, knowing what he did, but relief still crashed through me at the sight of him standing. Draken-stirred wind tossed strands of hair across his bluish-red spotted face. Blood. He'd bled tonight. He tipped his head back, looking up at the top of the Rise to where I stood. My breath caught, even though I knew he was only checking to make sure I was still alive.

Not because he cared.

Or because he still found me impressive.

But because of the ember of life.

Chest aching in a way I didn't want to look too deeply into, I took a step back when Orphine's head whipped toward the west and up, her lips peeling back in a low rumble of warning. I turned to the endless star-strewn sky. A cloud obscured the incandescent light, rapidly expanding, except there were no clouds in the Shadowlands.

"Off the Rise! Off the Rise!" someone shouted.

A horn blew again somewhere down the wall, and Orphine launched from the Rise, flying upward—

A ball of silvery fire erupted from above, narrowly missing the draken. I dropped to the floor of the Rise, rolling onto my back as the fire slammed into the tower, shaking the entire structure. Wind whipped over the Rise as Orphine crashed into a crimson-hued draken. I froze, shocked as she dug her back talons into its sides and went for the throat of the much larger beast.

"Fuck," growled Rhain, grasping my arm. He yanked me to my feet. "We've got to get off the Rise."

"Why are they fighting?" My boots slid over the stone as he pulled me out of the parapet. The two draken were a mass of snapping wings and teeth as they spun through the air.

"Draken are bonded to a Primal, Sera." His head jerked up as the crimson draken shrieked. "Not to all Primals."

I knew that, but I couldn't believe I was seeing two of them go at it. "But I thought they weren't allowed to attack other Primals."

"That doesn't mean they can't attack the Court." He shoved me in front of him. "And that also doesn't mean that all Primals follow the rule."

I had a sinking feeling I knew what Primal this draken belonged to. "Kolis?"

Rhain didn't answer as we raced across the Rise, soon joined by Ector. The two draken fought above us, their spiked tails whipping through the air. The crimson draken twisted sharply, shaking off Orphine and sending her flying into the section of the Rise we'd been standing on. Shadowstone cracked like thunder. The impact sent a bolt of fear through me, worry for the draken, but Orphine twisted, thrusting her claws into the stone before sliding off the other side of the Rise. I looked ahead to where the stairs appeared.

"Fast," Ector shouted. "Faster!"

A gust of wind swept over us from behind, tearing at my cloak and gown. My head jerked over my shoulder, and my heart stuttered. The crimson draken flew over the edge of the Rise, coming up right behind us. The frills around its head vibrated as its powerful jaws gaped open. Terror exploded deep inside me. In the center of the darkness, silver light sparked from the back of its throat—

Silvery flames slammed into the crimson draken, knocking it off course. I stumbled as Nektas swept over the Rise, his massive wings arcing above us. He fired on the enemy draken, his attack unrelenting as he drove the shrieking draken to the ground below. The draken fell hard, sending several guards on the steps against the wall of the staircase to keep from tumbling off.

Rhain slowed, his grip still firm on my arm as Nektas swooped down, landing on the ground beside the fallen draken. He circled the other as it tried to gain its footing, his tail sliding over the patchy gray grass. He snarled, pawing at the ground with sharp, thick talons. The guards on the steps stopped. So did Rhain and Ector, and I felt a warm pulse in my chest as movement on the ground below snagged my attention.

The Primal of Death stalked forward, the sword at his side slick and glistening in the starlight. Glimmering bluish-red blood ran down his cheeks and from where his black shirt was ripped on his chest, but his steps were long and sure as Nektas let out a deafening roar. Farther down the Rise, Ehthawn landed next to his sister, nudging her with a wing as she glared down at the crimson draken.

And then it happened.

The crimson draken shuddered and sparked—tiny bursts of silvery light erupting all over its trembling body as its head kicked back. The thick, spiked tail was the first to disappear, and then the body shrank rapidly, talons and limbs becoming legs and arms, scales receding to reveal patches of burnt, pinkish-red flesh across its chest and stomach. Spikes sank into shoulders, and frills smoothed out, replaced by a cap of curly brown hair.

A nude man lay there, his body a kaleidoscope of charred flesh and deep, seeping grooves. Bile crowded my throat. How he was still alive, I had no idea. He rolled onto his back, away from Nektas, turning his head toward the Primal.

The draken's shoulder shook as a rasping, wet sound rattled out of him. He was laughing as he lay there—*laughing* as Death approached him.

"Oh, Nyktos, my boy," the draken scraped out between rough laughs. "You have something…you shouldn't have, and you know better. You're going to be in so much trouble when he—"

"Shut the fuck up," Nyktos growled and brought his sword down.

In one clean, steady strike, Nyktos severed the draken's head.

Under Ector's and Rhain's watchful eyes, I waited at the foot of the thrones, sitting on the edge of the dais. Nyktos had ordered that they take me back to the palace, and I thought the decision had a lot to do with all the dying and dead around me. He didn't want me using the ember in front of so many, and with the pulse of the fight lessening, I didn't want to risk not being able to control it.

The two gods weren't quite sure what to do with me, spending the trip back to the palace arguing over whether they should place me in my bedchambers or one of the cells that apparently existed beneath the throne room. I had different plans as I tapped the flat side of the curved shadowstone blade on my knee.

I wanted to be here when Nyktos returned.

That was possibly a ridiculous decision since it would probably be best if I made myself scarce. But I would not hide from what he knew I had been prepared to do, and I would not hide from him.

And he'd been injured. I wanted to make sure he was okay. How he surely felt about me now that he knew the truth didn't matter. Concern haunted each minute. There hadn't been nearly enough time on the ground with him to tell how badly he'd been hurt.

So, I sat there with Ector and Rhain, both guards keeping more of an eye on the dagger I held than anything else. They could take me out with eather, but they knew Nyktos didn't want me dead. They also knew how fast I was with a blade now.

Only Aios had arrived since we returned to let the other gods know that Gemma had awakened briefly when Hamid arrived—the man who'd reported her missing at court—but had fallen back to sleep since. During her moments of consciousness, Aios hadn't gotten the impression that Gemma was aware of what I'd done, but none of us could be sure.

Aios hadn't spoken to me, and that hurt a little. I liked her, but Nyktos was her blood relative, and even if he weren't, I had a feeling she'd still see nothing but a betrayer when she looked at me.

Breathe in.

I held that breath until my lungs burned and then slowly exhaled. Did I regret what I was willing to do to save my people, even if it would've done nothing to help them? How could I? How could I not? But my messy state of emotions wasn't even nearly the most important thing I had to deal with. Besides the fact that I could be entirely wrong about Nyktos not killing me, there was this other Primal who had sent dakkais and a draken in response to feeling me use the ember of life. And if that Primal were Kolis? The King of Gods? He may not be able to bring life into creation, but he was still the oldest and most powerful Primal. If he wanted me dead, I would be dead.

But the question was, how many more people had to die between now and then? I closed my eyes and saw the Kazin siblings. I hadn't used the ember of life that night, but it had throbbed intensely after I'd killed Lord Claus. I wasn't sure about the night Andreia Joanis had been murdered, but more than mortals or godlings had been killed. There had been gods. And there would be more.

The strange whirring sensation in my chest alerted me to Nyktos' return. I still didn't understand that feeling or why it even existed, but I opened my eyes and slipped the dagger into my boot seconds before he entered the throne room. He'd wiped the blood from his face, but there were still cuts across his cheek and throat. They no longer bled that strange bluish-red, but the wounds hadn't sealed like the one had when I stabbed him.

He wasn't alone. Nektas walked beside him, shirtless as he'd been earlier in the day…or night? I had no idea how much time had passed. Saion was also with him, his steps slowing as Nyktos stalked forward.

As I slid off the dais and stood on surprisingly steady legs, all I saw was how coldly he'd brought that sword down on the draken. Those flat, frozen, silver eyes were now fixed on me.

"We didn't know what to do with her," Ector admitted, breaking the tense silence. "I suggested returning her to her bedchamber."

"I thought the cell would be a more fitting place," Rhain commented from the other side of the dais as Nektas halted in the center of the aisle. "However, she's been sitting here this whole time waving the dagger you got her around, and since you appear to want her alive, that's why we're here."

The corners of my lips turned down. I had not been *waving* the dagger around.

Nyktos stopped several feet from me. "Were you injured at all?" he clipped out.

I shook my head. "But you've been—" I sucked in a startled breath as Nyktos suddenly stood in front of me, having moved faster than I could track. Before I could even twitch, he hooked an arm under my right thigh and lifted my leg. Surprise shot through me, and I started to tip sideways. He curved his other arm around my waist, steadying me. I had no idea what he was doing, but I couldn't move or think as I stared into his flat eyes.

"Uh," Rhain murmured.

Without saying a word or breaking eye contact, he slid his hand down my thigh. A sharp swirl of tingles followed the glide of his palm and my breath caught. He smirked as his cool fingers drifted over my now-exposed knee. What was he—?

His gaze held mine as he reached down, curling those fingers around the hilt of my dagger. He slid it free. "Don't really want another dagger in my chest."

"Oh. Okay," Rhain said. "That makes sense now."

Nyktos let go, and I stumbled against the edge of the dais. Air punched out of my lungs as he moved away from me. "I wasn't planning to."

"Really?" He tucked the dagger into his waistband at his back. "Isn't that *exactly* what you were planning?"

I snapped my mouth shut because what could I really say to that? His smirk deepening, he stared down at me, and it took everything in me not to try and defend the indefensible. "Was it Kolis who sent the dakkais and the draken?"

"Yes," he answered.

My gaze dropped to the tear in his shirt. Was the wound still bleeding? That warm pulse in my chest nudged at me. "So, he knows I'm here."

"He knows *something* is here," he corrected. "He does not know the source, and that's how I plan to keep it."

There was a stupid skip in my chest. "Because you believe your father did something else besides putting the ember of life in my bloodline."

His lips thinned. "I know he must have had a reason that goes beyond keeping the ember of life alive. If that were the case, he wouldn't have put it in a mortal's body. And until I figure out why he did what he did, Kolis will not get his hands on you."

A deeper, fiery sting lanced across my chest as I squeezed my hands together. I forced my voice to steady. "And until then?"

"We will see."

Meaning, if he discovered that the ember of life was simply just that, he could very well decide to end me. Though, I didn't think he would. He wouldn't do that to the mortal realm if there were even a slight chance that Aios was right. "That's not what I meant."

He raised a brow. "It's not?"

"Will Kolis send others here to discover the source?" I asked.

"We'll most likely have a short reprieve," he told me.

The draken's taunting words resurfaced. "And you? What will he do to you for hiding the source of this power?"

His features sharpened. "That's none of your concern."

"Bullshit."

Nyktos' eyes flared wide as eather slid into his irises. "Come again?"

"You said it was none of my concern. I said that's *bullshit*," I repeated, and the Primal's head tilted to the side. Behind him, Nektas quietly moved forward. "How many people died tonight?"

The Primal didn't respond.

"How many?" I insisted.

"At least twenty," Saion answered from near the front of the chamber, his voice echoing. "We're still waiting to hear if any in Lethe passed."

I shuddered. Twenty. And that didn't include those who were injured.

"Don't pretend as if you care about the people here," Nyktos snarled, taking a step toward me.

Every muscle in me stiffened as anger unfurled. "I am not pretending. I don't want to see people die because of me."

His chin dipped. "Only me. Right?"

A bitter, acidic taste and burn pooled in my mouth and unfurled in my chest as my hands flexed.

Eather pulsed in Nyktos' eyes. "Is that shame I feel from you?" He laughed, the sound nothing like the ones I'd heard from him before. "Or are you that good of an actress? I think you are." His gaze swept over me, his lip curling. "And I also think you forgot to list acting alongside making bad choices as one of your many…*talents*."

I sucked in air that burned my throat. What he was referencing didn't pass me by. He was talking about him and me on the balcony. The stab of his words cut deep enough that I forgot I wasn't alone.

"And now you feign hurt?" Nyktos shook his head as that lip curled again. The disgust there…it bore down on me. "That is beneath even you."

My jaw unhinged. "Stop reading my fucking emotions!" I shouted, and Saion peeled away from the wall, his eyes growing wide. "Especially if you aren't even going to believe what you're reading, you jackass!"

Nyktos stilled. Everything about him *ceased*.

And that probably should've been warning enough that I may have *finally* pushed too hard. But I was beyond…I was simply beyond *everything*. "Do you really think I wanted to do this to you? To anyone? It was the only way we believed we could save our people. It was all I'd been taught. For my entire life. It's all I've ever known." My voice cracked, and I drew in another sharp, too-tight breath. "I would say I'm sorry, but you wouldn't believe me. I don't blame you for that, but don't you dare insinuate that what I've done with you was purely an act or that what I'm feeling is fake when I've spent my entire godsdamn life not being allowed to want or even feel anything for myself! Not when I spent the last three years *hating* myself for the relief I felt when you didn't take me because it meant I didn't have to do what was expected of me."

Nyktos stared at me.

Silence drenched the room, and I realized that I was shaking. My entire body. I'd never spoken those words out loud. Never. My heart thundered as a knot expanded and grew in my throat, threatening to choke me. "I know what I am. I've always known. I am one of the worse sort. A monster," I whispered, my voice hoarse. "But don't you *ever* tell me how I feel."

Nyktos didn't even blink.

The draken drifted closer to Nyktos, his red-eyed stare shifting from me to the Primal. Nektas leaned in, speaking too low for me to hear. Attention remaining fixed on me, Nyktos' chest rose with a swift, deep breath.

A long moment passed, and then he finally looked away from me to focus on Nektas. "You should be on the wall just in case I was wrong about the reprieve."

Nektas shook his head. "Others are there. They are standing guard."

"I'd rather have you there."

"I'd rather not leave your side," the draken countered. "Not now."

"I'm fine," the Primal stated, his voice low. "I told you that three times now."

"Five times, actually." Nektas held his ground. "And I don't have to tell you that I know better."

All thoughts of what I'd just screamed at the Primal fell to the wayside. My attention shifted to the tears in his tunic. The splotches of darker material along his chest *had* spread.

Ector hopped off the dais. "How much of that blood is yours?"

"Most of it," Nyktos answered, and the draken gave a low growl of disapproval.

"Shit," Rhain muttered, joining Ector on the floor. "Are your wounds not healing?"

"Do you want to die tonight?" Nyktos fired back.

Saion widened his eyes as he stared at the floor, saying nothing more.

"I could try," I started, and Nyktos' head swung in my direction. "My gift—the ember. It worked on the wounded hawk."

"Besides the fact that the ember of life isn't powerful enough to work on me or a god," he said, "I'm not sure I'd trust you enough to let you try even that."

I flinched. I flinched *again*.

Nyktos' nostrils flared as he inhaled sharply, looking away. "I just need to clean up, which I plan to do now if that would make all of you feel better," Nyktos said.

"That is not what would make me feel better," Nektas replied.

"Too bad." Nyktos glared at the draken. He started to turn and then looked back at me, his jaw hard. He refocused on Nektas. "Put her somewhere safe, where she can't do whatever idiotic thing is surely filling her head. She assigns no value to her life."

I opened my mouth, but Nektas cut me off. "That I can do."

"Perfect," the Primal snarled and turned, his boots a heavy thud against the shadowstone floor as he stormed out of the throne room.

As soon as I could no longer see him, I turned to Nektas. "How badly is he injured?"

"You don't have to pretend in front of us," Ector retorted.

Spinning toward him, I lifted a finger and pointed it at him. "What in the fuck did I just say about not telling me what to feel? That goes for you, too," I said, and Ector's brows flew up. I turned back around. "That goes for all of you."

Everyone, including the draken, stared at me.

Saion cleared his throat. "He was swarmed on the docks and the beach. The dakkais got in a lot of hits."

Rhain exchanged a concerned look with Ector. "How bad?"

"Bad enough that he needs to feed," Nektas answered. "And stubborn enough to ride it out."

"Hell." Ector ran a hand over his face.

My stomach pitched as I remembered what Nyktos had told me over our first breakfast. "What happens if he doesn't feed and rides it out? Will he turn into…something dangerous? He mentioned something along those lines before."

Nektas tilted his chin. "He's weak enough that he could tip over into that."

Rhain cursed again.

"But even if he doesn't, he's still weakened," Nektas continued.

"And that's the last thing we need right now."

I shoved a tangle of hair back from my face. "Why won't he feed?"

Nektas's gaze met mine. "Because he's been forced to feed until he's killed. That's why."

My lips parted. I took a step back as if I could somehow put distance between what Nektas had said and me. But I thought about the breakfast that morning, how I'd thought that he had been held against his will. I closed my eyes. "Did Kolis hold him prisoner?"

A long stretch of silence passed before Nektas said, "Kolis has done all manner of things to him."

The heaviness in my chest felt like it would drag me down to the floor. "How…how do we get him to feed?"

"We don't," Rhain said. "We just hope he rides it out."

"Actually, I think we can get him to feed now," Nektas shared, and I opened my eyes to find him watching me. "He's mad enough at you that he'd probably feed from you."

I blinked once and then twice. "I'm…I'm not sure how I feel about the ease in which you suggested that."

The draken raised his brows. "But?"

But Nyktos was weak, and it was the last thing they needed. He needed to feed, and if I had been ready to possibly be burned alive by a draken after killing Nyktos, I could prepare myself for this.

"Okay." I sighed.

Those unnerving red eyes latched onto mine. "Is it truly your choice? You can say no. No one here will make you do it, nor would we hold it against you."

I had no idea if anyone would hold it against me—they had far bigger things to use in that way. I could say no, but if Nyktos had never discovered the truth, I would've offered myself. And, deep down, I knew it had nothing to do with the deal. It would've been because I didn't want him to hurt.

"It's my choice," I said, looking up at Nektas. "I'll try. I'm sure I'll say something that will anger him."

Nektas smiled.

"Are you sure about this?" Rhain asked. "She came here to kill him."

"*He* brought her here," Nektas corrected swiftly, surprising me. Though, I wasn't sure what that changed. "Do you have a better idea?"

Rhain glanced at me. "No." A pause. "What if he kills her?"

"Well," Ector drawled as he walked past me. "Then I guess we don't have to worry about her trying to kill him."

"I'm not going to try to kill him," I snapped.

"*Now*," Ector tacked on.

"Come." Nektas motioned for me to follow him, and I got moving, shooting Ector a narrow-eyed glare.

Saion gave me a thumbs-up as we walked past him. "Thoughts and many prayers."

I didn't even dignify that with a response. I followed Nektas to the back stairwell, my heart surprisingly calm. We started up the stairs when I asked, "Is Orphine okay?"

"She will be," he said, and that was all we said until we neared the floor.

"I'm kind of surprised you suggested this," I admitted. "What if he's mad at you?"

"He told me to put you somewhere safe." Nektas opened the door and held it for me. "That is what I'm doing."

My brows pinched as I walked through. Nektas stopped in front of the door to my bedchamber. "He won't answer if you knock, but I am sure the door between your chambers is unlocked."

I stared at my door. "You really think this will work? Maybe he's too mad to do it."

"Let me ask you a question." Nektas waited until my gaze met his. "Would you have followed through if you never learned that killing him would not have saved your people?"

I opened my mouth. The word *yes* slithered up my throat, but it didn't go any further than that. It wouldn't go past my tongue because I didn't know if I would have. I couldn't say yes.

"That's why," Nektas said, pushing open the door. "I think he knows that, too."

I wasn't so sure about that, nor could I dwell on the realization of what I'd admitted and what it meant. I walked into my room, my gaze immediately landing on the door to his bedchamber. I didn't waste time just in case some small inkling of common sense invaded me. I only stopped long enough to toe off my boots and stockings. A fine mist of dakkai blood coated them, and I didn't want to track it through the chambers. I went to the door between our rooms and turned the knob.

Nektas was right. It was unlocked.

A faint shiver curled down my spine as the door cracked open, revealing a short, narrow passageway and an empty, dimly lit bedchamber beyond. My heart was still calm as I closed the door behind me and I crept forward, the stone floors cold under my feet. I entered the bedchamber that smelled of citrus, and as I suspected, it was empty except for the necessities. A large bed and some bedside tables. A wardrobe and a few chests. A table with one chair. A long settee. That was all.

The steadiness in my chest faltered as my gaze shifted to the halfway-open door on the other side of the bedchamber. I caught a glimpse of a porcelain tub. I moved deeper into the cavern-like space, my throat drying as I saw Nyktos in the bathing chamber.

He stood in front of the vanity, wearing only unbuttoned breeches that hung low on his hips, grasping the rim of the sink with white-knuckled fingers. He dragged a damp towel across his bloodied chest, his teeth bared as he hissed in a pained breath. The wounds would've been fatal for a mortal, significant and shocking. And the fact that he seemed unaware of my presence told me exactly how weakened he was. For a moment, I could only stare at the shimmering blood coursing down the defined lines of his stomach. How was he still standing?

"Nyktos," I whispered.

He froze at the sink, head bowed. The blood-soaked towel stopped moving across his chest. Slowly, he lifted his head and looked over at me. Knots formed in my stomach. There was a paleness there that hadn't been before, settling into his skin. The glow behind his pupils was fainter than I'd ever seen it.

"I clearly recall telling Nektas to put you somewhere safe where you couldn't get yourself into trouble," he said.

"Yeah, well, he thinks he listened to you."

"He did not."

I swallowed as his unblinking stare latched onto me. His eyes…gods, they were so *flat*. "You need to feed."

"And you, the utter last person I want to see right now, need to leave," Nyktos spat.

My spine went rigid. "You need to feed," I repeated. "That's why I'm here."

His head moved to the side, the movement odd and animalistic. Predatory. "Did you not hear me?"

"I did." I inched closer, stopping when his lips peeled back, revealing his fangs. My heart tripped a little. "But I wouldn't be here if you fed like…like other Primals."

The towel slipped from his hand, drifting to the floor. He didn't seem to notice. "And how would you know what other Primals do?"

"I…I don't, but I imagine they'd make sure they weren't weakened," I said. "And are able to protect their people."

His hand lifted from the sink, finger by finger as he straightened and turned toward me. Nothing about the way he moved was normal. It was too smooth. Too focused. "You truly have no fear of death, do you?"

"I…I always knew I would meet an early death one way or another," I admitted.

"How?" His voice…it was more shadow than anything now, thick and icy. "How did you know you would die?"

"I figured it would either be by your hand or one of your guards if I…"

"If you actually succeeded in weakening me? If I fell in love with you?" He *glided* to the opening of the bathing chamber. Goosebumps broke out over my skin. "If you managed to kill me?"

I nodded.

His head straightened, moving in that eerie, fluid way. He stared at me for a long, tense moment. The hollows of his cheeks became more prominent. "You need to leave."

"I'm not going to."

"Leave!" he roared, and I flinched at the guttural sound as a tiny kernel of fear took root. A tremor ran through him. "If you don't leave, I'm going to feed from you, and I'm going to fuck you while I do it," he warned.

A disturbing rush of silky heat appeared upon hearing his words. Something I would need to evaluate deeply. "Is that a promise?" I raised a brow. "Or just more talk?"

Nyktos made a sound, a low growl I never would've expected to come out of his throat. The tiny hairs on the back of my neck rose as instinct urged me to back away. "*Reckless*," he hissed.

"I think you know that *is* one of my talents."

Eather pulsed in his eyes, bright and brief. "I may kill you. Do you understand that? I haven't fed in…decades. I don't trust myself right now. Do you understand, *liessa*?"

Something beautiful and powerful.

Queen.

I lifted my chin, letting the hair slide behind my shoulders. His now-lifeless eyes tracked those strands as I revealed my neck. "You're not going to kill me."

"Foolish," he purred, his lips parting as his torn chest rose and fell rapidly.

"Maybe, but I'm still standing here."

"So be it."

I took a breath. That was all. One single, short breath, and Nyktos was on me, his hand buried in my hair, tugging my head back. He struck as fast as the vipers near the Cliffs of Sorrow, sinking his fangs deep into the side of my throat.

Chapter 38

The sudden dual bursts of stinging pain caused my entire body to jerk. The fire of his bite shot through me, startling in its intensity. Nyktos' grip on my hair and shoulder was tight as he pressed into me, my back coming against a wall. I gripped his arms, my nails digging into his cool skin.

There was nowhere to go—no escape. A scream built in my throat, but there was no air to give it life. I couldn't breathe through the fire clawing at my insides. My back bowed when he drew deep and hard against my throat, drawing my blood into him in staggering pulls.

And then it…*changed.*

Seconds, only seconds had passed from the moment his fangs pierced my flesh and the vise-like grip on my shoulder eased. The fire of his mouth against my throat didn't fade as his fingers now curled around the back of my head, but it became something else—something as overwhelming and powerful as the pain. The burn of his lips moving greedily against my throat built into a sudden, throbbing ache in my blood, settling in my breasts and between my thighs. The strength of it—the pounding, heated rush was shocking. It invaded my muscles, tightening them until they curled and spun.

Nyktos groaned, pushing into me, his fingers spreading across the edges of the bodice and curling around the center tie. He shifted, thrusting a strong thigh between mine. I felt him then, long and thick against my lower stomach.

I'm going to feed from you, and I'm going to fuck you while I do it.

I shuddered as a rush of damp heat flooded me. My eyes were open, but I saw nothing as his mouth tugged on my throat. My blood was on fire, my head falling back against the wall, cushioned by his hand. I moaned, and he sucked harder. I felt the pulls of his mouth all the way to my core. My body reacted out of instinct. Instead of trying to get away from him, I slid my hand up to the soft strands of his hair and tugged him closer, holding his eager mouth to my throat, wanting to be…devoured by the intensity brewing in my body. Wanting to be devoured by *him*. I moved without thought, rocking against the hard length of his thigh. The tension deep inside me erupted without warning, the pleasure lashing out in sweeping waves. I trembled and shook as I rode the powerful release.

I panted, gasping for breath and shuddering. As soon as the ripples abated, the pulsing tension built once more at my throat and under his lips as he continued feeding. It traveled through my body in a series of sharp tingles. My heart raced as the acute tension built again at my core.

He made another sound against my throat, a deep, rumbling growl that should've concerned me, but I was far past the point of being cautious. I pulled on his hair. His fingers dug into the thin material of my bodice. I jerked, gasping when he pulled hard on the front of the gown. The sound of tearing cloth scorched my ears, sending another bolt of arousal through me. He tore the gown from the bodice to the waist, freeing my breasts and my upper stomach. The sleeves of the ruined gown slid down my arms. A ragged cry parted my lips as the tips of my breasts brushed against the coldness of his blood-slickened chest. Letting go of his hair, I shrugged off the sleeves of the gown. The material pooled at my hips.

I wanted to feel more. I wanted to feel him. I *wanted.*

Nyktos lifted his head away from my throat, and suddenly I was staring up into swirling quicksilver eyes. They were so bright and so full of life. Neither of us spoke as my attention dropped to his parted, ruby-red lips. My gaze moved lower to his blood-streaked chest and flesh that had already begun to heal and seal itself closed. And lower still, to those once-jagged wounds that were now pink welts across his tightly coiled stomach muscles.

What my blood did for him was nothing short of miraculous. Maybe even more so than the ember of life. Or at least it felt so in that moment.

I looked even lower and felt a little weak. But I didn't think it had anything to do with him feeding. The throbbing length of his cock was visible through the flaps of his breeches and the head jutted up toward his navel. The tip beaded pearly liquid as it twitched.

Nyktos looked at me, his swirling gaze so intense that it was like a physical caress against my breasts and belly. I looked down at the shimmering bluish-red blood smeared above my navel and across my breasts and nipples.

His hand slid from my hair, dragging the curls forward over my shoulder. Strands fell across a breast as his fingers curved around the heavy weight. A breathy moan left me, and those eyes flew to mine.

It took me a moment to remember how to speak. "Did you take enough?"

"It will have to be enough," he answered, his voice thick with smoke and need and…hunger. He drew a thumb over the hardened nub of flesh and then stepped back from me. I felt the loss of his heat immediately as he stared at my partially exposed body, the hollows of his cheeks unforgivable. "Has to be."

I glanced at the wounds on his chest. The one I had inflicted on him the night we'd found Andreia had healed immediately.

He hadn't taken enough.

But I'd be lying if I said that was the only reason that propelled me forward. That it had nothing to do with all that *desire* for him—desire that had nothing to do with a duty that no longer mattered.

I wanted this. I wanted him. Me. For no other reason than for myself.

And he wanted this, too, even if he hated me.

Heart thumping, I reached down and slid the gown over my hips, taking with it the flimsy undergarment. I stepped out of the pile of clothing and stood before him completely nude.

He shuddered. "Sera…"

Throat dry, I placed my hand between my breasts, sliding my fingers down my stomach, drawing his stare to where they came to a stop just below my navel. His lips parted, his fangs appearing once more. The sight of them caused a throbbing ache in my throat, a reminder of the pleasure-pain of his bite. "You haven't taken enough."

Nyktos said nothing as his chest rose and fell rapidly.

"You promised." My pulse thrummed as I slipped my fingers between my thighs and against the damp heat. I sucked in the same breath he inhaled sharply, my cheeks warming. "You promised to feed from and fuck me."

He went completely still as I touched myself, dragging a finger through the wetness, remembering exactly what his fingers felt like inside me. I pushed my finger inside—

Nyktos moved so fast, he was like a streak of lightning in the midst of a violent storm. He was on me, catching my hand and drawing it away from me. His mouth closed over my finger, wringing a breathy moan from me as he sucked on it. His eyes flew to mine, and he let go, the hunger in his stare sending a wave of tiny bumps all over my skin.

"I did," he said, need thickening his voice. "I did warn you exactly what would happen."

"You did."

One side of his lips curled, and then he struck once more. This time, his fangs sank into the flesh of my breast, just above the rosy skin of the areola. The shock of pain was just as intense as before, just as stunning in its completeness. I couldn't think past it as his arm came around my waist and he lifted me, his mouth closing over the skin, the nipple. He sucked and drank *hard*, sending a shockwave of temporary pain and then brutal, shattering pleasure through me. He caught my head before it fell back, holding me against his body. I felt the head of his cock against my throbbing center as he turned.

I was barely aware of my back pressed onto something soft and warm. I clasped the back of Nyktos' head, holding him there. All I could focus on was the cool weight of him coming over me, the feel of his hungry mouth on my breast and how he shifted, shoving his breeches down while he fed, as the chamber spun and whirled, and my body *sparked* and ignited.

Drawing on the skin and taking more of my blood into him, he reached up, dragging his thumb across my lower lip. I turned my head, capturing his thumb with my mouth. I sucked as deep and hard as he did at my breast.

The rumbling groan he let loose sent another burst of pleasure through me. There was a strange taste on his thumb, something that reminded me of honey but thicker, smokier. Only distantly did I realize it must be his blood. I reluctantly released his flesh. He traced the line of my jaw and throat and then slid his palm over my other breast to the flare of my hip, eliciting a shiver from me when he settled between my thighs. I dug my fingers into his hair and skin at the feel of him, hard and cool pressing against my heat. He reached between our bodies, guiding himself. My breath halted and then sped up as I felt him pushing in. The stretch was a sublime sting of pain. I gasped, my hips tilting. He halted for a moment and then thrust in fully. My head kicked back as I cried out, shuddering.

The deep draws on my breast slowed as he remained buried deep inside me. His mouth eased, and then he ended the intoxicating pull and drag sensation I felt in every part of my body. The wet, cool slide of his tongue over my tingling nipple drew another raspy sound from me. He lifted his head, and my eyes opened. Our gazes met and held for what felt like a small eternity, and then he looked down at where our hips met.

"Beautiful," he whispered, and my chest—my heart—immediately swelled. A drop of blood from his lip—a drop of *my* blood—splashed off my other breast. Dipping his head, he dragged his tongue over the swell of flesh, catching the bead of blood. And then he kept going, closing his mouth over the puckered flesh there. I moaned, hips jerking.

Nyktos' groan was ragged, and he looked down again, the hand on my hip tightening. He shifted his body and watched himself withdraw, inch by inch, and then press back into me to the hilt. My moan of pleasure was lost in his as my back arched. My eyes closed again. For a moment, my senses were overwhelmed. Nyktos was a tremendous presence in my body, stretching me until nothing but the feeling of decadent fullness remained, curling my toes.

"Oh, gods," I whispered. Slipping my hands to the cool skin of his shoulders and biceps, I felt the fine tremor work its way through him when he slid a hand under my head. Opening my eyes, I sucked in air.

He was so incredibly still, his features sharper, taut. Bright flecks of eather churned in his silver eyes. Under his skin, shadows swirled. "Nyktos?"

A shudder rolled through him and the dark, hazy outline of shadow wings formed over his shoulders. Thick cords of muscle stood out along his neck as he stretched his head to the side and fought his true being. Who he was under the skin. I touched his cheek, and those wisps of eather slowed.

Another shudder rocked him. "I…I've never felt anything like this."

A knot formed in my throat. This was his first time experiencing this, and I didn't know what to do with that knowledge. It stung my eyes, partly because this felt like a first for me, too, and I didn't understand why. Still, I wanted him to know that.

"Me, neither," I whispered, and his eyes lifted to mine.

He stared at me. His features were too heavy with need for me to read anything else from them. "Don't lie to me now, even if you do so in such a pretty way."

"I'm not lying," I swore. I wanted him to believe me. It was the truth. "I've never felt this either. Never."

A muscle ticked along his jaw. "I don't have very much control right now," he stated thickly. "I don't want to hurt you."

"You won't."

A pulse ran through him, every part of him, and I felt it deep inside me. "You don't know that. I don't."

"You didn't when you fed," I reasoned, smoothing my thumb across his jaw. "You won't now."

"Your faith in me…" His hand curled into my hair. "Is admirable but reckless."

"Your fear is misplaced," I returned, drawing my legs up to his hips. Both of us lost our breath. Pressing my knees against his sides, I rolled him onto his back, an act that was only successful because I caught him off guard—an act that punched the air from my lungs at the exact moment it sent pleasure thundering through me as the change in position intensified the feel of him, somehow bringing him even deeper. I planted my palms on his chest, steadying myself. "But I am *reckless*."

Nyktos' answering growl spun its way around me. "Good gods…" He stared up at me as my hair slid forward, brushing his chest. The wounds were gone there, and almost completely invisible on his lower stomach.

Relief spun through me as I looked up at him. His eyes were a kaleidoscope of silver and white. His features had lost some of their sharpness, but I could still see the shadows under his skin, causing a beautiful marbling effect. I moved tentatively, rocking forward. "Is this…is this how you plan to kill me?"

"No." I lifted until just the tip of him pressed in and then slid back down until there wasn't an inch between us.

"You sure?" he asked. "Because I think you are." One of his hands went to my waist. The other gathered up one side of my hair, holding it back as I rolled my hips. His heavy-hooded gaze held mine and then shifted to the mass of curls he held, before moving to my breasts and finally to where we were joined. "And I think I'm going to enjoy this manner of death."

Heart thumping, I let my head fall back as I reached up, curling my fingers around his wrist. I drew his hand to my mouth, where I pressed a kissed to the center of his palm and then slid his hand down, over my breast. I shuddered as I rocked in a slow, torturous tempo, still dragging his questing, exploring fingers down over my belly, to where we were joined. I pressed his fingers against the tight, sensitized bundle of nerves there, crying out as a sharp curl echoed from deep inside me.

"Fuck," he groaned, his hips rearing off the bed, lifting both of us. "You feel too good, *liessa*."

Liessa.

My head snapped forward, and my eyes opened. His words, the friction of each withdrawal and subsequent return, his teasing fingers built a storm of sensations that quickly turned into a swirling knot of deep tension. I was close, my fingers spasming around his, and my nails digging into his shoulder as Nyktos followed my lead, his hips rising to meet mine. Soon, there was no real sense of rhythm as we moved against each other. It was pure instinct, driven by a shared need, one that pushed us closer and closer to an edge that I toppled over. I called out his name as the tension broke, and waves of release rippled through me. I slid forward, both hands on his chest as he thrusted faster, angled deeper. Shocks of pleasure cascaded through me when he wrapped his arms around me, pulling my chest to his. Holding me tight, he rolled me under him, his hips thrusting deeply, just once. He came, his head buried in my shoulder as he shuddered through his release.

I held him through it, running my fingers up and down his back even as sharp, swift aftershocks still rocked my body. He remained there for an indefinable amount of time, his weight braced on an arm but still heavy. It was time that I cherished—soaked in. The closeness, how we were still joined. The nothingness between us, and his scent and mine. The way I was Sera in these moments, and he was Ash to me. That was what I devoured. Greedily. Us. Because like at the lake, I knew it wouldn't last.

And it didn't.

Nyktos slowly lifted his head. My hands stilled on the length of powerful, corded muscles lining his back. He stared down at me. Was he counting my freckles again? Seeing if they'd mysteriously changed? Or would he kiss me? I wanted him to kiss me.

His lashes swept down, shielding his eyes, and then he rolled off me onto his back, lying beside me on the bed.

I didn't move. Not for several minutes. I couldn't. It took everything in me to push the knot back down my throat, to hastily stitch up the cracks racing across my chest. Had I honestly thought he'd kiss me? After what he'd learned? He wanted me—my blood and my body. He needed that as badly as I needed to know what it felt like to have him inside me. That didn't include kissing. Kissing felt far more…intimate and forbidden now.

Swallowing through the burn, I looked over at him. He was on his back, one arm tossed above his head, and the other resting in the space between us. He wasn't staring at the ceiling. He was looking at me.

"How?" Nyktos demanded. "How can you be so convincing?"

I tensed, thinking at first that he was talking about what we'd just shared. But then I realized that he wasn't looking at me. He was watching, prying into me. Reading. "You're reading my emotions."

"All things considered, that act doesn't even register against what you planned," he replied. "Does it?"

"That doesn't make it any less rude," I retorted.

"I suppose not, but you didn't answer my question. How are you so convincing?" Nyktos asked. "Were you also taught that?"

A wave of prickly heat washed over me. "I was not taught how to force emotion."

One eyebrow rose. "But weren't you? Tell me, Sera. Would that not be a part of the seduction? Of leading me to love you? To make me believe you feel something for me?"

Guilt crowded some of the anger, but not all. "First off, we didn't know you could read emotions. If we had, then I probably would've been schooled on how to feel something so deeply that even I began to believe it was real."

His eyes flared a bright silver.

"Secondly, why would I fake anything I'm feeling now? There'd be no point. It wouldn't save my people, even if I succeeded," I pointed out. "And, finally, need I remind you not to tell me what I'm feeling?"

Nyktos' jaw hardened, and a long moment passed before he turned his head away.

I stared at the harsh lines of his face, fighting the urge to yell. To just scream until my throat went raw. Somehow, I managed not to. "Did you take enough blood? Honest?"

A heartbeat passed. "More than enough."

"Good." Tangled hair fell over my shoulders as I sat up.

He went on alert in an instant as I looked around for something to put on. The clothing was ruined, but at least all I had to do was walk through a door. I started to scoot toward the edge of the bed—

"Where do you think you're going?"

Stopping, I looked over my shoulder. "To my bedchamber?"

His eyes narrowed. "Why?"

"Why…wouldn't I?" My heart tumbled. "Or am I supposed to be sent somewhere else? To those cells you referenced?" I stiffened. "If so, can I at least find some clothing you didn't ruin?"

A strange thing happened then. He seemed to relax. And a faint grin appeared, softening the angles of his features. "Yeah, I did ruin that gown."

I stared at him, caught between disbelief and a mess of a hundred other emotions. "I'm not sure why you're smiling about that."

"It will be a favorite memory for years to come."

My eyes narrowed on him. "Well, I'm glad to hear that, but it's not like I have a lot of clothes for someone to be tearing them off me."

His molten silver eyes shifted to me. "You weren't complaining when I did it," he purred. "If I recall correctly, you were quite eager to get rid of that gown yourself."

I was, but that was beside the point. Was he teasing me? Or was he…? My pulse kicked up. He couldn't be. I dared a quick peek below his waist, and a shock went through me. He was more than just semi-hard and that was…well, that was *impressive.* Was that a Primal thing? Muscles deep inside me clenched as I lifted my gaze back to his.

His eyes met mine and then lowered. "You are sitting next to me, gloriously naked, and I am *intentionally* staring."

"I can see that," I remarked acidly, annoyed by him… and myself, because I did nothing to shield myself from his stare. I did nothing to stop the fact that I enjoyed that he was staring.

One side of his mouth tipped up again as he drew his teeth—his fangs—over his lips. "My mark on your *unmentionables* is quite fascinating to me."

I looked down and sucked in an unsteady breath at the sight of the purplish-pink patch of skin and the two puncture wounds. A bolt of sharp-edged arousal darted through me as I remembered the push of his cock and pull of his mouth. "Pervert," I tossed out half-heartedly.

"Can't even argue with that." He turned his head away. "I'm not putting you in a cell."

"You're not?"

"Why would I?" he countered, closing his eyes. "You should rest. So should I. We need to be prepared for whatever comes next."

Kolis.

I swallowed again, somehow forgetting about that the moment I decided to feed Nyktos.

"Rest means sleeping, Sera, which usually requires that you lay down, unless you're able to sleep sitting up. I would find that impressive if so," he said. "But it would also be distracting."

I opened my mouth and found myself at a loss for words. "You want me to sleep beside you?"

"I want you to rest. If you're beside me, I don't have to worry about what you may or may not do."

I wasn't exactly sure what he was worried about me doing if I wasn't here, but being beside him when he was in such a vulnerable state as sleep seemed like the last thing he'd want since he obviously believed that the guilt I felt wasn't real. That my unwillingness to carry through with my duty was just *pretty* lies. "Are you not concerned?"

"About?"

Shaking my head, I looked away from him. "Oh, I don't know. Me attacking you?"

Nyktos chuckled deeply.

My brows flew up. "I'm not sure why you find that suggestion funny."

"Because it is."

I didn't move.

"Go to sleep, *liessa*."

That word again—one I knew could no longer mean something beautiful and powerful to him. It couldn't mean Queen. I would never be his Consort now. A word that was now a mockery. Or worse yet, never meant anything to him.

An unexpected, dark pain flared in my chest at that realization—at how much it bothered me.

Anger exploded as quickly as the hurt did. "You know what?"

He sighed. "What?"

"You can go fuck yourself." I knew it was a childish thing to say, but whatever. I rose from the indecently large bed, making it to my knees—

Nyktos wasn't nearly as at ease as I believed. He moved shockingly fast, one arm clamping down on my waist as his other hand curled around my chin from behind, tilting my head back. My heart stuttered at the feel of him against my backside, rigid and throbbing, his breath coasting over my ear. My heart skipped another beat because I knew how easy it would be for him to unleash his anger on me, and yet I felt no fear, only warmth.

His body felt *warm.*

My eyes widened as I relaxed into his hold. The chest against my shoulders, the hard stomach against my back, and the thick length of him—it was all *warm.*

"Do you want to know why I find your suggestion funny?" Nyktos asked before I could speak. The arm around my waist shifted, and I felt his fingers on my lower stomach—his *warm* fingers. "Do you?" he demanded in my silence, his thumb sweeping along my lower lip, and his other fingers inching down to the wide vee of my legs.

"No." I wet my lips, snagged between the need to point out how he felt and an entirely different, truly inappropriately timed need. "But I'm sure you're going to tell me. You do like to talk."

His answering chuckle was deep and smoky, rumbling through me as his fingers wandered even lower, skimming the tight bundle of nerves. My hips twitched, and he let out another laugh, this time softer. "You do like my fingers inside you, don't you?"

The tips of my breasts tightened when he dragged a finger over the sensitive part. This time, my hips jerked. He made a deep, rough sound, his finger sliding through the fresh wave of gathering dampness.

"I think there's something else you like more than my fingers," he said softly, parting the swollen flesh. "Isn't that right?"

I rocked back against him out of reflex, my toes curling as he worked his finger inside me, and the hardness pressed against my ass. "So?" I challenged. His hips moved behind me, against me. "And you know what I think? You forgot what you were going to say."

"Oh, trust me, *liessa,* I didn't forget." His breath coasted over the side of my neck and the bite mark there. Another bolt of awareness went through me.. He continued rocking against me as his finger moved idly in and out of me—as I followed those movements, and with each pass, his cock made its way lower until I felt it bumping against his hand and me. "I was just letting you forget."

I stilled.

Nyktos shifted then, pressing me down onto my hands and then my forearms and belly. My pulse pounded as his weight came over my back. With one hand still under my chin and the other hand still between my thighs, it forced my head back and my hips arched. His finger still moved as his thumb swirled around the apex, dragging ragged moans from me.

"It's funny because you cannot hurt me." That strangely warm breath of his still hovered over the mark on my throat. "You can never weaken me to the point that you'd ever be a real threat."

My breath caught as the meaning of his words penetrated the haze of arousal. I knew what he was saying. I was no real threat because he would never love me.

And maybe it was the reckless part of me that spurred my words. Maybe it was that hurt in the center of my chest. I turned my head toward him. "You sure about that?"

The sound he made was a cross between a laugh and a growl. Then his head snapped down. I stiffened as I felt the sharp tips of his fangs on my throat, just above the marks already there. He didn't pierce my skin, though. He just held me there as the—*oh, gods*—as the heated, hard length of him replaced his finger, pushing in and spreading me once more. The feel of him stole my breath. The utter, absolute dominance in how he held me there with his fangs. The unending press of him filled me with a wicked, wanton flood of heat.

There were no slow, tentative movements now. He fucked me as he pressed his fingers against me, working the bundle of nerves. Each powerful push caused his fangs to scrape my neck, but he didn't break the skin. Not once. And, gods, I wanted him to, but there was no way for me to seize control as I had the first time. He was in total control this time, and the fighter in me, the shameless part, knew that and submitted.

And it was *glorious.*

Gods, he…he was a fast learner.

Nyktos' thrusts were deep and hard, leaving no room for anything but the feel of him. His hips pumped against my backside as he kept me in that position, head tipped back, throat vulnerable, hips arched. And when I felt his thumb pressing against my lips, I opened my mouth and let him in.

And then I bit him hard.

"Fuck," he grunted against my throat.

A throaty laugh left me as I closed my lips around his thumb, sucking on the flesh I'd bitten. Only a heartbeat later, I realized that I'd drawn blood. My shock over my actions was quickly swept aside by the swirl of tingles across my tongue, and the taste of honey but smokier. It was his *blood.* Not much, maybe a drop. I swallowed, shuddering at the decadent taste. I should be disturbed by the fact that I'd tasted his blood, but I moaned around his thumb, rocking my hips against him.

His hand came down on my ass in a light smack that sent another sinful burst of pleasure through me. "Very naughty," he murmured.

Then he took me. He claimed me in a way I hadn't known I wanted to be claimed. His body pounded into mine, frenzied and raw. Release hit me, sending wave after wave of pulsing and spiraling pleasure through me. I cried out as my head kicked back against his shoulder. His hand finally shifted then, thrusting the mess of curls out of my face as I shook and spasmed. He followed me over the edge with a hoarse shout, his incredibly large body shuddering all around me.

Nyktos held me there, his chest sealed to my back as his head moved. His lips touched my skin, and then I felt the kiss against the mark he'd left there. It was I who shuddered then, and I immediately knew that neither of us would ever be the same again.

Chapter 39

I woke, temples aching slightly and knowing I was alone before I even opened my eyes. It was the absence of his body wrapped around mine. We'd fallen asleep like that, on our sides, my back to his chest, and his arms folded around me.

In the quietness of his chambers, I didn't know what to think about that—what to think about anything. Things were…well, they were a mess. Everything. From what my ancestors had learned and what was bound to happen to Lasania—all of the mortal realm and eventually Iliseeum—to Nyktos' father being the real Primal of Life and placing the ember of life in me, the truth of Kolis, and this…this thing between Nyktos and me.

At least he'd fed. Was that why his body had felt warm? Or was it something else? I had no idea. But he apparently had no plans to lock me in a cell.

I'd understand if he did. Who wouldn't? But I didn't think I could take that. He was right, though. I was no real threat to him, and that had nothing to do with the pointlessness behind attempting to kill him.

Something cold pierced my chest as I turned my cheek, inhaling his scent. I opened my eyes to the bare walls. What was I going to do now? I couldn't repair things between Nyktos and me because what was there to repair? I wasn't even sure the Primal was capable of something like love. And I didn't know if I was. But I…I wanted his friendship. I wanted his respect. I wanted him to be Ash, and I wanted to be Sera. But that would never happen. I couldn't save my people.

Or what if I could? What if this ember of life had been placed in me for another reason? But what could it be? And what would happen to those who lived here until we figured it out? There'd be more attacks, and maybe, eventually, Kolis himself would arrive. The King of Gods would come after Nyktos. I had a sickening feeling that he already had in the past. And whether or not Nyktos believed me, I cared about what happened to him—what happened to the people here.

What were my options? Find a way to turn myself over to Kolis? He would kill me, and that would possibly hasten the death of the mortal realm if what Aios said was true. It would only buy the Shadowlands extra time. Maybe. This wasn't being stuck between a rock and a hard place. This was being crushed by both.

But nothing would come from lying in a bed that wasn't even mine.

Head aching, I sat up and winced at the tenderness. It had been a while since I had engaged in such activities, and it had never been like that. I looked down, biting my lip at the puckered, puncture wounds on my breast as I gingerly prodded the skin at my throat. It too was tender but not painful. A fine shiver rolled through me as I started to rise, only then noticing the robe laid out at the foot of the bed. I stared at it in disbelief. Nyktos must've retrieved it. And I…

I smacked my hands over my face. That hurt. But what hurt worse was his godsdamned *thoughtfulness* even now. And I had planned to take that kindness and twist it. I had planned to kill him. And it didn't even seem to matter if I would've gone through with it or not. It was the intent that counted.

Wetness gathered behind my tightly closed eyes as tears burned the back of my throat, a sob filling my chest. *I will not cry,* I told myself. *I will not cry.* Crying solved nothing. All it would do was make my headache worse. I needed to pull myself together and get up and figure out what the hell to do now. I focused on Sir Holland's breathing instructions until the pressure behind my eyes lessened, and the burning, choking feeling receded. Then I got up and slipped on the robe. I forced one foot in front of the other, leaving behind Nyktos' empty, cold chamber that had briefly been full and warm.

I had just stepped out of my bathing chamber after making quick use of it when Paxton knocked on the door. The young man stood beside several pails of steaming water, his head bowed so his sheet of blond hair hid most of his face. "His Highness thought you might enjoy a warm bath," he said, hands clasped together. "So, I brought up hot water."

Surprised by the gesture for a multitude of reasons, and unsure of how Nyktos had known that I'd returned to my chamber, I *almost* needed to smack my hands over my face again. I didn't. Instead, I opened the door wider.

"That was very kind of him—and you, to bring all of these up here."

"He carried most," Paxton said, and my brows lifted as I popped my head out the door. The hall was empty. The young man peeked at me, and I caught a glimpse of deep brown eyes. "He had to go to court, Your Highness."

"You don't have to call me that," I replied before I could remember what Bele had instructed.

"You will be his Consort. That is how I should refer to you."

My throat dried. Paxton obviously hadn't heard. What would he tell the people here?

Paxton's chin went up a notch. "And you are a Princess, right? That's what Aios told me."

"I am." A wry grin tugged at my lips despite everything. "But only for one percent of my life."

That drew a quick, curious glance from Paxton as he picked up two pails. "You were born a Princess?"

"Yes." I reached for one of the pails.

"Then you're a Princess for a hundred percent of your life," he said. "And I got the pails. You don't have to carry them."

"I can carry them."

"I've got them." He eased past me, carrying the pails to the bathing chamber. He was careful to keep the buckets level and unaffected by his limp.

It was hard to just stand there and do nothing when I had two functioning arms. "How about I just pick up one, then?"

"I'd rather you not."

I already had the pail in hand. His sigh when he looked up and spotted me was quite impressive. "How long have you lived here, Paxton?" I asked, changing the subject.

"For the last ten years," he answered, his grip on the pail quite steady for such small arms. "Since I was about five. Before that, I lived in Irelone."

So, he was fifteen. I turned as he hurried back into the hall to grab two more. "Is your family here?"

"No, Your Highness." He passed me, leaving two more buckets in the hall. I resisted the urge to grab both and only picked up one. "My ma and pa died when I was a babe."

"I'm sorry to hear that." I joined him in the bathing chamber, where he took the water from me and proceeded to pour it into the tub.

"I don't even remember them, but thank you anyway." He disappeared back into the hall, returning quickly with the final bucket.

"How did you end up here?" I asked.

"My uncle wasn't so keen on having another mouth to feed, so I was on the streets, lifting coins when I could." Paxton poured the water into the tub. "I saw a man in a finely cut cloak and thought he'd be a good mark." He straightened. "Turned out to be His Highness."

I blinked. "You…you pickpocketed the Primal of Death?"

Paxton peeked through his hair. "I *tried*."

I stared at him. "I don't know if I should laugh or applaud you."

A brief grin appeared as he began picking up the empty buckets. "His Highness had roughly the same reaction. In my defense, I didn't realize who he was."

"So, he brought you back here?"

"I think he took one look at me and felt sorry." Paxton shrugged, empty pails swaying. "I've been living with the Karpovs ever since."

I had no idea who the Karpovs were, and I had a feeling there was a whole lot more to the adventure that'd led the orphan boy to the Shadowlands. I also thought about how the entirety of the mortal realm would be shocked to learn that the Primal of Death was far more generous and forgiving than the vast majority of humanity, who would've likely turned the young pickpocket over to the authorities.

Which was as surprising as it was disheartening.

"I heard about you, you know?" Paxton said, drawing me from my musings.

Tension poured into my body, causing the pain in my head to flare. "About what?"

"What you did last night—out on the Rise," he said, and a tiny bit of relief seeped into me. "Everyone's been talking about how the mortal Consort was up there, shooting arrows and killing those beasts." Something akin to approval filled his wide eyes, but the relief was short-lived. "We will be proud to call you our Consort."

Paxton hastily bowed and left, closing the doors behind him as I stood there, hating myself a little more.

"Ugh," I muttered. "I'm the worst."

Tired, I wandered back into the bathing chamber and rummaged through the bottles and baskets on the shelves. I picked up a white compressed ball of salts that carried a citrusy scent that reminded me of Nyktos, inhaling the tarty notes of bergamot and mandarin. Lowering the ball into the water, I watched it immediately fizz, spreading foamy bubbles across the surface of the tub.

Rising, I quickly glanced at the mirror. The bite on my neck wasn't visible through the clumps of curls. I turned, shrugging off the robe and hanging it on the hook inside the wardrobe. I placed a fluffy towel on the stool and took a moment to twist the length of my hair up, shoving a half-dozen pins into it to keep it dry. There was no way I had the energy to deal with wet hair. Air hissed between my teeth as I stepped into the warm water and sank down. Muscles I didn't even realize were tense and sore immediately loosened. Knees bent, breaking the surface of the water, I wiggled down and let my head rest on the rim of the tub. I was a lot more tired than I realized, and I didn't know if it was because of Nyktos' feeding or everything else. Probably all of it.

My eyes drifted shut, and I let my thoughts wander as the heat of the water, the comforting scent, and the silence eased the ache in my head, lulling me. I felt myself drifting to sleep.

A distant, soft thud invaded the tranquility, pulling me from the blissful nothingness. I pushed against the foot of the tub, scooting up as I pried open my eyes—

There was a flash of black. That was all. A glimpse of something thin and dark coming down in front of my face. I shoved my arm up out of reflex. The strip caught and jerked me back, my fingers snagging as he pulled the material tight around my throat.

Chapter 40

A wave of disbelief slammed into me a moment of utter stillness where my brain and body hadn't caught up to what was happening yet. *Why* this was happening.

The shock of the material digging into my windpipe despite my fingers being in the way threw me out of the frozen state. There was a rough curse above as the sash twisted. My heart lurched in my chest as my shoulders were jammed against the back of the tub. Eyes wide, I tried to drag in air, but only a thin stream worked its way into my throat. I turned, reaching back and grasping an arm—a warm, hard wrist. Out of instinct, I dug my fingers in. The man cursed again, a deep and guttural sound as my eyes darted wildly over the black walls of the bathing chamber. His grip loosened a fraction, allowing a larger burst of air into my lungs and I gripped the binding, keeping it from completely sealing around my throat.

"Don't fight," the man rasped, slamming a hand down on the top of my head. "It will be easier if you don't fight."

Don't fight? My heart slammed erratically as my shoulders slid down in the tub. If he got me underwater, I was done. I knew that. My chin went under, and panic crowded my thoughts. *Think, Sera. Think.* I planted my feet against the tub, bracing myself. *Think, Sera—* My gaze landed on the stool. Wood. If I could break it, it could be a weapon.

"I'm sorry," the attacker ground out. "It has to be done. I'm sorry—"

Letting go of the attacker's arm, I threw myself against the side of the tub. Water sloshed over the rim as I stretched, fingers brushing the towel—

The attacker jerked sideways, causing my feet to slide along the tub. The damn towel snagged on something, causing the stool to topple. Wood clattered off stone, and he shoved me down harder. I went under, sputtering a mouthful of sudsy, warm water. Panic and fear careened into anger—pulsing, pounding, red-hot fury, and that rage burned through the burst of terror and cleared my thoughts. I pushed as hard as I could off the foot of the tub with everything in me.

The hold on me shook under the burst of strength. I broke the surface, water and hair streaming down my face. Coughing, I threw my head back, connecting with a chin.

"Fuck," the man grunted, slipping backward.

Ignoring the sharp pain shooting down my spine, I kept moving as the attacker tried to regain his footing in the water pooling around the tub. I twisted sideways, throwing an arm over the side of the tub. The porcelain pressed against my bare skin as I shoved my head under the sudden gap between the sash and my throat. I clamored over the side of the tub, following it onto the wet floor. Gasping for air, I spun around on my knees, but I didn't make it very far.

A body crashed into mine, pushing me to the floor, a knee digging into the center of my back.

"Get off me!" I shouted. And for a brief, terrible moment, I was thrust back to that morning with Tavius, when he'd held me down just like this. The bitter taste of panic threatened to return, to overwhelm me.

No. No. No—

The man's weight suddenly left me as he cursed. I didn't know if he'd slipped in the water or not, but with my arms free, I grabbed hold of the leg of the stool. The reprieve was too brief. Hands clamped around my neck as I swung the stool around, welcoming the savage rush of satisfaction I felt when the edge of the stool connected with what sounded like the side of his head. The grip on my neck fell away, and I heard a shout. Scrambling forward, I rose to my knees and slammed the stool down hard on the edge of the tub. The impact cracked it in two, leaving me holding a leg with a jagged end.

The man grabbed me, but I was wet and slippery, and he couldn't keep hold. With a scream, I twisted at the waist, slamming the broken wood into flesh—whatever part of him I could reach. It was his stomach—the side. The man howled, stumbling backward and slipping in the pools of water. He went down hard, the side of his head cracking off the bathtub. He fell to the floor, unmoving, and I saw him for the first time. Dark, curly hair. Pink skin. Middle-aged. I thought he looked vaguely familiar as a burst of icy wind whipped through the bathing chamber, charging the air. I yanked the wood from the man's side and rose into a crouch, looking up just as shadows peeled off the shadowstone walls and raced out from the corners of the chamber, seemingly called forth as the doors flew open.

"*Nyktos*," I whispered, sinking onto my knees.

The Primal was in front of me within a breath, barely sparing the man by the tub a look. Shadows pulsed under his thinning skin. Bright streaks of eather churned through his eyes. "Sera."

For a moment, I thought I heard genuine concern in his voice, saw real fear in his stare, but that had to be a byproduct of my fright.

"Are you all right?" His hands folded over my upper arms.

Swallowing hard, I nodded. "How did you know?" The moment I asked the question, I remembered. "My blood."

"I felt it." He leaned in and swept back the hair plastered to my face. His features sharpened even more. "Your…fear. I tasted it."

Booted steps drew to a halt outside the bathing chamber, and I heard Saion growl, "*Fates*."

I glanced over Nyktos' shoulder to see Ector in the doorway beside Saion. His face paled as he took in the scene before him.

"Having your blood in me has come in handy." Nyktos' gaze lowered, halting on my throat. His jaw hardened.

"Exactly how much does my blood let you feel of my emotions when I'm not around you?"

"Only if what you're feeling is extreme."

"Feels a bit intrusive," I muttered.

Silvery, swirling eyes met mine. "Part of me is astonished and somewhat bemused that you could even feel anger about *that* right now." A pause as his stare returned to my throat. "The other half is…" He didn't finish, but thick tendrils of shadow spilled across the floor, forcing Ector to take a step back. The god's head snapped in the Primal's direction.

His reaction… Was he truly concerned? Did it matter if he was? Because I…I was valuable to him right now. No, not me. What I carried inside me was important. Of course, he would be concerned about losing the ember of life and whatever else his father may have done.

"Get me a towel." Nyktos shifted, shielding my body with his, but there was so much hazy darkness gathering around him that I doubted either god could see much of anything. "Not that one," he said as Saion neared, reaching for the one that had been on the stool. "One that hasn't been touched."

"Of course." A moment later, Saion handed a towel over.

Nyktos whipped it around my shoulders, but he didn't let go. He held the edges closed and brushed aside several more soaked strands of hair. The eather was all too bright in his eyes and in the streaks cutting through the shadows churning around him.

"He tried to strangle you?" Nyktos' voice was soft—too soft.

"He tried," I said, suppressing a shudder. "He failed, as you can see."

That didn't seem to ease the Primal as his fingers grazed my throat, the touch tender. "Your skin had better not bruise."

My eyes shot to his. He'd said that as if he could somehow will it into reality, and I wasn't sure why he cared.

"I'm okay," I repeated, clasping the towel just below his hands. "I mean, I'm pretty sure I'll never take another bath again in my life, but I'm okay."

Nyktos stared at me, brows slightly pinched.

"That's…that's Hamid," murmured Saion, and I caught a glimpse of him turning to where the man lay. "What the fuck?"

The name was familiar. It took a moment. "The…man who came to court to report Gemma missing?"

The man groaned, jerking my attention over Nyktos' shoulder.

"He's still alive," Saion said at the same time Ector stepped forward.

Nyktos twisted away from me. "Don't—"

It happened so fast…a bolt of silvery-white energy arcing across the bathing chamber to slam into Hamid. I sucked in a startled breath, jerking back. Nyktos folded an arm around my waist, catching me before I toppled over. He gathered me against his chest and stood, bringing me along with him. The aura of eather swallowed the man, crackling and spitting, and then there was nothing left but a fine dusting of ash.

"I don't know if I'll ever be able to use this bathing chamber again," I murmured, and Saion's brows kicked up as he looked over at me.

Nyktos drew in a deep, forced breath as the shadows scattered away from him, retreating to the walls and corners. "You killed him."

"Was I not supposed to?" Ector lowered his hand. "He tried to kill her, and for *reasons*, you are not too keen on that idea."

"I would've thoroughly enjoyed his death *after* I spoke with him." Nyktos pinned a glare on the god, and it was then that I realized the man hadn't just been killed. His soul had been destroyed. "There will be no questioning him now."

"Shit." Ector apparently realized the same thing. He dragged a hand through his hair. "I might need to think before I act."

"You think?" Nyktos snapped.

Ector cringed. "Sorry?"

"You're cleaning up this mess," Nyktos directed Ector then led me from the chamber.

"Gladly," Ector remarked. "I think I'm going to need a bucket and a mop. Possibly a broom…" He trailed off under the Primal's glare. "Or I could just use some towels and stuff."

I started to look over my shoulder, but Nyktos led me toward the chaise as Rhain entered the bedchamber, drawing up short.

"Do I even want to know?" Rhain asked, sword in hand.

"Hamid just tried to assassinate Sera," Saion answered from the doorway to the bathing chamber.

Confusion marked Rhain's expression as he sheathed his sword. "Why in the hell would Hamid do that?"

"That's what I would like to know." Nyktos sat me down on the chaise. Flames roared to life from the quiet fireplace, causing me to jerk. My wide gaze slid to him. "Primal magic," he said absently as if he'd only lit a candle. "Where is your robe?"

"I…I don't know."

He grabbed a throw blanket and then stopped. "You don't need to let go of the piece of wood, but you do need to let go of the towel," he said softly, and I blinked, realizing I was still holding the broken leg. "No one is looking."

At that moment, I honestly didn't care if the entire Shadowlands Court saw. I let go of the towel, and then the warm, soft weight of the blanket settled over my shoulders. I curled my fingers into the edges with one hand because I wasn't exactly ready to part with the only weapon I had.

"I wish I had my dagger," I murmured to no one in particular.

Everyone, including Nyktos, looked at me as if I'd possibly suffered some injury to the head. I sighed.

"How did he even get in here?" Rhain turned to the doors, stalking back to them. He checked them over. "There appears to be no forced entry."

"I left the doors unlocked." I briefly closed my eyes. "I thought someone would be guarding it."

"Same," Rhain murmured, looking over his shoulder at Nyktos.

I stared at the Primal, equally confused. Had he not made sure someone was outside to ensure I didn't do anything?

A muscle ticked in Nyktos' jaw. "I hadn't quite gotten to that part yet."

"He's had a busy morning," Saion chimed in. "First, assuring you and the others clucking around him like mother hens that he was okay, and then he had to check on the damage to the Rise."

I didn't know what to think about him not making it a priority that I was a…a prisoner. "Was there damage to the Rise?"

"Minimal," Nyktos answered.

"And were there more deaths?" I asked.

He looked back at me. For a moment, I didn't think he'd answer. Or that maybe he would accuse me of not caring. "There were injuries, but none that should be fatal."

Exhaling softly, I nodded. That was good news, at least. "So," I drew the word out as I looked up at the Primal. "A man who was a complete stranger just tried to kill me."

"Appears that way," Nyktos agreed flatly, sweeping his thumb over my chin before seeming to catch himself. He dropped his hand and rose. Several moments passed. "Did he say anything?"

"Only that…that he was sorry and had to do it," I told them.

"Why would he think he had to do that?" Rhain asked. "Hell, I never would have expected something like that from him."

"Did you know him well?"

"Well enough to know that he was a quiet man and kept to himself. Kind and generous," Rhain said. "And he hated Kolis as much as any of us."

I zeroed in on that. "Did he live here long?"

Nyktos nodded. "He was a godling that never Ascended—didn't have enough eather in him for the change to take hold, but his mother wanted to be a part of his life. She was a goddess."

"Was?" I whispered.

"She was killed several years ago." Nyktos didn't elaborate.

And he didn't need to. "Kolis?"

"He destroyed her soul," Nyktos told me, and my chest hollowed. "I don't even know what caused it. She was in a different Court at the time. It could've been anything—a perceived slight or a refusal to obey him. He made sure Hamid learned the details of her death."

"Gods," I whispered, sickened.

Saion glanced at me, his gaze straying to my throat—to the mark Nyktos left behind. I shifted the blanket higher. "Is it possible that he somehow found out what she plans to do?"

I stiffened.

"That's impossible," Rhain countered. "No one would dare speak of what she plans."

"*Planned*," I mumbled, but no one seemed to hear me.

"You know damn well that none of us would've disobeyed his orders. We wouldn't want to piss him off." Ector popped his head out of the bathing chamber. "And unlike me, Nyktos would think before destroying the soul so he could continue to fuck with us after we're dead."

But what would be the reason for a mortal I've never interacted with to feel as if they need to kill me? Then it occurred to me. "He came to visit Gemma. I guess during the attack or afterwards," I said, and Nyktos turned to me. "Aios said that Gemma was only awake briefly. Not long enough to discover if she knew what had happened to her. Is it possible that she knows and said something to Hamid when Aios wasn't there?"

"That's possible," Nyktos stated.

"Gemma is still here." Ector brushed past Saion, holding a pile of towels in his arms. "She was asleep when I checked on her, and that was right before I met up with you all downstairs. So, that was…what? Less than thirty minutes ago?"

Nyktos turned to Rhain. "Find Aios and see if there was a time that Hamid was alone with Gemma. Have Aios stay with her, even if she is still asleep. Then I want you to check out Hamid's house and the bakery he worked at. See if you can find out anything of interest."

"Of course." Rhain glanced at me, bowed, and then quickly left the room.

I was still thinking of what Gemma could've told Hamid. "But if Gemma realized that she died and I brought her back, why would that cause Hamid to try and kill me? He was concerned about Gemma. Wouldn't he be happy that she's alive?"

"You'd think. That's a good question I would've loved to have answered." Nyktos sent a pointed stare at Ector, who studied the floor as if it were of great interest. Nyktos shifted his focus back to me. "Are you sure you're okay?" he asked, and I nodded. He still came back to where I was sitting. "Let me see your neck again."

I sat still as his fingers brushed my hair back, grazing my shoulder, desperately trying not to think about how he'd touched me before—how he'd held me. His gaze lifted to mine, and when he spoke, I thought his voice sounded thicker, richer. "I don't think it will bruise."

"Are you reading my emotions *again*?"

He said nothing as he let go of my hair, his fingers brushing my cheek—his *warm* fingers.

"Oh, my gods." I shot up.

Nyktos eyed the broken leg I held as if he were half-afraid I'd use it against him, which was absurd enough that it actually made me want to use it. "What?"

"Your skin. It's warm," I told him, having forgotten that until now. "It's been warm since last night, after you..." I trailed off as Ector looked over at us, his expression curious. "Well, since last night. Is it because you fed?"

Nyktos frowned. "No. That wouldn't have changed it. My skin has been cool for as long as I can remember. Kolis's skin most likely felt the same way."

"Well, it's not that way now," I told him. "Can't you tell?" When he shook his head, I looked over at the two remaining gods. "Haven't any of you noticed it?"

Saion coughed out a laugh. "Why would we?"

"It's pretty noticeable."

"If one of us is touching him," Ector returned. "And none of us walk around touching him. He doesn't like to be touched."

I lifted my brows and looked over at Nyktos. "I didn't get that impression."

"Yeah, well, he enjoys your kind of touching," Ector stated. Shockingly, I felt my face heat.

Nyktos turned to the god. "Do you have a death wish today?" he growled, and I began to wonder the same thing.

"I'm beginning to think I do," Ector murmured and then shifted the bundle of towels. "But let me touch you. See if she's telling the truth."

I rolled my eyes. "Why would I lie about that?"

"Why would we not question everything that comes out of your mouth now?" Nyktos shot back.

A hundred different retorts burned my tongue, but every part of me locked up as I stood there. His accusation was warranted, but the coldness in his tone reminded me so much of my mother that it rattled me to my core.

Ector moved toward Nyktos as the Primal stared at me, his features unreadable. Forcing myself to remember Sir Holland's breathing instructions, I focused on Ector.

The god touched Nyktos' hand. Immediately, Ector's eyes went wide. "Holy shit, your skin *is* warm."

"That doesn't make any sense." Nyktos was still staring at me. I could feel it. "It…it has to be your blood."

"If it is, it's not like I did it on purpose."

"I wasn't suggesting that."

"Are you sure—?" I sucked in a stuttered breath, dropping the wooden leg as a sharp ache darted across my skull and along my jaw, leaving a webbing of shivery pain in its wake.

Nyktos stepped toward me. "Are you all right?"

"Yes," I bit out, pressing a palm against the side of my face. I squinted at the suddenly too-bright lights.

"Does your head hurt?"

"Or your face?" Ector asked.

"A little." I drew in a shallow breath as the throbbing ache settled deep in my temple and under my eyes. "It's just a…a headache. I'm fine. Shouldn't we be heading into—whoa," I murmured, blinking as the floor felt like it rolled slightly under my feet. "That felt odd."

Nyktos was suddenly beside me. He clasped my arm, and I barely felt the jolt of his touch. "What did?"

"The floor," I said, and his frown deepened.

"Are you dizzy?" Nyktos asked, and I started to nod, realizing that was rather dumb as the pain deepened. "I took too much of your blood—"

"It's not that," I told him. "I've had these headaches before—sometimes in my temples and under my eyes. Other times in my jaw."

His brows snapped down. "How often have you gotten them?"

"On and off. Only this…this intense once before. I think there may be something wrong with one of my teeth. There's been a bit of blood when I brush," I told him.

Ector lowered the towels and stared at me. "When did that start?"

"The blood?" I winced.

"Any of it," Nyktos demanded.

"I don't know. A couple of years ago. It's not…it's not a big deal. My mother gets them sometimes, too. The headaches. So maybe it's just that."

Nyktos' features were strangely stark as he stared down at me, too. "I'm not so sure that is the cause."

"Then what would it be?" I asked.

"Impossible," Saion breathed, and I'd never seen the god so unsettled.

"I know what you're thinking, but it's impossible."

"What?" I forced out around the throbbing ache. "What is impossible?"

"What I'm thinking *is* impossible, but I think I know what might help," Nyktos said and then turned to the gods. All it took was for him to send them one look, and they left the chamber. "Why don't you lay down? I'll be back shortly."

For once, I didn't argue with him. I nodded. He started for the door and then stopped. "There will be a guard outside this chamber," he said, his head lowered slightly. "You'll be safe."

Nyktos slipped from the room before I could say anything, and with how badly my head ached, I couldn't even read into that or what he'd thought was impossible. Remembering where my robe was, I went to the wardrobe and managed to slip it on. On the way back to the bed, I did stop to pick up the broken wooden leg. There was blood on the end of it, and a guard stationed outside or not, I wasn't taking any chances.

I climbed into bed, all but burying my face in the mound of pillows. I wasn't alone for long. Nektas arrived shortly after the Primal had left. He didn't say a word, and my head hammered too much to be bothered by his silence.

The draken was currently out on the balcony, having left the door half-open. Every so often, when I had my eyes open, I saw him pass in front of the door as if he were checking on me.

It wasn't all that long before he entered the chamber and announced as he had before that Nyktos was arriving.

"Can you sense him?" I asked, half of my face still planted in the pillows. Nektas nodded and stopped in the middle of the room. "Is it…the bond?"

The question earned me another nod.

"Do you like being bonded to a Primal?"

He nodded once more. "For most of us, it is a choice." Nektas looked at me then, his gaze unblinking. "We undertake the bond of our own free will, and because of that, we see it as an honor. As does the Primal."

For most of us? "Did the bond transfer from his father to him?"

"No. It doesn't work that way. When his father died, it severed the bond. Those who are bonded to Nyktos have done so by choice."

"And the ones who don't fall into the *most of us* category?" I asked, wincing as the throbbing in my head told me to be quiet.

Nektas didn't answer right away. "The bond can be forced, as nearly all things can. Some draken aren't given that choice."

"What…what about the draken last night? The crimson-colored one?"

"I do not know if he chose the bond or not, but I do know that Kolis does not give a choice."

The door opened before I could ask how Kolis or any Primal could force a bond. Nyktos stalked in, carrying a large tankard. His gaze immediately landed on me and didn't stray. "Thank you," he said to the draken. And then to me he said, "How are you feeling?"

"Better."

"She lies," Nektas advised.

"How do you know?" I muttered.

"Draken have an acute sense of smell." Nyktos sat beside me. "Along with sight and hearing."

"Pain has a smell?"

"Everything has a scent," Nektas answered as I eyed him wryly. "Every person has a unique scent."

"What do I smell like?" I asked.

"You smell of…" He inhaled deeply as my lip curled. "You smell of death."

I stared at him from my pile of pillows, mouth hanging open. "That was rude."

Nyktos cleared his throat as he lowered his chin. "He may be speaking of me."

"I am," the draken confirmed.

I glanced at Nyktos and then realized what he meant. Warmth crept up my throat. "I did bathe—"

"That will not wash away such a scent," Nektas countered.

I stared at them. "Well, that's...even more rude to point out."

Nektas tilted his head, and his nostrils flared when he inhaled once more. "You also smell of—"

"You can stop now," I told him. "I changed my mind. I don't need to know."

He looked a bit disappointed.

"I brought you something to drink that I think might help with the headache," Nyktos said. "It doesn't taste the greatest, but it works."

Pushing myself up, I reached for the tankard. "Is it some kind of tea?" I asked, curling my fingers around the warm cup. "Sir Holland made me some when I had a headache this bad before."

"It is a tea, but I doubt it's the same," Nyktos answered. "This should bring you relief."

"His tea made the headache go away." I sniffed the dark liquid. "Smells the same." I took a sip, recognizing the sweet and earthy, minty flavor. "Tastes the same. Chasteberry? Peppermint? And other herbs I can't remember? And let me guess, I need to drink all of this while it's still warm?"

Surprise flickered across Nyktos' face. "Yes."

"It's the same, thank the gods." I took a larger drink and then forced myself to down the remaining contents.

"That was…impressive," Nektas murmured.

"It also hurt a little," I rasped, eyes and throat stinging. "But it works, so it's worth it."

Nyktos took the empty tankard from me. "Are you positive that it's the same tea?"

"Yes." I snuggled back down onto my side. "It's the same. Sir Holland had given me an extra pouch of the herbs in case the headache returned."

"Did he say why he thought the tea would help?" Nektas asked.

"Not that I remember." I shoved my hands under a pillow. "My mother has migraines, so maybe he thought I was experiencing the same and figured it would help."

"That doesn't make sense." Nyktos frowned as he placed the tankard on the nightstand. "There is no way a mortal would have knowledge of this type of tea."

I raised a brow, already feeling the pounding lessening. "Is the tea special or something?"

"It would not be known in the mortal realm." Nektas glanced at the Primal and then his gaze landed on me. "You're sure this Sir Holland is mortal?"

"Yes." I laughed. "He's mortal." I glanced between the two of them. "Maybe the tea is more well-known than you all realize."

"Maybe you're wrong about this Sir Holland being mortal," Nektas returned.

"When exactly did the headaches start?" Nyktos cut in. "You said a couple of years ago?"

My gaze shifted back to him. "I don't know. Maybe a year and a half ago? Close to two?"

"That's not a couple of years ago," Nyktos pointed out.

"Sorry. My head felt like it was being ripped in two when I was being interrogated about it earlier."

Nyktos' lips twisted as if he were fighting a smile. "And they weren't always intense like the one today?"

"Right. Normally, I can ignore them, and they eventually go away. This is only the second time I got one this severe."

Nyktos studied me closely, his gaze tracking over my face as if he were searching for answers. "And the bleeding when you brush your teeth?"

"Infrequent," I told him. "Do you think it's something to do with a tooth? My stepfather once—"

"It's not a tooth infection," Nektas cut in.

"Can you also smell infections?" I retorted.

"Actually, yes, I can," he said.

"Oh." I sank a little deeper into the pillows. "That sounds kind of gross."

"It can be," the draken confirmed.

"Whether or not an infection smells poorly isn't important," Nyktos said, and I narrowed my eyes. "What you're experiencing also isn't a migraine."

"I didn't realize the Primal of Death was also a Healer," I muttered.

He shot me a bland look. "You're already feeling better, aren't you? Truly, this time."

"I am."

"That's it then." He glanced at Nektas, and the draken nodded. "I think what you're experiencing is a symptom of the Culling."

"What?" I jerked upright, wincing as the throbbing intensified for a moment and then faded. "That's impossible. Both my parents are mortal. I'm not a godling—"

"I'm not suggesting that you are," Nyktos cut in, a grin appearing and then disappearing. "I think the ember of life that was placed in you is giving you similar side effects as the Culling. You're the right age for it."

"A bit of a late bloomer," Nektas added.

I frowned at the draken. "I don't understand."

"Godlings go through the Culling because they have eather in their blood. The ember that my father placed in you is eather. That's what fuels your gift, and it would be powerful enough to evoke symptoms—ones that can be debilitating without the right combination of herbs that was discovered ages ago by a god who had a knack for mixing potions. Took hundreds of years, or at least that's what my father told me. A potion born of necessity since no other known medicine worked to ease the headaches and other symptoms that came with the Culling," Nyktos explained. "It's given to every god when they begin to go through the Culling, and to every godling we're aware of." The corners of his lips pulled down. "Which is why I would love to know how a mortal knew of this potion."

So would I. But there were way more important things I wanted to know. "Does this mean I'm going to go through the Ascension?"

"It shouldn't," Nyktos advised. "It is only an ember of life—an ember of eather. More powerful than what would be found in a godling, but you're not a descendant of the gods. It is not a part of you. You'll probably have a couple more weeks or months at most of these symptoms, and then they will go away. You'll be fine."

I was relieved, especially after what I had learned from Aios about the Culling. Toying with the edges of my hair, I looked over at Nyktos. As the aching continued to fade with each passing moment, it was replaced by many questions and words I wanted to speak.

Nektas cleared his throat. "If you'll excuse me."

The draken didn't wait for a response, leaving the chamber—leaving Nyktos and me alone. The Primal watched me like he always did, but there was a guarded quality that had never been there before.

"If you start to feel the headache again or any other symptom that doesn't feel normal, the tea will stop you from experiencing more severe symptoms," he said. "So don't wait."

"I won't." I twisted a curl around my finger.

He sat there for a moment and then started to rise. "You should get some rest. I know the tea can make you tired."

"I know, but…"

Nyktos arched a brow, waiting.

I drew in a deep breath. "I want to talk to you about—"

"About last night?"

"Well, no, but I suppose that's part of it."

"What happened last night won't ever happen again," Nyktos stated, and my fingers stilled in my hair. The finality of his words fell like a sword. "You will be safe here. You will be my Consort as planned."

My hands slipped from my hair. "You still want me as your Consort?"

A tight smile twisted his lips. "This has never been about what either of us wants. It has only ever been about what must be done. And if we do not proceed, that alone will arouse too much suspicion."

My heart started thumping. "I will be your Consort in title only?"

His head tilted. "Do you expect anything else? Do you think my interest in you overrides my common sense? Especially after learning of your treachery?"

The breath I took scorched my insides. "I don't expect anything from you. I don't expect your forgiveness or understanding. I just want a chance to—"

"To do what? Explain yourself? It is unnecessary. I know all that I need to. You were willing to do anything to save your people. I can respect that." His features were as hard as the walls closing in around me. "I can also…*respect* how far you were willing to go to fulfill this duty of yours. But for what purpose? Love has never been on the table."

I knew that. Gods I knew that after everything he'd gone through. I just hadn't been willing to fully admit it to myself. It wasn't love I sought. It was never that. Still, it was hard to speak what I wanted to. The words were so simple, taken for granted by many. "Friendship," I whispered as heat swamped my throat. "There's friendship."

"Friendship? Even if I considered such a thing, I would never think of you. There is no way I could ever trust you. That I would not doubt or question every thought or action. Not when you were shaped and groomed to be whatever it is you believed I wanted. Not when you are just a vessel that would be empty if not for the ember of life you carry within you."

I jerked back, my skin, body—everything—going numb.

Nyktos' eyes flared bright, and then he turned from me. "As I said, you will be safe here. You will be my Consort in title only as we figure out exactly what my father planned for you. But this is all. There's nothing else to discuss. Nothing else to be said."

Chapter 41

I sat by the unlit fireplace the following morning, staring at the burnt kindling that remained. I idly rubbed my palms over my knees. The breeches had been laundered and returned earlier, along with breakfast. It had been Davina who arrived, and the draken hadn't said much. I wasn't sure if that was normal or if she had heard the truth despite Nyktos' warnings to keep it quiet.

The one good thing that had come from the mostly untouched food was the butter knife that had been brought with it. The knife wouldn't do any damage to a god, but I was sure I could make it hurt when it came to a mortal, so I swiped it, slipping it into my boot.

I hadn't slept well the night before, even after the potion. The thought of eating anything didn't rouse interest.

I remembered the last time I'd felt this *hollow*. It was when I'd taken that sleeping draft. It wasn't just Nyktos. It was the truth about Kolis. It was the threat I posed to the Shadowlands. It was me. It was Tavius and Nor and Lord Claus and all the others. It was how much I missed Ezra and Sir Holland. It was how I wanted to tell my mother that I was never the cause of the Rot. And it was…it was how badly I wanted Nyktos to be Ash.

Weary, I toyed with the edges of my braid. It was also the knowledge that the past could never be undone. It couldn't be forgiven. It couldn't be forgotten.

A knock on the door dragged me from my thoughts. I rose.

"Yes?"

"It's Aios."

Surprised, I stepped around the chaise. "You can come in."

The door opened, and she wasn't the only one who entered the chamber. Bele, who had been in the hall when Davina had arrived earlier, walked in, too. Apparently, she was on guard duty, and I wasn't entirely sure if she was there to keep me safe or to keep others safe.

"I need you to come with me," Aios announced.

I tensed, suspicion rising. "To where?"

"Should be nowhere." Behind her, Bele stood with her arms crossed over her chest. My gaze snagged on her weapons—all far better than a paltry butter knife. "I told her Nyktos wanted you to remain in your chambers, but as always, Aios doesn't listen."

The redheaded goddess wasn't listening now. "Gemma is awake."

"Oh." I glanced between the two. "That's good news, isn't it?"

"Yes," Aios answered while Bele shrugged.

"Did she say why she went into the woods?"

"She'd spotted a god who had been at the Court of Dalos and feared she'd be recognized. So she panicked, ran into the Dying Woods, quickly got lost in them, and then saw the Shades. She hid from them for a bit until they found her, but that's not why I'm here," Aios said. "She claims that she has no knowledge of what happened afterward—of what you did."

"That's also good..." I trailed off as Aios's jaw hardened. "Or not?"

"I think she's lying. I think she knows exactly what you did and said something to Hamid," Aios explained. "I told her what Hamid had done, and she lost it, saying it was her fault. That's why I'm here. I want you to tell her what you did."

"In case anyone wants to know, I don't think that's a good idea," Bele announced.

"No one wants to know," Aios replied. "I think if she is confronted with the fact that we know she died, she'll tell us what she told Hamid."

I wasn't sure if that would work, but I was willing to try. It would be nice to have an answer to something. However... "You trust me to leave the bedchamber?"

Aios's nose wrinkled. "What would you do that I should worry about? Are you planning something?"

"Else," Bele added.

"I'm not," I stated.

"And you have no weapon, correct?" Aios asked.

"No." I really didn't count my butter knife as a weapon.

"Then why wouldn't I trust you?"

My brows lifted. "Besides the obvious?"

"My question exactly," Bele added.

Aios sighed. "Look, it was clear—to me at least—that you didn't want to do what you believed you had to. That doesn't mean I agree with your actions or that I'm not disappointed. You seemed to make him…" Her chin lifted. "Anyway, it's not like we don't have explicit experience in carrying out terrible deeds because we believed we had no other choice."

For a moment, I couldn't speak. "Have you ever plotted to kill someone who offered nothing but kindness and safety?"

Aios's stare met mine. "I have probably done worse. All of us have," she stated flatly. "Now, will you come with me?"

I blinked. "Yeah—Yes."

"Thank you." Aios wheeled around, the skirt of her gray gown fluttering at her feet.

Tugging down the sleeves of my sweater, I followed her out into the hall, my thoughts consumed by what Aios could've done that was worse. What Bele could've done. Because she hadn't disagreed with that statement. It wasn't until we reached the second floor that I asked, "Where is Nyktos? And how much trouble will you two get in for letting me out of my bedchambers?"

"He's in Lethe," Bele answered as we walked the wide, quiet hall. "There was some kind of incident. Not sure what exactly. I don't think it's serious—" she said when I opened my mouth. "But I'm hoping he doesn't find out about this little excursion."

"I won't say anything," I told them.

"I'd hope not," Bele remarked, stopping in front of a white door. She opened it without knocking, stalking in.

Aios shook her head at the startled gasp that came from within the small chamber. I followed Aios in, getting my first real look at Gemma.

Good gods…

She was sitting up in bed, hands in her lap, and her injuries…they were gone completely. No deep cuts along her forehead or cheeks. The skin of her neck was unmarred, and I would bet her chest appeared the same.

I never really got a chance to see what my touch did. Most animal wounds weren't as noticeable, and I hadn't seen the one that had ended Marisol's life. This ember…gods, it was as miraculous as what my blood had done for Nyktos.

Walking forward as Bele closed the door behind me, I saw that Gemma's hair, free of blood, was a light shade of blonde, only a few tones darker than mine. And I'd been right. She couldn't be much older than me, if that. Which meant she had lasted in the Dalos Court longer than most because she hadn't been in the Shadowlands that long.

Gemma looked at Aios first and then her gaze settled on me. Her entire body stiffened.

"I brought someone I think you need to meet," Aios said as she sat on the bed beside Gemma. "This is Sera."

The woman hadn't taken her eyes off me. A tremor went through her. Her brown eyes were impossibly wide. I came to stand near the bed.

"I don't know if you recognize me," I started. "But I—"

"I recognize you," she whispered. "I know what you did."

Aios sighed. "Well, that was far easier than I expected it to go." She twisted toward Gemma. "You could've just told me the truth."

"I know. I know I should've, but I…I shouldn't have said anything to Hamid. He's dead because of me. That's my fault. I'm sorry. I didn't mean to say anything." Tears tracked down Gemma's cheeks as she shook. "I was just so caught off guard and wasn't thinking—I know better. Gods, I know better than to say *anything*."

"It's okay." Aios went to place a hand on the woman's arm, halting when Gemma flinched. "We're not going to hurt you." Behind me, Bele made a low sound of disagreement, and Aios shot the other goddess a look of warning. "None of us is going to hurt you."

"It's not you all I'm afraid of."

"I know. It's Kolis," Aios said quietly, and my gaze shot to her. The empathy in her voice came from a place of knowledge, as did the haunted look I'd seen in her eyes.

Gemma's trembling ceased, but she paled even more. "I can't go back there."

"You don't have to," Aios promised.

"But it's my fault that Hamid attacked her. There's no way His Highness will let me stay here now." Her grip on the blanket bleached her knuckles white.

"Did you tell Hamid to attack me?" I asked.

She shook her head. "Good gods, no."

"Then I doubt Nyktos will hold you accountable," I told her, and her eyes shot to mine. The hope and the fear of believing in that hope was clear in her stare. "He won't force you to go anywhere you don't want to," I said, and I knew without a doubt that was true. "You don't have to be afraid of that either."

Aios nodded. "She speaks the truth."

An ache pierced my chest at how evident it was that she wanted so desperately to believe that. "Only time will prove my words right, and I hope you give it that time and don't do anything…reckless again," I said, fully acknowledging the irony of me suggesting against something irresponsible. "What did you tell Hamid?"

Her chest rose with a deep breath as her stare dropped to her hands. "I…I knew I was dying," she said softly. "When the other god found me? I knew I was dying, because I could barely feel his arms when he picked me up. And I…I know I died. I felt it—felt myself leaving my body. There was nothing for a couple of moments and then I saw two pillars—pillars as tall as the sky—with this bright, warm light between them."

Tension crept into me. She was speaking about the Pillars of Asphodel and the Vale. Had Marisol experienced the same? I knew her soul would not linger for long. And if so, did she realize that she had been brought back? I swallowed, hoping that Ezra had been able to steer her away from that belief or, at the very least, ensure that she never spoke of it. If she did, it could place both of them in danger, especially if it got back to a god who served Kolis.

"I felt myself drifting toward it and then I was pulled back," Gemma said. "I knew someone had brought me back." Her head turned to me. "I knew it was you. I felt your touch. And when I looked at you, I just knew. I can't explain it, but I did. It's you he's been looking for."

"Kolis?" Bele demanded, and Gemma flinched again at the sound of his name. The woman nodded. "How did you know?"

"I was…" Gemma pulled the blanket closer to her waist. "I was his favorite for a bit. He kept me…" She swallowed, stretching her neck, and Aios closed her eyes. "He kept me close to him for a while. He said he liked my hair." She reached up, absently touching one of the light strands. "He talked about this…power he felt. He spoke about it all the time. Obsessed over it and how he would do anything to find it. This *presence.* His *graeca.*"

"*Graeca*?" I repeated.

"It's from the old language of the Primals," Bele answered. "It means life, I believe."

"It also means love." Aios's eyes had opened. She frowned as she glanced at me. "The word is interchangeable."

"Like *liessa*?" I said, and she nodded. "Well, obviously, he is referencing life." I imagined Kolis still believed that he was in love with Sotoria. "He felt the—the ripples of power I caused over the years. We know that."

"Well, we suspected that," Bele corrected. "But we weren't sure until the other night when the dakkais showed."

I shifted my weight. "And that is what you told Hamid?"

Gemma blew out a ragged breath. "I never understood what he meant when he spoke of his *graeca*. Not until I saw you and realized that you had brought me back. I told Hamid that it must be you that Kolis was looking for. That you were the presence he felt, and that you were here, in the Shadowlands." She shook her head as she swallowed again. "I knew what happened to Hamid's mother. He shared that with me. I should've been thinking. Hamid…he hated Kolis, but he was also afraid of him. Terrified that he would come to the Shadowlands and hurt more people."

"So that's why," Bele mused, tossing her braid over her shoulder. "He thought he was protecting the Shadowlands by making sure Kolis didn't have a reason to come here. He sought to remove the lure. Kind of can't fault him for that line of thinking."

I stared at her. "Considering that I was the lure he sought to remove, I kind of do fault him."

"Understandable," the goddess quipped.

But I also understood Hamid's line of thinking. I could easily see myself doing the same. And I could also see how being the object of one's murderous intentions, no matter how noble, wasn't something that could be forgotten.

It was how I knew that Nyktos would never forget. Not that I needed to know what that felt like to know.

Chest heavy, I pushed those thoughts aside as a question rose that I felt it best not be asked in front of Gemma. Why hadn't Kolis come to the Shadowlands?

Gemma spoke, drawing me back to her. "I didn't think his *graeca* was a person. He never spoke of it as if it were something living and breathing. He talked as if it were an object. A possession that belonged to him."

Well, Kolis didn't seem the type to view living and breathing beings as anything other than objects.

"Did he ever say what he planned to do with his *graeca* when he found it?" Aios asked.

"I think we know the answer to that," Bele replied dryly.

I had to agree. Kolis couldn't conjure life. He would see the ember of such power as a threat and want to eradicate it.

"No. He never said anything to me, but…" She looked over at us. "He was doing something to the other Chosen. Not all of them, but the ones that disappeared."

My gaze sharpened on her. *They are simply gone.* That was what Nyktos had said. "What do you mean?"

"There was just some talk among the other Chosen who were still there. The ones that had been there the longest. Kolis did something to them."

"The ones that disappeared?" Bele asked, stepping forward.

Gemma nodded. "They weren't right when they came back," she said, and a chill swept over my skin. "They were *different.* Cold. Lifeless. Some of them stayed indoors, only moving about during the brief hours of night. Their eyes changed." A far-off look crept into hers. "They became the color of shadowstone. Black. They always looked…hungry."

Something about her words tugged at the recesses of my mind. Something familiar.

"They were frightening, the way they *stared.*" Gemma's voice was barely above a haunting whisper. "The way they seemed to track every movement you made, every beat of your heart. They were as terrifying as he was." Her grip eased on the blanket. "He called them his reborn. His Revenants. He said they were a work in progress." She laughed, but it was weak. "I heard him saying once that all he needed was his *graeca* to perfect them."

Aios glanced over her shoulder at Bele and then at me. It didn't seem like Gemma had more to share, but if she did, the three of us sensed that we wouldn't learn it today. The woman looked as if she was close to shattering. Once Aios assured her that she was safe to rest here, and it looked like Gemma believed her, we took our leave.

I stopped at the door, something occurring to me. I faced Gemma as Aios and Bele waited for me in the hall. "I'm sorry."

Confusion marked her face. "For what?"

"For bringing you back to life if that was not what you wanted," I told her.

"I didn't want to die," Gemma said after a moment. "That's not why I went into the Dying Woods. I just…I just didn't want to go back there. I didn't want to be afraid anymore."

Out in the hall and several feet from Gemma's door, I stopped. The goddesses faced me. "What do you think the reborn are? These Revenant things?"

"I don't know." Bele turned, leaning against the wall. "I haven't heard anything like that before, and trust me, I've tried to find out what has happened to the missing Chosen."

"I really hope the phrase *reborn* doesn't mean literally." Aios rubbed her hands over her upper arms. "Because I don't want to think about Kolis having found some way to create life."

"And that it might some way, possibly, involve you." Bele jerked her chin toward me.

"Thanks for the reminder," I muttered, but it did make me think of the question I'd thought of while in Gemma's room. "Why hasn't Kolis come to the Shadowlands? Why didn't he come himself when I brought Gemma back?"

"He hasn't stepped foot in the Shadowlands since he became the Primal of Life," Bele answered. "I don't think he can. Don't look too relieved by that," she said, catching the breath I exhaled. "As you saw, he doesn't need to come here to make his presence known. And we don't know for sure if he really can't."

I nodded, thinking over what Gemma had shared. "So, Kolis definitely knows about the ember of life—he may not know how it came into creation, but he knows it exists. And he thinks he can use it somehow, which I'm guessing Eythos didn't take into consideration."

Aios tipped her head back. "At this point, I doubt even the Fates know why he put the ember of life in your bloodline."

I stiffened as what she said struck a chord of familiarity in me. Frowning, I searched my memories until I…I saw Odetta in my mind. "The Fates," I whispered. "The Arae."

"Yes." Aios looked over at me. "The Arae."

My heart started pounding as I twisted toward her. "My old nursemaid, Odetta, told me that I was touched by Death and Life upon birth—she claimed that only the Fates could answer why. I always thought that Odetta was being, well, overdramatic because how would she know what the Fates may or may not have said or known? But what if she was speaking the truth? What if the Fates do know? Is that possible?"

"As far as I know, the Fates don't know everything." Bele pushed off the wall, her eyes lighting up. "But they do know more than most."

"Where is Odetta now?" Aios asked.

"She passed away recently." An ache cut through my chest. "She should be in the Vale. Can the draken somehow reach her?" I asked, remembering what Nyktos had said. "Wait. If the Fates know what Eythos planned, then wouldn't Nyktos have known that, too? And gone to them?"

Bele laughed. "The Primals cannot make demands of the Arae. They cannot even touch the Arae. That's forbidden to keep the balance. It wouldn't have crossed Nyktos' mind. I doubt it would've even crossed Kolis's, and he usually has no care for rules, whatsoever."

"We need to find Nyktos," I said, looking between the two of them. "He needs to know about these reborn and Odetta."

"Do you know where he is in Lethe?" Aios asked as she started walking. I followed.

"I do, but I'm on guard duty."

"Then we take her with us." Aios looked over at me. "You're going to behave yourself, right?"

I sighed. "I don't understand why everyone expects me to do something—" I cut myself off as both of them looked at me. "You know what? Don't even answer that question. I will behave myself."

"Nyktos is going to be so irritated," Bele muttered as we reached the spiral staircase and started down the steps.

That he would be. I didn't want to return to my chambers, to be left with my thoughts and the hollowness I felt, but… "How much trouble will you be in?"

"None once he hears what we have to say." Her palm glided over the smooth railing.

"You only say that because you've never done anything to anger him."

"True." Aios laughed as we rounded the first floor and the vast foyer came into view. "But what's the worst he will do?"

Bele snorted. "His disappointment alone is unbearable—"

The massive doors to the foyer swung open without warning, slamming into the thick shadowstone walls.

Bele jerked to a halt in front of me, throwing out her arm and blocking Aios from going any farther. "What the hell?"

I stopped behind them as a figure walked through the opened doors. Everything in me stilled as I took in the faint, radiant aura surrounding *her*.

The goddess, Cressa.

Chapter 42

Cressa wore a different gown, one the color of the peonies that had been scattered across the Sun Temple's dais. Under the bright light of the chandelier, the fabric was nearly translucent. I could see the indent of her navel, the darker hue of the tips of her breasts, the—

Okay, I saw a lot of her.

What I saw didn't matter. That bitch had been there when Madis slaughtered that babe. My hand slipped to my right thigh, only to come up empty.

"What in the hell are you doing here?" Bele demanded.

Cressa's gaze swept toward the stairs, her rosy lips curving into a smile. "Bele," she said, and I saw red at the sound of her voice. "It's been a while." Her chin tipped down. "Aios? Is that you? You look…well. I'm sure Kolis will be thrilled to hear."

Aios stiffened, then everything happened fast. Cressa threw up her hand, and there was a flash of intense, silvery light. Eather. The bolt of energy charged the air as it streaked toward the staircase. Bele pushed Aios aside as I snapped forward, grabbing her by the shoulder, but the blast of power ricocheted off the shadowstone.

"Aios!" I shouted as the eather smacked into her, forcing out a pained cry. The silvery energy rolled over half of her body in shimmery ripples from her stomach to her feet. The goddess crumpled, nearly taking me down with her as I fell back onto my ass.

Aios was limp in my arms, boneless, but the ember of life didn't pulse in my chest. "She's alive," I whispered hoarsely as I eased her onto her side. "She's alive—"

"Stay down," Bele ordered and then whipped around, gripping the railing. She launched herself over it, landing in a nimble crouch on the floor below.

I stayed low, one hand on Aios's shoulder, and peered through the railing. Bele rose, a silvery aura surrounding her as she stalked forward, sword in hand. I squeezed Aios's shoulder, hoping she could feel it, and then I began inching down the stairs, really wishing I had something better than a stupid butter knife. There were countless weapons in the chamber behind the thrones, but there was no way I could get to them unless I went back upstairs and took the other stairs. That would take too long. Anything could happen.

"I would love to play with you." Cressa remained where she was, arms at her sides. "But we really don't have time for that."

"Oh, you're going to fucking make time." Bele struck, thrusting out with the sword as a flare of eather left her other hand.

Cressa was shockingly fast, darting out of the way of both blows. She spun, grabbing and twisting Bele's arm. Bele dipped under it and kicked out, catching Cressa in the side. The goddess stumbled, letting out a husky laugh. "That hurt." She straightened, tossing back her mane of dark hair. "But not as much as this will."

"You're right. This will—" Bele jerked, her words cut off.

Cressa laughed again. "You were saying?"

For a moment, I wasn't sure what had happened, but I saw Bele look down. I followed her gaze to the…the tip of a dagger protruding from the center of her chest. Disbelief seized me as Bele's grip loosened on the sword and it fell to the floor with a thud that sounded like a crack of thunder. That dagger—oh, gods, it was shadowstone. It was deadly to a god if it pierced their heart or head, and that blade had to be close. It had to be right *there*. And there was no way Cressa had thrown it.

My head jerked around toward the atrium. I didn't see anyone, but someone else had to be here. Someone must have come in through one of the other entrances.

"Bitch," Bele whispered, staggering back.

"Thank you." Cressa smirked.

Bele turned to the stairs, going down to one knee. The ember in my chest warmed, causing my breath to catch. She was wounded. Badly. I knew that dagger had to come out. She would be virtually paralyzed, unable to heal and completely vulnerable, until someone removed it.

I had to get it out. I rose from where I was crouched, keeping an eye on Cressa while knowing there was someone out of my line of vision. Bele shook her head as she fell forward onto one hand, panting. "Get out—"

Cressa struck, her bare foot catching Bele under the chin and snapping her head to the side. The kick would've killed a mortal. It could've possibly snapped Bele's neck. She dropped forward, unconscious but in much worse shape than Aios. She wouldn't heal with that dagger in her. I *had* to get it out, and then I would shove it so deep into Cresa's heart, the bitch would choke on it.

Cressa's gaze shot to the stairwell. "Hello," she said, stepping over Bele, that mocking smile spreading across her lips. "You must be her. The mortal, would-be Consort to the Primal of Death. The entire realm has been wondering why he would choose a mortal, and I think we have our answer. Don't we, Madis?"

A rush of air stirred the wisps of hair at my temples. I spun as a blur came over the railing, landing behind me. I caught a brief glimpse of pale skin. A white tunic trimmed in gold. Amber eyes. Long, midnight hair—

Sharp, sudden pain exploded along the side of my head, and then there was nothing.

The shock of my body dropping to a hard floor jerked me back into consciousness. My eyes flew open to see a raised dais and two shadowstone thrones.

I turned my head slightly, wincing as a throbbing pain bounced inside my skull. I blinked, clearing the tiny bursts of white light from my eyes. Slowly, the forms of Aios and Bele came into focus. They were between two pillars, Aios on her side and Bele lying on her stomach, the dagger still protruding from her back. They had been dragged in here.

"She's awake," a female spoke. "You obviously didn't hit her all that hard."

Cressa.

I flipped onto my back, ignoring the flare of pain radiating down my spine.

"Well, I did drop her onto the floor." Madis leaned against a pillar, arms crossed over his chest. "You should be grateful I didn't accidentally kill her, considering how weak mortals are."

"But is she really all that mortal?" Cressa countered. My stomach twisted as she was suddenly before me, thick black hair cascading over her shoulders. "Are you?"

I gingerly sat up, curling my right leg toward me. I swallowed hard, trying to ease the dryness in my throat. "Last time I checked, I was mortal."

Cressa smiled just enough to reveal the tips of her fangs. "No. If it's you we've been looking for, I'm not so sure about that."

A wave of unease shuttled through me as she rose and drifted back several steps.

"But if you're not? Well, our bad." Cressa looked down at me with pitiless golden eyes. "We'll find out soon enough if you were what the *viktors* were protecting."

"*Viktors*?" I glanced over at Bele and Aios. Was there a way I could get to them—to Bele, at least, to remove the dagger? I would have a far better chance doing that than attempting to make it to the chamber behind the thrones.

Cressa arched a brow.

"He needs to get here soon." Madis looked at the mouth of the throne room. "Nyktos and the others will only be distracted for so long."

My heart turned over heavily. "What did you do?"

"Led a couple of dozen Shades into the city," Cressa said, and I felt my stomach pitch. "That escalated far quicker than I thought it would. He'll be busy for some time, cleaning up that mess."

Good gods, I didn't even want to think about the kind of horror the Shades would bring down on the people. But Nyktos had to know—he had to feel my emotions, wouldn't he? Had I felt anything extreme? I didn't think so, and for the first time, I cursed my inability to feel true terror easily. I glanced at Bele again.

"Don't even think it, mortal," Cressa warned.

My gaze shot up to her. "I have a name."

"Do I look like I give a fuck?"

"Do I look like I give a fuck that you don't?" I shot back.

Her head tilted, and her eyes narrowed. She took a step forward.

Madis unfolded his arms, and I tensed as he pushed off the pillar. "Careful. If it's her, and you kill her, you're going to wish you were dead."

"Gods, I hope it's not you," Cressa sneered, but I wasn't paying attention to her.

They didn't want me dead. I thought about what Gemma had said about Kolis and the missing Chosen that had come back *different*. "Why does it matter if I live or die?" I asked, drawing my other leg up. I shifted forward. If they couldn't kill me, then I could make a run for Bele.

"You'll find out soon enough," Madis replied. "But trust me when I say you better hope it's not you. Whatever Cressa wants to do with you—and she has a very active imagination…"

"I do," Cressa confirmed.

"Will pale in comparison to what awaits you," Madis finished.

"Did you all plan to say that?" I said. "I bet you two spent eons waiting for the perfect moment to be embarrassingly cliché."

Cressa's lips thinned. "You're going to test me, aren't you?" Her gaze flicked up, beyond me. "*Finally*."

I looked over my shoulder to the entrance of the throne room and saw gold. Hair and skin like sunlight, eyes like two citrine jewels.

It was a tall god with golden hair and eyes that matched. He strode into the throne room, his long legs encased in black, the white shirt he wore left untied at the neck. A smile appeared as he spotted me. "Well, hello," he drawled, and I tensed. The god knelt in front of me. His gaze swept over my features.

"What do you think, Taric?" Cressa demanded.

This was the third god. They were all here.

"I think you finally succeeded." He stared, reaching for me. "Hell, just like he described. This has—"

I reacted without thought, unsheathing the butter knife when he gripped my arm. Twisting into Taric, I thrust the knife as hard as I could—

The impact of the knife meeting the flesh of his chest rattled the bones in my hand and arm. The knife snapped in *two*. My mouth dropped open as I jerked the ruined blade back. I'd known it wouldn't do much damage, but I hadn't thought it would do *that*. Good gods… I lifted my gaze to Taric's.

"Was that a butter knife? Really?" A fair brow arched. "Did that make you feel better?"

I swung again, aiming the broken end at his eye.

Taric caught my wrist, twisting sharply. I gritted my teeth at the bite of pain. My fingers spasmed open. The useless knife slipped from my hand.

"She's a fighter," Taric commented, placing his palm against the side of my head as I went to jab with my elbow. "*Stop.*"

My elbow connected with the underside of his jaw, snapping his head back. Cressa laughed as Taric grunted. He jerked his head straight, eyes flared wide. "I said *stop*," he commanded.

I pulled back, attempting to gain enough space between us so I could use my legs—

The god cursed under his breath and rose, gripping my shoulders and yanking me to my feet. I tore free, backing up. I took a quick look around to make sure the other gods weren't near. They remained by the pillars.

Taric sighed. "You really want to try this?"

"No," I admitted, bracing myself. "But I will."

I struck first, but he caught my wrist and pushed—pushed hard. I flew backward, skidding across the floor. I hit a stone pillar with enough force to knock the air out of me.

"You're just delaying the inevitable," Madis commented from the sidelines as Taric stalked toward me.

Pushing off the wall, I spun and kicked out, aiming for his knee, but where he'd been was now nothing but empty space. I stumbled, barely stopping myself from falling.

"You cannot fight me."

I whirled, finding the god standing behind me. Shooting forward, I swept up with my fist—

He was gone again.

"And this is getting boring already."

Catching myself, I spun once more. He again stood in the middle of the room, arms folded across his chest. Now I was starting to get angry. Kicking off the wall, I gained speed and pushed into the air—

Arms snagged me from behind, and a frustrated shriek left me. "I am a *god*."

"Congratulations," I snapped, throwing my head back. I connected with his face. The blow sent another pulse of pain through me, and I swung my legs out—

Taric let go.

I fell, twisting at the last second so I landed on my knees. I popped to my feet and turned. The god gripped me by the throat, lifting me. His fingers dug into my skin as I kicked out. He pushed forward, slamming my back into a pillar. I sucked in a breath of pain when he lifted me off the floor and planted his forearm against my chest. He pressed in with his body, pinning me so we were at eye level.

"Look at me," he demanded, and his voice…gods, there was something about his voice. It crawled over my skin, trying to find a way in. "*Look at me.*"

I *felt* his voice digging into me with razor-sharp nails and brushing against my mind, demanding that I obey. That I do whatever he requested. And a part of me wanted to cave to it. But I fought the urge—

"Interesting." Curiosity filled Taric's tone as he gripped my chin, forcing my eyes to his. "The compulsion is not working on her."

"It has to be her," Cressa exclaimed. "Let's take her and get the hell out of here—"

"We need to be sure." Taric's hand slipped away from my throat and curved around my chin. "And there is one way I can confirm it."

"You know it's her," Cressa argued, coming forward. "You're just being greedy. Stupid."

"Possibly." Taric smiled, baring his fangs. My heart stuttered at the sight of them. "But I always wondered what the *graeca* would taste like." He jerked my head to the side roughly. "Seems like someone else already found out." His laugh hit my throat. "Oh, the King will be so very displeased by that."

There was no warning, no time to prepare. He struck, sinking his fangs into the same spot Nyktos had. He pierced my skin, and it *hurt*. The pain was hot, scalding my senses as he drew deeply on my blood, tugging harder than I thought possible. It didn't ease. It didn't become something heated and sensual. It was an endless, throbbing pain that sank even deeper with each wave, going past my skin to my blood and bone. Panic exploded in my gut as I struggled against Taric, but the god was too strong. And he was fastened to the side of my neck.

My entire body went stiff against the wall as mental fingers scratched at my mind and then sank deeper, clawing at me—digging into my thoughts, my memories, into the very core of my being. I didn't know how he was doing it, but he was peeling back layers, seeing what I saw, hearing words I'd spoken and those others had said to me. He was amid my thoughts—

Pain exploded, this time *inside* my head, deep and throbbing. It felt like my skull was being shattered. A scream tore through me. Starbursts flooded my vision as my throat sealed off, silencing the scream. Agony fired down my spine, burning through my nerve endings. I couldn't breathe through it, couldn't think, or hide from it. There was no veil to retreat into, no empty vessel or blank canvas to become. The pain settled deep in me, taking root, and tearing me apart. A metallic taste pooled in the back of my mouth. Pure terror dug in its claws. Nyktos was wrong. I *could* be terrified. I was right then. I couldn't take this. My fingers dug into Taric's skin. I couldn't take—

The clawing, digging *touch* retreated suddenly. Taric jerked away, and I didn't even feel the painful withdrawal of his fangs or when I hit the floor. I lay there on my side, eyes wide and muscles spasming, over and over as the fire faded from my skin and eased from my muscles.

"Is it her?" Cressa demanded, sounding first far away and then closer with each word.

My vision cleared as the burning sensation left my blood, and my muscles loosened. Dragging in air, I curled my fingers against the floor as the fiery pain still burned from my neck and chest.

"Oh, gods, it is," Taric exhaled. "But this is far more…" He staggered to the side, looking down. "What in the hell?"

The floor was *vibrating*. I watched the darkness gather in the alcoves and peel away from the walls, racing across the floor toward the entryway. I tried to lift my head, but the muscles of my neck were like limp noodles. A blast of thunder shook the entire *palace*. No. That wasn't thunder. That was a *roar*. A draken.

A gust of icy wind whirled through the chamber, the air charging with power.

Taric took a step back and turned to the front of the room as the air crackled and hissed. Pulling every ounce of energy I had in me, I sat up, leaning heavily against the pillar. Panting, I inhaled sharply, and the scent…the citrusy, fresh scent reached me. My breath hitched.

Nyktos.

The churning mass of shadows appeared in the archway of the chamber, and what I saw looked nothing like the Nyktos I knew.

His skin was the color of midnight streaked with the silver of eather, as hard as the stone the palace had been built from and just as smooth. The flesh swirled all over, making it difficult to see if his features were the same. The twin, sweeping arcs behind him were no longer wings of smoke and shadow but solid and similar to those of a draken, except his were a seething mass of silver and black. Power sparked from his eyes—eyes filled with so much eather, no irises or pupils were visible.

This was what I had seen glimpses of. What existed beneath the skin of a Primal. And he was terrifying and beautiful.

Nyktos rose into the air, wings stretched wide, arms at his sides, hands open, and eather dancing across his palms. "On your knees," he commanded. "*Now.*"

Chapter 43

All three gods dropped to one knee before Nyktos, their heads bowed in submission. They didn't hesitate.

"You dare to enter my Court?" Nyktos' voice boomed through the chamber, shaking the entire palace. I saw Aios stir out of the corner of my eye, but I couldn't take my eyes off him. He drifted forward, his wings moving silently. "And touch what is mine?"

"We didn't have a choice." Cressa gasped as wind poured through the ceiling, whipping her hair around. She lifted her head. Her skin had turned the shade of bleached bone. "We—"

"We all have a choice," Nyktos growled.

Cressa was jerked backward and then up into the air. I caught a glimpse of Aios sitting up and scrambling toward Bele as Cressa's body stiffened. Her mouth stretched wide in a silent scream, and just like with the guards at Wayfair, Nyktos didn't need to lay a finger on her. Deep, unforgiving cracks appeared in once smooth cheeks. She didn't crumble slowly. She exploded, shattering into a fine, shimmering dust.

"And you chose wrong," Nyktos said, his head snapping toward Madis. "Join your sister."

The god turned, but a shadow came in through the open ceiling—a large, gray-and-black shadow. *Nektas.* The draken landed on his forelegs, his front talons slamming down on the edge of the dais. His wings swept over the thrones as he stretched his long neck forward. The thick frills around his head vibrated as he opened his mouth. Silver fire poured from it, swallowing Madis within seconds.

When the fire receded, there was nothing where Madis had stood. Not even ash.

Hands touched my arm, startling me. My head jerked around to see Saion crouched there. "Are you okay?" His concerned gaze fell to my throat. "Sera?"

"Yeah," I said hoarsely, seeing now that Nyktos hadn't arrived alone. Ector and Rhain were coming through the alcoves, swords in hand. "Bele." I turned my head to where she and Aios lay on the other side. I felt a flare in my chest, one that turned my skin cold. Bele was on her back, the dagger lying on the floor. Aios was bent over her, clasping the other goddess's face.

Nektas's rumble of warning snapped my head around. Taric was on his feet, the trace of eather inside him erupting from within, whirling down the bare skin of his biceps and forearm, crackling and spitting silver sparks. The light swirled out from his palm, stretching and solidifying, taking the shape of a…*sword.*

A weapon of pure eather.

Good gods.

"Really?" Nyktos sounded *bored.* He descended fast, landing in front of Taric in the span of a heartbeat. His wings tucked back as his hand clamped down on Taric's wrist. The sword jutted out to the side, spitting and crackling. "You should know better than to try to use eather on me." His voice was so cold, so full of shadows. "All you're doing is pissing me off."

The glow of eather faded from Taric, the sword collapsing into nothing. The god stood there, his skin paler under the shimmer of gold. "Do you even know what you have here?" He started to turn his head toward me.

"Don't look at her. If you do, you will not like what happens next." Letting go of Taric's wrist, he folded his hand around the god's throat, forcing his head away from me. "And I know exactly what I have."

"Then you should know that he will stop at nothing to get to her," Taric sneered, his gaze tipping toward me once more.

"Oh, man, this is going to be bad," Saion murmured.

"What did I say about looking at her?" Nyktos questioned softly—too softly. A shiver tiptoed down my spine. Taric's entire body jerked as a hoarse shout parted his lips. Red filled the whites of his eyes. I shrank back against Saion, smacking a hand over my mouth as blood poured from the god's eyes. Taric let out a high-pitched whine as his eyes…*melted,* streaming down his cheeks in thick globs.

"Can't say I didn't warn you," Nyktos said.

I shuddered, bile crowding my throat. I'd never seen anything like that. I never wanted to see anything like that again.

"Fuck," Taric rasped, trembling. "Kill me. Go ahead and do it, *Blessed One*. It won't matter. He won't stop. He'll tear apart both realms. You of all people should know." Taric kicked his head back, baring blood-streaked teeth as he laughed. "Kill me. Take my soul. It will be nothing compared to what he does to you because you can't stop him. Neither could your father. He'll have her—" Taric howled as his entire body spasmed.

At first, I didn't know what'd happened, and then I saw Nyktos' wrist flush against Taric's navel. His hand…

His hand was *inside* the god.

He dragged his hand up Taric's stomach, carving straight through flesh. Shimmery, bluish-red blood spilled down the front of the god's shirt. The sounds…the sounds he made…

Nyktos leaned in, speaking directly into Taric's ear. "You underestimate me if you think I can't do worse to you." The Primal smiled then, and my skin iced over. "I can smell her blood on your lips. There is nothing that I will not do to you because of that."

Taric's body stiffened as Nyktos' hand sliced straight up the center of his chest, cutting through his heart. Nyktos twisted his hand and then jerked it free. Taric fell forward, hitting the gathering pool of blood with a fleshy smack.

I barely breathed as the Primal turned around. Those all-white eyes landed on me. Our gazes connected. Saion's grip on my arms tightened and then loosened as Nyktos' chest rose. The shadows trailing along his legs evaporated as the eather receded from his eyes.

In a heartbeat, Nyktos was kneeling before me. He appeared as I knew him. Flesh a warm, golden bronze, and no wings. Eather still whirled madly through his eyes, and his skin thinned when he took in the throbbing side of my throat. He lifted his hand—his blood-soaked hand. I sucked in an unsteady breath.

Nyktos halted, his fingers inches from my face. His gaze flew to mine. He lowered his hand. "I won't hurt you," he said. "Ever."

I swallowed. "I know." And I did know that. I *always* knew that, but the words…they just spilled out of me as I locked stares with him. It was like Saion wasn't behind me, still holding my arms. "But I was. I—I was *terrified*. That god. Taric. He did something. He got into my head and saw me. He saw everything, and it—" I sucked in air, feeling pressure clamp down on my chest.

"I know. He went through your memories. Not all gods can do it," he said. "It's a brutal way of discovering what you want to know. He didn't have to bite you to do it, but it's always painful regardless." The lines around his mouth tightened as his gaze searched mine. This time, he lifted his other hand and cupped my cheek. His hand was still warm. "Don't forget, Sera. You are not afraid. You may feel fear, but you are *never* afraid."

Letting out a ragged breath, I nodded and then felt something hard brush my fingers. I looked down to see Nyktos pressing the hilt of the shadowstone dagger into my palm. The one he had given me and then took away. My fingers twitched and then closed over the hilt. I looked up at him. He said nothing as his hand slipped away. Having the weapon in my hand brought forth a sense of calm, easing the tightening in my chest and clearing my thoughts. I knew it said something that he'd given it to me. Not that he trusted me now, but it was as if he knew I needed it. Knew it calmed me. And it meant something that he'd given it back. It meant a lot.

"Thank you," I whispered, and Nyktos closed his eyes. His features tensed—

"Nyktos," Rhain called, his voice sounding as if it were full of gravel.

Opening his eyes, Nyktos looked over his shoulder. "What…?" He trailed off, rising slowly. "No."

I saw Ector first. He was pale, eyes strangely glassy in the starlight. Then I noticed Aios, rocking back and forth, her cheeks damp. *The pulse.* I'd felt it. Slowly, I lowered my gaze to Bele. She was too still, too pale. My heart clenched as I pitched forward.

"No," Nyktos repeated, walking stiffly toward them.

"The dagger was in her too long. Or it hit her heart when they moved us," Aios said, her voice shaking. "She was fighting it. I saw her fighting it. She didn't—" A ragged sound silenced the rest of her words.

Nyktos lowered himself beside Bele. He said nothing as he touched her cheek. His chest rose. There was no breath and no words, but the pain was etched into his features, brutal and heartbreaking.

A soft trilling sound drew my gaze to Nektas. He remained on the dais, lowering his head between his front talons. Red eyes met mine.

"I…I can help her," I said, my heart speeding up.

Nyktos shook his head. "You have an ember of life in you. That is not enough to bring back a god."

I rose, swaying slightly. Saion was there, his hands still on my arms. "I can try."

The Primal shook his head.

"Can't she try?" Aios said, her breath catching in a shudder. "If it doesn't work, it doesn't. And if there's a ripple of power, we can be prepared. We have to try."

My steps were unsteady, weak, but I felt the ember warming in my chest, throbbing. "I want to try." I lowered myself beside Nyktos. Only then did Saion let go. "I need to try. They came for me. She died because of me."

Nyktos' head snapped in my direction. "She did not die because of you. Do not take that on yourself," he ordered. A moment passed, and then his gaze flicked beyond me to others I hadn't known were in the chamber. "Make sure the guards on the Rise are ready for…well, for anything." He looked to Nektas.

The draken lifted his head, calling out. That staggered, high pitched sound echoed throughout the chamber and was then answered. A shadow fell over the opening in the ceiling, and then another as nearby draken took flight.

"Try," Nyktos said.

Drawing in a deep breath, I set the dagger on the floor beside me and placed my hands on Bele's arm. Her skin had turned shockingly cold. I didn't know if that had anything to do with her being a god, but it felt strange under my fingers. The hum of the eather coursed through my blood, hitting my skin. A soft glow stretched out from under the sleeves of my sweater to cover my hands. *Live,* I thought. *Live.* I wanted it to work. I wasn't sure that Bele even liked me, but she had tried to defend me. She hadn't stepped aside and let the gods take me. She didn't deserve to die like this, and…

And *Ash* didn't deserve to have another drop of blood inked into his skin.

Live.

The silvery light washed over Bele and then seeped into her skin, lighting her veins until I could no longer see her underneath the glow. Nothing happened. Aios lowered her head, shoulders shaking, because nothing had—

The glow flared and then expanded, rolling out from Bele in a wave, an intense, powerful aura that became a shockwave. Wind roared around us, tugging at my clothing and hair. The floor shook—everything rattled as a bolt of light streaked across the sky above the open ceiling. *Lightning.* I'd never seen lightning here.

The aura faded. The wind and shaking ceased.

Nektas made that soft trilling sound again, and Bele's chest rose deeply as if she were drawing in a deep breath. I lifted my hands, too afraid that I was seeing things. But her eyes twitched. Lashes fluttered up, revealing eyes the color of starlight, bright and silver.

"Holy shit," Rhain whispered.

Nyktos jerked, placing a hand on the crown of her head. "Bele?"

Her throat worked on a swallow. "Nyktos?" she whispered hoarsely.

It worked.

Thank the gods, it had worked.

A shudder of relief went through the Primal and me and then the entire chamber. Aios snapped forward, picking up Bele's hand, holding it tightly between hers.

"How are you feeling?" Nyktos asked, his voice rough.

"Tired? Really tired. But okay, I think." Confusion filled her voice as she looked over at me. "Did you…did you try to stab that bastard with a butter knife?"

"Yes," I said, the word coming out as a laugh. "Didn't work too well."

"Crazy," she whispered, swallowing again. "I…saw it."

"Saw what?" He smoothed a hand over her forehead.

Her eyes closed. "Light," she whispered. "Intense light and…Arcadia. I saw Arcadia."

I clasped both of my hands together, holding them to my chest as Bele's muscles relaxed, and her breathing deepened.

"Bele?" Nyktos called, taking his hand from her cheek. There was no answer.

"Is she all right?" Aios asked.

"She sleeps," Nyktos replied, staring down at the goddess. Several long moments passed. "That is all."

"That is all?" echoed Ector. His laugh was abrupt. "That is not all." He was on his knees, the eather pulsing intently behind his pupils as he focused on me—as he stared at me with a mixture of awe and fear.

Slowly, Nyktos faced me. "What you did is impossible. An ember of life shouldn't have been enough for what you did," he breathed, searching my features as if he were looking for something. "You didn't just bring her back. You…you Ascended her."

Chapter 44

I found myself in Nyktos' office for the first time, and as I suspected, it had the bare minimum, just like his bedchamber.

His desk was massive, made of some sort of dark wood that glinted with a hint of red in the lamplight, the narrow lamp the only item on the desk. One chair sat behind the desk, and the only furniture in the room was a credenza, an end table, and the settee I was sitting on. The lounge was a light gray color and thickly cushioned. I felt as if I were sinking into the seat. Like it could swallow me whole as I stared at the empty bookshelves lining the walls.

Nyktos was checking in on Bele, who had been placed in a chamber on the second floor. I wasn't sure how much time had passed, but there had been no alarms from the Rise alerting us to an impending attack. That didn't mean any of us relaxed. Saion couldn't stand still, moving from one side of the room to the other every couple of minutes. Ector did the same, walking in and out of the office. Both kept stealing glances at me—nervous ones. I looked over at Ector, who now stood inside the office. He stared at me and then quickly averted his gaze.

"Can I ask you two something?" I said, wincing a little at the soreness in my throat.

Saion turned, facing me. "Sure."

"Are you scared of me?"

Ector's head jerked up. He said nothing. Neither did Saion for a long moment, but he finally spoke as he stared at the shadowstone dagger Nyktos had returned to me. I had placed it on the arm of the settee, within hand's reach. "What you did in there should be impossible."

I drew in a shallow breath, tucking my legs close to my chest as I sank further into the cushions.

I hadn't just brought Bele back to life.

I'd *Ascended* her.

"Why would that make you scared of me?" I asked.

"We're not scared," Ector answered, leaning against the open doorframe. "We are…unnerved. Unsettled. Disturbed. Un—"

"Got it," I cut him off. "What I don't understand is why it makes you all feel any of that. I couldn't have Ascended her." A limp curl fell across my face. "I don't even fully understand what that means for a god."

Saion took a step forward and stopped. "Normally? If this were hundreds of years ago and a Primal of Life Ascended a god? It would mean—what is the right word?" He glanced at Ector. "It means entering a new stage of life. A transition."

"What kind of transition? What can a god transition into?" As soon as I said that, my heart dropped. I remembered what Nyktos had told me. Primals were once gods. "She's a Primal now?"

"No," Ector said and then frowned. "At least, I don't think she is. Her eyes changed. They were brown before. You saw them. They're silver now. Just like a Primal. And that shockwave of energy that came out of her. That's what happens when a god Ascends. But she's not a Primal."

"*But* she's no longer just a god," Saion said, crossing his arms. "There was a shift when she breathed; when she came back. A burst of energy I felt. We all felt it. I'm willing to bet she's more powerful now. I wasn't around when the Primals Ascended but…"

I looked at Ector. "You were."

He nodded slowly, his jaw working as he crossed the room and leaned against the desk. "That's what it felt like. That energy. Not as huge as when a Primal enters Arcadia and a new Primal rises. I don't think it would've been felt in the mortal realm, but it was something. She may not be a Primal, but she's Ascended, and that's a big deal. A very unexpected big deal."

I sensed that there was more to it. "And a bad thing?"

"For the Primal Hanan it could be," Nyktos answered, coming

through the open doors and startling me. My gaze cut to him. He'd changed his shirt and now wore a loose white one untied at the neck and untucked. He was weaponless, but what weapons did he need? "Bele Ascending means that she could challenge his position of authority over the Court of Sirta, and he would've felt that."

My stomach flipped as I slowly shook my head. Hanan was the Primal of the Hunt and Divine Justice. "I don't know what to say."

"There's nothing to be said. You brought her back." Nyktos approached me, stopping a few feet away. The wisps of eather in his eyes were faint tendrils. "Thank you."

I opened my mouth but came up empty for several moments. "Is she…she's okay still?"

"She sleeps. I'm beginning to think that's common after such an act, as Gemma did the same." His gaze lowered. "You haven't cleaned up?"

Nyktos had ordered that I be placed here, so that's where I'd been. He seemed to remember that because he stiffened and then looked at Ector. "Can you grab me a clean towel and a small bowl of water from the kitchen?"

Ector nodded, pushing away from the desk. Nyktos remained where he stood. "Aios is with Bele, but she told me what Gemma shared with you all."

"Good." To be honest, I had already forgotten everything that Gemma had shared and what I'd realized afterward. "Did she tell you about Odetta?"

"She did."

"Can we speak with her?"

"She passed too recently for that," he said, and disappointment seized me. His features softened. "Her death and new beginning are far too recent. It could cause her to yearn for life, which would disrupt her peace."

"I understand." A bittersweet emotion swept through me. I would've liked to have seen her, but I didn't want to risk her—wait. My eyes narrowed on him. "You're doing it again."

"Sorry," he murmured, turning as Ector returned, carrying a small white towel and a bowl. "Thank you."

The god nodded. "I'll wait for Nektas." He pivoted and then stopped, turning back to me. His gaze met mine as he placed his hand over his heart and bowed at the waist. "Thank you for what you did for Bele. For all of us."

I went completely still.

"You're surprised by his gratitude?" Nyktos asked, placing the bowl on the table beside the untouched glass of whiskey someone had poured for me. "And I'm not reading your emotions. Your mouth is hanging open."

I snapped it shut as I watched him wet the end of the towel and then kneel in front of me. "What are you doing?"

"Cleaning you up."

"I can do that." I started to reach for the towel as Saion moved to stand by the door.

"I know." He knelt in front of me. "But I want to do it."

My heart—my foolish, silly heart—leapt. And if I were alone, I would've punched myself in the chest. This desire of his was likely born of gratitude. Not forgiveness. Not understanding. I lowered my hands to my lap. "So…um, why is Ector waiting on Nektas?"

"Because just in case Odetta *did* know something, I summoned the Fates—the Arae."

My heart skipped. "I thought the Primals couldn't command the Arae?"

"That's why I've summoned them. They may not answer, and if they don't, I cannot force them to."

I exhaled slowly. "Do…you think Odetta knew something? That the Fates were involved?"

"It's possible." He carefully brushed aside the half-undone braid. "The Arae usually move unseen, but…"

I peeked up at him. His jaw had hardened, and the eather burned brighter in his eyes. He stared at my throat, lines bracketing his mouth.

"He will burn in the Abyss for all eternity." His gaze flicked to mine and then shifted away as he gently dabbed at the wound. "Odetta could've known something about the Fates being involved." He refocused. "As we've witnessed recently, stranger things have happened. Either way, we'll know within a couple of hours if the Arae will answer."

I desperately tried to ignore the brush of his fingers and his fresh, citrusy scent. "How do you think Kolis or Hanan will respond to this ripple of power?"

Nyktos appeared to mull that over. "Honestly? Kolis had to know that Taric and the other gods had come. By now, I'm sure he realizes they are dead. Bele's Ascension will probably have left him and the other Primals…unsettled."

"She doesn't like that word," Saion commented.

I shot him an arch look.

Nyktos moved onto a new section of the towel, dunking it into the water. "I think Kolis may hold off for a bit until he can figure out what he is dealing with."

"And Hanan? How do you think he will react?"

"Hanan is old. He knows the truth about Kolis and my father." He brushed the towel over the wound, and I jerked a little at the fleeting burst of biting pain. His gaze flew to mine. "Sorry."

"It's fine," I whispered, feeling my cheeks warm. "It's nothing."

Nyktos stared at me for a long moment and then returned to cleaning the blood from my neck. "Hanan keeps to himself. I don't know his thoughts on Kolis, but it is unlikely that he will be thrilled by what he felt. Bele *will* be a threat to him. The other Primals will worry about the possibility of something occurring to them, as well."

"Would that happen to any god I brought back?"

"That's a good question," Saion chimed in. "I'm thinking probably not? Like a god would have to be primed for it. Possibly already fated to Ascend."

"Agreed," Nyktos said. "Though, we can't be sure when we don't really even know how it was possible."

"But why would it not have been possible?" I wondered. "Death is death. Life is life. Aren't gods and mortals alike in that sense in a way?"

One side of his lips curved up, and every part of my being affixed to his faint grin. It faded too quickly. "But it's not. A god is an entirely different being, and it requires a lot of power to do that. *A lot.*" He rose, picking up the bowl. "Did Taric or the gods say anything to you?"

I thought over what they'd said as Nyktos placed the bowl and towel on the desk, my thoughts going to those they'd slayed.

"What?" Nyktos turned back to me.

"Like you said after you learned about the ember, I think they were searching for me in Lasania. Or searching for the ripple of power," I told him. "They said they'd find out if it was me these *viktors* were protecting."

"*Viktors.*" Nyktos glanced at Saion and shook his head. "Been a long time since I've heard of them."

"Same." Saion frowned as he studied me. "But it kind of makes sense if she had *viktors*, especially depending on what exactly your father did."

"They are…mostly mortal, born to serve one purpose," Nyktos

explained, sitting beside me. "To guard a harbinger of great change or purpose. Some are not aware of their duty, but they serve nonetheless through numerous mechanisms of fate—like being at the right place at the right time or introducing the one they've been destined to oversee to someone else. Others are aware and are part of the life of the one they're protecting. Sometimes, they're called guardians. In all the time I've heard of them, I've never known there to be more than one to protect any given person."

"And do you think that the mortals killed by those gods were these *viktors*?"

"It's possible. It's not easy for a god or Primal to sense them. They'd have marks, just like godlings and descendants of gods have," Nyktos explained. "You'd have to suspect that they could be that to even sense for it. And I…I didn't."

And why would he at the time? All he knew was that his father had made this deal. He hadn't known what his father had done. "And by *mostly mortal*, what do you mean?"

"He means they're neither mortal nor god. But they are eternal, like the Fates," Saion said.

My brows lifted. "Well, that clarifies everything."

Saion smirked. "They are born into their roles, much like a mortal is born, but their souls have lived many lives."

"Reincarnated like Sotoria?" I asked.

"Yes, and no." Nyktos leaned back. "They live like mortals, serving their purpose. They die either in the process of doing that or long after they have served, but when they die, their souls return to Mount Lotho, where the Arae are, and are given physical form once more. They remain there until it is their time once again."

"When they're reborn, they have no memory of their previous lives, only this calling that some may or may not figure out. It's a way for the Fates to keep the balance equal," Saion said. "But when they return to Mount Lotho, their memories of their lives return."

"All of their lives?"

The god nodded, and I blew out a long breath. That could be a lot of lives to remember—a lot of deaths and losses. But also a lot of joy. If the Kazin siblings were *viktors*, did they know their duty? What about Andreia or the ones whose names I did not know? What about the babe?

What if that was what Sir Holland was?

My breath snagged in my chest. Could he be a *viktor*? He'd

protected me by training me, and he never gave up. Never. And he knew about the potion. It…it made sense. And because it did, it made me want to cry.

I let my head fall back against the cushion. This was a lot to digest. It had been a lot in a short period of time.

"If you want to bathe or rest, there is time," Nyktos offered.

I glanced at him, feeling a tug in my chest as our gazes collided. "I would like to stay here until we know if the Fates will answer. I don't want…"

I didn't want to go back to my chamber. I didn't want to be alone. I had too much in my head—too much inside of me.

A silence fell over the room, and I closed my eyes. I didn't remember falling asleep, but I must've dozed off. The next thing I knew, I felt a soft touch on my cheek—a *poke*. Blinking open my eyes, I realized that my head was lying on Nyktos' thigh, and I was staring into the crimson-hued eyes of a young boy, maybe nine or ten years old with shaggy, sandy blond hair.

Crimson eyes with thin, vertical pupils.

"Hi," the child said.

"Hello," I whispered.

His head tilted, his small, elfin face perplexed. "I thought you were dead."

What the…?

"You're not."

"No?" At least, I didn't think I was.

"Both of you sleep," the boy stated with a nod of his head. "He didn't hear me enter. He *always* hears me."

Nyktos stirred, apparently hearing him then. His thigh tensed under my cheek.

Jerking sideways, I placed my hands on the cushions and unfurled my legs. The child watched me with a very serious expression for someone so young.

"Reaver," Nyktos said, voice rough with sleep. "What are you doing?"

I nearly choked on my breath as I stared at the light-haired boy, trying to reconcile the sight of him as a draken with that of a child. It was somehow odder than seeing Jadis briefly as a little girl.

"I was watching you all sleep," Reaver answered.

My lips pursed.

"I'm sure that's not the only thing you were doing," Nyktos

replied, leaning forward. Out of the corner of my eye, I saw his hair slide over his cheek. "You must have a reason for being in here."

"I do." He stood straight in his sleeveless tunic and loose pants, the same gray color as the tunics Nektas often wore. "Nektas sent me to get you. He's in the throne room."

"Okay. We'll be there in a minute."

Reaver nodded curtly and then glanced at me. "Bye."

"Bye." I gave him an awkward wave I wasn't even sure he saw as he darted from the room on small, fast legs. "He is…"

"Intense?"

A strangled laugh left me. "Yeah." I scooted to the edge of the settee. "Sorry," I mumbled, thinking he probably didn't appreciate me using him as a pillow. "About sleeping on you."

"It's okay," Nyktos said after a moment, and I looked over at him. He was staring ahead, his expression unreadable. "I didn't mean to sleep, but you needed the rest. Both of us did." He rose then, looking down at me. "If Nektas sent him, that means the Fates answered."

My heart tripped over itself, and I stood so rapidly I got dizzy. I stepped back, bumping into the settee.

Nyktos reached out, placing his hand on my arm. "Are you okay?"

"Yes."

His eyes searched mine. "Do you have a headache?"

"N-No. I think I just stood up too fast."

Nyktos stared down at me. "I think it's the blood." A muscle ticked along his jaw. "Too much has been taken from you. Your body hasn't had a chance to replenish."

"I'm fine," I insisted as I started to step away but stopped, taking in the tightness of his features. "Don't feel bad about feeding from me."

He was quiet.

"You needed the blood. I'm glad I could do that for you," I told him. "If I'm a little dizzy because of blood loss, that's on Taric. Not you."

Still, he said nothing.

I was starting to feel a bit foolish. Perhaps I had misread him. "Anyway, I just wanted to make that clear. We should get going—"

The only warning I got was the scent of citrus and fresh air. I hadn't even seen him close the distance between us, but I felt his palm against my cheek, and his mouth on mine in the same heartbeat.

Nyktos kissed me.

The feel of his lips—his *warm* lips—was a heady shock, and the way he tugged at my lower lip with his fangs sent tiny, hot shivers through me. I opened for him, kissing him back just as fiercely as his mouth moved against mine. The way he kissed me was hard, demanding. Claiming. He sent my senses spinning. I was dizzy again, but this time, it was all because of him. The kiss left me rattled, and I didn't want him to stop. I started to reach for him—

Nyktos lifted his mouth from mine and stepped back, his hand lingering on my cheek before falling away. He looked as shaken as I felt, his features stark, eyes a storm of eather, his chest moving in deep, rapid breaths.

"That…" Nyktos swallowed, briefly closing his eyes. When they reopened, the eather had slowed. "That changes nothing."

Nyktos' words lingered just like his kiss did as we left his office and walked to the throne room.

There was a twisting motion in my chest as if someone had reached inside and started squeezing my heart. But there was something else at my core. Something small and faint that reminded me of hope. I didn't know what to make of either emotion, but as we neared the chamber, I shoved those feelings aside to dwell on later.

Rhahar and Ector stood at the archway of the chamber. They were not alone. An unfamiliar man stood with them, his sandy-blond hair brushing broad shoulders adorned in a belted, light gray tunic. His face was weathered and sun-warmed. Beside him stood a goddess. I knew what she was at once. It was the ethereal quality of her features and the faint luminous glow under her light brown skin. Her hair was the color of honey, a few shades lighter than the gown she wore, and her eyes were the brightest blue I'd ever seen. As we approached, the man placed a hand over his heart and bowed at the waist, as did the goddess.

"Penellaphe?" Surprise filled Nyktos' tone.

"Hello, Nyktos." She straightened, stepping forward. She glanced briefly in my direction. "It's been a while since we've seen each other."

"Too long," he confirmed. "I hope all is well?"

"I am." Penellaphe's smile was brief, fading as she looked at me again.

Nyktos followed her gaze. "This is—"

"I know who she is," Penellaphe cut in, and my brows lifted. "She is why I'm here."

"I am?"

She nodded, looking back to Nyktos. "You summoned the Arae."

"I did, but…"

"But I am not the Arae. You'll understand why I've come," she said, stepping back. Her hands clasped together. "One of the Arae waits inside for you. For both of you."

Curiosity marked Nyktos' face as he looked over at me. I nodded and Penellaphe turned to the male. "Wait for us here?" she asked.

"Of course," he answered.

She inclined her head. "Thank you, Ward."

I peeked over at him as we passed. I couldn't tell if he was a godling or a mortal, but I didn't see any aura in his eyes. Rhahar and Ector moved aside as Penellaphe drifted past them. I picked up my pace as Nyktos glanced over his shoulder, his steps slowing. I caught up with him, entering the now-candlelit chamber.

Nektas approached us, his long hair tied back, and Reaver at his side.

"Thank you." Nyktos paused to clasp the draken's shoulder.

"We will wait for you in the hall," Nektas answered, nodding in my direction as he put a hand on the back of Reaver's head, ushering the young boy forward. "We will wait for both of you."

A knot formed in my throat. I didn't know why. Maybe it was because Nektas had acknowledged *me*. I swallowed hard, looking toward the thrones and the dais. Maybe I just needed more sleep or—

Everything in me stopped. My legs refused to move. My head emptied because what I was seeing—*who* I saw standing before the dais, cast in the soft light of the candles and the stars—brought me up short. It made no sense. None at all. My eyes had to be playing tricks on me.

Because it couldn't be Sir Holland.

Chapter 45

"I don't understand," I whispered, moving once more and then stopping a few feet from Sir Holland.

"You know him?" Nyktos had shifted closer as he stared down at the man before us.

"She does," Sir Holland confirmed, his dark eyes searching mine. "I've known her for most of her life."

"He trained me," I whispered. I wanted to touch him to see if he was real, to hug him, but I couldn't move. "It's Sir Holland. I don't understand how this is possible."

"You can just call me Holland," he told me. "That is my name."

"But you're…why are you here?" Confusion pounded through me as Penellaphe glided past him, entering the airy chamber. "Are you a *viktor*?"

"No. That honor is not mine," he said.

"He's here because he's a Spirit of Fate," Nyktos stated coldly. "He's an Arae. One who's apparently been masquerading as a mortal." He eyed Holland. "Now I understand how you had knowledge of a certain potion."

"He's not a spirit." To confirm this mostly for myself, I reached out and pressed a finger against the rich brown skin of his arm.

"Spirits of Fate—the Arae—are like gods." Nyktos reached over, pulling my hand away from Holland. "They are not like the spirits near your lake."

Holland's gaze followed Nyktos' hand, one side of his lips curving up.

Stunned, all I could do was stare. That pragmatic part of my mind kicked in. Out of everyone, Holland had always believed…he had always believed in me. His unwavering faith now made sense. It was still a shock, but after learning the truth about Kolis, I knew I could process this. I could *understand.* And the knowledge that he was okay helped. Tavius hadn't done something terrible to him. So many questions rose. Mainly, I wanted to ask if he'd always known that I could never fulfill my duty, but I recognized that now was so not the time for that. "So, you weren't sent to the Vodina Isles?"

"I was, but I didn't go," he answered. "I knew my time in the mortal realm had come to an end. I came here to wait."

"Because you knew we…we would come to speak to you?"

He nodded.

That was…well, *unnerving.* How much did Holland know? More than I probably wanted him to. I swallowed.

A thought occurred to me. "This is why you never seemed to age."

"It wasn't the liquor," he said.

"No shit," I murmured.

Penellaphe laughed as she came to stand beside Holland, the gown settling around her feet in a puddle of silk. "Is that what he said?"

I nodded, staring at the man I'd considered the closest thing to a friend. A man I'd trusted. Someone who wasn't mortal. I didn't know yet if I should feel betrayed or not. "There is…there has been a lot I haven't understood, but this, I really don't get."

"I think I might know," Nyktos said, drawing my gaze. He was watching Holland as if he were a few minutes away from pitching him through the open ceiling. "The nursemaid spoke the truth. The Arae had been present upon her birth and you, being one of the Arae, learned of the deal somehow and took the place of the one who was supposed to train her." He paused. "To kill me."

"To kill," Holland corrected.

"Did it not occur to you to inform her of the pointlessness behind that endeavor?" Nyktos demanded, and I was glad he'd brought it up.

"I couldn't. All I could do was train her."

"I should thank you for that part," Nyktos replied, and I could already tell that wouldn't happen. "But you're Arae. You're not allowed to intervene in fate."

"He didn't." The goddess smiled, and Nyktos shot her an

incredulous look. "Not technically," she amended.

"I never directly interfered," Sir Holland said, and I really needed to stop thinking of him as a knight when he was basically a *god*. "That's why I couldn't tell you who I was or that the Rot wasn't tied to the deal. If I did, then it would have been considered interference. I was pushing it when I gave you the tea."

"You were pushing it by even being around her. So, it sounds an awful lot like semantics." Nyktos folded his arms over his chest. "Does Embris know about this? Of your involvement?"

My heart skipped. *That* was why Nyktos didn't sound exactly thrilled by this reveal. If Embris knew, the Primal could tell Kolis about me.

"If I had truly intervened, he would have known. But he's currently unaware of the deal and who the source of power is."

"Wait. How is that possible?" I asked, realizing something I hadn't before. "If the Arae answer to his Court, how could he not know about the deal—about everything?"

"Because the Arae don't answer to Embris. They just live there," Nyktos explained, angling his body so that the side of his hips brushed my arm. "Fate answers to no Primal."

"Unless we overstep," Holland tacked on. "By *directly* interfering."

I had to agree with Nyktos that it sounded like semantics, but I had more pressing questions. "Why did you even get involved? You were with me for so long. The number of years…" Did he not have a family? Friends? Those he missed? Or had he gone back and forth?

"It was a long time," Penellaphe spoke up. "Those years were a very long time."

"I did it because I knew I needed to. It wasn't easy, being gone for so long and so often, but this was bigger than me. Bigger than all of us." Holland leaned against a pillar and lifted his gaze to Nyktos. "I did it because I knew your father. I knew him when he was the true Primal of Life. I considered him a friend."

I glanced up at Nyktos, but nothing could be gained from his expression. "Did you know what was to become of him?" he asked.

Holland shook his head. "No. The Arae cannot see the fate of a risen Primal." Grief crept into his voice. "If I could have, I don't know if I would still be sitting here today. I don't…I don't think I could've sat by and done nothing."

My brows knitted together. "You would've intervened? What is the punishment for that?"

"Death," Nyktos answered. "The final kind."

I shuddered as my gaze swung back to him. Fear rose. "Is it okay that you're here?" I felt the brush of Nyktos' fingers against mine. The touch surprised me, but the soft hum of contact was calming. "Should you leave?"

"The Arae can do nothing to intervene in your fate," Penellaphe advised. "Not anymore."

Her words…they felt like an omen, leaving me chilled.

"Then you know why we summoned you. Can you tell us why my father did this?" Nyktos asked. "Why he would put such power into a mortal bloodline—what he hoped to accomplish from that?"

"The better question is *what* your father did exactly," Holland countered. "As you know, your father was the true Primal of Life. Kolis couldn't take *everything*. That would be impossible. Embers of life still remained in Eythos, just as embers of death remained in Kolis. And when you were conceived, part of that ember passed onto you. Just a flicker of the power. Not as strong as the ember that remained in your father, but enough."

Nyktos shook his head. "No," he said. "I never had that ability. I have always been this—"

"You wouldn't have known if you had that ember until you went through the Culling. But your father took that ember from you before Kolis could learn that you had it in you," Holland explained. "Eythos knew that Kolis would've seen you as even more of a threat. One that his brother would've extinguished."

Nyktos' eyes began to churn slowly. "My father…" He cleared his throat, but his voice was still hoarse. "He took it from me to keep me safe?"

My heart squeezed as Holland nodded. "He took that ember, along with what remained in him, and put it in the Mierel bloodline." Dark eyes focused on me. "That is what is in you. What remained of Eythos's power and what had passed on to Nyktos."

I opened my mouth, but I was at a loss for words. Nyktos' equally shocked gaze met mine. "I…I have a part of *him* in me? And his father?"

"You have the *essence* of his power," Penellaphe said, and my head swung back to her.

"That still sounds really weird…and uncomfortable," I said.

Penellaphe glanced away, her lips twitching before her gaze met mine. "That does not mean you have a part of Nyktos or his father in you or that it would somehow make you some sort of a descendant," she confirmed—and thank the gods for that because I was about a second away from vomiting a little in my mouth. "You just have the essences of their powers. It's like…how do I explain this?" Her brow wrinkled as she glanced at Holland. "It's like when a god Ascends a godling. The godling shares their blood, but they are not related to that god or any of that god's bloodline. The only thing that could happen is the essence could…recognize its source."

"What—what does that mean?" I asked.

"This would be even harder to explain, but I imagine it's a lot like two souls meant to be one, each finding the other." She was looking at Holland again, and my heart gave another leap. "Both of you may have felt more comfortable around each other than you would others."

The breath I took was thin as I leaned back against the dais. There was no denying that I had felt far more comfortable around Nyktos than I did anyone else. That I never really feared him. "I…I felt this…warmth in me when I first saw you. A rightness." I twisted toward Nyktos. "Not the night in the Shadow Temple, but in The Luxe. I never said anything because I wasn't even sure what I was feeling, and it sounded silly. But the night in The Luxe, I had a…a hard time walking away from you. It felt wrong. I didn't understand it." I turned back to Holland and Penellaphe. "Could that be why?"

"And here I thought it was my charming disposition," Nyktos muttered under his breath. I shot him an arch look. "I felt something similar. A warmth. A rightness. I…I didn't know what it meant."

My eyes widened. "You did?"

He nodded.

"As I said, it would be like two souls shaped for one another coming together," Penellaphe said.

Two souls coming together. Was that why I *interested* Nyktos so much, despite his intentions to never fulfill the deal? Why he was able to find peace in my presence? Could it also explain why I had been drawn to him even when I believed I had to end him? For me, maybe in the beginning. But now? I didn't think so. It was him—*who* he was. His strength and intelligence. His kindness, despite all that he'd seen and surely suffered. His loyalty to his people—those he cared for. It was how ending a life still affected him. It was how he made me feel. That, for the briefest moments, I wasn't a monster. That I was someone. Me. Not whatever I had been shaped into.

But for Nyktos? It really didn't matter. He knew what I'd planned.

Whatever had guided his interest was irrelevant. "And you don't know why my father did this? What he thought it could achieve?"

"I had a…prophetic vision before your father struck this deal with a mortal King," Penellaphe stated, sending a ripple of surprise through me. "It had never happened before, so I didn't understand what I saw. I didn't understand the words in my mind, but I knew they carried a purpose. That they were important. Especially when I told Embris, and he took me to Dalos." She swallowed thickly. "Kolis questioned me quite extensively."

I tensed, having a feeling her *questioning* was more like an interrogation—a painful one.

"It was as if Kolis believed he could somehow force an understanding out of me. A clarification." She shook her head. "As if I were hiding knowledge from him. But I couldn't make sense of what I saw or heard."

"That's not how they work—visions and prophecies. They are rare and the receivers of them are only messengers. Not scribes." Holland reached over, taking her hand in his. He squeezed, and I couldn't help but wonder if there was something between them. I'd never known him to be with anyone, but obviously, there was a lot I hadn't known.

"Kolis eventually gave up." Some of the shadows cleared from Penellaphe's eyes as she smiled at him. "Afterwards, I went to Mount Lotho. I figured if anyone could make any sense of it, it would be the Arae."

"We weren't much help at first. We *hate* prophecies." Holland laughed dryly. "It wasn't until Eythos came to ask what, if anything, could be done about his brother, that I recalled the prophecy and Kolis's interest in it. We shared it with him, and Eythos seemed to have some sort of understanding."

"What was it? This prophecy?" Nyktos asked. "Can you tell us?"

"What I saw was just disjointed images. People ruling in the mortal realm that didn't appear mortal—places I don't think yet exist."

"Like what?"

"Like cities forever laid to waste. Kingdoms shattered and rebuilt. Great and…terrible wars—wars between Kings…and between Queens." Her brows pinched. "A forest made of trees the color of blood."

Nyktos frowned. "The Red Woods?"

She nodded. "But in the mortal realm, and full of death. Steeped in the sins and secrets of hundreds and hundreds of years."

"Well," I said, exhaling slowly. "None of that sounds good."

"But I also saw her. I saw *them.* A Chosen and a descendant of the First." The eather burned brightly in Penellaphe's eyes as they met mine. "A Queen of Flesh and Fire. And him, a King risen from Blood and Ash, who ruled side by side with man. And they…they felt *right.* They felt like hope."

I really had no idea who they were or what that meant, but I would have to take her word for it. "Did you see anything else?"

"Nothing that I can understand enough to tell, but I remember the words. I'll never forget them." She looked down as Holland squeezed her hand once more and then let go. She cleared her throat. "'*From the desperation of golden crowns and born of mortal flesh, a great primal power rises as the heir to the lands and seas, to the skies and all the realms. A shadow in the ember, a light in the flame, to become a fire in the flesh. When the stars fall from the night, the great mountains crumble into the seas, and old bones raise their swords beside the gods, the false one will be stripped from glory until two born of the same misdeeds, born of the same great and Primal power in the mortal realm. A first daughter, with blood full of fire, fated for the once-promised King. And the second daughter, with blood full of ash and ice, the other half of the future King. Together, they will remake the realms as they usher in the end.*'"

She paused, looking up with eyes as bright as polished sapphires. "'*And so it will begin with the last Chosen blood spilled, the great conspirator birthed from the flesh and fire of the Primals will awaken as the Harbinger and the Bringer of Death and Destruction to the lands gifted by the gods. Beware, for the end will come from the west to destroy the east and lay waste to all which lies between.*'" She exhaled unsteadily. "That's…that's it."

I started to speak and then stopped, glancing up at Nyktos. There was a thoughtful pinch to the set of his lips and a whole lot of *what the hell* to the arch of his brow.

"That sounds…" Nyktos blinked slowly. "That sounded intense."

Penellaphe laughed lightly. "Isn't it, though?"

Nyktos nodded slowly. "I think it's safe to assume that the latter part is referencing my uncle. He is the great conspirator—the rightful Bringer of Death. He, along with my father, were born in the west." Nyktos looked down at me. "They were born in the mortal realm. Roughly where present-day Carsodonia stands."

"And the last part of the prophecy means that he will destroy all the lands, from west to east, including the mortal realm?" I wiped my hands down my thighs.

"Depends on how one defines *Chosen*," Holland said. "It could be speaking of those chosen to serve the gods or…or those like you, chosen for a different purpose."

"And the 'birthed from the flesh and fire of the Primals' could mean a rebirth of sorts," Nyktos said. "Not an actual birth."

"Okay. I get that, but how can that be referencing Kolis?" I asked. "How can he be awakened when he's already…" I trailed off,

"Unless he goes to sleep," Nyktos murmured, looking over at Holland and the goddess. "That will never happen."

Holland head inclined. "Prophecies…they are only a possibility. So many things can change them, and from what I understand, not every word is to be taken literally. The problem is, we do not often know which words should be."

I snorted at that. "The first part? The desperation of golden crowns? Could that be referencing Roderick Mierel? He was desperate if not yet a King at the time the deal was made."

"I believe so," Holland confirmed. "Eythos made the deal with Roderick shortly after he learned of the prophecy. But again, so many things can change a prophecy. That can change the meaning and the intention behind every single word."

"Well, that's great," Nyktos muttered, and I almost laughed.

Holland's smile was sympathetic. "There is never just one string that charts the course of a life or how that life will impact the realms." Holland opened his hand, spreading his fingers wide. I gasped as numerous strands appeared, no thicker than a thread and shimmering a bright blue. "There are dozens for most lives. Some even have hundreds of possible outcomes. You." His gaze lifted to me, and I swallowed. "You have had many strings. Many different paths. But they all ended the same."

A chill skated down my spine. "How?"

"Sometimes, it's better not to know," he answered.

Penellaphe drifted closer. "But, sometimes, knowledge is power."

I nodded. "I want to know."

A brief, fond smile appeared, and then Holland said, "Your paths have always ended in your death before you even saw twenty-one years of life."

I went numb. Before age twenty-one…? That was…gods, that was soon.

Nyktos stepped forward, partly blocking me. "That's not going to happen."

"You may be a Primal,"—Holland's attention shifted to him—

"but you are not a Fate."

"Fate can go fuck itself," Nyktos growled. His skin had thinned, revealing the swirling shadows underneath.

"If only." Holland's smile was faint, clearly unbothered by the storm brewing within Nyktos. "Death always finds you, one way or another." His focus had returned to me. "By the hands of a god or a misinformed mortal. By Kolis himself, and even by Death."

I stilled, my heart lurching.

"*What*?" Nyktos snarled.

"There are many different threads," Penellaphe said softly, looking up at Nyktos. A great sadness had settled into her features. "Many different ways her death could come at your hands. But this one." She lifted a finger, nearly touching one of the shimmering strands—a thread that appeared to have broken off into another shorter thread. "This was not intentional."

"What are you talking about?" Nyktos demanded.

"She has your blood in her, doesn't she?" she asked.

Nyktos went so still, I wasn't sure he even breathed. My gaze darted between them. "I don't have his blood. He hasn't—" I sucked in a breath. The night Nyktos had fed from me. I'd bitten his thumb and drew blood. I'd tasted it. I saw the moment Nyktos remembered. I twisted toward Holland. "It was just a drop. Barely even that."

"But it was enough," Holland stated. "The ember of life in you is strong enough to cause you to have the symptoms of the Culling, but it wasn't strong enough to push you into the change. The symptoms would've eased off, but not now. Not with the blood of a powerful Primal in you. You will go into the Culling."

"No." Nyktos shook his head, twists of eather swirling in his eyes. "She can't. She's not a godling. She's mortal—"

"Mostly," Penellaphe whispered. "Her body is mortal. As is her mind." She looked at me, her eyes glistening. "But what has always been inside of you is Primal. It doesn't matter that both of your parents were mortal. You were born with an ember of not one but two Primals inside you. That's what will attempt to come out."

"That can't happen." Nyktos thrust a hand through his hair, dragging the strands back from his face. "There has to be a way to stop it."

"There isn't." I gripped my knees as I looked between Holland and the goddess. "Is there? No special potion or deal to be made?"

Holland shook his head. "No. There are some things that not even the Primals can grant. This is one of them."

"She won't—" Nyktos cut himself off as he turned to me. I'd never seen him so pale, so *horrified.*

"This isn't your fault." I stood, surprised that my legs weren't shaking. "I did it. You didn't. And it's not like you had any way of knowing that would happen."

"So reckless. Impulsive," Holland murmured.

A laugh choked me. "Yeah, well, you've always known that is my greatest flaw."

"Or greatest strength," Holland countered. "Your actions could've given whatever it was Eythos believed upon hearing the prophecy a chance to come to fruition."

Both Nyktos and I stared at him. "What?"

"Look closer at this thread." Penellaphe lifted a finger once more to the string that had broken off. "Look."

Nyktos' head lowered as he stared. At first, I saw nothing, but when I squinted… I saw it—the shadow of a thread, barely there and ever-changing in length, stretching farther than any of the other threads and then shrinking to the length of the others.

"What is that?" I asked.

"It's an unexpected thread. Unpredictable. It is the unknown. The unwritten," Penellaphe explained. "It is the one thing that not even the Fates can predict or control." The corners of her lips turned up. "The only thing that can disrupt fate."

"And what is that?" Nyktos asked, his hands closing into fists at his sides. "And how do I find it?"

"It can't be found," she said, and I was one second from screaming my frustration. "It can only be accepted."

"You're going to need to give us a little more detail," Nyktos snapped.

"It's love," Holland answered. "Love is the one thing that not even fate can contend with."

I blinked.

That was all I could do.

Nyktos appeared to be as dumbstruck as I was, unable to formulate a single response.

"Love is more powerful than fate." Holland lowered his hand, and all but one thread disappeared. Only the broken one, and the shadow of an ever-changing string remained, glittering in the space between us. "Love is even more powerful than what courses through our veins, equally awe-inspiring and terrifying in its selfishness. It can extend a thread by sheer will, becoming that piece of pure magic that cannot be extinguished by biology, and it can snap a thread unexpectedly and prematurely."

"What exactly are you saying?" I asked.

"Your body cannot withstand the Culling. Not without the sheer will of what is more powerful than fate and even death." Holland looked to Nyktos. "Not without the love of the one who would aid her Ascension."

What Aios had told me about the godlings and the Culling resurfaced. "You're talking about the blood of a god. Saying that I would need the blood of a god who *loves* me?" I couldn't believe I was even speaking the words.

"Not just a god. A Primal. And not just any Primal." Penellaphe's blue eyes fixed on Nyktos. "The blood of the Primal the ember belonged to—that and the pure will of love can unravel fate."

Nyktos jerked back another step, the shadows churning around his legs, and I…I sat down again. Or fell down. Luckily, I landed on the edge of the dais. Heart twisting and squeezing, I watched Nyktos' head slowly turn toward me. His eyes were as bright as the moon as he stared down at me, and I didn't need his power to read emotions to know that he was horrified.

And I didn't need to be a Fate to know that I truly would die.

Nyktos could never love me.

Even if I hadn't planned to kill him. Nyktos was incapable of love. It was simply not in him. He knew that. *I* knew that.

"This isn't fair," I said hoarsely, angry at *everything*. "To do this to him."

"To do this to *me*?" he rasped as silvery streaks of eather appeared in the shadows swirling around him. "This isn't fair to you."

"It's not fair to either of you," Penellaphe stated softly. "But life, fate, or love rarely is, is it?"

I wanted to punch the goddess for telling me what I already knew.

But I drew in a deep breath, briefly closing my eyes. There was a lot of information to digest—a lot of knowledge that was ultimately irrelevant and overshadowed by the fact that I would die, sooner rather than later—and painfully, too. Anger sparked in me again, and I latched onto it, holding it close. The burn of that was familiar and felt better than the sorrow and hopelessness.

"There is more," Holland stated.

I laughed. It sounded strange. "Of course, there is."

"You have had as many outcomes as you've had lives," he told me.

"Many lives?" I repeated.

Holland nodded, and then the shimmery cords appeared once more. Dozens of them.

"What does that mean?" Nyktos' gaze flicked from the strings to Holland. "Her soul has been reborn?"

Holland also stared at the strings. "Fate doesn't know all because the actions of one can alter the course of fate. Just like she altered the course with a single drop of blood." He looked up at Nyktos. "Just like your father altered fate, as did the Primal Keella, when they stopped a soul from entering the Shadowlands, leaving it to be born over and over."

"You're speaking of Sotoria," I said, and he nodded. "What does that have to do with this?"

Holland's gaze shifted to me. "You are a warrior, Seraphena. You always have been. Just like she learned to become."

Tiny bumps rose all over my skin. "No."

He shook his head. "You have had many names."

"*No*," I repeated.

"You have lived many lives," he continued. "But it is that one, the first one, that Eythos remembered when he answered Roderick Mierel's summons. He always remembered her."

Nyktos had once again gone deathly still. "You're not saying what I think you are."

"I am."

"Eythos could be considered impulsive by many, but he was wise," Holland said, sadness creeping into his eyes. "He knew what would come of Kolis's actions. Kolis was never meant to be the Primal of Life. Those powers and gifts could not remain in him. What he did was unnatural. Life cannot exist in that state. Eythos knew they would fade, and they have. That is why no Primals have been born. Why the lands in the mortal realm are beginning to die. Why no gods have risen in power. He knew that Kolis's actions would be the end of both realms as we know them."

"Your father wanted to keep you safe," Penellaphe restated. "But he wanted to save the realms. He wanted to give the mortals and the gods a chance. He wanted to give you revenge," she said, looking at me. I shuddered. "So, this is what he did. He hid the ember of life, where it could be safe and where it could grow in power until a new

Primal was ready to be born—in the one being that could weaken his brother."

"I can't be her. There's no way. I'm not Sotoria. I'm…" My words faded as the rest of what she'd said broke through.

A new Primal was ready to be born…

"'*Born of mortal flesh, a shadow in the ember,*'" Nyktos repeated slowly, and then his chest rose in a sharp breath. "What Holland said about no gods rising in power is true. That hasn't happened since my father placed the ember in your bloodline. But you did it."

"I…I didn't mean to," I started. "But I think that's the least of my concerns right now."

"You're right. That is the least of our concerns right now, but it is what *that* means." Nyktos turned to the Fate. "Isn't it? *It's* her."

Holland nodded. "All life—in both realms—has only continued to come into creation because the Mierel bloodline carried that ember. Now, she carries the only ember of life in both realms. She is why life continues." Holland's eyes met mine and held. "If you were to die, there would be nothing but death in all the kingdoms and all the realms."

The floor felt as if it were shifting beneath me. "That…that doesn't make sense."

"It does." Slowly, Nyktos turned back. His gaze met mine, and he didn't look away. He didn't blink. "It's *you*." A sort of wonder filled his features, widening his eyes and parting his lips. "You are the heir to the lands and seas, skies and realms. A Queen instead of a King. You are the Primal of Life."

Coming March 15, 2022

THE WAR OF TWO QUEENS

From #1 New York Times bestselling author
Jennifer L. Armentrout
comes book four in her Blood and Ash series.

War is only the beginning…

Discover The Blood and Ash Series by Jennifer L. Armentrout

From Blood and Ash
Book One
Available in hardcover, e-book, and trade paperback.

Captivating and action-packed, From Blood and Ash is a sexy, addictive, and unexpected fantasy perfect for fans of Sarah J. Maas and Laura Thalassa.

A Maiden…
Chosen from birth to usher in a new era, Poppy's life has never been her own. The life of the Maiden is solitary. Never to be touched. Never to be looked upon. Never to be spoken to. Never to experience pleasure. Waiting for the day of her Ascension, she would rather be with the guards, fighting back the evil that took her family, than preparing to be found worthy by the gods. But the choice has never been hers.

A Duty…
The entire kingdom's future rests on Poppy's shoulders, something she's not even quite sure she wants for herself. Because a Maiden has a heart. And a soul. And longing. And when Hawke, a golden-eyed guard honor bound to ensure her Ascension, enters her life, destiny and duty become tangled with desire and need. He incites her anger, makes her question everything she believes in, and tempts her with the forbidden.

A Kingdom…
Forsaken by the gods and feared by mortals, a fallen kingdom is rising once more, determined to take back what they believe is theirs through violence and vengeance. And as the shadow of those cursed draws closer, the line between what is forbidden and what is right becomes blurred. Poppy is not only on the verge of losing her heart and being found unworthy by the gods, but also her life when every blood-soaked thread that holds her world together begins to unravel.

A Kingdom of Flesh and Fire
Book Two
Available in hardcover, e-book, and trade paperback.

Is Love Stronger Than Vengeance?

A Betrayal…

Everything Poppy has ever believed in is a lie, including the man she was falling in love with. Thrust among those who see her as a symbol of a monstrous kingdom, she barely knows who she is without the veil of the Maiden. But what she *does* know is that nothing is as dangerous to her as *him*. The Dark One. The Prince of Atlantia. He wants her to fight him, and that's one order she's more than happy to obey. *He may have taken her, but he will never have her.*

A Choice….

Casteel Da'Neer is known by many names and many faces. His lies are as seductive as his touch. His truths as sensual as his bite. Poppy knows better than to trust him. He needs her alive, healthy, and whole to achieve his goals. But he's the only way for her to get what she wants—to find her brother Ian and see for herself if he has become a soulless Ascended. Working with Casteel instead of against him presents its own risks. He still tempts her with every breath, offering up all she's ever wanted. Casteel has plans for her. Ones that could expose her to unimaginable pleasure and unfathomable pain. Plans that will force her to look beyond everything she thought she knew about herself—about him. Plans that could bind their lives together in unexpected ways that neither kingdom is prepared for. And she's far too reckless, too hungry, to resist the temptation.

A Secret…

But unrest has grown in Atlantia as they await the return of their Prince. Whispers of war have become stronger, and Poppy is at the very heart of it all. The King wants to use her to send a message. The Descenters want her dead. The wolven are growing more unpredictable. And as her abilities to feel pain and emotion begin to grow and strengthen, the Atlantians start to fear her. Dark secrets are at play, ones steeped in the blood-drenched sins of two kingdoms that would do anything to keep the truth hidden. But when the earth begins to shake, and the skies start to bleed, it may already be too late.

The Crown of Gilded Bones

Book Three

Available in hardcover, e-book, and trade paperback.

Bow Before Your Queen Or Bleed Before Her…

She's been the victim and the survivor…

Poppy never dreamed she would find the love she's found with Prince Casteel. She wants to revel in her happiness but first they must free his brother and find hers. It's a dangerous mission and one with far-reaching consequences neither dreamed of. Because Poppy is the Chosen, the Blessed. The true ruler of Atlantia. She carries the blood of the King of Gods within her. By right the crown and the kingdom are hers.

The enemy and the warrior…

Poppy has only ever wanted to control her own life, not the lives of others, but now she must choose to either forsake her birthright or seize the gilded crown and become the Queen of Flesh and Fire. But as the kingdoms' dark sins and blood-drenched secrets finally unravel, a long-forgotten power rises to pose a genuine threat. And they will stop at nothing to ensure that the crown never sits upon Poppy's head.

A lover and heartmate…

But the greatest threat to them and to Atlantia is what awaits in the far west, where the Queen of Blood and Ash has her own plans, ones she has waited hundreds of years to carry out. Poppy and Casteel must consider the impossible—travel to the Lands of the Gods and wake the King himself. And as shocking secrets and the harshest betrayals come to light, and enemies emerge to threaten everything Poppy and Casteel have fought for, they will discover just how far they are willing to go for their people—and each other.

And now she will become Queen…

Sign up for the Blue Box Press/1001 Dark Nights Newsletter and be entered to win a Tiffany Lock necklace.

There's a contest every quarter!

Go to www.TheBlueBoxPress.com to subscribe.

As a bonus, all subscribers can download FIVE FREE exclusive books!

Discover 1001 Dark Nights Collection Eight

DRAGON REVEALED by Donna Grant
A Dragon Kings Novella

CAPTURED IN INK by Carrie Ann Ryan
A Montgomery Ink: Boulder Novella

SECURING JANE by Susan Stoker
A SEAL of Protection: Legacy Series Novella

WILD WIND by Kristen Ashley
A Chaos Novella

DARE TO TEASE by Carly Phillips
A Dare Nation Novella

VAMPIRE by Rebecca Zanetti
A Dark Protectors/Rebels Novella

MAFIA KING by Rachel Van Dyken
A Mafia Royals Novella

THE GRAVEDIGGER'S SON by Darynda Jones
A Charley Davidson Novella

FINALE by Skye Warren
A North Security Novella

MEMORIES OF YOU by J. Kenner
A Stark Securities Novella

SLAYED BY DARKNESS by Alexandra Ivy
A Guardians of Eternity Novella

TREASURED by Lexi Blake
A Masters and Mercenaries Novella

THE DAREDEVIL by Dylan Allen
A Rivers Wilde Novella

BOND OF DESTINY by Larissa Ione
A Demonica Novella

THE CLOSE-UP by Kennedy Ryan
A Hollywood Renaissance Novella

MORE THAN POSSESS YOU by Shayla Black
A More Than Words Novella

HAUNTED HOUSE by Heather Graham
A Krewe of Hunters Novella

MAN FOR ME by Laurelin Paige
A Man In Charge Novella

THE RHYTHM METHOD by Kylie Scott
A Stage Dive Novella

JONAH BENNETT by Tijan
A Bennett Mafia Novella

CHANGE WITH ME by Kristen Proby
A With Me In Seattle Novella

THE DARKEST DESTINY by Gena Showalter
A Lords of the Underworld Novella

About Jennifer L. Armentrout

1 New York Times and International Bestselling author Jennifer lives in Shepherdstown, West Virginia. All the rumors you've heard about her state aren't true. When she's not hard at work writing. she spends her time reading, watching really bad zombie movies, pretending to write, and hanging out with her husband, their retired K-9 police dog Diesel, a crazy Border Jack puppy named Apollo, six judgmental alpacas, four fluffy sheep, and two goats.

Her dreams of becoming an author started in algebra class, where she spent most of her time writing short stories…which explains her dismal grades in math. Jennifer writes young adult paranormal, science fiction, fantasy, and contemporary romance. She is published with Tor Teen, Entangled Teen and Brazen, Disney/Hyperion and Harlequin Teen. Her book *Wicked* has been optioned by Passionflix and slated to begin filming in late 2018. Her young adult romantic suspense novel *DON'T LOOK BACK* was a 2014 nominated Best in Young Adult Fiction by YALSA and her novel *THE PROBLEM WITH FOREVER* is a 2017 RITA Award winning novel.

She also writes Adult and New Adult contemporary and paranormal romance under the name J. Lynn. She is published by Entangled Brazen and HarperCollins.

On Behalf of Blue Box Press,

Liz Berry, M.J. Rose, and Jillian Stein would like to thank ~

Steve Berry
Doug Scofield
Benjamin Stein
Kim Guidroz
Social Butterfly PR
Ashley Wells
Chelle Olson
Hang Le
Malissa Coy
Chris Graham
Jessica Johns
Dylan Stockton
Kate Boggs
Dina Williams
Justine Bylo
Richard Blake
and Simon Lipskar